BOOKS BY GARY JENNINGS

Aztec (1980)
The Journeyer (1984)
World of Words (1984)
Spangle (1987)
Raptor (1992)
Aztec Autumn (1997)

GARY JENNINGS

THE
CENTER RING

⊰⊹⊷ SPANGLE VOLUME II ⊶⊹⊱

FORGE®

A TOM DOHERTY ASSOCIATES BOOK
NEW YORK

THE CENTER RING: SPANGLE VOLUME II

Copyright © 1987 by Gary Jennings

A Forge Book
Published by Tom Doherty Associates, Inc.
175 Fifth Avenue
New York, NY 10010

Forge® is a registered trademark of Tom Doherty Associates, Inc.

ISBN: 0-812-56472-3
Library of Congress Catalog Card Number: 86-47687

First Forge edition: March 1999

Printed in the United States of America

0 9 8 7 6 5 4 3 2 1

For Gail Van Dyken

Prologue

"Well, here we are, on 'the other side of the pond,' " thought Zachary Edge—alias Colonel Ramrod, circus sharpshooter—as he looked back from the shore at the sooty steamship that had landed them here at Livorno, Italy. Others of the troupe were still coming down the gangplank. "And we're sure as hell more of a circus than the miserable mud show I joined back in Virginia."

Florian's Flourishing Florilegium of Wonders had been only a pitiful caravan of shabby wagons, threadbare (and hungry) artistes, one elephant and one mangy lion when, after Appomattox, it struggled north through a Virginia ravaged and impoverished by the just-ended Civil War. Along the way, the circus had endured and survived many a deprivation, near-starvation and all manner of disastrous accidents. But it had also recruited other performers and attractions until, by the time it reached Maryland, it was no longer just a "mud show" but a fairly creditable and prosperous circus. At Baltimore, Florian had bargained with a reluctant Captain Schilz of the coalship Pflichttreu for passage to Europe—because that was where Florian reckoned to build his Florilegium into a nonparell show indeed.

The crossing had been slow and, even in mid-ocean, not without further tragic incidents. However, just before docking, the circus had acquired two more members, and valuable ones, when Florian persuaded the Pflichttreu's musically-inclined engineer Carl Beck and its sailmaker Dai Goesle to "jump ship" and sign on as, respectively, the Florilegium's bandmaster and canvasmaster. This had not pleased Captain Schilz.

Now, when the whole troupe was on shore and out of earshot of the captain's fulminations about "betrayal," Florian went alone into the wharfside building marked DOGANAED IMMIGRAZIONE. He carried all the "conduct books" bearing every person's personal particulars, plus the brief laudatory comments added by Captain Schilz before his disillusion-ment. Sarah Coverley had had to invent that data for three Chinese foot-jugglers, but the had at least been able to put down their signatures—very elegant little scribbles of ink—which was more than some of the company could do. Abner Mullenax, Hannibal Tyree and Quincy Simms signed only with an X and a thumbprint. Sunday and Monday Simms, thanks to Jules Rouleaus tutelage, were able to write legibly, if childishly.

ITALIA

1

THEY ALL WAITED, WITH the wagons, animals and stacked luggage, on the vast, cobbled lungomare that stretched from the harborside to where the streets of Livorno city began. Around them, the cobbles were overlaid with tarpaulins spread by come-home fishermen, selling the night's fresh catch to housewives, domestics and even grandly attired ladies who pointed, beckoned, inspected and bargained without getting down from their carriages. Some of the troupers passed the time by walking about in small circles, awkwardly and tentatively, and occasionally stamping their feet.

"Feels funny, walking here," Yount grunted.

"You are a tenderfoot," explained Stitches. "Look you, after a long time on a smooth and springy deck, you step on the hard, unyielding land, you'll walk like on eggs for a while. Anybody newly come ashore is a tenderfoot."

They had not long to wait there. Florian emerged from the customs house looking most satisfied, and saying, "No problems at all. They may have been a little amused to find among our company three persons named A. Chink, but they made no issue of it. We are cleared to land.''

"They don't even want to count our armaments?'' asked Fitzfarris. "Examine the animals for disease?''

"No. And no quarantine. Not even a tariff to pay. I think Italy is simply too new and inexperienced at being a wholly unified nation to have had time yet to promulgate a welter of rules and red tape and tiresome petty clerks.''

"All right. What now?'' asked Edge.

"First, tov!'' Magpie Maggie Hag said firmly.

"Yes, first a good bath,'' Florian agreed. "And not in a tub of salt water, for a change. Ladies and gentlemen, I shall make an extravagant gesture, perhaps my last for some time. Follow me to yonder hostelry.''

He pointed. The Hotel Gran Duca, on the inland side of the lungomare, was an imposing three-story structure, built of stones to match the other harbor-works architecture. It had the appearance of being able to cater to any kind of traveler, by land or sea, for on one side of the main building was an extensive stable, coach house and yard, on the other a ship's chandlery and seamen's slops shop.

"I shall engage rooms for us,'' said Florian, "and order baths drawn and command that the dining room be laid for a noontime colazione. We will spend our first night in Europe in sybaritic luxury.'' All the women gave little cries of pleasure. "Meanwhile, Zachary, would you apply to the hotel stalliere and have his men run our animals and wagons into the stable yard? Arrange for feed and cat's meat—and a place for Abdullah and Ali Baba and the Chinks to bed down nearby.''

It was with some hesitancy that Edge went to the task of accosting his first Italian. But he found the hostler to be fluent in numerous languages, and so worldly that he evinced no least surprise at being asked to tend—besides eight horses—an elephant, a lion, three pigs, two black men and three yellow. When those arrangements were made, Edge went around to enter the hotel by its front door. The Gran Duca's lobby was an immense hall of rather gloomy magnificence, all dark mahogany furniture, wine-velvet draperies and upholstery.

Besides the people being loudly convivial in the adjoining taproom, there were more sober ones occupying the lobby's armchairs and divans: well-dressed women chatting over tea-cups, well-dressed men perusing newspapers, smoking enor-mous cigars or just snoozing. Since Edge was wearing his only passable street attire—his old army tunic and trousers, boots and cocked-brim hat—he felt very much the country hick in these surroundings.

Then he heard a call: "Signore, per favore. Monsieur, s'il vous plaît," and he turned to see a small, very shapely young female stranger waving to him.

She was dressed all in pale yellow—full crinolined skirt, an almost naughtily low-cut bodice, pert little kiss-me-quick hat, and she was just lowering a pale-yellow parasol as she came toward him—so she gleamed like a sunbeam in the dark hall, and the bright shine of her attracted the admiring gaze of every male idler, the stony stare of every woman. She had long, wavy hair the red-brown color of polished chestnuts. The brown irises of her eyes were so flecked with gold that they looked petaled, like flowers, and there were dimples about her mouth that made it appear ready to smile at the least excuse. She came up to Edge—and she came up only to his chest in height. Also, she had the tiniest waist of any woman he had ever seen, but it obviously was not made so by any kind of corset; she moved too lithely and her breasts moved too naturally. She looked up at him with that barely contained smile lurking on her lips, and she cocked her pretty head as if debating what language to employ. When Edge doffed his hat and inquiringly raised his eyebrows, she said:

"You are Zachary Edge."

"Thank you, ma'am," he said solemnly, with a nod of acknowledgment. "But I already knew that."

She looked a trifle disconcerted at his not having said, "At your service," or some such stock rejoinder. The dimples around her mouth wavered slightly and she tried a different language.

"Je suis Automne Auburn, monsieur. Du métier danseuse de corde. Entendez-vous français?"

"Well enough, yes, but why don't we stick to English?"

She reestablished the dimples, gave her bronze curls a brazen toss, twirled her parasol in a wanton way and said in broadest cockney, "Ow, orright, guv'nor. Oy'm an equilibrist, nyme of Autumn Auburn, and—"

"I don't believe it."

"Why, 'ere 'tis in print!" she cried, and whipped a folded newspaper from under one arm. "The *Era*, see? The circus trydesheet. Sixp'nce a copy, but oy'll give yer a free dekko. Look there in the h'adverts. *That* cost me five bleedin' bob."

She pointed to a column, and Edge read aloud, " 'A FA-THER OFFERS to managers: his young daughter, fourteen years old' . . ."

"Nar! Not that 'un." She tugged at the paper, but he kept reading, and kept a straight face:

" . . . 'Fourteen years old, who has only one eye, placed above the nose, and one ear on the shoulder. Interested parties apply this paper.' " He handed the *Era* back to her. "I'd have taken you for older than fourteen. But then, you freaks often do look—"

"*Will* 'ave yer jollies, wontcher? 'Ere. This 'un's moyn." She pushed the paper at him again, and he obligingly read:

" 'MISS AUTUMN AUBURN, la plus grande équilibriste aérienne de l'époque—ne plus ultra—affatto senze rivale. Frei ab August, this year.' Well, miss, I admire the linguistics. I count five languages in just those few words. But I still refuse to believe that anybody ever got christened Autumn Auburn."

She coyly ducked her head, and let her smile become a confiding laugh. "Ow, it ayn't me real nyme, o' course." She looked up at him through her luxuriant eyelashes. "But if Cora Pearl—'er wot was plyne Emma Crouch back in Cheapside—if she could myke 'er forchune in gye Paree by callin' 'erself Cora Pearl . . ." She twirled her parasol. " . . . I sez to meself, 'ow come little Nellie Cubbidge carn't do th' syme wiv a nice nom-dee-chamber like Autumn Auburn?"

"I don't believe that atrocious dialect, either. I heard enough genuine lime-juicers on the boat."

She laughed again, and said, in an English accent that was

merely melodious, "Are you armor-plated against teasing, Mr. Edge? You don't even smile."

"You do it so much better, miss. I'd like you to do the smiling for both of us, the rest of our lives."

For a moment that was silent but richly reverberant, they looked at one another. Then she gave a small, come-awake shake of her head and turned hoyden again.

"Give us a job, guv, and oy'll larf me fool 'ead orf."

"How did you know who I am?"

She resumed her normal voice, but still sounded mischievous. "I know everything about you. I saw the circus carrozzoni come in, and I ran to question the portinaio. He said everybody in the troupe had gone to the baths, except the Signor Zaccaria Ayd-zhay, who apparently does not bathe. I refused to believe that anybody ever got christened Zaccaria Ayd-zhay, so I made him let me look at your conduct book. You are an American, and you will have your thirty-seventh birthday on the twentieth of September, and you are the equestrian director of Florian's Flourishing Florilegium et cetera. And all those particulars were written in a feminine hand, so you have a wife...or a lady friend..." She paused, as if waiting for him to say something, then added lightly, "I cannot imagine how you got one, if you are averse to bathing."

"Is your name really Nellie Cubbidge?"

"Crikey, would I invent *that?*"

"Then I'll call you Autumn, if I may. And if I'm not mistaken, an équilibriste is a ropewalker . . . ?"

"Rope or wire. Slack or tight. And I have my own rigging."

"It's Mr. Florian who does the hiring, but I'll break his neck if he doesn't hire you. Now that that's settled, may I offer you a drink of something, in the bar yonder, to seal the contract?"

"To be honest, I'd rather you offered me a bite of something."

"Well, we're all convening in the dining room for a colazione, which I take to mean a meal."

"Ooh, lovely."

"Come and help me, in case I need Italian spoken, to tell the desk clerk to add you to the dining roster. Then, if you'll excuse me just briefly, I'll abandon my lifelong aversion and go take a bath."

"Ooh, lovelier yet."

"And I'll join you at the table, to introduce you to your new colleagues."

When the company assembled, the dining-room servants shoved together several tables to accommodate them. Everyone was in Sunday-best clothes, such as those might be, and Clover Lee was redolent of Dixie Belle Extract of White Heliotrope, and Carl Beck was redolent of the unidentifiable odors of the hair-raising lotion Magpie Maggie Hag had compounded for him. Hannibal, Quincy and the Chinese, of course, were eating with the stable hands. And Monsieur Roulette was being served in his room, said Florian, adding that, after the meal, the hotel's physician would be giving him an examination. So there were fourteen at table, but Edge fetched an extra chair to set between himself and Florian, then went to escort Autumn Auburn from where she waited in an alcove.

He presented her to the troupe with the prideful air of a connoisseur who had discovered an unrecognized objet d'art in a shop of common trinkets, and Autumn good-humoredly did her best to look maidenly grateful for that deliverance. Every man in the company beamed admiringly at her. And, although Autumn was better dressed than any of them, so did the women—all but two. Sarah Coverley and little Sunday Simms had instantly read Edge's glowing face, and they regarded the newcomer with a certain melancholy. Florian greeted her warmly, and so did most of the others. Carl Beck, when he was introduced, gazed at Autumn intently. "Fräulein Auburn, the very image you are of some other beauty I have met, or seen a picture of, but who it was I cannot think."

Sunday, on shaking Autumn's hand, merely murmured, "Enchantée." But Sarah, in her turn, lightly remarked, "Zachary, I congratulate you, but I am disappointed. Miss Auburn is not a klischnigg."

Edge said gruffly, "I decided I ought to step aside from your stampede of dukes and counts."

"A gentleman would have waited," she said, but still lightly, "until he was trampled by at least the first of them."

Autumn, whose brown-gold gaze had gone back and forth between them during that exchange, said, "Madame Solitaire, it must have been you who did the writing of his conduct book."

"Yes. And I can assure you, my dear, that he will conduct himself to your utmost satisfaction."

"Oh, my dear, you should have written that in the book. Now I shall have to judge for myself."

"Touché," said Florian. "Now, down swords, ladies. A man of any manhood abhors being discussed in the third person, as if he were a mute or a ninny or a dear departed, and Colonel Edge is none of those."

"Coo! You're a real colonel?" Autumn said to Edge, with exaggerated chagrin. "And I only called you mister."

"Sit down, everybody," said Florian. "Here is our antipasto and—not champagne, not yet—but a decent vino bianco. No doubt you are acquainted with the local provender, Miss Auburn. Are you lodging at this same hotel?"

"Not exactly," she said, as she eagerly helped herself from a platter. "In the hotel's coach house, in my own caravan. So I've been staying here at stable rates. On stable rations, come to that."

"Well, we ought to inform you, before you decide to join out," said Florian. "This is our first lodging under roof in a long time, and perhaps our last. But let us not talk business until we are well nourished. Tell us how you came to be here."

Between voracious partakings of the cold meats, pickled mushrooms and artichoke hearts, Autumn replied with staccato economy, "Old story. Goat show. Circo Spettacoloso Cisalpino. Folded on the tober here. Governor did a Johnny Scaparey. Stranded us all. Some of us stayed. Not much choice. Played to the summer seasiders. Passed the hat. Hat usually came back empty. Now the season is over. Still stranded."

The waiters brought the soup course, tureens of fragrantly steaming cacciucco, and started to remove the platters of antipasto. Autumn hastily said, "Prego, lasciate," to halt them, then said to the table at large. "Please, you have paid for all these tidbits. If you are not going to finish them, might I . . . ?"

"Wait you, missy," said Stitches. "There is plenty more will come, now just. You need not fill up on the preliminaries."

"I didn't mean for me. I thought—if I could have them wrapped—there are some other hungry kinkers, castaways from the Cisalpino, who'd be thankful to you all."

Florian instantly gave orders in Italian and the waiters bowed in acknowledgment. Autumn went on:

"I'm luckier than the others. I've my own rigging and my own transport. Actually, I had an offer to come on the Circo Orfei, but they're away up in the Piemonte somewhere. The hotel people here have been noble about my stable bill, but they won't let me hitch my nag to my van until it's paid up. So I was simply hoping to survive until the Orfei gets to this neighborhood, if it ever does."

"Orfei good show," said Magpie Maggie Hag. "Famous all over. Also prosperous. They no scarper. Better you go with them."

Edge frowned at her. Florian gave her a painted look and said. "Confound it, Maggie. I wanted to defer any shop talk, but . . ." He turned again to Autumn. "I'll concede that the Orfei family would probably pay you more, and more regularly. We can offer only part pay and promises."

"We should also confess that we don't always eat this well," said Edge, indicating the platters of red mullet and bowls of spaghetti that the waiters were just setting on the table.

"I am free, white and twenty-one," said Autumn. "Isn't that how it is phrased in your country, Colonel Edge?"

"Twenty-one," Sarah echoed faintly into her glass of wine.

"And I can make up my own mind," said Autumn. "If there's a place for me, Mr. Florian, I'll be glad to accept it."

Pepper exclaimed, "That's talkin' Irish, alannah, even if ye be a Sassenach. Hitch your wagon to a rising star." She lifted her wine glass and broadened her brogue. "In Paris we'll be toastin' ye in fine shampanny, whilst we sashay in carriages up and down the Chumps Elizas! Won't we, Pap?" When there was no immediate answer, she said sharply, "*Won't we*, Paprika mavourneen?"

"Oh," said Paprika, startled out of her contemplation of Sarah's wistful face. "Yes. Yes, indeed, Pep."

"Also, Mr. Florian," said Autumn, "if you're the only one of the troupe who speaks Italian, I might be of help in that regard, too."

"Are you fluent?" He held up a cruet from the table—a double cruet, of oil and vinegar, its two necks bent in opposite directions. "In dictionary Italian, this is an ampollina. Do you know the idiomatic name?"

Autumn smiled her dimpled smile and said, "It's the su-ocera e nuora, the mother-in-law and daughter-in-law. Because both the spouts cannot pour at the same time."

Florian smiled approvingly back at her. "Zachary, you have indeed found us a treasure." He turned to Fitzfarris. "Sir John, until you acquire some languages, I shall have to do all the dealing with authorities, and every necessary patch-work, and all the talking on the show."

"I'll start learning as fast as I can," Fitz promised.

"Meanwhile," Florian went on, "this afternoon I shall visit a printing shop and order plenty of new paper. Zachary, you and I must also work out a new program, to accommodate the addition of Miss Auburn and the Chinamen. Also, before anything else, I must visit the Livorno municipio, to arrange a tober for tomorrow. How long we will show here—before we move on inland—that depends, of course, on how well we do here."

He looked around the room, at the well-dressed, heartily eating and comfortably chatting other diners, as if estimating their eagerness to be entertained and their ability to pay for it.

"If I might suggest something," said Autumn, and waited for Florian's nod. "Ask the municipio for permission to pitch

in the park of the Villa Fabbricotti. Our ragtag dog-and-pony
Cisalpino couldn't get it, but that park is in the most fashionable part of town.''

''Thank you, my dear. You are proving more valuable
every minute. Can you by any chance play a cornet?''

She laughed and said no, and Carl Beck spoke up. ''Your
Kapellmeister I am. A band of musicians I require, nein?''

Florian raised his hands helplessly. ''We have an energetic drummer, a neophyte accordionist and a spare cornet.
Im Kleinen beginnen, Herr Beck, but we shall hope to
build—''

Stitches Goesle waved his fork around the room and said,
''Deuce, there is all these dagos can sing like Welshmen just,
and can play any instrument you put in their hands.''

''True enough,'' said Florian. ''But most Italians, except
the upper classes, have a dread of traveling any distance from
home. No, here in Europe . . . well . . . Paprika, Pepper, Maggie, I'm sure any of you can tell the canvasmaster.''

The younger women deferred to Magpie Maggie Hag, and
she said, ''Slovaks you want. Slovaks the niggers of Europe.
Every circus uses. They work roustabout—teardown, driving,
setup—then they play band music. So poor their country is,
they leave there, work circuses all over Europe. Get money
in pocket, take it home to families, come out to work circuses
again.''

''Upon my Sam!'' said Goesle. ''So much the better. Let
us hire Slovaks, Carl, to be your band *and* to be my crew.
Looking at your canvas I was, Mr. Florian, and I have an
idea that will double your tent's capacity.''

''Well, until we know what kind of crowds we'll
draw . . .'' Florian began, but Carl Beck spoke up again.

''Also I wish the *Gasentwickler* for the *Luftballon* to get
started. Extra hands for the making of it I will need.''

''Gentlemen, gentlemen,'' pleaded Florian. ''I thought I
had made it plain to you both, that we are starting this tour
with pitifully small capital. Until it is replenished—''

''What can cost the *Gasentwickler*?'' said Beck. ''Some
metal, some wheels, some gum hoses. No great expense. For

working it, the iron filings from any smithy we can get. Only will cost much the carboys of vitriol.''

"Herr Kapellmeister, right now, *any* expense is too much expense.''

Beck looked at Goesle and said, "Our sea pay we have.'' They nodded at one another, and Beck looked to Florian again. "Ein Abkommen. Slovaks you provide, Dai and I investment make in canvas, sheet metal, Musikinstrumente, all necessary. The quicker we have good show, good band, good chapiteau, the quicker we all prosper, nicht wahr?''

"Indubitably,'' said Florian. "And I thank you both for your gesture of good faith. But I fear such a gentlemen's accord would not persuade any Slovaks to join in it. They are a laborer class, and thinking is the one labor they cannot do. The notion of working for shares would be too subtle for their simple intellects. They comprehend only coin in the hand.''

"But they're also accustomed to the holdback,'' said Autumn. "Don't you pay that way in the States?'' She blushed slightly and said, "I seem to be sticking in my oar frightfully often. But our Johnny Scaparey left a crew of Slovaks also marooned here.''

"The holdback, yes,'' murmured Florian, regarding her appreciatively. "Circuses everywhere do it, and so did I, in the solvent years of weekly salary days.'' For the benefit of the inexperienced, he explained, "Every new hand always had his first three weeks' wages withheld, not to be paid until the end of the season. It's an old custom, partly to discourage the good hands from defecting to some better-paying outfit, but partly also a philanthropy—to ensure that the drunkards and wastrels among the crew have at least money to get home on when the show closes.''

"There you are, then,'' said Pepper. "The Slovaks will cost you only their keep, and glad they'll be to get that. They won't know we can't pay 'em. They'll suppose it's merely the old holdback. And if, after three weeks, we still can't pay 'em . . . well, we'll have worse worries than that, me boyos.''

"True, true,'' said Florian. "And we do have funds enough for sustenance. Very well. Herr Beck, Mr. Goesle, you shall have your Slovak crew and bandsmen. You may proceed with your plans.'' Those two immediately put their heads together, while Florian again addressed Autumn. ''You mentioned that some other kinkers had got the shove. What acts? And are they equally hard up that they might join out on a holdback basis?''

''Well . . .'' Autumn said. ''Now you'll think me a dog in the manger. Finding a place for myself and leaving them out. But I truly don't know that you'd want the others.''

''Try me.''

''The only ones that are still in town are the Smodlakas. A family act. Slanging buffers.''

At least half the people at the table looked blank. Florian translated for them, ''A performing dog act.''

''Three mongrel terriers,'' said Autumn. ''Nothing to look at, but jolly good they are. The Smodlakas had Serb names for them—unpronounceable, of course—so I always called the tykes Terry, Terrier and Terriest, and now those are the only names they'll answer to.''

Florian laughed, and asked, ''And what is the drawback to our hiring these Serbians?''

''Well, they include two children, younger than any on your show. A six-year-old girl and a boy of seven or so. It was for the Smodlaka family that I wanted the table leavings.''

''Are the brats mere appendages, or do they work their way?''

''They do. As exhibits. They're both albinos. White hair, white skin, pink eyes.''

''True albinos? Why, there's the beginning of a sideshow for us again, Sir John! A pair of Night People to present alongside our pair of White Pygmies. Why in the world, Miss Auburn, would I *not* want such a family?''

''Because Pavlo, the father, is such an absolute bastard. Everyone on the other show detested him.''

''Aha,'' said Florian softly, and flicked a collusive glance at Edge. ''How does his bastardy manifest itself?''

''He mistreats his family. He never even speaks to the children, and when he addresses his wife he always barks, just like one of his terriers. He's been known to hit her, too. And Gavrila is such a sweet, soft person that everyone hated Pavlo for that.''

"Zachary?" said Florian. "Our replacement focus?"

"If you say so, Governor. When he gets totally insufferable, we can always feed him to his own dogs. We may have to. For somebody who can't pay wages, you're fixing to take on one almighty expense just for sustenance.''

"Speaking of sustenance," said Florian. "Here are the sweet and the bitter to top off our meal. Zabaglione and espresso. Miss Auburn, can you find all those people for us? The Slovaks and the Smodlakas?''

"They're scattered around the city. If I might have an escort . . .''

"I'll go with you," Edge said, before any other man could volunteer. "But let me take you to meet Jules Rouleau before we go. I want to hear what the doctor says about his recuperation.''

When the meal was concluded, Florian left a heap of paper money for the waiters. Mullenax and Yount raised their eyebrows at that, so he admonished them, "Being poor is a disgrace only if it makes you *act* poor. Anyway, that mancia is not as lavish as it appears. A lira is worth just twenty Yankee cents. Which reminds me. All of you new arrivals ought to change your American money and begin to practice at calculating in lire.''

The whole troupe went to the hotel desk to do that. The Gran Duca's resident physician was waiting there, a Dottore Puccio, so Florian led him to Rouleau's room, accompanied by Edge and Autumn, and Carl Beck and Magpie Maggie Hag trailed along.

"Madonna puttana," muttered the doctor, when he lifted the sheet of the invalid's bed and saw the bran box. "È una bella cacata." Autumn tittered at that, but did not translate for Edge.

Dr. Puccio had reason to exclaim. The bran in the box had been replenished from time to time, as the marauding mice or rats or both had eaten at it. But the grain was intermingled with the rodents' droppings and a goodly admixture of coal-fire soot. Toward the bottom of the box, where the bran had got matted by the drizzle of the various medicaments applied to the leg's flesh wounds, it had also gone quite green with mold.

The leg was likewise a ghastly-looking object when he lifted it from the box: shrunken, discolored by the bran and wrinkled like a twig. The doctor continued to mutter—"*Sono rimasto . . . cose da pazzi . . . mannaggia!*"—as he swabbed the leg clean and then prodded and manipulated and scrutinized it. Still, the leg was whole, and it bent only in the places where it should, and its flesh wounds were now only scars.

Dr. Puccio looked around at the others in the room, with a threatening scowl, and in perfect English demanded, "Who prescribed this lunatic treatment for the injuries? No physician, surely."

"The bran box was my doing," Edge confessed. "It worked once for a horse I was reluctant to shoot."

The doctor snorted at him, then glared at Florian. "Signore, you did not inform me that I was being called to examine a veterinary patient." He raked his gaze around the others again. "Aside from this *merdoso* box, what attentions were given?"

"Cleaned wounds with carbolic," said Magpie Maggie Hag. "After, used basilicon ointment, Dutch drops, cataplasms of emollient herbs."

"Gesù, matto de legare," said the doctor to himself. Then he announced angrily, "None of this should have been done. Utter stupidity, peasant remedies, horse cures, unforgivable meddling." The troupers looked contrite and Rouleau looked worried. But the doctor gave an Italianate shrug of shoulders, arms, hands and eyebrows, and continued:

"Nevertheless, it all worked. You people could not possibly know why, so I shall tell you. None of those ridiculous old-wife nostrums of yours, signora, could have prevented the fomites and miasms of corruption from getting into the wounds. This patient should rightly have died of the frenzy fever. As for this—this *merda*—these recrementitious husks of grain"—he disgustedly sifted a hand throught the bran—"you might as well have packed the limb in sawdust. *Except.*

Surely you were all too ignorant to expect it, but the bran spontaneously generated these aspergillus fungi.'' He fingered the nasty mold in the box. ''It is known to physicians— *but only to physicians*, not to dilettanti lay persons like yourselves—that certain of the aspergilli have a subjugating effect on the fomites of disease. This green mold, this particular green mold, this alone, healed the patient's limb and preserved his life.''

''We did good, then, hey?'' said Magpie Maggie Hag, and she cackled.

Dr. Puccio gave her a sour look. ''Good is the prognosis, at least. The leg will require frequent massage with olive oil to restore its muscularity and flexibility. It will be two or three centimeters shorter than the other leg. You will walk with a limp, signore, but you will walk.''

''I am by trade an acrobat, Dottore. Will I leap again? Jump, bound, vault?''

''I doubt it, and I disencourage it. After all, the limb was not set and mended by a professional, but by ignorantes, however well-meaning.'' He gave another daunting look around at them.

''But you have a whole new career, Monsieur Roulette,'' said Florian. ''As an aéronaute extraordinaire. Chief Beck here is about to commence the construction of a gas generator for the *Saratoga*.''

''Zut alors! Then my accident has liberated me forever from the dull, flat ground. I must be grateful to it. And to you, Zachary and Mag, my ignorant, meddling amis.''

The visitors left the room and, in the hall, Carl Beck said. ''Bitte, Herr Doktor. A work of advice, if I may request? You shall already be perceiving that my hair is thinning.''

''Yes. What of it? So is mine.''

''Your professional opinion of this medication I merely wish to ask.'' Beck pulled from a pocket the bottle of potion Magpie Maggie Hag had given him.

''Is *that* what I have been smelling on you?'' The doctor turned to the gypsy. ''What is it?''

With a good imitation of his own supercilious air, she said loftily, ''Old-wife nostrum.''

For the first time, the doctor's eyes twinkled. He uncorked Beck's bottle and sniffed at it. "Aha! Yes! Per certo. I can distinguish the secret ingredients. But fear not, signora, I will not divulge them. Ja, mein Herr, this therapeutant should serve the purpose as admirably as anything known to medical science."

"*Danke, Herr Doktor,*" Beck bowed to him, then to Magpie Maggie Hag. "I was not disbelieving, I assure you, gnädige Frau. But it is a comfort from a professional an expertise to have."

Trying not to laugh aloud, the others departed. Edge and Autumn went on, out of the hotel, he carrying for her the ample paper sack of leftovers from the meal. Florian and Magpie Maggie Hag watched them go, and Florian asked idly, "What do your gypsy instincts say, Mag? About the hiring of the new people?"

"I dukker yes, hire them all. All except that rakli."

"The girl?" Florian blinked. "Surely you can't see any danger in Autumn Auburn."

"No. Beautiful, loving rakli, her. Make fine artiste. For Zachary, make fine romeri."

"Wife? Well, well. Do you foresee jealousy from—?"

"No. Even Sarah be not jealous of so good a rakli. In Autumn Auburn, no danger, only hurt."

"Oh, damnation, Mag! Save the mystic ambiguity for the jossers. How am I supposed to interpret that?"

She shrugged. "I dukker no more than that. No danger, only hurt."

In the piazza, when Autumn put up her pale-yellow parasol, and the late afternoon sun shone even more sunnily through it onto her auburn hair and piquant face, Edge could not help exclaiming, "You are the prettiest thing I have ever seen."

"Grazie, signore. But you've been in Italy less than a day. Wait until you've seen a sampling of the signorine in these streets."

"I'll never see them. Your dazzle is too bright. Will you marry me?"

She pretended to ponder the question, and finally said, "Mrs. Edge. It sounds like a female sword swallower."

"Anything is an improvement on Miss Cubbidge. But if you insist, I'll become Mr. Auburn."

"I don't insist on anything, Zachary, including marriage. Why don't we, for a while, do what the common folk call 'practice to marry'?"

He gulped and groped for words. "Well . . . fine. But that's an even blunter proposal than mine was."

"I hope it doesn't frighten you off. I am not a wanton, but neither am I *achingly* respectable. I wanted you the moment I met you, despite the grumpy greeting you gave me."

"That was self-defense. The sight of you nearly knocked me over."

"Then we both knew from the start. Would it not be foolish of us to delay through all the trivia of flirtation and courtship and being teased by our friends and the publishing of banns and . . ."

"Yes. Why don't we go back to the hotel right now and—"

"No. I may not be righteous, but I will be fair. I will make you look at what you could be wooing instead. There—look at that lissome lass. Is she not gorgeous?"

"She's no trial to look at, no, ma'am. But I'd lay money that she'll be fat before she's forty."

"How do you know I won't? Very well—that one. You cannot fault her. The girl with flowers in her hair."

"Autumn, you have flowers in your eyes. Stop pointing out prospects. I've got the one I want."

"Ah, lackaday. Impetuous man."

"Can we turn back now?"

"Certainly not. We are on a mission for the Governor. Meanwhile, Zachary, leave off staring at me and look about you. This is your first day in a new country, on a new continent. You should be devouring the sights like any Cook's tourist."

Now that Edge and Autumn had come a considerable way inland from the harborside smells of coal smoke, steam, salt and fish, Livorno was more of a treat for the nose than for the eyes. The advancing twilight was made misty and sweet by the wood smoke that drifted from kitchen doorways. From every front garden and window box came the tart, pungent, no-perfume-nonsense smells of old-fashioned flowers: zinnias, marigolds, chrysanthemums. Autumn even showed Edge a little city park that was pure fragrance: a cool-smelling fountain in a grove consisting entirely of aromatic lemon trees. Even now in the early fall they were all still laden with fruit that was evidently public property. Numerous urchins were climbing the trees to pick the lemons, filling cans and jars with water from the clear fountain, mixing the fruit juice and the water to make lemonade to peddle on the streets.

There were beggars everywhere, even in the most elegant neighborhoods, and not all were as enterprising as the lemonade children. Most of them merely squatted or lay about on the sidewalks, their sleeves or trousers or skirts pulled up to exhibit awful sores. They plucked at the passing Edge and Autumn, and uniformly, monotonously whined, "Muoio di fame . . ."

"I perish of hunger," Autumn translated. "Don't feel sorry for them. More than half are ablebodied humbugs, and even the real cripples could find work mending nets on the docks."

So Edge gave alms to only one beggar, because that one looked genuine and because he did not pester them. In fact, he was identifiable as a beggar only by the card hung around his neck: CIECO. He wore opaque eye goggles and he was being hauled along the street by a dog straining at its leash, trotting its master too rapidly to give him much opportunity to accost anybody. Edge almost forcibly had to stop them to put a copper into the man's hand. The blind man breathlessly gasped, "Dio vi benedica," shook his head despairingly, pointed to the dog that still scrabbled to keep going, and told Edge something.

Autumn listened, laughed and said, "Give him a bit more, Zachary. He says he used to have a well-trained lead dog. It would stop of its own accord whenever it saw a good prospect for a handout, and it would wait patiently while he unfolded the sad history of how he used to be a prosperous tanner, until he fell into one of his vats and was blinded by the acid. But that dog died, and this new one is hopeless. He says, 'Now, when this dog stops, I often find myself telling my life story to just another dog.' '' She laughed again, and so did the blind man, ruefully. ''Do give him more, Zachary. Those coins are only centesimi. Give him a whole lira.''

As they walked on, Edge remarked to Autumn that the Smodlakas were residing in quite a fancy district for troupers out of work. But then she led him around behind one of the mansions, and he saw that the Smodlakas were inhabiting only one end of a woodshed on the property. The head of the family, a man about Edge's age, with a great deal of blond hair and beard, was sitting on the shed's doorless doorstep, moodily whittling at a stick.

He looked up at Autumn's approach, gave no greeting, but made a wry face, hacked gloomily at his stick and said in English, ''One must have something to do when one is doing nothing.''

''Instead of splinters, you could at least carve a doll for the children. Pavlo, this is Zachary Edge, equestrian director of a new show that just landed from abroad. He is here to offer you a try at a place on the show.''

''Svetog Vlaha!'' the man exclaimed. He bounded to his feet, pumped Edge's hand and bawled greetings at him in a number of languages. Edge replied, ''Pleased to meet you,'' so Smodlaka spoke mostly English from then on, including the command he bellowed into the shed's dark interior, ''My darlings, come! Come and give welcome!''

Edge was really looking forward to meeting the albino children and even the downtrodden wife, but what came hurtling out of the dark, making joyful noises, were three small, scruffy mongrel dogs. Smodlaka immediately gave orders—''Gospodín Terry, pravo! Gospodja Terrier, stojim! Gospodjica Terriest, igram!''—and the dogs began skipping around Edge, one upright on its hind legs, one walking upside down on its forefeet, the other merrily turning head over heels.

Autumn gave Pavlo a look of vexation, leaned into the shed and called, ''Gavrila, children, you may come out, too.''

When the first of those ventured shyly to the doorway, twisting her hands in a patchwork apron, Pavlo interrupted his commands to the capering dogs—"Woman, fetch wine!"—and she whisked back out of sight as if he had tripped a spring.

Pavlo continued to bark like a dog at the dogs, while they, as silently and efficiently as the Florilegium's three Chinese, went on with their frantic cavorting. The woman appeared again after a minute, bearing a leather wineskin and three painted wooden cups. Without command, she filled and handed the cups to Autumn, Edge and her husband, then resumed twisting her apron. From behind the breadth of that apron, one on either side, peered out faces like wax topped by hair like flax.

"My woman," grunted Smodlaka, barely inclining his head in her direction. "Her hatchlings." He clashed his cup against Edge's and took a slurp from it.

"They have names," said Autumn. "Gavrila, this is Zachary Edge. Zachary, the little ones are Velja and Sava."

"Zdravo," they all said, and shyly shook his hand.

The mother was as Slavic blonde, fair-skinned and blue-eyed as the father, and she was quite a pretty woman, in a broad-faced and chunky-bodied way. But the two children were so extremely bleached as to be indistinguishable of sex, and their waxen faces appeared almost featureless—pale nostrils, pale lips, pale brows and lashes—except for their startling eyes: red pupils centering silvery-gray irises that flashed bright pink when they caught a ray of light.

Gavrila warily eyed her husband before asking the visitors, "Have you yet eaten, gospodín, gospodjica? We have bread, cheese. We have wine. We have everything."

"We have dined, thank you," said Autumn, and handed her the paper bag. "Here are some more goodies to supplement your everything, dear. Now we have other errands."

"But you have not yet seen my darlings' entire routine," Pavlo protested. The dogs were still frenetically doing their act, now leaping over one another in a complicated dancelike sequence.

"Take your *darlings*," said Autumn, "and your family, and show them to Monsieur Florian at the Hotel Gran Duca. I'm sure he will like them and engage them. Do you know where I can find the Slovaks?"

"Prljav," Smodlaka said contemptuously. "They are all doing beggar work at the railroad depot. Carrying bags, hoping for mancia. Debasing themselves."

"While you sit and whittle in unblemished prestige," said Autumn. To Gavrila she said, "I'll hope to see you and the children on the show tomorrow. Come, Zachary, I know where the station is."

It was not far away. Like most railroad depots, it was fairly new and—because a railroad, for all its noise and dirt, was a proud acquisition for any community—had been erected in the very heart of the city, built big and ornate, faced with Carrara marble. It overvaulted two immense marble platforms, alongside two sets of tracks, one incoming, one outgoing, and that area of the station looked neither new nor proud: already begrimed with soot and shadowed by a permanent pall of smoke hanging under the girdered glass roof.

One train had just come in from Pisa, and the passengers were elbowing, pushing, all but fighting each other to get out of the compartments and dash to relieve themselves in the depot's toilets. Edge was interested to notice that the European locomotives were coal-fired, like the steamship *Pflicht-treu*. The engines puffed out less voluminous smoke clouds than did the wood-fired American trains Edge was used to seeing—and evidently fewer sparks; these locomotives did not wear the big, bulging spark catchers atop their smokestacks. But their effluent of smoke and ash was greasier, filthier and more inclined to befoul the train's coaches, passengers, station surroundings and even the countryside along the right of way.

After the desperate egress of its passengers, the train disgorged an astonishing quantity of luggage they had brought: satchels, trunks, carpetbags, portmanteaux and a great number of huge, flat wooden crates. Each was of a size to contain a

sizable tabletop, but evidently did not, for it required only a
single porter to lift it from the luggage van to the platform.
Edge looked more closely at one of the boxes and saw that
it was stenciled CRINOLINA.

"Does that mean what I think it means?" he asked Autumn. "There's nothing in that big crate but hoopskirts?"

"Just one," she said. "One gown's collapsible hoop. One
to each crate. How else would you expect a woman to transport her wardrobe's understructures? Ah, look. One of those
porters is Aleksandr Banat."

She beckoned to a short, squat, shabby man, who instantly
came to her, doffing his shapeless cap so he could tug his
forelock. Autumn spoke to him in Italian, and he replied with
grunts and an occasional word in the same language. Then
he tugged his front hair so hard that he bowed. Then he motioned for Autumn and Edge to follow him, along the depot
platform to where the tracks emerged into daylight.

"He says he and all his fellow Slovaks are living in squat-
ters' shacks beyond the freight yard." Autumn explained.
"Pana Banat is sort of the chief of them. You may have
noticed that he has a whole inch and a *half* of forehead. He
also has some Italian and even some grasp of English."

They picked their way over tracks and sleepers and
switches and between sidelined coaches and goods wagons.
On the outskirts of the rail yards, they came to a veritable
township of shacks built of cast-off materials—rusty old corrugated metal, pasteboard, canvas, but mostly leaned-together
CRINOLINA crates. The populace of ragged, dirty men and a
few ragged, dirty women either sat about in listless boredom
or stirred tin cans hung over scrap fires or picked vermin from
the seams of their rags or sullenly regarded the newcomers.
Banat went among the shanties and came back with half a
dozen men. They could have been his blood kin, they so
closely resembled him—dark, hairy, barrel-built. Banat, with
flourishes, introduced them individually and effusively, but
Edge could grasp only that all their names were prefixed with
Pana, and all their names sounded like gargles.

"He says Pana Hrvat can play the cornet," Autumn translated. "And he himself can play the accordion, and Pana

Srpen even *owns* a trombone, and Pana Galgoc and Pana Chytil can play various other instruments. Anyway, they're all eager to work. Crew or band or both.'' She gave Banat instructions. ''Pana Banat will round up all of them—there are five or six more—and take them straight-away to meet Pana Florian.''

But first Banat led Autumn and Edge out of the shanty warren, back to the city proper, so they would not have to retrace their way through the rail yard, for darkness was coming on. They found themselves in a mercantile, working-class part of Livorno, where the night and the nighttime sea fog were oozing together through the narrow, crooked streets. The municipal lamplighters were hurrying at their work, to keep apace of the darkness. The lamps they kindled shone blurrily through the mist, lighting the shopfronts and street stalls and pushcarts of knife grinders, pasta makers, coral carvers, cheesemongers, mallow gatherers, birdseed sellers, porcelain menders, all still crying their wares and services to the passersby hurrying home for the night.

Then there came down the street a considerable number of people walking together in a clump. As they passed a lamp standard they became recognizable as a crowd of beggars—all ragged and filthy, some covered with sores, others crippled and hobbling, a few actually shuffling on all fours—but there was something even more odd about the man leading the bunch and walking normally.

''It's Foursquare John Fitzfarris,'' said Edge, and hailed him. ''We've been out collecting new troupers, Fitz. What in God's name are these you've been collecting?''

''Damned barnacles,'' said Fitz. ''I came out for a walk, because in every new town I like to find out some of the best places''—he grinned—''and all of the worst ones. Instead, I found myself leading this scurvy beggars' parade.'' He glared at the mob of old and young, male and female. They were not plucking at his clothes or whining ''Muoio di fame''; they were simply studying him in a sort of dumb wonderment. ''I've thrown them every copper I possess, but I can't get rid of them. I think they think I'm one of their own.''

Autumn made inquiry in Italian, and a couple of the beggars muttered replies. She said to Fitz, "They're hoping to discover how you got your face half-blue like that. It seems you're unique among the profession. No doubt they want to try it themselves."

"Goddamn," growled Fitz. "I'd like to *show* them how it was done. Serve them right. I never saw such an assembly of frauds. At times in my life, I've been on the cringe myself, so I know the real from the fake. See that one there? With all those revolting ulcers and scabs on his face and arms?"

"They look real to me," said Edge. "And horrible."

"That's the scaldrum dodge. You slap a thick layer of soap on your skin, then sprinkle it with vinegar. It blisters up, looks gruesome as hell, like advanced leprosy or something. Now, that fellow yonder, he's a bogus epilept. Falls down in the gutter, throws a fit of flailing and foaming, draws a sympathetic crowd of good Samaritans. Then that skinny woman—his wife, maybe—she slithers among the Samaritans and picks all their pockets. I'd like to hope I'm not going to have this rabble trailing me all through Italy."

Autumn immediately gave the crowd a blistering of Italian invective. They quailed and dispersed and trickled away down various alleys. Fitzfarris thanked her wholeheartedly and said from now on he wouldn't come outdoors without his cosmetic mask, and he accompanied Edge and Autumn back to the Gran Duca. When the three made their way through the front door, they found the lobby full of people who were not the usual well-dressed loungers.

"Florian's holding court," explained Mullenax, who was looking on and smoking a twisty black Italian cigar. Its rank aroma did not quite disguise Mellenax's own ripe breath, which suggested that he had early found the hotel's bar-room and well availed himself of it. "He's been lookin' at the conduct books of all them new folks you sent, Miss Auburn. He's already done hired the dog couple, and got 'em a room here. Now he's talkin' to all them workmen."

Edge asked Autumn, "Reckon I ought to help him with the sizing up of them? You can interpret for me."

"No," she said firmly. "We have practicing to do, remember?"

So, early though it was, they said good night to Fitzfarris and Mullenax and retired forthwith. Edge had been allotted a room to himself, and they went there instead of to Autumn's caravan, because she wanted to take advantage of the hotel's bathing facilities. A maid was sent running to draw the bath, and she shortly came back to lead Autumn there and assist in the ablutions. Autumn went fully dressed, except for her hat and parasol, because she had no dressing wrapper and the bath was a considerable journey distant through the halls. For the same reason, she returned to Edge's room completely dressed.

"Not to provoke any scandal," she said to him, "I have just now had to undo all my buttons and laces and things, and then, after the bath, to do them all up again. A tiresome business, being modest."

"Then let us be immodest," he suggested, "and really scandalous. Allow me to do the next undoing for you."

For the first time in his life, Edge had the ineffable delight of undressing with his own hands a delectable woman clad in the numerous layers and elaborations of European street attire. For the rest of his life, he would never forget the novelty, the nuances, the intricacies of that night's particular preliminary to the making of love. It was like a chaste defloration to be enjoyed before the actual union—like gently loosing the petals, one by one, from a peony or a camellia or some such many-petaled flower.

While Autumn submitted to his ministrations, she wore—in addition to everything else she was wearing—that mischievous about-to-smile expression of hers, complete with dimples. She stood patiently in the middle of the lamplit room like a child being readied for bed by her nanny. Edge being no nanny, his denuding of her took quite a long time, but it was for him a deliciously anticipatory time. And, as he went about it, his combination of painstaking carefulness and fumbling eagerness seemed to excite Autumn as well. She trembled, slightly but perceptibly, whenever she felt his touch on her body.

Edge began, after some study and deliberation, by unhooking and lifting away the amber bead garniture that edged her costume's low neckline. When that decoration was removed, the pale-yellow percale beneath was loose enough to reveal the shadowed cleft between the upper rounds of her breasts. That made Edge pause and gaze in pure appreciation for a minute, and *that* made Autumn take a deep, tremulous breath, and *that* made her breasts all the more interesting to observe. Then Edge collected himself and considered the next step, and decided it was to undo the extremely tiny imitation smoked pearl buttons of her sleeves' embroidered cuffs. They were maddeningly difficult for his man-sized and inexpert fingers, but next were the larger buttons that closed the percale blouse at the back, and they were easier. However, when they were undone, something was still holding the two halves of the blouse together between Autumn's shoulderblades. She had to assist for the first time—reaching her hands behind her to show him how a hook-and-eye worked. Then, to help further, she shrugged loose of the blouse and peeled it down her arms and threw it onto the bed.

The next layer under the blouse was a complex of sateen-and-elastic straps running over her shoulders, crisscrossing her white cambric chemise to attach to her yellow percale skirt. Edge investigated and discovered that the loops could be unbuttoned from the skirt's waistband. Then the lacings of that band around her waist had to be untied. Then another lacing all the way down the back of the skirt had to be unthreaded from the eyelets of seams concealed by a ruffle. When those things had been attended to, Autumn unwound the yellow skirt from around her and tossed it, too, onto the bed. She was still enveloped from waist to ankle by the contraption that had supported the bell skirt—horizontal hoops of stiff wire hung from each other on tapes, graduated in size from small at her hip level to extravagant at ankle level. But only another unbuttoning from the arrangement of straps was required, and the hoops collapsed around her feet in a ring of concentric circles. She stepped out of that enclosure, kicked it to one side and kicked off her little yellow kid slippers at the same time.

Autumn was still by no means naked, but she was rather

more naked than most women would have been at that stage of the proceedings. She wore no corset cover, and no boned corset under it to pinch her waist smaller, and no padded ''dress form'' to lend her a false bosom. She did not require any such artificial enhancements. Though she continued to stand like an obedient child being readied for bed—and stood perhaps no taller than one of the Simms girls—Autumn Auburn could not have been mistaken for a child. Above and below the waist that Edge could almost span with his two hands, her breasts and hips and buttocks were beautifully of woman proportions.

The next visible layer of dress was the sleeveless, waist-length white cambric chemise held up by narrow shoulder strings, and a full underskirt of tiered Valenciennes lace, the cheap machine-made sort. When Edge untied the ribbons that bound the skirt about her waist and it crumpled to the floor, it revealed another layer of apparel underneath. Autumn still wore a pair of drawers—finely pleated, edged with Hamburg lace—and garter-supported stockings of Richelieu-ribbed lisle, rather gaudily striped blue and white at the thigh tops, but of pale yellow the length of her legs, and with vandyke work ornamenting the ankles.

Edge did the rolling down of the stockings one at a time and very slowly—both to enjoy the gradual, exceedingly provocative revelation of her bare legs and to enjoy the tremor his slow motion induced in Autumn herself. She was hardly trembling for shame; her legs were not anything to be ashamed of; they would have graced any classical statue of a dancing nymph. They were firm with muscle, but not muscular, most delicately molded, sheathed in peach-colored skin that was as inviting of caress as real peaches are. Edge would have expected the soles of a ropewalker's feet to be tough and callused, but Autumn's were as velvety to his touch as were her calves and thighs, and he realized they probably *had* to be kept soft—sensitive to every quiver of the tightrope.

When the stockings were off, he rose to his feet and looked her over, with both satisfaction and calculation: the next layer had to be the ultimate. She now wore only the scanty chemise on her upper body and the drawers below. When he lifted the chemise up over her head, that brought her arms up, too. So he observed that Autumn did not subscribe to the practice of Pepper and Paprika: retaining the tufts of hair under their arms to excite the male rubes. Autumn was clean-shaven and smooth there, and in each armpit was a minor constellation of auburn freckles. That seemed a trifle odd, since she had not a single freckle on her face or throat or shoulders or—as was obvious when the chemise came off—anywhere else on her upper body. Edge would later deem it an appealing feature of Autumn's, and one known only to him: that all of her few small brown freckles were neatly tucked under her arms, and no others interrupted the pearly perfection of her body. But right now he was too pleased contemplating the more evident and even more appealing features of her.

The lifting off of her chemise made her breasts bounce merrily, as if they rejoiced to be free of even that light confinement, and they were a sight to make a man rejoice along with them. But Edge devoted only a moment to that. As he bent to take hold of the elastic waistband of the girl's last concealing garment, he bestowed a quick passing kiss on each of the auburn buds perkily upraised from its auburn halo. Then he slid the skimpy garment down past the triangle of auburn curls, still damp from Auburn's bath—and he kissed there, too, on the way—down to her pretty feet, and he kissed each of those as she stepped out of that final bit of cloth goods.

Kneeling where he was, Edge could now observe that Autumn was delightfully flower-petaled in her most secret part, as well as in her eyes. Her thighs were slightly apart, and she was aroused and invitingly open down there, and there peeked out dainty, glistening ruffles of soft pink, like the fluted edges of dew-damp petunia blossoms. After a minute or so of his simply gazing adoringly at that part of her, Autumn said in a shaky voice, but teasingly, "You did not quite finish the job. I am still not *entirely* naked." She lifted up her waves of auburn hair to show him the tiny imitation smoked pearls clipped to her earlobes.

"You can leave those on, if you want," said Edge. "If

you don't want to be *entirely* immodest and shameless and scandalous.''

"Oh, but I do!" she cried, unclipping the eardrops and tossing them away. "I do!" she sang, flinging herself on the bed. "I do, I do!"

2

AS AUTUMN smiled and slowly spread her legs, the crowd roared *"Brava!"* and then *"Bravissima!"* as she gracefully slid down to a stride split on the tightrope, and Bandmaster Beck tinkled a sweet descending arpeggio on his string of little tin bells.

It was a straw house—a *"sfondone!"* Florian had declared it, with some astonishment but with great satisfaction. He *had* got the Livorno authorities' permission to pitch in the park of the Villa Fabbricotti—"and for a trifling five percent of the ticket receipts," he reported. "They'll even trust me to do the calculations. I begin to believe that *all* the officeholders in this young Kingdom of Italy are still too new at their posts to have learned the clerkly delights of obfuscation and extortion."

Early in the morning, Florian and Canvasmaster Goesle and Crew Chief Banat and the dozen other Slovaks had driven the animals and wagons to the ungrassed athletic field in the park, and set up the chapiteau and the seats and tamped the ring curb. The roustabouts knew their business—they even chanted a Slovak version of the heeby-weeby as they worked—and the only helper they needed was elephant Peggy. Florian did not lay a hand to a mallet or a rope; he participated only to the extent of pointing and suggesting and approving. He smiled broadly, in fact, watching the Slovaks hammer two stakes at a time into the ground, six men to each, all swinging the sledges in a rhythmic blur that made a burst of noise like a fast drum tattoo.

The artistes of the company ambled out of the Hotel Gran Duca after a leisurely breakfast and took their time about arriving at the *tober* and getting into costume. Meanwhile, there was yet no paper to post about town, and no time to get a notice into any local newssheet. So, as soon as Peggy had finished her part in erecting the pavilion, she was attired in the red blanket and became Brutus. Hannibal got arrayed as Abdullah, and Florian rehearsed him in a few simple words of Italian. Abdullah set out proudly—''speakin' furrin, fust time ever,'' as he put it—beating his drum and bawling, ''Segue al circo! Al parco! Al spettacolo!''

And by show time that afternoon, the city folk had come swarming—well-dressed gentry from the Fabbricotti neighborhood roundabout; middle-class merchants and their families from downtown; seamen, naval cadets, fishermen and dockworkers from the harborside—and all paying in lire, not in barter goods.

Gavrila Smodlaka said shyly to her new colleagues, ''Gospodín Florian must possess some magic. The other show never drew like this. Gospodja Hag, did you work some gypsy enchantment?''

''No,'' said Magpie Maggie Hag. ''But if there be ever any magic anywhere around, Florian he will grab onto it.''

There had been warm applause for the come-in spec, even though the ''All hail, you ladies, gentlemen'' was sung in English; and for the violent voltige of Buckskin Billy, Dauntless Reinsman of the Plains; and for Barnacle Bill and his talented pigs; and for the Smodlakas and their even more talented dogs; and for the Chinese antipodists performing first in trio, then with Brutus and the teeterboard and the surviving Simms children; and for Pepper and Paprika on the perchpole—and quite hysterical acclaim when the little old birthday lady, ''Signora Filomena Fioretto, bisnonna di settenta anni,'' turned out to be the vivacious Madame Solitaire. But not until Autumn Auburn danced out upon her tightrope did the audience so boisterously proclaim its enthusiasm.

Now she was stretched in her stride split, one leg forward along the rope, the other backward, balanced there with no assisting prop except the pale yellow parasol. Her ring dress was very simple: a low-cut sleeveless blue léotard, flesh-colored tights on her legs, flesh-colored soft slippers on her feet. And the costume was unusual in being not spangled at all. Instead, Autumn had lightly oiled her bare shoulders and arms and bosom, and on the oil had sprinkled random dustings of a gold and silver glitter powder. "It is called diamanté," she told Edge, when he admired the effect. The effect was that, when she moved, she gave off no sharp slivers of light, but the exposed portions of her own flesh gleamed and glinted in a manner even more provocative.

Bandmaster Beck rang several upward-lilting arpeggios on his little bells as Autumn levitated from her split, slowly scissoring her legs together again and levering herself upright on the rope. She did a pirouette there, then twinkled along the rope to its platform end and threw up her arms in an exuberant V. The Slovak who had provided his own trombone and the Slovak who had been assigned the cornet blared some kind of Slovak hurrah. For the first time since Edge had been on the show, he not only heard, he *felt* the concussion of the massed clapping and shouts and whistles and cheers.

Every female of the company had been watching Autumn's début performance with the eyes of cats. Paprika murmured, half in admiration, half in envy, "But she is magnificent, that one. And she is beautiful." She turned to Pepper. "You and I got no such applause."

"We might do," her partner replied through her teeth, "if our act wasn't going all to ballyhack. I wish you'd put your mind again on your under-stander, and not up every other woman's winkle."

"Vulgar cow," said Paprika, and strode away. She went to the other side of the ring, where she engaged Sarah in close converse. Clover Lee had been standing with her mother, but she gave Paprika a chilly look and sidled away from them.

Edge had run into the ring to take Autumn's hand as she came down her ladder, and they both threw up their arms, to a renewed burst of clapping. Then Equestrian Director Edge blew a shrill blast on his whistle, and that brought four canvas-trousered Slovaks trotting into the ring. Two of them began dismantling the tightrope apparatus, two began working the ropes at the center pole to prepare the hoist for Pepper's solo hair-hang. Meanwhile, the meager band began a

stately *passamezzo,* and Sunday, Ali Baba and Florian also
entered the ring. While Florian commenced the next introduction—"Adesso, signore e signori!"—the Simmses went
into their capers, intended to keep the audience entertained
during the few minutes of working confusion. Ali Baba collapsed onto the ground, his body in a knot, his chin incredibly
propped on his buttocks, his hands and feet sticking out from
impossible places, while Sunday did flying flip-flops back and
forth over him.

"I surely do like that diamanté costume of yours," Edge
said to Autumn, when they were out of the ring. "You looked
like a fairy sprite up there. Also, I owe you a deep bow. I
truly had not expected you to be such an absolute marvel of
an artiste."

"Oh, I have done better performances," she said, professionally self-critical, but then she laughed. "The fact is, damn
it, I'm *sore*. You and I are going to have to moderate our
enjoyments, Zachary, at least on the nights before a show."

"I was worried we might not *have* any more nights. I was
biting my knuckles the whole time you were up there. My
God—splits and jumps and somersaults—landing on a half
inch of hemp . . ."

Autumn flicked a drop of perspiration from her forehead
and said disparagingly, "Zachary, that rope is only a scant
eight feet off the ground. I want Stitches to put my rope right
up under the roof."

Edge looked back at the rig. It was like a very tall sawbuck,
only with a rope substituting for the buck rail. A long-legged
X of wooden beams on either side of the ring held the rope
taut between them, and those X's were braced by a cadrolle
of pulleys and guy ropes outside the ring curbs. One of the
croisé supports was built taller than the other, and provided
a bit of platform, so Autumn could stand and lean there to
rest between exertions. Behind it was the ladder for her ascent
and descent. The shorter X support on the other end of the
rope was her "croisé de face," painted white just above the
rope, to give her, even in poor light, a distinct guidon on
which to fix her eyes and concentration.

"You listen, lady," Edge said sternly to Autumn. "You

want to ask *Stitches* to put you up higher? The equestrian director also gets consulted on projects involving any danger."

"Then regard it, my dear, like a director, not like an anxious papa. If I ever fell, I assure you, even eight *inches* off the ground, I should be irredeemably disgraced . . . Pepper, you lunatic mick, what in the world are you doing?"

"Yours is a difficult act to follow, Sassenach woman," growled Pepper. She was waiting for Florian to conclude her lengthy introduction. Meanwhile she was doubled over, had got one hand inside her tights, and was groping at a rather intimate area of herself. "But one thing I know—dagos have an appetite for spice." She got hold of what she was after, the cache-sexe at the crotch of her fleshings, and yanked it out, then hastily rearranged her costume and grinned wickedly. "So, begod, I'm going to flash them the upright grin."

"Ecco! L'audace Signorina Pepe!" Florian finally announced, and the music blared into a fanfare, and Pepper casually tossed the cache-sexe to Edge and danced blithely into the pista.

Yount the Quakemaker, who would go on next, came to stand with Edge and Autumn. They watched as two of the Slovaks hauled on the rope that lifted Pepper by her chignon, and the two musician Slovaks played the music she had earlier sung to them. At that, Yount said in amazement, "Miss Autumn, how come them foreigners of yours know that song: It's 'The Bonnie Blue Flag.' "

"It's 'The Irish Jaunting Car,' " Autumn corrected him, "And that Irisher is jaunting, right enough."

Pepper had extended her arms and legs sideways as soon as she was raised from the ground, and she stayed in that cruciform position all the way up to the lungia boom from which she hung. Then, before starting her acrobatics, she clapped her legs together, and her tights of course creased in the cleft between them. Since her tights were flesh-colored all over, except for their tracery of green sequins, she looked quite unabashedly nude up there. The women in the audience made sotto voce comments and the men made rather loud ones. But the remarks were all admiring, not appalled or denunciatory, as they would have been in the part of the world Pepper had recently come from.

Clover Lee grumbled, "Florian would give *me* Hail Columbia if I went on without my cache-sexe. And her, he's not even watching. Where did he go?"

"The king is in his countinghouse," said Fitzfarris, beside her. "I think he's been running to the red wagon between every two acts, just to finger the heaps of lire. But here he comes again."

"Sir John," Florian said immediately, without even looking up at the focus of everyone else's attention, "we'll break for intermission right after the Quakemaker, so you can start getting your sideshow ready. Let's see . . . you won't need Ali Baba. I want to send a message back to the hotel, and the lad can run a note to—"

"Send my woman," said Pavlo Smodlaka. "She speaks Italian, needs no note. And I have already commanded her to change into street dress. Woman! Come here!"

"Very well," said Florian. "Gavrila, I told the Gran Duca that only Monsieur Roulette would be staying there tonight. But happily we can now afford to keep all our rooms, and I see no reason to deny ourselves that comfort. Will you tell the management to expect our whole troupe back tonight? And for some nights to come. Only the stable facilities we will no longer require. The colored gentlemen and the Slovaks, they will bed down here on the tober to attend all the animals."

"You have the message, woman," said Pavlo. "Go." And she went, like a shot.

Florian took out his mason's pencil and his pocket notebook, and began intently scribbling and muttering to himself, "Item—translate all songs from English. Item—have Mag make ruffs for dogs . . ." From time to time, he distractedly scribbled the pencil in his beard, marring its silveriness.

Sarah slipped close to him and said quietly, "Since we're keeping the rooms, might I drop into yours tonight? I would like—"

"Oh, not tonight, not tonight," Florian said, without interrupting his memoranda, apparently even unaware of who had spoken. "Consultation tonight. All our executive people. Into the wee hours, most likely."

Sarah looked crushed. Fitzfarris shook his head and glanced about at the others nearby. Paprika was smirking in a smug sort of way. Clover Lee was frowning, but Fitz could not tell whether she was annoyed by Florian's rebuff of her mother or his not noticing and raising hell about Pepper's flagrantly revealing attire.

Anyway, by now, the audience was more enthralled by Pepper's daredevil performance than her brazen self-exposure. As she spun and twisted up there, thirty perilous feet above the pista, the crowd was ooh-ing and aah-ing. So was Monday Simms, in her own way. Fitzfarris, going out the back door to ready his sideshow, found Monday peeking in, from behind a fold of the canvas, and ardently rubbing her thighs together.

"I told you not to do that, kid," he snapped.

Monday started and gave him a shamefaced look. Then that turned to a look of genuine appeal, and she said, in a slurred voice, "Yes, and you told me there's better games to play. So show me 'em."

"You keep that up and somebody will, I guarantee it."

"You," she urged.

"Be damned if I'll take advantage of a little tan puppy. I prefer my women older and more experienced. Come see me when you're grown, kid. Right now, get your sister and get set to play pygmy."

She burst out, "How'm I s'posed to get experience if you won't give me it?" But then she clamped her mouth shut— Autumn had emerged from the back door, regarding them with some surprise—and the girl ran off around the side of the tent.

Fitzfarris shrugged and said to Autumn, "Every female in the company seems to be suddenly in heat."

"Oh?"

"And it's your fault."

"Oh?"

"I don't know why it happens, but I've observed it everywhere I've been. As soon as there's a striking new girl in town, so to speak, every other one starts stoking up her biological urges.''

''What's all this about urges?'' Mullenax said jovially, as he lumbered up to them, wearing his new lion-trainer uniform.

Autumn only said, ''I'd have thought Monday Simms was too young to have any kind of urges at all.''

''It's the black blood in her,'' Fitzfarris said. ''The tropical races mature early.'' And he went on his way.

''He's right, y'know,'' said Mullenax. ''A doctor told me once, it's the niggers all the time eatin' the watermelon that does it. He said watermelon is a powerful inspirer of them urges.''

''What utter nonsense,'' said Autumn.

''You think so? You got niggers in that England where you come from? You got watermelons?''

''Negroes, not many. Watermelons, very seldom.''

''Then who're you to say nonsense? You watch that other high-yaller gal—that Sunday Simms—watch the way she yearns at your man. Awright, to git Zack Edge you cut out Ma'am Solitaire, but niggers can cut, too. Lemme tell you, niggers cut with *razors*.''

''Abner, are you drunk?''

''Miss Auburn, I'm goin' in the lion's cage this afternoon. And I've decided it's time I try that head-in-his-mouth business. You think I'm go' do that *sober*?''

There came a tumult from inside the chapiteau, as Pepper finished her performance. But her applause was not quite the tumult Autumn had been accorded, and Pepper wore a disgruntled look when she was wafted down to the ground and the Slovaks helped her unhook her chignon from the rig. She gave the crowd only a cursory couple of bows, then ran out, so the musicians awkwardly let her music trail off, and Florian had to pounce into the ring to commence his introduction of Obie Yount, ''il Creatore del Terremoto.''

On her way to change her clothes, Pepper encountered Quincy Simms. She stopped short, and speculatively looked him over, and said, ''Hey, gossoon, what do you weigh?''

He studied, as if she had set him a deep philosophical

question, and finally said, "Law', mistis, I dunno."

"Well, can't be much. Do you think you could do them contortions of yours while holding to a bar, up in the air?"

He studied again, and finally said he "specked" he could.

"We'll see. Meet me after the night show, and don't change out of your tights. We'll practice."

The Quakemaker, when he had gruntingly lifted and rolled and tossed cannonballs, and had gruntingly had one dropped on his neck—*two* Slovaks, for the effect, gruntingly doing the lifting of it up the ladder—and had lain grunting and grimacing while Lightning the Percheron walked the boards across his chest, got a respectable roar of acclaim, mixed with cries of *"Bravo!"* and *"Bravissimo!"* and here and there *"Fusto!"*

While he took his bows, he said sidelong to Florian at his elbow, "I know what 'bravo' means. But what is 'fusto'?"

"Literally, it means a tree trunk. But it also means 'bravo,' only, um, more so. Surely, when you were in Mexico, you heard the word 'macho.' Same thing. A 'fusto' is a real man's man."

"No fooling?" Yount said in wonderment. And as soon as he could make a graceful exit from the chapiteau, he went directly, manfully, man's-manfully to Paprika Makkai, and inflated his chest and bulged his biceps and said without a trace of timidity, "Mam'selle, would you walk out with me?"

"Miért?" she said, startled out of her other languages.

"My chum Zack says Livorno is a nice town to walk around in. I thought you and me might take a stroll after the show. Maybe have supper together somewhere."

Paprika eyed him thoughtfully, while she recovered her aplomb—and while he manfully maintained the fusto inflation of his chest—then let her eyes go to Sarah, who was hiding a smile. "Why, you are most gracious, Sergeant. I think that would be a pleasing thing to do. But of course we must have a gardedám . . . a chaperon."

"Oh. We must?" His chest deflated a bit. "Well, all right."

"If Madame Solitaire might be persuaded to accompany

us? I believe, madame, you have no other engagements . . .''

The musicians were playing a thin but lively march as Florian proclaimed the interval—and the availability of Magpie Maggie Hag's divinatory servicies. The people chattered and laughed among themselves as they evacuated the pavilion. But quite a few stayed inside and moved down to the front benches to consult the gypsy. Edge observed that, as usual, they were all women. But most of these appeared to be in advanced stages of pregnancy, so they could hardly be wanting advice on how to snare a man. Even more unusual, Magpie Maggie Hag was now carrying a little notebook, like Florian's, and she wrote something in it each time she and a woman had their heads together. Edge took an opportunity, when one big-bellied woman had departed and another was ponderously approaching the gypsy, to ask her what all these imminent mothers wanted to consult her about.

''What you think? They ask if they are going to have a boy or girl.''

''And how do you make your guess?''

''What do you mean, *guess?*'' she said, indignant. ''I am Magpie Maggie Hag! I no guess. Of ten women, nine want boy.''

''And they want to see it in writing?''

''No, no. That is for later, just in case. Here in Europe, circus often stay long enough one place that baby *comes*. If it what I said, boy or girl, mama and papa have much joy, maybe come give me gift. If it not, they maybe come angry at me. So I show them writing, say I no dukkered wrong, you *listened* wrong. Always, see, if I tell woman is boy coming, I write girl. If I tell her girl, I write boy. Now go away. No pester. I making much money.''

Edge chuckled, patted her on the head, and went away. Out in the front yard, Florian was just finishing his oration on the contents of the museum wagon—and these Europeans *did* seem fascinated, as he had said they would be, by the moth-eaten mummies, simply because they were the relics of creatures mostly foreign to these shores. Next, Florian pointed to Fitzfarris, standing nonchalantly on an upended fruit crate—''Un' uomo bizzarro, Sir John il Afflitto Inglese''—and at the sight of the Afflicted Englishman several of the working-class folk in the crowd muttered and made the sign of the cross over themselves. But Edge's attention was taken by a different sight, to him equally bizarre. He went to find Autumn, to ask her, "Do the Italian people smoke *paper?*" and waved a hand around to indicate the many men and women who were apparently doing just that.

She looked faintly surprised that he was so surprised, and said, "You don't have the sigaretta in the States?"

She explained that it was really nothing but a short, thin, mild cigar, only wrapped in paper instead of a tobacco leaf. The sigaretta was becoming popular for occasions like this, or between the acts of the theater, when there was time for only a short smoke, and a whole cigar or a full pipe would be wasted. Women especially liked them, said Autumn, because they were not so odorous as cigars and were more graceful to hold in the hand.

"And now, good people," said Fitzfarris, when the crowd had got its fill of studying his affliction, "allow me to present my fellow monsters. First—here, step up, girls—behold! The world's only pair of genuine White African Pygmies in captivity!"

"I Pigmei Bianchi!" Florian translated, and kept on doing so, as Fitzfarris spun his fancies:

"And now, observe the exact and diametrical opposites in the catalogue of human races—heads up, kids—the Night Children!"

"I Figli della Notte!"

"Born in a cavern, reared in a cavern, never seeing God's sunshine until just a few months ago, when they were by chance discovered and brought forth from their immurement. Regard them well, for their delicate pale skin and sensitive pink eyes cannot long bear this daylight, and they must quickly retire to their accustomed darkness, or suffer most cruelly . . ."

When the wispy little Smodlakas had scampered off, presumably to shelter in darkness, Fitzfarris trumpeted, "And now, let me introduce to you, ladies and gentlemen, *Little Miss Mitten!*"

This caught Florian unprepared, and he stumbled for a translation, "La Fanciulla Guanto . . . er . . . Mezzoguanto . . ."

But the crowd was already laughing, for Fitzfarris had yanked a hand from his side pocket, and the hand was wearing a mitten, brightly painted with eyes, nose and an upper lip on the hand part, a lower lip on the thumb part. He immediately started wiggling his thumb to make the glove appear to talk, meanwhile himself saying—but not moving his own lips—in a high-pitched, shrewish-female voice, "Kept me waiting long enough you did, cuss you, John!"

In his own voice, lips frankly moving, Fitz apologized, "Only saving the best for last, my dear." He then embarked on a few minutes of quarreling with his own hand, in those two voices, and bantering antique jokes, and letting himself be the butt of them all, and giving Miss Mitten all the snappy "Punchinello lines." But the effect was unfortunately diminished by Florian's having to translate both ends of the duologue, and in one voice. Thus, when Fitzfarris plunged the obstreperous mitten back into his pocket (it crying from there in muffled bleats), then brought out his tin swazzles—"Any of you folks can perform the same trick! Amaze your friends! Be the life of every party!"—he sold disappointingly few of them.

So Florian waved a signal to the Slovaks and Hannibal at the tent's front door, and they began playing "Wait for the Wagon" and the jossers threw away their cigarettes and surged back inside the chapiteau.

The second half of the afternoon's program went off without the crowd's enthusiasm waning in the least. Barnacle Bill may have been a bit tottery in his swagger, and his German commands a bit blurry, but he got in and out of Maximus's cage—and in and out of Maximus's jaws—unscathed, and not even pretending to be scratched, for Florian had decided against reinstituting in the act the late Captain Hotspur's "bloody arm" trick. Brutus the elephant dragged a dozen burly and humiliated stevedores around the ring. Abdullah the Hindu juggled, among his many other items, several live and wriggling mullets from Livorno's own waters.

Colonel Ramrod now used one of the Henry repeating carbines for his first trick, and used Sunday and Monday Simms for assistants. He had been pleased to find, in Gran Duca's amply stocked chandlery store, the cartridge ammunition the Henry required. He had pulled the bullets, poured out some of the powder to make a less powerful propellant, and replaced the bullets in the shells. Also, Abdullah had taught the Simms girls to do a rudimentary juggling act, standing well apart and flipping saucers from one to the other so there were always one or two in the air between them. As they tossed the saucers, they stood so that Colonel Ramrod's spent bullets would land harmlessly in the back yard. Across the ring, he worked the carbine's lever and trigger, with indolent ease, and blasted the flying saucers to powder until the girls had no more to throw.

Then, using his familiar old Remington revolver, he shot, from various positions, the five gourds the girls propped up on the ring curb (dried gourds were plentiful and cheap in the Livorno markets), demolishing the fifth one, as he always did now, by aiming with his little mirror and firing bird shot backward over his shoulder. Meanwhile, Clover Lee had taught Sunday how to snatch up surreptitiously one of the spent balls and to stand firm and wear an apprehensive expression and flinch backward when Colonel Ramrod fired the sixth shot "into her teeth." And the audience broke its enjoined breathless silence with a crash of applause.

"All right, I owe a bow, too," said Autumn, when he came out of the ring. "I had no notion that *you* were such an accomplished artiste. I should have suspected, though, when I learned you had the closing spot."

"Florian and I have already decided that you should have it from now on."

"Zachary! I didn't mean to sound bitchy-hinting. I'm *glad* you are as good at your work as I am at mine. I would not want to be billed above my man—or even to feel in secret that I deserve to be. Equal talents but different talents, that's us."

"And I say vive la différence."

"Coo! And 'e's a cultured gent, as well!"

* * *

During the grand-walkaround finale, the Slovaks played the music well enough, but fewer than half of the performers now constituting the troupe could sing the words—"We loved each other then, Lorena"—so most only hummed or mouthed along. The people of the audience did not seem to feel cheated by that. They departed still in good humor, dispersing into the park or climbing into waiting carriages or hailing vetture on the parkside streets or simply sauntering off along the pavements. Magpie Maggie Hag left at the same time, returning to the Gran Duca to see that Rouleau got fed and then to give him his olive oil massage. Yount and Paprika and Sarah hurried away to the wagons to change into street clothes, and then they also strolled off the tober, Yount looking inordinately proud and fusto in the company of two pretty women.

The three of them almost immediately got lost in some of Livorno's more intestinal alleys, but the women did not mind. They dawdled along the narrow and twisty streets, stopping to examine the produce for sale in stalls and on pushcarts, and counting on their fingers to convert the prices of those things into currencies they were better acquainted with.

"Five centesimi!" Sarah exclaimed, at a greengrocer's cart. "That's—let's see—one cent. Look, Paprika, a *whole basket* of grapes for *one penny!* And here . . . greens enough to make a salad for an entire family, only a penny!"

"And here," said Paprika, at a poulterer's. "A pair of plump chickens, only seventy-five centesimi for the two. That's . . . hetvenöt heller . . . fifteen cents in your money, Sarah."

"No wonder Florian was so eager to get here. Why, we can live like royalty on a beggar's income."

After a while, Yount made bold to remind them that they had to be back at the park in time for the evening show. So they went into the first place they found with a TRATTORIA signboard. The proprietor managed to convey to them that he served nothing but a selection of pasta dishes, and they accepted his recommendation of fettuccine alle vongole. The trattore also, without being asked, set down a straw-clad bottle. Yount poured some of its contents into their glasses, and took a taste, and made a face.

"What is this stuff?"

"Chianti," said Paprika, sipping hers with enjoyment.

"What's it good for?"

"Whatever do you mean?"

"Something that tastes this sour ought to be good for curing some ailment."

"Idiota. It is a Tuscan wine."

"It sure ain't elderberry."

"Tuscany is this region of Italy we are now in. Chianti is one of its proudest products. The tartness of the wine is to make you better appreciate the buttery and salty taste of the pasta and the clams."

"Oh." Instructed, now, he attacked his meal as two-fistedly as a strongman ought to do, and Sarah was not far off his pace. But Paprika only picked at her food, evidently preferring to take this opportunity for serious conversation—or rather, to deliver a homily. And Yount gradually found his own gustatory pleasure dwindling, for what Paprika had chosen for a subject was the inadequacy of males as lovers. Perhaps Paprika was being kind, Sarah thought—talking in generalities about "men," rather than saying straight out that she wanted to discourage Yount's oafish wooing. Even if that was so, Obie Yount found it an uncomfortable experience, to hear his whole sex systematically denigrated.

"Men," said Paprika, "are clumsy in courtship, selfish and insensitive in the art of love. They neglect the infinity of subtleties that a woman best enjoys."

Through a mouthful, Yount said, "This sure is good macaroni, ain't it?"

"A man thinks of a woman as nothing more than a receptacle, to be filled with himself. She is expected to be thrilled just to be penetrated. But a woman can be immeasurably more thrilled by attentions to the outside of her, rather than the inside."

"Can I pour you some more of this Canty, Miss Paprika?"

"Not any man can ever know all the wonderfully excitable

little places on the outside of a woman's body. Only another woman can."

Sarah, eating with gusto, had been only amusedly glancing from one to the other of them. But her look became thoughtful, and stayed on Paprika, as she realized that she as well as Yount was being lectured. And Yount, for his part, began to find the experience more than uncomfortable; he was getting excruciatingly embarrassed. His two hands ceased shoveling fettuccine and found other occupations—one hand twining nervously in his beard, the other wiping sweat from his bald pate—when Paprika began to dwell on specific techniques and technicalities.

"Obie, have you ever, when making love to a woman, taken the time and trouble to admire the woman's . . . her chelidon, say, for instance?" She smiled salaciously. "Or her philtrum, perhaps?"

Yount looked warily about the restaurant. "Please, Miss Paprika. Some of these other folks might recognize low language, even in English."

"Don't be an ass. Answer me. When you make love to a woman, do you ever think to caress her chelidon? To stroke her philtrum?" Paprika's pink tongue came out and lasciviously touched her upper lip. "Have you ever *kissed* those places on a woman?"

Yount squirmed and said wretchedly, "Ma'am, I couldn't let myself say such *words* to a woman, let alone—"

"There. You see what I mean about males being dense? Would you be this much shocked, Obie, if the woman paid loving attention to *your* philtrum or chelidon? You have such places, too."

Yount wrung his beard and squeegeed his scalp. "Ma'am, please, could we change the sub—?"

"However, your own philtrum," she said, scrutinizing him mischievously, "is covered with hair."

"And decently clothed, too!" he burst out. "Why, I never heard such talk from a woman. Even in stag company, even in barracks, I wouldn't talk like you do about such things."

"Imbecile man, you do not even know what I am talking *about*. Here, I will show you those things."

Before Yount could leap up and flee, she was already showing them—not her own, or his, but Sarah's.

"This is the chelidon." Paprika reached over—making Sarah start slightly—to stroke her slim forefinger across the bend of Sarah's unsleeved arm. "The chelidon is the inside hollow of the elbow." Sarah quivered all over, as if she had been intimately fondled. "And this is the philtrum," added Paprika, stroking her fingertip down that little crease of Sarah's, and giving Sarah another frisson. "It is the indentation between the nose and upper lip."

"Oh," said Yount, settling onto his chair again.

"Do you honestly think that such anatomical terms—such innocuous words—are somehow lewd and nasty?"

"I reckon not," he mumbled, feeling foolish, not mollified. "But the way you talk about 'em is. Like you're lickin' the words as they come out."

"Sometime you should try licking the chelidons and the philtrum of a woman. She will probably be surprised. She will most certainly be pleased. And aroused. And responsive. She will account you an exceptional man. Nevertheless, no man has ever *been* a woman. So there is no way he can know all the delicate little nooks and crannies, the delicious places and things that yearn to be played with."

Yount said, "Hey." He had recovered sufficiently to be scandalized all over again. "Are you suggesting that a woman could be pleasured better by another *woman?* Than by a *man?*"

"I am not suggesting. It is a fact. It stands to reason. When a woman wants that sort of pleasure, why should she not seek it from one who knows best how to give it?"

"Why . . . but . . ." Yount groped for an adequate but inoffensive simile. "That would be like her buying a teapot without any spout."

"Ah, kedvesem, you men are so proud of that spout. You forget, the inside of a woman is only a place for childbearing, exactly like the inside of any sow or ewe, and a woman is no more humanly feminine or sensitive in there than those animals are."

"Now, that's got to be a lie," said Yount in horror. "I

ain't gonna talk as blunt as you do, but I will aver that I'm no virgin myself, and no woman ever *not* enjoyed my—my masculine apparatus. Miss Paprika, you are flat telling a lie.''

''I am flat telling the truth. A woman is sensitive only a finger's length or less''—she smiled—''inside her feminine apparatus. Sarah here will confirm that that is so.''

But Sarah only said faintly, ''I—I never thought about it,'' and Yount, appalled, made no further protest, so Paprika implacably went on at him:

''Even if you, teapot, have a spout like an elephant's trunk, its only real function is to deposit babies inside a woman. For sensation, for pleasure, for ecstacy, a finger in there is sufficient—or a tongue—and far more nimble, and far more capable of driving her nearly mad with—''

Yount abruptly stood up and waved for the proprietor. ''I reckon it's time we got back to the . . .'' He paused and said brutally, ''Back to the other circus freaks. Miss Makkai, if you intended to rid yourself of me, you have surely done that. I only hope you haven't curdled my feelings for every other woman in Creation.''

Thus it was that, immediately after the night show, Yount again dressed in civilian clothes and left the tober. He made his way to the nearest cab rank, where he managed, with vivid gestures, to inform a *vetturino* that he required a whorehouse. Arriving at such an establishment, he managed to inform the madam that he required a whore, whereupon he was ushered to a tawdry room containing Teresa Ferraiuolo. If Teresa Ferraiuolo shared Cécile Makkai's low opinion of the male half of humankind, she had sense enough not to make untimely pronouncements on the subject, and in any case could not have aired her opinions in English. However, after Obie Yount had departed—satisfied, gratified and to some degree reassured—Teresa Ferraiuolo went around to her sister inmates of the house, to warn them that those notorious perverts, ''gli Inglesi,'' were getting queerer all the time. This one, she told them, had insisted, between more routine and normal diversions, on being allowed to lick her elbows and her mustache.

*   *   *

At about the same hour, the Gran Duca's dining room was emptying of its late-dinner occupants, including most of the circus people. But Florian commanded the waiters to clear one large table for his conference with his Equestrian Director Edge, his Canvasmaster Goesle, his Bandmaster Beck and his Sideshow Director Fitzfarris. He also, when the other women of the troupe dispersed, asked Autumn Auburn to stay. So the six of them sat down around the table and the waiters took their orders for conferential lubricants.

Florian took out his little notebook and began ticking off items. "I will not bore you, lady and gentlemen, with a detailed treasurer's report. Suffice it to say that today's attendance was far better than I could have anticipated. I imagine we can mainly ascribe that not to our being the greatest circus ever to show here, but to our being foreign, hence a novelty. Whatever the reason, I believe we can profitably go on showing here in Livorno for another two weeks at least, before the receipts begin to tail off. Not to deplete our treasury too much, I shall continue the holdback on those firsts-of-May who have newly joined out, but I *will* be able to institute regular salary days for all the lifers. Meanwhile, Messieurs Goesle and Beck, you may proceed with those purchases we discussed . . . and with every expectation of being soon repaid for your out-of-pocket expenses."

"Already the drawings for the Gasentwickler I have prepared," said Carl Beck. "Tomorrow the buying of the materials I shall commence."

"Good," said Edge. "Maggie tells me that Jules ought to be moving to a wheelchair in a day or two, and at least hobbling with a cane not long after. It would be nice if we could have his balloon ready for tryout as soon as he's on his feet."

"Tomorrow also," said Beck, "additional Musikinstrumente for the otherwise unoccupied Slovaks I will buy, so they can be bandsmen—windjammers, as you say—during performances. For a start, I am adding only brass. I can buy them cheap at a monte di pietà pawnshop. Maybe later add woodwinds, more percussion."

"I leave that in your competent hands, Kapellmeister," said Florian. He went on, "Tomorrow our attendance should

easily equal today's and perhaps exceed it. The printers delivered our posters and throwaways this evening. I will have
some of our men out papering the city at dawn." From under
his chair, he got samples of the posters and handed them
around the table for all to admire.

"Wait you, Governor," said Goesle. "Better business we
cannot do. If we had had any straw on the ground today, the
jossers would have been sitting on it."

"Straw, yes. I have not yet been able to procure any, Dai.
But I have already contracted with a local mill for sawdust.
Very cheap. They'll deliver before show time tomorrow.
Have your roustabouts spread it over the pista and the seating
areas alike."

"Seven and seven times welcome it is," said Goesle. "But
Governor, if more people come tomorrow, Maggie the Hag
will be turning them away at the red wagon."

"No bad thing," said Florian. "Success breeds success. If
the town hears we are turning folks away, they'll be all the
more eager to see us."

"This poster," said Edge, "as well as I can make it out—it
seems uncommonly restrained. No strings of superlative adjectives. What has happened to your usual blowhard bombast,
Governor?"

"Ah, my boy, once you have the real goods, you no longer
have to do empty bragging. Leave the flummery to the would-
bes and the has-beens and the never-will-bes."

"Then it's a good poster, I reckon, for our classy show."

"Nevertheless, we will always find room for improvement," said Florian, and he consulted his notebook. "We
must work things out as we go along. For one thing, those
songs we sing. We could, of course, do local folk music. But
that would mean everybody's having to learn new tunes in
every country. I'd prefer to keep the old tunes and substitute
new words as necessary. Miss Auburn, could you spare me
the task, and do the rendering of them first into Italian?"

"Well . . . I'll try . . ."

"The words need not *say* anything, actually. What the hell,
they don't now. Just make sure that the opening chorus
sounds brash and sprightly, and Madame Solitaire's accom-

paniment is romantically sweet, and the closing chorus is a lingering farewell.''

"Crikey. You don't ask much, do you?''

"Now . . .'' Florian consulted his notes again. "Today's performances were necessarily inchoate, because we were in a hurry to put the show before the public. But we should be a *circus*, not a vaudeville of skits and tricks in a helter-skelter sequence. A circus should open with a flourish and close with a flourish. In between, it should be a well-considered alternation of the acts that entertain and the acts that thrill. Intervals of jollity relieving the spells of suspense and nail biting. So I have drafted a new program. See if any of you have any comments on it.''

He tore the page from his notebook and started it around the table, while he went on:

"Miss Auburn, yours is so clearly the most popular turn of all that it will henceforth close the show. The jossers will go home with pleasant memories of us, and will spread the good word. Colonel Ramrod, I am moving you up to close the first half of the program with your shootist exhibition. That will empty the crowd from the chapiteau at intermission in an excited mood, receptive to exploitation, ready to buy.''

"Buy what?'' asked Fitzfarris.

"For now, Maggie's services, your swazzles and your mouse-and-board game. Let us reinstitute that after the side-show presentation. The Italians are not simpering ninnies who will protest at a mouse's being put to worthwhile employment. Speaking of animals, Mag is already making ruffs for the Smodlakas' dogs, and new costumes for the Smodlakas themselves. When our wardrobe mistress is done with that, I will have her start on uniforms for your windjammers, Carl.''

"Still speaking of animals,'' said Edge. "I'd like to put the liberty act in the program before long. A couple of the horses are still wobbly from the sea voyage, but I'll get on with the training as soon as they've got their land legs.''

"And both Sunday and Monday,'' said Autumn, "have asked me to teach them wire-walking. If you're agreeable, Governor, I thought I'd give them a slant climb for a start.

If they're any good, they can go on to do a crossover."

"All right. Let me know if either shows any aptitude."

"Well," Autumn went on, "a slant climb should go up high and scary, so it can close with a slide-for-life. Come to that, I want to get my own rig up high, too."

"Confound it, Autumn—" Edge began, but Florian interrupted:

"My dear, I am in total accord. A thrill act should evoke as much thrill as possible. However, to point out the obvious, our chapiteau has only a single center pole. There is nothing up there to string your tightrope *between*. Until we have more room . . ."

Carl Beck interjected, "Ja! And my windjammers will a bandstand in the tent be needing. What we have now, richtig, they can from the back door lean in and play. But a proper band—"

Without force but with authority, Goesle said, "We are needing more room, Governor, for more than a bandstand and the missy's rope rig. There is no profit to having popularity if we have no place to put the crowds. Here is my thinking. At inconsiderable expense—one more center pole and some extra canvas—we can double the chapiteau's capacity. You have now a round tent. We simply split the round in half, move the two semicircles apart, each held up by a pole, and lace between them a sufficient rectangle of canvas, from peak to ground on either side . . ."

"You need not elaborate, Dai," said Florian. "A tent of middle and rounds is no novelty."

"I am not pretending that I invented it. I only say that I can do it, and cheap. I can give you an oval-shaped pavilion, plenty of seating room. And putting poles at either side of the ring means much more freedom for the performers—no impediment sticking up in the middle of their ring—and between the two poles can be slung Miss Auburn's tightrope. All sorts of capabilities. Also, I can arrange to incorporate in the tent a bandstand. Over the front door entrance, in the European style."

"Sehr gut!" Beck said approvingly. Autumn nodded and looked triumphantly pleased, and Edge scowled at her.

"I am well aware," Florian said patiently, "that a tent can be expanded. And naturally I have wanted to do exactly that. But we are talking more than one extra pole and some extra canvas. We are talking a considerable amount of additional seating."

"You will have to have it, soon or later," Goesle persisted. "Look you, what you have now—boards laid on boards, held together by the grace of God. That may have been necessary in America, where the seats had to be put up and taken down every day. But here in Europe, where they will stay in place for a week or more at a time, they must be more secure. I shall procure real metal jacks instead of your puny saplings, and the boards will be nailed to the stringers. The Slovaks tell me they can get me lumber, free gratis. I think they mean they will steal the railroad passengers' wooden crates, but I am careful not to inquire too close. Gratis is gratis."

"Nevertheless . . ." Florian muttered.

"Also," Goesle pressed on, "that piled-earth ring may have sufficed for your one-day American stands. Here it will have to be made and remade. From the gratis lumber I can also cut and shape the pieces for a permanent but portable ring curb. Brightly painted, padded on top. All these things I can do."

"Canvasmaster," Florian said earnestly, "these are all things I devoutly want done. However, consider. You can get canvas and lumber and jacks and everything else required. But then *they* require transport. We are also talking of more wagons and more draft animals. More harness, more feed, more animal tending, a bigger tober required everywhere we go . . ."

"Allow me to say a thing," Edge put in. "As you predicted, Governor, goods *are* cheap in this part of the world, at least compared to back home. I haven't priced big things like wagons, but if they're on a par with stuff like oats and hay and cat's meat, they shouldn't be out of our reach. As for the actual transport and tending, I might mention that Hannibal and Quincy give promise of becoming as good as Roozeboom was at hostling and wagonmastering."

"Yes," said Florian, nodding thoughtfully. "I don't know

how Abdullah did it, without a word of the local lingo—all I did was give him money—but he laid in good provender for the horses and the bull and the cat. And little Ali Baba, even with his atrocious *English*, somehow does a good job of supervising the Slovaks in their feeding and cleaning and care of the animals.''

''Well, there you are,'' said Autumn. ''If the crew are adequate and capable, Governor, you can't worry about the circus train or the tober being unmanageable.''

''It is managing the money outlay that mainly worries me. Zachary, do I take it that you, as equestrian director, support Dai's grandiose schemes for immediate expansion?''

''I think what I'd recommend is hedging our bets. Let Stitches go ahead with all those extras. At the end of our stand here, if it has paid us well enough to afford the new wagons and draft stock and other equipment, then we'll get them. If not, we'll probably have to dump all the new goodies and go on without them.''

''Satisfactory!'' said Goesle. ''Chance it I will. Because I am so sure of our success that I already have further plans for down the road. Our night-show lights are pathetic, and very soon I want—''

''Oh, lordy, lordy . . .'' Florian moaned.

''Hear you now!'' Goesle insisted. ''That Missy Pepper is complaining and rightly. The mere ground performers only get sprinkled with pellets and candle drippings. But *she* hangs by her hair close up to the chandelier, and she gets the drops of *hot* melted wax.''

Edge laughed and stood up. ''Well, you fellows can get on with the planning and arguing, but Autumn and I have to be clear-eyed and steady to perform tomorrow. We're off to sleep.''

As he and she left the dining hall, they could hear Carl Beck bringing up the matter of music again. ''. . . Not one of the dumb Slovaks can read notes, and anyway we have no notes to read. But at them *anything* besingen or brummen they can play. So, for the slow and graceful acts, I think Strauss. For the brisk and lively acts, Offenbach or Gottschalk . . .''

"You know something?" Edge said to Autumn, as they climbed the stairs. "All that hesitating and fussing and raising objections that Florian does? It's nothing but humbug. He's the greatest risk taker on this planet. He just wants us all to crank up our own enthusiasm for the outrageous ideas. And we always do."

"Oh, but I hope you have some enthusiasm left over," Autumn said seductively, "for other outrageous ideas."

She did her own disrobing this time, to save delay. And when she had peeled off all the concealed petals of fabric, she disclosed for Edge a small and sweet surprise. He stared—admiring, amused—and she said, "Well? You told me you liked the diamanté."

3

IT APPEARED that Livorno would not soon tire of the Flor-ilegium. The next day was another turnaway day, and so was the one after that, and the one after that. The Livornese were cheerful folk; whenever they were told there was simply no more room even for standing in the chapiteau, they shrugged and grimaced humorously and went away, to come again an-other day. Also, Aleksandr Banat reported that he recognized many repeat and re-repeat visitors among the crowds. Banat had appointed himself ticket taker and keeper of the front door at each performance, and he did that job so assiduously that Florian instructed the wardrobe mistress to dress him for the post—"as a merry-andrew, I think"—but Banat deemed that inelegant.

He pointed to the sign on a wagon and said. "Is Circo Confederato, no? Ought to be Confederato doorman."

"You have a point," said Florian. They went to the Quake-maker and asked if he still had his old Rebel sergeant's uni-form.

"Uh huh," said Yount, surveying the short, stout Banat. "It'll go around him all right, I reckon, but you'll have a helluva lot left over at each end."

However, Magpie Maggie Hag was able to alter the uni-

form to fit and, when Yount showed Banat how to wear the
forage cap properly atilt, it even disguised the man's lack of
forehead. Later, Banat went downtown to a monte di pietà
and bought some old, tarnished medals, polished them and
pinned them to the breast of his gray uniform. Thereafter, at
the chapiteau's front door, he greeted the incoming patrons
with soldierly dignity, and none of those ever remarked on
the anomaly of a Johnny Reb speaking an Italo-Anglo-Slovak
jargon and wearing the Order of the Netherlands Lion, the
Médaille Militaire and the Order of Guissam Alaouite.

Since the Florilegium was now far from what Florian had
once called Bible-thumping-bumpkin land, there was no ob-
stacle to its giving performances on Sundays. So the troupers
and crew alike worked two shows every day, seven days a
week. The weather stayed fine during their time in Livorno,
and the one rain that fell during that period fell in the middle
of the night. It waked Canvasmaster Goesle in his Gran Duca
room. He hastily dressed, strapped on his jingling belt of
knives, fids, awls and other implements, ran downstairs, woke
a vetturino at the hotel's cab rank and had himself galloped
out to the park. But he found, when he got there, that Banat
had already rousted out his crewmen to loosen the tent's guy
ropes and to spread tarpaulins wherever the rain threatened
to dampen the sawdust.

"That man Banat is quite competent," Goesle reported to
Florian next day, "and glad of it I am, by Dafydd. He even
knows to make the roustabouts half-hitch the end of every
rope back upon itself, so the ends won't trip anybody or get
frayed from being trodden on. Not much misses Banat, and
the other Slovaks readily obey him. Only one of the dozen—
lout named Sandov—is a slacker and a whiner and an absolute blockhead. But Banat says, if you will allow it, he will
get rid of the misfit."

"I hope this Sandov is not one of the bandsmen."

Goesle shook his head. "There is singing he does sometimes. Bawdy songs, I judge, from the way the others giggle.
But he has no voice at all. It grates on a Welshman's ear."

"Very well, then. Banat has my permission to get rid of
him."

Meanwhile, whenever the roustabouts were not patching the chapiteau's old canvas or doing routine yard tidying or attending the animals or, during performances, playing music or shifting rigging or running props in and out of the pista, they were being worked even harder in their "off time." They did fetch the free lumber, as they had promised (much of it was stenciled CRINOLINA), and Goesle set them first to sawing curved sections from it and nailing the pieces together, while he himself, with palm and big needles and waxed twine, sewed heavy leather into cushions and stuffed them with rags. The wood became twenty sturdy curved boxes, each a foot high and deep, and some six and a half feet long. Goesle had the men paint them in gaudy Italianate stripes of red, white and green, then affixed the padding to their upper sides. The boxes, laid end to end, made a handsome circular curb enclosing the forty-two-foot pista, except for a four-foot gap facing the tent's back door, for the entrance and exit of horses, the elephant and the cage wagon. Nevermore would anybody of the Florilegium have to dig and heap up and tamp an earthern curb. And nevermore would the Florilegium leave one, when it moved on, for the local children to play circus in.

Next, Goesle turned to the improvement of the chapiteau's rickety seating arrangements. He began by sending the Slovaks out again to liberate more lumber, while he went to the Gran Duca chandlery to look for metal jacks. That well-stocked shop did not disappoint him, because it kept those items in stock for the many aging ships that had to use such underpinnings to prop up sagging decks. So Goesle brought Florian to haggle in the vernacular, and they got a good price by buying more of the things than any one ship's master ever had to have.

During the while that Goesle kept the Slovaks busy at carpentry, he would occasionally spare them to rehearse under Bandmaster Beck, playing the old instruments and learning to play those newly acquired from the various local Mounts of Pity. One bandsman at a time was usually all that Beck required, because, having no sheet music, he had to sing or hum to each separate musician each separate instrument's part of every tune he wanted learned—"Like so it goes: boompty-tiddly-deedly-boomp." Then, after the cornetist and the horn player and the trombonist and the tuba player and the accordionist had each learned his individual part, Beck would beg from Goesle two men at a time, then three, and so on—and call in Hannibal and his drum—and rehearse them gradually at playing in unison. It was a system that might have daunted even such professional conductors as the brothers Strauss, but somehow the amateur aspirant Beck made it serve.

Also, whenever any number of the Slovaks were not working for Goesle or practicing music, Beck would have them shearing sheet metal or bending tubing or riveting and soldering together fairly intricate bits of his hydrogen generator. That was perhaps an even more ticklish business than his piecework music instruction. Beck himself was proceeding mostly by inspired guesses, and he had to impart those notions to untaught mechanists who could no more read his exquisite drawings than they could read sheet music, and with whom he had no language in common. But here again—"This pipe like so should go: hammer boompty, bend it, boomp again"—he made his impromptu system work, and the generator began to take coherent shape.

In the process of acquiring a Gasentwickler and a passable circus band, Beck also acquired a nickname. One day, one of the Slovaks hailed another—"Hey, Broskev! Pana Boom-Tiddly-Boom wants you!"—and it was not long before everybody on the show knew its Kapellmeister and chief engineer as Boom-Tiddly-Boom Beck.

While all that industrious construction and creation went on, the performing artistes happily enjoyed what was for them comparative indolence. Although they had to work before the public two times a day, and in their spare time practiced to improve their old tricks, and experimented with new ones, and instructed the young apprentices, and saw to the upkeep of their props and animals, they were unburdened of most of the "housekeeping" drudgery that had formerly been their responsibility. They rejoiced in being well fed by the Gran Duca's dining room, at dependable intervals, and in being able to resort to the hotel's hot baths as often as they wished, and in having their laundry done by washerwomen invisible belowstairs, and in being able to call on the hotel maids for clothes mending and pressing and button replacing whenever Magpie Maggie Hag was busy, as she almost always was these days, designing and making new costumes.

Best of all, they found they could count on enjoying a regular weekly salary day. And, since they no longer had to spend their stipend just to keep their acts and the whole Florilegium in existence, they could use the money for personal acquisitions. Few of them, however, squandered their first wages on nonessentials. The benign autumn days were getting shorter, the nights were getting chill and damp and winter was not far off, so most of the purchases were of sensible civilian clothes. Florian advised the women, though, that Livorno's shops and tastes were as provincial as those in Virginia, and recommended that they postpone all expensive indulgences until they got to the fashionable and cultured Firenze.

Abner Mullenax treated himself to a new eye patch. He discarded his old army-issue patch and had one custom-made for him by a local tailor—of fine black silk inset with a little star pattern of rhinestones. He still looked like a pirate, but now a prosperous one, or an eccentric one. The three Chinese managed to buy vast bundles of spaghetti, and at every mealtime they would make their own fire on the lot, first to boil the pasta, then to fry it to greasy crispness. And they ate with gusty sighs of satisfaction, as if they had rediscovered something they had long been yearning for. Several people remarked that the Chinese might more sensibly have bought themselves shoes, but the three men seemed to disdain footwear, and even politely refused offers of hand-me-down shoes from other troupers, and continued to go barefoot, whatever the weather or the conditions underfoot.

For his part, Florian was sufficiently emboldened by Livorno's unabating patronage of the show and the unabating receipts at the red wagon that he did not wait for the close of the stand to make his decision about investing in additional transport equipment. Indeed, he went at it with some extrav-

agance. He bought four new closed-van wagons—not really
new but in good condition—one to carry the chapiteau's
added canvas and seat planks and stringers and jacks and
ring-curb sections; one for the Slovaks to ride and bunk in;
one to accommodate the Smodlaka family and dogs, plus
Hannibal, Quincy and the Chinese; one to carry wardrobe,
musical instruments and props and, on the tober, to give the
artistes a real dressing room for the first time. That van he
even equipped with a small coal stove to keep them warm
this winter while they dressed, and on which Magpie Maggie
Hag could cook whenever they were not near a town or an
inn at mealtimes.

The already overworked roustabouts now had to devote
their every least remaining spare moment, usually late at
night, to painting the new wagons to match the rest of the
train and to putting a glossy new coat of black on Florian's
rockaway. But they did the job stolidly and uncomplainingly—all of them except the already notorious malingerer
Sandov. One of the Chinese antipodists turned out to be an
accomplished calligrapher and, though he could not at all
comprehend the words or letters, he beautifully copied them
from one of the old wagons onto each of the new ones, and
even onto the wooden panels that enclosed Maximus's cage
when it was on the road: FLORIAN'S FLOURISHING FLORILE-
GIUM, etc., etc.

Because those new-bought wagons would be immensely
heavy when they were loaded, Florian bought two horses to
draw each one, and he did not stint there, either. Somewhere
he found a stable that had for sale eight of the Pinzgauer
Tigerschecken horses bred in Austria: white horses spotted
with black—not splotched like American pintos, but polka-
dotted exactly like Dalmatian dogs. They were horses hefty
enough for draft work but gorgeous enough for Edge eventually to work into his liberty act.

The artistes were now performing in a new order-of-
appearance that Florian had devised to make for a better alternation of acts amusing and acts thrilling. Since the revised
program gave Autumn Auburn the closing spot, and Pepper

Mayo did her hair-hang several acts earlier, the disparity of applause the two women received was not so blatantly apparent. Nevertheless, it was apparent enough to Pepper, and she seethed and sulked—especially when Florian finally took a good look at her act, saw the scantiness of her dress and commanded her to resume wearing the cache-sexe under her tights.

"It's not that *I* mind ogling the vertical grin," he said. "And clearly the worldly Italians do not. But if I let you perform so, Pep, I can hardly refuse anyone else. Next thing we know, Clover Lee or the Simms girls will be wanting likewise to wink at the jossers—or the Quakemaker to flaunt his cod—and we can't have *everybody* baring everything God gave Adam and Eve."

So Pepper, fuming and fizzing, flounced off to continue her training of Quincy Simms in secret. They simply went some distance from the tober into the park, she tied a rope around the boy's waist, threw the rope over a tree limb and hoisted him a little way off the ground. There he practised doing the serpentine twinings and knottings of himself without any support under him.

His sisters were also getting extra training, from Autumn, in the rudiments of ropewalking. Since Sunday and Monday would have had to do that either barefooted or in their only shoes—the bright yellow spring-heel shoes, which would have been impossible—Autumn spent her own money to buy them each a pair of unpadded ballet slippers, and got Goesle to make a long, springy balance pole weighted with lead at either tip. The training began with each girl's teetering back and forth along the narrow edge of a two-by-four borrowed from the carpenter Slovaks. Eventually Autumn exchanged that board for a one-by-eight, and made the girls walk the one-inch strip. When they progressed to a half-inch rope, pegged only a foot above the ground, both Sunday and Monday had already become commendably surefooted.

At other times, Monday Simms continued to take riding instruction from Sarah, who told her, "I have made a decision. Since Clover Lee and I already do rosinback routines on Snowball and Bubbles, I want you to start riding Zachary's horse Thunder, and start learning the very ladylike and genteel art of haute école.''

"Ma'am?'' Monday said blankly.

"It means 'high school.' In other words, a very well-educated horse and rider. It's not like a thrill act, like our basse école rosinback acrobatics, or Buckskin Billy's galloping voltige. It's a subtle sort of fancy stepping, and you may think it tame by comparison. But it will be highly regarded by every spectator who recognizes fine horsemanship. It is done on this English saddle, which I just bought for that purpose.''

"That's a saddle? Looks more like a pancake.''

"I guess it does, compared to one of those cavalry rocking chairs. But you'll soon realize what freedom its lightness allows the horse, and what excellent control its smallness allows to your legs. Mount up, and I'll show you some of the steps Zachary had taught this horse long before he ever saw this circus.''

Monday vaulted aboard, and Sarah handed her a light riding crop. "Start him at a lope—not full run, just a Canterbury gallop—then touch his off shoulder with the quirt. That's called 'checking' him.'' Monday cantered halfway around the pista, touched Thunder and he instantly changed leads, reversing the order in which he put down left and right feet. "Touch him again,'' Sarah called. Monday did, and Thunder resumed his original gait. As the girl went past her, Sarah called, "Now check him every fourth step, and then every second step.'' The horse circled the ring again, changing step so frequently and smoothly that Monday cried delightedly, "He's dancing!''

She added, when she brought the horse to a halt beside Sarah, "O' course, I nearly fall off this-here pancake every time he checks.''

"You'll soon learn to ride with the changes. Now, if the band plays a polka, and you put Thunder to a canter, and keep checking him in that order—fourth step, second step, fourth step, second—it will look to the audience like Thunder is dancing a perfect polka. As soon as you've learned that one, I'll teach you the other sequences of checks that will make him dance the waltz, the schottische and so on.''

"Swine!" roared Pavlo Smodlaka, when one day he came raging to Florian, to report that Mullenax's pigs had viciously attacked his terriers. The children Sava and Velja had first intervened, he said, but they were too frail to separate the combatant animals. Pavlo had had to bestir himself and wade in to break up the fight, ''before the filthy swine could maim or kill or eat any of my darlings—or the children—but the dogs' pelts are much scratched and their nerves are in a terrible state! I demand that those prljav pigs be butchered!''

Since Florian was aware that the pigs had also become so corpulent that they could hardly do their own ladder climbing and other tricks, he spent the rest of the day preparing a convincing argument for retiring Hamlet & Co. from show business, then went to confront Mullenax, only to find that the predicament had already been resolved.

"Them pigs? Funny you should mention 'em, Guv'nor. I just this afternoon got rid of 'em. Gettin' rambunctious they was, and too big to be cute any more. Anyhow, all this time, I only been workin' 'em until they was well fatted up for eatin'.''

"You *ate* them?"

"Naw. I couldn't eat no old friend. Knowin' who it was, anyway. I gave 'em to the hotel kitchen.''

"You simply gave them away?"

"Well, more of a trade.'' Mullenax winked his one eye, which was quite spectacularly bloodshot. "The management's givin' me unlimited credit in the hotel grogshop as long as we're in town.''

Florian cleared his throat. "Er, Barnacle Bill, I sometimes worry . . .''

"Now, now. Nothin' to worry about, Guv'nor. That act's gone, yes, but I'm workin' up a real special 'nother one with Maximus. It'll outshine old Ignatz's bogus-bloody arm for damn sure. What I'm gonna have the lion do is jump through a *hoop of fire*. With me right there inside the cage holdin' it for him.''

"Well, yes, that would be grand. The trick is not unheard of, but not many trainers can accomplish it. Not even the most dedicated and sober ones.'' Florian slightly stressed the word ''sober.''

''I can do it. Me and old Maximus. See, he's got a lot livelier now that he's gettin' good vittles regular. And he already knowed to jump over my whip when I yell 'springe!' So what I did—I got a little curved piece of wood from Stitches. Propped it in the cage, made him jump over that. Maximus, I mean, not Stitches. So, after he got used to that, I added two curved pieces on both ends of that first piece. He jumped between 'em, over the older piece, just fine. So every few days I been puttin' him through a wider and higher curve of wood. All of this takes time, but one thing Ignatz taught me was patience. One day soon, I'll have that wood a complete circle around Maximus, and he won't balk at all.''

''He might when you set fire to it.''

''No, I'll do that slow and cautious, too. Dab just a little bit of coal oil at the top of the hoop, set it afire, have Maximus jump *under* it. When he realizes it don't hurt, I'll gradually bring the fire down and around the circle—everywhere except at the very bottom—because if he ever gets singed, I'll either get chawed to bits or we'll have to start over from the very beginnin'. Anyhow, if it works, it'll look to the crowd like Maximus is jumpin' through *a whole burning hoop of fire*. Nobody'll notice that the bottom of the circle ain't never fired.''

''Yes. Well. I shall look forward to it. You will be acclaimed and renowned. As you say, the secret is being patient—and careful—and sober. Above all, sober.''

''Guv'nor, I can tell you truthfully. I ain't never seen Maximus anything *but* sober.''

The Florilegium's program still lacked what Florian regarded as indispensable to a circus: a clown. But Florian could at least console himself that Pavlo Smodlaka, though neither a clown nor a midget, was Tiny Tim Trimm's veritable replica in loathsomeness and an ideal replacement for Tim, in that the other troupers were all nicer to each other just for having Pavlo Smodlaka around to abhor. The man was dependable. Three shows out of four, the trained-dog act would conclude like this:

As the audience broke into applause, Pavlo and Gavrila would skip from the ring, hand in hand, smiling broadly, their three terriers frisking around them as they bowed their way backward out of the tent. Outside the back door, Pavlo would fiercely slap Gavrila's face, contort his own in a sneer, and snarl at her, "Prljav krava!"—or as often in English, "Filthy cow!" Then they would link hands again, skip smiling inside again, while the still-clapping crowd beamed fondly at the husband-and-wife artistes working so joyfully together. The two would bow their way out again, and outside he might slap her again, or cruelly yank one of her braids so hard that she staggered, and growl something like, "You planted your fat bottom right in the line of view between Terry and the best-dressed people in the seats!" or "Why do you always stand in the posture of a new-dropped turd?" If the applause continued long enough to summon them inside for several bows, the alternating smiles and abuse could go on for quite a while.

Only once did the company have the pleasure of seeing Gavrila openly defy Pavlo. After one evening's performance, when the crowd was clearing out, Florian brought an elegantly attired, high-hatted gentleman around to the backyard. The two approached the new dressing-room wagon, from which all four of the Smodlakas were just emerging in their street clothes, and Florian said:

"I have the honor, my friends, of introducing to you il Conte Ventimiglia. He begs a favor of you. The count's hobby, he tells me, is photography. He has a fully equipped daguerrian studio in his villa, and he is compiling a collection of photographs of, um, curiosities. He would like to borrow your little ones overnight—to add their pictures to his collection."

"Pictures?" Pavlo said delightedly. "But is that possible? To capture a picture of the dogs performing in such rapid motion?"

"No, no," said Florian. "Not the dogs, the Night Children. Sava and Velja."

"Si!" the count said eagerly. "I figli della notte. Svestito. Tutto nudo. Affine di fare posture—ah—speciale."

"Er—nude?" said Florian, disconcerted. "Special poses? Count, you did not earlier mention—"

"Bah, only the hatchlings," said Pavlo, looking disappointed. But then he looked shrewd and said, "This count will pay? For this borrowing?"

Suddenly and ferociously, Gavrila spat, "He will do no such thing! Let him undress our children? Put them in *special poses*? Oscenità! Not while I live!" She curved her arms around the boy and girl and swept them away to their wagon.

Pavlo scowled darkly as he watched them depart, but then turned back to the count and gave him a shrug of resignation.

"Che peccato," murmured the Conte Ventimiglia. He brooded for a moment, while Pavlo also departed, then said to Florian, "Ebbene, per caso—i pigmei bianchi?"

"Sunday and Monday?" said Florian, now regarding the hobbyist with open distaste. "I had not suspected the nature of your collection. Nevertheless, here comes Sir John, the girls' guardian. I will at least relay the request to him."

He did so, and Fitzfarris said coolly, "As you know, Governor, I'm trying to learn the language. Tell me. How does one say in Italian 'go shit in your fancy hat?'"

Ventimiglia made a face of frustration, brooded some more, then gestured toward the dressing wagon. Its door stood open, and visible inside was Magpie Maggie Hag. With a heavy flatiron she had heated on the stove in there, she was pressing a costume she had just completed.

"Ebbene," said the count, with a wan sort of hope. "Per caso la strega?"

Fitz stared at the man in appalled fascination, and said to Florian, "Old Mag? This bug must really be desperate for perversion."

"Well," Florian chuckled, "just for the hell of it . . ." He called the gypsy to the van door and, trying not to laugh, solemnly put the proposition to her.

Magpie Maggie Hag still held the flatiron; it was smoking slightly. She came down the wagon steps with surprising speed for an old crone. She was too short to reach the count's face with the iron, but she gave one of his bare hands a sizzling blistering before he had the good sense to turn and run. The last seen of Ventimiglia, he was fleeing the tober and the park with Magpie Maggie Hag in literally hot pursuit.

"Good for Mag," said Florian, laughing. "And good riddance. That one was only a papal count, anyway, not real nobility."

"I'm glad to know it," said Fitz. "I was looking forward to meeting some real nobility over here."

Jules Rouleau was by now making daily visits to the tober in a wicker wheelchair lent him by the Hotel Gran Duca. His first visits were brief, but, as his long-unused arm and chest muscles strengthened, the visits became day-long, during which he wheeled himself around the lot, in and out of the chapiteau, faster than he could have walked.

"But I *will* be walking, par dieu," he said. "Sarah bought me a fine malacca cane, and in my room each night I take a few more steps. I limp, of course, mais merde alors, I am happy enough to be upright again. Even able to take a real bath, instead of having women sponge at just the accessible parts of me. An acrobat I will never be again, but an aéronaute, oui. I observe, Maître Beck, that you have made laudable progress with the machinery."

"Ja. The Gasentwickler should not too much longer require to complete. But the gas-making chemicals, I think, not until Florenz will we be able to buy. So there in Florenz the Ballonflieger you will become."

"Merci, maître. Grand merci."

"Call me now Boom-Boom," Beck said shyly. "Everybody does. More freundlich und Familie it sounds."

"Bien, Boom-Boom."

"Now, friend, allow me some ballooning instruction to impart. I know you have before on a tether gone aloft. But when to float free you wish, certain accessories you must employ. Around the basket will be hung many bags of sand ballast. To ascend faster and higher, one after another the bags you will drop. Nein, nein—not *drop*, verstehen—or somebody on the ground you maybe kill. *Empty* from a bag that sand. How much and how often you will learn to judge."

"Bien. And I already know about pulling the cord of the clack valve to release the gas, little by little, to descend."

"Richtig. Then if to ascend again you wish, you empty more sand. By up and down going, various breezes you will find, in various directions blowing. Thus, by choosing your breeze, the Luftballon actually *steered* can be, wherever you wish to go, then back to your starting point. The Zirkusplatz or wherever. Slowly release all the gas and like a feather down you come." Beck smiled and added, "I should say, all these things not from experience or genius I know. I have been reading many Bucher."

"C'est bandant, Boom-Boom. I sincerely thank you for all you have done—and for the masterly instruction also."

But it was Boom-Boom Beck who required some instruction in one of his other vocations, that of bandmaster.

"For the entrance of the elephant a ponderous music I have selected," he told Florian and Edge. "From Liszt's 'Battle of the Huns.' For your horses, Herr Edge—what else?— Strauss's 'Thunder and Lightning.' "

"You may have to play substitutes on short notice," said Florian. "Johann Junior is forever touring all over Europe, and we're likely to meet him anywhere. He's said to be a tight man about money, and he may demand payment for our using his music. But for now, let us rehearse to it."

So one day, in the free time between the afternoon and evening shows, Edge brought into the pista the horses he had already trained to perform without riders or harness—Snowball, Bubbles, his own Thunder, and the three unnamed horses acquired from the bummers back in Virginia. They all wore brilliant blue saddle blankets, liberally sequined and fringed with tassels, and spangled halters that held high blue plumes above their heads: costumes designed by Magpie Maggie Hag and fabricated with the help of Stitches Goesle.

Right now, Goesle had the Slovaks helping him round and taper and smooth the three sections of a new, second center pole for the soon-to-be-expanded chapiteau, and making a tall-spiked gum-shoe to support the new pole, and forging a bail ring for it—but Florian and Beck persuaded him to part with the musicians among those crewmen. The windjammers fetched their instruments and Bandmaster Boom-Boom conducted them in a rather raucous rendition of the "Thunder and Lightning'' polka. Edge stood at ring center and, with loud cracks but only gentle taps of his long whip, conducted the horses as they trotted or cantered around the pista— pranced, danced, pirouetted—formed in rank and reared all together or mingled in intricate patterns of crisscross and figure eights.

But after just a little while of this, Boom-Boom waved his band to silence and called indignantly to Edge, ''Herr Direktor, your horses are not at all moving in time to my music! Cannot you train them to listen better? It is a great confusion of rhythms between us and them. Ein Mischmasch.''

Florian smiled tolerantly and said, ''Excuse me, Herr Kapellmeister, but even the sweetest music means no more to any animal than a concert of jackdaws. It is *you* who must watch the performance and conduct in tempo to *them*. The horses, the bull Brutus, even the human acrobats and aerialists and jugglers. You must also be prepared for frustrations and emergencies. If, say, you have allotted thirty seconds of a cancan for one of the terrier's tricks, and the dog fails or balks at it, you will have to stretch or repeat that music. At all times, it must look to the jossers as if every performer *is* intelligently and skillfully performing in time to your music. In actuality, it is you who must exert that skill. Just the way you ring those little arpeggios on your string of tins in time to Miss Auburn's rope-dancing.''

''Herr Gouverneur, those are random notes. This is a Strauss polka. And, mein Gott, a polka is in strict two-quarter meter, with its tempo specified by its composer. Do you expect me to make it drag or race—ritardando, accelerando— from moment to moment?''

''Yes. Rubato—it is no sin. Composers far superior to the Strauss brothers have often marked their scores rubato, to allow the conductor that freedom of varying tempo. You will simply apply rubato to Johann's polka. And to all other music you play for artistes in motion: Liszt for the elephant, Wagner marches, schottisches, whatever. I told you it takes skill. I am confident that you will provide it.''

Beck looked duly flattered, but grumbled nevertheless, ''Wagner and Liszt and the Strausses—if them we encoun-

ter—for using their music they will not make you *pay*. Into
the pista they will leap and with their bare hands *strangle*
you they will.''

"I doubt it," Florian said calmly. "I have heard Wagner
and Rossini operas, and one Strauss operetta, sung by divas
who made the conductor and the whole orchestra sweat to
keep abreast of them. One other thing, Carl. I mentioned also
emergencies. Keep an eye on me or Zachary, as well, whichever of us is in the pista. If we make this signal"—he raised
his arms and crossed them in an X above his head—"it
means the canvas is on fire or something else baleful has
occurred. You will immediately switch from whatever you
are playing to Mendelssohn's 'Wedding March.' ''

Beck looked horrified. "Not circus music that is! Schwab-
belbusen that is! To listen to Mendelssohn is like with warm
water being wetted."

"Perhaps. But it will instantly alert all the performers and
crew. We can fix whatever is wrong, or hide it, or evacuate
the chapiteau if necessary. My long-time associates know
what the 'Wedding March' signifies, and I will so inform
everyone else on the show."

Florian had told the company to hope for perhaps two
weeks' stay in Livorno. It turned out to be more than four
weeks of straw houses before they found themselves performing one night before a less than sfondone crowd. When the
show commenced, Florian swept his gaze around, saw the
two or three upper tiers of planks quite empty and made a
decision on the instant. As soon as he had introduced the first
act, Abdullah and Brutus, he went to the backyard, found Dai
Goesle and said:

"Stitches, we'll strike it tonight. Bust the lacings right after
the audience leaves. Pisa is only some fifteen miles northeast
of here, an easy overnight run, but I won't ask you to go
tonight. Ordinarily, I'd have had an advance man there already and arrangements made."

"Glad I'd be to roll this very night, Governor."

"Thank you, Dai, but no. You wouldn't know where to
make the haul from the main road to whatever tober Pisa
allots us. It would be senseless for you and the whole crew

just to loiter about, unable to unload. No, we'll all get a good night's sleep and depart early in the morning. My rockaway can make better time than the rest of the train. I should have everything arranged with the Pisa municipio before you all arrive, and I'll be at the roadside to guide you in. There may even be time before dark to do the setup.''

"Or to start it, anyway," said Goesle. "Mind, I'll be putting the middle between the rounds of the chapiteau for the first time. It may take some few setups and teardowns before we can do it swift like.''

"True. So I won't schedule a performance for the next day, either. That will give us extra time for papering the town and stirring up enthusiasm.''

During intermission, the whole troupe got the word of their imminent departure from Livorno. When the show resumed, Sarah Coverley was watching her protégée Monday Simms putting Thunder through a passable haute école of cross step, Spanish walk, piaffe and half-passes, when Paprika came up to her to say confidentially, seductively, "Angyal Sarah, this will be our last night in the Gran Duca, and we may not have such luxurious and—private—lodgings again for a while. Let us spend this last night here, you and I, together.''

Sarah blushed noticeably, but she kept her eyes on the pista and said indifferently, "Whyever should we do that?''

"Oh, talk girl talk. Shop talk. Perhaps entertain each other.''

"Entertain?'' Sarah said absently, still watching the haute école.

Paprika said, with a pretense of impatience and scolding, "Kedvesem! Nemi érintkezés.''

"You know I don't speak Hungarian.''

"Kedvesem means darling. Nemi érintkezés means the sort of mutual entertainment I have in mind. I also know that you are neither stupid nor ignorant. You understand very well what I mean.''

Now Sarah's eyes were closed. In a small voice she said, "Yes.''

"Then let us cease playing hide-and-seek. Have you ever

been kissed, Sarah, or licked or caressed at your philtrum or chelidon?''

''I really don't remember,'' Sarah said in a firmer voice, and she finally turned to face Paprika. ''But I am not a prude, and I was never the typical American wife—'one position, under the covers, lights out.' I have enjoyed those caresses— in every other part of me. And I have always been satisfied to have a man do them.''

''But you do not have a man at present. You truly *are* Madame Solitaire. Zachary has jilted you. Florian is preoccupied with business. Who, then? Pavlo the Gross?''

Sarah had to smile at that, and grimace. She said, ''I grant that you are a coquette who would tempt anybody of either sex . . .'' She let her voice trail off.

''You can pretend that I am a man, if you like,'' Paprika suggested impishly. ''I do not care what goes on in your *mind*. Only in your—''

''No.'' Sarah shook her head. ''You said we have private lodgings. We do not. Clover Lee shares my room. Pepper shares yours.''

''Those are your only reasons for saying no?'' said Paprika, visibly brightening. ''Not sanctimony? Not priggishness? Only lack of privacy?'' Sarah blushed even more deeply. ''We can easily ask the night porter to rent us another room.''

''It's still no, Paprika. Clover Lee might go looking for me. Probably in Florian's room, and God knows what uproar that might cause. Pepper would certainly know why she'd been left to sleep alone. She would probably kill both of us in the morning.''

Indeed, Pepper was watching them from the farther side of the pista, watching with the eyes of a viper. When she saw Sarah leave the tent, she went to stand beside the Quake-maker, who was waiting to go on next, and engaged him in conversation, and glanced to make sure that Paprika saw *them*. She chattered only trivialities, but Yount was pleased at this unaccustomed familiarity, and she nestled against him to put their faces close together, and they both smiled a lot.

Paprika was still watching them, and now it was she who watched with the eyes of a viper.

Late that night, any passersby in the hotel corridor outside the room of Pepper Mayo and Paprika Makkai could have heard their voices through the closed and heavy mahogany door.

"Ye cheeky ginger-hackle! The little Clover Lee thistle-down would have none of your letch. So now, purely to spite her, ye'll play firkytoodle with her *mother!*"

"It is not for spite, sárkány! Sarah is a beauty, too!"

"Blaflum! Very froncey she may be, but she's half again as old as you are. Mutton dressed as lamb."

"Menj a fenébe! She is anyway a woman. I am at least being true to my nature. You are making moon eyes at a *man!*"

"If ye continue to scunge after that Sarah biddy, then may the fiend ride through the both of yez, booted and spurred. Meantime, I'm working up a new act. I guarantee I'll steal the show and outperform the two of yez into oblivion. Also I'll be showing that Obie boyo more than moon eyes, bedad!"

The eyes they both showed, next morning, were red from anger, weeping and lack of sleep. But the other artistes did not look much more sparkly, for Florian had pounded on their doors at first light, so that they could have a hearty breakfast and still be early on the road. Early as it was, though, they found that Stitches Goesle was already up and had been busy.

"In the ships' chandlery next door, just," he said. "Buying blocks and tackle for the new center pole. Such things may be hard to come by, inland."

Most of the troupers ate sleepily and fumblingly, but Florian bolted his breakfast and hurried to the hotel desk to settle the accounts. When he paid the bill in full—without quibbling about each and every item on the long tally, as any Italian guest would have done—the Gran Duca's manager was pleased to accept from him the now thirty-eight conduct books of troupe and crew. He carried the stack into his office and when he came out each book contained his exquisitely scripted declaration that its bearer had behaved irreproachably during his or her stay in Livorno. He called the names, to hand each book personally, with a deep bow, to its owner.

"Signor Rouleau . . . Signorina Makkai . . . Signor Goozle . . ."

" 'Tis pronounced Gwell," growled Stitches.

"Signorina Mayo . . . Signor, uh, Cheenk . . ."

Florian said impatiently, in Italian, that he'd take the rest of the books, their owners all being out at the circus ground.

When the company went out the front door—porters wheeling Rouleau in the wicker chair and carrying out considerably more luggage than these guests had arrived with—there was a sleepy but doughty Aleksandr Banat waiting with the dressing-room wagon. They all, except Edge and Autumn, managed to crowd themselves and their luggage and Goesle's big coils of rope and heavy wire, turnbuckles and pulleys into or on top of that wagon. As the two polka-dot horses hauled it off toward the Fabbricotti park, Autumn and Edge went around to the Gran Duca's stable yard and the stalliere hitched Autumn's ribby old horse to her little van. They stowed their luggage and Edge's armaments inside, then climbed to the driving seat and Edge took the reins.

He commented, "From the glimpse I got inside, this is a dandy little cottage on wheels."

"I bought it from a family of tinkers who had decided, for some reason, to settle and stay in one place. It housed the whole family, so it's more than ample . . . for me . . . alone . . ." She grinned at him.

"Oh, I don't require any hints, my lady. I can hardly wait to set up housekeeping with you."

Edge headed directly through the city for la Strada Pisa, and reached it simultaneously with the circus train coming from the tober. As it passed from right to left in front of Edge and Autumn, the Florilegium now made quite an impressive parade: eleven vehicles, all of them gaudily painted—except the gleaming black rockaway—four of them drawn by matched and spectacularly handsome two-horse teams. Behind the wagons, the circus's one spare horse towed Beck's not yet completed but at least already wheeled Gasentwickler, and Peggy lumbered last of all, swathed in a new, betasseled, gold-lettered, gloriously scarlet covering. Edge saw with mild surprise that Pepper sat conspicuously beside Obie Yount on the wagon he was driving, and Yount looked mightily pleased about that. Jules Rouleau was stretched out comfortably atop the tarpaulin that covered the balloon in its wagon, where he was best insulated against jolts and jouncing.

Edge turned onto the Strada Pisa behind the elephant, then flicked the reins to urge Autumn's old nag up past the train, and fell in behind Florian. As soon as the train was off Livorno's cobbled part of the strada and onto a hard-packed, smooth dirt surface, Florian put his horse to a brisk trot and his rockaway began to draw away from the rest of the procession. After a couple of miles, the rockaway had gone out of sight in the morning ground mist, and the little cottage on wheels was leading the train.

Riding up front there, with all of Italy before him, feeling very much the professional equestrian director of a circus that was no longer a mud show but a real circus, with his beloved sitting close beside him, with prospects of their seeing new and exotic places, Zachary Edge was more pleased with life and the world than he had been since before the war, or maybe since much longer ago than that.

He took from his frock-coat pocket a box of Sigarette Belvedere—Autumn had given him a quantity of them as his birthday present, a week or so ago—struck a match, lit a cigarette and took a deep, satisfying inhalation. He had earlier considered the Italian men sissified, smoking these little tubes of tobacco, but when he tried one he found it tasty and pleasurable. It was also a safer thing to smoke than a pipe, around the circus's hay and straw and sawdust. When one's leisurely smoke was interrupted by urgent work to do, a cigarette could simply be stepped on, but the emptying of a pipe took time and scattered sparks broadcast. Edge smoked only cigarettes now, and so did most every other smoker in the company, including Pepper and Paprika. Abner Mullenax and Magpie Maggie Hag smoked the twisty, black, rank Italian cigars. Only Obie Yount, perhaps thinking it better sustained his "fusto" status, stubbornly stuck to his pipe.

The view of Italy that Edge and Autumn were at this mo-

ment observing from the Strada Pisa was not much of a view.
The road was as straight as Autumn's tightrope, crossing the
extensive coastal plain of the Toscana region, and that plain
was as flat as Kansas. The road itself was pleasant enough to
drive on, lined on both sides and completely overarched by
evergreen, flat-crowned umbrella pines. But, when the ground
mist finally wisped away in midmorning, there was nothing
to be seen beyond the trees but flat farm fields, with the
farmhouses so far away that only occasionally could one be
glimpsed. Now and again, the circus train met a farm cart
headed for Livorno, or was passed by one going toward Pisa,
and the occupants gave the troupers cheerful waves. But those
were the only people to be seen, for the farm fields had already been harvested of their wheat and barley. Oddly,
though, between the bleak, brown expanses of stubble, there
was frequently a field of brilliant yellow flowers, so profuse
that they made a solid yellow blanket over the ground. Edge
asked Autumn if she knew what kind of crop that might be.

"It's what they call here colza. In England we call it rape-
seed. You'll see it all over western Europe, winter or summer.
Whenever a grainfield gets poor and scanty, the farmer lets
it rest for a year and plants only colza on it. Somehow—
don't ask me how—that makes the ground rich and fertile
again."

"Well, right now, those patches of colza are the only pretty
things in this landscape."

"No farmer would plant colza just for its prettiness. He
doesn't think of beauty; he knows only fertile and fallow. He
is tied to the land; shackled to it." She leaned her head on
Edge's shoulder. "Thank goodness we are not. We can just
enjoy the prettiness and then move on to the next prettier
place. Aren't we lucky?"

"I've begun to think I'm the luckiest man in the world."

"But you shouldn't smile about it. You look much handsomer when you are not smiling."

"Confound it, woman! People are always telling me that.
Do I have to go around glooming like Job, just so I won't
cause comment?"

"Oh, I can tell when you're happy, Zachary, whatever face

you wear. When we first met, you told me I could do the smiling for both of us, for the rest of our lives. And I can, too, because I am the luckiest *woman* in the world.''

4

''I CAN scarcely believe our good fortune!'' crowed Florian, when he met the train, as promised, just outside Pisa. ''The municipio is renting us the city's Campo Sportivo for our tober. Very near to the famous Leaning Campanile. I gather that some visiting Livornese have highly praised the show. And, when I showed the authorities our impeccable conduct books, I did not even have to ask. They *volunteered* that ideal location. Well, let us not waste time. Follow my carriage.''

The troupe had not stopped along the road for a noontime meal; they had munched on snacks they carried, so it was now only midafternoon. Edge followed Florian, and the rest of the train followed him, across the bridge over the river Arno and then along a broad road skirting the main city, a road much crowded with other vehicular and pedestrian traffic, most of which came to a stop to gawk at the entry of the Florilegium, while other folk, in a hurry or uninterested in circuses, loudly cursed the jamming of the road.

This part of Pisa could have been the outskirts of Baltimore: all dingy warehouses and industrial buildings. But when the train had turned from the outer road into the city itself, the troupers could see, over the warehouse roofs, the skewed belfry of the Leaning Tower and the dome of the cathedral, almost as high as the Tower. Those tops of the two tallest buildings in Pisa remained in view all the way to the Sports Field, which was an oval racetrack with roofed wooden stands on either side and a neatly mown grass infield ample enough for the circus to spread itself out more than comfortably.

''Smooth as an English manor lawn,'' said Autumn.

And proudly Florian said, ''I told you, Zachary, that we would be a low-grass show in time.''

When most of the wagons were ranked in what would be
the backyard, with the dressing-room nearest to what would
be the back door, Stitches Goesle—sparing not even a glance
for the Leaning Tower in the near distance—bawled for the
roustabouts to start unloading the tent and baggage wagons,
and to unhitch and grain the horses, and to feed the lion and
elephant. Florian stayed on the lot to help Goesle supervise
the setting up and to get his first look at his expanded chapiteau. So did Carl Beck, to start the internal rigging as soon
as he could. But the artistes, being no longer involved in that
hard labor, had the afternoon to themselves, And Autumn,
though she had worked in Pisa several times before, cheerfully went as guide to Edge and those other troupers—
including even Magpie Maggie Hag, Hannibal Tyree and the
three Simmses—who were eager to take a look around the
city.

They strolled back to the broad road, through a gateway
in the ancient city wall, then down a cobbled avenue, across
two or three narrower streets, to emerge in the many-acred
expanse of the Piazza dei Miracoli. They looked about, and
most of them looked dazzled. Tucked off in a far corner of
the piazza was the Jewish Cemetery and—in Edge's opinion—the high wall around it was distinctive for its plain sim-
plicity, because the four other structures on the vast green
lawn flaunted more pillars and arches and pinnacles than he
had ever seen in all the years of his whole life. And surely
nobody anywhere could ever see so many at one time as
could be seen here simply by swiveling one's gaze from left
to right.

The immense cathedral, besides being unstinting of columns and arches, was horizontally striped by alternating
courses of black and white marble—rather aptly, thought
Edge, like alternate layers of devil's-food and angel cake.
Similarly striped was the huge, circular baptistery, a little way
distant from the cathedral's façade. Edge told Autumn that it
looked to him like a spare dome—complete with ornamental
pillars and arches and pinnacles all around it—left over from
some other massive church building.

"Not to me," she said, with a smile. "See, it's got that

little cupola on top, like a nipple. I always think of the baptistery as the exposed giant breast of some pagan Titan goddess buried under all this holy Christian ground.''

The far-famed Leaning Tower was also of black-and-white stripes of marble, pillared and arched around every one of its seven tiers and the belfry on top. Edge had been seeing engravings of it ever since his childhood geography classes, but the tilted campanile was far more impressive in actuality than in any mere picture. Now *that*, he thought, could be a Titan's wedding cake. Some jealous rival Titan had reached down, grabbed it and given a malicious yank, so that now the cake was stretched painfully high and uniformly cylindrical, all the way to where the belfry perched, and it seemed about to topple sideways off the Titans' wedding reception table.

Hannibal asked Autumn, ''When it s'posed to fall over, ma'am?''

''Well, it has stood like this for about six hundred years,'' she said. ''I don't think you have to worry about standing beside it this minute. Nevertheless, it goes on leaning a fraction of a millimeter more each year.''

''So it's *bound* to fall sometime,'' said Clover Lee, with awe.

''Sometime, but not today. We people are too lucky.'' Autumn gave Edge a glance and a smile. ''Florian and Zachary and I all say so. Would any of you care to climb to the top? There's a spectacular view. I should warn you, though: there are nearly three hundred steps.''

''Hell with that,'' said Mullenax. ''There's a saloon right across that next wide street yonder. I'll wait for y'all there.''

Fitzfarris lazily said he would, too, and so did Magpie Maggie Hag, saying she was too old and rickety for mountaineering. The rest paid their admissions—along with a few other tourists, all Italians from elsewhere in the country—and trudged up the stairs. Edge and Yount and some others ascended warily, holding to the wall and going up practically hand over hand, because they had the eerie sensation of being continuously and irresistibly drawn toward the tower's lower side. Only those whose acts and lives depended on an unerring sense of balance went up with agility and assurance.

But the view from the balcony that encircled the belfry was worth the climb. Westward, they could have seen all the way to the sea, and southwest to Livorno, but for the haze of Pisa's multitude of smoking chimneys. To the north and east, mountains were visible, an inspiring sight after the plain they had just crossed. To the south, the greater part of Pisa lay spread out before them. The city was about twice as big as Livorno, and much more richly studded with ornate palaces and churches and towers and citadels.

An ancient docent was posted on the balcony and, like something run by clockwork, he droned facts and figures about il Torre Pendente, first in Italian, then in English, concluding with the information that "in order to establish the laws of velocity and acceleration of falling objects, Galileo Galilei—from the downward side of this very balcony—dropped cannonballs and lesser weights . . ."

"Hoy," Quincy said under his breath, looking over the balustrade at the insectlike figures on the lawn below.

"Cannonballs, eh?" boomed Yount, grinning, having at last heard of an Italian with whom he had something in common. "Fetched 'em all the way up here to drop 'em? Where might I meet this Gali-Gali and shake his hand?"

The docent only blinked, and Autumn laughed. "Probably in heaven, Obie. He's been dead for more than two hundred years. Come to think of it, though, you might not even find him there. The Church denies heaven to men who are *too* strong."

"Shucks," said Yount, disappointed.

"Perhaps of more interest to the females among us," Autumn went on, "that widest avenue you see to the east is where you'll find the fanciest and most fashionable shops. It goes right on across the river bridge and farther yet. Plenty of shops. Just don't bankrupt yourselves before we get to Firenze, where—"

Pepper said, "Och, the sun is about to go down, and I'm thinking we'd better get down, too." She looked behind her, warily, at the seven sizable bells in the belfry. "If they ring the Angelus, or whatever these dagos do, it's lifelong deaf we'll be."

"Not to worry, signorina," said the aged docent. "The bells have never been sounded since they were hung here. The vibration might be too much for the Torre Pendente."

They went, anyway, to be back on the tober before dark. Each of them gave the old man a few coppers of mancia, and again many of them negotiated the staircase with caution and queasiness. They found Fitzfarris, Mullenax and Magpie Maggie Hag loitering about the base of the tower, all three of them exceedingly aromatic of breath.

As they approached the Campo Sportivo, Florian came across the racetrack to meet them, saying wearily, "The crew and I will be working for a while yet, so we'll be having a late supper. But I took time out to go and engage rooms at a hotel. You people might want to haul your luggage there, freshen up, take dinner at a decent hour. The hotel is not quite as magnificent as the Gran Duca, but it is convenient. La Contessa Matilde. Go back to the first corner and turn right."

"Well, all our hotels got noble names, by damn," said Yount. "Miz Sarah, you and Clover Lee ought soon to be meeting your counts or jukes at *one* of 'em."

Sarah gave him a wan smile. They and the others just now seeing the transformed chapiteau—much larger and more imposing than it ever had been—took the time to walk completely around it, admiring and marveling. Then most of them piled their personal belongings into an empty wagon.

Edge said to Autumn, "If you'll forgive me for letting you dine unescorted, I'd like to stay and get acquainted with the new setup."

"Of course, my love. I'll take your luggage along with mine."

The pavilion was still the same height as before: some thirty-five feet. But, with the fifty-foot-wide new canvas laced between the parted halves of the old round tent, it was now an oval spanning a splendid hundred and twenty feet from end to end. The old and new center poles protruded above bail rings at either side of the inset panel. Clearly that had required some alterations in both the old and new canvas—and still did. Two roustabouts were atop the tent peak, one clinging to each pole top, both of them busily stitching at the canvas and relacing ropes about the bail rings. From the ground, Dai Goesle was giving rapid-fire instructions which Aleksandr Banat, beside him, translated to them in a bellow.

Goeslé saw Edge appraising the work, and paused to say, "When we tear down here, I shall ask Florian and you, lad, for a day's layover. I should like to spread the canvas all on the ground and paint it. Look you now, 'Tis an obvious patchwork, new-canvas-colored and old-canvas-colored. I suggest stripes all over, but we can discuss that. At all events, a thin coating of oil paint will improve the chapiteau's rain resistance and life span. Also, I will have the artistic Chink paint the circus's name—big, *big*—above the marquee. What think you of the marquee, Zachary?"

Instead of having merely left a side panel unlaced so it could be pinned back to make a front door, as had heretofore been the practice, Goeslé had made two neatly hemmed slits, ten feet apart, in his new center canvas, from ground level to a height of eight feet. That flap was raised outward and supported on two new, candy-striped poles, like the roof over a front porch: a much more inviting entry-way. Edge could look in and see the pavilion's similarly cut back door just opposite, beyond the ring, which now had no center pole in its actual center to impede his view.

To make a sort of avenue leading patrons to the front door, Goesle had erected a four-foot-high plank platform on the left—where Fitzfarris would present his sideshow and mouse game and ventriloquy during intermissions. On the right, the red wagon and the cage wagon were parked end to end. Patrons would first encounter the red wagon's ticket booth, then could view the museum at the rear of that wagon, then move on and regard Maximus, then move on beneath the marquee and into the chapiteau. Both sides of the avenue were lined with Roozeboom's old pole torches, for the nighttime shows.

"Go you along inside, Zachary," said Goesle. "You will hardly recognize it,"

He hardly did. The pista looked much bigger than forty-two feet across, with no pole in it. The two center poles stood four feet away from the curbing on either side, leaving ample room for the come-in and the closing specs to parade around the outside of the ring. Canvasmaster Goesle and Chief Rigger Beck had strung guy wires outward and sideways from high on the two poles, to brace them, and those wires disappeared among the seat planking, heavily staked and turnbuckle-tightened at ground level.

Mathematically, the addition of the fifty-foot center canvas should have increased the chapiteau's seating capacity by half again. In reality it nearly doubled the capacity. The old tiers of seats, their stringers now firm on real iron jacks, curved around the semicircular ends of the tent, and Goesle's new, matching tiers of planking covered the straight sidewalls. But there was a good deal of space remaining between the old seats and the center poles and the canvasmaster had not wasted that. He had made still more plank seats and placed them all at ring-view level, to fill in the space. To all the front seats were attached, at intervals, Roozeboom's tin-reflector oil lamps.

"For the time being," said Florian, who was supervising the interior work still going on, "we'll let the jossers race each other for those front seats, or fight for them. But eventually Stitches wants to build comfortable folding chairs—what a circus calls its 'starback' seats—to occupy that best viewing space. And we can charge a higher ticket price for them than for what we call the 'blues'—the plain planks further back."

In some awe, Edge looked around, at what appeared to him to rival the pictures he had seen of the vast Roman amphitheaters of old. For a moment, he thought Goesle had extended the seat planking right over and across the tent's front door. But then he realized that the wooden construction up there, braced on jacks, was a stand for the circus band, neatly fenced about and provided with stools.

"Our chief rigger is almost finished with hanging the show," said Florian, gesturing upward.

Edge looked up and remembered how he had once thought that being inside the Big Top was like being inside a *Saratoga* sort of balloon. Now he might be inside a canvas cathedral, the space up there was so immense and airy, and the chapiteau top looked so much higher than it really was. The guy wires glinted where they converged on the center poles. The old pole wore its lungia boom, canted out at a slight angle over the pista. A roustabout was clinging there, affixing to the boom's end a block and fall for the hoisting of Pepper by her hair. Florian was gesturing to him instructions on how to rig the hoist in such a way that it would not tangle with the chandelier, also hanging up there.

The new pole had, on its ring side, a small wooden platform, with a rod-and-rope ladder dangling from it to the ground, and it took Edge a moment to recognize that the platform was Autumn's resting stand. At this moment, Boom-Boom Beck was kneeling on it, and he and a Slovak on the other center pole were adjusting the turnbuckles and tension of the tightrope that crossed the fifty-foot space between them. On the old pole a bright white spot had been painted at what would appear to be Autumn's eye level, for her guidon. The rope was exactly twenty-seven feet off the ground, but it seemed sky-high to Edge.

"Miss Auburn is a consummate artiste," said Florian, though Edge had not spoken. "As surefooted on a rope as on the pista sawdust. And an artiste wants her work or his work displayed to best advantage. You love the little lady, yes. But Zachary, if you want to have her go on loving you, take my advice. Do not attempt to be her *keeper*."

"You're right," said Edge. "It'll chill my gizzard every time she goes up there, but I'll try not to show it. To change the subject, let me ask you something. Since we don't now have a pole or any such thing in the middle of the ring— excuse me: in the pista—why are those men digging a big hole there?"

"For a grave," said Florian.

Edge stared and said incredulously, "You tell me not to worry about things. And you're expecting somebody to *die*?"

"Somebody already has. I hoped you would not notice."

"*What?*"

"An unfortunate accident, but an expendable someone. You recall that useless layabout named Sandov? When we unfurled a bale of canvas during the setup, he rolled out of it, quite stiff. We could have used him for a stringer jack.''

"Governor, that doesn't sound to me like any accident.''

"Not a mark on the body. He simply got baled up while he was napping, and suffocated.''

"That story smells a little tall. How could his chums not notice him napping on the canvas they were furling?''

"Ahem. Let me put it this way, Zachary. The identical accident has happened many times . . . during many tear-downs . . . at many circuses. That it seems always to happen to an unlovable and worthless person I prefer to ascribe to coincidence. I will ask, though, that you do not mention this incident to anyone else. None of the performers has ever troubled to count the roustabouts, I think, and certainly nobody could tell one of them from another.''

Edge somberly shook his head. "Of course I won't say anything. Hell, who am I to make a fuss about men dying, deservedly or otherwise?''

"Please remind me, however, when we get to the hotel, to scrap the man's conduct book,'' said Florian. "In case some meddlesome authority demands to see a match-up of books and their owners.''

So, when Florian, Edge, Beck and Goesle finally trooped to the Hotel Contessa Matilde, and were the only persons eating in the dining room at that hour, and some of the other troupers came just to sit and keep them company, the only subject discussed was that of the circus's come-in music.

"I've tried and tried, Governor,'' said Autumn, "but I have to confess that I just cannot concoct Italian lyrics to fit your accustomed 'God Rest Ye Merry' tune. Anyway, that's an old English song, and not many continental audiences will even recognize it. So I consulted with Kapellmeister Beck''—Beck nodded gravely—"and, with your permission, we'd like to use 'Greensleeves' instead. It's English too, of course, but it's known and loved all over the world.''

"It is,'' Paprika concurred. "I have heard it played on cimbaloms in Hungary.''

"Commendable initiative, my dear Autumn,'' said Florian. "But isn't it somewhat treacly for a come-in?''

"No, sir. Our talented bandmaster has done a very merry

and bouncy arrangement of the melody''—Beck looked modest—''and I did new lyrics, not so soppy and sentimental.'' She handed a piece of paper across the table. ''I don't claim it's *Die Meistersinger*, but it's simple enough that anybody can memorize the words.''

Florian, chewing, scanned the little quatrain she had written in Italian, quietly beating the measure of ''Greensleeves'' with his knife and fork, then put down the utensils to applaud all by himself. ''A fine job of work, my dear. We'll assemble the company and the band to rehearse it in the morning. Zachary, I repeat, you found a true jewel when you found that little lady. I bid you: treat her tenderly.''

''I try,'' said Edge, a trifle glumly, thinking of the high rope.

5

THE CHAPITEAU'S pista was again a level and unblemished circle of sawdust by the time the Florilegium prepared to open its first show in Pisa. Magpie Maggie Hag, in a sort of blur of movement, dealt out tickets from the red-wagon booth, and scooped in the lire and centesimi, and shoved out change—or most of it—and the incoming patrons scarcely glanced at the museum or the lion in their rush to claim the best seats, and the pavilion quickly filled, from front benches to those in the uppermost rear. After Banat dropped the marquee flap to close the front door, he reported to Florian, with what he evidently supposed was a snappy Confederate salute, ''Almost one thousand tickets I took,''

''Glory on us!'' said Pepper, overhearing. ''Faith, we'll soon be rich as Crazes.''

Florian laughed. ''Then let's not keep the good people of Pisa waiting, Irisher. Around to the backyard wid ye, for the come-in.''

The Grand Entry and Promenade was now led by Brutus, so that Abdullah, on her back, could add his bass drumming to the band's music right from the start. Except for the elephant and the horses and the capering terriers, everybody in the procession sang Autumn's words to Beck's rollicking rendition of "Greensleeves":

> Circo-o è allegro!
> Circo-o è squisito!
> Circo ha cuore d'oro,
> E benvenuto a-al Circo!

As Autumn had said, everyone in the audience knew the tune. By the time the parade was on its third circuit of the pista perimeter, the crowd had got the words as well, and was singing along in a roar that almost overwhelmed the windjammers' utmost efforts.

Florian and Edge had rearranged the program so that now the liberty horses did the come-in already wearing their plumes and spangles and tasseled blankets, and Colonel Ramrod could turn them into the pista while the rest of the parade went out the back door. The band swung smoothly into "Thunder and Lightning" and, at the crack of the sjambok, the horses went smoothly into their routine. Edge was exceedingly glad, this first time under the new high rigging, that Autumn was not going up there until the very end of the show. He would doubtless be nervous enough while he watched that, but at least he was not rattled and addled *before* doing this opening liberty act, or his later sharpshooting and his still-later Buckskin Billy voltige.

When the elephant reentered, after the horses' departure, she strode majestically and Abdullah boomed his drum doomfully to the "Battle of the Huns." The band went into a brisker music—a medley of von Suppé overtures—while Brutus did some of her solo tricks. The tug-of-war with volunteers had been cut from the act. Instead, Monday, Quincy and the three Chinese cartwheeled into the pista, beckoned Brutus onto the teeterboard and, as she seesawed happily, did their poses and pyramids and leapfrogging on her back. When Brutus carried Abdullah and the Simmses off again, the Chinese stayed in the pista to do their antipodal kicking and twirling of each other, to the incongruous accompaniment of some frantic Russian dances by Glinka. Next, Pepper and

Paprika did their perch-pole performance, to one of Liszt's Hungarian rhapsodies.

The band went silent while Florian called and coaxed "Bisnonna Filomena Fioretto" from the stands, and introduced her with all his usual flapdoodle. Sarah had now learned by rote to say her thanks in Italian when the cringing old lady was presented with the little cake and candle, and also to make her astounding request for a birthday horseback ride. She did so, over the soft music of "For He's a Jolly Good Fellow," in a cracked and quavery voice that served to mask any infirmities of her pronunciation.

When the horse ran away with the old lady, the act went over more spectacularly than ever before—numerous real old ladies in the seats actually swooned—and the crowd's gasps of relief and gusts of hilarity and thunders of applause were correspondingly greater when Filomena stood up on the horse's rump and shed all her grandmotherly black and stood revealed as Madame Solitaire. For the first time in a long time, Jules Rouleau, seated on the washtub near the back door, again sang, "As I sat in the circus and watched her go round . . ." After Sarah had taken her bows, she went, towelling herself, to congratulate Rouleau on finally "kicking sawdust" again after his long layoff. The band began "The Irish Jaunting Car" and Pepper went aloft for her hair-hang. Sarah was still chatting with Rouleau when she was suddenly spun around and kissed on the mouth.

"Pompás! Magnificent!" cried Paprika, hugging her tightly.

"It's—it's hardly the first time you've seen the act," Sarah said breathlessly.

"Ah, but your voice, your bit of Italian this time. Almost *I* believed it all real and true! You are öszintén müvési. Does one say in English you are a mistress of your art?"

"Well . . . er . . ." said Sarah, but then Paprika was kissing her again, long and passionately, while Rouleau looked on with one eyebrow lifted.

They were being watched from aloft, too, as Sarah saw when at last she was loosed from the embrace. Paprika followed her glance, but only mockingly smiled upward. Pepper, still and rigid in mid-air, was staring down at them with that hair-strained rictus grin and eyes of green ice. Beck was desperately putting all manner of trills and flourishes into "The Irish Jaunting Car," waiting for her to start her performance. Pepper did not, until both Paprika and Sarah had vanished through the back door. Then she threw herself into her spins and convulsions and swing-overs with such frenzy that Beck had to put the "Jaunting Car" to a headlong gallop.

Late that night, in the Contessa Matilde dining room, most of the troupers, at the several tables they occupied, prattled gaily about the success of their various acts, and how much better they could perform in the new, unimpeded pista, and with appropriate band music, and what an appreciative audience the Pisans were. But Pepper and Paprika sat at different tables. Sarah sat at yet another, not saying much and moodily picking at her supper.

Neither did Edge have much appetite, though he sat beside his Autumn, and she was as pleased and excited about the day's triumphs as any of the lesser artistes. Her tightrope act had brought the audience to a standing ovation at both the afternoon and evening shows, and now she was repeatedly trying to convince Edge that his own voltige act was, in fact, much more dangerous than her own. "I have to avert my eyes, Zachary, when you slide from the saddle of a galloping horse, and under its belly, among those churning hoofs, and up the other side into the saddle again." That did not much reassure him. Autumn had looked so tiny and so vulnerable and so fragile away up there under the tent roof, doing feats that had made him gulp even when she was doing them a mere eight feet off the ground. He could only hope that in time he would get over his dry-mouthed, clammy-palmed anxiety whenever she was aloft.

Much later that night, Jules Rouleau was just falling asleep when his hall door quietly opened and someone slipped into his nearly dark room. "Qu'est-ce que c'est?" he mumbled. "Surely not another massage at this hour?"

"It's not Maggie. It's me—Sarah. I need your help, Jules."

"Qu'est-ce que c'est?" he asked again, but now wide

awake and startled. In the dim light that reflected into the room from the kitchen courtyard downstairs, where the scullions were still cleaning up, Rouleau could see that Sarah was taking off her clothes.

She said shakily, "You—you watched that girl Paprika kiss me. Not just the quick kiss that show people often give one another, but like a—like a lover."

"Chérie," he said, sitting up in the bed, his own voice a little unsteady as Sarah continued to undress. "You could never have deluded yourself as to the nature of those two flagrant toms."

"No. But P-Paprika has lately been courting *me*. And when she kissed me today, I almost—no, I *did*—I enjoyed it. I was aroused by it."

"That can happen," Rouleau said, with what sangfroid he could muster. "But why come to me? Why are you taking off your—?"

"Jules, I need a man. Just to prove to myself that *I* am not a tom. I beg of you, Jules . . ." She was naked now, and slid under the covers beside him.

Rouleau shrank away, saying almost in panic, "Chérie, you embarrass me. You have long known that I am—in my way—what Pepper and Paprika are in theirs."

"You have at least a . . . male body. Please, Jules!"

"To me it would be . . . not *you*, you understand, dear Sarah . . . but the act itself would be abhorrent. There are other males on the show, masculine males, who would rejoice in obliging—"

"I have lost Zachary, and Florian is consumed with business, and any other man would swagger and brag and gossip. You are an old friend. Do it just once, for friendship's sake."

"I simply *cannot*, Sarah. You know I would do for you anything in my power. But that, it simply is not."

She pondered for a moment, then said diffidently, "Could you not pretend—pretend that I am a boy?" She turned so her back was to him, and nestled herself close against him. Rouleau groaned slightly, slid down from his pillow to curve his body to hers, and put his arms around her—but only at the waist, being very careful not to touch anything palpably female about her. "Now," Sarah said softly. "Try to imagine that I am . . . anyone you would prefer." She reached back to take hold of him, but he recoiled.

"Do not do that, please. It is too plainly a woman's hand. Do not even speak. I shall—I shall try . . ."

Except for the creaking of the bed, there was no other sound in the room for a long time, while Sarah tried with little movements of her bottom to entice Rouleau to an arousal of what stubbornly remained flaccid. She could feel him beginning to perspire but nothing else.

At last he broke the silence. "It is no use, Sarah. I am sorry, very sorry, but . . ."

"Perhaps if I did this?" she said, and slid downward in the bed. Her voice was muffled under the covers when she said, "Boys do this, don't they?"

Rouleau feebly groaned again, but let her try. And she tried with passion and energy and skill and patience, but to no effect.

"Je suis désolé, Sarah. It is hopeless."

After a moment, still under the covers, she said meekly, "Would you—could you do that? To me?"

"No!" he said, and violently moved away from her. "That, I will not even attempt. I am again sorry, Sarah, but I am certain I should be sick. You would feel more than ever rejetée."

Like a wounded animal, she crept upward in the bed again, and laid her head on the other pillow.

"Would you just hold me, then? Nothing more. Only hold me until we fall asleep."

He did, but still gingerly, touching no place feminine. The room was full dark now, the scullions having finished their late cleanup and put out all lights, but Sarah did not sleep at all. She was still wide-eyed when the darkness lightened slightly toward dawn and the rattle and clash of pots and pans began again, as the cooks came back on duty to prepare for breakfast. Rouleau's arms were still around her, so she considerately did not stir until he awoke, and that was quite late in the morning.

Thus it was that Clover Lee, heaping her breakfast plate at

the dining room's luxuriantly provisioned buffet sideboard, naïvely said to Florian, beside her, "Mother didn't sleep in our room last night. Was she with you?"

"Er . . . no," said Florian. "Not last night, no." The question had caught him unawares, or he might have equivocated, because Pepper and Paprika were next in line at the sideboard.

Pepper rounded on Paprika, her face contorted, but Paprika said, "You *know* where *I* was. In our room and in our bed. Remember? We kissed and made up. Five or six times, and very nicely, too."

Diplomatically, Florian and Clover Lee sidled off to a far table.

In a tight voice, Pepper said, "And *you* know bloody well how deep I always sleep afterward. Ye could have gone anywhere, wench!"

"Don't make a ridiculous scene, kedvesem. I don't go lurking about in the middle of the—"

"Och, ye lurk about her in the clear *daylight!* But let us just ask herself. Here's the hussy now." Sarah came into the dining room, noticeably red-eyed and tousled. Pepper rushed up to her and demanded, "Where *did* ye sleep, then, if not where ye belonged?"

Sarah snapped, "None of your goddamned business!" and walked around her.

Pepper hissed, ground her teeth, turned and threw her plate—whether at Sarah or at Paprika could not be told, because she missed. An innocent Milanese traveling salesman, taking only a continental breakfast of buttered panino, marmellata and coffee, found himself with a lap full of hot salsiccia and scrambled eggs. He sprang up, bellowing, "Fregna! Sono fottuto!"—but Pepper had stomped out of the room.

She was not seen again—and Paprika looked everywhere—until the band was already tuning up for the afternoon show. Then Pepper and Yount, cozily arm in arm, came strolling onto the Sports Field among the crowd that milled about there. Yount was flushed of face and pate, his beard was in some disarray. Pepper no longer looked furious, but serene, and the bodice of her green street gown was misbuttoned here and there.

"Pep!" cried Paprika, in something of a sob. "Hurry! We have another straw house. You've barely time to change for the come-in."

"Lardy-dardy," Pepper said offhandedly. "It's getting in practice I am for undressing and dressing in a twinkle. Ain't that so, ducks?" She gazed at Yount adoringly.

Yount went pinker and said, "Uh, well, I reckon that's commendable in a woman. Punctuality."

"Whisht, I've always come quickly. And often," said Pepper, while Paprika stared in horror. "Obie, macushla, would ye like to precede me in the dressing room?"

"No need, Miss Pepper. I only got to step out of these clothes. I got my Quakemaker leopard skin undern—"

"Losh, it's forgetting I was." And she giggled lasciviously. "Ah, well. Tooraloo for now, love, 'til next time."

Yount lurched away. looking almost tipsy, and Pepper tripped lightheartedly up the little stair of the dressing wagon. Paprika followed.

"You were just quizzing me and tormenting me, weren't you, Pep? All of that was színlelés—pretending—wasn't it?"

Pepper murmured, but to herself, "Musha, look at me. Did I come all the way from the hotel clad awry?" She began unbuttoning.

"Pep! Tell me none of that was true. You and that dumb ox."

Pepper looked at her, finally. "Nay, instead I'll tell ye an old tale the tinkers do tell. This jackeen comes to Biddy Early, d'ye see, and he asks the witchwoman for a talisman that will keep his pretty wife faithful to him. Biddy tells him he already *has* such a thing. Jackeen says what? She says 'tis a magic ring, boyo. Jackeen says where is it, then? Old Biddy says 'tis 'twixt your woman's legs. As long as ye keep your finger in that ring, never cuckolded can ye be."

"Oh, Pepper, dearest one, I've not been unfaithful. I've no more than flirted. And never with a *man*, never since I've known you."

"Shall I tell ye, then," said Pepper, stepping with sensuous slowness out of her last garment, "what ye've been missing?"

"Pep, you didn't!"

Silence.

"Did you?"

Silence, as Pepper slipped sinuously into her tight fleshings.

"You only teased him," Paprika said hopefully. "Perhaps you let him stroke the velvet . . ."

Silence, with a dreamily reminiscent smile.

"Please, Pep," Paprika said despairingly. "Don't say that you actually let him thread the needle!"

"Again and again. He ain't called the Quakemaker for nothing."

Paprika was weeping now. "You swore you would never—"

"Arrah, don't go having the sterics. 'Twas not as terrible as the only other time a man took me. I've told ye about that. How me uncle Pete Rovie bundled me school frock over me head and skewered me like a chicken—in the wrong hole, even, he was that dim-witted. But with dear Obie, now, I do think I might even learn to *prefer* doing it proper, like." And she swept out of the wagon, leaving Paprika in tears.

So it was Paprika who was truant from the Grand Entry, ashamed to show her puffy face and its ruined makeup and her general air of misery. In consequence, she got a severe scolding from Florian, and another when she went through her perch-pole routine as stiffly as an automaton.

When the afternoon audience had dispersed into the twilight, most of the performers and crew busied themselves with seeing to their equipment, props and animals, and Autumn said to Edge, "Would you come with me, Zachary? Herr Beck is rearranging my rig for a practice session, and I'd like to show you something."

He walked with her inside the chapiteau. Up on the bandstand, Dai Goesle was affixing pole lamps he had bought that morning in a Lungarno shop. None of the windjammers really needed them, since none but Boom-Boom Beck could read music, with or without light. But Magpie Maggie Hag had created for the bandmaster a uniform that made him look as impressive as a Feldmarschall, and he wanted it to be visible. Beck was visible at this moment, but in work clothes. He and a couple of Slovaks had disconnected the farther end of Autumn's tightrope from its guidon-marked center pole, brought it down at an angle across the pista and were securing that end to a heavy stake.

"I'll be rehearsing Sunday and Monday in their slant climb," said Autumn. "They should be ready to make their début at it by the time we get to Florence. But what I wanted to show you . . . Well, every time I look down when I'm up there on the rope, I see you watching me, all pale and tense. I thought perhaps, if you just climb to the platform with me"—she gestured to the rod-and-rope ladder—"it might relieve you of some of your apprehensions."

"All right. Yes, it might."

"Go ahead. I'll follow you up."

Like the rankest of rubes, Edge started to climb the rope ladder as he would any ordinary wooden one. But as soon as he had both hands and both feet on the rungs, the ladder abruptly slanted outward so that he was hanging almost horizontal. He found himself braced that way, unable to proceed, as if he were climbing the *underside* of an ordinary ladder.

Autumn laughed tolerantly and said, "Not like that. There's a knack to it. Drop down and I'll show you." He did, shamefacedly, and watched her demonstrate. "You actually climb up the side of it. See? The rope against your body, hands and feet around either side of it to the rungs." She went up as swiftly and agilely as a monkey, though she did not at all resemble a monkey in any other respect. "Now you try," she called down from the resting stand.

Edge did it, though slowly and awkwardly, feeling as if he had suddenly doubled in weight. He was so intent on placing his hands and feet alternately on the rungs that not until he stood beside Autumn on the tiny platform did he look down, and he almost reeled. Hands locked on the center pole behind him, he exclaimed:

"Jesus, woman! It's like looking down from Natural

Bridge! It looks a damn sight higher from here than it does from down there, and that was fearsome enough.''

"Oh dear. I hoped this would cure you of worrying about me.''

"And look yonder," he said in awe. "You have to cross that gap between here and the other pole where the white mark is. It looks as wide as the Mississippi!''

"I don't *have* to do it. I do it because I have a talent for it. Because it's what I do best.''

"Now that's a flat untruth," said Edge' relaxing slightly. "I can list any number of things you do—''

"Zachary!''

"Well, it's a fact. All right, you've fetched me up here, and I've looked, and I still can't promise I'll ever get case-hardened about your performing up here. It's only because I love you that I worry about you. But, as you say, it's your work and your art.''

"And my pleasure. Up here—especially when the crowd and the band go all hushed and suspenseful—I don't think of danger or the altitude or the need for precision and caution. My body goes on performing while I do nothing but *listen*. Up here, everything murmurs so sweetly. You listen, too, Zachary. Do you hear? The canvas just above us quietly ruffling, the guy wires humming, even the center pole vibrating enough to sing gently . . .''

"Autumn, I love you too much to let my worrying worry you. Too much ever to do anything to hinder or handicap you. So *that* I never will. No conditions, no thou-shalt-not's, no meddling.''

"You are a considerate lover. Maybe that's why I love you, too.''

"Right this minute, I'm a slightly dizzy lover. Do I go down the same way I came up?''

"Same way. Feet and hands on opposite sides of the rope.''

When they were down, and Autumn had skipped off to change into practice clothes, Edge stayed. When there was no one in the chapiteau except Slovaks, he climbed up and down the ladder several more times. He would never get monkey-agile at it, he decided, but at least he could do it now less like a fearful and feeble old codger.

Outside, in the front yard, Paprika found Sarah loitering not far from where Florian was conversing with a well-dressed stranger.

"Sarah, kedvesem," Paprika said. "Pepper and I have come to a final, definite parting of the ways. I have taken a separate room at the hotel. Perhaps now I could persuade you—"

"Hush!" Sarah said irritably. "Florian has a distinguished visitor. I am trying to hear what they say."

The stranger was saying, ". . . Elder brother is of course il Direttore, but I am the one brother who speaks English. And we assumed, seeing your affisi—'Confederate American Circus'—that you yourself would be American."

"I am honored by the visit, signore. During my earlier days in Europe, I never had the good fortune to encounter your circus or any of your family. We can speak in Italian, if you prefer."

"No, no, sta bene. English is good practice for me. I enjoyed your show, Signor Florian. Small but well organized and pieno di energio—how would one say it? Full of vim?"

"Here is our equestrian director, signore," said Florian, as Edge came to join them. "Also our tiratore and voltige rider, as you have seen. May I introduce you? Signor Orfei; Colonel Edge." The two men bowed and shook hands. Florian went on, "A visit from one of the famed Orfei family is compliment enough. That you speak a compliment, as well, is high praise indeed."

The visitor said, "One likes to pesare—size up, do you say?—size up the competition."

"Now you flatter us," said Florian. "We can hardly be competition for the Circo Orfei. Yours must be the oldest circus in continuous existence in all of Europe."

"We believe so. It was more than a hundred and thirty years ago that an Orfei—he was a monsignore of Holy Church, can you imagine?—fell in love with a gypsy girl, shed his vows and vestments and ran away with her. On the road, he played flauto music and she danced, for coppers thrown. Until they accreted other wandering show folk. But for many decades, Signor Florian, the Circo Orfei was only a gypsy caravan train, much smaller than yours is now.''

''An inspiriting story, signore,'' said Florian. ''And I warn you, I hope to emulate the Orfei's growth and success.''

''I wish you buona fortuna. Some circus proprietors fear and fight competition. I personally believe that the more and better circuses there are, the more of them the people wish to see and enjoy and compare. I did not come here, I assure you, to dissuade you from competing. We are showing now in Lucca, just nineteen chilometri from here, so I am making a courtesy call on a colleague.''

''Perhaps you would like to look around? The colonel and I will be pleased to escort you.''

''Grazie, but I have already circulated, sconosciuto. One sees best that way. And I observed immediately one thing odd. You have no teloni del giro.''

Florian translated for Edge, ''High fencing around the whole tober.'' And to Orfei, ''I am familiar with the European practice of fencing to block the view of everyone not a paying patron. Actually, that would be better employed in America, where the natives are incurably nosy. Here in Europe, the people are more polite, and do not go prying into our privacy of the backyard. If and when I find fencing desirable, I shall have it built. But there are a great many other things taking priority.''

''Senz'altro. Si capisce.'' Orfei leaned both hands on the ivory handle of his ebony cane. ''While I am here, signori, may I essay one inquiry? Your funambola, the Signorina Autunno, she had made application to join the Circo Orfei. I would certainly not deprive you of your finest act. However, if the signorina still wishes . . .''

Edge bristled, but Florian spoke first. ''I think not, signore. The fact is, she and Colonel Edge here have—ahem—become as close as your apostate ancestor and his gypsy love.''

''But I don't own her,'' said Edge. ''You can speak to her yourself, and in private.''

''No! Never! Colonello, I am an Italian. I charge you: remember Romeo e Giulietta, Dante e Beatrice, Monsignore

Orfei e la zingara. Interfere with a love affair? I could never hold up my head in Italy again!"

"Much obliged," Edge murmured.

"As a matter of plain fact, signori, our program is already somewhat overcrowded. My elder brother is occasionally too enthusiastic in hiring, and too sentimental to dismiss anyone. But one of our best trapeze artistes, his contract is soon to expire, and I think he would like to move elsewhere."

Florian said, "I should be more than pleased to have a trap act, but we have no rigging for it."

"Maurice LeVie—a Frenchman, but he speaks also Italian and English—Maurice owns his own rig. Nickel-plated. Beautiful. Also his own horse and van for transport."

Florian whistled admiringly. "Could I afford him?"

"One hundred fifty lire each week."

Florian whistled again, not so admiringly. "Thirty dollars. That's twice as much as I'm paying my equestrian director here."

Edge said, "Don't concern yourself with that. A good trapeze act ought to be worth that and more to us. And I won't grudge his making a salary bigger than mine. I've been up there in the tent peak once, and I'm damned if I'd *cavort* up there for any amount of money."

Orfei said, "Perhaps you signori—and any others of your company—will honor our show with a visit in Lucca. Maurice closes the first half of our program, before the intervallo. You can see him perform, and judge his worth, and get back here, all in one day."

"Good idea, that," said Florian. "We will have a day's layover here after the close of this stand, to do some furbishing. Thank you for the invitation, Signor Orfei. The colonel and I and our sideshow director will see you in Lucca."

The Florilegium's stand at Pisa lasted only ten days in all, but it was by no means what Florian would have called a bloomer stand back in the States or a bianca here in Europe. It was a succession of well-packed, often turnaway houses. Evidently every person resident in Pisa attended, and every tourist and traveler passing through, but, with the chapiteau's vastly increased capacity, ten days sufficed to entertain them all. During that time, the circus suffered no accidents or internal strife, though everyone noticed how Sarah avoided Paprika's company, and Paprika and Pepper avoided one another, except when necessary at performances.

When, at the night show on the tenth day in Pisa, the chapiteau seats were only two-thirds occupied—mostly, said doorman Banat, by patrons he recognized as repeaters—Florian gave orders for the teardown that very night. Early next morning, all the canvas lay spread out flat on the now brown, trampled and sawdusty oval of grass where it had stood. Stitches was walking, barefoot and bent over, ruling chalk lines on the canvas to guide the barefoot Slovak painters waiting with buckets of the colors chosen: green and white.

"I am using only the thinnest possible wash," Goesle announced to those of the company looking on, "to preserve the canvas's flexibility, and not to diminish the lovely glow of it when it is lit inside at night. Also, the paint will dry by tomorrow."

Edge hitched Snowball to the rockaway, and he, Florian and Fitzfarris set off at a brisk trot through the morning ground mist on la Strada Lucca. This road was lined on both verges with immense chestnut trees, leafless now, so their limbs meeting above the road resembled the ogive arches and groins of some kind of churchly edifice. Also, the bark of the chestnuts' trunks peeled and curled like a multitude of scrolls. Edge could entertain the illusion that he was riding through a medieval monastery's library. Beyond the trees, the land was still flat, but no longer just fields of stubble and colza. There were orchards of twisted, tormented-looking olive trees, and vineyards of grapevines similarly warped, knotty and contorted.

Fitzfarris said, "If somebody was to ask me right now for a capsule description of Italy, I'd call it a gnarled land."

"Oh, you'll see a variety of landscapes before we leave Italy," said Florian. "Alabama cotton fields, Vermont stone quarries, Minnesota iron mines. Louisiana rice paddies, Virginia timber forests, snow-capped Adirondacks . . ."

They arrived at the Circo Orfei's tober—on a Campo Sportivo almost identical to Pisa's, set between two projecting bastions of Lucca's high and thick old city walls—just before the afternoon show began. So Florian hurried Edge and Fitz along the circus's midway: a row of booths topped by canvas banners portraying, with unabashed exaggeration and artistic license, the attractions to be found within: La Dama Obesissima, Ercole il Potente, Il Ragazzo Pinguino . . .

"Very Fat Lady, Hercules, Penguin Boy," Florian translated, as they went by. "He'd be one of those flipper-armed children."

The Orfei's chapiteau was no bigger than the Florilegium's now was, but it was painted all over with varicolored stars, and flew pennons and burgees emblazoned "Orfei" not only from its two center pole tops but also from the points of all its surrounding side poles. And there were numerous other tents around and behind the big one. The two most prominent bore banners: one crowded with pictures of animals around the word Serraglio; the other showed a gauzily veiled dancing girl and the words Ballo del Tabarin.

"Menagerie and Music Hall," said Florian. "The latter being, no doubt, a rawhide girly show for men only."

The smaller tents had only small signs, all the same: È Vietato l'Ingreso. "No admittance," said Florian. "The troupe's dressing rooms, cook tent, smithy, that sort of thing. And look, there are even donnickers for the patrons." He pointed to two privy-sized boxes off to one side of the tober, marked Uomini and Donne. In the circus's backyard, beyond all the no-admittance tents, were ranked and filed numerous tinker-style caravans similar to Autumn's, with little tin chimneys trickling smoke.

"This is some spread," murmured Edge.

"Don't let it daunt you, lads," said Florian. "Ours will be as grand someday. Grander."

At the front door, a haughty Harlequin took their tickets and a haughty Columbine handed each of them a well-printed program of several pages. Fitzfarris examined his with professional interest, noting that it carried advertisements for numerous Lucca merchants and services. As at their own chapiteau, Florian, Fitz and Edge entered this one under the bandstand. It held three times as many musicians as Beck commanded—all of them ornately (and irreverently) uniformed as the Pope's Swiss Guardsmen—and they were thundering a medley of operatic marches for the come-in.

.   "Just look at that," said Fitzfarris, marvelling, when they found their numbered starback chairs. "The back door has velvet curtains and a fancy proscenium arch."

The Grand Entry and Promenade that came through it was even more splendiferous. It was led by the equestrian director, dressed not gaudily but in formal riding dress: glossy top hat, "pink" swallowtail coat, well-cut breeches and gleaming high boots. Besides the multitude of artistes strutting in the procession—spangled and flowing-cloaked and profuse of ostrich plumes—there were four elephants, two camels, twenty or more caparisoned ring horses, a lion and a tiger and a leopard, each in its separate cage wagon.

There were also nonfunctional tableau wagons, richly carved and gilded, bearing painted panoramas and appropriate props, depicting such events as Columbus discovering the New World, Marco Polo discovering China and various other Italianate historical highlights all the way back to Caesar discovering Britannia. To judge from the tableaux, Columbus and Polo and Caesar had been greeted in every new land by numbers of native women only diaphanously clad in gauze and gossamer. Edge stood up and peered to get a better look at those wagons as they made their way around the farther curve of the pista. Their inner sides consisted only of laths and chicken wire and two-by-four buttresses. Edge sat down again and remarked on this.

"Common practice," said Florian. "Every circus promenade goes counter-clockwise around the outside of the pista. Why waste work and expense to adorn the left side of the wagons?"

The last of the procession was still trickling out through the back-door proscenium when the first performers erupted inward through it—a violently harum-scarum tumbling act. "I Saltimanchi Turchi!" bellowed the equestrian director before the band bellowed, even more loudly, the overture to Rossini's *Il Turco in Italia*.

Signor Orfei had complimented the Florilegium's "well-organized" show, but this one was much more so. It had to be, there was such an abundance of it. While one act was making its bows to a storm of applause, another performer or troupe would be already going into action. Edge watched enviously but closely, making mental notes, as the equestrian director, ever cool and suave, managed all that teeming cast of characters and animals, plus props and rigging and the roustabouts (every one deft and unobtrusive, wearing black coveralls) who carried and rolled and hauled the varied equipment in and out of the pista.

There was not a fumbled performance in the whole first half of the program, nor a slow-paced one. Even the four elephants came in at a lumbering trot, unaccompanied by any bull man, and went briskly through their strength-and-balance tricks without any evident commands except an occasional snap of the equestrian director's whip. Seemingly of their own accord, they closed with the dramatic "long mount"— the lead elephant rearing on her hind legs, those behind rearing to put their forefeet on each other's rumps, all up curling their trunks and trumpeting triumphantly.

Meanwhile, the Slovak roustabouts were loosing the ropes to let dangle from the chapiteau's peak the glittery, nickel-plated rigging of "Signor Maurice, il intrepido acrobata *a-e-ro*-batico Francese!" and a small, dark man skipped into the pista. He was enveloped in a scarlet cape, which he doffed with a magnificent, twirling flourish. He was slim almost to skinniness, and the tights were spangled electric-blue all over. He twinkled up the rope ladder as nimbly as Autumn had done.

Edge said to Florian, "He's got *two* trapeze swings up yonder. How can he use them both?"

"When was the last time you saw a trap act, Zachary?"

"Damned if I remember. Sometime well before the war."

"Ah, then you have a treat in store. Since then, Monsieur Léotard in France has revolutionized the art, and every other aerialist in the world is following his lead."

Maurice LeVie's performance was indeed something new to Edge, and to Fitzfarris, too. They had previously seen trapeze artistes do nothing more than the twists and flips and swingovers possible on any gymnasium's horizontal bar— only with the bar suspended high in the air. Maurice likewise did those things first, but then—as the band played Strauss's "Bal de Vienne"—he hung by his knees from his bar and set it swinging, faster and farther and higher with each swing. Suddenly he let go with his legs and launched himself through empty air—the entire audience gasped—to catch the other bar with his hands. The impact started that trapeze swinging, and now the bespangled Maurice literally flashed back and forth, like blue lightning, between the two high-swinging bars, sometimes catching hold with his hands, sometimes with his bent knees, sometimes only by his toes. And in the empty space between the two bars he did daring rolls and twists and tumbles, as if he were absolutely weightless. At the very last, Maurice stood erect, heel to toe, on one of the still perilously swinging bars, held up his arms in the V and continued to swing, balancing there, with no support but centrifugal force, while the audience went wild.

Fitzfarris exclaimed, "We've got to have him, Florian!"

"We will, if he'll have us. Let's get out before the crowd does."

In the front yard, Fitzfarris went off to inspect the midway attractions, while Florian and Edge went to the red wagon and found there the same one of the brothers Orfei that they had already met. He invited them in, set chairs for them beside his desk, gave them each a cigar and a glass of good Barolo wine, and said, "Well? Would you wish to speak to Monsieur LeVie, Signor Florian?"

"I think it unnecessary. His work speaks for itself. And he must be fatigued at this moment; I would not disturb his rest. If I might just see his conduct book?"

"Certo," said Orfei, and opened a desk drawer containing scores of those things, shuffled among them, brought one out and handed it to Florian. "Everything in it is praise and commendation. Nothing whatever in it to discredit the man. Except, of course, that." And he pointed to something on one of the little book's pages.

"Of course, that," said Florian, but he seemed to pay little heed to whatever it was, skimmed quickly through the other pages, and gave the book back to Orfei. "Have you mentioned to him our interest in acquiring his talents?"

"I have, signor, and he was most enthusiastic. It would be a challenge and a delight, he said—his very words—to employ his trapeze in helping to hoist a new, small show to greatness. And he was not being either egotistical or condescending. Maurice really is a gentiluomo—how would you say?—a jolly good fellow."

"Done and done, then," said Florian. "I expect our Florilegium to be in Firenze six or seven days from now, and I shall hope to have a three-week stand there, at the very least. Unless Maurice changes his mind in the meantime, we shall trust in his joining us whenever it is convenient to him."

"Maurice will not disappoint you, signore. He will be there."

"And the Circo Orfei? Whither bound?"

"Siena next, then we move southward for the winter, perhaps as far as Egypt."

"After Siena, Rome, I suppose?"

"Dio guardi, no! At least, we will not go there again until and unless Rome becomes one with the rest of the Kingdom of Italy. The Province of Rome is the last remaining Papal State. Perhaps vindictively, the authorities have become oppressive and censorious. Puritanical, if one may apply that word to Holy Church. The Roman carabinieri nearly jailed me and my brothers for dressing our bandsmen like the Swiss Guard. Believe me, they would make you shroud all your females in shapeless smocks. They would monitor every jest and joke. No, no, I advise you, friend Florian, stay clear of the Holy City and its environs."

"Thank you. We will. A pity, though. Few of our troupe have ever visited there."

"Oh, visit, by all means. No one should miss seeing Rome, and mere visitors are not interfered with. Also, I should tell you that the Roman people are not as sanctimonious as their overlings. If you pitch at Forano, just north of the State border, and if Rome hears good notice of your show—eppur si muove—the people will readily travel the fifty chilometri of railroad to attend.''

"I thank you again, Signor Orfei," said Florian, getting to his feet. "You have been most helpful and generous and hospitable. I hope it will be in my power to repay somehow—"

"Only continue to give a good show, signore. Keep the circus, as an institution, in good repute. If we all do that, we all help each other."

When Florian and Edge emerged from the office wagon, the crowd had all gone back into the chapiteau for the second half of the performance, and the midway was empty of every josser except Fitzfarris. He said dismissively, "The freaks are all pretty much standard stuff. And that rawhide hootchy-cootchy is as tame as milk. We've got girls a damn sight handsomer, and I could put on a damn sight racier show . . . if you'd let me, Governor, and if I can talk our ladies into doing it."

"If they have no objection, I have none," said Florian. "But that will have to wait until we've got a separate annex tent, to keep it private and discreet."

The three were mostly silent on the way back to Pisa, each of them mulling over the things he had most admired and envied at the Circo Orfei, and calculating ways and means to adapt those things to his own work, concerns and responsibilities in the Florilegium. It was after dark when they got back, so since they could not inspect Goesle's canvas paintwork until daylight, Florian drove directly to the hotel. The other troupers, most of whom had spent the free day shopping and sightseeing all over town, were having dinner for a change, instead of a midnight supper. The new arrivals joined them at the tables, and handed around the Orfei programs— Florian called them "Bibles"—for the others to admire, and regaled them with accounts of the wonders they had seen, and with their avowed intentions of making the Florilegium, before much longer, "even bigger and better than the Circo Orfei!"

*   *   *

Next morning, they checked out of the hotel and rode with their luggage to the tober, where they were sincerely thrilled by the great spread of canvas on the ground. It no longer looked like drab, ordinary canvas, but like something fresh from a toy shop—broad green and white stripes from peak to bottom, the stripes converging into points atop the semicircular ends of the tent, and an elaborate cartouche above the marquee entrance flap, within which panel the Chinese artist had painted in vivid black-outlined orange, with frills and garnishes, FLORIAN'S FLOURISHING FLORILEGIUM. Everyone made fulsome and congratulatory comments to Goesle—everyone except Magpie Maggie Hag. She looked at it and said, "Red?"

"Red?" echoed Dai Goesle. "Are you perchance colorblind, Madame Hag? There is green and white yonder, and a bit of orange and black."

"I see too good," she said. "There is red on it." With which she went and got inside one of the van wagons.

Goesle shook his head, turned to Banat and said, "Order the men to bale it, stow it and get ready to roll, now just."

"If Maggie's dukkering something," Edge muttered to Florian, "oughtn't we to make sure there's nobody asleep on the canvas?"

"Hush," was all that Florian replied.

The troupe's final packing and other preparations for departure were briskly and quickly done. But, once the train was on the Strada Mare-Firenze, Florian's rockaway set a decorous pace. Florence was some sixty miles distant, a three-day run without hurrying. There were other towns along the way, but Florian considered most of them not worth setting up for.

"So we will spend tonight at Pontedera," he told Rouleau, riding with him. "In a hotel or albergo if it has one. If not, we will camp out as we used to do. The next day's run will bring us to Empoli. That town is the junction point of two main railroad lines, so there we will set up and show. The local populace ought to give us two or three days' attendance, and perhaps some of the rail travelers will stop off to see us, besides."

The circus train arrived at Pontedera at twilight, and the town did boast two decent inns which, between them, had food enough to feed the whole company and rooms enough to accommodate all who would not be sleeping in the wagons in the stable yard. Magpie Maggie Hag was one who stayed outside, not even emerging from her seclusion to eat dinner. Autumn and Edge, also, after dining at one of the inns, elected to sleep in her little cottage on wheels, the first time they were occupying it together.

"Compact, cozy and pretty," said Edge, taking a good look around the interior, most of which was painted a cheery sunshine yellow.

"It was rather too cozy," said Autumn, "even for me alone, when I had to carry all my rigging in here. I'm glad Florian gave me wagon room for all that gear."

In one corner was a small coal-oil stove, for heating or cooking, with a tin stovepipe going up through the barrel roof. There were cabinets and cupboards for stores and wardrobe and linens. There was also Autumn's trunk and hand luggage, Edge's dunnage bag, his several weapons and their possibles kit. The one bed, along the van's left wall, was cleverly hinged under its middle. With its outside half folded over the other, toward the wall, it presented its underplanking for a table, and there were two chairs to set at that table. When the tabletop was flipped open again, it revealed a palleted and blanketed bed big enough for two. In both walls of the van and in its entrance door were outward-opening windows curtained with yellow chintz. There were window boxes for them, empty of flowers in this season, with hooks enabling the boxes to be hung inside when the van was on the move and outside when it was stationary. On the wall were two other things: an oval mirror, rather wavery and uncertain of reflection, in a chipped stucco frame; and on the facing wall a much better-framed photograph of the French ropewalker Mme Saqui, autographed "to Mlle Auburn" in English and in a loopy, childish hand, "When this you see— Remember me."

Edge had brought from the albergo a bottle of Capri wine "to toast this blithesome occasion." Autumn fetched two goblets from a cupboard and they did that, happily, clinking their glasses, as they sat at the table. When they had finished the wine, they opened the table into its bed aspect and celebrated the occasion even more intoxicatingly. They were still in one another's arms when, early the next morning, they were awakened by an awful scream.

Edge bounded to a window, threw it open and stuck his head out. Not far away stood the dressing-room wagon, its door open, and Pepper Mayo was running away from it, emitting shrieks like a banshee. Clover Lee was also visible, coming down the steps of that wagon, very slowly and stiffly, as if she were sleepwalking.

"Clover Lee!" Edge called anxiously. "What's going on?" Autumn was now beside him at the window. From various other wagon doorways and windows peeked out bewildered black, yellow and Slovak faces.

Clover Lee continued her trancelike pace until she was close enough to tell Edge, in a voice devoid of any emotion or inflection, "Mother didn't sleep in our room again last night. When none of the others coming down for breakfast knew where she might be, I said I would look in the wagons. Pepper said she would come with me . . ."

"Well?"

"We found her in there." She waved vaguely toward the wagon.

"Is something wrong with her? Is she ailing? Hurt?"

Clover Lee shook her head, and her eyes filled with tears. She struggled for a less explicit language, and finally managed to say, "We found her . . . avec Paprika . . . les deux toutes nues . . . dorment . . . en posture de soixante-neuf . . ."

Edge understood the words, but not the import. When Autumn saw the blank look on his face, she whispered in his ear. Edge colored slightly, but recovered and said to Clover Lee, "You might save yourself some surprises and shock, girl, if you weren't always snooping and meddling in your mother's private doings."

"Don't call her my mother any more!" said Clover Lee, with a sudden resurgence of spirit. "I won't be daughter to any rotten *tom!*'' And she too went running off toward the albergo.

So when the circus train took to the road, there were now four females—Sarah, Pepper, Clover Lee and Paprika—riding in vehicles as far apart as possible and avoiding other people's eyes. The rest of the troupers rode in an embarrassed silence, reluctant to talk to their wagon companions because it might look as if they were bandying low gossip or ribald jokes about the morning's incident. When they arrived at Empoli and Florian had visited the municipio, then directed the train to its allotted tober beyond the railroad yards, and the crew began the setup, everybody was still feeling constrained to only necessary remarks, questions and responses. There were not even many cries of wonderment and delight when the tent went up, far more handsome and impressive in its new paint than when it had simply lain on the ground.

The company's stiffness prevailed until show time the next afternoon, when the chapiteau filled to capacity with the local residents, mostly sooty railroad workers and their families. Then all the troupers forced smiles onto their faces for the come-in—and all the subsequent acts were done with seemingly carefree panache, even Pepper's and Paprika's perch-pole act. But then, while Sarah was doing her Pete Jenkins, Pepper went and got Obie Yount, and with him in tow confronted Paprika.

"I want the Quakemaker here to tell ye a thing," Pepper said grimly. "Obie, did you and me ever go to bed together?"

Yount's eyes bulged, and he appeared to have swallowed his tongue.

"Did you and me ever do *any* kind of kerfuffle? Anything more than walk and talk and maybe hold hands once or twice?"

Yount gulped several times before he could say, "Why, no. Never, Miss Pepper."

"Is that the truth, Obie?" Paprika said wretchedly.

"Honest to God, Miss Paprika. After what you once told me, I damn sure wouldn't want to have anything to do with . . . er . . . I wouldn't presume to poach on any private preserves.''

Paprika burst into tears. ''Oh, Pepper, why did you pretend—?''

''Hoping jealousy would bring ye back and bind ye. Didn't work, did it? Come! Now we'll have a word with your new sweetmeat!''

When Sarah finished taking her bows and acclaim, she found Pepper and Paprika waiting for her near the back door.

''I've told Pap and now I'll tell you, too, ye bawd,'' said Pepper, almost snarling. ''My new act will put the both of yez in the shade. Out on the pavements. Just watch! Yez'll get what the Connaught men shot at!'' And she danced out into the pista, where Florian was introducing ''l'audace Signorina Pepe!''

She first went through her familiar hair-hang performance, slant-eyed, grin-masked, to the band's ''Irish Jaunting Car.'' But when she had been applauded for that, she held up a hand to the crowd, as if to say, ''Wait a bit, and watch what's next.'' Abdullah commenced a slow, suspenseful, rumbling roll on his drum, while the roustabouts lowered Pepper almost to the ground. There Quincy was waiting. Pepper, with both hands, grasped the loose end of the rope tied around his waist, and the Slovaks again began to haul her aloft.

''No, Pep!'' cried Paprika from the sidelines, audible even over the continuing drumroll. ''The weight is too much!''

But nothing untoward happened while Pepper and her small black burden were drawn up close to the lungia boom. Nothing happened until Quincy began his contorting and knotting of himself. The strain of that drew Pepper's face into a more than usually broad grin, and the grin was still on her face when, all in one instant, she swung Quincy's rope and slammed him against the center pole—where, surprised and dazed, he clung—and Pepper's whole scalp tore loose from her head and she plummeted to the pista with a deadweight thump and an explosion of sawdust around her, and the entire audience screamed at the sight of what was even more gruesome than her fall: her bright hair still hanging from the lungia ring and drizzling blood.

Abdullah's drumroll was drowned out as Beck immediately set the band to blaring the "Wedding March," and Edge and Florian ran into the pista. While Florian waved for the crowd to be calm and quiet, Edge lifted the limp body in his arms and, as unobtrusively as possible, carried it out the back door. Behind him, the band music subsided enough for Florian to be heard shouting, "All part of the act, signore e signori! Niente paura, the lady will be back in a moment, siano persuasi, amici! . . ."

Edge and his burden—its loosely lolling, bald and bloody head still grinning, its eyes no longer pulled aslant, but bulging and staring—were intercepted in the backyard by Paprika and Sarah, both of them weeping and wringing their hands.

"Oh, Pep, dearest!" sobbed Paprika. "I never meant—"

"Be quiet!" snapped Edge. "She can't hear you. And don't look at her!"

From the chapiteau came the music from Mozart's *Magic Flute*, meaning that Monday and Thunder were going into their high-school precision paces. Florian burst from the tent's back door, calling, "Zachary! How bad is it?"

"As bad as can be. Her back and neck are broken. Probably a lot of other things, as well."

Paprika let out a louder wail. Florian rounded on her and said brusquely, "Get to the dressing wagon and get out of your tights, quick! Zachary, take Pepper's off her!"

"Don't you dare!" sobbed Paprika, clutching at Edge's arm. "You leave her alone. And leave her with me."

"No, miss!" Florian said severely, while Edge stood, undecided, still cradling the body. "You are going back in there, into the pista, Paprika, to take Pepper's bows for her. Those dago peasants won't know the difference."

"What?" she exlaimed. "Vérszopó! You are a ghoul—a vámpir!"

"No, miss," he said again. "It is the least you can do— and the most you can do—and the last thing you'll ever be able to do for her. Strip, I said!"

Edge took Pepper to the dressing-room wagon and gently laid her on the floor inside. Sarah and Paprika, both still crying, but only softly, climbed in after him. Sarah helped Paprika out of her orange tights, while Edge clumsily peeled off Pepper's green ones. Neither of the girls wore anything underneath, except the little cache-sexe pads. Edge took note, in an abstracted sort of way, that Pepper was exceedingly beautiful—so long as he kept from looking at her terrible face. Paprika was beautiful all over, and he could not help noticing that, for she flung away her cache-sexe and was totally naked.

"Pepper would have wanted it so," she sniffled, seeing the looks Edge and Sarah gave her. She added, trying to smile, "I'll flash the vertical grin at the jossers, sure and I will!" and she began to slip into the green fleshings. Edge brushed the sawdust off her costume, while Sarah did what she could to repair Paprika's smeared makeup.

Florian was outside the wagon, fidgeting. As soon as Paprika emerged, he hustled her again through the chapiteau's back door. When they had gone through the flap of canvas, Sarah and Edge heard a gust of applause for Monday's haute école act. That was succeeded by a greater roar of applause as Florian presented the resurrected artiste—"Ancora una volta, l'audace Signorina Pepe!"—miraculously whole and healthy.

"God, how ghastly," Sarah murmured, between sobs. "The show must go on." She turned to look at Pepper's bare body, shuddered and turned back to Edge again. "And it was all my fault, Zachary. All *my* fault. *All* my fault."

"Get hold of yourself, Sarah," Edge said gruffly. "I'd stay and try to comfort you, but I'm on next."

She was crying forlornly when he dashed for the chapiteau. Florian was beginning the introduction of "il infallible tiratore scelto, Colonello Calcatoio" and everything seemed back to normal in there—except that off beneath the stands, out of sight of the audience, Rouleau was tenderly holding Paprika while she wept against his shoulder. Also under the stands, Sunday was trying to comfort a quivering Quincy, who mumbled, "Hoy . . ." over and over. His other sister stood nearby, but she was simply looking dreamily up at the lungia and rubbing her thighs together. Edge followed her gaze, but there was nothing to see up there; the roustabouts had made quick work of removing Pepper's last remains.

Colonel Ramrod managed to get through his shootist performance without missing any of his targets and without anyone else getting killed. The intermission followed, and, when Magpie Maggie Hag did not come in to do her stint of palm reading, Edge and Florian went to look for her. They went out the back door, brushing past the Slovaks rolling Maximus's cage into the pista, and found the old gypsy in the dressing-room wagon. She had done the laying out of Pepper: washed her clean of blood, closed her eyes and somehow smoothed the hideous grin off her face, so the dead girl looked pleasantly composed. She had garbed Pepper in one of her street gowns, and had even somehow reaffixed the torn-off hair, and combed it, so it looked quite natural.

"Good work, Mag," said Florian. "Now let me and Zachary put her in one of the other wagons—so the artistes can change in here—and I'll ask Stitches to do up a shroud for her. We'll bury her after the night show."

Edge lifted the limp body, and Florian reached to support the head, but rigor mortis had already begun to set in there, sufficiently that it no longer flopped loosely.

"Do you think we ought to have a show tonight?" Edge asked, as he carried the body to one of the tent wagons. "I don't know if everybody's going to be able to finish this one."

"Yes, everybody will," said Florian. "Just as they went on performing after Captain Hotspur died."

"Ignatz didn't die right in front of them. Or quite as horribly. And he was a middle-aged man, not a pretty young woman."

"We could have lost someone even younger, if not so pretty. Had Pepper fallen on top of Ali Baba, she would probably still be alive and he certainly would not. She swung him to a safe grip on the center pole just as she dropped."

"Yes. I wonder if that was only a convulsive twitch or a deliberate act of heroism. Still, it won't make anybody feel better about her death."

"Nevertheless, circus artistes have remarkable resilience. I grant you, Pepper's partner may be too overwrought to perform for some time, but Paprika has no act now, anyway, with her under-stander gone. So tonight I'll move Clover Lee's rosinback turn to the first half of the program . . . if that is all right with you, equestrian director.''

"You're the Governor. And I can be as resilient as anybody."

"Good. Let's see . . . I'll spot Clover Lee right after the Chinks' antipody, so she'll lead right into her mother's Pete Jenkins. Maybe move the Quakemaker up, too, to fill the gap where the hair-hang was." He went off, muttering to himself, "Must remember to tear up her conduct book . . . cancel her room at the albergo . . ."

When they buried Rosalie Brigid Mayo under the pista late that night, the sometimes-Reverend Dai Goesle conducted the obsequies. This time he gave the funeral no nautical flavor, nor even Dissident Methodist. Somewhere in Empoli he had procured a Roman Catholic missal, and he employed that version of the Order of the Burial of the Dead. He even pronounced the Latin correctly enough to satisfy the other Catholics present—Paprika, Rouleau, the four Smodlakas and most of the Slovaks—who all crossed themselves in unison at the fitting moments. When each of the company dropped a bit of earth onto Pepper's shroud and it came Florian's turn, he again murmured the Roman epitaph, "Saltavit. Placuit. Mortua est." The service was marred by only one circumstance, which not many failed to notice. Sarah, Paprika and Clover Lee stood equidistant around the grave—that is, as far apart as they could get. Sarah wept quietly, but the other two did not. They kept their dry, cold eyes fixed on Sarah, not even lowering their gaze when it was time to bow heads in prayer, regarding her with accusation and disgust.

6

THE NEXT morning Clover Lee came to breakfast in the Empoli albergo bearing a piece of paper, and handed it to Florian.

"Again, Mother did not sleep in our room," she said

calmly. "This time I was damned if I'd go looking for her. It wasn't until just now that I noticed some of our luggage and gear were gone, too. Then I found this under her pillow."

Florian unfolded the paper, pursed his lips and looked unhappy, tugged at his tuft of beard, then read aloud to the others in the room, " 'I am sorry for everything. Good-bye, dear child, and good luck. Tell everybody else the same. Your loving mother.' "

"*Should* I go looking for her?" Clover Lee asked, unconcernedly.

Florian shook his head. "Futile. Her grouch bag must have been quite full by now. And, this town being a rail junction, she could have gone north, east, west or south. No, she did as she wished to do, and we shall respect her decision. What about you, Clover Lee? Will you stay on with us?"

"Of course. She may have deserted me, but I won't desert the rest of my family."

So, when the show went on that afternoon, every artiste— including Peggy—stretched his or her performance by a few minutes, to make up for the paucity of acts. During the intermission, Fitzfarris—who by now had memorized his patter in comprehensible Italian—expatiated at greater length on his few freaks, and drew out his ventriloquized banter with Little Miss Mitten and actually sold a good number of his swazzles, while Magpie Maggie Hag had no scarcity of pregnant women's palms to read during that extended interval.

But at the nighttime show, when Florian saw that the chapiteau was not quite full, he said to Edge and Goesle, "Bust the lacings tomorrow, but you can take your time about it. I'll leave early and drive on ahead to arrange for our tober in Firenze. I'll take the Simms and Smodlaka kids with me, to start them posting paper. Then I'll meet you somewhere along the road and we'll camp for the night."

"Florence is only about twenty-five miles from here," said Edge. "We could easily push along—"

"No. This time . . ." Florian paused dramatically. "This time we are going to *make parade!* Into the city and up and down its main streets, before we haul onto the tober. Not the great Orfei nor any other European circus observes that flamboyant American tradition. It will astound the Fiorentini.''

Next day, Edge found that the mere twenty-five miles to Firenze was slow going, for the road became all twists and tight turns and switchbacks as it wound along the tortuous Arno River valley around the foot of Monte Albano.

''Curious climate here in Italy,'' he remarked to Autumn. ''Down in the lowlands the ground mist rose in the morning and burned off before noon. Now that we're in hilly country, the ground mist starts in the afternoon.''

The train was still some five miles from Firenze when Edge saw, through the misty twilight, Florian's rockaway at the side of the road.

''This is where we'll spend the night,'' said Florian. ''There's easy access to the river, for watering the stock. And that village you just passed through ought to be able to supply Mag with anything she needs for cooking us a meal.''

''Any problems about getting us a stand?'' Edge asked.

''And what did you do with the children?'' asked Autumn.

''No problems at all,'' said Florian. ''Got permission to pitch in the city's newest and fanciest park. The kids are still posting—it's a big job. After all, Firenze is at least twice the size of Pisa. I booked rooms for the kids in a pensione for the night.''

Very early the next day, for the first time in Edge's experience, the train was prepared for ''making parade.'' Florian brushed his frock coat and top hat while he gave the orders. Hannibal was sent to give Peggy a good scrub in the river shallows; then he anointed her all over with neat's-foot oil, polished her toenails and garbed her in her red blanket. All the horses were combed and brushed to a high shine and the liberty horses were caparisoned in their plumes and spangles. The wooden sides were removed from Maximus's wagon. The Smodlakas' terriers were adorned with their frilly ruff collars. All the artistes—even Rouleau—put on their freshest ring dress, but, because a chill wind was sweeping down the river, those in fleshings donned cloaks over them. Beck and his windjammers polished their instruments and put on their band dress, and Banat wore his bemedaled Rebel uniform. Fitzfarris applied the cosmetics to hide his one marketable attribute, and he, Goesle and the roustabouts took over the job of driving the eleven wagons behind Florian's rockaway.

When the train arrived in the outskirts of Firenze, a neighborhood of shacks and shanties, the occupants of which came to their doors with wide eyes and open mouths, Florian halted and called, "Take your places!" Edge mounted one of the saddled horses, threw his cloak back from his shoulders to show his resplendent Colonel Ramrod uniform and moved up to take the lead ahead of the rockaway. Beck and his bandsmen disposed themselves atop the tarpaulin of the balloon wagon. Hannibal, with his drum, climbed up to Peggy's neck. The other performers perched in graceful attitudes on the roofs of various vans and threw off their cloaks. Barnacle Bill stood, legs braced apart and arms akimbo, on the top of Maximus's cage. Terry, Terrier and Terriest were let down to the road and instantly began throwing somersaults and cartwheels. So did the three Chinese.

Beck and his band began blaring the *William Tell* overture, as Colonel Ramrod led the parade along the Via Pisana, a street of rather better residences. From every house window popped out the heads of the adult inhabitants to watch this most novel spectacle, and from every door popped out children to caper and cheer and point—eventually two mobs of them, one dancing backward in front of Colonel Ramrod's horse, the other prancing behind the elephant. As Beck and company went on through their repertoire, Edge kept watch for the lampposts and other objects bearing the Florilegium's posters, leading the way to the Arno's south bank, where a broad, paved thoroughfare ran alongside and well above the green, opaque, swift-flowing water.

"Yonder across the river," Florian yelled to him, "that's the Cascine Park where we'll be setting up. But now we'll keep going along this Lungarno Soderini."

The riverside Lungarni served a dual purpose, Florian later explained. They were embankments only recently piled up and faced with stone, primarily to contain the Arno's frequent floods. But their paved tops had also become favored promenades for strollers, riders and carriages, especially for those people who came in summer to admire the spectacular sunsets reflected in the river beneath the succession of elegantly proportioned bridges.

At any rate, most of the bridges were elegantly proportioned. But Edge gaped in wonderment when the Ponte Vecchio came in sight. The river ran under it, so it was a bridge, all right, but like none other he had ever seen. It might have been a village suspended in a mirage, it was so clumped and clustered all along its length with two-, three-and four-storey buildings, arches, tile roofs, chimney pots at crazy angles, lines of laundry, men with fishing poles leaning out of some of the windows. Most of the houses hung out sideways from the bridge, as if just barely clinging there over the water. Only when Edge passed the southern end of the bridge—the crowds strolling onto and off it had stopped in surprise—could he look along its length and see that, though the Ponte Vecchio was crammed with awninged shops and stalls on both sides, it was indeed a passage from one bank of the Arno to the other, unroofed and open to the sky the whole way.

Meanwhile, the Florilegium was somewhat forcibly making a right-of-way for itself along this south side of the river. The ever-increasing throng of children preceding it made other people and vehicles retreat into side streets as the parade passed. All along its route, people peered from the windows and doorways of the very tall and ornately decorated buildings it was now passing. Across the river, as well, the walkers and riders on the Lungarni over there came to a standstill, the people shading their eyes, pointing, calling each other's attention to the phenomenon.

The Florilegium artistes tirelessly smiled and waved from their wagon and van-roof perches. A few of the townsmen closest to the parade doffed their hats and half-bowed, a few of the women half-curtsied, as if uncertain whether they might be seeing some new kind of entourage accompanying the visit of some new kind of royalty. Some of the townswomen, though not many, turned away or pressed their children's faces into their voluminous skirts, to shut out the sight of the skimpily costumed circus females. Jules Rouleau, seated with Paprika atop the dressing-room wagon, laughed when he heard her grumble through her smile. "That's right, hide, Signora Tub-of-Lard there. I'm posturing up here, chilled to the marrow, pimpled with libabör and risking pneumonia, purely to affront your matronly modesty."

The band had twice or thrice repeated every piece of music it knew, when Edge espied a circus poster stuck on the balustrade of a bridge ahead. Having to dodge among the children milling about in front of him, Edge turned his horse onto the Ponte San Nicolò—a wide bridge, with no accretion of buildings on it—and the bandsmen took a breather while the Florilegium crossed the river. They lifted their instruments again, and pitched into *William Tell* when the parade came off the bridge and proceeded up the Viale Amendola directly ahead, where still more gawkers watched from the pavements, from windows, from halted vehicles.

When the viale debouched into a broad, circular piazza, the posters guided Edge half-left and into an avenue that led westward again, more or less paralleling the way they had come along the other bank of the Arno. A couple of times, the parade had to thread its way through a street so narrow that the watchers in its windows had to duck inside when the wagons passed. The Florian's postermarked route took the procession between two crumbled stumps of ancient stone pillars, the remainder of what had been the Porta di Prato in what had been the city's walls in olden times. Beyond were the young trees, lawns, graveled roads and walkways of the Pratone delle Cascine.

"It means the Dairy Farm," said Florian, when the train had gone some way within the park and halted on the grassy oval inside another racetrack. "A dairy farm is what all this area used to be, until the city grew up around it and appropriated it for a public park."

"I'd like to meet the man who designed those lamps for it," said Edge, pointing. Every one of the park's countless lamp standards rose from a cast-iron base that consisted of three clawed paws clutching the ground.

"Yes," said Florian, chuckling. "If the man ever encountered some such three-legged beast, I'd like to ask him where, so I could acquire it for the show.''

The artistes climbed down from their parade perches—Rouleau requiring some assistance—while the three terriers and the three Chinese collapsed on a grassy bank, panting and cramped from their having flip-flopped and cartwheeled all the way here. The brass players of the band were gingerly feeling their lips, bruised from the jolting of their band wagon while they played, and a couple complained that they had even suffered some loosened teeth.

''Well, they don't need lips or teeth to do their roustabout work,'' said Florian. ''Goesle, Banat, get the whole crew started on the unloading and setting up. Abdullah, undress the bull and get her ready to pull her weight. Then you and the Chinks keep all those ragamuffins clear of the area. I am going back to town to fetch our own kids and to book hotel rooms for us. You others, who have no chores to do, may wish to change into street dress and amble about the city while it's still daylight.''

Several of the artistes did that, including Edge and Autumn. He and she, arm in arm, turned to the right on leaving the park, and walked among the townsfolk promenading along the Lungarno Amerigo Vespucci.

''I know who Vespucci was,'' said Edge. ''America was named after him. But you'll have to explain everything else, my dear. I'm especially intrigued by that peculiar bridge yonder.'' He gestured past the two intervening bridges to the third, the Ponte Vecchio, a mile away but easily visible, bulking above the others and glowing like red gold in the afternoon light.

''It is reserved to the shops of goldsmiths and silversmiths,'' said Autumn. ''That highest story, on the upstream side of the bridge, used to be a private passage for the royals and nobles to cross from the Uffizi Palace, when it was the government offices. They could get to the royal residence on the other side of the river, the Pitti Palace, without having to elbow their way through the squalid common folk on the bridge and the streets.''

Themselves having no great prejudice against mingling with the common folk, Autumn and Edge crossed the bridge, jostled by the crowd, marveling at the gold and silver and vermeil works on show in the row of shop windows or being personally displayed and loudly advertised by the artisans who had created the pieces. Then they recrossed the bridge, along the opposite row of shops, Autumn gasping or sighing at sight of this or that bijou, and Edge wishing he could afford to buy every one of them for her.

When they came off the bridge, and into the Piazza della Signoria, Autumn said, "Over there on the farther side of the square is the spot where two famous fires were lighted."

"Famous fires?"

"Four hundred years ago, a man named Savonarola was jilted by his childhood sweetheart, so he fled to a monastery, but that only increased the bitterness in him. He came here to Florence as a missionary, and preached against lust and vanity and pleasure and wine bibbing and all those good things. He convinced the Florentines that they were damned unless they reformed. So, one Carnival day, they made a tremendous bonfire here in this piazza and threw into it all their more worldly possessions—mirrors, perfumes, wigs, dice, portraits of the most beautiful courtisanes—everything that hinted of dissipation. Florence must have been a bleak city after that orgy. Then, about ten years later, the Florentines had had enough of Savonarola and his perpetual carping. They made another fire here in the piazza and burned *him*. Let that be a lesson to you, Zachary Edge. Don't ever try to reform the Florentines."

"I'd never dream of trying to reform anybody. A reformed rakehell is the most obnoxious of human beings."

"I am so glad you agree. Before Savonarola arrived here, the ruler of Florence was a man affectionately known as Piero the Gouty. One gets gout only from high living. So I like to think that Florence always has been and always will be a place of luxuriant sensuality and hedonism."

There was one memorable thing Edge had already noticed on that first day, and would notice it on every other, and would always remember it as his most enduring impression of Firenze. It was the way the sunlight, even at midday, seemed never to fall direct and harsh down onto the city, but fell always aslant, caressingly, making every crumbled old stone wall as vivid and distinct as the deliberate relievo of palace façades, and making the narrower streets into mysterious, dark crevices from which one emerged into courtyards or piazze or gardens so warm-colored that they seemed preserved for eternity in purest amber.

When Edge and Autumn got back to the Cascine racetrack, just as night fell, the setup was all but completed. Under the work lights of basket torches, sputtering and dripping gobbets of fire, the roustabouts were doing the finishing touches to the chapiteau, going around it adjusting the tension of guy ropes and hammering a stake more securely here and there, and growling throatily every time they made any move.

Edge asked, "Stitches, why are your crewmen growling like that? Do their teeth still hurt?"

"No, 'tis by my order. I am trying to get us all trained, now just. I have told everybody, even the Governor—and now I tell you—whenever any of us feels like uttering a profanity in public, he is to growl instead."

"All right. But why?"

"Look you." Goesle pointed to where two nuns and a crocodile of small children in school uniforms were watching the work. "There'll be more of that—nuns and nannies and schoolmarms bringing their tykes out to watch us set up or tear down. For an educational experience a little out of the ordinary, y'see. And then maybe the bull Peggy acts balky and somebody will let fly—in no telling what language— with something like 'You goddamned two-tailed son of a bitch!' And the schoolmarm will find that a trifle *too* educational for her kiddies, and we'll get a delegation coming by here to complain about morals and suchlike."

Florian came out of the chapiteau, dusting his hands, and said to Goesle, "As soon as your Slovaks are finished here, get them out slapping up more paper—all over town—all night, if it takes that long." To Edge and Autumn he said, "Most of the artistes have already gone to the hotel to dress for dinner. If you two would like your luggage taken over there, pile it in my carriage and follow me. It is in easy walking distance of here. The Hotel Kraft on the Via Solferino.''

''Oh, good,'' said Autumn.

Edge asked, ''An English-run hotel? German?''

''No,'' said Florian, ''though there are plenty of foreign-owned hotels. This city's population is only one-third actual Florentines. Another third are expatriate English and a third are other foreigners—Americans, Russians, Germans, Frenchmen. The Kraft is owned and operated by Italians. But its clientèle is mostly of visiting show folk—theatrical, operatic, circus, pantomime . . .''

At the hotel, when Edge and Autumn had washed and refreshed themselves in their room, they met Florian and Carl Beck in the hall, and the four took a table together in the dining room downstairs, among the several tables at which their fellows were already eating. Edge looked around, to see if he could identify any other show folk on sight. Nobody was actually leaping about or striking attitudes—everyone in the room ate sedately and conversed quietly—but several obviously *were* of some theatrical occupation, for their faces were leathery and dyed almost orange from years of wearing stage makeup.

''I told you this is a cosmopolitan city,'' said Florian, taking a folded newspaper from his coat pocket. ''This afternoon, I was able to buy from a street-corner news vendor the latest issue of *The Era*, imagine that. After dinner, I'll peruse the Situations Wanted, to see if there's anyone at liberty here in Firenze who might be useful to us.''

''May I look at it, Governor?'' asked Autumn. ''I always like to see if there are any names I know.''

Florian handed it over, and Autumn began to leaf through the pages. Carl Beck was saying, ''. . . Into town tomorrow morning. For the acid and other chemicals I will go seeking.''

''Well, don't make the balloon gas your overriding priority,'' said Florian. ''When that trap artist arrives, you'll have to think about ways to hang his rig so it doesn't interfere with Autumn's. I wish he were here already, so we'd have him on the program right from tomorrow's opening show.''

"He is here, Monsieur Florian," said a dandily dressed gentleman sitting alone, with a cup of cappuccino, at the next table. He stood up and bowed. "Maurice LeVie, à vos ordres. I arrived this morning, I watched you make parade in the American style. I was much taken by it."

"We are very, very pleased to meet you," said Florian, beaming, as he and Beck and Edge also stood. "Didn't recognize you out of pista dress, monsieur. Allow me." And he made introductions all around. LeVie shook the men's hands and kissed Autumn's. The trapeze artiste was small and trim, and seemed composed not of quicksilver, as he had looked in performance, but of all sharp points: sharp nose, sharp chin, sharp widow's peak in his glossy hair, and extremely sharp, darting eyes.

"Do join us," said Florian. "Some wine, perhaps?"

"Merci, no wine," said LeVie, sliding his chair over to their table. "My profession, comprenez, forbids me to risk either tipsiness or the morning-after."

"Of course."

"I had the opportunity," LeVie went on, "to admire all of you, especially your so-lovely ladies, when you rode in. Here in the hotel, I have taken the further opportunity—incognito—of observing your Confederate American company at closer range."

"Aha," said Florian, humorously wagging a finger at him. "And if you had observed, say, that we ate our petits pois with a knife, or exhibited other American barbarities, you would have remained incognito and slipped quietly away."

LeVie smiled—his mouth made a sharp V—and shrugged his pointy shoulders. "Say only that I am satisfied. Indeed, that I am happy to join—your expression is 'join out,' I believe. I shall present myself and my appareil at the tober in the morning, to assist you in the hanging of it. Also, Monsieur le Chef de Musique, you will wish to know my motifs d'accompagnement."

"Ja. Ja doch," said Beck, apparently awed by the man's confident professionalism.

"I would like to ask you one thing, Monsieur Maurice," Florian said almost diffidently. "Understand, now, I have no desire to mar the purity of your solo performance. But we have in our troupe a young lady—a beautiful and accomplished young lady—who is temporarily without an act. Her perch-pole under-stander was incapacitated by an accident. But the young lady can also do a trap turn.''

''Old style or Léotard?'' LeVie instantly asked.

''Old style only. She has been in the States for some years, and the Americans are woefully behind the times in that regard. But I wondered if perhaps . . .''

''I could teach her the leaps? Work her into un jeu duel?''

''Only if you think it would enhance your own act. Otherwise . . .''

''Is the young lady in this room at this moment? Do not call, please, merely indicate.''

''That is she,'' said Florian, nodding toward another table. ''Elle des cheveux roux. Cécile Makkai.''

''Ah, oui. Une demoiselle charmante. And that orange hair should nicely complement my blue fleshings. Always I wear blue, messieurs.''

Edge remarked, ''Paprika is partial to orange tights that match her hair.''

''Splendide! And what a perfect nom-de-théâtre for her.''

''She is Hungarian,'' said Autumn.

''A delightful race, especially the females of it. I concur in your suggestion, Monsieur le Gouverneur. If La Paprika is willing, I shall take her to be my partner.''

''Fine,'' said Florian. ''I will introduce—''

''In the morning, s'il vous plaît, make all the introductions.'' Maurice stood up again. ''For now, avec permission, I am always early to bed, even when ha *ha!*—it is a solo turn.''

When he had saluted and left the room, Florian murmured, ''Brisk little chap, isn't he?''

''He also seems to have an eye for the ladies,'' said Edge.

''His conduct book recorded nothing disgraceful.''

''I only meant—if he's a ladies' man—in fairness, shouldn't you have mentioned Paprika's, uh, proclivities?''

''Why warn him?'' Florian said carelessly. ''Either he will soon perceive her nature or—who knows?—with a handsome male partner, Paprika may just possibly change her inclination.''

''Per piacere, signori, signorina . . .'' said a new voice, a hoarse and husky voice. Another short, slight, but much paler man was addressing them. ''You are of the Florilegium, no? I saw you conversing with Monsieur Maurice. He and I once worked at the same time on the Zirkus Ringfedel. I thought . . . if you are hiring . . . I happen to be between engagements. I am Zanni Bonvecino.''

''A joey, eh?'' said Florian, looking him up and down.

''A sad-face, Governatore,'' the clown said. He had the mournful voice for it, thought Edge.

''A toby, then,'' said Autumn, regarding him closely.

''Si, signorina. I notice you have there *The Era*. You will find my inserzione there, inquiring for employment.'' While he talked, the clown had taken two empty plates and two knives off the table. Now, a knife in either hand, he was spinning a plate on each point, keeping both the dishes horizontal as they twirled. He seemed to be doing this absentmindedly, as another man might twiddle his thumbs while talking. ''I also do Harlequin merriment, humpsty-bumpsty, droll patter, impudent repartee, funny songs. I can even do the Lupino mirror.''

''Not until we get another joey, you can't,'' said Florian. ''We have none at all, at the moment.'' The clown was now spinning one of the plates behind his own back, and the other he passed back and forth, still serenely spinning, under one of his legs. ''What sort of patter do you do, Signor Bonvecino?''

''Improvviso, or I make it seem so. On arrival in any new town, I go immediately to the local hairdresser. He always knows all the town gossip, and freely tells it. So my patter makes laughingstocks of the local notables and despicables. I deride the scandals, the pomposities, the peccatuccie, whatever offers, in whatever the local language.''

''Maraviglioso,'' said Florian.

''Erfinderisch,'' said Beck.

Edge asked, ''How often do you get shot at, friend?''

''Signore,'' Autumn said abruptly, and leaned forward.

"Are you perhaps related to one Giorgio Bonvecino?"

"No, signorina." He let the plates spin off the knives, and put the utensils back on the table.

"Are you sure? He was a—"

"Quite sure, signorina. I *am* Giorgio Bonvecino."

Autumn's eyes widened, and she said almost reverently, "I heard you sing with La Diva Patti in *Sonnambula* at Covent Garden."

"I had that honor, sì, and others. Unfortunately, I lost my voice when a mistress lost her temper. She kicked me in the throat. Fortunately, I did not lose also the several languages in which I had learned to sing. I told you, I do know funny songs. They are Zanni Bonvecino's parodies—I do not have to exaggerate to make them so—parodies of the arias for which Giorgio Bonvecino was once famous."

"Good heavens," murmured Florian.

"Ah, well," said the clown. "She might have kicked me elsewhere to even worse effect. Here is my conduct book, Governatore. Will you look at it?"

"No hurry," said Florian, tucking it unopened into a pocket. "Are you stopping at this hotel?"

"No, Signor Governatore. I have a cheap pensione."

"I will engage a room for you here with the rest of us. Welcome to the troupe, Signor Bonvecino."

To everyone's delight, the next day's two shows were both turnaways, even with the vastly bigger chapiteau—and the company put on the best show Edge had yet directed or watched. The Florentine audiences, too, were among the best the Florilegium had entertained. As the troupe made its Grand Entry and Promenade, the crowd joined in, at about the second go-round, to sing along with "Circo-o è allegro!" and never let their enthusiasm flag from then on.

After Colonel Ramrod's liberty act, the new clown Zanni came on to exchange banter with Florian. That was all in Italian, but Edge recognized some words—"Robert Browning" and "Daniel Dunglas Home" and "medium" and "humbug"—and those particular mentions drew the loudest laughs from the crowd, so Edge assumed Zanni was dealing with local gossip. The whole time the clown was talking back to Florian, he was doing his plate spinning, this time with the two plates atop long, whippy slivers of bamboo, so the feat was even more magical than it had been at the dining table.

In the pista, Zanni looked quite different from the unemployed toby who had humbly approached Florian the night before. He wore a tight-fitting Harlequin costume and tiny cock-and-pinch hat. Just a few touches of greasepaint had completely altered his face—a dark lining to accentuate his eyelids, his eyebrows redrawn in little quirks like caret marks, his mouth slightly broadened by rouge—and he had combed his hair downward all around, in the style of an old-time knight's page. After his repartee routine with Florian, he repeatedly ran into the pista between other acts, to help acrobat Sunday and contortionist Ali Baba entertain the crowd during those intervals. While Zanni cavorted, flickered and pirouetted, he held his elbows high and seemed to dance weightlessly on his tiptoes. He also appeared to be taking some perverse enjoyment in his antics: his face and graceful movements combined glee and mischief, so he rather resembled a faun or satyr. Then he would contrive to trip over something, and look suddenly graceless and disgraced, and he would fold, kneel, bow his head into his arms, the picture of abject humility and melancholy.

When there had to be a long interval between acts, as for instance when the cage wagon got rolled in, Zanni would cartweel into the pista, clasp his little hat to his breast and announce loudly, ''Il gran tenore Giorgio Bonvecino canta 'M'appari' ''—or some other aria. He would proceed to sing it, with no more hand wringing or gesticulation than any stage tenor would have done, but the Florentine patrons were familiar with opera and they remembered the once-great tenor, though they did not now recognize him. When Zanni sang in his gruff, broken, often-cracking voice, the audience took it as a genuine and expert burlesque. They laughed so hard they nearly reeled off the stands, and at the finish they applauded and bravoed for the mimic as appreciatively as they would once have done for the real Giorgio Bonvecino.

Every other act went equally well. For the first time in

public, Maximus vaulted through his fire hoop—though Edge
had had some apprehensions about that, because Barnacle
Bill's breath was so spirituous that he might well have gone
up in flames himself when he lighted the hoop. Maurice
LeVie was again blue lightning on the trapeze, and sent the
patrons out at intermission smiling and chattering excitedly.
Sir John took advantage of their happy frame of mind—after
showing them his "tattoo," the museum, the Night Children
and the White Pygmies—to sell them scores of his ventriloquy swazzles and then to inflict on them his long-unused
mouse game. Fitz was getting his mice now from a cage trap
the Hotel Kraft had obligingly let him set in its kitchen, and
he had memorized enough additional Italian to shout seductive come-ons and congratulatory payoffs.

The Confederate doorman Banat had taken it upon himself
to insititute a new system of doorkeeping. The jossers had
only to show him their tickets on first entering the chapiteau.
Not until after intermission, when they swarmed in again, did
Banat actually take their tickets—this to ensure that none of
the vagrant promenaders attracted by Fitzfarris's shouts
sneaked in with the paying customers.

In the program's second half, the Simms girls now did the
slant-climb. Holding the long, limber balance pole, Monday
stepped tentatively, as if fearfully, onto the tightrope angled
down from the center pole to a stake under the first rank of
seats. Then, still pretending awkwardness and trepidation, she
went slowly, step by tremulous step, while Abdullah rumbled
a suspenseful roll on his drum, until she was all the way up
to the rope's top turnbuckle. Cautiously, she turned around
up there and started down, just as Sunday, with another balance pole, started up from the bottom. The audience whispered and mumbled: what would happen when the two girls
met in the middle? When they did, it occasioned a quick
twinkle of feet and poles—for one moment during the crossover, each girl was standing on the rope on only one foot,
and the two were exchanging poles—then they were past
each other, and Monday came trippingly down to the ground
while Sunday went to the top.

Then Florian bawled to the audience, "Allora . . . il scivolo di salvezza! *The slide for life!*'' (In private he, Autumn and the girls called it simply the go-down.) Sunday turned to face the descent, let go one hand from her balance pole, let herself suddenly plummet from the rope—to a concerted gasp from the crowd, and a *boom!* of Abdullah's drum ''taking the fall.'' But somehow her free hand shot up and grabbed the pole again, from under the rope and on its other side, so the pole became a supporting bar. Holding to that, dangling under the rope, she slid down in a rush—to a loud glissando from the band—to be caught by Edge at the bottom. He gave her a squeeze of reward, and she gave him a glowing, adoring smile.

The closing spec was done to new music. Autumn had despaired of ever being able to translate ''Lorena'' into Italian that would fit the meter—and in fact declared that, though the music was stirring, the words were not *worth* translating. So Florian decreed that the show would henceforth close with the national anthem of whatever country they were in. Tonight the final Promenade marched, with all the artistes waving and smiling, many of them capering, to the music of ''La Marcia Reale.''

Twice a day, day after day, the artistes continued to perform before sfondone houses. Despite that rigorous regimen, most of them were at the tober every morning to continue their ceaseless practice of old turns, tryouts of new ones, and the teaching of apprentices. Clover Lee was now essaying every rosinback posture and spin and leap from horse to horse that both her mother and Captain Hotspur had ever done. Hannibal Tyree, whenever he was not practicing juggling every sort of object that came to hand and was not rehearsing with the band, was working with Obie Yount to train Brutus to *lose* in a tug-of-war with the Quakemaker. The Smodlakas had got Goesle to build them a midget Roman chariot, and were teaching the dogs to open their act by trotting into the pista hauling one of the albino children in it.

Edge labored to train the polka-dot Pinzgauer horses to join his liberty act, meanwhile rehearsing Monday and Thunder in ever more precise refinement of their haute école two-steps, travers, renvers, courbettes and caprioles. Rouleau, not yet having anything of his own to do, went on teaching Sunday new acrobatic tricks, and Quincy worked on new routines with the three Chinese, the elephant and the teeterboard, and Sunday went doggedly on with her language lessons. She evidently had determined to rival Florian in multilingual prowess: she was not only studying French (and good English) with Rouleau, she was also beginning to learn Italian from Zanni Bonvecino and German from Paprika—whenever Paprika was not being initiated by Maurice LeVie into the mysteries of Léotard-style trapeze work.

Besides feeling it the duty of an equestrian director to have some knowledge of all the acts under his command, Edge was fascinated by the trapeze practice, and often wandered into the chapiteau of a morning to watch Maurice and Paprika at it.

"But the damned bar is so damned heavy, kedvesem," Paprika complained, during one of her early lessons. "Mine was never so heavy when I had my own aerial rig."

"Your bar had only to support you, mam'selle," Maurice said patiently. "And your weight kept it steady at all times. These two bars are heavy for good reason. A lightweight trapeze would jiggle and sway when swinging loose. If the bar is not always perfectly straight, horizontal, parallel to the ground when you or I lunge for it, you or I or both of us could miss our grip, and fall, and be dead. Hence the heaviness."

Edge already knew, from supervising the hoisting aloft of the rig, that each of the bars—wound along its length with lint bandage fixed by sticking plaster—had a five-pound nickel-plated knob beyond the rope on either end of it. He also knew, from seeing Goesle make the things for Paprika, that both she and Maurice wore tight wristbands for added strength there, and on both hands sail-maker-style "palms" of suéde leather, with holes cut for their fingers.

"No, no, no!" Maurice shouted, on one occasion when Edge was observing. Maurice was on one platform and Paprika on the one opposite. "Do not lean forward to anticipate the bar when it swings to you. Lean *backward* as you seize it, and remain leaning backward as you leave the platform. That way, you are putting your weight on the bar from the start of your swing. You will not feel so much tug of gravity—you will not feel so heavy—at the bottom of your arc.''

The chief crewmen of the Florilegium, Goesle and Beck, were also on the Cascine tober every morning, and also hard at work. Carl Beck had procured, from pharmaceutical merchants in the city, the various chemicals he required for his Gasentwickler. Now he spent most of his spare time in empirical tries at determining the proper proportions of those ingredients—and Rouleau could only fidget impatiently, because Beck insisted, ''Not until I know what I am doing will I let you try what you can do as a Luftschiffer.'' Beck also had some of the bandsmen-Slovaks building something for himself, the nature of which he declined to disclose until it was done. Meanwhile, Dai Goesle and some other crewmen were putting planks and hardware together into some object Fitzfarris had requested, but the purpose of which he refused to reveal even to the builders. Magpie Maggie Hag, as usual, was sewing costumes—now for the Simms and Smodlaka children, who had outgrown their older ones.

Only during the three-hour intervals between the afternoon and night shows did the troupers indulge themselves, a few times a week, in dressing in street clothes and wandering through the city. They ogled the local architecture, toured museums and galleries, browsed or bought in the luxury shops or the cheap flea markets, strolled in the Boboli Gardens, or rode in a vettura to see the view that Boccaccio and Lorenzo de Medici and Shelley and other immortals had seen from the hill of Fiesole.

Mullenax spent most of his leisure time in whatever workingmen's Italian bettola he happened to chance upon, because he could count on the other tipplers' standing him free drinks when they learned that he was the lion tamer Barnacle Bill. Edge, Fitzfarris and Yount spent a few hours each week in Doney's Café, the favored watering hole of Americans resident in Firenze. There they would sit over wine or espresso and review with the other expatriates the latest news from the States. American highwaymen had now moved from the roads to the rails; in Ohio a train had been stopped by armed bandits, its baggage car and passengers robbed. The whole South was being overrun and bullied and ransacked by Yankee and Free Negro "carpetbaggers" . . .

But as a general thing all the circus folk preferred to roam among the native people and native scenes, and even found some scenes that the Baedeker guidebooks neglected to mention. One day, Autumn took Edge to show him the venerable house where the great Dante was "believed to have resided" before his banishment from Firenze. Edge regarded it with due gravity. But then, when they walked along the street behind the house, the Via del Proconsolo, Edge noticed that every single shop was devoted to the display and sale of formidable canvas corsets and belly flatteners, and even uglier abdominal furniture constructed of india rubber, leather and cork—trusses, hernia belts, scrotum supporters—and he mildly suggested that the city fathers might have located Dante's presumed residence in a more high-minded neighborhood.

Maurice and Paprika, even when they were sightseeing with other artistes, never ceased discussing the finer points of trapeze work. When they were out walking with Edge, Autumn and Florian one day, and a drizzle of rain began to fall, Maurice was moved to say, "Mam'selle Paprika, we will never go aloft on a day of really heavy rain. Should the rain seep in through the canvas"—he nodded to Edge—"our equestrian director will not *let* us take the risk, or the Mam'selle Auburn either, for the bars and the platforms and the tightrope will probably be slippery."

The group ducked out of the drizzle into the Uffizi Gallery, where Botticelli's painting of *Spring* inspired Maurice to add, "Pleasant weather can be as hazardous to us, mam'selle, as the rainiest or iciest weather. On a merely balmy day, it can be actually *hôt* up there close under the peak. I have known trap artistes to faint and topple during their exertions, and others to sweat through the suéde palms so they lost their grip and fell."

Later, at the Hotel Kraft's dining table, Maurice was reminded of another caveat: "Never eat before a performance,

Mam'selle Paprika. It is wise to be as light as possible in the air. But more important—should there occur an accident, an injury, then swift surgery may be necessary. If ever that happens to me, I should dearly hope to be put to sleep while I am cut open. And no physician can administer the mercy of ether or chloroform unless the patient has an empty stomach.''

Notwithstanding LeVie's expert tutelage, Paprika never became as proficient as he was at the "flying" part of the trapeze act, but she did not have to be. As eventually worked out, their act commenced with only Paprika being introduced by Florian—"L'ardumentosa acrobata *a-e-ro*batica, Signorina Paprika!''—and she went lightly up the rope ladder to her platform, untied the trapeze bar, swung it out and—to the band's playing the sprightly Hungarian cigány "There Is But One Girl''—while the bar continued to swing, did every sort of pose, flipover, knee-hang, toe-hang and even a handstand on the bar. She concluded her solo turn by swinging again to the platform and flinging up her arms in the V for applause. At that moment, a ragged, dirty, drunken man came staggering and stumbling from the stands.

He argued profanely with Florian and Edge, and struggled with the roustabouts who dashed into the pista. But the drunk always broke loose of restraint, ran to climb the rope ladder—pretending several times to slip and almost fall before gaining the platform, releasing Paprika's hooked-back trapeze and launching himself out on it. As he swung back and forth, sometimes by just one hand, sometimes fearfully clutching with both arms and both legs, Paprika looked aghast and the band played a cacophonous hash of Wagner's *Flying Dutchman* overture. But then the drunk began shedding and dropping his ragged clothing, piece by piece.

At the instant Pete Jenkins hung revealed in his electric-blue spangles, and the crowd laughed at its own credulity, and the band rippled smoothly into the "Bal de Vienne,'' Paprika swung out on her trapeze. Maurice performed acrobatics on one bar while Paprika imitated him on the other. Then she retired to her platform and Maurice did his blue-lightning tumbles and twists and twirls as he hurtled back and forth between the traps. At the climax of the act, both Maurice and Paprika were on the bars, swinging faster and higher, faster and higher—until both let go of their traps (thunder of bass drum), whizzed past each other in a dual mid-air somersault, caught the opposite bars, hauled themselves up to sit casually on them, waving and smiling, to a frenzy of cheers, clapping, whistles, bravos and bravas.

At one afternoon show's opening, the artistes in the come-in spec were surprised to hear their "Greensleeves" music sounding even louder, bouncier and more jingly than usual. They all peered up at the bandstand every time they promenaded past it, but could discern only that there was one more uniformed Slovak up there than usual. Nobody could see, over the projecting edge of the stand, what instrument that windjammer might be playing, and Bandmaster Beck only smiled smugly down at them. Whatever it was that he had added to the band continued to augment all the music for all the subsequent acts, with jingles, rat-a-tats, hollow clunks, brassy clashes and strange, unearthly shimmers of sound. Not until the crowd emptied at intermission could Florian and Edge climb up the seats adjoining the bandstand, to investigate.

"An old Bavarian plaything it is," Beck said proudly, as they stared at it. "The Teufel Geige, by name—Devil's Fiddle. My Slovaks I showed how to make it."

The Devil's Fiddle was only an upright pole, five feet tall, at the bottom of which was attached a coiled spring that rested on the bandstand flooring. Fixed here and there along the pole were cow bells and sleigh bells of assorted sizes, a tambourine, some hollowed-out blocks and a brass cymbal.

"Not even a trained musician it requires. Anybody can play it," said Beck. "With a single drumstick, this or that piece of the Teufel Geige he strikes. Extra resonance and reverberation, the spring at the bottom gives. Or, for loudest crescendo and fortissimo, the player simply up and down bangs the whole pole. On the spring, the Apparat bounces, and all the attachments together go bing-bong, tinkle-jangle, tock-tock, boom, crash, clash . . ."

"Ingenious, you Bavarians," Florian murmured. "I'm

glad that some of the Florentines got the opportunity to enjoy it.''

"Some?" said Beck. "Then closing here in Florenz we are?"

"It is time. We have had more than three good weeks, but no turnaways these last few days, and today even some empty seats. Besides, it's getting damned cold. We will emulate the Orfei and head south.''

"Let us, then, with a grand flourish go out," said Beck. "Make posters, please, Gouverneur, announcing a Luftballon ascension for the final day, between the afternoon and nighttime shows. Weather permitting, be sure to add.''

"You think you are ready, Carl? And Monsieur Roulette? Very well. I shall have the paper printed overnight and posted tomorrow. The next day will be our last in Firenze."

Ascension Day, as the eager Rouleau irreverently referred to it, dawned clear and cloudless. Early that morning, Beck and five of his Slovaks unloaded the *Saratoga* from its wagon and carefully unfolded the silk bag and its netting and its ropes outward across the grass from the racetrack's infield oval. While four of the men went to fetch the Gasentwickler, the other hung sandbags around the outer rim of the upright wicker gondola. Early though the hour was and much as Beck might have wished to do this first inflation unobserved, in case of embarrassing incident or failure, quite a crowd of Florentines had gathered, including a number of nuns marshaling crocodiles of schoolchildren. So the roustabouts grunted and growled instead of blaspheming while they worked.

"These ascensions you will only in important cities be able to make," Beck warned Rouleau, who stood leaning on his cane beside the bag-hung basket. "And then perhaps only once or twice on opening or closing day, for a special attraction. I had not realized, until I experimented, how much of the chemicals for each inflation are required. So much and so heavy that with us the supplies we cannot carry, but must purchase on the spot. Observe.''

The Gasentwickler consisted of two very big, metal-sheathed boxes, each on its own set of four wheels. They were currently connected by a length of six-inch india-rubber hose. Boom-Boom unscrewed and lifted open a sort of hinged iron manhole on top of one of the boxes and bade Rouleau look inside.

"This tank the generator is. Lined with lead, to resist corrosion of the acid. You will also see that random and staggered shelves it has inside, for better distribution of these iron filings." The five Slovaks came up, each bowed under the weight of a heavy sack. One man at a time hefted his sack to the manhole and poured its contents into the tank, shaking and waggling the mouth of the bag to scatter the filings over the inside shelves. The men made several trips, pouring in—Rouleau lost count—fifteen or twenty sacks of the filings. Then they came again, now with buckets of water, and filled the box to within a couple of feet of its top. Beck closed and screwed down the manhole cover, while the men went away again and began returning with immense glass carboys of what looked like more water.

"Oil of vitriol—sulphuric acid," said Boom-Boom. "Much experimenting this required, to determine the amount and correct procedure of adding it."

Into a copper funnel at one end of the generator tank, the men slowly poured, one by one, five carboys of the acid. Then there was a long wait, timed by Beck with the watch he had borrowed from Florian. Finally he gave a nod and the roustabouts slowly poured in three more carboys. Another long wait, another nod, and the men slowly poured in two more carboys.

"The Wasserstoff—the hydrogen gas—by now is generating," said Beck. "The slow addition of the oil of vitriol prevents too rapid generation, for the tank's walls it might strain. Now is passing the gas through this thick hose into the other box. Feel."

Rouleau put a hand to the hose between the two machines, and jerked his hand away again; the rubber was almost burning hot.

"That is why the second Apparat, the cooler and purifier, we must employ. In there, over and around a grid of tubing full of cold water, the hot gas circulates. Then through a second chamber, charged with lime water, it bubbles, losing all impurities and useless gases. Now the connection I make—observe—of this outflow hose to the fitting at the bag's appendix. And in between, a force pump we have, to hasten the pure hydrogen's passage from Gasentwickler to Luftballon.'' He beckoned, and a Slovak came to start energetically working the pump handle.

By now, the whole Florilegium company had gathered to watch, as avidly as the jossers. But it took a long time before anyone could see that anything was happening inside the *Saratoga*, and it had to be taken on faith that something was noiselessly happening inside the Gasentwickler. But then the limp vermillion-and-white silk stirred gently. A wrinkle unwrinkled here. A small fold unfolded there. After twenty minutes or so—the roustabouts taking turns at the force pump—it was evident that the bag's upper layer of silk was some inches above the ground it had been lying on. In an hour, the silk had formed a dome, still amorphous and earthbound, but higher than a man's head. Two hours after that, the *Saratoga* was fully inflated, towering tall and broad and proud above its gondola, contained by its netting, restrained by its anchor ropes—and all the watching circus folk, city folk, nuns and children were chattering excitedly.

Beck disconnected the hose coupling from the balloon's appendix, then set his men to flushing out the two generator boxes with many, many buckets of water before the machines were rolled off to the circus's backyard, out of sight. Edge noticed that balloonist Rouleau had been buttonholed by Fitzfarris, Monday and Sunday Simms. Fitz was talking and pointing—to the balloon, to the girls, to himself and to Rouleau, who listened with apparent interest. Only the final exchange of that colloquy were audible to Edge as he passed them.

''. . . Do it, won't you, girls?'' Fitzfarris asked.

''Mais oui,'' said Sunday. ''Il commence à faire une grande aventure.''

''Bien,'' said Rouleau. ''Then do it we shall.''

By the promised time of the ascension, just before sun-

down, not only the entire Cascine Park but also the farther
bank of the Arno and the balconies, windows and rooftops
on both sides of the river were packed with oglers elbow to
elbow. All those nearest to the Florilegium's red wagon were
waving lire notes and clamoring for tickets to the final show.
Edge remarked to Florian that the city appeared to have suddenly renewed interest in circus entertainment, and maybe it
would be profitable to stay here a while longer.

"No," said Florian. "It's always better to depart while you
are a novelty, and interesting, rather than after you have become a fixture, and stale. Besides, Firenze would be expecting to see a balloon ascension every day now, and that is
impractical."

Now there came a tumultuous band fanfare from inside the
tent. Beck and his band emerged, drummer Hannibal and the
Devil's Fiddle player included, all marching to the exuberant
music of "Camptown Races." Behind the band strode Jules
Rouleau, without his cane, subduing his limp as much as
possible. Over his yellow-and-green fleshings, he wore Colonel Ramrod's yellowlined black cloak, and the train of it
was carried by Autumn and Paprika, also in their pista costumes. Arriving at the *Saratogas'* gondola, Rouleau shed the
cloak with elaborately swirling flourishes, to disguise the fact
that the two girls were discreetly assisting his climb into the
basket.

The band music muted so that Florian, with a poster rolled
into a makeshift megaphone, could bray a long harangue at
the crowd—on the perils of aerial journeying, the courage
and skill of Monsieur Roulette, his doing this ascent purely
to thank the city of Firenze for its generous hospitality, etc.,
etc. While all other eyes were on Florian and the *Saratoga*,
Edge happened to glance toward the chapiteau's front-door
marquee. Fitzfarris, wearing his makeup to cover his blue-
ness, was directing a couple of Slovaks in hauling out the
object he had had Goesle construct for him. It was a large
wooden cube that looked like nothing more than a furniture
crate painted black and ornamented with gilt stars, crescent
moons and other cabalistic designs. When the men set it a
little way out from under the marquee, Edge could see that

there was a narrow, shallow tin gutter tacked around the outer four edges of the crate's top.

Florian finished his introduction, the band blared a theme from Corette's *Le Phénix*, some roustabouts cast off ropes, and the vast crowd let out an "Oo-ooh!" that must have been heard as far away as Fiesole. But the balloon went up only slowly, as it had done in Baltimore, the Slovaks paying out the haul-down rope so that Rouleau, when he was some three hundred feet up, could make the crowd gasp again when he insanely vaulted out of the gondola. Then he did his acrobatics on the rope ladder slung over its side, but—in deference to his fragile leg—he did not prolong that exhibition. When he climbed back inside the basket, the crewmen—not he, this time—let go the haul-down rope, and Rouleau took it up with him, coiling it into the basket, as the *Saratoga* soared free.

Still rather slowly, or so it seemed from the ground, the balloon went higher and drifted off to the northward. The watchers could barely see the distant Rouleau now busy at the gondola rim—emptying one of several sandbags—and the balloon more swiftly dwindled higher, until it caught a breeze from the opposite point of the compass, drifted back over the Cascine Park and southward across the Arno. Evidently Rouleau was determined to test what control he had over the craft, for he took it higher, then lower, then higher again, by alternately dumping sand and opening the clack valve, to float in various directions at various levels of the sky. Boom-Boom Beck conducted without looking at the band, so he could keep an eye on the balloon and nod with admiring approval of Rouleau's maneuvers.

Finally, with the slow, deliberate, inch-and-pinch caution of a sea captain berthing an immense ship, Rouleau brought the *Saratoga* down and sideways, aiming for the tober again. It was hardly to be expected that he would make a pinpoint landing on his first try, but he did get close enough and low enough to drop the free end of the haul-down rope, and the Slovaks rushed to seize it and tow the balloon toward touchdown. The crowd roared and applauded as the *Saratoga* was slowly dragged earthward. Then the band gave another blast

of fanfare to attract the people's attention, and Fitzfarris bellowed through the paper megaphone:

"Ebbene, signore e signori! . . . Attenti! . . . Un pezzo della
arte magica! . . . Osservate!"

The jossers lowered their gaze from the balloon to ground
level and saw Fitzfarris languidly puffing on a large cigar,
then gesturing with it to his gilt-and-black platform. On it
stood Monday Simms, in a graceful pose, wearing little else
but a few strategically placed patches of sequins.

"Osservate!" Fitz continued. "La fanciulla che sparisce!"

"The girl who vanishes," said Florian, for anybody who
needed a translation. "What is Sir John up to now?"

Keeping an eye on the balloon being brought down hand
over hand by the roustabouts, Fitzfarris went on bellowing
his broken-Italian to hold the people's attention:

"Osservate vigilantemente, signore e signori! . . . In un is-
tante, la fanciulla . . . sparirà!" The *Saratoga*'s gondola was
only a few feet above the ground when Fitzfarris bawled
more loudly, *"Signorina . . . sparisca!"* and waved his cigar
toward her.

There was a not loud but concussive noise—*fwoompf!*—
and a bright flash of flame, succeeded by a billow of white
smoke that rolled upward from the four sides of the platform,
briefly hiding the girl, and the front ranks of the surrounding
crowd recoiled from the small explosion. The smoke rolled
up and off the platform and away into the air . . . and there
was no Monday Simms standing there any more. The crowd
made a murmur of marveling disbelief, but Fitz gave them
no time to discuss the phenomenon. He was already shouting,
"Ecco!" and pointing to the gondola just now touching the
earth. "Ecco! La fanciulla magica!"—and the people looked
and blinked and gasped, for there in the basket, just come
down from the sky, standing in a graceful pose beside Monsieur Roulette, stood the very girl they had just seen disappear
from the platform on the solid ground.

"Trust Sir John," said Florian admiringly, "to find a new
use for pretty twins."

"I'm only surprised," said Edge, as the crowd burst into

renewed applause, "that he didn't think of some way to make money from the trick."

In a way, Fitz had, for the nearmost of the jossers clamored even more loudly for tickets to a show that so freely displayed such wonders as they had just seen. When Goesle and his men loosed a section of the rope fencing to let them through, there was a stampede for the red-wagon counter where Magpie Maggie Hag presided. Fitzfarris threaded his way through the throng and, smiling triumphantly, came up to Florian and Edge.

"Found some of that stuff the stage magicians call lakapodum powder," he said. "Thought I'd put it to good use."

"Lycopodium," Florian corrected him.

"Whichever it is, what is it?" asked Edge.

"A sort of fungus," said Florian. "Dried and powdered, it is used in fireworks—or for such effects as we have just seen."

"Touched my cigar to it," said Fitz, "and at the same time touched a spring latch that dropped Monday through a trapdoor. I won't do that trick too often, though, because now I can't show the White African Pygmies without giving away the gimmix."

"No matter," said Florian. "You'll have more time at intermission to work your mouse game, and you ought to do a booming business. We have certainly got a turnaway crowd."

Even those folk who were turned away from the ticket counter, though they looked mortally disappointed when the more fortunate ones swarmed inside the chapiteau, loitered about the tober to watch Monsieur Roulette pull the *Saratoga*'s ripcord and collapse the balloon. They stayed on to watch him and the Slovaks carefully fold all the silk and net ropes and hoop and basket, and stow the apparatus in the wagon. They stayed on to gamble at the mouse game during intermission. They even stayed on until the show was over—and the come-out audience loitered, as well—to watch wistfully while the roustabouts and elephant dismantled the entire chapiteau, while the artistes went by ones and twos into the backyard dressing wagon, and emerged in street clothes and went off to the Hotel Kraft for one last supper and one last night's sleep in Firenze.

7

THE JOURNEY south from Firenze might have been plotted on a map with a dash-dot-dash line, the dashes representing the road runs of about twenty miles apiece, and the dots being the villages, towns and cities to which each of those runs brought the circus train. Florian had laid out the route to follow the interlinking river valleys west of the Apennine mountain chain running the length of the peninsula. This necessitated a sometimes meandering and circuitous progress, but it was preferable to suffering the winter cold and fogs of the mountains, the steep and twisty roads up and down them and the lack of grass or hay up there for the stock to pasture on.

All the circus folk were sorry to leave the beauties and pleasures of Firenze, but, at the end of the very first day's run, when they came to the outskirts of San Giovanni Valdarno, they were heartened by the town's looking promising in a peculiar sort of way. The road ahead was flanked by high mounds that flashed gemlike glints of ruby, emerald and sapphire in the late-afternoon sunlight. "Look at that, by damn," Edge remarked to Autumn. "This place is surrounded by hills of jewels." But as they got closer, the glittery hills proved to be only heaps of many-colored broken bottles—the refuse piles of a grappa distillery. The rest of San Giovanni was likewise all industrial and ugly—the workshops of ceramics makers, gravestone carvers, harness-and-saddleries.

The train's southward route almost regularly alternated colorful and pleasant places with dreary and ugly ones. The troupers were much more taken with their next stop, the city of Arezzo. It was built on a hill rising from lowlands of grainfields, orchards and vineyards. To the eyes of those approaching, it looked as if the city, contained and delimited by an encircling medieval stone wall, had had no place to grow but upward, piling terrace upon terrace of buildings and thereby lofting its biggest edifice, the Citadel, to the topmost height of all. But the next stop, Cortona, was another disappointment—a grim, silent town, all ramparts and fortifications. And the next stop was another treat for the eyes and spirits, a hamlet beside the lovely lake of Trasimento, shimmering silver in color.

"However, it was not always that color," said Florian, and he addressed Hannibal Tyree in particular. "This is where your namesake, Hannibal of Carthage, battled against the Roman consul Flaminius. A hundred thousand men died hereabout, and it is said that their blood made the lake red for years afterward."

When, late one afternoon, the train approached the high walls of Perugia, Florian was waiting—he having, as usual, hastened on ahead to deal with the municipal authorities. This time, he called the company together to tell them, "Once again, we will be pitching on the local racetrack, and it is only a little way from here, outside the city ramparts. However, we will be sharing it with a fair already in progress."

"Oh, hell," said Fitzfarris. "Oughtn't we to give this place the go-by, then?"

"Certainly not," said Florian. "The fair will be no competition for us. Rather, it will be an added attraction—part of your midway, so to speak, Sir John. And the fair and circus together will definitely draw good crowds. But I do think we ought to make it clear that we are something more rare and special than a commonplace provincial fair. I propose that we make parade again, all around the city, before we pitch."

So the Florilegium entered Perugia as it had entered Firenze, with flamboyance. The band played numerous times through its repertoire, the women waved and smiled and—though the evening was chilly enough that they wore their cloaks—occasionally bared a glimpse of their fleshings or their real flesh. The procession followed the broad main avenue that circled the city, sometimes outside, sometimes inside the old walls, and the Perugians gathered alongside the avenue or peered down from the ramparts or leaned out the windows, with loud noises of welcome.

The circuit of the city being some two miles in extent,

night had fallen by the time the circus got back to its starting point, and Florian's rockaway led it south toward the Hippodromo. There was no trouble in finding that, for one half of the racetrack's infield oval was brilliantly lighted by the fair's lamps and torches set around tents, stalls, booths and one immense wooden construction too big to be under cover. The fair was also loud with voices, noise and music—several different musics being sung or played simultaneously. The circus wagons drew up on the unoccupied half of the infield, the bandsmen changed from uniforms into work garb and joined the other roustabouts in starting the setup, while Florian went back into the city to seek a convenient and suitable hotel or inn.

The artistes next got out of costume into warm street clothes and went sauntering through the fair, for many of them had seen fairs only in America, and those had consisted mostly of the local folks' showing off to each other their champion livestock, homemade quilts, garden produce of the giant-pumpkin sort. This Italian fair seemed more like a vast sideshow, every participant offering some kind of entertainment, or something to eat or drink, or a game to gamble on, or some odd product for sale.

Edge and Autumn went first to inspect the tremendous wooden thing they had noticed on arrival. It was a wheel as high as a house—or, rather, two wheels fixed together side by side with crossbars at intervals, and from those crossbars were hung half a dozen little two-seat gondolas. People sat in those, looking brave or merry or terrified, as the wheel ponderously turned, the gondolas always hanging level while they went up, over and down. The turning was done by a man on a platform at the wheel's hub, profusely sweating even in the chill night air, as he toiled to turn a crank extending from the axle. An accordionist on the ground played raucous musical accompaniment.

"Those are the new swinging boats," Autumn said. "I first saw one of those machines in Paris. Now they're popular everywhere."

They went on through the milling, noisily excited crowds, up and down the rows of torchlit tents, stalls and booths, those variously identified by fancily painted or merely scrawled signboards: Museo di Figure di Cera, Sala de Misteri, Tomba della Mummia . . .

"Wax Museum," Autumn translated. "Hall of Mysteries. The Mummy's Tomb. These are all known in the trade as entresorts—entertainments that the public pays simply to walk through. And their proprietors are called voyageurs forains, meaning they're not much better than gypsies."

She and Edge stopped to buy a hot salsiccia. The charcoal brazier was attended by an old woman who sat on a stool with her feet in a basket to protect them from the cold ground. For a very few centesimi, she handed each of them a greasy, sputtering sausage impaled on a sliver of wood. As they walked and ate, they could see others of their company eyeing and trying the fair's offerings. Fitzfarris was making a particularly close scrutiny of the entresorts, paying to walk through one after another.

"Now what in the world is this?" asked Edge, as they came to a stall that was only a many-slatted wooden rack all covered with hair. There was hair of every human color—including aged gray, white and silver—bunched in swatches like horsetails, some short, some long, some straight, some curly.

"Just what it looks like," said Autumn. "False hair for sale. There's a customer trying some on." She pointed to where, at one side of the stall, a woman was trying to match the rusty color of her own scanty hair, holding to her head one horsetail after another, peering into a cracked small mirror hung there on a nail. "She'll braid it in among her own—a switch or a rat, we women call it—and pay for it by the gram or kilo, depending on how much she needs."

"I'm glad you don't need any such thing," said Edge. The swatches reminded him too much of what Pepper Mayo had left hanging from the circus's lungia. "Where does the hair come from, anyway?"

"From poor women—or dead ones. From streetwalkers who have fallen clear to the gutter. From workhouses, almshouses, hospitals, lunatic asylums, morgues . . ."

"Jesus, I'm *really* glad you don't need any. But maybe we

ought to mention this booth to Boom-Boom Beck.''

"You are wicked.'' She laughed. "Now I think I will go back to the caravan, Zachary. I do believe that sausage has disagreed with me.''

Edge looked alarmed. "I'd better walk along with—''

"No, no. I am not ill, dear, only queasy. Bit of a headache, too. You go on and see everything there is to see.''

So he did, for he had seen and heard something in one booth that interested him. The booth contained mainly a clutter of what Florian called "slum''—trumpery gimcracks and souvenirs—plaster Madonnas, cheap penknives, chromos of the Last Supper. But among those things, prominent in a place by itself, was a round box of genuine cloisonné, the lid of which the old man in the booth lifted every time someone passed by. And when the box was opened, it played, in a thin, twinkly way, the music of "Greensleeves.'' Edge went close to look at it, the old man raised the lid and the music pinged and jingled.

"Bella, no, la scatola armonica? Un oggetto di mia nonna . . .''

He went on at some length and, after he had repeated himself several times, Edge grasped that the box was suitable for snuff or small jewelry, that it was a bequest from the old man's old grandmother, that the music-machinery in the base of the box had been made, very long ago, by an English master of such instruments. When "Greensleeves'' slowed to a lugubrious plunk-plonking dirge, the old man showed Edge the winding key on the bottom of the box. Then he named a price indicating that he highly valued either the work or his dear grandmother's memory. Edge named a price quite insulting to both. They haggled until Edge—not wanting to pay too cheap a price for a gift for Autumn—finally agreed on a figure and paid it.

On the way back to the tober, Edge fell in with Fitzfarris, who said he had had a stroke of what might be good fortune, but he waited to broach it until they found Florian, busily rounding up all who would be staying in the albergo he had engaged.

"I've found me a tent for my rawhide show," Fitz announced.

"A top for your annex," Florian automatically corrected him.

"There's a fellow here, speaks a little English, and with my little Italian we got to colloguing. He's showing a dismal old mummy, and he wants to sell out and fold up. The top is no bigger than an army hospital tent, but plenty big enough for me to stage a hootchy-cootchy. And it's pretty dingy, but Stitches can paint it up to match the chapiteau. Anyway, I can get it at a reasonable price—and he'll throw in the mummy. What do you say, Governor?"

"What do you want with the mummy, if it's no draw?"

"Oh, hell, this dago doesn't know anything about presentation. He just lets the damned thing lie there. I'll have Mag put some suggestive scanties on her, I'll concoct a history for her . . ."

"Her? It's a female mummy?"

"Who can tell? It's all shriveled—and I mean *all*. I can bill it as a morphodite, if I want to. It's the tent I mainly want."

"It's fine with me, then, Sir John. Go get it."

So Fitzfarris acquired the tent, and Goesle and his men began darning its canvas and replacing its old ropes with new ones, and at the plains town of Foligno and the hill town of Spoleto, in each of which the Florilegium played for two days, Fitz included his mummy among the phenomena of his sideshow. Magpie Maggie Hag, with her clown paints plus ointments and powders borrowed from the other women of the troupe, had enlivened and plumped out the mummy's furrowed face so that it looked, if not gorgeously feminine, at least rather more human than tree bark. She had hidden the bald brown skull under a vaguely pharaonic hat and clothed the body in a gauzy gown embroidered with her notion of an Egyptian design. The gown left the withered arms and legs visible to demonstrate that this was indeed a mummy, but the bosom was padded to give some added semblance of its being a female mummy. Meanwhile, Fitz had had Zanni Bonvecino write for him a rigmarole in Italian, and had memorized it.

"La Principessa Egiziana, signore e signori!" He went on to aver that she was six thousand years old and "of royal rank, as indicated by the luxurious linen which still covers her shapely body."

That was *all* he said about the exhibit in those two towns, as if uncaring whether or not the jossers marveled at the exhibit. But, by the time the Florilegium arrived at the sizable industrial city of Terni, Fitz's new top was all painted and set up on the midway. So, at the first show's intermission in Terni, Fitz presented his "Egyptian princess" with a bit of extra patter that Zanni had provided, and spoke it in a confidentially low voice:

"Any gentlemen in the audience who identify themselves as physicians or surgeons, and who might wish to examine more closely the physiological details of this amazingly preserved young female body, may apply at the specially restricted pavilion yonder, after the close of our main performance, and upon the payment of a small additional honorarium . . ."

A surprisingly large number of the adult males in that audience proved to be physicians or surgeons, willing to spend five lire just to satisfy their professional interest in ancient Egyptian anatomy.

The next town on the route, Rieti, provided another abundance of doctors to patronize the mummy's tent. But they—and their women and children, too—were almost as much beguiled by another addition to the show. For the first time, Colonel Ramrod introduced the eight polka-dot Pinzgauer horses into his liberty act. That meant that he had in the pista, all at one time, a herd of fourteen horses, handsomely blue-blanketed, plumed, spangled and tasseled by Magpie Maggie Hag. There was one difference in their dress now: each horse's blanket bore on its right side a large number, from 1 to 14.

After Colonel Ramrod had put individual horses and teams of them and ensembles of them and all of them through their several tricks and patterns and dances, the close of the act consisted of their cantering counterclockwise in a mixed bunch around the inside of the pista curb. Then, as the eques-

trian director flicked his whip in signals known only to him
and to them, the horses began to fall into single file. The
horse bearing the number 1 drew ahead of the other, number
2 moved up, and so on—until the horses composed a complete circle, 1 to 14, cantering around and around their master,
and looking properly proud of themselves. The audience paid
the supreme compliment of sitting silent for a moment, in
stunned admiration, before breaking into a storm of applause.
Then the carousel-like circle broke, and the horses—seemingly of their own accord—cantered through the curb opening
and out the back door, still in numerical order.

The Florilegium's next run, up the Salto River valley, took
three days and nights. There were no towns big enough to
pitch in, and the alberghi and locande along the roadside had
kitchens and larders sufficient to feed the company, but no
beds enough for them. So the artistes and senior crewmen
took their meals in the inns, and retired to wagons and pallets
afterward. On one of those nights, Fitzfarris put to Paprika a
persuasive suggestion, but evidently not persuasive enough,
for she was heard to snarl at him:

"You ask me to do rawhide? Csúnya! I have been wondering what to do with my perch pole. I think I will shove it
up your végbél."

Whereupon Fitzfarris applied to the younger females: Clover Lee, Sunday and Monday. "It will be a tableau," he
pleaded. "You only *pose*. More or less. And it's *biblical*.
What could be more praiseworthy than illustrating the Scriptures?"

"Well . . ." said Sunday charily.

"Splendid! You and Monday will portray the daughters.
Now, what do you say, Clover Lee, to the very grown-up
rôle of a Hittite matron?"

In that time of no performances and no other distractions,
Magpie Maggie Hag did the costumes for Fitzfarris's planned
biblical tableaux, while he rehearsed in their rôles the three
girls, plus two Slovaks he had conscripted besides. With
Zanni's help, he also sketched out the lettering for a sign-

board, and got the Chinese painter to do it "artistically" for him.

When the circus set up in the castle-topped town of Avezzano, Fitz did not immediately display that sign, and during his sideshow presentation at intermission he did not, this time, invite any doctor to an intimate showing of the mummy. Instead, having concluded the sideshow, he announced in words again provided by Zanni:

"After the main show, there will be presented, in the smaller pavilion you see yonder, for the modest entrance fee of just ten lire, a special educational performance for gentlemen only. You will see and be thrilled by a vivid tableau taken directly from the Holy Bible. It unfortunately cannot be performed before women and children. (You gentlemen, I am sure, know the indelicate frankness of certain parts of the Good Book.) This educational show must be discreetly and privately presented *only* to those adult male students of the Bible who will not be shocked or scandalized by seeing the Holy Scriptures . . . ahem . . . laid bare."

Immediately after the closing spec, Clover Lee, Sunday and Monday ran to change in the dressing wagon—the two Slovaks had only to shed their working overalls, as they were wearing the basics of their costumes underneath—and then to Fitz's annex, where they all ducked inside under an unpegged piece of canvas at the back.

Florian and Edge came sauntering out of the chapiteau, and Edge said, "Good God, will you look at that?" He pointed to the mob of men besieging the annex tent, where Fitzfarris was feverishly selling tickets. There evidently were as many Bible students in Avezzano as there had been physicians and surgeons elsewhere. These all were elbowing each other to crowd through the tent's front flap under the now prominently displayed signboard:

SPETTACULI BIBLICHI
E SCOLASTICHI
I La CONCUPISCENZA di *David* e *Bathsheba*
II-Il *Stuprato* di LOT per sue FIGLIE

When Edge and Florian also squeezed inside the top, Fitz-farris turned away all the other men still clamoring and waving their money—assuring them that tickets for the second tableau would go on sale as soon as the first Bible study session was concluded. The small tent was packed chocka-block already, except at its far end, where hung a drab piece of spare canvas for a curtain. Now Fitz pulled a string that slid the curtain aside, disclosing an elevated wooden platform. Behind it, on the inside of the tent canvas itself, the Chinese artist had painted his Oriental notion of the landscape of Israel. At the same moment, one of the conscripted roust-abouts invisible "offstage" began playing on the accordion his Slovak notion of what David, King of the Israelites, would have played on his harp.

The first tableau commenced, but it was not really a tab-leau, for there was some action to it. There climbed upon the platform the other Slovak, clad in a silver-painted pasteboard breastplate and a pleated short skirt, below which his legs were bare and hairy. Next Clover Lee appeared, clad in a short frock of almost transparent gauze. While those two nuz-zled and pawed each other, simulating a fond leavetaking, Fitzfarris began reciting in Italian below the platform:

"The men of the city went out to fight against Joab. And, by the treachery of David the King, Uriah the Hittite departed from his wife Bathsheba." The armored Uriah retired from the platform, leaving Bathsheba in throes of exaggerated grief. There was a brief interruption of the music as, out of sight, its player relinquished the accordion to Uriah the Hit-tite, and himself climbed onto the platform, wearing a short-skirted chiton, hairy legs and a gilt pasteboard crown.

As the music resumed, Bathsheba recovered and began making gestures of scrubbing her blonde-tufted underarms. "And it came to pass," intoned Fitzfarris, "that David, from his roof, saw a woman washing herself." The Slovak David made his eyes bug out at her. "And she came in unto him, and he lay with her." David and Bathsheba lunged together, and embraced and slavered over one another, as Fitz slowly pulled his string and the canvas curtain slowly obliterated the scene. "But the thing that David had done displeased the Lord."

It had not at all displeased the crowd of Bible students. They all shouted lusty encouragements and bawdy suggestions to the illicit lovers as the curtain closed entirely.

Florian and Edge, at the rear of the audience, threw open the front-door flap of canvas and they were the first out. Most of the rest of the crowd exited only as far as where Fitz had reappeared, so they could each throw him ten more lire to see the second tableau. That caused some squabbling with turned-away patrons who had impatiently waited outside, but Edge and Florian left Fitzfarris to deal with that. They went around to the back of the top to intercept Clover Lee as she slid out from under the sidewall.

"Er . . . Clover Lee, my dear," said Florian. "Since the departure of your mother, I consider myself as being in loco parentis. And I would be remiss in that duty if I did not express my mixed feelings about your appearing in such a *raw* rawhide exhibition."

Clover Lee giggled. "I don't mind showing myself. It's even kind of exciting, to feel all the heavy breathing going on in there, and knowing none of them can get near me. Except that hairy Slovak. You might tell Sir John—no, I'll tell him myself—to make his damned David stop drooling on my boobies."

She skipped blithely off toward the dressing wagon, and Florian and Edge shrugged at one another.

"Well," said Florian. "No hope of squeezing back in there to see what Sir John has put the Simms kids up to. We'll have to wait until tonight."

"Maybe longer than that," said Edge, looking up at the low gray clouds from which snow was beginning softly to fall. "Do you reckon Fitz has offended the Almighty?"

The snow came only in fitful flurries during the rest of the day and did not prevent the people of Avezzano from making the nighttime house another sfondone. But Florian kept sticking his head outside the chapiteau during the first half of the program and finding the snowfall heavier each time. Edge kept a roustabout posted up on the trapeze rig, to alert him if the snow should drift in upon it. It did not, and Maurice and Paprika went through their performance without mishap. Theirs was the closing act before intermission, but Florian informed the audience that, since the snow was quite thick on the ground outside, he would suggest that they keep their seats. So, while Magpie Maggie Hag circulated among the stands, doing her predictions for pregnant women, a disgruntled Fitzfarris had to display his Tattooed Man self, his White African Pygmies, his Night Children and his Egyptian Princess from the middle of the pista—where he could work neither his Little Miss Mitten swazzle sale nor his mouse game.

The second half of the program also went without incident, including—when the lookout crewman reported it safe—Autumn's tightrope performance that closed the show. But before the troupe could complete a single circuit of the "Marcia Reale" closing spec, many of the jossers were already marching for the front door, and all the rest soon followed, and everybody went running for home or for carriages and wagons, not one of them lingering to attend the annex's Spettaculi Biblichi.

"Shit," said Fitzfarris, glaring out from under the marquee.

"No, that's snow," Edge said humorously, and he turned to Dai Goesle. "The body heat of the crowd kept the snow from accumulating on the chapiteau, Canvasmaster. But now that they're gone, what do we do?"

"No problem," said Stitches. "Look you, I will set a couple of Peggy's bales of hay on a slow burn in here, and leave a couple of my men to tend them through the night. That will keep the canvas clean and dry."

There was no snow falling next day, but the town streets and the circus tober were so slushy and muddy that Florian gave orders for immediate teardown. However, the Florilegium—and most particularly Fitzfarris—had no better luck at the next town, Sora. It was bad enough that Sora was a paper-mill town, as nauseously stinking as Baltimore had been, but no sooner had the afternoon show begun than a drenching rain began to fall. Then a wind began to blow. Then both rain and wind got fiercer. Between the noise of the elements and the distressed flopping and booming of the chapiteau canvas, even Florian's bellowed introductions of the acts were overwhelmed.

Edge had again posted a roustabout in the peak and, long before Maurice and Paprika were scheduled to go on, that Slovak descended from his perch to report that the trapeze rig was soaking wet and so was he. Edge put out the word to the company that both the trapeze and tightrope acts were to be canceled, and that everyone else should stretch his, her or their act to fill. Meanwhile, Florian herded half a dozen crewmen out into the howling storm. He directed them in hauling all the heaviest circus wagons to the windward side of the chapiteau, and rigging extra guy lines from the canvas to those wagons.

"At least we won't have to fear a blowdown," he informed Edge when he returned, sodden and dripping. "Not unless the storm gets a lot worse."

"Couldn't make much difference," said Edge. "The people are already pretty damned damp from the water blowing in under the eaves and down from the bail-ring openings."

Damp or not, the audience chose to remain inside during the intermission, as Florian recommended. And so Magpie Maggie Hag and Fitzfarris again had to do their stints indoors. Later, after the closing spec, Florian made another announcement to the crowd: that the storm appeared to be slackening, and that all who wished to wait until it stopped entirely could remain in the chapiteau and be entertained—at no extra charge—by a concert of "canti spirituale" performed by Genuine American Negroes.

"The Happy Hottentots, signore e signori—Gli Ottentotti Felici!"

There came into the pista Sunday, Monday, Ali Baba and Abdullah, all of whom had hastily changed into street clothes. They sang, and quite sweetly, a long medley of "Sometimes I Feel Like a Motherless Chile," "Joshua Fit de Battle Ob Jericho" and the like, accompanied pianissimo by the band—pianissimo because Boom-Boom Beck had not much rehearsed his windjammers in this music. Meanwhile, Fitzfarris sulked and fumed at the repeated cancellations of *all* his money-making innovations.

It was not until the Florilegium pitched in Cassino—a town that seemed to cower under the massive, majestic Benedictine abbey on the mountain overlooking it—that Fitzfarris was able to resume his annex show. Florian and Edge were too busy with other matters to attend the tableaux presented after the first circus performance. But after the nighttime show, when just about every man in the audience flocked to the smaller top, Florian and Edge made sure to get themselves standing room for "The Ravishment of Lot by His Daughters."

"And it came to pass," Fitz recited, "when God destroyed the cities of Sodom and Gomorrah, that he sent Lot out of the midst of the overthrow."

The offstage accordion started wailing a Slovak notion of the orgiastic music that would have been a staple in Sodom and Gomorrah. The canvas curtain opened, revealing the other Slovak, wearing a shapeless burlap robe, carrying over one shoulder a burlap bag. "And Lot went up and dwelt in the mountain, and his two daughters with him."

Sunday and Monday appeared on the platform, wearing diaphanous, all but all-revealing frocks, and conspiratorially put their heads together. "The firstborn said unto the younger: Come, let us make our father drink wine." Lot produced from his bag a bottle of grappa, and swigged from it, and reeled about the platform, and fell supine with a crash.

"And the firstborn went in and lay with her father." Sunday lay down only chastely beside Lot, but the fact that Monday looked on with a gloating expression and suggestively chafed her thighs together could have made the jossers imagine that they were watching a most indecent coupling there on the platform floor.

After a moment, Sunday crept away again, Lot awoke and arose and staggered about. Fitzfarris spoke again, "The firstborn said: Let us make him drink wine this night also." Lot brought out his grappa once more, and drank heavily, and fell down. "Go thou in, and lie with him." Sunday gently shoved her sister down beside Lot, and Monday lay not quite so chastely; she was perceptibly writhing and rubbing her legs together. The Sodom-Gomorrah accordion music went crescendo, and the curtain began edging across the scene, as Fitzfarris bawled his last line—"Thus were both the daughters of Lot with child by their father!" The assembled Bible students exploded in hurrahs and shouts of "Ha coglioni duri, questo padre!" and "Lui si è rizzato!"

But those cries were drowned by a louder, very angry bellow of *"Desistiate! Infedeli!"* The jossers all turned and craned to see the source of that—and quailed when they did. Two men who had been wearing heavy overcoats, although the evening was mild, now flung those open to display their cassocks underneath, as they went on roaring in outrage, *"Scandalo! Dileggio! Putridità!"*

"Damnation," growled Florian. "I should have foreseen something like this, right here in Saint Benedict's bailiwick."

The men in the tent, averting their faces, poured fearfully outdoors and away, leaving only the two irate priests, Florian, Edge and the bewildered-looking Fitzfarris.

"What's eating these birds?" he asked, as they continued to shake their fists and shout invective at him.

"I fear, Sir John," said Florian, "that we may be in trouble." He spoke in Italian to the two, and gamely introduced himself as the circus's owner, therefore the party to blame. That did not appear to mollify the padres, still fizzing and sputtering. "It seems," Florian translated to Fitzfarris, "the word of your show spread far and wide since this afternoon. The abbot-bishop delegated these two functionaries to come and investigate. They didn't much like what they found. They predict that the bishop will like it even less."

"Hell," said Fitz. "What can a bunch of preachers do to us?"

"Here in Italy, the Inquisition still wields considerable authority," said Florian. "I might also mention a unique method of execution once practiced here. A condemned man had his abdomen slit, his intestines drawn out and slowly cranked around a wheel, while he still lived and looked on."

Fitzfarris gulped, and said, "Oh, come on, now . . . Florian, tell them I was only quoting from the Bible. Well, I was, wasn't I? Or did that Zanni pull some kind of dirty trick in his translation?''

"No, you read aright," said Florian, and he conversed briefly with the seething clerics. "Now they're quoting, too—from Shakespeare—that the Devil can cite Scripture to his own purpose."

"This is a lot of balls," said Edge. "These two busybodies waited until they'd seen all there was to see before they started to fuss."

"Hush up, Zachary," said Florian. "The two of you clear out of here. I've taken responsibility, so I'll take any castigation that's coming. Go on, get out."

They went, but they stayed close by, in case Florian needed rescue—or his entrails replaced. After some time, they saw the two priests emerge from the annex into the light of the torches outside it. They clapped on their pileus caps and strode briskly off the tober, their cassocks and overcoats flapping. A moment later, Florian also came out, evidently unscathed.

"Well, what happened?" Fitzfarris asked.

"Oh, I made a contribution to the diocesan charity fund."

"That's *all*?" said Edge. "That got us off the hook? Heresy, blasphemy, whatever the hell it was?"

"The thing is," said Florian, "they spotted the trace of bay in the complexion of the Simms girls, and correctly surmised that they are mulattoes."

Fitz was staggered. "You mean those dago buck-nuns complained about *miscegenation*? Two pretty buffalo gals frolicking with a *Slovak*!"

"Oh, the padres didn't so much mind seeing a white man cavorting with two mulattoes. Their objection was more theological than moral."

"What?"

"You see, those sons that Lot begat on his daughters were Ammon and Moab. Much later, among King Solomon's wives were Ammonite and Moabite women, descendants of that episode on the mountain, and it is established that Saint Joseph was lineally descended from Solomon. The Church theologians are bothered enough by the possibility that Jesus's mother's husband could have been a product of that incestuous coupling ages before. And now—when you introduce a couple of high-yellow girls into your reconstruction of the epic—you appear to be smearing the Holy Family with a tar brush besides.''

"I'll be damned."

"Maybe not. If you'll promise not to show the Lot and Daughters tableau again while we're here in Cassino, the good fathers have promised they'll pray for you.''

"I'd like to tell the good fathers one thing," Fitz said sourly. "Let them pray into one hand and piss into the other, and see which fills up faster."

As the Florilegium moved on from town to town, Stitches Goesle and Boom-Boom Beck, in their free time, continued to make improvements in their departments of the establishment. Beck somewhere found and purchased a snare drum and a tenor drum, and conscripted another Slovak into the band to play them, for they served better than Hannibal's big bass drum to sound a suspenseful roll during a thrill act or a brisk rataplan during clownish knockabouts. Goesle, for his part, built a pair of what the longtime circus folk called donnickers, and he designed them to be portable—three walls and a hinged door, enclosing a single-hole bench, the whole of which could be collapsed flat for transporting—and had the Chinese artist paint ''Uomini'' on one door, ''Donne'' on the other. At every new tober, as soon as the tents were set up, he put roustabouts to digging pits at a suitable distance, over which to set the two privies.

The Florilegium had been only briefly and not seriously incommoded by the mild mid-Italy winter and, as the circus traveled southward from those wintertime latitudes, springtime was moving northward from the Mediterranean. The two met in the town of Caserta, where every flowering plant was in bud, and the plane trees lining the long, broad avenue leading to the old Royal Palace were already in brilliant green leaf. It was there at the avenue that Florian, after his ride on ahead, met the circus, to report:

"The Caserta authorities will have none of us. They decline to grant us a tober in the town."

Edge said, "Do you mean they already got wind of Fitz's hootchy-cootchy? Are we going to be banned everywhere from now on?"

"If that is so," said Autumn, "why are you grinning, Florian?"

"Because King Victor Emmanuel just happens to be temporarily in residence here at La Reggia"—he gestured to the avenue and the vast, colonnaded palace visible at the far end of it—"instead of in Firenze or his palace at San Rossore. And the king's authority supersedes the local. When I called at the municipio, I was referred to a court steward."

"My God," said Edge. "Has even the *king* heard of the rawhide?"

"If he has, he'll want to see it," said Florian. "I won't tease you any longer. I am smiling because we are moving up in the world." He raised his voice to the rest of the train. "Gather around, everybody!" When all the principals of the company had assembled, he explained, "It seems that King Victor Emmanuel has a passion for circuses, but has never seen an American one. His Majesty invites us to pitch in the park of La Reggia here, and to stage a command performance for him and his court."

There were various exclamations, Clover Lee's the loudest: "At last! Counts and dukes!"

"Even a crown prince, my child," said Florian. "The king is accompanied by his son Umberto. Very well, everybody, let us first oblige His Majesty by making parade as we go up the avenue."

So they did, and the day was warm enough for all the troupers to strip down to their pista costumes, and they all did their most graceful postures and movements, and the band played its lustiest. As they got close to the palace, some French doors opened in an upper story, and a number of uniformed, gold-braided and bemedaled figures emerged onto a balcony to watch. At that, Beck broke off whatever music his band was playing, to roar out "La Marcia Reale"—and all the men on the balcony doffed their cockaded hats.

A pair of palace flunkies in antique wigs and knee breeches trotted out of a ground-level door to direct the train into the two-mile-long park. The servants ran on ahead and finally stopped to indicate that the circus was to pitch on a grassy lawn among fountains, fishponds, temples and statuary. As the roustabouts began unloading the wagons and preparing to set up, Florian told Beck:

"The command performance will take place tomorrow, at whatever hour best suits the court's convenience. After tomorrow, His Majesty will graciously allow the local town and country folk into his park for our subsequent performances. Meanwhile, Chief Beck, I don't know if it is possible to find chemicals for the balloon's generator in a town this size. But why don't you hasten into Caserta and see what you can do?"

"Ja wohl," Beck said, and began to bellow at his Slovaks.

"It looks like some nabob is paying us a visit already," said Autumn, drawing Florian's attention to the royally carved and ornamented gold-and-white coach which just then drew up at the edge of the tober area.

Two guardsmen first alighted, then handed down from the coach a short, plump, bluff-featured man in an elegant military uniform, with the big rosette of the Order of Annunziata above rows of medal ribbons. He was bald, even of eyebrows, from his forehead to the caput of his head, but he compensated for that with an imperial beard and thick, upturned mustaches that extended like a frame far on either side of his face.

"Bless my soul, it's His Majesty himself," said Florian. "Clear out, everybody. Colonel Ramrod, you stay to welcome him with me. And you, Miss Auburn, to interpret for Zachary."

The other troupers dispersed about their busness—all but Clover Lee, who retired only to a respectful distance, and there began practicing flip-flops and cartwheels to display her legs and under parts to best advantage. His Majesty seemed to appreciate that, for his porcine little eyes were on her even while Florian and Edge were bowing and Autumn curtsying to him, and Florian murmuring, "Benvenuto, Maestà."

The king shifted his connoisseurial gaze to Autumn, as

Florian introduced her and Edge. Then the four of them together, followed closely and watchfully by the guardsmen, strolled to where the roustabouts were laying out the tent poles.

"The king says," Autumn translated to Edge in an undertone, "that he is interested in the mechanics of our trade. Because, he says, the King of Prussia has personally observed the methods by which circuses move from place to place, and has applied some of those methods to his Prussian Army. The king thinks his own army might learn something from the technicalities of circus stowage and transport and general efficiency."

When Hannibal commanded the elephant to haul upright the first center pole, Florian waggishly told Victor Emmanuel, "Regard, Your Majesty—that one we call the *king* pole. As Your Majesty is to your kingdom, so is the king pole the mainstay of our chapiteau. Because, when it is erect, it becomes the fulcrum that enables the levering upright of the second center pole . . ."

The king smiled, making his mustache tips almost meet between his eyes, and spoke at length.

"He is admiring big Peggy's obedience and skill," Autumn told Edge. "He says he is a lover of animals. He is putting together the first zoölogical garden Italy has ever had. And he is especially proud of having acquired a whole herd of Australian kangaroos."

When the chapiteau's roof canvas was hauled up by its bail rings to the peaks of the two center poles—the roustabouts doing the heeby-weeby chant—the king asked something of Florian, who immediately started scribbling with his mason's pencil on a piece of paper.

"His Majesty asked for the words of that chanty," Autumn told Edge, and laughed quietly. "Perhaps he thinks that is the secret of circus and Prussian efficiency. It is amusing to imagine the whole Italian Army marching off to battle in cadence to 'Heeby-weeby-Maggie-*moo*-long . . .' "

At any rate, the king's curiosity seemed satisfied. He took the paper and parted from Florian, Edge and Autumn, after many mutual bows and compliments, returned to his coach, detailed two liveried attendants to remain on the scene, and was driven away.

"His Majesty requests that our performance be at three o'clock tomorrow afternoon," said Florian, flushed with pride and pleasure. "These equerries are to provide anything we might need. And at every mealtime while we are here, they will escort us to one of the palace's dining rooms, and the Slovaks, Chinks and blacks to the kitchens."

Both of the equerries hovered about until the crew erected the seats in the chapiteau. Then the two men conferred, and one of them set off at a run toward the palace. Shortly afterward, a number of wagons and servants came through the park bearing more suitable seating.

Florian said, "I should have realized that a royal court can't be expected to sit on planks. Chief Goesle, please remove those foremost benches."

That was done, and in their place the servants set a tremendous high-backed thronelike armchair, then, on both sides of and behind it, some dozens of exquisitely gilded and tapestry-upholstered chairs. Meanwhile, the crew and artistes completed what work they had to do, saw to their animals, laid out props for the next day, then washed themselves and dressed in their best civilian clothes. Leaving only Aleksandr Banat, who insisted that a circus needed a watchman even when it was installed in a royal park, the rest of the company rode in the wagons with the servants back to the palace and were shown, according to their station, to either dining room or kitchen.

The dining table provided for the artistes and crew chiefs was ablaze with candlelight from chandeliers and candelabra, shining on porcelain, crystal, silver and damask. There was a footman behind every chair, and a constant procession of other servants—commanded by a maggiordomo—bearing tureens of various soups, platters of many meats, bowls of pasta and vegetables, ice-filled buckets in which reposed bottles of wine, still and sparkling, white, rosé and red.

Zanni Bonvecino exchanged some banter with the servants—they seemed slightly distressed by the familiarity—just long enough to assure himself that none of them except the maggiordomo comprehended the occasional English word he addressed to them. Then, when the maggiordomo was briefly out of the room, Zanni leaned across the table to say confidentially to Clover Lee:

"I would strongly recommend, signorina, that you be careful how you comport yourself when our royal host is about."

"I beg your pardon?" she said stiffly.

"He is a notorious womanizer, and not at all subtle or discreet about it."

"Oh, tut," Paprika put in. "Sheer gossip. They say that about every royal male."

"Well, ten or so years ago," said Zanni, "when he was merely King of Sardinia and came to visit Paris, I was present—only as a singer, of course—at a gala given for him by the emperor and empress. I personally heard him commit two frightful breaches of manners. On being introduced to a certain lady of the French nobility, he announced quite loudly that he already knew her well, having once bedded her in Torino. Later, when we entertainers were preparing to perform, he asked the Empress Eugénie, again in no hushed voice, whether it was true, as he had heard, that in France the female dancers never wore—er—undercoverings. If so, he said, then France would be absolute heaven for him. Needless to say, he has not been invited back to Paris since then."

After dinner, the troupers only slowly made their way to the palace's outside doors. By ones and twos and groups, they idled to traverse and admire as many rooms as possible of the reputed twelve hundred in the palace. They did not venture above the ground floor, but there every room was of museum opulence and preservation: all gold and marble and velvet and monumental staircases and priceless antique furnishings and immense hanging tapestries and ceilings clustered with stucco putti and curlicues. Clover Lee murmured dreamily, "I should not mind living here . . ."

Back at the tober, they discovered that Beck and his assistants had returned from town—and by some magic or miracle or sheer Bavarian tenacity, he *had* procured sufficient carboys of acid and barrels of iron filings, and was setting everything out in readiness for the balloon's inflation on the morrow.

*   *   *

Well before three o'clock the next afternoon, the *Saratoga*
was towering impressively above the highest trees in the Reggia park, the artistes were all in readiness and even the windjammers had finished their interminable tuning up. But the
king and court exercised the royal prerogative of being three-
quarters of an hour late, arriving in a train of elegant coaches,
broughams, clarences and landaus drawn by matched teams
of horses. Banat directed his fellow Slovaks in assisting the
guests from the carriages and—after they had all exclaimed
at the unexpected sight of the *Saratoga*—escorting them to
the chapiteau marquee. From there, Florian and Colonel Ramrod ceremoniously ushered them to their seats—the king to
the thronelike big chair, and to the others the handsome
young Crown Prince Umberto, various elderly or middle-aged
duce and conti and marchesi, plus officers of the army and
of the royal household, and many of their wives, daughters
and consorts, the men and women alike dressed as richly as
for a court ball. There were some forty people in all, the
smallest audience the Florilegium had ever played to—but
every artiste performed to perfection.

As he did everywhere, Zanni the toby made his verbal
clowning suit the place and occasion—*not* referring to any
of the present patrons, but to "Sophie's boy." Victor Emmanuel laughed long and loudly, and so did his retinue, for
Zanni was poking fun at the king's own bête noire, the Emperor Franz Joseph of Austria and his meddlesome mother,
the Dowager Empress Sophia.

The Quakemaker risked rupturing himself, showing his
feats of strength with the cannonballs, and of endurance when
his Percheron repeatedly plodded over him, but he still managed to "win" in the tug-of-war with Brutus. Even the Chinese antipodists seemed to realize the importance of this
occasion, and did upsidedown exploits more impossible-
seeming than any they had ever done before. Clover Lee did
her rosinback act with consummate grace, performing her
most spectacular tricks directly in front of the chair of the
young, slim, smiling Prince Umberto. Monday and Thunder
were picture-perfect in their haute école fancy stepping. The

Pete Jenkins flabbergasted this august audience as much as it had done any crowd of yokels, and, after the intrusive drunk became Maurice LeVie, he and Paprika became a faultless dazzle of blue and orange on the trapezes.

For a wonder, thought Edge, as the show proceeded, none of the animals—dogs, horses, lion or elephant—discourteously shat in the pista. It was customary to do what Florian called "rearing" the animals before any major performance, meaning to give them a mild purge and an opportunity to evacuate themselves before the show, but it did not always suffice. On this occasion, however, none of the beasts even made water. At intermission, Magpie Maggie Hag read the palms of several of the court ladies, and they tittered with delight, for she made only most glowing predictions. Sir John presented himself and his other freaks close to the seats, then entertained the guests with Little Miss Mitten, then let the gentlemen take a fling at his mouse game, punctiliously paying off the winners and, at the end, generously returning all the money of the losers.

During the second half of the program, Barnacle Bill was uncharacteristically untipsy, and Maximus got into the spirit of the occasion, growling and clawing bloodthirstily but performing as tamely and willingly as a dog. When the real dogs came on, Pavlo Smodlaka introduced a new turn. He borrowed the band's accordion and played a simple tune while the terriers singly, in twos, or all three, yapped in various tones to provide a passably harmonious "singing." During the shootist act, Colonel Ramrod missed not a shot, and at the last one, into Sunday's teeth, she did a wonderfully realistic backward jolt.

Abdullah the Hindu juggled an incredible simultaneous assortment of eggs, lighted candles, a bottle of wine and some horseshoes. Then, nonchalantly juggling several of those things with only one hand, he extended his other to the seats, offering to include whatever else he might be given. The *king himself* unsheathed and gave Abdullah his jewel-hilted sword. Unfazed, Abdullah added it to his blur of flying things, making the sword twirl and flash as it flew, finally catching it in his teeth, like a pirate. Buckskin Billy rode a voltige that should have broken every bone in his body, concluding with the "Saint Petersburg Courier," one foot on each of two wide-apart horses, the other horses galloping one by one between his legs. Last, Autumn Auburn gracefully did on the narrow, high tightrope the twirls and pirouettes and splits and back flips that other performers had done on solid, safe ground or on the broad backs of horses. Then the closing Grand Promenade was done with as much pomp as the opening one had been, and as if it were playing to a tent-bulging throng of people.

After their polite and sparse but appreciative applause, the king and his courtiers got up from their chairs to come to the pista and mingle democratically with the players and praise their performances and—with Florian or Zanni or Autumn translating where necessary—ask questions about their art and their way of life. Most of the questioners were eager to know the tricks the artistes *must* employ to do some of the apparently impossible things they did. But most of the artistes answered truthfully that they used no tricks, only experience and practice. However, when Prince Umberto and some other army officers inspected Colonel Ramrod's revolver and carbine, and congratulated him on his awesome marksmanship, Edge said nothing about the use of bird shot or blank charges for some of his effects. Florian watched with amusement as a fat, white-haired duchessa playfully squeezed the Quakemaker's bulging biceps. Then she asked him, in stilted English, what sort of companion he considered the best for the road.

Yount pondered, then said, "A stiff dose of constipation, ma'am. So you don't have to stop and tarry too often."

The dowager rocked, so Florian quickly and loudly inquired if any of the guests would be pleased to visit the annex tent and view Sir John's version of scenes from the Bible—adding that only the gentlemen would be likely to enjoy them to the fullest. King Victor Emmanuel leered and remarked that, while the ladies of his court might have forgotten much of the Bible since their catechism days, he would wager they could quote word for word from such smutty "backstairs books" as *Eveline* and *Schwester Monika*. The ladies, young and old, all tittered and put up their fans before their faces, but did not contradict him. So the whole court trooped outside and into the smaller top, and Fitz boldly launched into his recital.

Some while later, when both tableaux were done and the audience emerged from the tent, the men and women alike were smiling salaciously, and none of the women was being carried in a faint. Fitzfarris came out last, and Florian was waiting, to say, "Well?"

"Well, that fat, white-haired old bat invited me to dine privately with her tonight."

"That old bat is the Duchessa da Brisighella."

"And Clover Lee is invited to do the same with Prince Umberto. If that's all right with you, Governor."

Florian grimaced. "Clover Lee had told me flatly that she needs and wants no protecting. You might, though, Sir John."

"Ah, well. I told you once that I had looked forward to meeting titled Europeans. I can hardly repulse a duchess, however repulsive she is. But even if I'm profaning my chastity, by damn, I've regained my artistic integrity. I'm going to have our Chink artist add an imprimatur to my signboard. 'As presented at the Court of His Majesty Victor Emmanuel II.' I defy any more meddlers to interfere with my Bible studies—at least as long as we're in the Kingdom of Italy."

The balloon ascension was the closing spectacle of the afternoon. It drew awed and admiring cries from the gathered royalty—and from others besides. Though the town of Caserta was some way distant, the people in the park could hear shouts and oaths from that direction, and the hoofbeats and rumbling wheels of at least one runaway horse and wagon. When Rouleau brought the *Saratoga* down again—and again with surprising accuracy, so the ground crew did not have to run far to catch its trailing rope—and was hauled to the ground and took his bows, many of the royal gentlemen pounded him on the back, and many of the ladies caressed him more gently.

Then the courtiers made their adieux personally to each and every member of the company, even to those roustabouts in evidence. Servants now came from the carriages, their arms laden, and the king himself presented every female artiste with a huge bouquet of hothouse carnations and a fine, fringed silk shawl embroidered with a crown. To each man— even Hannibal and the three Chinese—he gave a silver cigarette case engraved with the royal arms. To each of the children—Sava, Velja and Quincy—he gave a small, stuffed velvet kangaroo. Then he wished the Florilegium a capacity crowd of the common folk during its stay, and he and his retinue returned to the palace.

That night, when the troupe went to the palace for dinner, Fitzfarris and Clover Lee were conspicuously absent from the table, and one other—Monday Simms—sat silent and glum. The rest chatted and praised the provender and joked and laughed. Then, when the servants brought in platters of ortolans broiled in black butter and capers, and everybody was silently admiring the dish, Autumn suddenly raised her head and tilted it as if listening to something far off, and said wonderingly into the silence, ''A clock just stopped somewhere.''

Everybody, including the servants, looked at her—some uncomprehendingly, some in surprise, but Magpie Maggie Hag's look was intent and searching. The dining room's maggiordomo smiled at Autumn and said, ''Signorina, it still ticks and tocks,'' and indicated the priceless ormolu clock on the mantel, its little pendulum busily waggling.

''No,'' said Autumn. ''Not in here. Somewhere else.''

''Signorina,'' the steward said patiently. ''There must be two, maybe three hundred clocks in this palace.''

''Nevertheless,'' said Autumn, ''one of them stopped. I know it. Just hearing it stop gave me a twinge of earache.''

The other troupers made dismissive noises and began to attack their broiled little birds. But Magpie Maggie Hag still gazed at Autumn, while the maggiordomo, to humor that guest's queer whimsy, snapped his fingers to the footmen standing at attention behind all the diners' chairs, rattled instructions in Italian, and the footmen departed the room in quickstep.

Autumn smiled her thanks to the maggiordomo and then, like the others, proceeded to eat. When they had finished the ortolans and were using their fingerbowls in preparation for the next course, Florian leaned over to say privily to Edge:

"I must impart something which His Majesty confided to me. He is preparing to make a military alliance with Prussia. I think it behooves us to turn around and head north again, if we wish to see Rome at all, and I'm sure we do."

"I'm sure," said Edge. "But what's the hurry? I don't see the connection."

"It is rather complicated to explain," said Florian. "All of the Italian peninsula is now a united kingdom, except for the Papal State around Rome. However, on the mainland is the Italian-speaking region of Venezia, which has been held by Austria for fifty years. Victor Emmanuel—and the Venetians themselves—wish that land to become a part of Italy. Meanwhile, Prussia envisions an equally united federation of the German-speaking peoples. That will require the conquest of Austria, among other acquisitions. A Prussian-Italian alliance almost certainly presages war against Austria, the Prussians striking from the north, the Italians through Venezia."

"So? Are you afraid they will conscript Hannibal and his elephant?"

"No. But unless we intend to spend years in Italy, we have only two means of egress to the rest of the continent. One is by ship again, God forbid. The other is through the alpine passes, and those of Venezia are the easiest. I want us to get through those passes before they are closed or under fire. If we turn north again, immediately after we close here in Caserta, we should have time to pitch for some while outside Rome—and make visits into the city—before we have to move on to Venezia and through it, in advance of the outbreak of hostilities there."

Edge said, "Well, Governor, I reckon you know best."

"And you of all people, Colonel, know that a battleground is no place for noncombatants." He sighed. "A pity, though. I had hoped to show Naples to all our company. Even more, I wanted us all to taste the sybarite life of the Amalfi coast." He sighed again. "But the old saying is 'Vedi Napoli, e poi mori.' I had rather *not* see Naples and not die. So we must simply work things out as we go along. Now that spring is upon us, we can go north again by a different route—over the highlands instead of the low—so we will at least see different scenery along the way.''

When dinner was done, the artistes left the dining hall leisurely, again ambling through the splendid rooms and corridors. Gavrila Smodlaka, wandering by herself into a great, banner-hung hall, was surprised to see Clover Lee there, looking slightly disheveled and very despondent, sitting on a tread of the broad staircase. In her usual self-effacing way, Gavrila said good evening, and diffidently asked if anything was wrong.

Clover Lee looked at her, sniffled and said distantly, ''Is that all there is to it?''

''Excuse. My English is not well. Is what to what?''

''Making love. Watching Prince Umberto gobble down the food and wine in a hurry, so he could tumble me onto my back, and then do a lot of shoving and bouncing and poking and sweating and hurting me. Is that all there is to it? I thought it was supposed to be an enjoyment.''

''Um . . . well . . . the prince is young. Not experienced. Too eager, perhaps. Did *he* appear to enjoy?''

Clover Lee made a mouth. ''He said 'grazie mille' and lit a sigaretta. Then he gave me this.'' She held up a small satin evening purse embroidered with the royal arms; it jingled as she did so. ''There are twenty little gold coins in it.''

''Scudi, those are. Twenty scudi—one hundred lire—perhaps twenty dollars American. Some men would not even have given you the thousand thanks.''

''Twenty dollars. Twenty minutes. That's all it took.'' Clover Lee added pensively, ''I wonder what my mother ever saw in men.''

''But she had older men,'' said Gavrila. ''Gospodin Zachary. Gospodin Florian. Perhaps you should, too. It makes better if the man is old and you are new.''

''I think you mean young. But if a young man is too eager, an old man wouldn't be eager at all.''

"If you think such, gospodjica, you will never know anything about making love. The older man, less greedy for his own pleasure, give most pleasure to the woman. Believe me or do not, but a man too old even to use his húy—excuse the word—can delight a woman to onesvesti. How would you say? To swooning, to delirium."

"To hell with that," said Clover Lee. "Let the men do the swooning, and let them pay for it. From now on, my female parts will be just a commodity for sale or trade, and on my terms. This time, for just twenty minutes, I got to play Crown Princess Clover Lee . . ."

"Tikh, little one. Someday you will meet someone to whom you will want to *give* yourself. Come now, walk with me, back to the tober."

Clover Lee got slowly to her feet. "It hurts some—to walk."

"Unfortunate it is," said Gavrila, as if she knew whereof she spoke, "a large part of love is the hurting of it."

"Then you can bet that I'll peddle my love for a higher price than twenty scudi a hurt." Clover Lee laughed a mirthless laugh. "And when I *give* myself, it'll be for a title that lasts longer than twenty minutes."

Meanwhile the dining hall's maggiordomo had hurried to catch up with the main group of sightseeing troupers. Looking as astonished as his professional dignity would permit, he came to Autumn and announced:

"The signorina has an exceptional sense of hearing. One of the footmen I sent searching has just returned and informed me that a timepeace *had* stopped, sì, just about the time the signorina mentioned that occurrence. A girandole clock in the western Tapestry Room. No mystery about it; evidently the palace orologiaio simply neglected to wind that one." He paused. "What *is* remarkable—the clock is two floors above and a hundred paces west of the dining hall where the signorina was seated."

Autumn laughed, a trifle unsteadily, and said, "Oh, well. I hope I haven't cost the clock man a reprimand."

"We'd all best be careful," Yount said jovially, "how we whisper secrets anywhere around this little lady." And the matter was dismissed, but Magpie Maggie Hag continued to look sidelong at Autumn from time to time.

8

THE FLORILEGIUM proceeded east from Caserta, a two-day run to Benevento. As they came into the town's outskirts, Edge and Autumn, in the lead, were keeping a lookout for Florian, when they found themselves catching up to another, even slower-moving procession.

"It's a funeral cortège," said Autumn. "Don't try to go around it. Decency requires that we trudge along with it. And from the number of carriages and black plumes, I'd say the deceased must have been somebody important. Benevento might look more kindly on us if we pay our respects, as well."

So the circus train, however bizarre an addition it made to the cortège, went along behind it and even turned when it did, into a cemetery. Edge pulled up some distance from where the black hearse and flower carts and mourners' carriages did, outside an impressive mausoleum bedizened with stone angels. Edge and Autumn and all the rest of the company got down from their wagons and vans, and stood with bowed heads while several priests and acolytes went through the lengthy ritual. Then the pallbearers removed a bronze coffin from the hearse and bore it into the mausoleum. After a while, they came out, but the chief pallbearer among them turned and shouted a question in through the open door: "Vostra Altezza non commanda niente?" Not surprisingly, he got no reply from the crypt, so he turned to the clerics and mourners and called, "Tornate a casa. Sua Altezza non commanda niente."

"He says everybody can depart," Autumn translated. "His Highness, whoever he was, has nothing further to command."

So the company hastily climbed back into and onto the circus train, and Edge hurried to lead it out of the cemetery ahead of the cortège, and resumed the road at a brisk trot. They found Florian waiting as usual, but this time with his big tin watch in his hand. "You had me worried," he said. "I'm no Maggie Hag—and *she* hasn't lately dukkered anything bad that I know of—but one could say that this town is replete with omens."

"With a name like Benevento?" said Edge. "I'm lame in Italian, but I'd read that as meaning 'fair wind.' "

"However, that was not always its name. It was first founded, away back in B.C., by a tribe that took refuge here after being trounced by the Romans—so they called it aptly Maleventum, for the ill wind that blew them here. It wasn't until some centuries later that the Romans took over the town and superstitiously changed the name to the exact contrary."

But nothing at all bad happened to the Florilegium in Benevento. And nothing worse than an occasional wheel slipping its rim or a bit of harness breaking happened to the circus train during its subsequent climb up into the Monti del Matese ranges of the Apennines, where it stopped to perform for a day or two in any town along the way that promised a profitable attendance. No real trouble occurred until they were high on a twisty, rutted, rocky road between two mountain towns: Castel di Sangro behind them, Roccaraso somewhere ahead.

"Those names sound ominous to me, Mr. Florian," said Sunday Simms, who was today riding beside him on the rockaway. "Castle of Blood. Razor Rock."

"You are getting your Italian slightly corrupted by your French, my dear," he said. "Sangro is merely the name of that river down in the ravine beside us. Castel di Sangro is just Castle on the Sangro. And Roccaraso means only Cut Rock. Probably a cliff or a mountain cleft—oh, *damn!*"

He reined Snowball to a sudden stop, and the rest of the train behind him had to stop so abruptly that some of the horses reared in protest. Just ahead of the train, the road swerved sharply around a shoulder of the mountain. Out from the shrubbery there, three men had stepped into the road, holding firearms at the ready, and the biggest of the men was holding up a hand, palm outward.

"Alto là!" he shouted. "Siamo briganti!"

They were beefy men, swarthy, bearded, dirty, ill-dressed and generally evil of aspect. Their extremely old flintlock shotguns, however, looked better çared for than the men, and just as wicked.

"Sit still and quiet," Florian told Sunday. "They are bandits."

"Niente affatto," said another of the men; looking insulted. "Siamo briganti!"

"All right, they prefer to be called brigands," Florian told Sunday. "Just don't do anything sudden or foolish."

"State e recate!" demanded the biggest man.

"Stand and deliver," Autumn translated for Edge, on the vehicle next in line. "They don't look scholarly, but they must have read a Walter Scott novel at some time."

"This isn't funny, damn it," said Edge. "All my weapons are inside the van."

The three were now shouting: "Abbassate!" "Tutti!" "Mani in alto!"

Florian spoke to Sunday, and they climbed down from the rockaway seat, holding their hands high, as ordered. By ones and twos, all the others of the circus company got down to stand in the road, hands up and empty. The brigands waved their shotguns and barked more orders.

"They want us all to stand where they can see our hands," said Florian. "Banat, please pass that instruction to the other Slovaks." But no one could translate to the three Chinese. Though they imitated the general hands-up pose, they jabbered among themselves, as if discussing what may have looked to them like a new California peculiarity of behavior.

"Che portate?" snarled one brigand. "Togliamo lo tutto— denaro, beni, cavalli, vagoni . . ."

"They want everything we've got," Autumn translated. "Money, goods, the horses and wagons . . ."

"Goddamn it," Edge growled again in frustration.

Then everybody heard a sort of mingled whiz and flutter in the ambient air, and all three bandits suddenly fell over backward, rigidly and simultaneously, as if they were some kind of circus act themselves. As their shotguns clattered to the road, so did the fistsize rocks that had hit each of them in the head. The bandits lay still and, for a moment, every-body else stood immobilized by surprise, hands still high. Then they looked about, and there was a chorus of glad exclamations, as they saw the three Chinese each gripping with a prehensile bare foot another rock, in case a second barrage was necessary.

"Well, I *will* be goddamned!" said Edge. He hastily kicked the fallen shotguns away from the fallen bandits, then he and Yount knelt to examine the men.

"One of 'em's turned black in the face," Yount reported to Florian. "I'd reckon his skull is cracked. The other two might recover. Do you want 'em to?"

"Not until we are well along the road," said Florian. "Pitch them all into the river ravine. If any of them survives and can climb out again, maybe he'll repent and reform."

The females all shuddered and turned their backs while the bandits were disposed of. Meanwhile, Florian went and grate-fully shook each Chinese by the hand, though Sunday mur-mured to him, "Properly, sir, you ought to shake them by the foot."

"I just wish I could speak to them. But one thing I prom-ise. From now on, these resourceful lads will no longer be treated as Chinks. They'll have a room in a hotel whenever we do, and dine with us like white men."

Fitzfarris said, "They may have to put on shoes, to be allowed in."

"Damned if they will," Florian said staunchly. "Any hotel that refuses them entry will lose *all* our trade. And, while I'm at it, I will also demand a room and a place at table for Abdullah and Ali Baba from now on."

L'Aquila was the next city interesting enough and popu-lous enough to keep the Florilegium for more than a couple of days. When the troupers first saw, at the city portal, the huge pink and white stone fountain with its ninety-nine faces spouting water into its immense basin and heard Florian tell the story—"It is said that this city came miraculously into being, with ninety-nine piazze, ninety-nine castles, ninety-nine churches and ninety-nine fountains. And at every sundown you will hear a bell in the Law Court tower toll ninety-nine times''—they all clamored to spend time enough in L'Aquila so that they could see all those marvels.

As soon as the circus was set up on its assigned tober there, Beck and Goesle came to Florian with the latest innovation they had produced between them.

"Regard, Herr Gouverneur," said Beck, holding out to him a handful of crumbly, pebbly, gray-white substance. "What would you call that?"

"Plain old lime, isn't it? The same stuff you use in your generator's cooling machine, Carl? What you pour in the donnikers, Dai?"

"Kalk it is, ja," said Beck. "Calcium. But a kind new to me. At a Fabrik in the last town, it was given to me. Carburetted calcium, it is called."

"And why are you showing it to me, gentlemen?"

"Because if water on this karburiert Kalk is poured, a gas it makes. Ethine gas, it is called."

"Boom-Boom has built this tank apparatus," said Goesle, indicating a thing that looked vaguely like a patent washing machine. "Put in that calcium stuff and some water, turn a valve and it feeds the ethine through a hose to a burner. Just by itself, the gas gives as good a light as any coal-oil lamp."

"However, Stitches on that has improved," said Beck. "A lamp he has built in which the gas flame makes incandescent a stick of *ordinary* lime and—"

"Limelight!" exclaimed Florian. "By damn, you fellows have been wanting it long enough, and so have I! But I thought it required all kinds of complicated equipment."

"So it does, if you are wanting an oxyhydrogen flame," said Goesle. "Which means a retort contraption that is complex and always eager to explode, besides. This ethine flame does not give quite so brilliant a limelight. But it has the advantage of being easy to produce—and safely—from the carburetted calcium that is cheap and can be procured in any fair-sized city."

"But this is magnificent!" crowed Florian. "Gentlemen, I can't thank you enough for your enterprise and ingenuity."

"We thought first to surprise you," Beck said proudly.

"Not to tell you, but tonight to *show* you. However, then we thought, ach, so bright it is, it might frighten the animals or even the artistes."

"Yes," said Florian. "I will inform everyone beforehand."

"And only dim I will start the light," said Beck. "From the bandstand I will the tank and valve operate. Up gradually I will make bright the light during the come-in."

"Splendid. And you, Dai, by all means, get on with making as many more lamps as you think we should have. Including at least one for Sir John's annex."

Goesle did. Before the circus departed from L'Aquila, it was peforming its nighttime shows in a blaze of pole lamps and footlights. Shining through the green and white painted canvas, the limelight added a pale-green luminosity to the orange light cast by the outside torches, so the whole tober became a beacon that drew the Aquilani like moths. Meanwhile, in one of the town's reputed ninety-nine squares, Goesle found a maker of eyeglasses, and Autumn went there with him to translate to the ottico his request for a lens much bigger than was ever used in any spectacles. The lensmaker was not taken aback; he only said, "Ah, per una lanterna magica?" and produced the item from his stock.

Goesle worked on his next lighting innovation, by trial and error, whenever he had time, while the Florilegium now moved westward, and he had his new limelight contrivance perfected in time to bedazzle the citizens of Cantalupo. It was a movable spotlight that cast a beam instead of a flood of light, and cast it as far as the very top of the chapiteau. During the performance, Goesle—wearing heavy gloves against the heat of it—could fix that specially brilliant glow on whatever artiste was performing, and thereby make less noticeable any roustabouts or other extraneous persons who had to be in the pista at the same time. He could also make the light follow every move of the galloping horses and riders, and even the hurtling trapeze artistes.

Rome was the circus's next destination. But, when the circus arrived at the nearest practical place outside the Papal

State, which was Forano, that proved to be not much of a town. There was a railroad depot alongside two sets of tracks, some tools and equipment sheds, some shacks occupied by the railroad workers, and a bettola in which they drank away their spare time and lire. The stationmaster said the Florilegium could set up wherever it pleased—there were empty fields all around—so Florian instructed that it be pitched a good distance from the noise, smoke and sparks of passing trains. "However, there is no need to make haste in the setting up," he said. "We have all earned a breathing spell."

He called the whole company together and told them, "The stationmaster says there will be a train to Rome in half an hour, at six o'clock. All who wish—including you, Abdullah, and little Ali Baba—may get your hand luggage and accompany me there. We will take a hotel and spend the next week merely luxuriating and sightseeing about the city. Canvasmaster Goesle, Chief Engineer Beck, Crew Chief Banat, you may also come to Rome whenever you are ready. Let the roustabouts come, too—in shifts, so there will always be some on watch here. Have every man bring paper to post, plenty of it. I want to see it on every one of the seven hills of Rome. Mark on those posters that our first performance will be a week from tomorrow."

So the artistes were all in street dress and waiting on the platform when the train arrived from the north, chugging, chuffing, rattling, spewing smoke, soot and steam. Some of those waiting—the Simms children and the Chinese, who had never before been so close to such a monster—cringed away from it, flattening themselves against the depot wall. But the pale little Sava and Velja Smodlaka cooly stayed at the edge of the platform, as did all the others to whom railway trains were no novelty. When the doors swung open, the troupers climbed into the compartments and, when the train clattered into motion again, even the first-time riders soon got over their nervousness. Indeed, they took delight in being whisked across the landscape at such a dizzy speed. The train was making nearly thirty miles an hour—half again more distance in a single hour than the circus train ordinarily accomplished in a whole day.

Jules Rouleau had appointed himself guardian of the children, and had shepherded them all into one compartment. He took note, with rueful amusement, that Monday Simms enjoyed the trip even more than the others, though she never looked out of the window at the countryside blurring past— farmhouses, barns, haycocks, ox-drawn plows, even the occasional glimpse of the brown river Tiber. Monday simply sat with her eyes unfocused and a trembly smile on her lips, clearly because the plush-upholstered seat vibrated more pleasurably than anything she had ever before felt in contact with her phenomenally excitable under parts.

There were no more stations after Forano, and the train did not slacken its breathtaking pace the whole way to its destination. But the houses visible outside became more numerous, with only yards or garden plots between them. Then they became clusters of houses separated only by streets and alleys. Then they became solid city blocks of soot-blackened stone and brick buildings, and crowded closer to the railway line. Less than an hour and a quarter after the troupe had boarded it, the train slowed but its noise increased, as it rumbled under an echoing, girdered glass roof, then racketed along beside a platform crowded with people dressed for travel, with railway men, porters, baggage carts, vendors hawking every imaginable sort of food, drink and curio. When the train at last juddered and jolted to a halt, Florian went along the passage from compartment to compartment, announcing, "We are here! Roma, La Città Eterna! Everybody out!"

They made their way through the crowded and noisy terminal, and came out at the edge of a piazza that was, by contrast, silent except for the sigh of a sundown breeze, and almost empty except for a waiting line of vetture for hire. Florian commandeered a sufficient number of those to carry all the troupers and their luggage, climbed into the front one and led the way to a hotel called the Eden, near the Borghese Gardens. Rome had about the same number of inhabitants as Florence, but the city was so much more open and sprawling that, to those visiting for the first time, it seemed extremely scant of both people and vehicular traffic on the streets. While the Hotel Eden's porters were carrying in the bags and the desk clerk was leafing through the conduct books, Florian bought a newspaper from the stand in the lobby, took a look at it and said, ''Oh, hell.''

''Something wrong, Governor?'' Edge asked.

''Well, no more than I expected. King Victor Emmanuel did sign that alliance with Prussia. Just a week after Easter.''

''Does that mean we cut and run? I'll round up the others before they get settled in.''

''No, no. There'll be war, that is certain, but I doubt that it can start instantly. I will not deprive us all of this chance to enjoy Rome. Instead, we will cut short our stand in Forano. Rome would no doubt have given us something like three weeks of sfondone houses. But after our week of holiday, we'll give only a week of circus shows, and then move on toward the frontier. Now, let us get out of these sooty traveling clothes and dress for dinner. The Eden sets a good board.''

As the company ate and drank voraciously and happily, there was sitting at another table a slender middle-aged gentleman with a very pretty girl who might have been his daughter. He waited politely until the artistes were on their coffees and liqueurs, then stood up, approached Florian and said in English:

''Forgive the intrusion, sir. But I heard you earlier, in the lobby, mention a circus. And just before dinner I saw a paper on a lamppost in the street.''

''Ah, then some of my crewmen have already come to town. Good.''

''So I assume, sir, that you are the Florian of that Florilegium. Perhaps I might introduce myself—a fellow showman. I am Gaetano Ricci, balletmaster, choreograph and teacher of the art.''

''A pleasure, Signor Ricci. Allow me to introduce the artistes of my troupe.'' He took Ricci from one table to another, and the balletmaster cordially shook the hands of the men and boys—even those of the Chinese and blacks—and kissed the hands of the women and girls. When Florian presented "the Signorina Autunno Auburn, funambola staordinaria," Ricci was moved to sigh and say:

"Signorina, I only wish my stage were as narrow as your rope."

"Good heavens. Why would you wish that, signore?"

"Because then not so many people would think that dancing and acting are so easy. I should have to endure fewer damned interviews with abysmally untalented hopefuls. But here ... allow me to present one who *is* talented." He led forward the young girl. "The Signorina Giuseppina Bozzacchi. Only twelve years old, but she has been training since she was five, and is now in my corps de ballet, and very soon will be una prima di tutto." The girl smiled and curtsied shyly, and a few of the male troupers dared to kiss her hand. Signor Ricci continued, "I invite you all to a rehearsal at any time, and you can see Giuseppina dance. My school is on the Via Palermo, behind the Teatro Eliseo."

"That is kind of you, signore," said Florian. "Our young ladies might well learn something to their advantage by seeing real ballet performed. In return, let me invite you and the signorina, any others of your pupils, to visit our circus next week as our guests."

After breakfast next day, Florian told the troupe, "There is one sight I wish to show you all. Some of you will have seen it before. But humor me. Then you can wander the city at will."

And he called for another train of vetture, and drove everybody to the Colosseum.

"I wanted all of you to see the birthplace of the circus," he said as they leaned backward and stared up in awe at the three-tiered façade of stone arches. Its dignity was just slightly diminished by the many lines of laundry strung between its columns by housewives of the immediate neighborhood. "Actually, the earliest such shows took place in the Circus Maximus, down there in the valley"—he waved toward the southwest—"but nothing of that remains to be seen. The Circo Massimo had fallen into disuse by the time this Colosseum was built. The Anfiteatro Flaviano, to give it its proper name."

As he led them inside the massive structure, he went on, "Sadly, it has decayed over the past eighteen centuries. There once were slopes of boxes and seats all around this vast ellipse, for perhaps forty or fifty thousand spectators. Away up there, on what is left of the upper cornice, you can see the holes for long poles that supported an awning of cloth—more cloth than would make a hundred *Saratoga* balloons—that protected all the seats from sun or rain."

"Incidentally," added Autumn, "it was only during *circus* performances that the Roman men and women did not have to sit apart in separate sections."

"Try to envision," Florian continued, "the chariot races, the battles between wild beasts, the duels between gladiators, the contests between Christians and lions, the acrobats and jugglers peforming by *hundreds*. In those times, this immense arena floor was not just packed earth, as you see it now, but polished marble—sometimes sanded to absorb the blood shed. Underneath the floor, invisible now, were the dressing rooms for the performers, the dens and ramps for the animals, the armories of the gladiators. Perhaps sometime they will be excavated and brought to view."

He gazed around as if he could see all those old-time events occurring again, and the Colosseum thronged with cheering crowds. "Ah, those were the days!" he said, and sighed. "Now that you have indulged me and my nostalgia, friends, go your separate ways. I recommend that you first stroll yonder, westward, and see the remains of the Forum, the center of the Empire, the heart of Rome to which all roads once led."

So that day they roamed about the weedy ruins of the Forum and the Palatine Hill. Over the following days, some or all of them visited most of the famous landmarks of the city. They each threw the traditional two coppers into the Trevi fountain, and squandered a great deal more money in the fashionable shops of the Via Condotti, and some of them rode to see the view of all of Rome from the Gianicolo.

"But this one is my favorite building in the whole city," said Autumn, leading Edge into the Pantheon as proudly as if she had just bought it. They stood in the middle of its

rotunda of majestic emptiness, directly under the round opening at the tip of the coffered dome, nearly two hundred feet
above their heads, from which a sunbeam slanted dustily
down to lay a tremendous golden oval on the curve of side
chapels at floor level. "That dome up there," said Autumn,
"is exactly as high as its diameter—a hundred and forty-four
feet. It was built more than seventeeeen hundred years ago,
but *still* it is the biggest dome in all the world unsupported
by ribs or braces or chains."

Edge asked fondly, "Is that why this is your favorite building?"

"I like things that last," she said simply.

Since the Hotel Eden was situated very near the top of the
Spanish Steps, the troupers generally took that route down to
the Piazza di Spagna and ambled from there to other quarters
of the city. But often they would stop at one of the popular
trattorie on or near that piazza, for a bite to eat, or to sip a
cappuccino, grappa, wine or the incomparable Tuscan mineral
water while they watched the other foreign tourists come and
go.

"The staircase is rightly named la Scala della Trinità,"
said Florian. "There are three landings, you see, and at the
top is the Church of the Trinity. But this piazza got *its* name
because long ago the Spanish Embassy was here; hence the
popular name for the stairs. And this piazza also has another
name. It is derisively called by the Romans 'il ghetto degli
Inglesi' because it is so constantly full of foreigners."

He and Edge were at that moment having a drink in the
Caffè Greco, just off the piazza. But Edge felt out of place
there, under the portraits of the great men who had been
patrons there before him—Goethe, Leopardi, Stendhal—and
he was vaguely uneasy at not having any idea as to which of
the many men drinking in his presence might sometime or
already be equally famous. Anyway, he found more interesting an old cart horse at the curb just outside the Greco's
window. It was having a feed of grain, and it was apparently
the Roman custom to provide a horse with an extraordinarily
long nose bag with only a little grain in it. This bag, at least,
hung almost to the pavement, so, after the horse had munched

one mouthful of oats, it had to toss its head and fling the long sack high in the air, to snatch another mouthful as it flopped down again.

Edge and Yount and Fitzfarris more often patronized Lepre's, where they could usually find visiting Americans with whom to discuss the latest news from the States. Similarly Dai Goesle several times squired Autumn Auburn to the Caffè Dalbano, frequented by visiting Britons, to get the news from home.

One afternoon Florian gathered all the females except Magpie Maggie Hag, and as many of the males as showed any interest, and herded them to Signor Ricci's rehearsal studio. The balletmaster seemed genuinely pleased to have them visit, and introduced them to the dancers in the hall—young men and women, younger boys and girls—all handsome, svelte and lithe, all wearing practice costumes.

"We are just now trying a new little story, 'Il Stregone,' " said Ricci. "I have set it to old music by Monteverdi, and it employs every dancer in my company. The principals are the Enchanter, the victim Princess, the wicked Stepmother Queen, and the gallant Prince who comes to the rescue. The girl whom you met the other evening, Signorina Giuseppina, you will see among the corps of Summer Blossoms in the palace garden. You must, of course, imagine the garden and all the costumes. But I believe the music and dance will set the scene for you."

He placed chairs for his visitors around the big bare room, sat down to a pianoforte and began to play, and the numerous ballerini and ballerine began dancing on the polished expanse of floor—pas seul, pas de deux, de trois, and so on. Whenever the principals tired or retired, the bevy of Summer Blossoms came on—variously de suite or tout ensemble.

Obie Yount leaned and muttered to Florian, "Damned if I can make any sense of all this prancing. Does it say anything to you?"

"Well, yes. That chap doing all those flutters with his arms, he is the evil enchanter, putting the princess under a spell, so that—"

"Why?"

"Why? Why what?"

"Why should he? Put her under a spell?"

"Well . . . er . . . well, it's what evil enchanters *do*."

"Oh."

"He puts her in this spell, you see, and— "

"Knew a fella back in Chattanooga, used to have spells."

"Confound it, Obie! Not *that kind* of spell."

When the performance was concluded, and the visitors had applauded, and the dancers were toweling the sweat off themselves, Florian said to Signor Ricci, "I am sure that all our ladies envy yours their grace and gossamer lightness. Of course, ours—performing on horseback or sawdust or a mechanical rig—do not have so many opportunities to show such qualities."

"A woman should *always* be graceful. Let us see. You circus ladies, stand up!" A little startled at his vehemence, they all complied. "Stand here before me and look feminine." Ricci nodded approvingly at Autumn and Paprika, but barked at the others:

"Regard! The Signorine Auburn and Makkai—how those two girls stand. Have the rest of you never troubled to take notice? Never tried to emulate their stance?" Clover Lee, Gavrila, Sava, Sunday and Monday looked guilty. "Do it now!" he commanded. "Stand with one foot just behind the other, the two pointed away from each other. That gives the best line to your legs. Now put your shoulders back, thrust your titties out. Do as I tell you!"

"Please, sir," whimpered little Sava. "I no have any titties."

"Until you have got them, pretend you do! That is better. All of you remember that posture, practice it, stand so every time you stand anywhere." To Florian he snapped, "For those who work on the ground only, put on them very short skirts and calf-high boots. That will make any girl look taller and willowy, make her legs look longer and slimmer and more shapely."

"Er . . . si, signore."

"Now, all of you, walk!" Ricci commanded the females. "Walk around me in a circle." They did so, trying still to keep their shoulders back and their titties outthrust. "Terrible!" he snarled. "Except for the rope artistes, all of you walk like ordinary women—stamping on the heel bones. Ghastly! Signorina Auburn, why have you never shown these slovens how to walk?" Autumn tried to make some reply, but he overrode her. "Take them away and teach them to walk, before they taint my own girls."

"Please, sir," Sunday said meekly. "When we've learned that, can we come back for other lessons?"

"Aha! One of you at least has the ambition to improve her grace and appearance. Anyone else?" All of them except Monday raised a hand. "Signorina Auburn, you need no improvement. The rest of you, if you are sincere, be here at ten tomorrow morning. Dismissed!"

And the entire circus company found themselves again outdoors, on the via Palermo, feeling rather as if they had just come through a whirlwind. During the few days that remained to them in Rome, those females who had been invited to attend Signor Ricci's classes conscientiously did so.

When the holiday was over, and the company returned by the railway to Forano, and the circus began giving its performances, Signor Ricci came to every nighttime show. The first time, he brought all his dancers—and Florian gladly, as he had promised, let them attend free of charge. Thereafter, Ricci came accompanied only by little Giuseppina, and he could be seen pointing out to her various aspects of the artistes' performances—because, he explained to Florian, a ballerina could learn something even from Clover Lee's rosinback routine and Zanni's extravagant fall-downs. And, after each nighttime show, Ricci stayed on the tober for an hour or more to continue his how-to-be-graceful instruction of the several circus females. Sunday Simms was the most attentive of those, and the most persevering at practice after he had departed.

Meanwhile, Rome provided every one of that week's shows with a straw house. There was daily a noontime train outbound from the city, and another at five in the afternoon, and each came to Forano with its coaches packed full of Romans. The people willingly whiled away the time before the performances—eyeing the museum and the lion and the mummy or gambling at Fitzfarris's mouse game or having their futures foretold by Magpie Maggie Hag. And, after the shows, they just as willingly waited—or the women did; the men spent more of that time attending Fitz's Bible-study sessions—until they could catch the six o'clock and eleven o'clock trains inbound to Rome.

Finally, one noontime, Florian sent a bunch of Slovaks to plaster the city with posters announcing a balloon ascension at sunset the next day. He also showed one of the posters to the Forano stationmaster and spoke persuasively enough that the man immediately sat down to his telegraph key. The next day's two trains from Rome each had two locomotives in tandem, pulling a double length of passenger coaches, and all of those were crammed with circusgoers. The two shows that day were more than sfondone, and Florian could hardly declare a turnaway of people who had come so far. So he had the roustabouts take down the chapiteau's sidewalls, and the overflow crowd could at least peer in under the seat stands. They did not seem to mind paying full-ticket prices for seeing the performance only distantly and narrowly. At any rate, everybody had a good view of the *Saratoga* going up, floating back and forth above the Tiber, and finally coming down, and their approving roar at that would have done credit to the Colosseum.

It appeared that the Florilegium could go on enjoying full houses indefinitely, but it was now the first week of May, and Florian was anxious to be starting out of the country. So the teardown was done, the wagons were packed and the train went northward. From now on, Florian announced, the circus would show only in major and populous towns, and for no more than three days in any of them. Viterbo was the next nearest and sizable city, but it was, like Rome, inside the censor-ridden Papal State, hence had to be slighted. So the first run was a long one, three days and two nights on the road, before the circus reached the town of Orvieto.

The troupers could see that place for half a day before they got to it, for Orvieto sat like a town on a table above the

floor of the plain they were traversing—the whole of it clustered atop a rock pedestal nearly an eighth of a mile high.
When they arrived at the base of that cliff, they saw that there
was a brand-new, steam-driven funicular tram to keep the
town above supplied with the produce of lowland farmers,
vintners and such. But the circus train had to toil its way up
a long incline of road that angled back and forth up the cliff
face to the city's Porta Romana, where Florian was waiting.

While the roustabouts did the setup on the assigned tober,
Florian invited everybody not working to come for a stroll
with him and see the truly unique feature of Orvieto. He led
them nearly to the drop-off of the rock pedestal on which the
town sat, gestured and said, "Il Posso di San Patrizio." The
Well of Saint Patrick was unique, indeed: a circular pit dug
down through the rock as big across as a circus pista. Its rim
was surrounded by men and women leading asses that carried
casks, barrels and enormous jars. When the troupers made
their way through that waiting crowd and peered over the
edge of the well, they nearly reeled with vertigo. The water
level was a dizzying two hundred feet below them, and the
men and women ascended and descended that chimney along
a spiral staircase hewn from the rock walls—or rather, two
concentric spiraling staircases arranged in a double helix, so
that the trains going down and coming up could do so simultaneously, never having to meet and pass each other. Not
only was the well pit a work of staggering dimensions; the
men who had dug it had done the extra incredible job of
hacking seventy-two "windows" from the pit wall through
the rock to the outer cliff face, to provide daylight for those
going up and down inside.

"It was dug more than three hundred years ago," said
Florian, "to ensure that the city had fresh water whenever it
was under siege. Ever since, the Italians have said of any
spendthrift that 'he has pockets as deep as the Well of Saint
Patrick.' "

As they all turned back toward the tober, Florian added,
"Speaking of spending, I have a suggestion to make. I, for
one, am getting too old and feeling too prosperous to continue
living the vagrant gypsy life when we are between stands. I

mean having to put up in seedy roadside inns or to sleep in an even less comfortable circus wagon. All of us now have some money put by. I suggest that we spend some of it to purchase traveling vans like those owned by Miss Auburn and Monsieur LeVie. We need not get one apiece—that would be costly, and make our train inordinately long—but a caravan house-on-wheels can be bought and shared by several people. I personally will be purchasing a van in consortium with Mr. Goesle and Herr Beck and Signor Bonvecino. I submit the idea for the rest of you to think about. And I will say one other thing. Either spend all your lire before we get to the frontier, or exchange them for good gold or gems. The Italian paper and coins will be worthless in Austria.''

Among the several discussions of the caravan idea, one took place between Maurice and Paprika. He said to her, ''My van is not large, but it could easily accommodate one other. And gladly.''

''Merci, mais non,'' she said.

''Pourquoi non? We are partners in the air. Why not on the ground? I have long wondered why you keep me at a distance. I know you have no other man.''

''And I will not have any. You are a worldly person, Maurice, and an understanding one, so I shall tell you. The fact is that I can get—satisfaction—only from a female. I have been that way ever since . . . well, there was something that happened in my childhood.''

''Ah, pauvre petite. Some kindly old uncle, no doubt.'' Paprika shook her head. ''An older brother, peut-être. It happens.'' She said nothing. ''Your father, then? Mon dieu! Que de merdeux—!''

''No, no! My father was a decent man. All he did was die.'' She looked away. ''It was my mother! My istenverte mother!''

''Qu'est-ce qui?'' Maurice gasped. ''C'est impossible!''

''No, it is not impossible,'' she said sulkily. ''And maybe it was partly my own fault. I was an only child, and willful. When my dear father died, I was just eleven years old, but I was determined to preserve his memory. I insisted that my mother not seek a new husband. So she said, 'Then you must take your father's place.''

"Surely she meant—''

"She meant *in* bed. And she made me do exactly that. Of course I could not do *everything*, but we . . . devised substitutes. And in some respects, she said, I was better than my father had been. Better than any man could be. She never did marry again. I was her lover—no, her *tool*—until I was old enough to leave home and make a life for myself.''

"And that . . .'' Maurice had to clear his throat. "And that has influenced you to love only women?''

"*Love them?*'' Paprika laughed like a vixen barking. "I hate them! I loathe and despise women, exactly as I loathed and despised that one. Unfortunately, I remain as warped as she made me. To this day, I can get sexual pleasure no other way. I know. I tried once with a man. And that was such a pathetic farce that I shall never try again.''

"But, chérie, consider. Une hirondelle ne fait pas le printemps. There are men and there are men.''

"No, Maurice. I will not demean and disgust us both. I know myself too well. I can only couple with another female, even though I feel no affection, nothing but contempt for her. And if, to indulge myself in that way, it requires that I corrupt some innocent girl or woman—why, then, I get even more pleasure from it. You asked. Now I have told you. Think what you will of me, but . . . can we go on being partners? In the air?''

"In the air,'' he said sadly. "Ainsi que les hirondelles.''

Before the circus left Orvieto, Florian, Goesle, Beck and Zanni had found and bought a very nice caravan for themselves, and a horse to draw it. The journey to the circus's next stand, Siena, took four days and three nights, and after those nights on the road—two spent sleeping in the wagons, one in an extremely dismal locanda—the other circus folk were ready and eager to procure vans of their own.

In Siena they found two more for sale. Pavlo Smodlaka, though he grumbled bitterly about having nobody to share his outlay, bought the better van to carry and house his family. The other vehicle was rather shoddy and smelly—it being the property of a squalid gypsy clan—but it was at least commodious. Hannibal Tyree and Quincy Simms consulted together—"We's got pockets like dat Saint Patrick's well"—then somehow managed to convey a proposal to the antipodists. The Chinese not only cheerfully proffered all their accumulated wages—but they then cheerfully and immediately started sweeping and swabbing the van's interior to make it habitable for its five new owners.

The remaining unhoused troupers had to live and sleep in whatever accommodations offered during the next four-day run, to Pistoia, and in that town they found no such vehicles for sale. When Yount and Mullenax loudly complained about their being "orphans" among the others' opulence, Zanni remarked humorously, "Well, you have arrived in a good place to put yourselves out of your misery. This town of Pistoia is where pistols were first made, and got their name."

However, after the stand there, another four-day run brought the circus to Bologna, and that was a big city where almost anything could be purchased. "A most beautiful and hospitable city," said Florian. "Why, the Palazzo Comunale, where I applied for permission to pitch, has a staircase specially built so horses could climb up to the council chamber in the olden days, when the council members were too haughty to walk up on their own feet."

"And Bologna's university," said Autumn, "has been hospitable enough to engage even *female* professors from time to time. One of them was so beautiful, they say, that she had to stand behind a curtain when she lectured, so the students wouldn't be too distracted to take notes."

"That reminds me," said Maurice. "A student of your own, lovely lady, has asked to study also with me. Your apprentice ropewalker, Sunday Simms. She probably does not realize it, but she is following the classic progression—from parterre acrobat to the rope to the trapeze. I told her I would require your permission."

"You have it, of course. Sunday is eager to learn all she can. Just in those few lessons from Maestro Ricci, she acquired a good deal of new poise and assurance. And she is indefatigable. When she is not practicing in the pista, she is at her books. Let us, by all means, encourage her every ambition.''

During the three days the circus showed in Bologna, it found the necessary two more houses-on-wheels. One was bought by the quartet of Yount, Mullenax, Fitzfarris and Rouleau. The other was bought jointly by Paprika, Clover Lee, Sunday and Monday Simms. Florian looked dubious when he heard of that arrangement, but Clover Lee privately assured him, ''I agreed to share the cost and the quarters only after I took Paprika aside for a *very* frank conversation, and I laid down some strict rules. Whatever mischief she tries to do outside the caravan, I can't control. But inside those walls, she is not even to *leer*.''

Of the artistes and managers, that left only Magpie Maggie Hag without a traveling house, but she did not want one. ''I have whole dressing and kitchen wagon now all to myself, all I need. I am gypsy, anyhow. Too much easiness no good for gypsy.''

She and others of the company spent their free time in Bologna making other purchases, because Florian told them, ''Buy for the road ahead. When the war starts, *everything* is going to get scarce and expensive, in Austria as well as here.'' So the wagons in which people no longer had to ride or sleep were stocked full of hay and grain for the horses and elephant, smoked meats for the lion, staple groceries for the humans, canisters of calcium carbide for the limelights, coils of rope, cans of paint and tar and coal oil and axle grease, harness and horseshoes and miscellaneous hardware, fabrics and thread and sequins for the wardrobe.

Carl Beck found and bought acid, iron filings and lime to stoke his Gasentwickler machines this one more time, because Bologna was the last big city the circus would visit in Italy, and he and Rouleau felt it merited a balloon ascension, which might well be the *Saratoga*'s last performance for some while to come.

None of the Bolognese seemed to share Florian's apprehension of impending war. Or, if they did, they did not let it inhibit their appetite for enjoyment. They packed the chapiteau at every show, and all but fought for the divinations of

Magpie Maggie Hag and the diversions of the mouse game at every intermission, and the menfolk crammed into the biblical-tableau top after every show, and a vast crowd came to attend the closing-day ascension of the *Saratoga*—and to exclaim both at that and at the accompanying magic of a pretty girl disappearing in a puff of smoke from before them, while the balloon was high aloft, yet reappearing in its gondola when it landed.

In fact, the Bolognese poured into the red wagon's coffers so much Italian coin and paper currency that the circus's departure, on the morning after tear-down, had to be delayed while Florian, Zanni and Maurice, each of them carrying in each hand a satchel full of lire and centisimi, scurried about to every money-changing establishment in the city. Unlike the happy-go-lucky circus patrons, the dour and sad-eyed old Jews who ran those establishments had either personal experience or a long racial memory of many a war, pogrom, revolution and financial crisis. Every man of them set a stiff (and identical) price for their alchemy of changing paper and copper to gold. Florian and his assistants accepted what they could get, and get in a hurry. Though they lost on the exchange, they returned to the wagons bearing an estimable cargo of specie that was legal tender anywhere in the world.

The circus train that finally departed from Bologna was now a train of which the tail end—that being literally the tail of the elephant—departed something like half an hour after Florian's rockaway pulled out of the tober. Besides the elephant and the rockaway and the tandem machines of the gas generator, the train comprised seven house-vans and six wagons drawn by one horse apiece, and four heavier wagons drawn by the double teams of polka-dot horses. The vehicles were so numerous that almost every man of the artistes and crew had to drive one. They all had to travel some distance apart, to stay out of each other's churned-up dust, so the train, from Snowball's white nose to Peggy's tufted tail, strung out for nearly a fifth of a mile.

*   *   *

At Modena, Florian said, "All right, everybody, I have already converted our main treasury into bullion. Now let us all get rid of every bit of pocket money we are still carrying." He and his three van mates spent theirs in stocking their caravan with wine, the good local Lambrusco. And most of the women spent their remaining lire to buy bottles of Modena's unique Nocino, a sticky-sweet liqueur made from walnuts.

Even though the troupers were hurrying to outrun the war, and putting on shows as they went, they did not neglect their free-time responsibilities. Goesle and Beck put their Slovaks to painting all the newly acquired caravans to match the rest of the train—blue bodies with white wheels, window shutters and trim. They left the Florilegium's name off those vehicles, however, in case any of their owners should have occasion to decamp to another show. Magpie Maggie Hag had tired of seeing Monday Simms do her stately haute école riding in a mere suit of fleshings, so now she rigged Monday out as a Cordobesa of her own native Spain: black velvet trousers with silvery conchas down the seams, soft boots, a white blouse with wide sleeves and a bright red bolero over that. On Monday's head, she set the low-crowned, flat-brimmed Cordobés hat that was intended for men but has always been one of the most flattering headpieces a woman could wear.

Maurice and Paprika began showing Sunday some of the rudiments of the trapeze art, making her wear at all times the safety lungia rope.

"No, no, no, kedvesem!" Paprika chided her. "Do not reach out with your legs when you prepare to alight on the platform. Always keep your hips forward—*hump it!*—so you alight gracefully."

"If you come feet first," Maurice told her, "you will find the bar dragging you backward off the platform. Clumsy, that, and dangerous. Only when you are swinging free and pumping—to swing faster and higher—only then, never otherwise, do you bend in the middle to bring your legs forward."

And little Quincy Simms was likewise trying to enlarge his

ring talents. He had begun following Zanni Bonvecino everywhere except to the donniker, and gamely trying to imitate his every comic turn except the aria singing. Zanni graciously favored the boy with some elementary advice, of which Quincy comprehended perhaps half.

"There are six basics in the clowning art: stupidity, trickery, mimicry, falls, blows and surprises. You should exclude the first from your repertoire, because you are a Negro. Stupidity would merely mark you as a lazy chuckleheaded Jim Crow; leave that to American circuses. Here in Europe—well, for example, in Paris there was a clown called Chocolat. Nobody watching him ever thought, 'There is a Negro clown.' Everybody thought, 'There is a great clown.' Now, if you wish to try the clowning art, you must become no longer *you*. A clown is not a person, not an object, he is what *happens*."

"Yassuh."

"And, damn it, don't open your mouth. For all I know, you are a genius, but you *talk* stupid. Bene, the first thing necessary is what we call avoir l'oeil—to have the eye. Try the basic clown tricks and watch. See which, in your case, best amuses the audience. Joey ribaldry or toby pathos, the horse laugh or the weary smile, joey cunning or toby helplessness, pure pantomime or a pista full of props, Joey knockabout or toby melancholy. Thus you find your particular bent, your métier, your magic. Then you *make fun of it*."

"Yassuh."

When the circus train left Modena, it had not gone far along the road to the north before it found itself again a conspicuous and incongruous part of another procession. It had got between two road-filling columns of the Italian Royal Army on the march—infantry soldiers under full field pack and shouldered arms, gaudier-uniformed cavalrymen on war horses slung with a superfluity of equipment, horsedrawn cannon carriages and caissons, supply wagons, ambulance wagons, all the necessaries for waging war. Florian passed the word back along the train for all the women to put on the crown-emblazoned shawls the king had given them, to proclaim the Florilegium's allegiance. Having no choice but

to travel along with the army, the circus people were somewhat uncomfortable and embarrassed, especially when various soldiers bawled comic comments at them, and others
bawled curses of complaint—because Peggy imperturbably
beshat the road, and the soldiers had to break step and break
ranks to avoid trudging through it.

But when twilight came, the circus train pulled off into a
meadow beside the road for the night. And when it resumed
its northward journey next morning, there was no more army
in sight. All that day, the train did not catch up to any, and
none overtook it. "The troops will all have moved off to east
and west from here," Florian guessed. "The river Po, about
twenty miles up ahead of us, is the Venezia border. Beyond
that will be the Austrian troops. We are right now in a po-
tential battle zone. So let us make haste—and ladies, don't
wear those shawls today."

Meeting no further impediment, the train reached the Po
at the next twilight, and found a bridge with a barrier and
a sentry post at either end of it. On the closer side, the station was candy-striped bright red, white and green, and
flew the Italian flag of those same colors, and was manned
by a squad of the Alpine Brigade—looking not exactly prepared for alpinism, since they wore high-fronted jackboots,
tall shakos and tunics encrusted with braid, frogs and ep-
aulettes. Florian leaned down and spoke to them in Italian,
and they raised the barrier without any fuss, except for
some you'll-be-sorry comments on the idiocy of leaving
sunny Italy for sullen Austria.

The flag and the sentry post on the other end of the bridge
were of Austria-Hungary's more somber black and yellow,
and the guards—of the Tirolean Rifles—were dressed in
trimmer, no-frills uniforms of silver-green. They likewise appeared indisposed to make any fuss about the Florilegium's
crossing their border. They did manifest Teutonic efficiency
to the extent of demanding the troupe's conduct books,
though they gave them only a desultory riffle-through when
Florian handed them over. Then they raised the barrier and
the circus train plodded past. The word went down the line—

"We are now in Venezia"—but nobody could see any immediate difference in the environment. The landscape here looked just as Italian; so did the people, the farmhouses, the vineyards and olive groves; when they bedded down by the roadside again that night, a farm woman who sold them a pail of milk spoke Italian while she did so.

Two days later, the circus pitched just outside the walls of Verona and, while the crew started the setup, Autumn led every female of the troupe into the Old Town—all of them twittering with excitement, even Magpie Maggie Hag—to show them the Capelletti house, from the balcony of which Giulietta had traded compliments and vows with Romeo Mantecchi. Florian chuckled as they trotted off and told the men of the company, "I fear they'll be a little disappointed with that landmark, but they should enjoy the rest of Verona. It is a beautiful city."

It was, the men agreed, as they strolled in through the Porta Nuova and along the broad, flower-bedded Corso. The city was red and gold and pink, except where the occasional house wall was entirely covered with a giant mural—David besting Goliath or St. George besting the Dragon or some such scene.

"I only regret that I cannot take us either east or west," said Florian. "Eastward, of course, there is Venice, and everybody should see Venice at least once in his life. Westward, though, on the other side of Lake Garda, there are two pretty towns that not even many Italians have ever heard of. They are side by side on a little hill, and they're both named Botticino. But one is Botticino Mattina and the other is Botticino Sera—the morning and the evening Botticino—according to when each of them gets the sun on its vineyards."

The circus women did return from their excursion looking a trifle disappointed. The Capelletti house had not just a balcony, but *two* balconies, and Autumn confessed that she had no idea which one the visitors should be adoring. Furthermore, when the women asked the whereabouts of Romeo's family mansion, Autumn confided that there were several houses in Verona that claimed that distinction—and anyway, according to Shakespeare's own countrymen, the whole Romeo and Juliet story was nothing but a bitter-sweet fable.

But no one had much time or leisure to pine over that disillusionment. Verona was having its annual Agricultural and Livestock Fair, so the town's population was swelled with visitors. The fact that many of the visitors were in Austrian uniforms did not dampen the other folks' festive mood. They spilled over from the fairgrounds to the circus grounds and packed the chapiteau at every performance during the three days it stayed.

"Why can't we stay longer?" Fitzfarris asked at the closing show. "We've been making money hand over fist. Good Austrian kronen. And hell, we're already in Austrian territory, aren't we?"

"The very territory that Italy is preparing to fight for—and to fight on," said Florian. "No, we keep moving."

That he was not being overcautious was demonstrated when, in the afternoon of the circus train's second day outbound from Verona, on a road that was gradually but steadily rising toward the distant highlands, the train found itself again in the midst of an army on the move. This time the Florilegium could not march with it, for the army was coming from the other direction, from the north, and was composed of Austrian infantry, cavalry and artillery. So the circus got entirely off the road to wait while it passed.

"Right around here," said Florian, "we are leaving Venezia and entering the Trentino area. Ninety-nine percent of the people here are Italian, but you'll see differences in the architecture. And every geographical feature has two names. That river alongside the road is the same Adige that it was in Verona, but up here it is also the Etsch. Our next stand will be in the town called Trento in Italian, Trient in German."

When the road was clear of soldiers again and the circus train resumed its journey, climbing all the time, the troupers did remark the change in the farmhouses along the way. They were still painted in passionate Mediterranean colors, but they had the heavy, overhanging roofs of alpine chalets. Whenever some passerby or farm worker stopped to gape at the sight of the train, he or she would shout a greeting in Italian, but he would be wearing lederhosen and she a dirndl. At last, four days' climb from Verona, the train came in sight of Trento/Trient—and a striking sight it was, for the town completely filled the breadth of the Adige/Etsch valley, and over the town towered the great isolated rock called the Dosso Trento. Although there were palaces and loggias of the Venetian style in Trento, most of the buildings had massive roof eaves, balconies set above high-snow level, and belfry caps on their chimneys.

Florian, waiting to guide the train to its tober, greeted the troupe with the news: "It has begun. On June sixteenth, the Prussians invaded the Austro-Hungarian province of Bohemia."

The predominantly Italian populace of Trento might have been undecided whether to cheer for Austria, to which they belonged by treaty, or for the other side, the Prussian ally of Italy. But one thing they could unreservedly cheer for was a circus, so they flocked to the Florilegium and forgot politics. The company enjoyed another well-received and profitable stand—but only for two days, then Florian moved them on.

They climbed higher yet into the mountains, to the town of Bolzano—or Bozen—and during the two days they showed there, they got the news that Italy, as expected, had joined Prussia in declaring war on Austria. When Florian called for the teardown this time, he told all the wagon and van drivers that they would now detour off the main road they had been ascending, and would instead take a secondary road that continued alongside the Adige River and went north-east by way of a town called Merano.

"What for?" asked Edge. "All the way here, I've been assuming we'd cross the Alps at the Brenner Pass. It's directly north of here, the road is good, the pass is not impossibly high and—hell—that's been the classic alpine crossing ever since the Ostrogoths."

"The classic invasion route to the south, yes. Therefore the likeliest route by which the Austrians will continue to pour cavalcades across—as an ex-cavalry officer like yourself must be aware. I don't want to sit on top of an Alp waiting for a whole army to get out of my road. We will go over the Paso de Resia instead. It is only a few feet higher, and a few days farther from here.''

Just before nightfall of the first day out of Bolzano, the train reached Merano, a town that seemed to be composed of nothing but inns. Florian announced, ''We will not show here. Merano is a resort for consumptives. They come for the rest cure, for the clear air cure, for the whey cure, for the grape cure. Probably they could not wheeze their way up into our seat stands. However, let us find enough inns to accommodate us all. Then everybody eat hearty and get a good night's rest in the feather beds. The road ahead will be hard, and empty of any amenities.''

After dinner, Autumn and Edge, before availing themselves of their bed's big, warm but weightless feather quilts, stepped out onto the balcony of their room. The moon was full that night, and its light made especially imposing the snow-capped sharp peaks all around Merano, but high above it. The rim of mountains, luminous blue-white with sharp black valley shadows, looked as hard-edged as a jagged piece of tin against the dark blue sky.

''Lovely,'' murmured Autumn. She gazed all about the horizon and, when her eyes came back to Edge, he saw that even in moonlight their flower-petal specklings of gold were visible. She said, ''You know, if you think about it, the moon is *always* a full moon. Only we can't see it.''

He said admiringly, ''I'd think, with the eyes you've got, you could see it all the time. Now me, I'm not so perceptive. It's only just this minute that I've noticed something. My shadow is black. Everybody else's shadow is black. Yours is rose-colored.''

Involuntarily she looked down, then laughed. ''Liar. Idiot.''

''Well, it looks so to me. Everything about you, my dear, looks flowery to me.''

The next stretch of road took five days and nights to negotiate. It got ever steeper and more twisty, making the horses labor and frequently requiring the troupers to get down and walk to lighten the load. It also made for chilly nights, even inside the caravans, even now in high summer, for they were nearing a mile above sea level. But the road at least stayed below the snow line, and nobody and none of the animals got intolerably fatigued, none of the wagons broke down, and—whether or not there were armies crossing the Brenner Pass—no marching columns blocked the way up to this one. In the forenoon of the sixth day, the troupers discovered that they were no longer climbing, but proceeding on a level piece of road. They came abreast of a small chalet, painted Austrian black and yellow, flying the Austrian flag, and a few Tirolean Rifle sentries came out of it—but only to wave a greeting. Florian halted the train there, went to have a few words with the guards and returned to say:

"Ladies and gentlemen, you are at the crest of the Lechtal Alps. This pass is called, behind us, the Paso de Resia— ahead of us the Reschenpass. We are leaving the cisalpine lands for the transalpine. And just in time, from what these good fellows tell me. The Austrians and Italians are furiously battling right now, somewhere in the vicinity of Verona, where we so recently were situated. From here, my friends, the road is all downhill, into the Tirol valleys of Austria—or, as the country prefers to be called in its own language, the Österreich."

⊶ ÖSTERREICH ⊷

1

THE REST OF THAT day, they descended the mountain valleys down which tumbled the river Inn, young and boisterous up here, a pale jade green in color because of all the oxygen it had absorbed from the snows higher up in the ranges. There were noticeable differences between this transalpine side of the pass and the cisalpine they had just ascended. Back there, they had been climbing through oak, beech and ash trees. On this side, the trees were mostly evergreen: pine, fir and spruce. On that southern side, the wild flowers had been mostly oleanders and verbena; on this northern side they were gentians and saxifrage.

There were a few very small villages sprinkled down the Inn's high valleys, all too small to have any accommodation for strangers. When the train stopped outside a hamlet named Pfunds, to pass the night, Florian said, "Maggie tells me we have just about used up all our provisions over these last days. I shall go and knock on doors and ask if I can buy bread, milk and cheese from some good Hausfrau. Come, Banat, and help me carry whatever I can get."

The two of them returned well laden. Magpie Maggie Hag

had made up a campfire, the Slovaks another, around which the artistes and crewmen sat as they ate their bread and cheese. Suddenly they all sat up a lot straighter, startled by a very loud, very weird noise—a sound commingled of rattle, hoot and shriek—from somewhere in the blackness of the pines on the other side of the road.

"Jesus jumping Christ!" said Yount.

The extraordinary noise sounded again. The elephant uneasily shuffled her feet, Maximus uttered a growl and the terriers could be heard yapping inside the Smodlakas' caravan.

"I bet it's a g'nome," said Sunday, shivering.

"A what?" said Fitzfarris.

"A g'nome. A sort of boogey-man. Monsieur Jules lent me a book about the Alps, and it said the Alps are full of g'nomes."

Rouleau sighed. "Your erudition, my dear, sometimes outruns your vocabulary. In English it is pronounced *nome*."

As if answering to the name, the appalling sound came again.

"Well, whatever it is," said Mullenax, "I don't think I can sleep with it squawlin' like that. Zack, you got your carbine loaded with scatter shot? Lend me it."

"You'd go after the thing? One-eyed? In the dark?"

"I'm the animal tamer, right? And in the dark, two eyes ain't much advantage over one."

Edge shrugged, got the carbine for him, and Mullenax went slinking off into the woods.

"I think Abner's fairly well loaded, himself," said Fitzfarris. "If he lets off that weapon in a careless direction, we're all liable to get sprinkled with bird shot."

But the creature, whatever it was, gave its clatter-howl screech again, and no gunshot followed. A few minutes later, the creature sounded off again, but the noise stopped abruptly in mid-yammer. All the people around the fires looked at each other questioningly. After a long silence, Mullenax came into the firelight, carrying a large, untidy black bundle.

"Didn't have to shoot him. Just whacked him off a branch with the gun butt. He's still alive, so I tied him with my belt.

I never seen nothin' like this critter, and I'm damned if I want him loose when he wakes up mad at me." He dropped the thing on the ground in the light, and everybody gathered to look. "Big as a turkey—but no turkey ever made such a noise, or ever had such a wicked bill as that."

The bird was mostly bronze-black in color, with shimmers of blue and purple, and its body did resemble that of an American turkey, complete to the fan-feather tail. But It had the head, beak and talons of a raptor. When it began to stir awake, it opened fierce hawkish eyes, over which were bright red-feather "eyebrows," and clacked a viciously hooked yellow beak, and again uttered that shattering noise, and everyone recoiled from it.

"Nothing supernaural or threatening," said Florian. "It's a kind of grouse. In every European language it is called something like cock of the wild or cock of the mountains. Back in Italy it would have been the gallo alpestre. Here, it's the Auerhahn."

"In Scotland it's the capercaillie," said Autumn. "Gaelic for cock of the woods."

"Is it good to eat?" asked Yount.

"Yes, indeed," said Florian. "At this season, anyway, when it has been feeding on berries and such. In the winter it feeds on pine needles, so it tastes like turpentine."

"Hey!" said Mullenax. "Ain't nobody goin' to eat a bird I bothered to take alive. He's for *showing!*"

"You'll never tame and train that thing," said Fitzfarris. "But we could put him in among my stuffed museum birds."

"Yes," said Florian. "Hereabouts, it is not an exotic, like a hummingbird or an opossum. But most city folk will only have seen an Auerhahn dead and stuffed. That's what we'll do: put it alive in the museum."

As the circus train continued on down the valley of the Inn, the scenery sloped up toward the sky on either side, and consisted of dense forests of black-green pines, from which wafted occasional wisps and toots of gray mist, like ghosts standing up to observe the passing procession. Here and there, the ranks of pines gave way to forests of fir trees, as ripply looking as a sea washing upon the mountain flanks.

Among all those dark evergreens, the infrequent deciduous tree—a linden or chestnut—flared as bright as a pale green explosion.

Every mile or so, the forest had been cleared for a house and pasture. The houses were of the solid alpine design: the front for the human inhabitants, the rear for stabling the livestock in winter, so their body heat would help warm the humans' quarters. The roof of every house was massive, its eaves overhanging all around, and a balcony encircled the house under the second-story windows—the balcony and every window sill overflowing with brilliant red geraniums. Over the front door was nailed a great wide rack of deer or elk antlers, and beside every house stood rows of beehives. The pastures behind the houses were so steep that it seemed impossible that any animals could stand on them to graze. But there were herds in plenty—as beautiful as show stock: horses of glossy brown with blond manes and tails, cows of a delicate silvery-dun color. And on these warm summer days, not just the colts and calves but even the full-grown horses and matronly cows bounded and cavorted about. There were sheep, too, but they were not so surefooted on the slanted pastures; the troupers laughed to see one of the sheep lose its purchase and tumble like a barrel downhill.

Since the weather continued fine, the troupe camped along the road every night, but frequently stopped at a Schenke or Gasthaus for a meal. Some of those inns were poor places and served the food of the peasantry, which seemed to consist solely of the Sterz, a cornmeal cake with strips of pork-fat cracklings laid on top. And in one of those taverns, a couple of the newcomers made the mistake of ordering the peasant beverage called Rhum—to discover that it was not even a distant relation of rum, but a vile distillate from potatoes, mixed with brown sugar, almost too awful even for Mullenax to drink. But other houses catered to richer travelers, and in those the viands were superb: jugged hare, roast wild boar, fish fresh from the Inn, immense dumplings, vigorous beer, gentian-flavored liqueur.

Around the campfires at night, the more experienced travelers explained to the newcomers various things about Austria:

"The Habsburgs who have long ruled this land," said Florian, "must be the oldest continuously ruling family in all of history. I'd guess that they have held one throne or another—as dukes, counts, kings, emperors—longer than any Egyptian dynasty ever did. Their family tree goes back to a Count Guntram the Rich, around the year nine hundred, who named the line for his Habichtsburg—Hawk's Castle. In their time, the Habsburgs have ruled everything from little duchies to the entire Holy Roman Empire. Right now, there is a Habsburg trying to rule a rather unruly Mexico."

"That won't last long," said Edge. "Maximilian only managed to sneak in there because the States were distracted by their war."

"And of course he went only because Franz Joseph commanded him to," said Florian. "After all, what does an emperor *do* with a younger brother? Try to find some second-rate job for him abroad. Maximilian had already made a mess of governing Venezia. The man is a simpleton."

"I was once among the singers summoned to entertain at Maximilian's court, when he was in Venice," said Zanni Bonvecino. "His wife is Charlotte of Coburg, and she is quite unbalanced. She is a rabid and perpetual housekeeper, forever dusting tables and things, like a demented chambermaid."

Carl Beck said, "And Franz Joseph to Elisabeth is married. Of our Bavarian Wittelsbachs she is, and for lunacy the Wittelsbachs are long notorious."

"Well, Franz Joseph had *one* damned good reason for marrying Elisabeth," said Florian. "She is said to be the most beautiful woman ever to wear a crown since Nefertiti."

"Nevertheless," said Paprika, "Elisabeth *is* a Wittelsbach—and eccentric at the very least. She is obsessed with her beauty and health. Always exercising, bathing in strange oils, eating strange substances. Also she detests court formality and royal duties, and despises her husband. I hear that she travels now as often as she can, and, even when she returns to her own domains, she spends most of her time in

Budapest, leaving Vienna and her own children to Franz Joseph and his iron mother, Sophia.''

"Let us say this for her, though," Autumn put in. "The Empress Elisabeth adores circuses, and she herself is a skilled rider. She has even done trick riding, and is said to take every opportunity to indulge her fondness for circuses. Goes about incognito like that sultan—who was he, Florian? The one that was always prowling among his subjects in disguise?''

"A Persian caliph. Harun al-Raschid.''

"I have heard that, yes," said Paprika. "Also that she now speaks Magyar to perfection, among all her other languages.'' Paprika paused to giggle. "Do you know, they say Elisabeth has a pet name for her husband. She calls him 'Megliotis.' Not just behind his back; to his face as well. And the poor fool *likes* it, because in classical Greek it would mean Majesty. But in Magyar that word would translate as something like 'Dead Standstill.' ''

"Well, standing still *we* should not be,'' said Florian. "Let us get to bed, and be early on the road tomorrow.''

He was off earliest of all, because on that afternoon the Florilegium would arrive at its first sizable Austrian city, Landeck, and Florian had to hurry there to arrange for the tober. So Edge and Autumn led the train, with no possibility of losing the way, for there was only the one road following the river Inn down the valley. Edge knew that the Inn eventually in its course became one of the major waterways of Austria, but it was still no more than what in Virginia would have been called a creek. However, the main road now began to be intersected by crossroads at intervals, and those crossed the Inn on high-humped covered bridges, each as solidly wooden-walled and roofed as any mountain house. Then, quite suddenly, another creek joined the Inn and made it more of a respectable river, and there at the meeting of the waters was Landeck, with Florian waiting at the roadside.

"We'll pitch on the Eislaufplatz. In the winter it is a skating rink. While I've been waiting for you, I have been doctoring these Italian-language posters. Let's have all the lads who are not driving start pasting them up while the rest of us go on to the tober.''

Landeck was an exceptionally clean city, especially as compared with some of those in Italy. There was not a scrap of litter to be seen, nor a single untidy house or yard, nor an unkempt person. Most noticeable, here as in the villages they had already come through, there were no beggars anywhere in residence. But Autumn told Edge that Austria was not entirely devoid of them; they had all migrated to Vienna, where the pickings were better.

Landeck appeared to have grown rather haphazardly around its centerpiece—an immense, square-towered castle—the buildings having accreted there first, then sprawled out over the valley and then up the surrounding mountainsides. The circus train had to wind a slow, tortuous course through the narrow streets, all the way to the other side of the city. So the crewmen posting the paper could pretty well stay abreast of the train while they worked. To the top of each poster, Florian had added with his mason's pencil, in big black letters: NIGHT DENKEN AN KUMMER! When the train pulled up at the sometimes ice rink and everybody piled out, Edge asked about the addition to the posters.

"It means 'Forget Your Worries,' " Come to the circus instead of moping. If we're in the Germanic lands long enough, I'll get those posters entirely reprinted. But the word 'circus' is recognizable enough."

"Does this town have something in particular to mope about?"

"All of Austria does. I have heard the latest war news. Austria's troops down south have soundly trounced the Italians, as expected. But its armies in Bohemia are steadily retreating before the Prussians, with heavy losses. And that was *not* expected. The Austrian soldiers are known to be better trained and disciplined than the Prussians, and they had recent combat experience against the French just seven years ago, while the Prussians have not fought a war in fifty years. But I am told that the Prussians have some terrible new weapons—breech-loading repeater rifles versus the Austrians' old muzzle-loaders, and cannons made of Essen steel instead of cast iron, so they can fire more rapidly and accurately. I gather that courage and experience don't count for much against superior firepower.''

''I can guarantee you they don't,'' Edge said drily.

But the Landeckers, however patriotically preoccupied they may have been, congregated to watch the elephant and the Slovaks erect the chapiteau and the smaller top, and a goodly number of them went to Magpie Maggie Hag in the red wagon to buy tickets for the morrow. Fitzfarris was also at the red wagon, but he was at the back of it—the museum part—and he called Florian over.

''I hope Abner's goddamned turkey bird is worth the showing,'' Fitz said angrily. ''This is the first time I've taken down the side panels since we put the bird in there. And just look what it's done to the rest of the museum!''

The rest of the museum was now quite nonexistent, except for a pile of scraps of fur and hide, wads of stuffing, scattered feathers, and three glass eyes, relics of the two-headed calf. The Auerhahn's wicked beak and talons had demolished every last exhibit—the birds, the animals, even the milk snake. The malefactor spread its fantail and glared out at them defiantly.

''Hell,'' said Florian. ''I should have known. When we heard that bird bellowing in the middle of the night and the middle of summertime, I should have realized it wasn't doing any mating call. It was defying any other birds to trespass on its territory.''

''It's sure got *this* territory all to itself now. Good thing the Chinks weren't still living in there. I ought to make Abner eat the confounded thing—raw—feathers and feet and all.''

''Well, we did toss the Auerhahn in the cage without any provender. Probably it got hungry.''

''All right, then *it* can eat *Abner*. Any creature that could make a meal of a three-eyed embalmed calf ought to really enjoy a one-eyed clodhopper pickled in alcohol.''

''Simmer down, Sir John. You have to admit that the museum was a rather shoddy makeshift. I'll have one of the Slovaks scrape the mess out of there, and then I'll work up a gruesome patter about the Killer Bird from the High Crags. Later on, as we go along, maybe we can pick up some more real live museum pieces. Hello . . . what's this?''

A uniformed, official-looking gentleman strode briskly onto the tober, gave the tents a contemptuous look, then made his way to Florian and superciliously addressed him in German. The two conversed for a minute, then the stranger strode inside the chapiteau.

''Who's he?'' asked Fitzfarris.

Florian made a face. ''A manifestation of the Teutonic efficiency I have been expecting and dreading. He'll have a title something like the Herr Inspektor of Diminutive Details, from the Department of Obstruction, in the Ministry of Public Meddling. We'll be pestered by another like him in every town big enough to support a typically layabout civil service. I'll deal with him.''

He went into the tent, where Stitches Goesle was watching the roustabouts put up the seating. The Landeck inspector was feeling a fold of the sidewall canvas, and looking critical of it. When Florian entered the inspector officiously snapped his fingers and commanded, ''Benehmenbüchern!'' Florian went out again, and to his caravan, and brought back all the conduct books. The inspector paged through every one of them— and carefully, reading every entry in every language, or pretending he was doing so. At least one of the words he recognized, for he looked up from that book and said, ''Kanevasmeister?''

Florian told him that the canvasmaster was the man in charge of the chapiteau. He pointed to Goesle, and the inspector asked that he be summoned. When Dai came up to them, the man said, ''Herr Goosely?''

'' 'Tis pronounced Gwell,'' Dai growled. To Florian he said, ''And who is this clinchpoop, then?''

''City inspector,'' said Florian, and he listened as the official went into a lengthy speech. He translated to Goesle, ''The inspector says our canvas is highly flammable, and there are no buckets of either sand or water for use in the event of fire.''

''Wait you, Governor,'' Goesle said indignantly. ''Why tell me these things? You know them as well as I do.''

"Of course. Let us simply seem to be discussing the matter."

"What is to discuss? I know of nothing that will stop canvas catching fire. If you want me to procure buckets, that I can do, given time and opportunity."

"This twit can forbid us to open the show, if he is so minded. Naturally he did not come around until after I had paid the city a fee for the tober, and we are all set up. So we could waste time, effort and money if we were simply to fold on command. That is the way such petty officials operate. Now you say something else, Dai, so I can translate to him."

"Say *what*, Governor? You can tell him from me that he can go from here before I will hit him with a stake mallet."

"Thank you, Dai." Florian turned to the official and delivered a long spate of German, with gestures. The inspector rubbed his chin and looked suspicious.

"What did you tell him, then?" Goesle asked.

"That the wagon carrying the fire buckets is not here yet. It threw a wheel rim on the road. But the buckets will be here—and filled—before we open tomorrow."

"He doesn't appear to believe you."

"He will." Florian took from his pockets a sheaf of tickets, with a number of Austrian gulden notes folded among them. These he presented to the inspector, with a laving of syrupy German compliments. The official took the tickets and money, but regarded them with even more suspicion.

"I think now," said Goesle, "you are going to be charged with bribery."

Just then Autumn came into the chapiteau, wearing street dress. "Dai, one of my rig's turnbuckles seemed loose, last time I—oh, excuse me. I didn't notice that you were occupied."

The inspector looked over at her, blinked and looked more intently at her. Then he whipped off his hat, bowed deeply to her and began backing out of the tent, meanwhile bowing likewise to both Florian and Goesle, and saying rapidly and obsequiously, "Gut gemacht! Alles in bester Ordnung sein. Verzeihen Sie, mein Herren! Küss die Hand, gnädige Dame . . ." and he was gone.

"What caused all that?" said Goesle, bewildered.

Florian said, "We finally convinced him that he will see the fire buckets here tomorrow."

"But he won't, Governor."

"He will, if he has to close both eyes to do it. I must say, a lovely lady arriving at just the right moment seemed to help convince him. Miss Auburn, he must have mistaken you for his empress in disguise. Remind me to have you around every time I have to deal with officialdom."

"Here is something else to remind you about," she said, producing a piece of paper. "New lyrics for the come-in spec. Boom-Boom and I worked them out together. Still to the tune of 'Greensleeves.' "

"Bless me, I had quite forgotten we'd need that," said Florian. He read and softly sang the words:

> Zirku-us ist Vergnügen!
> Zirkus vor Freude hüpfen!
> Zirkus hat Herz rein golden!
> Und alles zu Zirkus willkommen!

"We can all get together and practice them tonight," said Autumn. "Carl also has to teach the band a new march for the closing spec."

"Yes, that's right. The Austrian anthem. Well, I do thank you and him for these lyrics, my dear. Truly remarkable. To make German words rhyme and scan—even approximately— must put a strain upon the genius of Wagner himself."

By the next day's first performance, Zanni had done his accustomed snooping about the locality. So when, early in the show, he and Florian did their comic exchange, most of Zanni's jokes were topical. He made the audience roar when he poked fun at "die Sechsundsechzig Starken," the sixty-six local merchants who composed Landeck's civic promotion board. Zanni played that for all it was worth, because Starken could be made to mean either "men of big business" or "big fat businessmen."

Zanni also introduced a new element into the act: an assistant joey, in the small person of Quincy-Ali Baba Simms.

And Ali Baba got his first-ever laugh just by walking into the pista, for Zanni had done his makeup like that of the Sambo or Bones in an American minstrel show. Ali Baba's face was blacked even blacker with burnt cork, except for a watermelon-slice mouth. He wore a sober suit and white gloves. The effect was of a little Negro exaggeratedly impersonating a white boy exaggeratedly impersonating a Negro, and the crowd thought it hilarious at first sight.

During the comic-patter exchange. Ali Baba had little to do. Only when Florian, pretending fury at Zanni's retorts and insults, tried to chase the clown, Ali Baba would contrive to be hanging onto Florian's frock-coat tails, or just then bending over to adjust a shoe so Florian tripped over him. Ali Baba's real clown début came at the end of the act, when Florian finally got furious at *him* and chased him around the pista. At that, Zanni produced a plug hat from somewhere and set it on his head, but put it there upside down. Ali Baba, fleeing from Florian, did a high leap that took him over Zanni—and he somersaulted there in midair, so that for an instant he and Zanni were head to head—and came down beyond, on his feet, with the plug hat right side up on his own head.

Because he and Zanni had practiced and perfected that trick in strict secrecy, even the watching troupers burst into surprised applause, along with the audience. And the audience produced a kind of uproar that Ali Baba and the other Americans had never heard until now. The people clapped their hands in the ordinary manner, but they augmented that noise by loudly stamping in unison, so the noise was thunderous. It did not abate until Florian, Zanni and Ali Baba—especially Ali Baba, his grin nearly splitting his head in half—had returned again and again for bows.

The Landeckers did that simultaneous hand-and-foot acclaim for every act, but they did it loudest for one turn in particular. The troupers never could divine the reason, but every show in Landeck drew a house full of apparently fanatical dog-lovers. The Smodlakas' terriers got such deafening applause and cries of ''noch einmal!'' at the first show that Pavlo and Gavrila and the children had to repeat several tricks and then take repeated bows. At that night's show, in the limelight, with Goesle's spotlight following the dogs' antics, the act elicited the same response, and the Smodlakas obliged with even more encores.

When the same thing happened at every subsequent performance, Gavrila began to get almost embarrassed by the unceasing curtain calls. She would have bowed out of the pista after a number of encores, but Pavlo always gave her a black look that kept her, the dogs and the children performing until the pale Velja and Sava were drained almost transparent. And at the Florilegium's very last performance in Landeck, the Smodlaka act went on and on until even the terriers were half dead, and Colonel Ramrod had to shrill his whistle and crack his whip repeatedly before Pavlo would let his family and animals retire, then himself stayed to bask and bow and beam until the equestrian director almost had to drag him off.

"Confound it!" Edge snapped at him. "I've got to fit in five more acts before the closing spec, and then we've got to tear down, and you've hogged the pista for nearly half an hour."

"Cut short the prljav other acts, then!" Pavlo snapped back at him. "Not mine, that these good people like best."

Edge had an inspiration that he thought clever. "Has it occurred to you," he said, "that all the hoorah might have been led by some rival dog trainer? Keeping you on view long enough for him to steal all your signals and tricks for his own act?"

Pavlo started, gasped, "Svetog Vlaha!" and went almost as white as either of his children. He stooped, grabbed up Terry, Terrier and Terriest as if they were in imminent danger of abduction, and hurried them off to their caravan.

There was one other unscheduled incident that night, but it caused no trouble except some missed beats of Edge's heart. Autumn was nearing the end of her act, slowly inching her way upright from her stride split on the tightrope. Every eye was on the tiny, high-up, yellow-clad sprite, and so was the brilliance of Goesle's spotlight. The silence in the chapiteau was such that the hissing of the lights' gas flames could be heard. Then, for no reason anyone could see, Autumn lost hold of her little yellow parasol. It fluttered down out of the limelight, so it seemed to vanish from existence, but Edge was not watching that. He kept his anxious gaze fixed on Autumn, sure that his breathing and his pulse both stopped during the fraction of a second that she was put off balance by the loss of her prop. Autumn only barely wavered—probably no one in the audience even noticed—then she continued to inch her feet together from the split until she was again standing on the rope, and she skipped along it to the platform to take her bows and applause.

"It simply slipped out of my hand, Zachary," she said, when she was down. "Maybe I'm still not accustomed to the spotlight. It does give me a bit of a headache . . ."

Edge said only that he was happy it had not proved serious. He sternly restrained himself from saying anything critical or cautionary. But he was aware that Autumn's confidence in herself was no longer absolutely unshakable. Her flower-petal eyes had in them a new look. It was not fear or worry or apprehension; it was pure puzzlement. Autumn Auburn had made a mistake she had never made before, and she was wondering why.

However, she had brightened again by the close of the show, when the band was playing "Gott Erhalte Unseren Kaiser," and the troupe was doing its final promenade around the chapiteau. Marching beside Edge, who was leading his liberty horses, she said to him:

"Listen to that chune. Owlwise—"

"Owlwise?"

"Hush. I'm doin' me cockney. Owlwise in Stepney we used ter sing that chune, but wif bawdy words." So she sang along with Haydn's august anthem, for Edge's ears only, all the lyrics of "She Was Poor But She Was Honest," and they both laughed again.

Next day, the circus train went leisurely on down the Inn valley. There were no villages or towns big enough to merit making a stand, and the next sizable one would be Innsbruck, but Florian was in no rush to get there. He explained, "We take our time on the road, and Innsbruck is of a size to give us a good long engagement. Then we take our time going wherever we go from there. By the time winter is upon us, I want us to be in the Danube lowlands, and we will stay in those more clement lowlands until the spring.''

The troupers did not mind traveling at a sauntering pace, for the ever-widening valley was ever more beautiful to look at. Every village square and farmhouse yard glowed with garden flowers and the fields between were riotous with wild ones. "The Blumenmeer," said Beck. "So the Österreichers call it. The Blossom Sea. Especially in spring, when in flower all the orchards are: cherry, peach, apricot, almond. Now blooming only the Pappeln are.'' Those were the poplars, the trees mainly in evidence along the way. In this season, they were shedding such a snowstorm of white fluffs that the road was banked deep with them. The horses' hoofbeats were almost inaudible, but they kicked up clouds of the white down, and the wagon train left a high, long-hanging white trail behind it, like smoke, so that from a distance it could have been mistaken for a steam-propelled railroad train.

One evening, when the troupers camped by the roadside and applied to a nearby farmhouse for fresh food, the victuals they got included a basket of goose eggs. Fitzfarris, unnoticed, purloined one of those eggs and took it off somewhere. The next night, at the next camp, when Magpie Maggie Hag was preparing to fry some of those eggs, Fitzfarris happened to be standing by, and he suddenly said, in a voice of awe, "Good Jesus, Mag! Look at that one you just picked up.''

She did, and cried, "Devlesa!'' and dropped it, but Fitz nimbly caught it.

Others gathered, and Fitzfarris handed the egg around—"Just look at that!''—and the others all exclaimed or murmured over it. When Florian joined them, he asked lightly, "Have you discovered the goose that lays the golden eggs, Sir John?''

Mullenax said, "Damn near as good as. Look at it, Governor.''

Florian turned it over and over in his hand. It was an ordinary goose egg, except that its shell was not quite smooth. It bore an embossed figure: a neatly recognizable Christian cross slightly upraised from the surface.

Yount asked excitedly, "How could we find the one amongst them geese back yonder that laid this egg? If that goose makes a habit of it, we'd sure as hell have some curios to sell!"

"I don't think Sir John needs the goose," said Florian, his eyes twinkling. To Fitzfarris he said, "You figure this would be a good gimmix for the Auerhahn, don't you?"

"Aw, shucks," said Fitz. "You've seen this dodge before."

"Usually in the more backward communities, where the yokels are good game for superstition and miracles. What did you use, Sir John?"

"Drew the cross with wax, dipped the egg in some of Boom-Boom's leftover generator acid for a couple of minutes, then scraped the wax off. Governor, you talked up that bird real well in Landeck—made it sound like Sinbad's roc—but the jossers didn't look very impressed. So I thought: suppose we put a twig nest in that cage, talk up the creature as a miracle layer, peddle the cross-marked eggs . . ."

"Well, it's certainly worth trying. This is all Catholic country hereabout. But I fear you'll find our next audiences— the folk of Innsbruck—quite civilized and blasé."

"Anybody religious is easy game for religious flimflam," Fitz said confidently. "But if crosses don't sell, I'll do a patriotic flimflam instead. Make the eggs wear the Austrian coat of arms."

However, the circus arrived at Innsbruck to find that its people were feeling rather glum about patriotism and not very hopeful of miracles.

"The war news was slow getting up the valley," said Florian, when he met the train at the city's riverside outskirts. "While we were still at Landeck, the Austrians were so dismally defeated in Bohemia—at some place named Königgrätz—that they have retreated all the way south to the vicinity of Vienna, and Franz Joseph is asking Prussia for an armistice. Austria has lost the war."

"What will this mean to us?" asked Edge.

"Right now, probably scant houses and not very joyous audiences. I have secured a tober for us—in the Hofgarten—

but I do not think, at this solemn time, I will be so tasteless as to put up any of those forget-your-worries posters.''

He led the train along the river avenue, through the grounds of the university, skirting the constricted area of the Old City, over which gleamed the gold-plated balcony roof of the Schloss Fürstenburg, and on into the public park that stretched beyond the State Theater. While the roustabouts unloaded the wagons and prepared for the setup there, Florian resumed talking to Edge:

''As regards the immediate future, Austria's defeat probably will mean a depression of business, including ours. I hear that Franz Joseph has already agreed to let go of Venezia. That is a large and costly loss, and Prussia's Chancellor Bismarck is likely to demand even more concessions.''

Edge said, ''So Austria will mean poor pickings for us.''

''At least for a while. Not long. Austrians have a faculty for rebounding quickly from adversity, or developing an indifference to it. But I am looking farther down the road, so to speak, and I foresee future political upheavals.''

''Affecting us?''

''Affecting all of Europe, I fear. For a long time, Bismarck has been trying to unite all the independent Germanic states into one cohesive and invincible Deutsche Reich. Until now, two other empires—the French and the Austrian—have maintained a fair balance between them. And Louis Napoléon and Franz Joseph, between them, have pretty much managed the destiny of all the rest of the Continent. Now Austria has lost a good deal of power and prestige. Louis Napoléon won't weep over that, but neither will he smile on a Germanic nation getting itself unified and rising to power. Soon or later, France must act to crush Bismarck's ambitions.''

''Meaning another war,'' said Edge. ''Where, do you reckon?''

''Ah, I wish I could foresee *that* clearly, Zachary, so we could avoid the place and the occasion. We must simply make our plans as best we can, as we go along.''

''Per piacere, Governatore . . . Direttore . . .'' said Zanni Bonvecino politely, coming up to them. ''I heard you mention plans. I wonder if they might be elastic enough to include some new artistes.''

"Unfortunately, signore," said Florian, "we were discussing plans gone agley, as a poet once put it. Meaning tutti rotoli.''

"Ohimè. Then forgive my being presumptuous. But might I at least introduce some old friends to you? They saw us ride in.''

"Oh, by all means. Always pleased to meet fellow show-folk, even if I cannot . . . well . . .''

"Here are the Kyrios and Kyria Vasilakis, which is to say the Signor and Signora Vasilakis.'' They were a darkly handsome couple aged perhaps thirty. "Spyros and Meli—originally of Greece.''

"Kalispéra," said Florian. The Vasilakises immediately grinned brilliant ivory grins and began jabbering simultaneously. "No, no, please!" said Florian, laughing and making fending-off gestures. "Kalispéra is one of maybe eight Greek words I know, and the other seven are indecent.''

"Parakaló," said the male Vasilakis, with a shrug. "We spik some Angliká. Also other. Franks. Talian.''

"And this," said Zanni, "is a native Austrian, the Herr Jörg Pfeifer. All of us have worked at one time together on the Zirkus Corty-Althoff. My friends, allow me to present the Florilegium's Governor Florian and Equestrian Director Edge.'' They shook hands all around, and Zanni went on, "Jörg and Spyros and Meli were engaged to entertain during the annual Trade and Crafts Fair here in Innsbruck. But that fair has just now closed, early and abruptly, because of the bad news from the war front. So they are at liberty.''

"Ah . . . yes . . .'' Florian said uncomfortably. "And tell me, what do you all do?''

"I am a white-face," Pfeifer said proudly. He was a short, broad, gray-haired man of about sixty. "In the pista I am called Fünfünf.''

"He and I," said Zanni, "used to do the Lupino mirror together.''

"No! Is that a fact?" exclaimed Florian, his face brightening.

"And I," said Spyros, "I it fires, swallow swords." He pronounced the *sw* in both those words. "Wife Meli snake kharmer."

Zanni helpfully translated. "He *eats* fire and swallows *swords*. She is a snake charmer. They have their own equipment and snakes, and their own caravan. Jörg also has his own van, and a splendid wardrobe of the traditional white-face dress."

"Well . . ." said Florian. "As you all must realize, the war news is distressing to us, too. I don't expect that we will shut down like the Trade Fair. However . . ."

"I myself," said Pfeifer, "would seriously consider any salary offered, however much less than my usual five hundred francs a week."

Florian calculated, and murmured for Edge's benefit, "A hundred American dollars. I am sure you are worth every centime of that, mein Herr. So I would not demean you or myself by uttering such an offer as I would have to make."

"Utter it. I am a comedian. I can do no worse than laugh."

"One hundred fifty francs, Herr Fünfünf."

"Accepted." He turned to Zanni. "We will try doing the mirror at the very first show. Let us go and see how rusty we have become."

"A moment," Zanni said to him, then to Florian, "What of Spyros and Meli, Governatore?"

"We can hardly doom them to performing on Innsbruck's street corners, can we? But I must consult with our sideshow director regarding their salary. Will you take them along, Signor Bonvecino, and introduce them to Sir John?"

When the four had gone off toward the backyard, Edge said, "We no sooner run into hard times again, but you have to play Lord Bountiful. You're going to pay a joey as much as you pay Maurice LeVie?"

"Not just a joey, a *white-face*. I'd have been stupid to let him get away. The white-face is the most ancient traditional element in a European circus. But it would have been heartless to take him and then refuse the other two. Anyway, I got Fünfünf at such a bargain rate that we can afford the sideshow Greeks."

"What kind of name is Fünfünf? It sounds like a cat sneezing."

"Only a nonsense word. If it translated from the German at all, it would be something like 'five-by-five'—which is approximately the shape he will have in the pista: five feet high, five feet wide. You will see what I—oh, Christ Almighty, here comes another city inspector to poke around and find fault and want his palm greased. Go fetch Autumn for me, Zachary."

"I can't. She's feeling poorly. Of course, she'd never admit to any such thing, but I could see she's been looking not as sprightly as usual. I'm making her stay abed until Maggie Hag can take a look at her."

"I'm sorry to hear it. And sorrier that I'll have to deal with this jack-in-office all by myself. But I hope your dear lady's indisposition is only trivial and temporary."

Florian went to meet and greet the inspector, and strolled along with him as he scrutinized the rising tent, and peered at other things, and scribbled in a notebook. Florian kept up an amiable chatter of German, but the inspector only grunted in response—until Florian had the inspiration to remark that "this whole circus in on the square." The inspector gave him a keen look and asked if it was also "on the level?"

"By the plumb rule," replied Florian.

"Then the builder is smitten," said the inspector, shutting his notebook. When the two had exchanged certain discreet signs, he asked another question: "And if there be no stones for the builder?"

"Then refresh him," said Florian, "with money to bring him to the next lodge." There was a discreet transaction of another kind, and the inspector took his leave.

Edge was sitting on the let-down little steps at the back of the caravan when Magpie Maggie Hag came out the door. He stood up to let her descend the stairs, and said, "Well?"

She beckoned him a short distance from the van. "Has bad headache, says your romeri. Also weakness sometimes in her hands. It comes, goes, one hand, then other. But is not weakness, is numbness. I know. When she not look, I prick with pin, she no feel."

"What's causing it, Mag?"

"Could be many things. Some no matter, some matter much. But tell me. You not notice any difference in her?"

"Why . . . yes. She's been listless—downcast—ever since that night she dropped her parasol during the Landeck show."

"You not notice any other thing? From before that?"

"Well, how do you mean? Have *you* noticed something? When?"

"Long time ago. In Italy palace. When she heard clock stop."

"Oh, come on, Mag. That was peculiar, yes, but don't use it to start a rube routine on me. If Autumn is ailing, I want to know about the ailment, not listen to any gypsy-jinx talk."

"But that clock she did hear stop. Person's head can do strange things. And when head start doing strange things, should start wondering why."

"Damn, Mag! Are you saying she's sick in the head?"

"You not notice any difference in face . . . in how she *look?*"

"Well . . . yes. Her eyes have lost some sparkle. But wouldn't that be natural, if she's feeling puny?"

"Next time you look her eyes, look close. For now, make her rest. Not let her perform tomorrow. I have rub her hands with hot-pepper salve. Now I go mix potion for make strength. We will see."

Edge stood slumped for a minute, thinking, then squared his shoulders and entered the van. Autumn lay on the bed, propped against a pillow, with a pencil and paper in hand, and she was listening to the tinkly music of "Greensleeves" being played by the little music box Edge had given her back in Perugia.

"Rather than just lie here," she said, "I thought I would get a start on composing French words for the come-in—for when we get to Paris. Somebody else will have to put them into Magyar and Russian, for when we go—"

"You stop worrying about the circus," said Edge. "Concentrate on getting yourself well again, my girl." He pulled over one of the two chairs and sat down beside her.

"Oh, Zachary, you know how we women get the mopes and the fanteagues from time to time. If we simply quit work and downed tools every time—"

"I won't risk your having a female swoon thirty feet up in the air. You're not going on tomorrow. Not until Maggie has spooned some of her nostrums into you, and you get your strength back."

"But I am *the close of the show!* Florian will tear out his beard."

"No, he won't. Sunday and Monday can do the slant-climb, and that will satisfy the jossers that they've seen ropewalking. And now Florian has just hired a new joey that he thinks is something special. So we'll have a full program; the audience won't feel cheated."

"I shall not be missed at all?" she said, pretending dismay. "That is a worse prospect than taking a tumble."

"You'll be missed by me. And to hell with everybody else but you and me. I want you well again. I'll tie you to that bed if I have to."

She went on making protestations, but Edge was not listening. He was, as Magpie Maggie Hag had instructed, taking a very close look at Autumn. And there *was* something different about her—about her face—it was noticeable only now when he was seeking something to notice. It looked as if . . . but that was impossible, he told himself. A face couldn't *do* that. The most beautiful features might get ill, old, wrinkled, coarse, even scarred, but the change he now seemed to see was a physical impossibility for a face. Goddamn it, he thought, that old gypsy has spooked my eyesight.

"You just lie there," he said, "and luxuriate in idleness. I'll be looking in on you, and as soon as I get a chance to go downtown I'll buy some books for you. When Maggie brings her witch's brews, you be a good girl and choke them down, you hear?"

Outside again, Edge found Florian in conference with a gathering of men and women of various ages, the men in dusty-green lederhosen, the women mostly in varicolored dirndls. The conference ended with several of the people handing money to Florian, then they departed. Florian beckoned to Edge and said happily:

"Sir John is going to be in his glory. Not only does he have two new attractions for his sideshow—the sword swallower and the snake handler—he will also have a full and flourishing midway for the first time. Those people were seeking what we call faking privileges—permission to set up in our front yard here. And some even want to come on the road with us afterward. Every kind of joint and butcher."

"Joint? Butcher?"

"Souvenir joints, slum joints, candy butchers, pastry butchers. Like the stalls you saw at that fair in Italy. These folks were all peddling edibles, potables, craftwork, slum, every sort of thing—here at Innsbruck's Trade Fair—and they all got dispossessed when it folded. Now they are eager to cleave to us. Not much money in it for us, of course. I asked only a nominal fee from each of them for the faking privileges. I demanded no rake-off from their take. Still, they'll add bustle and color and vivacity to our front yard."

"If you say so, Governor."

"Well, surely you saw that some of those female cheapjacks are young and pretty. I especially admire them in their crisp native dirndls—making their bosoms so high and perky." He smiled appreciatively. "It used to be that only girl children wore dirndls, until their older sisters saw how fetching that frock-and-apron is. Virginal and seductive at the same time. I do believe there's no more flattering dress a pretty woman can wear."

"You sure are sounding exuberant, Governor. I reckon that civil inspector wasn't too incivil in his snooping."

"Oh, I got rid of him easily enough. We turned out to have some interests in common. Also there is an old Austrian custom called Freunderlwirtschaft. What I believe you Americans call 'you scratch my back and I'll scratch yours.' But you, Zachary, my boy, you are *not* sounding exuberant. Why?"

"I have to tell you, we've got to rearrange the main program. Autumn can't go on tomorrow. Maybe not for some while."

"My dear friend, I am sorry to hear that. You and she both have my condolences, and of course my hope that she soon gets better."

"Thank you. But the program?"

Florian considered only briefly. "Instead of Autumn coming on to close after the Simms girls we'll bring on Fünfünf and Zanni to do the Lupino mirror. That's always a guaranteed audience pleaser."

"I thought sure you'd move the trapeze act to the close."

"No. Herr Pfeifer has nobly accepted a comedown in salary. Let us at least pay him in program status. Let him and Zanni close the show with a slambang, knockabout spill-and-pelt."

"There'll be slamming and banging, all right, when Maurice and Paprika hear about this. You said you foresaw another war in the offing. I suspect it's closer than you think."

"Let us get it over with, then. I believe all the principals concerned are in the chapiteau right now."

Florian and Edge went in, and found Beck and his roustabouts hanging and testing the security of several aerial rigs at once. Maurice and Paprika were closely eyeing the men arranging their trapeze apparatus up near the roof peak, and Sunday and Monday Simms were just as closely watching other men tighten the turnbuckles of their rope slanted between peak and ground. In the middle of the pista's sawdust circle, heedless of all the work going on above and around them, Zanni and Fünfünf were demonstrating to little Quincy Simms a nicely carved wooden frame. It was big enough to have contained a grown man's full-length portrait, but it was only an empty and open rectangle.

Florian had to shout, above the noise, to the clowns and the aerialists. They left their several occupations and came over to him. Edge would probably have broached the news with some tergiversation, but Florian said bluntly, "Our show closer, Miss Auburn, is ill and will not appear tomorrow. Misses Sunday and Monday, you will go on as usual, next to closing. Herr Fünfünf, if you and Signor Zanni believe you have sufficiently mastered again the Lupino turn, you will follow the Misses Simms and close the show."

The two clowns said "Ja" and "Si" together.

Maurice essayed only a mild protest. "Surely, Monsieur le Gouverneur, the show should close with a thrill act. Meaning myself and my partner on the trap."

Florian said, "I usually have a reason for my decisions, Monsieur LeVie. Let that suffice."

Maurice shrugged in Gallic resignation, but Paprika flared in Hungarian high temper. "It does not suffice for me, kedvesem! After all our years of kicking sawdust together, you now deny me the close and give it to this . . . this first-of-May? Ó jaj, actually he appears more like first-of-December!" She scathingly looked the newcomer up and down, from his thin gray hair to his shabby attire of civilian suit and shoes. "Do you really expect me to accept second place behind this—this feeble old derelict?"

Before anyone else could speak. Herr Pfeifer quickly knelt, tugged off his heavy shoes and then, without removing any other of his confining clothes or even loosening his cravat, stepped in his stocking feet onto the Simms girls' slanted tightrope. Without balance pole or any other helping prop, he ran surefootedly up the rope to its top, where it was secured near one of the trapeze platforms. He vaulted nimbly onto that platform, unhooked the held-back trapeze bar, swung out on it, did a number of flipovers, knee-hangs and handstands—his incongruous street clothes bunching and coming awry and flapping—then swung back to land lightly on the platform, leapt from there again to the slanted rope and came *cartwheeling* down it. Back on the ground, not even breathing hard, he gave Paprika as haughty a look as she had given him, then sat down on the pista curb to put his shoes on again. Everyone in the chapiteau, from Florian to the least Slovak, was staring at him, stunned and speechless.

Paprika broke the prevailing silence, and she did it graciously. "Verzeiht Sie, Artistenmeister. What I said was inexcusable. I shall be proud to appear anywhere on any program in company with you. I abase myself."

"Never abase yourself, Fräulein," the old fellow said gruffly.

Zanni said, "Jörg also was once an aerialist."

"But then I fell. I broke some bones. And I lost my nerve."

"Ma foi," Maurice said in awe. "I should hate to compete with you whenever you recover it."

"Aber, Herr Fünfünf . . ." Sunday said timidly. "Aber . . . warum werden ein Clown?"

"I did not become a *clown*," he said. "I became a white-face. It is a higher calling even than aerialist. You will see tomorrow."

2

THEY ALL saw a great many new things on the morrow. By noontime, in the tober's front yard, two rows of what Florian had called joints lined the way to the chapiteau. Some of the stalls had bright banners stretched above them to extol their wares, and all had their wares prominently to be seen or smelled: Chinese paper parasols, steaming wurst and kraut, head-and-stick hobbyhorses, fresh-baked hot waffles, tortoise-shell combs, beer straight from the keg, goat's milk straight from the nanny, tin trumpets, layered tortes, decorative little lamps, sugar sticks, toy drums, cuckoo clocks . . .

Beyond the stalls, nearest to the chapiteau's front-door marquee, was Maximus in his cage, staring out with impassive dignity, except when he caught a scent of cooking sausage and wrinkled his nose in wistful sniffs. Across the way from him was Fitzfarris's "disappearance" pedestal, now doing duty as a stand for Spyros Vasilakis. He repeatedly took from a bottle a mouthful of naphtha, then blew it forth in a spray ignited by a burning pine splint in his hand, and so spouted a fountain of flame that made an advertisement for the circus visible all over the Hofgarten. Meanwhile, from inside the pavilion could be heard Kapelmeister Beck's entire band—cornet, trombone, tuba, French horn, accordion, Teufel Geige and snare, tenor and bass drums—rendering, with real Tirolean oom-pah-pah, every one of the circus's themes, from "Greensleeves" to "Bollocky Bill" to "Bal de Vienne."

Next forward of Spyros's stand was the red wagon, with

Magpie Maggie Hag at the guichet up front, waiting for ticket buyers. At the museum at the rear of the wagon were Sir John in his tattoo-concealing makeup and Jörg Pfeifer in street clothes, both of them shouting "Kommt! Hereine!" and such things. The Innsbruckers attracted by the fire eater's billows and seduced by the museum keepers' bellows into buying tickets then got to see Spyros close up and the lion in his cage and the Auerhahn glaring maniacally out through its museum wire netting. In a corner of the museum, and netted over to be safe from the bird's likely depredations, was its "nest" of woven twigs. Whenever a suffcient crowd of jossers had assembled there, Sir John would cease shouting and start expatiating—Pfeifer translating—on the frequent miraculous eggs to be found among those laid by the Auerhahn, and would take out and display one. The eggs now bore the embossed sentiment "Gott und Kaiser." Occasionally a knowledgeable spectator would sarcastically point out that a miracle even greater than the egg tribute to God and Emperor was its having been laid by a *cock* bird. But occasionally, too, a pious or patriotic onlooker would beg hard enough to persuade Sir John—who made sad grimaces of reluctance and sacrifice—to sell him the egg, and would pay a fancy price for it.

"It's a pity you can't be seeing it all," Edge said to Autumn. "The Florilegium is about as splendiferous as the Orfei now."

"Just as well I can't, I suppose," Autumn said wanly from her sickbed. "Even from a distance, the noise doesn't improve my headache. I *would* like to watch that white-face, though."

"That reminds me," said Edge, elaborately offhand. "Can I borrow your wall mirror? Fünfünf and Zanni are going to do something called the Lupino mirror, which means a fake one of some sort. But to lead into the act they need a real one."

Autumn gestured consent, with one hand, and Edge took the mirror off its hook. Autumn continued to move the hand, clenching and unclenching it, flexing the fingers. She murmured, "It's gone feeble again. What could be the connection between an aching head and a weak hand?"

"Don't worry about it. Maggie will soon have you hale and hearty and bonny again."

Autumn said, with a rueful laugh, "Gorblimey, I think she's making me drink that tincture she had Boom-Boom smearing on his head."

The Florilegium drew only a medium attendance that afternoon, not a scanty bianca, but not a sfondone crowd either. However, at intermission Florian said philosophically, "Well, at least we're making our nut," because the audience that spilled out onto the midway began indulgently spending money. They bought every sort of thing from Sir John's voice-projecting swazzles and the Auerhahn's eggs to the carte-de-visite of the White African Pygmies, and they kept Magpie Maggie Hag profitably occupied at palm reading and dream dukkering. The people also patronized the midway joints, eating and drinking, buying slum mementos of the occasion. During the sideshow, Sir John, with Florian interpreting where necessary, first showed off his own freakish face, then his old-standby freaks of Night Children, Pygmies, the Egyptian mummy, Little Miss Mitten, and in dramatic conclusion brought on his new pièces de résistance.

"The Gluttonous Greek!" he introduced Spyros, who bounded onto the platform clad in doomfully black fleshings. Inside the chapiteau, Beck took the signal to have his band crash into Wagner's "Magic Fire Music." Sir John went on, "This is a man who will eat anything, Herren und Damen, things that would kill you and me—including blazing fire and razor-sharp steel!"

Spyros took a gulp from what looked like a bottle of water, but was really olive oil to lubricate his innards. Then he unrolled a bundle of chamois skin to reveal a dagger, a short sword and a real cavalry sabre, all brilliantly nickel-plated. He hurled them, one by one, point first into the wooden platform to show that they were not bogus or telescoping blades. He retrieved the dagger first, wrenched it out of the wood, wiped it thoroughly with the chamois skin, threw his head back, opened his mouth and let the dagger slide down inside, to the hilt. Next he did the same, more slowly, with the short sword. Next he did the same with the long sabre, but with grimaces, grunts and eye rollings to proclaim the superhuman difficulty of getting it all the way down his gullet. Sir John had learned from Spyros that there truly was no trickery to this, except for one small and unnoticeable deception: the cavalry sabre's blade had been shortened from its standard length of thirty inches to twenty-six, which Spyros had long ago determined, by experiment, was the distance from his lips to the pit of his stomach.

"And now," announced Sir John, echoed by Florian, "der gefrässig Grieche will do the impossible! He will swallow all three blades at one gulp. Watch closely. You will actually see his Adamsapfel bulge and wriggle as the steel is forced past it." The Greek's Adam's apple did exactly that, and several women in the crowd had to be led away by their escorts. When Spyros extracted his armory, piece by piece, he again carefully wiped all the blades, and Sir John explained, "The Gluttonous Greek must cleanse the steel beforehand, because even a speck of dust could make him retch, and that would make the razor edge slice into his esophagus. He also wipes them afterward, but for the *swords'* protection. Because of the Greek's unorthodox diet, his stomach acids have become so powerful that they could corrode even Essen steel."

Now Spyros took a swig from a bottle of goat's milk, partly to wash down the olive oil, which could have caught fire, and partly just to moisten the lining of his mouth. Then he lit oil-soaked wads of cotton wool on short rods, stuck one in his mouth, closed his lips, brought out the wad extinguished and smoking, stuck another lighted one in his mouth, stuck in the extinguished one and lit it from the other in there. After several repetitions of and variations on the burning wads, he did what he had been doing previously—the less uncomfortable but more spectacular feat of taking a mouthful of naphtha, spewing it out and lighting it as it sprayed, so the great mushroom of fire went *whoompf!* over the heads of the people, making them cringe and duck and turn away from the undeniable furnace heat of the flames.

When they returned their attention to the platform, Spyros was gone and Meli stood there. She wore fleshings that were entirely covered with silvery spangles, like scales, making her a most fetching, curvaceous, sinuous serpent-woman. She wore her dark hair in two long braids, and there were two large, covered wicker baskets at her feet.

"Meli the Medusa!" shouted Sir John. "The only woman in the history of the world, since our Mother Eve, so beautiful and tempting that snakes come to her of their own accord. Venomous snakes, crushing snakes, no matter. She so charms them that they never do her harm. Or"—he paused impressively—"they have not *yet*." From inside the chapiteau came the single sound of the cornet, doing a tweedly, Oriental-sounding rendition of Rameau's "Zéphire." Sir John and Florian continued, "Notice, Herren und Damen, the prettily patterned but clearly vicious reptiles Meli the Medusa is now taking from one basket. The country dwellers among you will recognize them as specimens of the adder, the deadliest snake found in Europe."

They were not. If Meli had not earlier confided the truth to Sir John and Florian, they would probably not have been on the same platform with her and her pets at this moment. The snakes indeed were, to the lay observer, well-nigh indistinguishable from the venomous European adder, but in fact they were the harmless smooth snakes of Britain. Meli now had half a dozen of them twining about her arms and shoulders and throat, while she herself did an undulating, serpentine, suggestive dance to the tweedling cornet music. Finally the snakes found her two long braids of hair, slithered up along them, and the dance ended with Meli's head crowned, like Medusa's, with a coiffure of snakes intertwining and coiling about each other.

They were not *trained* to do that, she had explained, but did it naturally. They were arboreal snakes, always seeking to climb upward. The twining they did around her arms and neck during the dance was accomplished by her *preventing* their climbing, and, when she ceased to frustrate them, they simply slithered up to her highest point, the top of her head.

Now she reached up and disentangled them, returned them gently to their basket and covered it. From the other basket she lifted a different snake—or, rather, lifted the fore end of it, for it was a rock python eleven or twelve feet long, and heavy, and at midbody as big around as a man's thigh.

So Meli merely dragged out its foremost part and let it curl around one of her legs, and slide the rest of its length from the basket, and up around her—while she went again into her undulating, erotic dance. Part of the dance's eroticism was supplied by the python itself. In its climbing of Meli's body, it brought its big head and phallic length up from between her legs, before coiling around her hips and continuing on up her. Meli's dance necessarily got even slower when she was bearing the python's full weight. When she ceased to dance and threw up her arms in the V-posture and the audience broke into applause, Meli was wearing most of the snake as a massive belt around her middle, its fore length extending up her back so its head looked over her shoulder—the eyes coldly unwinking, the forked tongue flickering in and out. The chief secret about letting a python get you in its clench, she had explained to Florian and Sir John, was to make sure that most of it wound around your belly; any constrictor snake was not so likely to start squeezing in earnest when it was gripping soft flesh as when it was coiled around a bony part like the rib cage.

While Meli let her python pour itself back into its basket, Sir John produced his wooden apparatus and a field mouse and bellowed an invitation for all and sundry to rally around and join in his "Mauserennen." Florian let that game and Magpie Maggie Hag's divinations go on until some of the people not partaking began to look restless. Then he sent word to Beck to strike up the band again, and the crowd hurried back inside the chapiteau.

The second half of the program went well, and Pavlo Smodlaka this time did not prolong his slanging-buffers act—although this audience, too, seemed greatly to enjoy the talented terriers and to applaud them extravagantly. In fact, Pavlo hurried the act along and kept furtively scanning the stands for possible lurking spies. Several times he was so distracted that Gavrila or one of the children would have to give the dogs their next signal. And when the act finished, in record time, Pavlo allowed himself and his family only the briefest of bows before hurrying with them out of the tent.

Finally, when Sunday and Monday were taking the applause for their rope work, Zanni skipped into the pista, bringing with him this time Fünfünf, and Edge got his first look at what Florian said was "one of the oldest, most esteemed, ever-changeless characters of European circusdom." Zanni was attired, as he had been all during the show, in his Harlequin outfit, with just enough makeup to give his face its range of expressions from glee to mischievousness to despair. But Fünfünf was a complete transformation from the man Jörg Pfeifer—or from any mortal being, thought Edge.

He wore a one-piece, loose costume of bright red satin, lavishly adorned with silver sequins. It had tight, wrist-length sleeves that rose in high peaks at his shoulders. From those peaks, the dress hung as straight and waistless as a smock, until it forked into a pair of short, broad pants ending just above his bare knees. The costume did make his torso look almost perfectly square, as the name Fünfünf implied. Below it, he wore white slippers and calf-high white stockings. Above it, his entire face was white with greasepaint, and on that dead-white skin his eyebrows and lashes were blacked, his mouth rouged bright red and both his ears painted bright red as well. He wore a brimless, conical white hat which, blending into the white of his forehead, would have made him rather resemble a bald pinhead, except that the cap was jauntily tilted just a bit to one side.

The white, black and red makeup was both droll and demonic; Fünfünf could have been of any age, or ageless. Throughout the act, when his face was not comically-evilly impassive, it showed only two other expressions: eyebrows raised in disdainful hauteur or red mouth grinning sardonically wide. The bizarre makeup and dress, unvaried through generations of white-faces, seemed—even to Edge—imbued with the tyrannical authority of antiquity. So did Fünfünf's superior and domineering manner, as he ordered Zanni about, and derided him, and humiliated him, and made him grovel—and made the spectators roar with laughter. Like them, Edge had to laugh at the white-face, but he laughed with some unease, and he suspected that those others did the same. Though he had never seen a white-face before, he felt that the seriocomic figure was somehow eerily familiar—like a recognizable memory from childhood of that funny-frightening goblin or spook or bogeyman never encountered but always lurking to "get you if you don't behave."

Edge could understand only an infrequent word of the German the two joeys spoke, but the give-and-take could be inferred from the action—as now, when Fünfünf blindfolded Zanni and gave him instructions to walk, stop, turn left or right in response to whistled commands. With a tiny whistle, the white-face began to blow various numbers of tweets, and Zanni obeyed—only to have the malicious Fünfünf send him walking into a center pole, from which he ricocheted flat on his back (*boom!* from the bass drum). The white-face next sent him across the pista, to trip over the curbing and fall flat on his face (*r-r-rip!* from the snare drum). When Zanni got up, he scratched his head and ponderously cogitated, then smiled slyly. Meanwhile, Fünfünf had beckoned to little Ali Baba, who ran in with a bucket of water to set in the ring. Now, when the white-face whistled, Zanni looked smug and clever and obeyed the commands in reverse, turning left when directed to the right, and so on—and of course stepped into the pail with a splash (*cr-rash!* from the cymbal).

While the audience roared, Zanni angrily tore off his blindfold and, with the bucket wedged on one foot, stumped over to Fünfünf and kicked the bucket at him. But it remained stuck on his foot, so Zanni was flung on his back again (*boom!*) with that foot in the air, the pail upside down and emptying the rest of its water on him (*cr-rash!*). Fünfünf sent Ali Baba trotting off, then helped Zanni to his feet, pretended solicitude, dusted him off and—when Ali Baba ran in again, bringing Autumn's wall mirror—held that up for Zanni to resettle his little hat, pat his wet hair straight, smooth his eyebrows. Then Zanni bent closer to the mirror, shut his eyes and just stood there.

"Was gibt's?" asked the white-face. Zanni replied, with gestures—so that even Edge could comprehend—that he wanted to see what he looked like when he was asleep.

"*Kretin!*" snarled Fünfünf. He whipped off his own hat and beat Zanni over the head with it. When the white-face put his hat back on, he was dissatisfied with its placement, and bade Zanni hold the mirror for him. Fünfünf looked into it, bent and stooped this way and that, made it plain that he was dissatisfied with the mirror, and demanded a bigger one. Zanni and Ali Baba obediently scampered from the pista and through the back door.

After a moment, there came a loud smash and tinkle of glass out there. (Goesle had provided a scrap piece for the effect.) The audience began laughing in anticipation of Fünfünf's rage at the mirror's having got broken, but he appeared not to have heard. He merely waited in the pista, still finically adjusting his hat, striking attitudes, humming to himself. Then Ali Baba, looking terrified, crept into the pavilion again, lugging that big empty, rectangular wooden frame. Crouching on the far side of Ali Baba, hiding, Zanni also came creeping and looking terrified. The white-face noticed nothing until Ali Baba got near him, set the frame upright on the sawdust and stood to one side to hold it there.

"Ah!" said Fünfünf, and stepped in front of the "mirror." At the same instant, Zanni stood up on the other side of the frame.

"Eh?" said Fünfünf, raising his eyebrows and taking a startled step backward. At exactly the same time, Zanni opened his mouth, raised his eyebrows and took a step backward.

Fünfünf shook his head as if to clear it—so did Zanni—stepped forward again—so did Zanni—and bent to scrutinise his reflection—Zanni did the same. Fünfünf/Zanni slowly, very slowly raised a hand, adjusted his/his hat a millimeter to the left/right—then abruptly dropped his/his hand again. Already the jossers were falling about and nearly strangling with laughter, and so were most of the troupers looking on. The mirror effect was appreciable and enjoyable, whatever side of the pista it was viewed from. Since both clowns moved in such perfect synchrony, and both were visible to everybody, it was the viewer's choice: which was the real, which the reflection, which imitating which? After a good deal of this, Fünfünf totally turned his back on the mirror. So did Zanni. There could not possibly have been a signal between them, but, when the white-face slowly, furtively turned his head to look at the mirror over his shoulder, there was Zanni looking just as suspiciously back at him.

Fünfünf's movements and dodges got more and more convulsive and complex—interrupted by sudden freezes of position—but every one of them was faultlessly imitated by Zanni. At last, when the clowns evidently decided that to make the crowd laugh any more was to risk the people's having mass apoplexy—and when even Ali Baba was laughing so hard that the mirror was shaking—they somehow mutually agreed to end the show. Fünfünf suddenly sprang clear to the right of the frame, Zanni sprang to his left, and they were face to face with no pretended glass between. Infuriated, the white-face again began beating Zanni with his hat, but that was not enough; he snatched the frame from Ali Baba and brought it down over Zanni's head, astonishing the whole audience and troupe with the sound of real glass violently smashing. (One of the bandstand Slovaks provided that with another piece of scrap.) Zanni acted as if a genuine mirror had been broken over his head: he reeled and collapsed across the frame. Since the white-face was dragging that as he ran from the pista, he dragged the limp Zanni behind him, flopping and flailing, out of the chapiteau.

The two had to come back again and again to take bows to the people, who were wildly clapping hands and stamping feet, even while they continued to laugh and spill tears down their cheeks. At every other reentry, Fünfünf and Zanni brought Ali Baba with them to share the acclaim.

"Pure magic!" Edge shouted to Florian beside him. "The Lupino it's named for, was he an Italian like Zanni?"

"No. George Lupino. Englishman," Florian shouted back. "Quick, now. Call the closing spec while the crowd is still on the crest."

Edge's whistle shrilled over the noise, and the noise was

immediately increased by the band's thundering into "Gott Erhalte Unseren Kaiser." Edge took his part in the promenade, riding Thunder and, with his sabre, saluting the audience. But, the moment it was over, he flung his reins to a roustabout and hurried to the caravan to see how Autumn was.

She was fine, she said, feeling much better. In fact, she was out of bed and dressed, and pottering about the van's interior, doing little tidying-up chores. "You were right, Zachary. The bit of rest was all I needed." She came and kissed him. "You're a competent physician. The weakness is all gone, and the headache all but."

"Now, let's not hurry things," he cautioned. "That's a sure way to bring on a relapse."

"No, honestly, darling. I think I could be up on the rope for tonight's show. Certainly by tomorrow."

"Well, let's just try you," he said, with a sigh. This would be cruel, but it had to be done. "Come outside, dear."

He led her out of the van and around to the side of it. There he took down the rope slung for their wash and laid it in a straight line on the ground. "All right, walk that."

"Really, Zachary, this is an insult. A rope not an inch aloft?"

"Humor me, dear one. It's only a test."

She made a face of good-natured toleration and stepped onto one end of the rope, and started along it, and wobbled and was off it. "Oops. You see how the least layoff gets one out of practice?" She went back to the rope end, started along it again, squinting narrowly at it, and staggered and was off it again. She looked up at Edge, with an expression of bewilderment and chagrin. "Oh, Zachary, what can be the matter with me? I see *two* ropes . . . I can't focus . . . they blur back and forth . . ."

"We'll try again when your headache is entirely gone," he said gently, as he coiled the rope. "Now, will you humor me some more and get back to bed? I'll go and consult with my colleague, Dr. Hag. If she can't come up with some concoction to cure that headache once and for all . . . well . . . I think we ought to take you to a real, honest-to-God physician."

"Zachary, I have never had to go to a doctor in all my life." But she let him assist her, as if she were a fragile and ancient lady, up the steps and into the van. "I've always been as healthy as a horse."

"Then I'll be sure to find a horse doctor," he said, hoping to make her laugh. And she did, but it was not her old laugh.

Of the crowd that had emptied from the chapiteau out into the front yard of the tober, most of the males had made directly for the annex tent where Sir John bawled invitation to his "biblischer Bilder." But one of the men who did not, a very young man, came to where Florian was in conversation with his bandmaster. He said, "Bitte, Herr Florian" and introduced himself as Heinrich Mehrmann.

"From your speech," said Beck, also in German, "I take you to be from the north. Hamburg, perhaps?"

"Hamburg exactly. I am assistant to the Herren Hagenbeck."

"Du meine Güte!" Florian exclaimed. "It has been years since I have seen the family, or heard word of them. How is my old friend?"

"He is well, Herr Florian. I have often heard the elder Herr Hagenbeck speak of you. So, when I saw your train arrive here, I telegraphed to him. He sends his regards and best wishes for the success of your tour."

"Why, that was thoughtful of you, Herr Mehrmann. Are you traveling on business for him?"

"I was," the young man said rather dolefully. "The city fathers of Innsbruck had decided they wanted to have a zoölogical garden here, and they asked the advice of Herr Hagenbeck, because his Hamburg Zoo is so famous. He sent here his son Carl to help with the design and planning, and to recommend animals to start the stocking of it."

Florian turned to Beck to say, "In case you do not know, the Hagenbecks, senior and junior, do not believe in caging animals. In the zoos they design, they have areas separated by moats and fences from each other and from the viewing public. And in those areas, they recreate the animals' natural habitats, insofar as possible, where they can live untrammeled.''

"Anyway, everything seemed settled," said young Mehrmann. "And I have brought all the way from our Hamburg park and stables the exotics selected. But now, because of the verdammt war, Innsbruck has decided that this is no time to spend city funds on nonessentials."

"I can see their point," said Florian. "But I am sorry for you."

Mehrmann quickly asked, "Are you sorry enough, Herr Florian, to buy the animals yourself?"

"*Eh*? Why, lad, the war has pinched me, too. Of course I am desirous of adding to our menagerie. You saw what a scant few animals we have. But you also saw the empty seats in the chapiteau. Like the Innsbruck city fathers, I feel this may be a time of prudence and conservatism."

"But . . . if you acquired these exotics at a most bargain price, Herr Florian? In his telegram to me, Herr Hagenbeck der Älter himself suggested it. He knows you personally, he knows what it costs to bring the animals here, he knows it will cost more yet to take them home again, so he suggests it is best for all concerned to offer them to you—at any reasonable price you can pay."

"Well!" said Florian. "Well . . . this *is* a most tempting offer. But, my dear fellow, it involves more than just my purchasing the animals. I should have to hire extra keepers, buy cage wagons, horses to draw them . . ."

"I am empowered to sell you also the cage wagons and the very good horses which transported the exotics here," said Mehrmann. "Again at a bargain. And they came driven by their Slovak keepers, who are paid trifling Slovak wages, and I am instructed to give you leave to hire them away from us."

"Du meine Güte," Florian said again, this time in a marveling murmur. "Your offer is unbelievably generous, young Herr, and well-nigh irresistible . . ."

"Nevertheless, Herr Gouverneur," said Beck, with Bavarian practicality, "it must be pointed out that, as soon as you own the animals, this bargain ceases to be a bargain. Every week from then on, the additional wages must be paid. The animals should probably have a tent of their own. The meat markets and feed dealers, now and in perpetuity, will ask no bargain prices for their commodities.''

Mehrmann said, ''What more can I offer than everything in my keeping? Some things are beyond my capacity.''

''Of course, of course, my boy,'' said Florian. ''We are merely trying to make plain our own situation. But at least I could look at what you have—and *wish* I had them. Where are they?''

''Across the river, in the Mariahilf district. The Innsbruck councilmen, embarrassed at having caused so much bother, have made a small gesture of atonement by letting me use some city-owned stables over there.''

''Very well, I should like some others of the company to see them, too. Will you wait here, lad, while I round them up?''

Beck remarked, in English, as he walked away with Florian, ''Impoverished we are not. As you said at intermission, we are here our nuts employing—''

''I said *making our nut*, Boom-Boom. Circus jargon for earning at least our daily expenses.''

''Ja. And before, in Italy, we were prospering. Natürlich, for the bargaining effect, we can cry poor. But I hope you will not too cruelly of such a Jüngling take advantage.''

''I have known and traded with and respected Hagenbeck der Älter since before his son was born—the son who is now taking over the family business. I would not dream of mulcting any of them. But first let us determine if they have anything we want.''

In the circus's backyard, they found the company cleaning up and relaxing after the show. Magpie Maggie Hag was stitching a tear in somebody's costume. Pavlo Smodlaka was using a heated curling iron on his blond beard and tying up strands of it in his wife's curl papers. Meli Vasilakis was stirring her smaller snakes about in a tub of tepid water, taking them out one at time, carefully drying each one and then anointing it with warm olive oil. Jules Rouleau was holding

Autumn's mirror for Jörg Pfeifer, who was using lard to wipe off his makeup.

Abner Mullenax, watching that process, asked, "Jules, what is that greasepaint made of, anyhow?"

"Call it muck, ami," said Rouleau. "The joeys all do. The white is made by mixing melted lard with oxide of zinc and tincture of benzoin."

"And hard on the skin it is," grumbled the white-face. "I am glad I finally got old enough to deserve this wrinkled face of mine, but I have had it ever since I first started wearing the muck."

"At least hair you have," Carl Beck said wistfully. "Hair makes one not so old look."

"Oh, Zachary," said Florian, as Edge joined the group. "As soon as Fünfünf is finished here with Autumn's mirror, you can return it to her. We're going to town, so we can buy another to use as the prop."

Magpie Maggie Hag looked up from her sewing, and she and Edge exchanged a glance. He said, "Let the fellows use it as long as they want. I'll—I'll buy a really good one for Autumn . . . when she's up and about again."

"As you like. Anyway, can you leave your lady long enough to accompany us? Boom-Boom and I are off to inspect some exotics that are for sale. Barnacle Bill, I'll want you to come, of course, and—"

"What the hell are exotics?" Mullenax asked.

"Barnacle," Florian said patiently, "your lion Maximus is one. Exotics are show animals that are not native—like that Auerhahn—not familiar to the jossers. Abdullah, you come along, too. And Canvasmaster, will you also? We may have new tent making to discuss."

Florian took young Mehrmann beside him on the rockaway, to direct him. Edge, Beck, Mullenax and Goesle rode in one of the empty canvas wagons, and Hannibal drove. When they had crossed the bridge over the Inn, they proceeded through suburbs that got increasingly rural, and came eventually to a field containing stables, barns and fenced enclosures. Two exceedingly un-Austrian creatures came to one of the fences to peer over at them: a Bactrian camel and an

Indian elephant that could have been the twin to Peggy, except that this one had vestgial tusks. But when Edge saw what was in one of the other stockades, he breathed, "Godamighty!" At the same time, on the rockaway, Florian said to Mehrman, "Mein Gott, are those your draft horses, Heinrich? Why, even *they* are splendid enough to rank as exotics."

"Ja, thoroughbred friesisches Vieh. You begin to comprehend the bargain I offer, Herr Florian? For the price of ordinary draft nags, show-quality horses."

They were, indeed. The seven horses were as big as Obie Yount's Percheron, but not so bulky and much more graceful. They were shiny black all over, but the most striking thing about them was the natural waviness of their long manes and ground-sweeping tails, and the little wavy plumes of hair on their fetlocks, like wings on their feet. As soon as Edge got down from the wagon, he went among the Friesians, admiring and caressing and talking to them, and he almost had to be dragged away to see the other animals that the elegant black horses had hauled here.

Young Mehrmann waved toward the two animals peering at the visitors, and said, "Elefant, Trampeltier." Then he led them through a barn where his cage wagons had been lodged under cover. The cages were all much more commodious than the American-standard four by ten feet that Maximus lived and performed in. Mehrmann pointed and identified their occupants, "Tiger und zwei Tigerinen bengalisches," he said at the cage containing those cats, a male and two females, all in prime pelt and alert of eye. "Bär und Bärin syrisch," he said at the cage containing two good-sized bears of unusual color: brown flecked with silver.

"Syrian bears," Florian told the others. "The breed most amenable to training." He asked Mehrmann a question, and translated the reply. "They are three years old. Which means we'd get five or six good years of use out of them before—as is quite common with bears—they go blind, and get difficult to work with."

"Zwei Hyänen," said Mehrmann at the cage containing two specimens as handsome as hyenas could ever be, meaning ugly and scruffy.

"I've heard about them critters," said Mullenax. "How come they ain't laughin'?"

"It's only the spotted hyena that laughs, Barnacle Bill. These are the striped variety. Be glad. If we acquired the spotted ones, none of us would ever get another night's sleep."

At the next cage, Mehrmann said, "Zwei Zebras und ein Zwergpferd sudamerikanische." The one that was not a zebra was clearly an equine, dun-colored, but not much bigger than a large dog.

"Heinrich says it is a dwarf horse from South America," said Florian. "Colonel Ramrod, are you familiar with any such thing?"

"No. But I'd bet the joeys could do a lot with him in their act."

"Schimpansen," said Mehrmann at a cage that was pretty well filled with part of a tree, and the tree was hung with five or six chimpanzees, all of which began shrieking and gibbering at the visitors. "Zwei Strausse," said Mehrmann at the next cage. It had no solid roof, only bars across its top, so the two seven-foot ostriches could stand comfortably erect with their heads poking through.

The next cage was only half floored, the other half of it being a tank slung below the wagon's axles, full of water into and out of which four sleek creatures were frolicing. "Seelöwen," said Mehrmann, but Florian said rather scornfully, "Water dogs," and Edge said, "Me, I'd call them seals."

"Sea lions, to be accurate," said Florian. "Water dogs in circus parlance. Just as a camel is a hump, a zebra a convict, a hyena is a zeke, apes are the jockos. I can't remember all the other nicknames for other animals. Well, gentlemen, have you any comments you wish me to translate to Herr Mehrmann?"

"Oh, Sahib!" Hannibal said eagerly, and with his best Hindu servility. "Peg—I mean Brutus—she be powerful glad to have 'nother bull for company. Me too, Sahib."

Mullenax asked apprehensively, "Governor, was you plannin' on just exhibitin' these critters? Or—Jesus!—am I supposed to *tame* them bears and tigers?"

Florian said to Mehrmann, in German, "I did notice that your tom tiger has that bristly, lionlike mane that often betokens a bad cat."

Mehrmann shook his head. "He and his sisters are good ones. Already accustomed to persons entering their cage, soon ready to learn tricks. I would not deceive you, Herr Florian. These are Bengal cats, not the stupid and untrustworthy Siberians. Also they were captured in the wild, and so have a healthy respect for men—not domestically bred, hence contemptuous of their masters."

"Very well, the tigers would be acceptable. My bull man would be thrilled to have the elephant, and my equestrian director, as you noticed, is enamored of these Friesian horses. I personally do not adore a camel. I don't mind it spitting on its Slovak keepers, but it often causes complaint when it spits on paying customers. Nevertheless, it has the advantage of being able to travel on its own feet, and it looks good on parade."

Mehrmann had taken out a notebook and was listing the items mentioned. "Katze, Elefant, friesische Pferde, Trampeltier . . ."

"However, I definitely do not want the sea lions," said Florian. "It is too often difficult to find fish for feeding them, when on the road. Also their fishy smell permeates the entire train—everything from canvas to costumes—and is impossible to eradicate."

"Scheisse," muttered the young man. "I have to drag that tank wagon all the way back to Hamburg?"

"And the wagon full of chimpanzees," said Florian.

"But, Herr Gouverneur, what is a menagerie without jockos? All circus patrons *love* to watch their antics."

"True enough, lad, but I'm damned if I know why. When the beasts are not plucking nastily at each other's hides, they are playing obscenely with their own privates. Why a chimp is supposed to be intrinsically funny, cute and lovable is a mystery to me. But I once saw a small girl hand a peanut into a chimp cage—and have all her fingers bitten off. The way an ape's teeth are interattached in the jawbone, it is impossible to remove the dangerous eyeteeth without taking out all the others, and then the brute starves to death. No, I will not have any."

Mehrmann muttered some more, about being stuck with the two wagons most troublesome to deal with, but then said philosophically, "Well, it could been worse. On my next trip, I was supposed to be bringing here a rhino, a hippo, giraffes . . ."

"Maybe you can still interest the Innsbruck elders in your jockos and water dogs—if the price is right—as a nucleus for their zoo, whenever they do get around to building it. In the meantime, Heinrich, will you calculate your lowest possible price for all those other creatures, and their five wagons, and five of the Friesians to draw them, and the number of your Slovaks we'll be needing as keepers. My colleagues and I will be discussing the pros and contras of buying a menagerie in these precarious times, and what we can afford to pay for it if we do. Come to the tober tomorrow, and we will talk again."

3

FLORIAN ASKED Edge to ride with him on the way back. And, after some inconsequential remarks about the menagerie prospects, Florian said guardedly, "I dislike to pry, Zachary, but I and the whole troupe miss your lady Autumn. I don't mean as part of the program, I mean the much-loved girl herself. Is there anything any of us can do? Can you tell me what is ailing her?"

"I wish to Christ I knew," Edge said dully. "I only know what it's doing to her. And she's just beginning to realize—to admit to herself that it's no small affliction." He described the ropewalking test she had tried and failed.

"Well, loss of balance, loss of focus," said Florian, "even a light touch of la grippe can sometimes cause that."

"It's something a damned sight worse than the grippe. Florian, will you keep it to yourself if I tell you? Mag is the only other one who knows. Not even Autumn knows yet just *how* bad this is."

"Of course I will. But what could possibly be so—?"

"It's her eyes. Autumn's eyes. I don't know how to say this. It sounds ridiculous. But it's a fact, and it's terrible. Her eyes are . . . they're shifting."

"Shifting?" Florian puzzled over this for a moment. "Is that why you're not eager for her to have her mirror back? Do you mean her eyes are rolling wildly about?"

"No. They've gone out of alignment. Mag noticed it first. But now I can see it, too, and it's more obvious every time I look at her."

Florian meditated again, then said, "Zachary, I am not trying to make light of this. But you describe the girl as if she has gone cockeyed. Can you be more specific?"

"Yes, I can, goddamn it," Edge said fiercely, wretchedly. "One of her eyes has moved *lower on her face* than the other one. That's why she couldn't focus on the rope. That's why I took away the mirror. I can't let her see what she looks like. Her whole head has somehow begun to change shape. To get lopsided. I reckon that accounts for her persistent headache, but what accounts for the—for the disfigurement, I just don't know. I realize it sounds crazy and impossible, but *that is what is happening*."

"Sweet Jesus," said Florian. "That gorgeous girl. Zachary, I can't tell you how desolate I . . . but look here, man. This is clearly beyond Maggie's witcheries. We must get Autumn to a professional doctor."

"I figured to take her tomorrow morning. I was going to ask if you'd help. To find a good one, and then do the talking for us. And, please God, tell him beforehand not to look horrified, not to let Autumn suspect that she is . . . that she's changing from being beautiful."

"Yonder is the shop of an Apotheker," said Florian, for they were back in the middle of town by now. "Wave the other wagon to go on. We'll stop here and I will inquire about the local physicians and their specialities and their reputations. We shall want only the best."

Edge waited on the rockaway while Florian went in. He was gone for some time, and returned to say, "The apothecary recommends a Herr Doktor Köhn. Not far from here.

Let us go and make sure he can see us tomorrow."

Again Edge waited, nervously twiddling Snowball's reins, outside a very ancient-looking, half-timbered house. Florian was absent for an even longer while, but finally emerged, looking rather more cheerful than when he had gone inside.

"We have an appointment for ten tomorrow. I was fortunate enough to have a word with the Herr Doktor himself, not just a servant. He looks about as old as his house here— old enough to be experienced and wise, I judge."

"Did you warn him—?"

"Yes, yes. I told him exactly what you've told me. I don't know if he believed it. I don't know if *I* believe it yet. But he did hazard one optimistic guess. A mild apoplectic attack, he said, certainly will cause a lingering headache and may produce a partial paralysis of the face, but that can be merely temporary."

"Well, I'll hope so," said Edge, not sounding very hopeful.

When they arrived at the Hofgarten, Beck already had his band tuning up, and the outdoor torches were being lighted, and the joints on the midway were setting out their replenished stock, and the snack butchers were firing up their braziers and grills. At a Weissbier stand, Fitzfarris was drinking a seidl of the pale lager with a lemon slice floating in it, while he gallantly and laboriously tried to flirt with the barmaid. That very pretty girl, even prettier for being dressed in the summery freshness of a pink-and-white dirndl, pink stockings and shoes, was laughing at Fitz's inept attempt at German endearments, but looking pleased with them, nonetheless. At a little distance, Monday Simms was watching that byplay and looking sulphurous. When Florian came along the midway, she intercepted him.

"Governor, me 'n' Sunday wants a word with you."

"Certainly, my child. But can we make it a quick one? It is almost show time."

Monday beckoned Sunday from somewhere and went on, "We does like travelin' with you-all, and learnin' trades, and earnin' money of our own. But we thinks we *earns* it—and we tired of bein' treated like nigger trash."

Florian looked astounded by her vehemence, but, before
he could speak, Sunday said, "Excuse her, Governor. Monday has learned pretty good manners, but she sort of mislays
them when she gets excited. What she means to say—"

"I know what I means to say, sister! We done noticed that
these Europe people see us like foreigners. But so do they
see them Chinamen—even Clover Lee—even you, sir. They
see *foreigners*—not black or yeller or white foreigners."

"That is undeniably true," said Florian. "So, if all of us
foreigners are equally regarded by the natives, how have you
been slighted?"

"By *you-all*. 'Specially that—that high 'n' mighty Sir
John." At Fitzfarris and the barmaid she shot a look that
should have set their hair aflame.

"Ah," said Florian, trying not to show amusement. "Une
fille jalouse."

"Oui," said Sunday. "Still, she is right, you know, Governor. Sometimes we're Hottentots, and all the time we're
African Pygmies, which is degrading enough. But Sir John
has us doing that rawhide show, which is becoming unen-
durable. The men who pay to see it *sweat* at us and *pant* at
us, and the Slovak playing Lot is forever *feeling* us."

"We tries hard t' be better'n trash," said Monday. "We
does the slant-climb, and I does the school horse act and
Sunday does her acrobaticals and she's practicing good on
the trap, and I done axed Mr. Pfeifer if he'll teach me *real*
ropewalking, and he said yes, and—"

"Whoa. Aspetta. Halte-là," said Florian, raising his hand
in surrender. "You are absolutely right, I concede it, and I
apologize for my thoughtlessness in letting you be exploited
for so long. You are no longer orphan lambs, but estimable
young ladies, and you deserve to be treated with more dignity. I will lay down the law to Sir John. No more sideshow
for you, no more rawhide show. Would that appease you,
mam'selles, and would you accept my contrition?"

They said that it would and that they did. They went off
hand in hand, holding their pretty heads high—though Monday turned hers once, a to flash a look of black lightning back
at Fitzfarris and his pink-and-white charmer. Florian was just

then interrupting their tête-à-tête, to lay down the law to Sir John.

And that night, after the show, Florian, Fitz and most of the other chiefs of the Florilegium held council as to its immediate future. All the troupers except Edge and Autumn, who ate supper in their caravan, were taken by Florian to the five-hundred-year-old Hotel Goldener Adler. In an elegant dining room, they feasted on salmon-trout, pheasant, Knödeln dumplings, Inntaler wines and, for the sweet, a dish called Schmarrn. "The word means balderdash or swill," said Florian, "but order it anyway." And it turned out to be delicate crêpes scrambled together with whortleberries. When the others of the company had departed, sated and happy, Florian, Fitzfarris, Beck, Goesle and Mullenax sat on, over coffee and liqueurs.

"I'll repeat, Sir John," said Florian. "I am sorry that I yanked Sunday and Monday away from you so abruptly. But it was a move too long overdue."

"No great hardship," said Fitz. "The sideshow is still ample, and the Bible study group tonight seemed satisfied just to see David and Bathsheba. But I suppose Clover Lee will resign, too. I think she *likes* making the jossers' tongues hang out, but I doubt that she'll go on doing an act that two mulatto girls consider beneath their dignity."

"Quite so," said Florian. "And I have a suggestion. From now on, Sir John, suppose you confine the whole sideshow inside the annex top, and we'll make it an extra-ticket entry at intermission. More than that. After you've displayed the Tattooed Man, the Night Children, the Mummy, your Miss Mitten and the Gluttonous Greek, make Madame Vasilakis the blow-off, accessible only to adult males, for another extra fee."

"Have Meli do a biblical tableau? Eve and the serpent, maybe?"

"I'll leave that to you and her. And your fertility of invention. I will only remark that the sight of a toothsome female fondling a snake ... well, it excites certain other imaginings in the mind of even a spectator as elderly and jaded as myself."

All the other men around the table smiled and nodded. Fitzfarris looked thoughtful and said, "Um . . . yes. You don't think Spyros might object to his wife—er—performing for a private audience?"

"I doubt it. He is a Greek."

It was Stitches Goesle who raised a minor objection. "One thing, just. Since the war news, Governor, we have shown to houses only two-thirds of capacity. Yet you are planning now to charge *extra* for the sideshow that was formerly gratis?"

"It seems sensible to me, Dai," said Florian. "The fewer the patrons, the more we ought to get out of them, as long as they're on the tober. But I am not being avaricious. They'll soon be getting more for their money, even if they only pay to see the main show in the chapiteau. Unless young Herr Mehrmann proves impossible to bargain with—and he won't—I expect to acquire those animals of his, and soon to work some of them into the main program."

"That reminds me," said Fitzfarris. "I can arrange another addition to the program, Governor, and it won't cost us a kreuzer. You noticed that tap wench I was cozying up to?"

"Indeed I did."

"Well, there's a lot of girls just as pretty in the other stands and joints. They say they want to tag along with us when we hit the road again. And all those girls like to dance. Have any of you ever seen an Austrian dance called . . . something like 'the shoe-slapper'?"

"Der Schuhplattler," said Beck. "Not Austrian. *Bavarian* it is."

"Whichever," said Fitzfarris. "Anyhow, it's all jumping around and kicking cross-legged and slapping the thighs. Those girls really look good at it, flouncing their short skirts up and all. See, they don't have any work to do, once the crowd leaves the midway for the seats. So why not—even before the come-in spec—have those eight or ten girls out dancing the shoe-slapper in the pista? I suppose you know the proper music, Boom-Boom. Be especially nice if we could have them all in identical dirndls."

"A very good idea," said Florian. "And it needn't be a burden on our wardrobe seamstress. We'll simply outfit the girls all from the same shop downtown. I'll let you attend to that, Sir John. It ought to be a pleasant excursion for you in such company.''

Mullenax said grumpily, "Foursquare, you get to fool around with nicer animals than I do. Mr. Florian, you said you want to work some of them new animals into the show. Hell, I don't know how long it'll take me to train them things. Or even if I can, all by myself.''

"There are tricks to every trade, Barnacle Bill, and I happen to know a few pertaining to yours. Here . . .'' He picked up from beneath his chair and handed across the table a toy tin trumpet. "From our own midway. A gift for you and your musical bear.''

"Huh?''

"Until we decide what else we'll want your animals to learn, you can start immediately by leading one bear on a leash into the pista and ordering him to play that trumpet.''

"Huh?''

"Prepare it beforehand. Stick a cork down the bell of the horn, then fill the tubing with sugar water. The bear will take the horn in his forepaws, tilt it like one of your own jugs and drink from the mouthpiece. I'll wager *you* never had to be taught that trick, and neither will he. Meanwhile, unnoticed, Kapellmcister Beck tootles a simple little tune on his cornet. The audience sees a bear, at your command, playing a trumpet, Q.E.D.''

"Well, I'll be damned . . .''

"Also, gentlemen,'' Florian went on, "until we decide what else we'll do with them, some of those animals will at least promenade with us in the come-in and closing specs. The new bull, the hump, those superb black horses and the dwarf one. I'm not sure about the convicts; zebras are fractious little beasts. We'll see. Anyway, as soon as we've got the animals, here, Canvasmaster, will you and Maggie start making harness and trappings and regalia for the promenaders?''

"Aye, Governor. And when they're *not* in the pista or on the road? I assume they'll require quarters.''

"Yes. Can you start sketching a design for a menagerie

top that will accommodate them? Make it a walk-through:
the animals tethered or caged on either side of an aisle from
front door to back, so the jossers can stroll and ogle. Some
one of us who speaks the local language—perhaps Fünfünf,
while we're in these regions—can do a patter on the creatures' habits and habitats.''

Goesle was already doing an imaginary drawing with his
fingertip on the tablecloth, and muttering, ''I think no center
pole . . . a rectangle of quarter poles . . . sidewalls that can furl
up for airing it out . . .''

''To play music for a bear and Schuhplattler girls maybe
I am only required,'' Beck said, a trifle peevishly. ''Any of
my men can play those things. The men the entire *show* can
play without direction from me. Even if I am gone away.''

''Gone away?'' Florian echoed, with some alarm.

''Here in Österreich to poor houses we are showing. The
people all by the war are upshaken. But only thirty kilometers
north of here my homeland Bayern is, and Bayern by the war
not much affected was. Better business surely, if there we
go.''

''Yes, I had already thought of moving to Bayern—to Bavaria.''

''But I ahead of you go on, alone. Direct to my family's
home in München I go. There my Dampforgel on a wagon I
put—''

''By the Almighty!'' Florian exclaimed. ''I had totally forgotten. You own a calliope!''

''Steam organ, ja. It myself I made, and good it plays, but
not everybody appreciates. The neighbors always have despaired to see me home from my voyages come. This time,
though, the Dampforgel away I will bring, so rejoice they
will. You and circus northward go, I southward the steam
organ transport, we meet wherever.''

''A splendid idea, Carl, and a magnificent contribution it
will be. Let me see now, which wagon can we spare?''

''Nein, nein. Only a saddle horse give me. Better time I
will make—straight north across the Bayerische Alpen. In
München a proper wagon I will purchase.''

''All right. Take that nag that draws Miss Auburn's caravan. I've been meaning to buy her a better one, anyway. When you get to your family's place, you can give them the horse, sell it, turn it out to pasture, as you like. Then buy another good one to draw the calliope wagon. When do you plan to depart, Carl?''

''At your convenience, Herr Gouverneur.''

''Well . . . scant attendance or not, as long as we're set up here in Innsbruck, I'll give it at least the three weeks we planned on. Get the new animals accustomed to us, that sort of thing. If you're sure the band can function without you to conduct . . .''

''Tenez!'' Rouleau said suddenly. ''I trust I am earning my keep on this show, messieurs, as acrobatics instructor and scholarly tutor to the young folk, but I have few chances to participate as an artiste. Boom-Boom, ami, before you depart, I insist that you send me and the *Saratoga* aloft one time here in Innsbruck.''

Beck looked inquiringly at Florian.

''Why not?'' said Florian. ''Neither the aérostat nor the gallant aéronaut should be let to atrophy from disuse. Unfortunately, we cannot charge the public any extra fee for an exhibition so freely visible—but, yes, do that for Monsieur Roulette, Carl.''

''Merci, messieurs,'' said Rouleau.

''After that,'' Florian continued, ''and whenever you are satisfied with the band's competence, Carl, you may go. Autumn's old jade will serve to carry you over the Scharnitz Pass. But, when *we* leave here, our train will go on following the Inn, keeping to the easy ground through the river valleys. We won't pitch again until we are across the border of Bavaria. In Rosenheim. Yes. That is where we will set up, and we'll stay there until you arrive.''

Next morning, Goesle took a number of roustabouts, and Jorg Pfeifer for interpreter, in one of the canvas wagons, to see what the Innsbruck merchants could supply in the way of materials for making a whole new tent plus fancy tack for the animals. Fitzfarris took the balloon wagon, with eight merrily giggling midway girls riding on its soft bed, to get

them costumed for their pista début. Florian and Edge helped
Autumn—though she protested that she needed no help—to
the seat of the rockaway, and set off for the Herr Doktor
Köhn's clinic. If Florian noticed the change in Autumn's appearance, he had steeled himself to give no least sign of it.
On the drive into town, he determinedly tried to maintain a
cheerful atmosphere. He told the happy news of Carl Beck's
imminent journey to Munich to bring a real, ripsnorting calliope for the circus, and of Fitzfarris's having recruited a
corps of dancing girls. When he had exhausted those topics,
he joshed Autumn on her being the first of the Florilegium's
troupe to resist such homegrown treatments as Maggie's
gypsy brews and Colonel Ramrod's cavalry cures.

"I *don't* resist them," said Autumn. "It's going to a doctor
that *I* resist, but the colonel is ramrodding me into it." She
gave a small laugh. "This trip reminds me of an old cockney
song they sing on the halls in London:

> Every Saturday afternoon
> We loves to drown our sorrers,
> So we owlwise visits the waxwork show
> And sits in the Chamber of 'Orrors . . ."

Even the glum-faced Edge had to smile his crooked smile
at that, and Florian said, "You have a fine voice for the halls,
my dear. Is there more to the ditty?"
She nodded and sang the rest, laughing as she did:

> There's a beautiful statue of Mother there,
> Wot gives us pleasure rather,
> For we likes to think of 'er as she looked
> The night she strangled Father.

Two hours later, most of which time Florian and Edge had
spent chain-smoking cigarettes in the clinic's waiting room,
the door of Dr. Köhn's examining chamber opened and he
came to join them. They both respectfully stood up, and the
doctor spoke to Florian, who translated: "While your Frau is

getting dressed, Zachary, the Herr Doktor would like to put some questions.''

Edge asked anxiously, ''She's in a dressing room?''

''It's all right. The doctor says he took the precaution of removing the mirror in there.''

Köhn looked hard at Edge while he spoke again to Florian.

''The various procedures,'' said Florian, ''of inspection, palpation, percussion and auscultation reveal no organic disturbances. There had been no stroke of apoplexy. There is no paralysis. The Frau has a mildly elevated temperature and a neuralgic tenderness in one hand. The most important sign diagnostic is that one most evident—the asymmetry of Autumn's face. Also, the Herr Doktor remarks on some coffee-colored mottlings on the skin of her thorax. Has she always had those, Zachary? Could they be mere birthmarks?''

Edge shook his head. ''I've never seen any such thing. She always had skin like fresh cream. All over. But lately . . . lately . . . she has undressed only in the dark . . .''

Florian relayed that to the doctor, who waggled his bushy eyebrows, meditated, then spoke again.

''To your knowledge, Zachary,'' said Florian, ''has Autumn ever visited the East? Anywhere from, say, Egypt to Japan?''

''No. Has anybody? Autumn's told me how much she looks forward to seeing Russia, because she's never been east of Vienna.''

More parley between the doctor and Florian.

''Would you happen to know, Zachary—the other shows Autumn has been on—were there any Oriental artistes?''

''She's never said. But hell, Florian, *we've* got three of them.''

''True, true. That had slipped my mind.''

He spoke to the doctor, who immediately asked another question, which ended—after a brief hesitation that made it noticeable—with the word Aussatz. Florian recoiled and blurted the more common German word meaning the same thing: *''Lepra?!''* Even Edge could comprehend that one, and he also reeled, aghast. The doctor gave Florian a look of exasperation and hastened to speak some more. Florian sighed with relief and told Edge:

"He says he is only eliminating random possibilities. He wanted to know if those Chinamen showed any sign of that dread disease. He says Autumn's condition exhibits certain superficial similarities, but it *cannot* be leprosy—thank God— because there is one sure and certain symptom of that affliction—what the Herr Doktor calls foot-drop—which she does not have."

The doctor demonstrated. He lifted one foot from the floor and made it dangle from his ankle, toe down, meanwhile saying comfortingly to Edge, "Nein, nein. Nicht das."

"Danke," Edge said huskily. "It's good to know she doesn't have something that horrible. But then, what *does* ail her?"

Now Florian and Köhn engaged in quite a long colloquy, from which Florian emerged to say:

"The Herr Doktor is frank to admit that he simply does not know. There are several possibilities. One is leontasis ossia, which I take to be some kind of bone disease. Another is heteroplasia, which he says is an abnormal tissue formation. There are still other possibilities, neural in nature."

"Christ. Well, can he help her at all?"

After another bit of conversation, the doctor turned and went back inside his chambers. "He is fetching some medicine," said Florian. "Autumn is to take it, and remain indoors and at rest. No activity, no chills. He says the condition will persist, but she is in no immediate danger."

"No *immediate* danger?"

"He wants her to see a certain specialist when we get to Vienna, and he assures me there is no urgency about her arriving there. Whatever is wrong with her, it is chronic, not acute, not critical."

"Damn it," growled Edge. "Even if she's not dying or not getting any worse, I want her to have some relief from the continuous headache . . . and the uncertainty and the worrying."

The doctor returned to the room, and Autumn was with him. She was fussing with her auburn hair, and said to Florian a little tartly, "You'd better tell the good doctor that he's going to lose all his female patients unless he puts a looking glass in his dressing alcove."

Florian did so, or pretended he did. After his next exchange with Köhn, the doctor handed Autumn a number of very tiny envelopes and a slip of paper.

"Those powders," said Florian, "are something called Dreser's Compound. A very new drug, still in process of trial and evaluation, but the Herr Doktor deems it miraculous. You are to take one of the powders, my dear, whenever you have a headache or a fever or that neuralgic affliction in your hands. Guaranteed relief."

Autumn said, "Coo, ducks, old Maggie guarantees *hers*."

"Well, these at least come from the Herr Chemiker Dreser's laboratory, not from a witch's cauldron."

"Ask him, please, if I can take one now. My head *feels* like a witch's cauldron."

The doctor went to draw a glass of water. Autumn tipped one of the little envelopes into her mouth, then drank.

"And the slip of paper," Florian continued, "has the address of the Herr Doktor von Monakow, whom you are to consult at Vienna. He is fluent in English and he is a noted myopathist and neuropathist, I am told, but I am not told what those resounding titles signify in layman's language."

So they thanked Dr. Köhn, and Edge paid him, and the three headed back for the Hofgarten, and Florian again tried to maintain a cheerful air by jollying Autumn:

"Only a woman would contrive an ailment to baffle the most highly recommended physician in Innsbruck. Why, if you were a man, you'd have walked in there with an honest dose of the clap. Do you feel any effect from that medicine yet?"

"You know," she said, with some surprise, "I really do. The headache is going away. Already it is milder than it has been in ever so long."

Edge said, "Well, I'm glad the visit accomplished *something*."

Autumn patted his hand and said blithely, but with a sigh,

"There, there, my dear. If the sky falls . . . well . . . we shall catch larks."

When they got to the tober, young Herr Mehrmann was waiting, with a sheaf of papers under his arm. "Back to business," said Florian. "Zachary, when you have got Miss Auburn comfortably settled, will you join us in my caravan?"

However, by the time Edge joined them, Florian and Mehrmann obviously had concluded their transaction. Florian was signing, with his old stub of mason's pencil but with grand flourishes, one paper after another, and shoving them across the table to where the young man was scrupulously counting a heap of gold pieces. When the count evidently came out right, he said, "Abgemacht," took the signed papers and gave Florian a handful of booklets.

"The conduct books for the newly hired Slovaks," Florian told Edge. "We are getting one to drive each of the five new wagons, and to be keepers to their occupants, and a sixth to help Abdullah herd the bulls and the Bactrian when we're on the road."

When the young man had shaken hands with each of them and departed, Florian chuckled and said, "We are getting all the exotics for no more, I suspect, than the Hagenbecks paid the foresters and poachers who brought them in as cubs and pups and chicks."

"Still, that looked like a considerable outlay," said Edge. "Can we afford it?"

"We are a circus. We should strive to be better than other circuses. There is an old Austrian saying you ought to know, Zachary, since it is a saying of Austrian *cavalrymen*, who are notorious gamblers. 'You can play cards without money, but you cannot play cards without cards.' Now, would you kindly inform Dai Goesle that he can take any spare roustabouts while this afternoon's show is on, and go across the river to help bring our new men and menagerie over here. Tell him also to get paint for those new cage wagons, to match the rest of our train. And tell Banat that he will now be crew chief over six more of his compatriots. It's up to him to make room for them in the Slovaks' sleeping and traveling wagons. Meanwhile, I will discuss with Abdullah and Ali Baba the logistics of procuring extra hay, grain and cat's meat.''

"Right, Governor.''

"Oh, one other thing before you go, Zachary. No, two things. That horse drawing your van is getting rather superannuated. And Boom-Boom needs a not too frisky saddle hack to carry him on that errand for us. Let him have Autumn's old nag, and I'll get a replacement horse. However, since I know how much you admire those new Friesian blacks, why don't you hitch one of them to your van?''

"Thank you, Governor. That's a thoughtful gesture. Autumn will be pleased, too.'' Edge waited. "You said two things . . . ?''

"Er, yes . . . yes . . .'' Florian twiddled his pencil stub for a moment. "Zachary, you must be aware that you cannot forever keep Autumn ignorant of the—of the changes in herself. Soon or later, she is bound to encounter another mirror. And to see her face.''

Edge swallowed, nodded wordlessly, and went out.

4

BY THE TIME that afternoon's show closed, Goesle and his men had led the Hagenbeck animals and their keepers to the Hofgarten. It turned out that the new Slovaks were already acquainted with the Florilegium's Slovaks, all of them having variously, at one time or another, been crew on the same circuses, so there was no problem about their assimilation. As the new men ranked the cage wagons and tethered the uncaged animals in the backyard, Aleksandr Banat bustled among them, issuing trivial and unnecessary orders, luxuriating in being now the crew chief of fully seventeen underlings.

After the last of the audience had drifted off the tober and the artistes had got out of their ring dress, the troupers and the midway stallkeepers, as well, congregated in the backyard to see the new acquisitions—all of the company but Carl Beck and his bandsmen, whom he was rehearsing at being a band without a conductor.

"I tole you, Sahib Florian, ol' Peggy be happy to see new bull," said Hannibal, grinning at the great beasts as they delicately explored and whuffled over one another with their trunks, occasionally entwining them as in a handclasp. "Ol' Peggy must of thought she was the one and onliest elephant on dis earth. Hey, Mas' Sahib, what dis new one's name?"

Florian consulted the list Mehrmann had given him. "Mitzi. That's how she'll answer to commands, Abdullah. But for billing—well, it's obvious: Brutus and Caesar. Now, this camel—let me see—she is Mustafa, and that'll do for billing, too. We'll have Maggie deck her out in fringed shawls and halter and camel bells. Maybe a tassel on her tail." Mustafa curled her rubbery big lips in a sneer.

"Hey, Governor," called Mullenax, from beside one of the cage wagons. "While you're tellin' names, tell me which one of these critters is Kewwy-dee."

"What?" said Florian, puzzled. He went to look: it was the cage of the two Syrian bears.

"You told me the bear that plays the horn is Kewwy-dee. Which one of 'em is it?"

Florian still looked bewildered for a moment. Then he smiled, shook his head and murmured to himself, "Q.E.D." To Mullenax he said, "You'll just have to try them out, Barnacle Bill, and decide which one is better at the trick."

"All right. And he'll be Kewwy-dee. I'll call the other one Kewwy-dah, so I can tell 'em apart. That suit you, Governor?"

"Of course, Barnacle," said Florian, with amusement. "They're your property, after all."

Hannibal asked, "What we feed dese bears, Sahib?"

"That's one good thing about bears, Abdullah, they'll eat almost anything. But they prefer fresh food, not dried stuff like hay. So, in the manner of your former pigs, Barnacle Bill, they'll be our receptacle for table leftovers and such. But we'll also give them fresh fruits and vegetables whenever possible, throw them the occasional fish we may come acoss. And, during your training of them, reward each successful accomplishment with a morsel of bread and honey. Bears love honey."

Florian went on along the row of cages, looking at his list, and most of the troupers trailed along to listen.

"The tiger's name is Raja," said Florian, "and the tigresses are Rani and Siva. All good Bengal names, I assume. The ostriches are Hansel and Gretel. After a boy and girl in an old German fairy tale."

Clover Lee asked, "What about these awful-looking hyenas?"

Florian consulted his list and chuckled. "Anwalt and Berater. Both words just mean 'lawyer.' Wonderfully apt, I must say, for carrion-eating scavengers. But you needn't bother remembering the names. Even hyenas wouldn't answer to those." At the next cage, he said, "Now, these two zebras—"

"I'd like to call them Stars and Bars," said Mullenax. "After the bonny old Confederate flag. If that's all right with you, Governor. See, the one's got kind of a star on his forehead, and God knows they both got enough bars."

"Fine with me. That other little horse in there is listed as Rumpelstilzchen."

"Why?" somebody asked. "The name is bigger than he is."

"Rumpelstilzchen was a dwarf in another old folktale."

"A good name," said Jörg Pfeifer. "Let us keep it. Zanni and I can do some funny patter on the name, when we work the animal into our act."

"Also, Fünfünf, may I ask," said Florian, "would you do the patter in the menagerie for the jossers? You know the sort of thing."

"Ja, ja. These tigers are man-eaters, and took the lives of twenty African Schwartzen before they were captured, and—"

"*Hindu* Schwartzen, please. The tigers come from India. And of course Caesar gored a score of elephant hunters with his little tusks. And Rumpelstilzchen is the sole surviving specimen of the supposedly mythical leprechaun horse."

"Wie sagt man *leprechaun* auf deutsch?"

"Well . . . Kobold . . . Troll . . ."

"Ach, ja. And the camel is called the ship of the Sahara."

"This one is a Bactrian two-humper. Ship of the Gobi. But what the hell, the jossers won't know the difference. And would you mind wearing a suitable costume, Fünfünf? I'll have Maggie get it together—a pith helmet, bush jacket, boots. You can carry one of Colonel Ramrod's carbines while you're at it."

"Schon gut," said Pfeifer indifferently. "Right now, it is time for me to give Monday her ropewalking lesson."

He went off to the chapiteau and Florian turned again to Mullenax. "While we are discussing ferocity, Barnacle Bill, let me assure you that it is not all humbug, not by any means. Until you and these creatures get well accustomed to each other, treat them with the utmost caution. Be wary of the tigers even if you think they are fast asleep. Because of the striping around the eyes, you can never be sure if they are closed or only watchfully slitted. The bears you will *never* go near, or let out of their cage, unless they are muzzled. A strap muzzle won't impede the trumpet-tootling. Be careful also of the bears' claws, even though they have been blunted. I will have Maggie make a special metal codpiece for you to wear under your clothes from now on. If a bear takes a swipe at a man, it will always rake first at his testicles."

"Jesus," said Mullenax.

"Oh, yes. A bear is more to be feared and distrusted than any of the great cats. A bear can even trample you, and accidentally, because a bear does not see very well straight ahead. When you are working it, stay always just within its peripheral vision."

"Huh?"

"Stay just to its left or right front," Florian patiently explained. "Now, excuse me, I must have a word with Stitches."

He found the canvasmaster supervising a number of non-bandsmen Slovaks in the cutting of canvas for the menagerie tent. Florian thanked Goesle for having so expeditiously delivered the menagerie itself, then asked him, "Dai, while you're doing this canvas work, I wonder if you would oblige me by also making a banner line."

"It is a likelihood, Governor, if you'll tell me what it is."

"A series of colorful canvas banners, slung side by side. Each a rectangle—say, six by eight feet—lapped and hemmed top and bottom so ropes can be reeved through. I'll have our Chink artist paint them, each depicting one of the wonders of our show."

"No problem, Governor. I'll have a plenty of remnants left over. Now, look you, another thing. To save me and my lads a lot of time and laborious work, I am having a lumberyard in town shape the quarter poles and side poles for this new top. I know we've been Irish-prodigal of money lately, and not much coming in, but the locals asked a price so low it would have been a foolishness not to give them the job. What else I've been thinking: wood is plentiful and cheap here in this alpine country, and it might *not* be in other places. While we are here, why don't I have the locals also cut the pieces for folding chairs?"

"Aha! Our starback seats. At last."

"With the backs and seats and legs rough-cut, I can have my lads do the finishing of them, and the putting of them together, as we go along, whenever we have a spare moment."

"Commendable initiative, Dai. The extra prices we can charge for comfortable starbacks will eventually pay for them. Go to it."

Leaving Goesle to his work, Florian ambled in through the back door of the chapiteau to glance about at the rehearsal, practice and instruction going on. The pavilion was practically billowing its roof and sidewalls with all the noise inside it, for the bandmaster was at this moment conducting both the band and the eight midway-girl dancers in their performance of the Schuhplattler. The musicians were doing a blasting oom-pah-pah of brassy Bavarian folk music, and the girls, although they were cavorting on soft sawdust, contributed to the noise with the repeated thigh-slapping that the dance demanded. Florian noted with approval that all the girls *were* pretty, as Fitzfarris had said, and that Fitz had dressed them in dirndls of blue and white. Not only did the costumes match the colors of the Florilegium's wagons, they were also intended to please Kapellmeister Beck, because blue and white were the flag colors of his native Bavaria.

The others in the tent went on with their business, taking no notice of the oom-pah-pah and the thigh-slapping and Boom-Boom's frequent vociferations. High up in the trapeze rig, Sunday, securely belted to the lungia, was being swung to and fro in various postures by Maurice and Paprika. In the pista below, out of the way of the dancing, Jules Rouleau was teaching Ali Baba various new ways to tie his limber body into knots. Outside the pista curbing, the Quakemaker grunted and heaved at some new strongman equipment he was preparing to introduce into his act. Yount had somewhere found four more cannonballs—and these were solid, not hollow, two each of eight-inch and ten-inch diameters. He had also procured two stout iron rods with threaded ends, and screwed each of those into two of the soft lead balls. So now the Quakemaker had two sets of dumbbells, not in any way fake or gaffed, honestly weighing more than a hundred twenty-eight pounds and two hundred fifty-six pounds respectively. He was trying different ways to struggle erect—from flat on his back, from a sitting position, from a squat—while he lifted the lighter, then the heavier, then both dumbbells together.

"Con permesso, Signor Governatore," said the clown Zanni, as he brushed past Florian into the tent, carrying something limp draped over one arm. He went to where Rouleau was working with Ali Baba, and borrowed the boy from him. What Zanni was carrying turned out to be two arm-length tubes of black india rubber, each terminating in a white glove like those Ali Baba wore with his clown costume of minstrel-show blackface. Zanni showed him how to put the gloves-and-tubes on, then pulled down his shirtsleeves so that only his gloved hands showed. Then they went together to where the Quakemaker was taking a rest from his labors. They exchanged some words, and the strongman nodded. So Ali Baba bent over, seized a dumbbell bar with both hands, pretended titanic exertion, did fierce grimaces, and very, very slowly began to stand erect. The Quakemaker burst out laughing, inaudibly in all the ambient noise. Ali Baba's new gloves were wired inside, to stay clasped around the dumbbell bar as he slowly straightened and slipped his hands out of them—so the black rubber tubes slid out of his sleeves, making it appear that his skinny black arms were lengthening. Zanni even picked up the boy and lifted him higher, over his own head, making those black arms stretch impossibly longer and skinnier yet.

"A comic effect, no?" said Zanni.

"Yassuh," Ali Baba said, giggling. Then to Yount, "Kin I do dat, Mr. Quakemaker, eb'ry show, when you is done wid de dumbbells?"

"I reckon," said Yount, still laughing. "Here I'm busting my gut to show the folks a real strongman act. And you'll come along and make fun of it, and prob'ly get twice the applause. But hell yes, it's comical. Don't mind me and my professional jealousy. You do it, Quincy."

Between the two center poles, but only a foot off the ground, the tightrope was rigged. Ignoring the dirndled girls dancing and swirling and bouncing on either side of the rope, Monday was mincing along it, and Fünfünf, though he stood close beside her, had to shout above the noise.

"Since the Fräulein Auburn does a classic Seiltänzer ballerina act, and you will not wish to compete with her, you will learn a comic turn on the rope."

Monday shouted back, "I druther be classical and graceful and beautiful. Anybody can act funny."

"Ha! Think you so? I learned rope-dancing in a few weeks. Thirty *years* I have been striving to learn funniness. It will take all your skill, Fräulein—and all your grace and all your beauty—to do it right."

"If you say so," Monday said, not with great enthusiasm.

"On the ground you will practice dancing foolery, as we call it. You will learn the stork step, the chicken walk, the crab glide, the skip shuffle, the hesitation walk, all the others. Then you will translate them to the rope. Step down, now. Imitate me. This is the stork step. Come! Walk as I am doing."

Monday did so, but complaining. "All these-here pretty white gals flouncin' their pretty shapes all 'round, and I gotta walk all crooked."

"Hush! You are a stork. Protrude your tail more. That is better. Now get onto the rope and do exactly the same."

Three times, Monday tried stork-ropewalking, and slipped off each time. "It's 'cause I can't see my *feet*," she protested, "walkin' this stupid way."

"You are not supposed ever to watch your feet. Keep your eyes fixed on the white guidon daubed on the pole yonder." Monday sighed, but tried again, and was rather surprised that—*not* watching her feet—she could stork-step without falling off the rope. "Much better," said her teacher. "Much, much better. Only stick out your tail more. Remember you are a stork. More tail!"

"Mr. Meister," said Monday, through teeth clenched in her concentration, "could you anyways stop callin' it my *tail?*"

"Your sister," said Paprika, looking down from the trapeze platform, "is doing very well at funambulism."

Sunday also looked down and said, "Yes, she is."

"Like you, she has grown a figure, and quite a good one. Tell me, has she outgrown her habit of doing wichsen to herself?"

Sunday looked puzzled and said honestly, "I don't know." According to her decorous German dictionary, "wichsen" meant only to wax or to polish.

"A pretty girl should not have to resort to bringing herself off." That phrase also meant nothing to Sunday, but she could comprehend Paprika's next remark: "What she needs is a lover."

Sunday laughed and said, "What she *wants* is Foursquare John Fitzfarris."

"And you, Liebling, you want Zachary Edge. Too bad he is already taken."

"He is attached, but he is not married."

"Aha! You bide your time. Yes, you are young enough to wait. But perhaps, when your time comes, you would stand a better chance if you were instructed in more than the arts of trapeze. In the arts and wiles of love. I can be an instructress elsewhere than in the air, you know."

"I have heard," Sunday said coolly. "No, thank you."

"Brrr!" said Paprika, pretending to shiver. "You call that in English the cold shoulder, I believe. However, I can warm the coldest shoulder. And other things—"

But Sunday was swinging across to the other platform, where Maurice was standing and tapping a foot impatiently. He said a few words to Sunday, took her bar from her, swung across to where Paprika stood and said probably the identical words to her: "Kindly keep your girlish babillage for the ground, mam'selle. Up here we work."

"Hard work, indeed," murmured Paprika. Then she shifted her gaze from Sunday to Maurice and said, "Once you invited me to share your van. You never spoke of it again. *You* do not work very hard to attain your ambitions."

"You will recall, chérie, you rather effectually demolished that particular ambition."

"But, as you said then, une hirondelle ne fait pas . . . Have you ever considered deux hirondelles en même temps?" She looked across the intervening space at Sunday. "In Magyar we call it rakott kenyér. In your language it would be, I think, un homme en sandwich."

He looked where she was looking, then looked again at her. "I am a Frenchman, Paprika, therefore by nature tolerant of others' differing natures. But do not dream of courting your own partner. That is courting trouble."

"You courted *me*, Maurice."

"We were only the two of us then. What you now suggest is a triangle, and even in French farce, that is an overworked cliché for trouble. Cannot you direct your ambition outside the chapiteau? At least to the ground? Why not one of those lusty wenches dancing down there?"

"Utálatos! Those beefy trulls?" she said, sneering down at them. "No, Maurice, I sometimes think I must be getting old and wicked—like the old men who lurk around schoolyards. I seem nowadays to have a taste for . . . for the new and fresh and unawakened."

"Old, you are not. Wicked, perhaps. Perverse, beyond a doubt. If you loved—if you *could* love—mais non. Knowing what I know of you, I expressly forbid you to pursue this course. If we three are to survive up here, we must love each other, oui, but not *love* each other, do you understand me? This air up here is mine to command, and I will have it clean.''

Still gazing at Sunday, Paprika murmured, ''Forbidden, eh?'' and ran the tip of her tongue across her upper lip.

''Not another word now Take the bar. Show me a *passe ventre*. You were very slipshod at it this afternoon.''

Every night, when Edge came home to the caravan after the show, to help Autumn prepare their meal—they had not accompanied the other troupers to any hotel or Gaststätte for a long time now—she would eagerly inquire into all the details of the performance, and he would dutifully report:

''Well, that nitwit Pavlo is still whisking his dogs and family in and out of the pista, faster and faster every show, like he's working up eventually to a genuine disappearing act. I made a real mistake when I warned him to be leery of rivalizers.''

Or another day he would report: ''Fitz has got a prime replacement for Clover Lee and the Simms girls in his blow-off. That good-looking Greek woman does 'The Amazon Maiden in the Clutches of the Dragon Fafnir.' And she does it so naked that her, uh, vital parts are only covered by the coils of the python—even though it's moving all the time. I don't know how she and the snake manage that. I do know she'd be arrested for indecent behavior anywhere outside that tent. She carries on like she's being ravished by a man. Still, it's pretty to look at, too. The snake literally *dances* up her and down her and around her, in time to the accordion music.''

Or another day he would report: ''The new animals are marching in the specs just fine. Even the zebras, as long as I keep them close-haltered. And the other night, in the menagerie tent, Abner saw Peggy crawling *under* Mitzi's belly. She was only giving her back a brisk scratching, but Abner has made that into an act. Now he announces 'London Bridge!' and has the elephants do it in the pista. Abner's pretty smart with the animals; he's begun to win the trust of the tigers and bears, even. I do wish he wouldn't guzzle a whole bottle every time he has to get into their cages, but he says damned if he'd *get* in, otherwise.''

''I wish,'' said Autumn, ''I could see the show. There has been so much added since I took ill. I don't know why I shouldn't be allowed. That medicine has completely relieved me of the headache. Of course, I know I can't go back to performing yet, because I still can't focus my vision on anything as close as the rope. But things at a distance I can see perfectly well.''

''What about the—those discolored spots on your chest?''

''Still there, but they haven't spread or multiplied. I am sorry the doctor told you about those.''

''Damn it, Autumn, you and I have shared every least thing ever since we've been together. I don't like learning things about you from some third party. I'm still peeved that you took to putting out the lamps, just so I wouldn't notice.''

''I was afraid you'd take them for those liverish blotches that old ladies get, and decide I was growing old, and discard me.''

That was so patently a lie, and so witless a lie from one of Autumn's intelligence, that Edge did not even bother to suggest that it was also an insult to *his* intelligence, and his love and loyalty, as well. He said only:

''The doctor cautioned you not to risk a chill. But right now it doesn't get chilly until nightfall. I think, if you bundled up good, you could attend any afternoon show without danger. And sit in the stands with the jossers, if you see better from a distance.''

''Oh, I could!'' she said fervently. ''*May* I, Zachary?''

''I reckon so. Do me one favor, though. Wear a hat with a veil. If that demented Pavlo Smodlaka should spot you in the stands, he'd be sure he was being spied on, and that I'm responsible for the spying. Let's not drive him totally insane.''

''Anything you say, dearest,'' said Autumn, and kissed him.

But that night again, as had become her practice, she blew out the lamps before undressing for bed. Edge did not complain or even comment. He was gratified to have it so. Making love to Autumn in the dark enabled him to delude himself that he was making love to that radiantly beautiful and unblemished Autumn of other nights that now seemed long ago.

"Oo-ooh, how splendid!" Autumn gasped, the next afternoon, when they stood at the entry end of the circus midway. "Why, Zachary, it has become as grand as just about any other stand I have ever seen!"

Autumn was well and warmly clothed in coat, muffler, gloves and high boots. From her broad-brimmed Leghorn hat depended a riding veil, tucked into her coat collar, and within it her face was only a dim glow. At Edge's request, Florian had earlier gone along the rows of midway stalls, ordering their proprietors—somewhat to their mystification—to hide away any mirrors they had on display among their slum. But Autumn probably would not have noticed them in any case: she was so enthralled by the new additions to the tober.

Besides the banners and placards that proclaimed the wares of the midway joints—sausages, beers, cuckoo clocks and such—the Florilegium now flaunted its own banner line, stretched across the front of the chapiteau above the marquee entrance. The Chinese artist had proved a little uncertain of anatomy, both human and animal, but that had not inhibited either his imagination or his palette. In brilliant and unearthly colors were depicted, on one banner, a flamboyantly fanged and clawed and tangle-maned lion, strewing a jungle with bloody fragments of black Africans; on another Colonel Ramrod, anomalously slant-eyed, firing volcanoes of flame and smoke from a pistol in each hand and strewing a desert with bloodily punctured Red Indians; on another a bejeweled Hindu Indian juggling lighted torches while being upheld upon the meshed tusks of two exceedingly corrugated elephants; on another the three Chinese themselves, vividly yellow, engaged in upside-down and sideways and crosswise tortuosities that even they had not yet attempted . . . and so on: eight banners all together, almost audibly screeching for attention.

Sir John's annex top, off to one side of the chapiteau, had its own separate banner. That one displayed a very pneumatic-looking naked lady with an inhumanly ponderous bosom—the Oriental artist was clearly overawed by Occidental mammaries—her eyes bulging and her mouth gaping in a scream as she was simultaneously squeezed by the coils and scorched by the fiery breath of a reptilian, avian, leonine, winged and lasciviously leering dragon. It was by far the best-portrayed animal of all on the banners.

On the other side of the chapiteau was the new menagerie tent, striped green and white like the others, and Edge led Autumn there. She happily took a deep breath of the evocative mixture of smells—at once ammoniac and aromatic—of elephants, great cats, horses, warm hay, feed bins, sawdust and new canvas.

"Before each show," said Edge, "any josser that has bought a ticket, and doesn't want to patronize the joints, can come in here for a look-around. When there's enough of a crowd collected, Jörg Pfeifer expounds—mainly on what the menagerie costs in outlay of money, time, labor and loss of life."

"What *did* all this cost?"

"Florian won't tell me. I think he gave a part payment and a promissory note. The Hagenbecks know him and trust him."

He took Autumn down the middle of the tent and introduced to her the caged or tethered newcomers on the other sides of the aisle ropes: Mitzi-Caesar, Kewwy-dee and Kewwy-dah—those names required explanation—Hansel and Gretel, the lawyer hyenas, Raja, Rani and Siva.

"Oh, aren't they sublime, the tigers!" Autumn exclaimed. "We humans think we are nature's masterworks, but they *are*. The jungle cats, the house cat, every kind of cat is superior to all other animals."

"Come, come," Edge said chaffingly. "We humans are made in God's image." Then he was sorry he had said it, remembering what Autumn now looked like. But all she said was:

"The cats don't care about God. They worship nothing, they envy nothing and they fear nothing. If that is not superiority, what is?"

The horses were at the farther end of the tent, and there Clover Lee was brushing her old dapple, Bubbles. She greeted Autumn a little uncertainly, seeing her so muffled in concealment. But when Autumn responded in her usual clear accents, Clover Lee forthrightly asked after her health, then expressed the whole troupe's hope that their stellar colleague would soon be among them again.

"Thank you. I hope so, too," said Autumn. "The menagerie is wonderful, isn't it, Clover Lee? But surely it will be a long time paying for itself."

"Well," said the girl, grinning, "you know Florian. Unless he's perched out on a precarious limb, he just doesn't feel he's alive."

Edge said, "Yes, he's buying yet another big wagon and drayhorses. It turns out we'll need them to carry all the provisions for these animals on the road—and the new starback seats, when we've got them."

"And the European troupers keep telling him," said Clover Lee, "that we ought to have rolls of slat-fencing, like other European circuses, to put up around every tober. We do get a lot of sidewallers sneaking in, and that gripes Banat especially. But Florian says a fence is just *too* much to haul about."

Edge and Autumn left the menagerie and entered the chapiteau through its front door. Above them, inside the marquee, Boom-Boom Beck was just then tuning up his band, and he took up the cornet to play a bar of "Greensleeves" by way of salute, and Autumn waved up to him. She kept her head back, then, gazing wistfully up into the peak of the tent, until Edge gently ushered her onward. Goesle and his men had not yet assembled any of the folding chairs, so the "starbacks" were still only the benches nearest the pista. Edge seated her on one of those and stayed with her until it was time for him to go and cast his directorial eye over the lineup of the come-in spec.

He glanced over frequently and anxiously, during the show, to where Autumn sat among fat Bürgers and their fat Fraus and their pudgy Kinder. She appeared not to be feeling any ill effects of her first venture outside the caravan since the visit to the doctor. She applauded as vigorously as the jossers did, and, though Edge could not see her face, he knew she must be smiling to see so many new acts and so many refinements of the old ones.

Abdullah now did his juggling while dancing a-tiptoe from neck to neck of a dozen upright beer bottles, deliberately kicking over one of them every few minutes, until finally he was balanced on one toe on a single bottle, still imperturbably juggling fragile eggs and iron horseshoes at the same time. Zanni had introduced into his clown turn a balancing ladder, like the one Monsieur Roulette had used to have, except that this one was a breakaway ladder. Zanni stood it up with no support, and kept it standing and teetering while he did various acrobatics on it. Then one after another rung fell away when he stepped on it, so his posturing took him higher up the ever more rickety and wobbling ladder, until he was desperately cavorting on only the uppermost and last remaining rung. When that fell, so did he, but to catch the ladder's two uprights under his armpits, at which point he worked them like stilts to go arm-striding in giant steps around the pista.

Clover Lee had added a flock of white doves to her bareback act. She had bought the dozen birds in the market, then during seven days of training had worn a mantle while she rode, in the folds of which were sprinkled grains of wheat. During that week, the pigeons had learned to chase her as she rode, to get at the wheat, and when, on the eighth day, she discarded the cloak, they followed out of habit. Now, as Clover Lee circled the pista on Bubbles, doing ballet stands, jetés and entrechats, the white birds *were* her mantle, following close as she rode and, when she halted, fluttering to alight on her arms and shoulders.

Brutus did her old act under Abdullah's command, then Barnacle Bill brought on Caesar, and Florian announced in German, "The Bridge Over the Inn!" Brutus and Caesar constructed it by entwining their trunks, and Sunday Simms danced a little ballet up and down that span, while the band played a waltz. Then Florian announced, "London Bridge Is Falling Down!" and the waltz was interrupted by a cymbal clash, and the elephants suddenly parted, and Sunday bounded to stand gracefully on Caesar's head while Brutus crawled back and forth under Caesar's great belly.

Sunday also now participated in the trapeze act, but mainly to the extent of standing on one platform, in artistic poses, and giving the bar a shove toward Maurice or Paprika whenever they shouted for it, "Houp là!" All three of those artistes were now, by Maurice's recent decision, garbed in tights of varying shades of blue, richly spangled. Maurice, was still in electric blue, like lightning; Paprika wore a very dark blue, to show off her orange hair; Sunday was in very pale blue, to contrast with her abundance of jet-black hair. And, near the close of the act, Sunday was allowed one trick that brought all three blues together. Maurice and Paprika, on the separate bars, finished a succession of acrobatics with both of them swinging upside down by their knees. Paprika swung close to Sunday's platform, reaching out her arms. Sunday also reached out, the two girls' hands clung, and Sunday was swung dangling in a swoop to meet Maurice. The audience gasped as she somehow transferred her grip in mid-air from Paprika to Maurice, and he swung her through another arc to land lightly on her feet on the opposite platform.

"I just wish," Sunday shyly told Autumn, who went to congratulate her during the intermission, "that when we clasp each other's wrists up there, I didn't have to clasp Miss Paprika."

"Oh, dear," said Autumn. "Is she up to her tricks with you, now? Well, I suppose it should be no surprise. You are still an adolescent, but you have grown from a pretty child into a beautiful young girl. I take it you are not, um, inclined toward Paprika?"

Sunday's fawn-colored cheeks were tinged with rose, but she tried to sound worldly. "What she has suggested . . . the particulars . . . she says I'd enjoy them. Maybe I would. She ought to know."

"But?" said Autumn.

"But I'd rather save . . . save all that sort of thing for . . . for a man, when I'm grown up enough to have one. Miss Paprika says I might as well enjoy myself in the meantime, and it won't make any difference later on. To me or to . . . to any man. Would it, Miss Autumn?''

''I can't speak from experience. But I know it to be a common experience in the best boarding schools, even convent schools, yet the girls go on to make good marriages. Why do you ask? Are you thinking of obliging her?''

''She says she will see that I never get any further in trapeze work, if I don't.''

''Why, the ruddy bitch! That is far more monstrous than— than anything you and she might willingly do. Private acts are private business, but blackmail is a crime. Shall I speak to Zachary?''

''Oh, no, please,'' said Sunday, in alarm. ''Don't do anything to get that woman angry at me. I'll—I'll give it some more thought. But please, Miss Autumn, don't mention this to anyone else.'' And she ran off to the dressing wagon.

Autumn rejoined Edge, and said nothing about the conversation. They spent the rest of the intermission in the sideshow, and she was as delighted with that as the Innsbruckers were. Then later, after the conclusion of the main show in the chapiteau, she insisted on seeing also the Amazon Maiden and the Dragon Fafnir. When Fitz's canvas curtain closed on the final throes of that performance, Autumn laughingly said to Edge, ''My God, I thought you told me she *pretended* to be ravished.''

''Come around the back and meet her. You can ask her if she takes it seriously.''

Behind the curtain, Meli Vasilakis now had a dressing robe on and was putting the lid on the big snake's basket. When Edge had made the introductions, Autumn said, ''I hope Fitz never talks me into any such tableau vivant. I'd be terrified.''

''Is not kinthynos. Not danger. Python never hurt me. Also he is old age.''

''I wasn't thinking of the python. Maybe you didn't see the eyes of those *men* watching.''

''Vlepo,'' Meli said gaily. ''I have good house-band of jealousy.''

''House-band?''

''Spyros always watch while I work.'' Meli beckoned, and

he stepped onstage to be introduced to Autumn. "Any man look me too hard, get eye burned out. House-band Spyros *real* dragon."

They went off, carrying the python basket between them, and Autumn said, "They make a refreshing comparison to Pavlo and Gavrila."

"The Vasilakises don't have to be the only happy house-band and wife," said Edge. "I proposed marriage to you when we first met, and a dozen times since."

Autumn playfully put a fingertip to the end of his nose, and said, "You are in Germanic lands now, and I bid you, reflect. The German word trauen means to marry. Almost the same word, trauern, means to grieve. It can't be a coincidence."

"Damn it, be serious."

"All right. May I come to see tomorrow's show, too? Seriously."

"Seriously, no. The doctor warned against too much exertion, remember. I'll untether you again two days from now. That's when Jules is going up in the *Saratoga*."

The Florilegium had, all this while in Innsbruck, continued to draw less than capacity crowds. But the attendance improved suddenly and dramatically after Rouleau went soaring up and down the Inn River.

To that spectacle, Fitzfarris again contributed the magical disappearance from the midway and reappearance from the sky of the seemingly same pretty girl. The Simms sisters did not object to *this* as exploitation of themselves, because they much enjoyed the balloon rides, and alternated in the rôles of disappearee and reappearee. This time, it was Monday who leapt triumphantly from the basket when the *Saratoga* alighted. After she and Monsieur Roulette had taken a score of bows to the applause of the watchers who thronged the Hofgarten, he took her aside and said petulantly, "*Must* you do that thigh-chafing business the whole time we are aloft? Your sister does not do it. Your jiggling of the gondola makes it très difficile for me to gauge my landing on the correct spot."

Sunday was nearby and overheard, and she gave Monday a long look, as of speculation.

It had been Florian's posters announcing the balloon ascension that had brought the hordes of city people to the Hofgarten that day, but the increased circus attendance in subsequent days consisted of people who had had no notice of the spectacle. The unexpected appearance in the sky of something as uniquely beautiful as the *Saratoga*, visible for leagues around, piqued the curiosity of every country family in the whole Inn valley. Their farm harvests were safely in, and winter snows had not yet put them into hibernation, so wagonloads of country folk crowded all the roads leading to Innsbruck from then on, and they made directly for the tober.

"Well, I'm glad we stuck it out," said Florian, with satisfaction. "And I'm glad you stuck with us, Carl, to help provide this bounty. So we will stay on here until the crowds begin to dwindle again. Or until snow falls, which will have the same result. That means there is no need for you to make haste to München, but you may take your leave whenever you like. We will keep to the original plan, and be in Rosenheim awaiting you."

So, after conducting several more band drills and leaving innumerable instructions to be followed in his absence, Beck did depart. His colleagues tried not to laugh when he did. A seaman in a saddle would have been a quaint enough sight, but this one very much resembled Sancho Panza, with the swaybacked old nag under him and his plump legs sticking out sideways and his bald spot gleaming as long as he was in sight.

The Florilegium enjoyed many more weeks of prosperity before the first snow fell. It was a heavy fall that required the slow burning of hay bales in the chapiteau and annex tent all that night. No fire could be allowed in the menagerie top, but the animals' own body heat was enough to keep the snow from collecting on its roof. And next day Florian ordered teardown and preparation to get on the road to Bavaria.

He and Edge made a hurried trip into town that day, to request from the Herr Doktor Köhn an ample road supply of the helpful Dreser's powder. The doctor asked numerous

questions about Autumn's condition, and Edge's replies—
even his report that "her face gets ever more crooked"—
seemed satisfactorily to confirm the doctor's original opinion.
Florian translated; "He sees no possibility of accurate diag-
nosis until Autumn is examined by that Vienna specialist, but
he still says there is no urgency."

"I don't know whether to take that as hopefulness or hope-
lessness," Edge said. "Anyhow, since we're detouring away
from Vienna, ask him if he knows a good doctor any place
near where we're going, in case we need one. A doctor that
speaks English, if possible."

Dr. Köhn obligingly took from a shelf a thick directory,
thumbed through it, and wrote on a slip of paper a name and
address in Munich. Then he filled a multitude of little envelopes with the headache reliever, and wished Edge and his
lady "viel Glück."

When the Florilegium left the snow-blanketed Hofgarten,
it was now a train like that of any army battalion on the move.
The black rockaway was leading a blue-and-white procession
of ten equipment and supply wagons, six cage wagons, nine
house caravans plus the rolling Gasentwickler, two elephants
and a camel—and trailing those walking animals came the
ragtag, varicolored straggle of caravans and wagons of the
midway hangers-on. Fully a third of the train had crossed
the bridge over the Inn while a third was still on it and another third was still approaching it.

They were two days and two nights on the road—a snow-
covered road, banked high with snow on both sides—going
northeast to the border. There, at Kufstein, they crossed from
Austria into Bavaria, and again everyone marveled at the way
the border guards let them cross without challenge or hin-
drance. "I think," said Florian, "this time it's because the
Bayerischer sentries are pleased to see our wagons wearing
their national colors." Rosenheim was another day's journey
northward along the Inn, but now Florian put his Snowball
to a canter to take him on ahead. So once more Edge led the
train, alone on his driver's seat, because Autumn was—not

by choice but with resignation—riding inside the caravan, in the bed. Edge did not enjoy being alone any more than she did, but he was grateful for the snow under the wheels that cushioned her ride.

✦⇒ BAYERN ⇐✦

1

ON THE RIGHT SIDE of the road, as the circus train neared Rosenheim, was still the Inn River, very broad here, and on the left side were the flat, dreary, seemingly limitless swamps that the local folk called the Great Moss— but not in disrespect, for that expanse of salt and sulphur mud provided their livelihood. A city whose two chief industries were the export of salt extracted from those marshes and the attraction of clients to its numerous salt-mud and sulphur-mud spas could not be expected to smell too good, but at least it held out promise of a prosperous stand, for not even the recent war would have depressed the market for salt and health cures.

As usual, Florian came back along the road to meet his circus and lead it into town, announcing, "The city fathers have allotted us a good pitch in the Kaiserbad park, and I got some children to post plenty of paper last night."

But, when they were on the smooth-stoned streets of Rosenheim, Florian exclaimed, "What the hell have those brats done?" There were posters everywhere, indeed, but they were not the Florilegium's. He got down to examine one, and

so did Edge, who could discern only that the poster advertised
DER ZIRKUS RINGFEDEL.

"Isn't that something?" said Florian through gritted teeth.
"In just the time it took me to go and meet you, those bastard
Fedels have pasted over all our paper."

"Like that pipsqueak back in Maryland?" asked Edge.
"Are they going day and date against us?"

"Not even that," said Florian, with a snort. "It says, 'Wait
for the BIG ONE! The Greatest Show in Europe will arrive
in *No Time at All!* Save your money for the VERY BEST!' "

"I take it you're not the only sly showman in the business."

"But look at the date!" snarled Florain. "The Ringfedel
is not getting here for another six weeks! Oh, those Fedel
boys are sly enough, and they're notorious for underhanded
tricks like this, and they are loathed throughout the profession. Orfei warned me about them. And theirs is not even a
proper tent circus. They've got a railroad train, so they can
scoot in a hurry to any place that seems circus-ripe—or to
snatch it away from any rival circus. They don't even have
any canvas to set up; they simply show in auditoriums and
armories and such. You see what it says here: 'Herren und
Damen, why trudge through a snowy and muddy lot to endure
a hard bench in a drafty tent? Wait to enjoy the GREAT
RINGFEDEL in gemütlich comfort and warmth.' "

"How would they have known we were coming here?"

"Oh, hell, the Fedels employ more advance men than artistes, and pay them better. They're forever out spying everywhere. And you can wager that the Fedels will have a spy
pretending to be an innocent josser among our first audience.
He'll go snooping about with detective designs, so he can
report on our every act and innovation and gimmix and piece
of rigging, so the Fedel boys will know precisely how we
measure up as competition to them. And next a Fedel agent
in disguise will be slinking around our backyard trying to
hire our stellar performers away from us."

"They sound like Yankees. What do we do about this in-
festation?"

"Keep a sharp eye out, mainly. First of all, let us get the

company settled on the tober, and any who care to do so may repair to the Kaiserbad hotel for a good dinner. Meanwhile, even before we start to set up, I'll have Stitches send every spare roustabout through the city, to tear this paper and post ours. If they should encounter one of the Fedel paperhangers, well, they'll know how to discourage him. And we will re-paper every damned day, if we have to.''

However, once the Florilegium's posters were restored, they were not again interfered with, and the brief appearance of the Ringfedel's paper seemed not to have persuaded many Rosenheimers to stay at home and hoard their money and wait six weeks for a different circus. Although the opening day was cold and that night more so, and the tent *was* drafty and the tober soon *was* trodden into a morass, both of the first two performances drew sfondone houses, mainly con-sisting of the proprietors and employees of the local saltworks and spas, and the spas' less debilitated guests, and all their wives and children. Nobody complained of the inconven-iences attendant upon seeing a real circus under real canvas, and everybody roundly applauded—with much foot-stamping—every act and attraction. The people of Rosen-heim, in fact, took a specially excited interest in Sir John's sideshow Egyptian Mummy and spent a good deal of time huddled about it, speculating on what salts and brines had been used to preserve that cadaver.

"That gives me an idea," Fitzfarris said to Florian and Edge, as they watched the people clustered about the mummy at the night show's intermission. "Governor, you mightily admired what you called the Bible of the Orfei circus. Re-member? So why don't we print up a handsome program of our own? Use just a couple of pages to list all our acts. And then, to fill the other pages, sell advertisements."

"Advertise mummifying salts?" asked Edge.

"No. Advertise the healthful spas of Rosenheim. The Kaiser-bad here in this park, the Marienbad, the Dianabad, all the others. We could give them a real puff—'Marienbad's waters make sick folks as lively as Zanni the Clown!'—or as strong as the Quakemaker—whatever they'd like to see in print. And charge the bath owners a stiff price, because we'll go on using those German programs all over Bavaria and Austria.''

''A very good idea, Sir John,'' said Florian. ''I'll start soliciting the proprietors first thing tomorrow, and—''

He was interrupted by the approach of a man who might have been any random josser from the crowd, but who introduced himself, in German, as an unemployed circus hostler. Florian relayed that to the others. ''He says he was working most recently for the Ringfedel, but he quit because he despises the outfit. Colonel Ramrod, could you use an extra horse tender?''

''That man's no Slovak,'' said Edge. ''Why is he working a slop job?''

''The very question that occurred to me,'' said Florian. ''But I'll give him a trial chore, and see how he does at it.''

He and the stranger exchanged some words, then Florian took out a piece of paper and his mason's pencil. While he leaned against a midway stall's counter to write, he said, ''I asked him if he knows where the local telegraph office is. He says he does.''

Fitz asked, ''Who do you know in Bavaria to telegraph to?''

Florian did not reply until he had finished composing the message. He gave it to the stranger and gestured for him to run with it. Then he told the others, ''I telegraphed to our advance man, to advise him that we will omit showing in Munich, because I have heard news of plague there. I instructed him instead to hurry to other towns and book us good tobers in them—Fürstenfeldbruck, Landsberg, three or four more.''

''What advance man?'' asked Fitzfarris. ''I'm the only one you've ever had, and I haven't worked since we left the States.''

''There still is no advance man,'' said Florian. ''But no matter. I would bet my purse on your mouse game before I'd bet on that telegram's getting dispatched. The fellow is almost certainly one of the Fedels' spies. We'll never see him again.''

"Hell, we could have just flung him off the lot," said Edge.

Fitz asked, "Did you get word of the plague from Boom-Boom?"

"I have had no such word," Florian patiently explained. "And we *will* show in Munich, because now I am quite confident that the Zirkus Ringfedel will not try to rivalize against us there. You see, lads, there are persons who think themselves ever so clever, to pry into another's business by lurking and eavesdropping. But then they must *believe* the things they ferret out, however improbable, or what was the point of taking so much trouble to learn those things? The Fedels will convince themselves that I am privy to secrets they are not—that Munich is stricken and that those other places are plums for the picking. Preposterous, and any reasonable person could tell by looking at a newspaper and a map. A plague in Munich would be front-page news. The towns I listed are mere map dots, not worth our visiting. But those towns *are* on the railroad. Therefore, if the Fedels are so clever as to be fooled by their own snooping . . ." Florian smiled and spread his hands. Then he said seriously, "The fact remains, however, that we are traveling across a continent replete with circuses and competition. I *would* like to have a competent advance man out ahead of us."

The succeeding days were as busy and profitable for the Florilegium as the first had been. The good people of Rosenheim not only continued zestfully to patronize the show, they also manifested the famous Bavarian hospitality and *Gemütlichkeit*. Numbers of them begged leave to introduce themselves to their favorite performers among the troupe, and invited this one or that, or several at once, to parties and balls and restaurants and even meals in their own homes. Florian remained wary of spies and abductors, but he did not forbid the fraternizing; the only condition he set was that the younger artistes not go anywhere without a chaperon in attendance.

So the troupers happily accepted many invitations, although, after their free and easy circus life, they often were rather intimidated by the severely efficient domesticity they found when they visited any local household. Right inside every front door were felt pads upon which a guest was bidden to step and thereafter keep under his feet, not walking but sliding the pads with him, so as not to mar the highly waxed house floors—even to shine them more glossily. And many of the objects in every house, no matter how obvious their use or function, the visitors found tidily labeled: ''Handtuche'' stitched on bathroom towels, ''Topfe'' amd ''Pfannen'' lettered on kitchen cupboards, ''Guten Appetit'' embroidered on the table napkins. Fitzfarris solemnly swore that he had even seen a cuckoo clock in one house identified by name tag, ''Kuckucksuhr.''

Of course, it was the young, beautiful and unmarried females who got most of the overtures. Paprika declined all the enraptured young men who sent her flowers and sweets and notes, on the ground that she had to chaperon and interpret for the Simms sisters, whose un-Bavarian complexion did not at all repel Bavarian swains. Monday complained that Paprika constantly attended them only ''to stick a spoke in our wheels.'' Sunday took Paprika aside and quite bluntly pointed out that Rosenheim contained as many fetching women as eligible males. But Paprika only gave them a motherly, tolerant smile and continued to hover whenever the girls, Sunday especially, went out to dinner, or to a Varieté theatre or for a sleigh ride along the Inn.

There *were* women in Rosenheim, and the unattached among them were not bashful about introducing themselves to the unattached Florian, Maurice, the two clowns and, in droves, to the Quakemaker. The blacks, Chinese and one-eyed Mullenax, were the only troupers unbesieged. Mullenax, at least, did not seem to mind; he was happy to spend his off-hours in a Beisl or Weinstube, soaking up schnaps. When Obie Yount received his first scented billet-doux, and had Florian translate it, and learned that his admirer was a widow woman, he recoiled. He still retained his Dixie boyhood recollection of widows as elderly women, usually obese, wearing shapeless dresses and singing hymns. But Florian knew better and quickly disabused him of that misapprehension. So Yount accepted the invitation and many thereafter, finding that European widows—anyway, the ones bold enough to accost him—were of quite a different breed, and sang songs sweeter than hymns.

"There's one thing, though, that does gravel me when I'm bedding these hot-blooded widder women," he confided to the wallflowers of the company: the married men and other undesirables. "Every one of 'em has a needlepoint picture on the wall by her bed. It shows a grave with a weeping willow sagging over it, and there's a motto—Florian tells me it says 'Our Darling Departed' or 'Love Eternal' or some such sentiment—and the willow's fronds are wove from the late husband's own real *hair*. It's enough—well, it's almost enough—to make a man's pecker droop like the willow."

One evening between shows. Edge was approached by a man a few years younger than himself, who wore the uniform and insignia of a major in the Prussian Army. He introduced himself informally as Ferdinand, and said, "We have something in common, Colonel. I also participated, in a minor way, in your American War Between the States. On the other side, I must confess. The wrong side."

"No apologies, Major," said Edge. "I am neither a colonel nor a Confederate any more. But why do you say the 'wrong' side? It won, after all."

"Ach, Chancellor Bismarck predicted that from the beginning. But the Union Army was deplorably scant on gentlemen. One of my Yankee fellow officers stole my umbrella. Another stole my fine English barometer."

"You must have gone to war very well equipped."

"I went mainly to observe. And I did learn some useful things. I saw how your American stirrups have leather covers over them, to prevent their tangling in twigs and brush. When I came home, I recommended their adoption in the Prussian Army. All our cavalrymen now have them."

"And are you still observing, here in Bavaria?"

"Occupying. Only temporarily. I was engaged in the recent unpleasantness with Austria. My battalion remains on the border, and I am quartered in the Schloss here."

The Prussian officer and the Virginian ex-officer continued to chat of old war times, trying to fix on some battle they might both have been involved in. Then Ferdinand mentioned that "the literal high point" of his Union service had been his once going aloft in an observation balloon. Edge told him of the Florilegium's *Saratoga*, and regretted not being able at present to offer Ferdinand a ride in this one, but summoned the troupe's aeronaut to join the conversation.

"Monsieur Jules Rouleau, may I present major—?"

"Ferdinand, Graf von Zeppelin," said the man, with a stiff bow and a click of his boot heels. "I am much, much interested in ballooning, gentlemen. Perhaps you both would do me the honor of taking dinner with me at the castle?"

Edge again expressed regrets, not wanting to leave Autumn unattended, but Rouleau accepted with pleasure. Von Zeppelin raised a hand, and a uniformed orderly drove up with a fine landau, and the Graf and the aeronaut departed the tober.

"That's dandy," said Clover Lee, who had been looking on. "A Graf is a count, but do I get him? No. I've been courted by half a dozen young men here, and they've all turned out to be the sons of bath owners."

"Ferdinand already has a Gräfin back home in Berlin," said Edge. "He mentioned her. Never mind, Clover Lee. I'd bet that a Bad-owning family is wealthier than any of the nobility."

"I wouldn't know. My escorts have talked about nothing but Ella Zoyara."

"Who?"

"The greatest and most beautiful équestrienne in Europe, and she performed here a year or two ago. She wouldn't be flirted with, so I guess the local young blades settle for me as the next best thing."

"Then they're no judges of equitation. Or of beauty. You were as expert as your mother even before she left. Since you had those ballet lessons back in Rome, you have far surpassed her. In beauty, too."

"Well, I hope sometime we cross the track of that Zoyara,

so I can get a look at her. Meanwhile, I thank you sincerely, kind sir, for the compliments.''

When Rouleau returned from the castle, some hours later, he was accompanied in the landau not by von Zeppelin but by a plump, waxy-skinned, waxen-mustached and extremely well-dressed young man, whom he introduced to Edge as the Herr Wilhelm Lothar.

''Willi was among the distinguished company at dinner,'' said Rouleau. ''Florian has been wanting an advance man, and Herr Lothar is seeking employment congenial to his taste for travel. Will you be so kind as to show him around our establishment, Zachary, while I go to find Monsieur le Gouverneur?''

Edge complied, though he found the pudgy young Wilhelm—''Oh, do call me Willi''—almost amusingly perfumed and pomaded. While they went about the tober, and Edge showed him things and presented him to other troupers, Rouleau was enthusiastically telling Florian:

''. . . Perfect for the post. Speaks as many languages as you do, and has entrée everywhere. I wished to tell you privately, before you meet him, that Wilhelm and Lothar are but two of his names. He has a string of them, and they conclude with Wittelsbach.''

''No! Of the Bavarian royal family? Then what was he doing dining with an enemy Prussian?''

''Willi was only one of the many local luminaries present. Von Zeppelin keeps open house, so he probably did not know half of them. Anyway, Willi is apolitical; a dilettante; a social animal.''

''Well, the title-hunting Clover Lee, at least, would certainly be delighted to have such a princeling among us.''

''Er . . . I did say, ami, this is a private disclosure. Willi entrusted his identity to me in confidence. He is forbidden by the family to make public his lineage.''

''Forbidden! I know that family is famous for its eccentricity, but surely to forbid—''

''Even eccentrics can outcast one of their own. Willi is a remittance man, well provided for, so long as he keeps secret his familial affiliation. He is—que dis-je?—cashiered, defrocked, whatever it is that a family does with an embarrassing cousin.''

''He must be eccentric to the point of lunacy. I should not much care to have a certifiable lunatic representing Florian's Florilegium.''

Rouleau sighed and said, ''The other Wittelsbachs may be mad; Willi is only queer. Pas plus qu'est un enculé, if I must so vulgarly describe him. Are you being deliberately dense, mon vieux?''

''No, but I am relieved to hear the plain truth. An innocuous Ganymede is not necessarily disqualified from our employment. True, he will scarcely be acceptable to Clover Lee. But his, ahem, predilections need not interfere with the duties of an advance man.''

''Au contraire,'' said Rouleau, ''if I am correctly informed as to the numbers of—of his and my persuasion—among the European upper classes, Willi Lothar could be our passe-partout into high society, palaces, command performances . . .''

''Take me to meet him, I shall first try his fluency in Magyar.''

So Edge and Rouleau stood by, Rouleau looking proprietorially pleased, while Florian and Willi conversed as volubly and, to the bystanders, as incomprehensibly as any two genuine Hungarians. Then they switched languages, through Italian and French to some others that Edge could not even name. Finally Florian emerged from the colloquy to announce that Willi would indeed be joining the establishment, that salary terms had been agreed upon, that Willi's first task would be to design a printed program for the Florilegium and sell advertising space in it to the Rosenheim baths. After that, he would do his advance-man traveling in his own calash, driven by his own body servant, and his first trip in that capacity would be to Munich.

''Perhaps,'' said Rouleau, coloring slightly, ''since I am a flightless chicken until Boom-Boom is with us again, I might go along with Herr Lothar—to show him the ropes, so to speak.''

''Do so, Monsieur Roulette,'' said Florian. ''The young

man seems well experienced in dealing with officialdom, but he has probably never in his life haggled with a feed dealer or a meatmonger.''

No more than a week later, Willi Lothar proudly presented Florian with the printers' first proof of an exquisite, stiff-covered program printed in blue and black on several pages of good white paper. The inside two pages listed, with flamboyant descriptions full of superlative adjectives, all the acts and attractions of the circus. The surrounding pages contained almost equally perfervid advertisements for the Kaiserbad, the Ludwigsbad, the Marien-bad, the Johannisbad and several others, each attempting to top all the others' claims of miracle resurrections wrought by their mud baths, sulphur baths, chalybeate baths, esoteric methods of massage, water cures, galvanic cures, dietary cures, etc. Willi also handed to Florian the heavy purse of money he had earned from that endeavor.

''Magnificent! A promising beginning to your new career!'' said Florian. ''Tell the printer to run off two thousand copies of this beautiful Bible. And tell doorkeeper Banat that he is to treat these *like* Bibles—hand them out to the jossers as they enter the chapiteau, then collect the programs again as they leave, so we can use them over and over. Then you and Jules may depart for Munich whenever you like.''

Another week or so later, and hideously early in the morning, everybody on the tober was awakened, practically jerked bolt upright from bed or pallet or straw, by a great shrieking whoop of noise. Even the circus animals started up with roars, squawks, neighs, barks and trumpetings, expressing the same shock and consternation as did the exclamations of the humans:

''Ach y fi!'' cried Dai Goesle, as he leapt from his caravan bunk in his long underwear, colliding with Zanni Bonvecino, also leaping and crying, ''Che peto forte!'' But the third man in that caravan merely sat up in his bunk, smiled beatifically and said, ''Carl Beck has brought my cally-ope.''

''On the road, Jules and your new man I met,'' said Boom-Boom to Florian and all the others who had erupted into the frosty morning, wrapped in robes and blankets and rugs.

"Chopped wood, we all did, so to fire up the boiler of the Dampforgel I could, this last mile, for a nice surprise to give you all."

Most of the company growled a sour opinion of his nice surprise—"Christ, if the two elephants could sing," said Mullenax, "that's what they'd sound like"—and went back inside their warm vans and wagons. But Florian, Edge, Fitzfarris and a few others stayed outdoors, their breath steaming like the calliope, as they voiced their admiration of it. Not that it was very admirable to look at; Beck had built it to be purely functional, so it was only a massive, complex, convoluted heap of machinery bulking above the sides of the farm wagon he had fetched it in. Like a railroad locomotive, it had a firebox under a water boiler, but there its resemblance to a locomotive ended. From the boiler, copper tubes snaked all about, to culminate in a rank of various-sized upright pipes with lipped apertures, like those of a church organ, but there the resemblance to an organ ended. The keyboard was unique to the calliope: not dainty ivory keys but stout wooden ones, each about four inches wide, for they had to be played by hammering on them with the fists. The steam pressure inside the organ pipes was such that their stops were held closed by heavy springs, so the linkage from keys to stops made for a stiff action, to say the least.

The contraption stood up there, billowing clouds of mixed blue smoke and bright white steam, while Beck bent to the keyboard, beat his fists on it and ripped off a few snorting, wailing bars of "Les Patineurs." The entire menagerie tent again let out a bellow to rival the calliope's. And from the direction of the Kaiserbad came running several hotel employees and three Rosenheim policemen. All of them stopped at a safe distance from the smoke and steam, and shouted to inquire whether they should summon the fire brigade. Florian called back some words of reassurance, and they went away, but looking back over their shoulders and muttering among themselves.

"I think," said Florian, "we had better defer any further demonstrations for a more decent hour. Carl, can your Slovak accordionist learn to play this?"

"Anybody with strong arm can learn."

"Very well. Instruct him. I shall have Stitches and his carpenters erect a decorative wooden bower over the machine. As soon as that is done, gentlemen"—his voice rose as it did when he made an announcement in the pista—"we will up stakes here and proceed en grand cortège to *make parade into Munich!*"

2

EDGE RETURNED to the caravan from which he had forbidden Autumn to step, even when they were wakened by what had sounded like the Last Trump. She was now in her dressing gown and had lit the little coal-oil stove to start breakfast.

"I could see the calliope from the window," she said. "I should very much like to get a closer look."

"It's bitter cold out here, dear. The wind is coming right across the river ice."

"And it has been a week since I was last let out to see the show. Zachary, darling, I can't make you realize how damnably boring this captivity has become. I feel like Rapunzel in her prison tower. Even reading has become very difficult. Focusing on the page, I mean. Now I can do it only by closing one eye, and that gets wearisome."

Edge gnawed his lip, but said as brightly as he could, "Tell you what, Rapunzel. As soon as there comes another sunny day, even if it's cold, I'll furlough you again. Goesle has got the new starback chairs in place, so we'll reserve one for you. Wait until all the jossers are in, and the tent's warmed up some, and seat you just before the come-in. By then, we ought to have the calliope in the spec, so you'll get your close look at that, too. All right?"

"Jolly well all right," she said happily. "Rapunzel thanks her kindly captor." She turned to smile at him, and her bleared lower eye gave him a cheerful, ghastly wink that turned him colder than the wind off the Inn had done.

Goesle and his assistants now lavished their spare-time labor on the making of the casing Florian commissioned to go over and around the naked machinery of the calliope. They did such an elaborate job of fret-saw scrollwork that the steam organ—with a leather-padded seat for the organist— eventually was hidden within what could have passed for a flower arbor. Then, after painting the wagon and the enclosure blue and white to match the rest of the train, they pointed up the fancier bits of filigree with gilding. While they worked and the calliope was inaccessible to him, Carl Beck lazed away his free time in the Kaiserbad, easing the road-stiffness of his limbs by sitting for hours in a hot saline bath. But that made his *neck* stiff, for at the same time he was having to balance atop his head a tremendous glob of allegedly hair-encouraging sulphur mud.

What with one thing and another, Beck was not ready to fire up his Dampforgel again and introduce it into the show until the afternoon performance of the Florilegium's last day in Rosenheim. The day was cold but bright, so Edge helped Autumn bundle up in layers of warm clothing and a veil, then bade her wait in the van until the last minute before the come-in. Rosenheim had continued to give the show mostly straw houses, and this closing day brought a turnaway attendance. So the chapiteau was well crowded and tolerably warm by the time Edge ushered Autumn to her starback chair near ringside. The band oom-pah'ed into its Schuhplattler overture—again without a conductor, because Beck insisted on being the organist at the calliope's début—and the midway girls went into their boisterous dance.

A few minutes later, the dancing girls all gave an involuntary and excessively high leap—the seated crowds almost did, too—and the band's oom-pah'ing was totally obliterated, when there came a sudden cataclysmic roar-hoot-screech from outside the tent. After that first staggering impact, the noise became recognizable as the drinking song, "Wein, Weib und Gesang," but became no less deafening. A horse plodded in through the back door, hauling the high and glittery new wagon from which emanated both the uproar and the damp, scorchy smell of an immense steam laundry. Beck's wagon horse had had at least a little while of earlier proximity to the clamor to get accustomed to it, and the skittish zebras had been excused from this walkaround. But the other horses, the two elephants and the camel came in leaning backward as if they were being urged down a steep hill, and the caged creatures were all but beating on the bars. Not only the animals' drivers and tenders, but also every other trouper in the parade—except the invisible Beck and the beaming Florian—looked almost equally buffeted and dazed by the tempest of noise.

However—circus folk and fauna alike being infinitely adaptable to circumstances—by the spec's third circuit of the chapiteau, they all had evidently decided to take the noise as nothing more than exceedingly loud applause and were calm in consequence. The artistes waved and bowed and blew kisses to the crowd—which was applauding, though unheard—and the animals afoot stepped high and proud, and the caged ones relaxed to enjoy the ride. As Beck finally let the "Wine, Women and Song" wane and wheeze diminuendo, his Slovak driver edged the calliope wagon to one side, and let the rest of the spec precede it out of the tent. When the calliope let go its fierce grip of the music, the band picked up the tune, though sounding Lilliputian by comparison, so the Kapellmeister could step out of his fancy bower and take his bows to the now audible ovation.

"Unfortunately, the applause was not universal," Florian told Autumn, when he and Edge sat down with her during the intermission. "We will have to omit the calliope from tonight's performance, and it is just as well that we are leaving tomorrow. A delegation was waiting outside the back door when our spec emerged—irate Bad-proprietors, their house physicians, masseurs and what-not leaped out of the mud baths and into the nearest tree branches when Boom-Boom struck his first chord."

Autumn started laughing, and so did Florian.

"Humorous, yes, but not to Carl. He very peevishly demanded to know how he can possibly train his replacement organist before we get to Munich. I told him they can practice together on the road, whenever we're on an uninhabited stretch of it, but if any cows jump over the moon, he'll have to do the placating of their owners.''

After the intermission, Barnacle Bill came on, no drunker than usual, to put Maximus and the horn-playing Kewwy-dee and the bridge-making elephants through their turns. When he and they had taken their bows, Sunday, Zanni and Ali Baba did antics to amuse the crowd while the pista was cleared. Then the band played a polka to introduce the Smod-lakas' dog act, and the blond man and woman, the terriers, the albino children, came prancing and cartwheeling in. But when Pavlo took his commanding stance for the first trick, he gave no command. Instead, he turned very red in the face, pointed an accusing finger at part of the audience and bellowed, ''Is again here the spy!''

Dumbfounding his family and the equestrian director, he lunged from the pista in among the nearer starback seats, elbowing through the startled spectators and overturning some of them, meanwhile roaring, ''I see you, prljav snooper! I have every time seen you! Lady dress and veil don't fool Pavlo!'' Edge was angrily cracking his whip and blowing whistle blasts, but Pavlo crashed on until he loomed over the chair where Autumn sat, and with a snarl he snatched off her hat and veil.

Then he recoiled, turned pale, dropped the hat, whimpered, ''Svetog Vlaha . . .'' and crossed himself with an unsteady hand. Several of the jossers seated in the vicinity had been watching the madman, but their stares now fixed on Autumn. There were murmurs of ''Himmel'' and ''Schrecklich'' and ''Mein Gott,'' and more signs of the cross made. Other people farther off, thinking the interruption was part of the act, stood up and craned to see what was happening.

By now, Edge was at Autumn's side, helping her to her feet, and saying through his teeth to Pavlo, ''Get back in the pista, you son of a bitch, and keep the show going.'' Pavlo backed away, speechless, shaking his head in awe, and stumbled to the ring, where his family regarded him with fearful wonderment. As Edge helped Autumn through the stands to the back door, the band music resumed, and Gavrila could be heard, instead of Pavlo, giving the dogs their first cue: "*Gospodjica* Terriest . . . *igram*!"

Autumn, shaken and bewildered, kept saying, "What . . . ? What . . . ?" as Edge supported her and bore her along as quickly as possible through the backyard clutter and the inquiring looks of idle roustabouts. In their own caravan, he helped her take off her outdoor garments and then tenderly lowered her onto the bed.

"What . . . ?" she was still saying. "What was all that . . . ?"

"Compose yourself, little girl. I told you the man is demented by professional jealousy. And I'll make him sorry he is. But I've got to go on next—do my shooting. Then I'll have Florian take over as director and I'll skip my voltige act. Will you be all right until I can get back here?"

"Yes . . . yes," she said distractedly. "Don't neglect your duties But . . . what *was* all that . . . ?"

When Edge stepped into the pista a few minutes later as Colonel Ramrod, he found, for the first time since he had borne arms in any capacity, that the weapons were unsteady in his hands and, for the first time since his recruit training days, he had to concentrate hard to take accurate aim. But, by pretending that every target was Pavlo Smodlaka, he got through the turn without mishap. After he and his assistants, Sunday and Monday, had taken their bows, he asked the girls to take charge of the carbine and pistol. Then he gave Florian the whistle and whip, told him that Buckskin Billy would not be performing in this show and left the chapiteau, going first to pound on the door of the Smodlakas' caravan.

A few minutes afterward, when Edge entered his own caravan, Autumn was still on the bed, now with her face pressed into her pillow, but she had put a pan of water on the little stove. Because Edge's knuckles were scraped raw and bloody, he went to wash his hands before he touched her. But he paused there, and looked down into the pan, and went cold again. The window curtains were all open, and the van's interior was bright, so Edge could clearly see his reflection in the water.

"You brought me books and all sorts of other diversions,"

Autumn said miserably, her voice muffled by the pillow. "I wondered why you never brought another mirror. It occurred to me to look at myself in the water, in daylight."

Edge swallowed the lump in his throat, washed and dried his hands, and came to sit on the bed beside her. She hid her face deeper in the pillow and said something else.

"Turn your head, Autumn. I can't hear you."

She adjusted her position slightly. "You can listen, but don't look at me any more. Please. Dear God, what is happening to me, Zachary? I never knew—you never let me know—how awful it is. How could you bear to . . . to be near . . ."

"Autumn, nobody knows what it is. Not Dr. Köhn, Maggie Hag, nobody. But don't talk like you're something to be *tolerated*. Damn it, woman, I love you."

"You can't. I don't. Lying here . . . since I looked . . . I've been thinking. I'm in the right place. A circus. I may not be an artiste any more, but all I have to do is move across the pitch to the sideshow tent and . . ."

"I said don't talk like that." He stroked her cheek, the fraction of the "good side" of her face that she had turned toward him.

"But I am a grotesque! A gargoyle!" Abruptly she forgot her own troubles and exclaimed, "What have you done to your hands?"

"I beat the shit out of Pavlo Smodlaka."

"Oh, that was childish. You said yourself he is deranged. He didn't deliberately reveal—"

"I know. But he deserved a thrashing, if only for disrupting the performance. Anyway, I had to hit out at somebody, somebody atrociously malignant, and I can't reach God. You're worried and scared, but I'm worried and *infuriated*."

"None of which does any good. But what *can* be done?" Her one visible flower-petaled eye filled with tears.

"There's got to be something, and we'll find it. We'll collar every doctor in Europe, if we have to. I've got the name of another one in Munich, and we'll call on him the minute we get there." He held her until the eye closed and she slept.

*   *   *

Munich was two days' run from Rosenheim, and the Florilegium now at last left the Inn River and took a road toward the northwest. Along the way, Beck and his accordionist rode on the new calliope wagon, driven by another Slovak, and let it straggle well behind not only the circus wagons and animals, but also well behind the midway-joint vehicles. Even so, everybody in the train could hear the whoops and hoots and ululations of the Dampforgel, as Beck rehearsed the organist who would play it from now on. None of the draft horses and none of the livestock in the roadside fields actually stampeded, but cows, sheep and horses—and farm folk—did gaze wonderingly as the calliope smoked and steamed and agonized past them. And, when the troupe gathered around its campfires, Fitzfarris swore that he had seen wild creatures—elk, boar, wolves and Auerhahns—come to peer from the shelter of the roadside woods.

Florian reported to the company, "I happened to tell our new organist that, in the States, a calliope player is always known as the professor. So now he insists on being so called, and Banat is miffed, because it sounds more prestigious than his own title of crew chief. Nevertheless, American tradition accords the honorific, so all of you try to remember to address that Slovak as Professor, if ever you have occasion to speak to him."

"He'll soon be too deaf to hear it, anyway," said someone.

And someone else asked Florian, "Where are we to meet Jules and Willi, to lead us to our tober?"

"We made no arrangement, but I have little doubt that they will find us. *They* are not deaf."

When, about noon of the next day, the spired skyline of the city rose ahead of them, Florian halted the train. "Behold—München, meaning the Monks, for it was named to honor those excellent friars who perfected the art of making the best beer in the world. Now let us prepare to make fitting parade."

He moved the balloon wagon up to second place behind his rockaway, and all the bandsmen climbed aboard it, so their music could be heard, however briefly, before the calliope came along at the tail of the procession. The cage wagons had their weather panels removed, and the elephants and camel were draped with their fringed and tassled robes. Magpie Maggie Hag had even made big, fuzzy blue pom-poms to go on the points of Mitzi's tusks. The human artistes arranged themselves in attractive postures on wagon and van tops, but kept their cloaks around them until they should reach the lee of the big buildings that lined the city streets.

Florian blew his whistle, Beck gave the downbeat and the band swung into the "Auf der Heide" army march, and for behind, the calliope did the same. The Rosenheimerstrasse brought the circus into a district of the city that was all industrial buildings, almost all of them immense, block-square breweries. The air was thick with the cheesy smell of hops and barley fermenting, and seemed to be made even thicker by the music's reverberating between the high brick walls of those buildings. The workers crowded the windows and doors to watch—they could hardly avoid hearing—and to wave aprons and paddles and ladles. The parade then crossed the Ludwig Bridge over the river Isar into the city proper. Now it was on the broad avenue called the Thal, laid with streetcar tracks, so the circus's wagon drivers had to steer with care to keep off the rails. Several drivers of the streetcars themselves, hearing the circus approaching, had to hurry their horses to intersections and steer their "toast-rack" coaches off into side streets, whence they angrily shook their fists at the parade for interrupting their schedules.

But other people crowded the sidewalks to watch the procession, and waved and cheered and clapped. Jules Rouleau and Willi Lothar evidently also heard the circus hit town, for they met it at the big Isar Tower, both of them leaping from the crowd into the cab of Florian's rockaway.

"Willi got us a tober in the Englischer Garten," Rouleau shouted up to Florian. "No one but he could have done that."

Florian waved acknowledgment, but did not turn immediately toward that park. He followed the Thal through the big archway that pierced the Old City Hall—and when the calliope roared through that tunnel, it really roared—which brought the parade into the Marienplatz, Munich's vast central plaza, full of memorial columns and statues, and surrounded by buildings whose façades were all balconies, gables, mural frescos and niches in which stood more statues.

The train went from there up one street and down another, some of them broad, some narrow, all impeccably clean and none without its ample decoration of towers, fountains and statues, in addition to the decorative-enough buildings that flanked it. Every street was likewise crowded with Münchners delightedly waving welcome. The parade circled the massive theatres and museum, and the walls of the palace and its park, before emerging into the wide-open spaces of the Englischer Garten, six hundred acres of immaculate lawns, fine old trees and flower beds—now fallow and snow-dusted—and icicle-fringed cascades. There were not enough strollers in the park on a winter day to make a crowd, so the artistes hastened to wrap themselves in their cloaks again. Beck let his band cease playing to rest their mashed lips and aching teeth, and also the calliope organist, to rest his bruised fists.

When all the troupers had got down from their parade perches and the roustabouts were neatly ranking the wagons and vans, Rouleau told Florian, "Willi and I have not yet posted any paper, not knowing exactly when you would arrive."

"Well, get on with that, then. The crew will be busy with the setup, so hire some vagrant Kinder to do it. Have you engaged hotel rooms?"

"On reserve," said Willi. "I trust the Hotel Vier Jahreszeiten is satisfactory?"

"Oh, eminently," said Florian. "The Four Seasons is several-star deluxe, as I recall. You may be dangerously elevating our appetites to champagne, when presently we have but a beer pocketbook."

Willi gave a patrician sniff. "One should never lower one's taste to the level of one's trouser pocket. A person who has not a champagne palate seldom is offered champagne."

"Then go and order the rooms made ready. In the meantime, I shall treat the company to a champagne-palate meal at the Chinese Tower here in the park."

When Florian extended that invitation to the troupe, and most of them hastened to change into civilian garb, Edge said thank you but declined on behalf of himself and Autumn. "We'll just have a bite in the van, and we won't need a hotel room either. As soon as we've eaten I want to get her to this doctor"—he brought out the slip of paper—"Renate Krauss, on Prinzregentensstrasse. How do I find him?"

"Not him, her. A lady physician, most unusual. Anyway, Prinzregeten is the street from which we entered this park. You'll have no trouble finding her."

The park's Chinese Tower was outwardly a faithful simulation of an immense pagoda, but the restaurant inside regaled the troupe with a most Bavarian meal, and a sumptuous one—liver dumpling soup, grilled Waller fish, Sauerbraten, parsley potatoes, orange-sauced carrots, Spatenbräu beer, Virgin's milk wine and, for the sweet, a marvelously sculptured chocolate chalet, its marzipan roof snowed over with whipped cream. After that meal, the troupers had almost to be helped aboard the wagons for their return to the tober.

There Aleksandr Banat was waiting to tell Florian, "Visitor you have," and to hand him a business card printed in several colors.

"S. Schmied," Florian read aloud. "Chefpublizist, Zirkus Ringfedel. Ha! Fancy title for an advance man. Show him to my caravan."

"Not him, her," said Banat.

"Well, well, two rarities in one day," mused Florian, and, when he greeted her, he said in German, "An advance *woman* I have never met before, gnädige Frau. Or is it Fräulein?"

"Schmied will suffice," she snapped, looking annoyed. Florian studied her and decided that S. Schmied must have been a goodlooking woman before middle age and self-importance took their toll. She went on, in a slightly less aggressive manner, "I come to congratulate you, Florian, on the fine lie you fed us."

"Bitte? I have not communicated anything to your organization, neither truth nor falsehood."

"Oh, stop it, Florian. At your sly instigation, the Ringfedel is booked for the next two months into a succession of charming but negligible villages. We *would* neglect them, except that we so admire your cunning—to send us off into the hinterland so you can prosper here in München. So we will be good sports about it. Not only will we honorably fulfill those engagements, but also the Herren Fedel good-humoredly wish to reward their fellow showman for such a show of finesse.''

''Now *you* stop it, Schmied. I have just come from my Mittagesen, of which I over-ate to excess, and another serving of sweets might prove vomitory. Let us talk straight. By way of example, I shall begin. I freely admit that I expected interception of my telegram, and that I devoutly hoped someone would swallow it and choke on it. I do not apologize. It is revenge that makes the world go round.''

''Very well. You exacted your revenge. Now the Herren Fedel wish to acknowledge that, and extend their hands in friendship, and even offer you a gift, to avert any future quarrels between—''

''I warn you, Schmied, I may lose my meal into your lap. I know very well what good sports the Fedels are, and how honorable. It was your impetuosity, Chefpublizist Schmied, that made those backwoods bookings, and the Fedels are *bound* to them. Because you also had to arrange with the Bavarian National Railways the schedules of open track from town to town, the necessary shunting and so on—nicht wahr?—and the B.N.R. would not take kindly to your scrapping that schedule. From what I know of the Fedels, they are furious at this costly bungle of yours, and probably have threatened you with dismissal. So you are now here to give me a gift. What, pray? A blade between my ribs?''

She gave him a look that could have been exactly that, but managed to say, not too abrasively. ''We offer you the contract of one of our stellar exhibits. Wimper, we call him.''

''Eyelash?'' said Florian in English, then went back to German. ''One of the little people, I assume. Dwarf or midget?''

''Not a malformed noué, a genuine nain, perfectly proportioned, but in miniature. In his forties, and stands only one hundred centimeters tall.''

"Hm. About the size of a five-or six-year-old. Not really phenomenal for a midget, Schmied."

"But your Florilegium has none at all, as we are naturally aware. A five-year-old with a mustache, and smoking eine Zigarette, well, is not that better than none at all?"

"And you would simply sign him over?"

"Yes. To make us friends."

"Hogwash. This Wimper is a liability you wish to get rid of. What is his particular defect? Stealing? Concealing himself in the females' dressing room?"

"No." She sighed and shrugged. "Nothing more than the usual defect of his kind. He is a snotty little bastard."

"Hm. Well, perhaps we could use a new snot. Our other one has lately been acting most chastened and virtuous. Describe this snot."

"He pretends to be ein Volksdeutscher, and on his conduct book puts the German name of Samuel Reindorf. Actually, he is only a Polack, with a name like Hujek or something. That should describe him sufficiently. But in the pista or on the annex platform, he does a dancing turn, strutting like a real human being, invites a large woman from the crowd to be his partner, und so weiter, and the contrast with reality is comical. Though with us he travels by rail, he has his own caravan and horse."

"Very well. I shall consider accepting him, Schmied . . . and accepting a truce between our establishments . . . if you throw in eine Gratisaktie."

"Lieber Himmel! What else? The Ringfedel has not an unlimited supply of expendables."

"Come. I am sure you can think of something."

"You drive a hard bargain, Florian, for one getting *gifts*. However . . . well . . . there is the Terrible Turk . . ."

"Strongman, no doubt. I have a strongman."

"I can offer nothing more. As it is, my employers are not going to be jubilant. I might mention that the Turk also has his own van, horse, costumes, props . . ."

"Then give me a little time to think over your offer, to consult with my equestrian director, und so weiter."

"Let me know, then. I am at the Pension Finkh."

"The Fedels don't exactly pamper you when you are work-ing advance, do they? You'll be there a day or two longer? I shall communicate my decision as soon as I have made it."

"And you will have Wimper and the Turk as soon as you might want them," said Schmied, with the first smile she had allowed herself.

With a very similar smile, Paprika was saying dreamily, "After such a good meal as we just had, I always feel like making love. Don't you *ever* feel like that, little kedvesem?"

"Oh, sometimes, yes," Sunday admitted, but hastened to add, "Not on a full stomach, though."

The two had come to collapse on their caravan bunks after the feast at the Chinese Tower; Clover Lee and Monday had been dragged off for costume fittings by Magpie Maggie Hag. Now Parika and Sunday lay supine, almost inert, on their opposite sides of the van, sleepily staring up at the curve of the roof overhead.

"When, then, do you feel that way?" asked Paprika. "When you are being entertained by the Johnnies from the seats?"

"No. So far, none of those has much impressed me." Sun-day hesitated and slid a sidelong glance at Paprika. "It's odd, I suppose. I only feel—excited—that way—when I come down from a balloon ride."

"Nothing odd about it, angyal. It is quite usual to be tit-illated by any experience of high adventure or high risk."

"Is it?" Sunday said, with elaborate uninterest.

There was a spell of silence, then Paprika asked, "Will Jules be taking the *Saratoga* aloft here in München?"

"He hopes to, if the weather permits."

"And this time it is your turn to ascend, is it not?"

After another prolonged spell of silence, Sunday said, "Yes."

"Get dressed now, Fräulein Auburn," said the Frau Doktor Krauss, when the lengthy and thorough examination was done. "Join your young man in my office, so I can speak to you both at the same time."

Autumn said, "If—if the news is bad, I should prefer that he not know."

"And *I* prefer that you obey orders," Dr. Krauss said.

When the doctor was seated at her desk and the other two in front of it, she looked over the notes she had taken, then said to Autumn, "According to what I know of British history, you English have some Saxon blood."

"Is that what ails me?" Autumn said with a wan smile.

"If you are part Saxon, I should hope that you have the Teuton virtue of Gelassenheit—composure, imperturbability, even in adversity."

"We English call it phlegm," said Autumn, but her smile wavered.

"Whatever her virtues," Edge said impatiently, "let's hear the adverse part."

The doctor gave him a nod, and continued speaking to Autumn. "It is for that news that I would wish you to be gelassen. I must tell you that you are dying."

Autumn and Edge both rocked visibly, and Edge said, appalled, "Damn it, lady, *you* are sure enough gelassen."

Autumn gestured for him to subside, and said, "Frau Doktor, who among us is not dying?"

"Some sooner than others. I could have honeyed the words, Fräulein, but it would have been cruel. Now that you know the worst, the rest of what I say will seem trivial. Whereas, if I had begun gently, and worked up to that dire prognosis, you would have suffered at every word."

"Then please let me now have every word."

"The medical term fibroid phthisis will not convey much to you. There are tubercles forming and multiplying within your bones and unnaturally enlarging them—at present in the bones of your skull—and, sad to say, this form of phthisis does not respond to any known treatment."

"You said 'at present,' Frau Doktor. Will it spread elsewhere inside me? I am already a repellent sight. Am I to get uglier yet?"

The doctor dropped her eyes and cleared her throat. "You will think me facetious to say that this disease is cured only by death. And you will think me callous to employ the word 'fortunate,' but that I shall do. If the disease had struck first elsewhere, it would almost certainly have invaded one bone structure after another, making your life a torment of pain and helplessness. However—and by comparison, fortunately— it early attacked the skull. The growth there will continue, but not for long, because it is not only warping your face and head, it is growing also inside. Before much more deformation can be noticed, the bone will have constricted around a vital blood vessel or the vital lobes of your brain. You will be dead. And spared. Dare I employ the word 'grateful'?''

"Sweet Jesus Almighty," muttered Edge, slumping in his chair.

But Autumn still sat erect, her ravaged face calm. "Yes, I shall be grateful for that mercy, at least. Thank you, Frau Doktor. Can you estimate when? And will the headache become intolerable?"

"It should get no worse than can be palliated by the Dreser's Compound. I will give you a supply that will last . . . long enough. But exactly how long that will be, I could not predict without keeping you under observation, to ascertain how rapidly the tubercles are multiplying. And a stalwart Saxon would not wish to spend her last months—weeks, whatever—languishing in a clinic. Go and enjoy what remains to you of world and time. And go, as we say, mit Kopf hoch. Or as you English say, keeping a stiff upper lip."

As Edge numbly escorted Autumn out of the front door to the street, she murmured, "I wonder . . . why *do* we say that?"

"Eh?" mumbled Edge, from the depths of his daze.

Autumn let down the veil from the hat, to hide her face— and the tears now starting—and said, "It is the lower lip that trembles."

3

"HELL, YES, I'll rejoice to get a midget for the side-show," said Fitzfarris. "I don't care what kind of putrid character he may be. I've just lost half of my snake-charmer turn and the *whole* of my hootchy-cootchy."

"Is something wrong with Meli? asked Florian.

"Not with her, no. That python of hers. Right now—when we're in the biggest city we've been in yet—he decides to shed his skin."

"That incapacitates him from working?"

"You bet it does. He stinks to high heaven. Meli says it's a common failing with pythons, especially elderly ones. It'll be a week or two before he's presentable again, and I'm glad I'm not sharing the Vasilakis caravan. Anyhow, Meli can only do the Medusa turn in the meantime, with the small snakes. So yes, I'll take all the new exhibits you can get me."

"And Quakemaker, how do you feel about our hiring the Turk?" Florian asked Yount. "You have only to say no, and I'll cancel him."

"Well, Governor, my first thought *was* no. But I don't want to scotch anything that might improve our show. And I think a double strongman act might do that. Him and me, we can pretend a contest in the pista—see which can out-strong the other. Maybe even do some wrassling. If he's the tetchy type, we can take turns winning."

"No, don't!" said Fitzfarris, brightening. "That'll give me another shakedown besides the mouse game. I'll make a book on the outcome each time you wrestle. Only a fool would bet on such a proposition, of course, but there are always plenty of fools. Once I've got the bets down, Obie, I'll give you and that new hefty a secret sign to let you know who's to win."

"Here comes our equestrian director," said Florian. "We must have his consent, too." But first Florian asked Edge about the visit to the physician, and the state of Autumn's health.

"Same old story," Edge lied. "She's to keep on taking those powders. No prospect of her rejoining the show any time soon. But this Dr. Krauss says she doesn't have to stay so sheltered. She can at least come and watch the show when she wants to."

"Ah, that's something. We'll be happy to have her back among us even to that extent." Florian went on to tell Edge about the visit of the Zirkus Ringfedel's Schmied, and the possibility of acquiring two new artistes for the company.

Edge said he had no objection if no one else did, only remarking, "Obie, you sure aren't yet a total professional, if you still don't have any professional jealousy."

"Only thing I'll be jealous about," said Yount, "is if this Turk gets more of them widder women from the seats than I do."

"Then I'll send a messenger to Schmied," said Florian. "But not until tomorrow. Maybe cause her a sleepless night."

Edge made a quick inspection of the tober, found nothing requiring his attention, and went to rejoin Autumn in the caravan, where he found Magpie Maggie Hag keeping her company.

"I've told Maggie the verdict," Autumn said.

"Then why did you forbid me to tell Florian or anybody else?"

"Because there's no reason to make anybody else feel bad. I wish you didn't. Maybe it's not fair to Mag, either, but I confided in her because . . . toward the end, you . . . may have need of her. In the meantime, I want you to put on a brave face, and I . . ." She determinedly made a joke of it. "Since nobody could tell if my phiz is brave or not, I'll keep it veiled."

The gypsy grunted, "Not everything beautiful has to be pretty."

"You are a dear to say so, Mag."

"Me, I never pretty. So I not bitter because in old age I am not. Only women who once had beauty get crabbed and sour when it goes. You luckier than them. You die young and sweet, not old and bitch-mean."

Edge burst out, "Well, I'm damned if I can see any luck in this! And no amount of tent-show philosophizing—"

"For shame, Zachary!" said Autumn. "You owe Mag an apology. You know very well she has never humbugged any of us. And when you are thinking clearly again, you will have to admit that you and I have had wonderfully good fortune. It gave us more than a year together, and everything that happened was enjoyable. Partly because we were experiencing those things together for the first time. Nothing ever got repetitious and monotonous. Neither of us got stale and predictable. And now . . . now things will still be enjoyable, maybe even more so, because we'll know they're happening for the last time.''

Edge forcibly suppressed his urge to go about kicking things and breaking things, and instead mumbled, ''Yes. All right. I do apologize, Madame Hag.''

From opening day onward, the Florilegium was as well attended in Munich as it had been in Rosenheim, and so were the sideshow and all the midway stands. Florian and Beck were inclined to give much of the credit for that success to the calliope, which bellowed jolly music for an hour before the start of every show. Out here in the wide-open spaces of the Englischer Garten, it could be played without deafening or deranging any of the local populace, but it could be heard as far as the Marienplatz in the middle of town, where, Beck said proudly, ''Lorelei's music it is to the Münchners.''

Even while the Amazon-and-Fafnir rawhide show was temporarily suspended, the red wagon took in silver, copper, paper and the occasional gold maximilian or carolin, in such ample measure that Florian wore a perpetual small smile—it broadened when he paid the company on salary days—and everyone knew that the menagerie and other recent acquisitions were already pretty well paid for. Indeed, Florian encouraged still further outlays during the weeks in Munich. Goesle and Beck put new wheels on the wagons that needed them; and decorated *all* the wagon wheels with fret-sawed and wondrously painted ''sunburst'' panels, and added to and improved the night-show carbide lighting.

Jules Rouleau repeatedly pestered Carl Beck to take time off from those mundane chores and put his balloon in the air. But Beck very sensibly pointed out that the circus certainly needed no attendance booster at present, that to inflate the *Saratoga* right now would require more chemicals and more of his time than heretofore—cold weather, he explained, thinned the ambient air, so more hydrogen would be needed to lift the balloon—and also, which Monsieur Roulette could easily perceive for himself, that this winter in Munich was being an exceedingly windy one, hence unsafe for ballooning.

One day Florian said to Beck and Goesle, "I have for too long been running the Florilegium out of my hat and my vest pockets. Even the conduct books are now too many for me to keep track of. I need an office."

So Stitches and Boom-Boom redesigned the red-and-museum wagon, and supervised their Slovaks in the rebuilding of it. Since the wagon's only permanent occupant was the Auerhahn, the museum part got diminished into just a wire hutch for the bird, and the ticket end was expanded into a real office on wheels. Magpie Maggie Hag's guichet was still at the wagon's rear, but behind her now was a fair-sized room, with a window on either side, a desk with a coal-oil lamp, a desk chair and another chair for any business visitor, and a file cabinet for the conduct books, the new ledgers and the increasing other stationery the Florilegium was beginning to require for its operations and record keeping.

During all this time, Edge was doing as Autumn had bidden him, hiding his misery and faithfully performing his numerous duties. Because he was loath ever to leave Autumn's presence, he prevailed on her to attend as many performances as possible, where he could keep an eye on her—even if she was only a veiled and anonymous figure among the jossers. There was no recurrence of the earlier ugly scene; Pavlo was now, as Florian had remarked, a much improved and more temperate man, or at least was confining his nastiness to his nearest and dearest. Anyway, he no longer raced to get his act offstage, and had even added to it—dressing the three mongrels in miniature papier-mâché horse heads and false tails for their come-in with the tiny chariot, and putting them through an equine "dressage" before taking off the trappings and letting them do their regular dog act.

The other performers also and as always practiced refinements of their accustomed acts and essayed new ones. Barnacle Bill had got the tigers Raja, Rani and Siva trained to the point where he could snap his whip and they would bound atop three wooden pedestals in their cage. Then he would also get inside that cramped space, bark "Hoch!" and they would sit up on their haunches, pawing the air.

"It ain't much, but it's worth showing," he said to Edge. "It took me long enough. Next I hope to teach 'em to mosey back and forth past each other, from one stand to another. Once you got a cat on a pedestal, see, at least he's not likely to take a jump at you, 'cause it's an awkward position to spring from."

"All right, Abner. Put the tigers in at the next show," said Edge, backing away and privately thinking that Mullenax's breath might be his best protection against attack.

The clowns introduced two new bits of business into their act. One consisted of Ali Baba's riding into the pista on the dwarf horse, Rumpelstilzchen—which always got a laugh—but thereafter the animal did nothing except stand patiently while Fünfünf and Zanni made jokes about it. Their other new routine was more active and calculated to appeal to the Münchners' well-known affinity for earthy humor. Zanni and little Ali Baba put on pugilists' big practice gloves and did a ludicrously mismatched humpsty-bumpsty prizefight, trading innumerable fake but resounding punches, concluding the bout by collapsing "unconscious" together, each man's head to the other's behind. Then Ali Baba would suddenly jerk up his head, look aghast, hold his nose, flap his other hand as if clearing the air and shout in German to the haughty referee, Fünfünf, "I won!"

"How do you know?"

"Zanni just let out his dying breath!"

(Uproar of Münchner laughter and applause and foot-stamping.)

Even Autumn contributed to the circus's increasing variety and quality of acts by helping Jörg Pfeifer in the ropewalking instruction of Monday Simms. In the intervals between afternoon and evening shows, Autumn would come to the chapiteau where numerous artistes were rehearsing and the Slovaks were picking up litter, straightening the planks and chairs for the next show. If any of those people wondered why Autumn came always dressed in a street gown and heavily veiled, they were too circus-polite to inquire why, or even to refer to the oddness.

Pfeifer already had Monday working on the rope high up under the tent peak, and the girl was well accustomed to the altitude. She was costumed as a chimney sweep, in black tights, with her face sooted and her hair tucked up into Florian's oldest cast-off top hat. For a balance pole she carried a long chimney brush. Pfeifer stood on her resting platform and called his instructions out to her—usually an exhortation like "More tail! Stick out more tail!"—because her act, though it required artistic precision, was totally a comic turn, all angular movements, jerks, twitches and pretended near-falls. Autumn could not climb to the platform, and she would not presume to interfere between master and pupil, so, whenever she had a suggestion to make, she would call up to Pfeifer and let him relay it across the air to Monday:

"Herr Pfeifer, would you ask Miss Simms to pause for the crab glide and just stand perfectly still for about four beats before she goes into the skip shuffle?"

Pfeifer repeated it, and Monday stopped where she was, her long brush-tipped pole waggling slightly to maintain her balance.

"Now, while she is still," said Autumn, "would you tell her, Herr Pfeifer, to look all around the chapiteau, at everybody in here?"

Monday carefully did so, though seeming puzzled by the command. Then, no more instructions forthcoming, she went on through the skip shuffle, the hesitation walk and the rest of her turn. Not until she and Pfeifer had descended the rope ladder did Autumn explain:

"During that moment when you paused, Monday, did you take note that all the bystanders were looking at you? Herr Florian, Colonel Ramrod, even the Slovaks stopped working to look at you. Not at Zanni and Ali Baba practicing over there, not at Barnacle Bill in the tigers' cage yonder. They looked at *you*."

"Yes'm. I seen. How come you told me to notice?"

"You have just learned a subtle device of dramatics. When every other person in a crowded pista or on a crowded stage is in hectic motion, what rivets the attention of the audience is one figure maintaining perfect stillness. Remember that and whenever you want to, you can seize the audience for your own—better even than if a spotlight were on you.''

Pfeifer nodded in confirmation. ''That can make the difference between a mere performer and a real star artiste.''

''Aw, that I can't be,'' said Monday. ''Can't nobody but Miss Autumn be the rope star.''

Autumn bent and, through her veil, kissed Monday on the cheek, and said, ''Make me forgotten.''

One day, when the Florilegium had been showing in the Englischer Garten for three weeks or so, two well-traveled and weather-beaten house caravans turned from the park drive onto the tober. A few minutes later, Banat ushered their owners into the office wagon, where Florian sat discussing future routes with Willi Lothar, and Banat announced the newcomers as formally as a doorkeeper at a state ball:

''Shadid Sarkioglu the Terrible Turk! Samuel Reindorf the Wimper!''

''Ah, gentlemen, welcome, welcome!'' Florian said warmly. ''You make an impressive pair.''

They did that, the Turk being at least as big and bulky as the Quakemaker, so the Eyelash looked very much like an insect beside him. But they said loudly and at the same time:

''Efendi, a pair we are not! We took the same road, no more.''

''Do not couple me with this oversized and stinking Terrible Turd!''

''Well, at least you both speak English,'' said Florian. ''That is a pleasant bonus.''

''Had to learn many languages,'' said Sarkioglu, knuckling his immense black mustache. ''Nobody outside Türkiye speaks Türkçe.''

''And *I* learned many languages in boyhood, from my many tutors,'' said Reindorf, stroking his tiny brown mustache. ''Because I am a natural scholar.''

''A somewhat larger scholar than I was promised,'' said Florian, eyeing him. ''I might have known Schmied would lie about that, too. She said a hundred centimeters. I estimate that you stand a hundred and seven. Forty-two inches. Also, that is a false mustache you are wearing. If it were not for your thinning hair, you might be only a presumptuous Kindergarten brat.''

''Is there anything else you dislike about me?'' snarled the midget.

''Yes,'' Willi Lothar put in. ''Your professional name. It has no Mumm to it, Herr Florian. No zest, no spunk.''

''You are right, Willi.'' Florian pondered, then said, ''I think, instead of Wimper, we shall call you—yes—Little Major Minim. That is understandable in most languages.''

''Only a major? Scheisse! Tom Thumb is a general.''

''Be satisfied, Minim. Properly ranked by midget standards, you might not even make corporal.''

''Now I will tell you what *I* do not like,'' said Minim, with gritted teeth. ''This is called Zirkus Confederate, and that means Rebels, nicht wahr? Well, I would this minute still be a rich landowner in my native country''—he refrained from mentioning the country—''but for the Insurrection of '63, which overturned the natural order of society and forced me into exile. Therefore, *I do not like Rebels!*''

''You are no plantation slave, only a hired hand.'' Florian opened his new file cabinet. ''Here is your contract. Do you wish to take it and go?''

''No,'' the midget said sulkily. ''I need the salary. I am at your mercy. But do not expect me to like it.''

''Crew Chief Banat,'' said Florian, ''show our new colleagues where to spot their vans in the backyard. As soon as they are comfortable, introduce them to our equestrian director. Then come and fetch me. I shall want you to do your acts for me, Shadid, Minim.''

When they had gone, Florian muttered; ''By damn, the midget is a worthy successor to our last one. Or his reincarnation.''

''The big fellow seems decent,'' said Willi. ''Big men usually are.''

''He seems, yes. But the Fedels would not have let him go if there wasn't *something* wrong with him. We'll just have to wait and find out what.''

''Hot damn!'' exclaimed Yount in the chapiteau, when

Edge summoned him to meet his new co-strongman. "Just *look* at his dumbbells, his cannonballs, his teeterboard— everything *nickel-plate*!" He looked also at the Turk, who topped his own height to the extent of having a wealth of curly black hair; the Turk returned the look with mild brown eyes, and smiled tentatively. "Hell, Zack, you better ask him if he'll stoop to be co-strongman with *me*."

"Ask him yourself, Obie. He speaks English as well as you do."

"That is so," said Shadid. "I am told you have ideas for us to compete in tests of strength. Shall we discuss?"

They strolled off toward the other side of the pista, chatting like old friends. Edge turned to the other newcomer and said affably, "Now, what is it you do for a turn, Herr Reindorf?"

"It is insulting to have to prove myself, and I will certainly not prove myself twice. Florian said *he* wished to see me perform."

"Suit yourself," said Edge, but no longer affably. "Banat has gone to get him. I can wait."

He watched Yount rolling into the pista his homemade dumbbells and Stonewall's cannonballs—those things looking like Stone Age artifacts by comparison with the Turk's glittering equipment. The two strong men were joined over there by little Quincy Simms.

"Who is that?" asked the midget, staring in amazement.

"Young Ali Baba," said Edge. "Contortionist, acrobat and apprentice joey. He does a comic capper to the Quakemaker's turn. He tries to lift one of those ungodly heavy dumbbells and—"

"That is no Ali Baba," the midget said with contempt. "That is ein Neger." He turned to grin maliciously at Edge. "I thought you Rebels had lynched all your Neger people."

"Ready, Major Minim?" said Florian, arriving with Fitz-farris in tow. "This is Sir John, director of our educational exhibits. What are you going to show us?"

"Here in the pista? Nothing. I am a danseur. I must click my heels and stamp my feet. I cannot do that on sawdust and tanbark."

"All right. We can step across the midway to the annex,

which is where you will be performing on the platform. Exactly what dance do you do, Major?''

"Any dance. Any exhibition dance that can be done solo. Jig, hornpipe, flamenco, mazurka. After my solo, I beckon to the largest woman I can see in the audience. We dance together, and I make her look ungainly, fat, shambling, stupid. Gross.''

"Yes, I imagine you would. Sir John, we'll have the accordion player be his accompanist as well as Meli's. Banat, go get that man and have him report to the annex for a first rehearsal.''

Fitz said, "Major, your routine sounds nicely comical, but—''

"Comical? I do art!''

"Oh, surely, yes. But I think we might improve on it just a little. Suppose, after you've made a fool of the josser woman, you then do a real artistic turn with a proper dancing partner? Maybe one of our pretty shoe-slapper girls.''

Minim scowled, grumbled to himself and finally said, "I do not much care for embracing a pretty woman.''

"Oh?'' said Florian. "Would you prefer a male dancing partner?''

"Scheisse, no!'' Minim said fiercely. "I am no goddamned Schwule. You big persons are as thick in the head as in the body. What I mean is that, with a pretty girl of full size who really knows how to dance, I might compare unfavorably. That I should not like.''

"I see,'' said Florian. "Well, let us go and observe your dance, and then we shall confer. Equestrian Director, do you mind if we borrow the major for a few minutes?''

"Not a bit,'' said Edge, with feeling.

He spent the next half hour watching the two strongmen trying one another's props and discussing the alternation of their feats of strength, and Edge occasionally tossed in a suggestion of his own. When Florian returned to the chapiteau, alone, Edge told him:

"The hefties have settled on a routine. I like it; see what you think. Obie will be the brute caveman, with his rusty old gear, and Shadid will be a modern dandy, with his shiny apparatus. Obie'll pound his chest, play the rough and tough man's man, all fusto. And Shadid—this surprised me—he doesn't mind the rôle of mincing around and looking coy, even effeminate. For one thing, after Obie lets his big Lightning walk the plank across his chest, the Turk lies down under the plank to do the same—but calls in the little Rumpelstilzchen to prance lightly across him."

Florian said, "That is European artistry for you—compared to the American man's horror of looking unmanly. It sounds as if they will make a good duo."

"Of course, eventually Shadid shows himself as strong as the caveman. Lightning walks over him, too, and both men do the heavy lifts, and so on. And they'll close with one of them outdoing the other. One picks up every weight he can possibly lift, then the other picks him up, with the weights and all. Depending on which one Fitz signals to be the winner."

"Very good. Very good."

"How about Little Maggot Minim? What's his act like?"

Florian laughed. "He is funny as hell, without meaning to be, and without suspecting that he is. When he strikes a flamenco pose—and puts on that tormented scowl that every flamenco dancer seems to think essential—and then starts stamping his tiny feet and snapping his tiny fingers, it's a treat even for jaded old me."

"What about the girl partner?"

"He finally acceded to that, when Sir John suggested a girl of Minim's own size. Our Night Child, Sava Smodlaka. She is quite pleased to have something to do in the sideshow besides just stand around. Sir John is rehearsing them now."

"That sounds fine, too. Now, if we can all restrain ourselves from grinding that little maggot underfoot, I'd say we'll be making good use of the Ringfedel's rejects."

"Minim should be no more of a provocation to murder than Tim Trimm was. But I'm wondering why the Fedels let the Turk go. You've perceived nothing obnoxious about him?"

"Not yet. He's good at his work and he seems to be an obliging sort. I haven't seen any bad side to him at all."

Shadid Sarkioglu's bad side did not show itself until he went about the backyard, among the caravans and wagons, amiably introducing himself to every trouper and crewman he met. And then the bad side was shown only to the Vasilakises. Meli was doing laundry and Spyros was wringing things out and hanging them up to dry. Both of them were clad in worn dressing robes, because all their clothes were in the washtub. Shadid approached, a smile upcurving his monster mustache as well as his lips, and he stuck out a big, hairy hand and spoke his name.

Spyros said, "Kalispéra," wiped his wet hand on his robe and reached to shake the newcomer's hand.

But Shadid's smile vanished, he yanked his hand back, and his face went almost as dark as his hair and mustache. "Helleni?" he exclaimed.

"Yes, we Grik," said Spyros, his hand still out.

"Enemies! Exterminators!" Since Spyros had spoken in a sort of English, Shadid spoke in the same language. "Know, then, that I am a Muslim Turk of Morea. One Turk whom you infidel revolutionaries did not massacre."

"Ai, Kristos," Meli moaned.

Spyros said placatively, "No, no. Is true—Turkia, Hellas old enemies. But not us, friend."

"Friend? How dare you, chiti?" Shadid's eyes reddened and bulged. He shot out one hand, grabbed Spyros by the front slack of his robe and lifted him off the ground. "Hellene man is one thing only—the enemy to be destroyed by jihad!" He flung Spyros against the side of their caravan, whence he slumped to the ground, the breath slammed out of him. Meli cowered by the washtub as the infuriated Turk turned his red glare on her. "Hellene woman also is one thing only—to belong to the victor of the jihad, *if* the victor is merciful." He spun again and aimed a thick finger at Spyros, who was clutching at the wagon wheel to rise. "You! Stay there! In presence of a Turk, you are never to stand erect. Remember!" And he stalked away.

When he was out of sight, Meli helped Spyros upright and said urgently in Greek, "We must run and tell Kyvernitis Florian, and demand his protection."

Spyros shook his head, struggled for breath and said hoarsely, "No . . . no." And after a moment, "No one else saw. We must not stir up dissension."

"*We?*"

"If the Kyvernitis hired the Turk, he must want the Turk. Perhaps more than he wants us. Remember, wife, he hired us only because we were stranded. Shall we now demand that he choose between the Turk and us? We cannot afford to lose this employment."

"What do we do, then?"

"We must strive hard to stay out of the Turk's way. If he is not provoked by the sight of us"—he sighed—"perhaps there will be no trouble."

"Perhaps," Meli said, and echoed his sigh.

"Perhaps . . ." Edge dared to whisper to Autumn, as they lay in bed that night. "Perhaps that Dr. Krauss was wrong? Speaking as a layman, I'd say the last half hour or so proved you just about as healthy as any woman could hope to be."

Autumn laughed. "A layman, yes, you are." Then she said soberly, "Well, I truly am thankful that *that* function of mine hasn't been impaired."

The caravan was curtained and dark, as it always was at bedtime now, so they could not see one another, and, when they made love, Edge obeyed one unspoken rule: he would not stroke her face or hair. Otherwise they were in no way restricted or inhibited. What Edge could touch of Autumn felt as perfect and delightful and exciting as her body always had been, and she responded as passionately and happily as she always had done.

She said, "Maybe the thought that it might be the last time makes us even more eager to make it the best time for both of us."

"But if the doctor was wrong . . . just think . . . we could go on having such wonderful times forever. You know, a lady doctor is a rarity. So probably she had a hard time getting her medical education, and maybe she didn't get all of it. So perhaps she *was* wrong."

"Perhaps," Autumn said, with a sigh.

*   *   *

The very next morning, and very early, the caravan of the Vasilakises was shaken as violently as if one of the elephants had hold of it. Meli sat up with a little shriek and Spyros, on the outside of the bunk, was actually tumbled out of it. Cursing in fright and confusion, he staggered across the bucking floor, flung open the door and stuck out his tousled head.

The Turk let go the caravan corner he had been rocking up and down, and said, "Hey, Greek. I must go into town, buy some things I need."

"Ugh?" Spyros rubbed sleep from his eyes. "Well, go. Why wake us to tell?"

"I have no money. I am on holdback salary. Give me money."

"Ugh? What? We are not rich people, friend. Go ask—"

"A *friend*," Shadid said menacingly, "would not deny a friend." His mouth and mustache grinned, and he began rocking the van again.

"For God's sake, Spyros," Meli whispered from the bunk. "give it to him."

The caravan continued to toss, making it difficult for Spyros to open a trunk, find their grouch bag and extract two gold carolins from its not very heavy contents.

"Here," he said, bracing himself in the pitching doorway. "All we can spare."

Shadid let go of the van and roughly snatched the outheld coins. "You will learn, Greek, how much you can spare." And he went away.

Florian one morning assembled the cast of the sideshow: Fitzfarris, Spyros and his swords, Meli and her now-recovered python, the two Night Children and Little Major Minim—everybody but the Egyptian Mummy and the egg-laying Auerhahn cock—and took them to town to be photographed at the Studio Zimmer, so they would all have fine cartes-de-visite to peddle to the jossers. While they were thus engaged, Florian went to a printer and ordered new posters and new insert pages for the programs, listing the Florilegium's now considerably expanded roster of acts and attractions.

Sunday, Monday and Clover Lee finally got Florian's permission to go out with young men unchaperoned, provided they and their inviters all went out in a bunch. And, since none of the younger men ever turned out to be of royal or noble lineage, Clover Lee made sure that nothing compromising happened on those outings. Anyway, the gallants took the girls only to chaste entertainments like plays and operas and ballets in Munich's great theatres. And there the young men were perceptibly disgruntled because the girls paid no attention to them, but only to the performances, continuously whispering among themselves remarks like, "See that ballerina's fluttery little gesture—I could do that right in the middle of a one-hand walkover" and "See how the heroine goes all the way upstage before she turns to give the hero that look—very effective touch—must remember that."

One evening at dinner, Florian announced to those of the company present, "In this land, the whole of this month of December, even part of the next, is devoted to Christmas celebrations. Today, for instance, is the Feast of Saint Barbara and day after tomorrow will be the Feast of Saint Nicholas. I suggest that we all enjoy our own Christmases early and vicariously, because during the final traditional twelve days of Christmas we will have our biggest crowds ever on the tober."

So the troupers made even more frequent visits into town, simply as tourists and sightseers. They strolled the streets and ogled the enticingly stocked shop windows and bought things. They admired the public buildings' adornments of banners, ribbons, candles and torches, the multitudes of crèches and tableaux of costumed children in Nativity scenes, the carolers on street corners and the trumpeters on church towers playing accompaniment to the bells.

During all that season, when the Florilegium's "professor" let loose on the calliope before performances, he played medleys of old German carols and hymns, and did them very well, though it may have been the first time in history that "Silent Night" was audible for five miles around its source.

On the December 13 Feast of Saint Lucia, the circus offered only an afternoon show, because Florian knew that the entire population of Munich would be lining the city streets that night to watch their children do the Lichterzug, and the circus folk also went into town to watch. The children were all dressed in their best, and on high poles carried candle lanterns they had made of paper in the shapes of stars, cradles, snowflakes, little houses. Shyly but sweetly singing carols, they marched all about the central city, to come at last to the Maximilian Bridge. There, rank by marching rank, they dropped their lighted lanterns into the Isar River. Some of the paper things instantly dissolved and sank, but a whole flotilla of them survived to go bobbing, whirling or sedately cruising downstream, bright motes in the darkness.

On Christmas Eve the circus did not show at all, because on that day every Bavarian family stayed at home, trimmed the Christmas tree, sang carols, exchanged gifts and feasted. Florian reserved for that afternoon two of the splendid rooms of the Eberlsbräu restaurant in the Karls Tower—one room for the artistes, one for the crewmen—and treated them all to a lavish holiday spread. Edge and Autumn attended that party, but took a table a little apart from the others, so Autumn could lift her veil whenever she took a bite of food or a sip of wine.

From Christmas Day through the succeeding twelve days, as Florian had promised, the Florilegium enjoyed turnaway crowds, and even the people turned away at the ticket booth remained on the tober to squander money on the midway joints and Fitzfarris's mouse game. For these days, which would be the circus's last in Munich, Florian made a change in the show program. Pfeifer and Autumn had declared Monday Simms ready to make her début on the tightrope, so Florian decided to give her the coveted closing spot. Since Pfeifer had trained her, he could hardly complain because the Lupino mirror act was thus relegated to next-to-close, and neither did Zanni protest.

Only Sunday Simms may have felt some resentment and envy of her sister, because Florian canceled their preceding slant-climb as being "anticlimactic" to Monday's new solo turn. Sunday being still only a minor figure in the trapeze performance, she now had no act at all, except her function as a fill-in acrobat. But she did not let any unsisterly feelings show on her face when she watched the sooty and ragged little chimney sweep do her rope clowning—to the band's fitting music from Strauss's "Cinderella"—and then heard the crowd applauding and cheering and stamping their feet as they had done for no previous act that day.

Monday, up there on the platform, swept off her battered top hat to let her glossy hair tumble free, and took bow after bow, and smiled broadly and whitely through her soot. Only a few knowing eyes on the pista level could have perceived that she was also briskly chafing her thighs together, quite ecstatic from the combined efforts of loud acclamation and femoral frication.

Paprika, standing beside Sunday, said with amusement, "She is doing wichsen again." Sunday said nothing and continued to clap as vigorously as the crowd and the other troupers were doing. "Don't feel bad, kedvesem," Paprika added. "You will outshine your sister when you are ready to take full part on the trapeze."

Sunday grumbled, "If I ever get the chance."

"You will get your chance. When I decide you are ready to realize *all* your capabilities. Ready for . . . anything." Sunday turned, then, and looked at her long and thoroughly. Paprika returned the look and asked, very businesslike, "Perhaps after the next balloon ascension?"

Sunday studied her for a while longer and finally said, "Perhaps."

When Monday came down from her platform, flushed and bright-eyed, Florian and Edge were waiting to congratulate her on her smashingly successful début, and Edge handed her an immense bouquet of flowers.

"Ooh," she said. "One of them Johnnies from the seats?"

"No," said Edge. "From somebody who really knows and appreciates good rope work."

Monday opened the little envelope pinned to the bouquet, took out the card and, when she read it, her eyes got even brighter, because now they had tears in them. She gave the card to Florian, stood on tiptoe to kiss Edge on the cheek and told him, ''Pass that-there on for me.'' Then, carrying the flowers, she danced away to take her place for the Grand Promenade forming around the pista.

Florian read the card aloud. '' 'To Mademoiselle Monday. Make me forgotten. Do not forget me.' Signed . . . 'Autumn.' '' And he turned away so Edge would not see his own misted eyes.

On the ninth or tenth day of Christmas, Chefpublizist Willi returned from his advance run, to report that he had booked tobers in every appreciable community to the northeastward, clear to Regensburg, and had engaged a team to start posting paper in Freising, the first stop on the route. So now Carl Beck, although he still maintained that a balloon ascension would be unlikely before spring, at least acceded to Rouleau's entreaties to purchase in Munich all the iron filings, acid and other generator supplies that would probably be unobtainable in lesser cities.

The countryside was heavily snowbound when the circus train filed out of Munich, but the meticulously efficient Bavarians had plowed and swept clear all the major roads. The troupers and crewmen who had to drive the vehicles sat bundled in coats and blankets and every other covering they could devise. Those who did not have to ride outside stayed in their caravans most of the way and kept their little stoves burning, so the wagon train left hanging in the cold blue air a trail of bluer smoke. The camel uncomplainingly walked barefoot all the way, as it would have done in its cold native land. So did the three Chinese scorn shoes, as always, even when they had to get down on the frozen ground for some reason. But Hannibal and the Slovak bull man had thoughtfully provided sheepskin boots, the wool inside, to strap and buckle onto the elephants' big feet. One trouper who did not have to ride in the wind and cold was Autumn Auburn, but she insisted on resuming her seat beside Edge. And she clearly took delight in riding there, as if even a featureless desert of snow was worth seeing by one who probably was seeing it for the last time.

Of course, the land was not entirely featureless. Frequently a family of red deer would stand bright against the snow, or there would loom up from the white fields a multicolored and onion-domed church or a sprawling abbey or the jagged ruins of an ancient castle. The towns the circus stopped in, whether just to spend a night or to set up and show, were medievally picturesque—gabled houses with half-timbered or weathered stone fronts and steep roofs dotted all over with dormer windows. The smaller towns booked by Willi were good for only a week's stand apiece, but Freising provided a profitable two weeks and Landshut three. None of those places, however, did Beck regard as worth the effort of sending the *Saratoga* aloft, nor did Rouleau even suggest it.

During that remainder of the winter, the Florilegium experienced no overt misadventures, problems or troubles of any significance, though some occurred covertly. Shadid Sarkioglu continued to molest the Greeks; he particularly enjoyed waking them early and shockingly by making their caravan bounce and, when Spyros came to the door, demanding money.

"But you on salary now," Spyros protested, when it happened in Freising.

"All spent, and I must entertain a lovely lady from the seats. Give me money."

Spyros did so and continued to do so. But his repeated compliance in no way lessened the Turk's enmity and malice. On the street or on the tober, whenever Shadid and the Vasilakises met, he would snarl—or, after a while, a mere glare from him would suffice—to make Spyros and Meli hasten to sit down somewhere or kneel and pretend to adjust a shoe, until he had passed. The Turk somehow managed to time all these occurrences when no other trouper was near to notice, and the Greeks meekly refrained from mentioning their persecution to Florian or anyone else.

One other peculiar circumstance did get reported to Equestrian Director Edge, but he was inclined to dismiss it as trivial. Doorman Aleksandr Banat came to complain—as well as Edge could grasp from his hash of languages—that the circus was being cheated by an epidemic of sidewalling: children sneaking into the show without buying tickets.

"That doesn't sound like the scrupulously honest Bavarians," said Edge. "Even their kids are unnaturally honest."

"Almost every town, every tober, after every daytime show, I see him, chase him, never catch him."

"Them, I reckon you mean. And only at the afternoon shows, eh?"

"*After* afternoon show, Pana Edge. Always little boy."

"Little boys, Banat. Plural. But after the show? Do you mean they sneak in and hide somewhere to wait for the evening show?"

This was too much for Banat's comprehension. He could only shrug and repeat, "Always little boy come, I see, I chase, I no see no more."

"Well, usually it *is* little boys, seldom little girls. Catch them if you can, Chief, but we won't thrash you if you don't."

Banat again shrugged helplessly and went away, muttering.

4

BY THE time the Florilegium finally approached the lovely old city of Regensburg, it was early springtime and no longer too cold for the troupers to peel down to their performing costumes. So they did that and made parade into the city, again preceded by the band and trailed by the hooting calliope. The streets were tortuous and so narrow that the buildings seemed to lean and almost touch rooftops high above the cobbles, but Florian led the way through every passable one of them, even when that left no room on either side for spectators, except in doorways and windows. The parade continued on across the Stone Bridge—where the Regensburgers crowded the parapets to watch and wave and cheer—to the more open suburbs beyond the Danube, then back across the bridge to the city.

"Is this town particularly fond of chickens?" Edge asked Autumn and Magpie Maggie Hag, who was riding with them.

"There's a plaque right in the middle of the bridge with what looks like chickens engraved on it."

"In memory of an old legend," said Autumn. "Do you see the cathedral towers sticking up above the roofs ahead? Well, centuries ago, the two architects building that cathedral and this bridge were competing to see who could finish first. The devil came to the bridge builder and offered a bargain. If the architect would promise him the souls of the first three to cross the Danube on this Steinernebrücke, the devil would see that it was finished before the cathedral was. So they struck the bargain, and the bridge was finished first. The architect of the cathedral was so chagrined that he killed himself by jumping off one of its unfinished towers. If you look close, among the gargoyles on those towers you'll see the stone effigy of the man falling headfirst down it. But meanwhile, when the bridge was dedicated, its architect cheated the devil by sending first across it only three cocks. So that event is still memorialized in the plaque."

Magpie Maggie Hag asked, "The chickens maybe white and blue?"

"Heavens, I've no idea," said Autumn in surprise. "*Is* there such a thing?"

The gypsy said, "Never see such. But I dukker now white and blue birds. I dukker no good from them."

"Well," said Edge, "we've got quite a few birds now. The Auerhahn, the ostriches, Clover Lee's doves. None of them blue and white. We'll keep a wary eye out, but I must say birds don't sound very menacing."

When the circus reached its tober in the Dörnberg-Garten, most of the troupers hurried to change clothes and proceed to the nearby Goldenes Kreuz Hotel, where Willi had engaged rooms.

One who did not hurry there was Jules Rouleau. Instead, he went to interrupt Carl Beck's directing of the Slovaks who were starting to unload the wagons.

"I have soared now, ami, over many waters great and small. The Baltimore harbor, the Arno, the Volturno, the Inn. Surely you will allow me to ascend above the mighty Danube."

"Ja, ja, ja," said Beck. "I will no longer postpone. In complicity with your desire, even Johann Strauss you now have. A new waltz dedicated to the Danube he has recently composed, and already the most popular of all his works it is. As soon as the sheet music I can acquire, and my Kapell can rehearse, the ascension will be made. Tell Herr Florian the poster announcements to prepare."

And so, although the circus did a thriving business right from opening day and had no need to promote attendance, Regensburg was soon plastered with new-printed posters. They proclaimed that, on Easter Sunday, the twenty-first of April, when of course there would be no circus performance, the city would instead be treated (weather permitting) to a spectacle never before seen by its citizens. Fitzfarris immediately began canvassing the Apotheken of the city until he found one that stocked the lycopodium flash powder, so he could add his vanishing-girl fillip to the occasion. And Zanni Bonvencino proposed yet another side attraction for that special day.

"All I need is that tub," he said to Florian and Edge, indicating the old wooden washtub that had served the circus for so long and in so many capacities. At this moment, it was serving its basic function; Clover Lee was rinsing out a set of her fleshings in it. "And I shall purchase some geese."

"Eh?" said Florian, and Clover Lee looked up from her work with equal puzzlement.

Zanni said, "This Dörnberg park will not accommodate the entire city populace to see the balloon lift away. The Stone Bridge is the next-best vantage for watching the ascension, so it will be crowded also with spectators. When those onlookers get stiff necks from gazing upward at the *Saratoga*, they can relax by looking down at the Danube. And there they will see me in my tub, being towed along the river by my geese."

Clover Lee laughed, and Florian said, "A comical turn, indeed, signore. But the Danube is a swift and turbulent river, and still bloody cold even now."

"No fear, Governatore, I have no wish for a dunking. I shall keep to the shallows close in to shore."

"And hey, Zanni, buy *white* geese," said Clover Lee. She turned to Florian. "I can do a rosinback turn at the same time, along the broad street that runs beside the river, with my white doves all trailing along."

"Why not?" said Zanni. "Che sarà maraviglioso. All of us together—myself, Monsieur Roulette, Sir John, Clover Lee, the Mademoiselles Simms—we shall make that a day, Signor Florian, to be remembered in the annals of the circus."

"Oh, and Zanni," said Edge, reminded of something. "Make sure there's not a blue feather on any of those geese."

During the couple of weeks remaining before the epochal day, the circus folk passed their free time in strolling through Regensburg's narrow streets and teeming market squares and along the riverside promenades onto the Steinernebrücke to look down on the midstream Danube islands. More than one of them, on returning to the tober, made sure to go to Carl Beck—who was daily rehearsing both his band and the calliope professor in "The Beautiful Blue Danube" waltz—to tell him that the Danube was actually a muddy brown color and not notably beautiful, with chunks of winter's ice still careening down it. After hearing that six or seven times, Beck began snarling at his informants, "Until Vienna wait and to Meister Strauss himself tell it!"

On several occasions, Florian took three or four troupers to the riverside Wurstküche for its famous sausages and beer. He had to make several trips, taking just a few guests each time, because that restaurant was so tiny and so perpetually crowded with local folk. Each time, before entering, Florian would direct the guests' attention to the date chiseled in the little building's stone wall: 1320.

"I'll be damned," said Fitzfarris. "In America we revere anything that dates back even to George Washington's day. But this place was feeding people when Dante and Robert the Bruce and Marco Polo were still alive."

"And I'll bet," said Mullenax, when they went inside, "that they got stifled by this identical same smoke, 'way back then." The single, soot-encrusted room had its stone cooking hearths on one side, rude trestle tables on the other, and under its low beams hung a dense, oily and aromatic gray smoke, so a patron had to stoop to see beneath it. "But, by Jesus, the provender can't be beat!" Mullenax added, when he tucked into the Weisswurst and Sauerkohl and quaffed the amber Bischofsbräu.

Zanni procured his white geese, eight of them, and Stitches made little harnesses for them. Zanni took the birds and the tub to the small pond in the center of the Dörnberg-Garten and began rehearsals. After enduring a painful number of pecks and pinches, he got them all tied to the tub with thongs of varying lengths, and then, carrying Mullenax's heavy sjambok, folded and wedged himself with considerable effort into the wooden vessel. It took him a while of snapping the long whip at the geese to accustom them to going all in the same direction. Even then, some of the geese paddled while others beat their wings and tried to take off, but the overall result was to haul the tub at least slowly across the water in the direction Zanni aimed for, and the several watchers cheered from the pond bank.

"We will go better on the river, with the current helping," said Zanni. "And that confusion—some birds swimming while others try to fly—well, that only adds to the comic effect I desire."

Holy Saturday came, fair and windless, giving promise that Easter Day would be as clement. And Paprika's eyes sparkled as brightly as the day when she said softly to Sunday, "After the *Saratoga* descent tomorrow, everyone else will repair to the hotel to while away the holiday. So you and I can have the caravan to ourselves."

"Yes," said Sunday, returning the woman's smile so boldly that Paprika gasped with delight.

But then Sunday went to find her sister, and said, "How would you like to go up tomorrow, instead of me?"

Monday blinked and grinned, but then said with a tinge of suspicion, "You ain't go' miss that ride just out of sisterly love. What's it go' cost me?"

"Nothing. It will earn you something," said Sunday. "Another sort of sisterly love.'' She explained, as well as she could from mere hearsay.

Monday looked surprised, but not greatly shocked. After only a brief consideration of the prospect, she shrugged indifferently. ''Don't sound too hard to take. And maybe I'll learn some tricks to bait John Fitz with. Anyhow, it's worth it, I reckon, just for the extry balloon ride.''

''And remember not to talk at all,'' said Sunday. ''Don't say a word the whole time, whatever happens. She'll never know us apart except by . . . well . . .''

''I know, I know. I can't talk as prissy nice as you do. Awright, I'll keep mum. Unless you lying to me, and I find out this kind of frolic *hurts*.''

Carl Beck stoked up his generator early on Easter morning, and by noon the *Saratoga* stood brilliantly red and white and gigantic above its anchor ropes. By that hour, too, it seemed as if every Regensburger of every age and sex and condition was outdoors. The people earliest out had crammed onto the Florilegium tober and throughout the Dörnberg park roundabout, and so got to enjoy the band's repeated rendition of ''The Beautiful Blue Danube,'' interspersed with other spirited tunes, while the balloon preparation went forward. The rest of the population packed into every other open space that gave an unimpeded view of the sky—the several other city parks, the squares, the whole length of the Steinernebrücke and the Oberer and Unterer islands upstream and downstream of the bridge. So, when the band hit a caesura and dramatically stopped playing and the balloon soared aloft, it seemed to be impelled by the breath of the city itself, exhaled in one concerted and prolonged sigh from some forty thousand throats. Then the band resumed, louder than ever, the ''Blue Danube'' waltz, and the city gave a thunderous cheer.

Clover Lee, in provocatively nude-looking fleshings and gold-spangled léotard as bright yellow as her flowing hair, and Zanni, in his tight Harlequin costume, and the calliope in its gaudy wagon, with steam up but sitting silent, were at the riverside ferry slip well upstream of the city's center. The équestrienne, the joey and the professor waited until the *Sar-*

atoga had been up for half an hour or so, letting it have the undivided admiration of the Regensburgers as it variously dipped lower, rose higher, moved up and down the Danube, back and forth from city to suburbs.

Then Zanni, with the assistance of the ferry men, put his tub and geese overside from the riverbank, and the men helped him squeeze himself tightly into the tub, while the geese honked and squawked and beat their wings and churned their feet against the current. Zanni uncoiled his incongruously big whip, gave it a brisk snap, the ferrymen let go—and the geese, willy-nilly, went off in an impetuous swoop downriver, having to hurry to keep the tub from running over them. With a similar sudden swoop, the calliope launched into "The Beautiful Blue Danube," loud enough to be heard above the circus band by the spectators away inland in the park.

At the same moment, Clover Lee put Bubbles to a lope, then to a canter, just to keep pace with Zanni. The helpful ferrymen then unlatched the coop of doves she had left with them. The birds burst out in a white explosion that resolved itself into a white cloud fluttering and trailing behind the girl. From the ferry slip, the promenade sloped upward from the water level, so Clover Lee quickly lost sight of Zanni down there. But she was too busy to look at him, anyway, beginning the ballet stands and steps and acrobatic postures and somersaults.

At the circus tober, the bandsmen gratefully ceased playing when the distant calliope outbellowed them. Simultaneously, Florian yelled—he now had a proper tin megaphone to yell through—"Achtung, Herren und Damen!" directing their gaze to the platform on which stood a pretty and smiling fawn-colored girl. While he bawled the patter about magic and mystery and vanishment, Fitz leaned against the platform, negligently holding a lighted cigar. Sunday had to keep her smile from widening into a grin when she saw Paprika, not looking in her direction at all, but with her rapt eyes on the gondola in the sky. Then Florian concluded, "Schau mal!" and Fitz languidly moved, and there was the *poof!* of flash and smoke, and the panel dropped from under Sunday's feet.

She lit lightly on the ground and hunched down so the panel could slip shut again. Then she snaked through the open back of the platform and under the chapiteau sidewall. She hurried to the caravan she shared with the other females, and there changed into a calico gown belonging to Monday, before she appeared again among the troupers outside.

Meanwhile, the people lining the riverside promenade had brought their gaze down from the vermilion-and-white balloon to the gold-and-white spectacle of Clover Lee gracefully cavorting as she was borne along at the head of her flock of doves. And the people packed elbow-to-elbow on the Stone Bridge brought their gaze down to the comical spectacle of Zanni, already soaking wet from the river spray, flailing his tremendous sjambok, his tub bobbing and pitching and yawing close behind the frantically paddling geese, and all of them bearing down headlong toward the bridge pillars. Those spectators on the promenade and the bridge had their mouths wide open, but their cheers—or whatever else they might have been shouting—could not possibly be heard over the tumult of the calliope, even by their closely pressed neighbors.

Zanni and his geese sluiced between two of the bridge pillars like wood chips sucked down a drain. The people lining the downstream parapet leaned over to see them squirt out the other side. To Clover Lee, who was also past the bridge by now, Zanni's swift progress was discernible from the fact that the watchers' heads slowly lifted as their gaze followed him down toward the Unterer island, where he had planned to steer to shore. So Clover Lee turned Bubbles, during which slowdown the doves clustered and buffeted each other to find space to land on her head, shoulders and arms. Then Clover Lee cantered back the way she had come—shaking off the doves into a trailing cloud again—and repeated her bareback performance, with variations. She continued to do that, up and down the promenade, until the balloon's shadow swept over her as it softly descended and wavered toward touchdown on the tober.

The city cheered as the *Saratoga* came down and disappeared from the view of most of the watchers, sinking be-

neath the city's rooflines. The people crowding the
Dörnberg-Garten went on cheering as it settled among them.
The roustabouts were right there, to seize the rope Rouleau
threw out, and Paprika was also there, extending a hand as
Monday suddenly stood up in the basket—eliciting noises of
amazement and delight from the onlookers—and Paprika
gently assisted her to step out. The people enthusiastically
kept clapping their hands and stamping their feet on the
ground, but Paprika murmured, "Now don't detract from
Jules's applause, kedvesem. Let him take his bows, too. Here,
I have brought a cloak. You must be chilled." And she
wrapped it about the girl and hustled her off toward their
caravan, while Jules proudly preened in the crowd's unabating loud acclamation.

"Ó jaj, you are cold," said Paprika, when Monday shed
the cloak in the caravan. "Your skin is libabör all over, and
it is usually satin. But I will massage you back to warmth."
She continued to chatter, as if she were far more nervous
than the girl about what might happen next. "Quick, take off
your tights and lie down. I shall strip also. Bare bodies are
warmer than anything . . . Ó jaj de szép!" She made that ex-
clamation on an in-caught breath of admiration, as Monday
peeled off her fleshings, then discarded the only other thing
she wore, the little cache-sexe pad.

Paprika said "Ó jaj de szép" over and over as she stared
with wide and shining eyes. Monday stood somewhat uncomfortably, one moment covering herself with her hands, then
hesitantly baring her body again. Paprika shook herself and
said, "Ó jaj de szép means simply 'Oh, my, how beautiful!'—but I should not speak Magyar words you do not
know. Since you have some German, I should use for the
endearments—for the intimacies—only German words, ja?
But lie down, lie down, I shall be right there."

Monday slowly stretched out atop the bunk's covers, herself still uncovered, and her eyes stayed on the woman, just
as Paprika's stayed on her. Paprika kept on distractedly talking, while her fingers trembled and fumbled at her own clothing.

"I remember from a long time ago that you told my former

partner that you were ashamed of your—your Flaumhaar
down there between your legs. Do you recall, Sunday? You
told her it was like a scattering of little peppercorns. And it
is, it is, but it is *enchanting*. It conceals nothing, it leaves
your Schamlippen beautifully visible. Vulnerable. Oh, dearest
Süsse, you should never be ashamed of it." She laughed
shakily and said, "For contrast, look at mine."

Monday looked, for Paprika had now shed all her lower
garments and wore only her blouse, at the buttons of which
her fingers fluttered. Monday looked with genuine curiosity
and interest, because one of Clover Lee's rules for the caravan prohibited any occupant's baring herself completely in
the presence of another.

"You see? My pink Flaumhaar is *all* you see there. It
might as well be a cache-sexe, so little it reveals. Ah, but
within it . . . I am almost ashamed to admit . . . my little ruby
Kitzler has become as hard as a man's Ständer, just from
gazing at you." Again she laughed shakily, but merrily.
"And you too, Liebchen—ha-*ha!*—look down at your
breasts. Your darling dark Brustwarzen have also pushed out
stiff, and that is from gazing at *me*, nicht wahr?"

Monday hesitated, then nodded, then swallowed audibly.

"We are much alike, you see? Why did you wait such a
stubborn long while to find out? Ach, this verdammt thing!"
Paprika impatiently yanked her blouse apart, its buttons flying, and ripped it off. Breathing as if she had been running,
she lay down close beside Monday, as close as the whole
length of their bare bodies could get. "Oh, Sunday Süsse, we
will be so good for each other!" She took Monday's face
between her two trembling hands and opened Monday's quivering lips with the passionate pressure of her own.

Clover Lee, carrying the coop of recaged pigeons, took
care to ride from the ferry slip the long way around the
fringes of the city to get back to the Dörnberg-Garten. But it
was slow going, for even the back streets were jammed with
people dispersing after the show, going home or to church or
just leisurely sauntering. When she arrived at the tober and

gave Bubbles to a roustabout, Florian asked how her part of the spectacle had been received.

"Couldn't have been better," she said. "Everybody that wasn't watching Zanni was watching me. All the applause we could want, even if we couldn't hear it over the calliope."

"I suppose the professor will be a while, getting that machine back here," said Florian, looking at the jossers still in the park. "What about Signor Bonvecino?"

"It'll take him even longer, I bet, having to come through the middle of town. He said he was going to give the geese their liberty after their performance but I hope he'll remember to bring back our washtub."

"Well, small loss if he doesn't. It has been a glorious day. Come along, now. We're all off to the hotel, to change into our best dress and then convene for a sumptuous Easter dinner."

"Usually," said Paprika, "one of a woman's Brustwarzen affords her more pleasurable feelings than the other." With her fingertips she tenderly tweaked each of Monday's, and the girl's body twitched. "I shall kiss and lick and suck them alternately, so we can know which one pleasures you the more." After a little while, during which Monday gasped and wriggled, Paprika lifted her head, smiled maternally and said, "The left one. Deliciously sensitive, ja?" Monday bashfully returned the smile and nodded. "Very well, now you do the same to me, Sunday dear, and guess—from my responses— which of mine."

When Florian, in new-bought clawhammer coat, ruffled shirt and well-cut trousers, descended from his hotel room to the dining chambers he had reserved, he looked about, then commented to Jörg Pfeifer, "I am wondering what became of your fellow comic. Seeing how crowded the streets still are, I'd have thought he would come directly here to the hotel."

"Probably went to return his props to the tober," said Pfeifer. "He's a conscientious sort."

"Well," Florian said, "there's no hurry about sitting down

to table. I notice some others are not here yet. Mademoiselle Paprika, Barnacle Bill, one of the Simms girls . . .''

"Enough," Paprika said breathlessly, breaking the long and mutually probing kiss they had been exchanging. "Enough of these preliminaries, or I shall go crazy. Feel here, how my Kitzler is standing to salute you. Put your hand here, so. Ah-h. Now open that place with your fingers, gently, like the wings of a butterfly. Ja. And within . . . ah, there!'' Paprika writhed in delight, but was conscious that Monday was also vibrating. "Ah, it excites *you*, does it, merely to touch me there? But, my dear one, you are doing wichsen to yourself, like that dolt of a sister of yours. Let me do it for you, while you do for me. Open your legs just a little. Ja, yours is as pert and juicy and eager as my own. Let us together . . . ja, ja, like that . . . Ach, Gott!''

Florian rapped a spoon on a wine decanter until he had the attention of the assemblage, and announced, "Some of us are still tardy, but there's no sense in letting the viands get cold. Be seated, ladies and gentlemen. And Dai, perhaps you'd invoke an Easter grace upon the board.''

While lay preacher Goesle was doing that, Florian went to the adjoining room where the roustabouts were dining, and called Aleksandr Banat away from the table. "I hate to interrupt your meal, Crew Chief, but I need a trustworthy messenger.''

Banat, chewing a mouthful of something, nodded trustworthily.

"Several troupers have yet to arrive, but I am mainly concerned about Zanni. No one seems to have seen him since he went to the river. Would you run to the tober, Banat? The equestrian director and his lady remained there in their caravan. Inquire of Zachary whether Zanni has returned. If he is not to be found, hurry back here and tell me.''

"Du lieber Himmel," gasped Paprika. "We have each reached the Höhepunkt half a dozen times, and never yet moved from lying side by side. Let us do Mundvögeln. Do

you know Mundvögeln?'' Monday shook her head, only
slowly, because her tousled hair was heavy with perspiration.
''I shall show you.'' Paprika changed position on the bunk.
Monday jerked convulsively at the first warm, moist sensation, and cried out. ''Put your arms around my hips,'' said
Paprika, her voice muffled, ''and rest your head between my
thighs. This will drive you wild, so hold me tight.'' Monday
kept on convulsing—and crying out—until, burying her face
in Paprika's pink fluff, she discovered for herself a new use
for her mouth. Thereafter, they both thrashed and rolled
about, but quietly, all their noises cried inside each other.

After searching everywhere on the tober, in the chapiteau
and the annex, even in the midway stalls and booths, Edge
and Banat ran to the backyard and flung open every closed
wagon. At the caravans, they knocked on each door before
throwing it open. At one, Edge's knock elicited a startled
response. ''*Pokol!* Ki a csuda?''

''Is that you, Paprika?'' Edge called urgently. ''Is Zanni
in there, by any chance?''

There was a moment of stunned silence, then what sounded
to Edge like two voices giggling, but only Paprika's voice
answered, and angrily, ''Certainly not! What kind of question—?''

''Sorry to bother you. It's just that Zanni's missing. Never
showed up for dinner.''

Paprika called something else, but Edge had turned away.
Banat was saying, ''Not in other vans, Pana Edge. Nowhere
is he.''

''You run and tell Florian to turn out all the other men.
I'll start for the river right now. It'll be getting dark before
too long.''

''I suppose,'' Paprika said lazily, ''we ought to show ourselves at the dinner. And I suppose we ought to arrive separately, not to cause comment. But not just yet. Let us lie
here and rest together a little while. All this time, I have done
all the talking, spoken all the endearments, never let you say
anything. And I shall frankly tell you why. It was nervous-

ness, as if I were some sheltered maiden and this were my very first time. In a way, it was. Always before, for me, it meant no more than taking a drink of water when one is thirsty. This is the first time ever that I have felt... You know, someone said to me, some while ago, that if I could ever know *love*—and I only laughed and made some jocular reply. I did not believe I *could*, ever. But now, with you... oh, Sunday, Sunday Süsse! Still, I must not too boldly declare myself. Perhaps you have only casually indulged, and it may take you some time to decide whether you, too... anyway, at least we have now let down the barrier. There can be many more such times, Sunday dear—opportunities for us to learn every secret part of each other, and where and how best to do what, so we pleasure each other in the highest degree." She laughed happily and hugged Monday more warmly. "But right now... what we have done already... nothing nicer I could conceive."

Monday started and raised her head, to say dazedly, "Conceive? Miss Paprika, ma'am, do that mean one of us done *made a baby?*"

Paprika's whole body jerked, as if the tangled bedclothes had suddenly discharged an electric shock. She flailed away from Monday and leapt from the bunk. She stood beside it, rigid, trembling, staring down at the girl.

"You are not—" she said, in a voice choked with astonishment and rage. "Not—"

"You wasn't s'posed to know," Monday said contritely.

"Isten Jézus!" Paprika's face flushed to the exact color of red paprika.

"I traded. For the balloon ride."

Paprika's flush spread, all the way down her breasts, and she said in a terrible low voice, "Never in all my life have I been so insulted, so humiliated, so demeaned."

"And you *didn't* know, Miss Paprika, so why you get mad? Sunday and me is triplets, not no bit different nowhere on our bodies. Wasn't it just as much fun as it would of been with—?"

Paprika snarled wordlessly and, as if Monday had been a sudden intruding stranger, she seized up a pillow to cover her slick-shiny belly and its matted pink fluff. With her free hand, she gestured violently for Monday to go.

"But—Miss Paprika," the girl beseeched. "*Is* I go' have a baby from doing what we done?"

"You *stupid* néger bitch! Get . . . out . . . of my *sight!*"

Monday slid off the bunk, as far from Paprika as she could get, and grabbed the nearest street frock at hand, one of her sister's, and hastily pulled it over her head, stepped without stockings into her shoes, and fled the caravan, buttoning the dress as she ran.

5

EDGE HAD not gone far from the park when he met Mullenax ambling toward it, and asked him, "Are you coming from the hotel, Abner? Has Zanni shown up there?"

"Aw . . . the hotel. The dinner. I knowed I was forgettin' somethin'," drawled Mullenax. The local grogshops had not closed for the holiday. "You lookin' for Zanni? Hell, he must be in Vienner by now, or wherever that river goes."

"You saw him? Where?"

"Like I said, whizzin' downriver. I watched from the bridge, with the rubes. Wherever that joey ends up, he'll end up mightily bedraggled. Last I seen, that tub was rollin' over 'n' over, dunkin' him under every time. He wanted to make them folks laugh, and by damn he *did.* Say, is there any of that-there dinner left?"

But Edge had already hurried away. When he emerged from the narrow streets at the old Wurstküche, at the near end of the Stone Bridge, he turned right and trotted down the riverside promenade, peering anxiously over the water. But the water was all he saw, with still some chunks of dirty ice ripping along in the brown turbulence, and beyond the water the tangled underbrush of the Unterer island. He tried stopping some of the people still peaceably promenading, but his few words of German and his gesticulations produced only uncomprehending shrugs and apologies. So he trotted on and kept peering until he was past the island's end, and the Danube's farther shore was dim in the fading daylight. If Zanni had made that bank, he was too far away to be seen. So Edge turned and retraced his steps, and about halfway back to the bridge he met Florian, who said:

"Almost everybody, male and female, is out searching. I left Sir John posted at the hotel, to send us word in case Zanni does get there. The Quakemaker and the Terrible Turk have climbed down from the bridge onto the island, to comb it from stem to stern."

"I tried asking the passersby," said Edge. "Not with much luck."

"I have asked, too. A few who watched Zanni's perfor- mance said they tried to shout and wave warnings to him. They thought him foolhardy—or suicidal."

"So do I, now that I've had a close look at that river. He only practiced in a quiet pond. If he'd tried it here first, he'd have changed his mind in a hurry."

"My fault, mainly," Florian said gloomily. "I really should have paid more attention. I did have qualms, when I saw how tightly he had to stuff himself into that vessel . . ."

"And Maggie dukkered something about birds. But white and *blue*."

"Eh?"

"Never mind. Let's get back to the bridge and see if Obie and Shadid found any sign of him."

As they went, Florian said, "Fünfünf is taking it hardest. So, to give him something to occupy him, I sent him to in- form the Polizei. They have a river patrol—a steam launch, and good lanterns, if a night search is necessary."

When they reached the bridge, they hastened out onto it, for they could see Yount and the Turk laboriously climbing one of the high center pillars, and carrying something from the island up to the parapet, where several other troupers and a knot of city folk had gathered.

"All we found was this," said Yount, panting. He and Shadid were muddy to the waist, and much scratched else- where. What they had found was the wooden tub, its staves now loose and clattery. "It don't look good for Zanni, Gov- ernor. There was only three of the geese still tethered to this thing, and dead. Pretty near stripped of all their feathers, besides. Any water that can drown something as feisty as a goose ain't going to be very easy on a mere man.''

They were all silent for a minute. Then Edge asked Florian, "Should I spread the word that we'll stay shut tomorrow?"

"No, no," said Florian. "Alive or injured or dead, Zanni would not want that. The news is bound to get around the city, but we can't have the people *pitying* us. No, spread the word to the company that they're all to strain to look as jovial as possible. To prepare to perform at their tiptop best—and maybe at length, to make up the slack if Zanni is still missing tomorrow.''

"Have *you* seen Zanni, sis?" demanded Fitzfarris, springing up from his armchair in the hotel lobby as Monday moped in through the front door, her dress unkempt and her hair a mare's nest.

"No," she said dully. "Somebody else was lookin' for him, a while ago. Is he lost? It's my sister I'm lookin' for.''

"Yes, he's lost. And Monday is out with the others, hunting—''

She almost shouted, "*I'm* Monday, cuss you, John Fitz!"

"Well, excuse me all to hell. But that's Sunday's dress you're wearing, unless I'm mistaken about that, too. And you're not wearing it very securely. Kid, you look like you got dragged through a knothole backwards. What've you been up to?''

She wailed, "Oh, John Fitz, I'm scared I'm go' *have a baby!*'' Several of the lobby loungers and desk clerks stood up or leaned around columns to see better.

"Hey, now . . .'' said Fitzfarris, embarrassed, glancing about at the spectators. "Try not to have it here. Get on upstairs.''

"*You* don't care!" she wailed, even louder, then burst into tears and flung herself upon him, clutching his shirt front.

"Hey, now . . .'' Fitz said again, helplessly patting her back and giving a gruesome grin to all the people staring. "Sis, I sure do thank you. You've made my reputation in Regensburg. Come on. Let me help you to your room.''

She subsided to sobs and sniffles as he half-supported her up the stairs and asked solicitously, "Who—I mean, what makes you think you're in the family way?"

Monday hiccuped and said, "I ain't sure why. But ain't that what 'conceive' means?"

"Yes. But you're not sure *why*? Well, I've heard that that happened once before. Only I hope the Holy Ghost didn't leave the Virgin Mary looking as scraggly as—"

"I ain't no virgin no more!" she wailed. A passing hotel maid shrank against the banister to let them by, giving Fitzfarris a scathing glare as she did so.

"Je-sus . . ." he muttered. When they got to the upper floor, he asked which way her room was, took her there and led her to the bed. "Kick off your shoes and lie down." She threw herself supine, threw one arm across her eyes and lay there, still sobbing. "Wouldn't you be more comfortable if you buttoned that dress less crooked?"

Without looking, she used her free hand to work at the buttons, and mumbled, "What happened?"

"You tell me."

"I mean to him. What happened to Zanni?"

"I'm sorry to say that he hasn't come back from his ride on the river. We're afraid he's drowned. But don't you trouble about that right now. I gather you've got troubles of your own. *Did* somebody take advantage of you, Monday?"

She sniffled and said faintly, "Yes."

"Some stranger? Or one of your Johnnies from the seats? Or somebody from the show."

More faintly, "Show."

"Damn. Then I think I'd really rather not know who . . ."

She moved the arm so she could look at him, and said, not so faintly now, "You're jealous?"

"Well, more concerned than jeal—"

She flung the arm across her face again, wailed, "Oh; you don't care one bit!" and resumed weeping.

"All right, all right, I'm jealous, I'm jealous. And I guess you'd better tell me who he was, so I can—I suppose *something* will have to be done."

She peeked out at him again. "Awright. It was—it was him. It was Zanni."

Fitzfarris looked at her long and hard. "Come on, sis. The truth."

"It *was*. That's why I axed what become of him."

"You stumbled into the hotel just a minute ago. Zanni's been gone since noontime."

"It was afore he went. I just been layin' and cryin' all these hours. But it was *lots* of times afore that."

"Now, Monday, it's convenient to accuse somebody who maybe never can deny it, but that's a mighty scurvy thing to do. If you want to protect the real culprit, then I wash my hands of—"

"It *was* him. Ain't you never wondered how come Quincy got took into the clown act with the real joeys? I *axed* Zanni to give my li'l brother a real act to do. And he said awright, he would, if I would . . . if I would . . . and he's been doin' it to me ever since."

"Son of a bitch," said Fitz, but still uncertainly. "Zanni's always been such a courtly fellow. Are you sure you didn't dream all this, kid?"

"I can show you," Monday said simply. Her dress was unbuttoned all down the front, and now she flipped the two halves open, so he could see her entire: the fawn-colored flesh, the dark-brown nipples, the black peppercorn tufts and the dried white flakes clinging there.

Downstairs, Florian said to the several troupers and crewmen who had returned to the hotel with him, "Well, I don't know where Sir John has got to, but the desk porter says Zanni never arrived. Anyhow, I've instructed the porter to send everybody to the dining room as they come in. Since our dinner was so tragically interrupted, we'd all better have a bite now to sustain us."

"I don't have much appetite," said Edge. "And I want to get back to Autumn."

"I ain't hungry neither," said Yount. "But I could sure use a stiff drink, and I bet Terrible could, too. We're both pretty chilled and sore."

So Edge departed, and the others went to the dining hall, and still others did, too, as they came back from the several fruitless searches.

"You little liar," said Fitzfarris, rolling away from Monday and showing her the red stain on the sheet. "Taken advantage of, were you? Scared you were pregnant, eh? Well, now you *can* worry."

She looked anything but worried, smiling with satisfaction and triumph. But she tried to put on a solemn face as she said, "We never done it that way. We done what Miss— what Mr. Zanni called mumfergle. Do you know that way?"

"I never learned much Italian," he said drily.

She said, with some hesitation, "Well, I reckon it would work on you, too. On that."

Fitz said skeptically, "Was Zanni built different some way?"

"Uh, no. No. It's just . . . well, let me try . . ."

She changed position on the bed and, after a moment, Fitzfarris murmured in wonderment, "I'll be damned." Some while later, when he was breathing normally again, he said, "Did you really think you could have got pregnant, doing that? Didn't your mother ever tell you girls how you *do* get pregnant?"

"Uh huh. I reckon mammy told us everything she knowed to tell. But surely no woman in Virginny ever even *heard* of mumfergle. I never did, until just . . . so how was I to know any different? I didn't mean to trick you with no lie."

"Well, one thing is certain. I can't call you kid any more."

"No. I'm a woman. *Your* woman, now."

"Are you sure you'd want to be? Obviously I'm no better a man than that Zanni. Letting you—"

"But you're *my* man. Whatever I do with you, it's on account of I want to. Could we maybe, from now on, be a real pair, you and me? Out in the open, like Colonel Zack and Miss Autumn? Even if I'm a nigger?"

"If ever you call yourself that again, I'll slap you around, like a real husband." He sighed, but not unhappily. "I never thought I'd take me a child bride. But I won't skulk to do it, like Zanni. Yes, Monday, from now on . . ." She squealed and hugged him. "You'd better break the news to your sister. I'll tell the others. It'll mean some changes in traveling arrangements. Let me get dressed and get back downstairs."

"So it's up to the Strompolizei now," Florian said resignedly. The pickup meal finished, he and a number of the men of the troupe were drowning their sorrow in schnaps, wine and beer. Several of the women had also taken a bracer of strong drink, then had retired to their hotel rooms or caravans to mourn in seclusion. "Ah, here comes Sir John. Man, we were a little worried that we'd lost you, too."

"No, I was—uh—doing my good deed for the day. Monday Simms came in all fagged out, and I helped her to bed. Hand me that bottle, will you, Maurice?"

"If, as you say, Florian, the show must go on," said Rouleau, "the *Saratoga* is still almost fully inflated. Boom-Boom would have to give it only a small recharge. But we can have another ascension tomorrow."

"Good idea. Show the flag, so to speak. Fünfünf, have you any routine you can substitute for the Lupino mirror on such short notice?"

"Nothing as good. But Major Minim . . ." Pfeifer turned to the midget, whose head barely topped the table. "You could take Zanni's place in the farcical prizefight with Ali Baba."

Minim snapped, "I will not be made fun of!"

"You'll do as you're told!" said Florian, just as snappishly. "In this extremity, we will not coddle your precious artistic pretensions. We must all work things out as we go along, and that includes you."

Minim snarled viciously into his glass, but made no more demur.

"Tell you what else, Governor," said Yount. "Me and Terrible can string out our wrassling with a new touch we've practiced. Just leave the lungia boom angled out from its center pole, dangling its rope where we can get at it. What we do, we take turns swinging across the ring, like jungle apes, and kicking each other all to hell."

"Good, good. Every little bit helps. But that rope will still be hanging there, Maurice, when your trap act starts. It won't be in your way?"

"It should not be any bother," said LeVie. "Come to think of it, that can add a touch to my Pete Jenkins. When my drunken pignouf is struggling with the roustabouts, Paprika will look down disdainfully and even haul up the rope ladder. Then my pignouf will have to do a comic climb up that extra rope, to get to the platform."

"Good, good."

"If you have no more instructions for me, Efendi Florian," said the Turk, "I must go and clean up. I have a rendezvous tonight with a lady who admired the way I climbed the bridge." He and his mustache grinned. "For that, I must go and get money, also."

"Say, Shadid," Fitzfarris said. "To entertain ladies as often as you do costs like hell. I know. If you don't want to plunder your grouch bag all the time, maybe you'd like to make some money real easy. How about selling me your caravan and horse?" The Turk looked interested, and the other men looked curiously at Fitzfarris. "I'd deduct the price of my present caravan share, and you could move in there with Obie and Abner and Jules."

"Make an offer," said the Turk. "I do not need a whole house to myself. Quakemaker? Roulette? You would not object?"

They both said, "No, not at all," and gave it as their opinion that the absent Mullenax would not mind, either, since he was usually too drunk when he came to bed to notice who else was in the van. So Fitzfarris and Sarkioglu did only a brief dicker, and Fitz paid over the money, and the Turk went off to his assignation.

"I'll tell you fellows why I'm moving out," said Fitz.

"None of our business," said Rouleau. "No need to explain."

"It's your business then, Florian," said Fitz. "Since you're sort of the Simms kids' guardian, I probably ought to have your blessing. Monday and I—"

"Say no more. That girl has been mooning after you for

ever so long. If she's finally caught you, I will only say that congratulations are in order, and that this news does much to brighten an otherwise dark day." Florian raised his glass and gave Fitz the traditional German toast, "Hoch soll'n Sie Leben, dreimal hoch!" And the other men followed suit, with comments not so dignified:

"No wonder you looked wistful when Terrible left, Fitz," said Yount. "A woman of your own will stop *you* bucking the tiger."

"Well, here is hoping she can tame him," said Pfeifer. "I would not wager on it."

LeVie said, "Ah, but love, like religion, can accommodate every sort of eccentricity."

"Ach, Mumpitz," said Beck. "With his tall tales, Sir John always her can subdue."

"C'est vrai," said Rouleau. "I overheard Fitz saying his prayers before bed the other night. And you know what? He was lying!"

Monday was still supine, still wearing nothing but a beatific smile, when Sunday entered the room, sat down beside her and said wearily, "So many things have been happening that I forgot to worry about you and your adventure. Have your heard about Zanni?"

"Uh huh," Monday said dreamily, still smiling.

"I've been out tramping the streets, trying my German on everybody I met, but nobody knows anything." Sunday blew out a long breath. "Well." She cast a sidelong glance at her naked sister and said, "Well, from the look of you, the adventure wasn't intolerable."

"No, ma'am!" Monday said emphatically. She sat up, clasped her arms around her knees and beamed even more radiantly. "Every bit of this whole day's been downright nice. And I got you to thank for it."

A trifle uncomfortably, Sunday said, "Well, I just came up to make sure you were all right. You seem to be. Don't you want to come downstairs and get something to eat?"

Monday giggled. "Sister Sunday, you wouldn't believe how full I am. And all I've done *learnt* today."

"Oh, my. From her? I hope it hasn't made you what she is."

"Not nohow! You told me true, and I'm obliged to you. It got me John Fitz. How 'bout that?"

"What got you John Fitz?" asked Sunday, bewildered.

"What-all I learnt. Things that might get *you* your Mr. Zack. Listen here." And Monday, with relish, told everything that had happened since she stepped out of the balloon gondola, and Sunday's eyes went wide with amazement as the tale unfolded.

Only once did she interrupt: "So you gave the game away."

"I'm sorry, sister. I truly did mean to keep quiet."

"It doesn't matter. Soon or later, she'd have found out. I figured she'd have a fit, then."

"Did she ever. Well, after I skedaddled out of there . . ." and the tale went on, and Sunday's eyes got ever wider.

The next day, there was still no sign of Zanni Bonvecino and no word from the river police, and most of the artistes were frantically busy, rehearsing new bits to prolong their acts, and Beck and his roustabouts were pumping additional gas into the *Saratoga*, and the tober was overrun with jossers waiting, well before noon, to buy tickets to the two o'clock show. Clearly, the whole town had heard of the circus's presumed tragedy and, apparently, everybody in town had come to see how the circus was bearing up under it. What with the troupers' busy doings and their attempt to show only smiling faces to the jossers, they took no notice of the one face so implacably furious that nothing would ever make it smile again.

There was a turnaway house, of course, and the crowd that managed to get in seemed to find nothing lacking in the performance. Perhaps their applause for each act was done even more vigorously, out of sympathy as well as appreciation. Everything in the show went well until the closing act of the first half. Paprika had neither looked at nor spoken to Sunday all day long—they had both taken care to go separately to the dressing wagon to get into their blue fleshings—and Sunday was just as pleased to have Paprika silent, instead of in a Hungarian rage. The two still did not speak when they were up on the platform, and Sunday dutifully swung out or hooked back the trapeze bars, as Paprika went through her solo turn to the band's playing of "There Is But One Girl."

Then, when Paprika took her bows and the band went into "The Flying Dutchman," there emerged from the crowd the drunken Pete Jenkins, with all the attendant hullaballoo before he got up to the trap and revealed himself as Maurice and turned into blue lightning. After his dazzling solo, he and Paprika went into their duet to the "Bal de Vienne," and Sunday continued to monitor the bars according to their "houp là!" commands.

The audience's attention was abruptly distracted from the act by some obtrusive activity at the chapiteau's front door. Several uniformed policemen had entered, and Banat was officiously trying to bar them because they had no tickets, so Florian trotted over to intervene. After a moment, he beckoned for Edge to leave his post in the pista and join them. The jossers got so intent on that business—knowing it must pertain to yesterday's tragedy—that not many of them saw what now occurred on the trapeze rig high above.

It was time for Sunday's brief participation in the act. Paprika came swinging toward the platform on her bar, hanging by her knees, her arms extended. Sunday reached out and leaped, their hands seized one another's wrists, and Sunday was swung in a swoop and, just at the bottom of the arc, Paprika bared her teeth at Sunday and let go of her wrists. The smaller girl was strong enough to hold on for only another fraction of a second, not time enough to gain the altitude or momentum to reach Maurice as he swung in approach. Her grip broke and Sunday went flying, passing close enough under Maurice to see the horrified look on his face.

Florian was saying to Edge, "The Polizei found a body far downstream, and have fetched it back to Regensburg. They say it is waterlogged, bloated, much ravaged by the river fish. It could be someone else. They want us, as the circus's chief authorities, to come at once and see if we can identify it."

Only about half of the more than one thousand people in the chapiteau were watching what happened aloft, and only a few of those gasped in realization that Sunday's free flight was unintended, that she had been hurtled toward a plunging crash into the farthest tiers of seats. But Bandmaster Beck was observing, as always, to keep his music matched to the act. Almost before Sunday's brief flight ended, he had wig-wagged the band to break off and blast into Mendelssohn's "Wedding March" at an emergency jog-trot tempo.

Edge was saying to Florian, "What's the damned hurry? Tell the police to curb their damned efficiency and wait. Tell them we'll break for intermission right after—Jesus Christ!"

Hearing the disaster music, he and Florian whirled to look. The whole audience was now clamoring in distress and dis-belief. Sunday was still aloft, and her slim blue body was jerking wildly about. In midflight, she had caught the rope left dangling for the strongmen's act, and she had hit it with such force that it and the lungia boom were flailing, the rope's lower end cracking like a whip over the nearer jossers' head, but Sunday was holding fast. Maurice had alighted on the platform above her, and dropped the rope ladder, and was rapidly descending it. Paprika still hung by her knees from her bar, and swung almost placidly back and forth, watching, and no one could see what expression her face now wore.

"*Blue* . . . birds . . ." Edge said to himself, as he and Flo-rian went running.

Maurice got to a rung of the ladder on a level with Sunday, and though she was still dizzily oscillating, managed to reach out and grab the rope and gentle it to steadiness. Then he helped Sunday shakily put out one leg, then her other, to the ladder's rungs, and finally clutch it with her hands. Maurice keeping close, Sunday weakly descended, and her legs nearly gave way beneath her when she touched the pista ground. Florian and Edge were waiting there—and the police as well. Sunday pointed up at Paprika, but had to pant and gasp and sob for a minute before she could get the words out: "She tried to kill me. She deliberately let go of me."

The crowd did not hear the words, and the policemen did not comprehend them, but every face in the chapiteau followed Sunday's arm and stared accusingly up at Paprika. Away up there, she was now pumping her body, swinging in longer, swifter swoops and going higher each time—and, incongruously, the band kept the "Wedding March" in perfect rhythm with her. Then, at the top of a swoop, Paprika relaxed her bent legs and swan-dived into space. Her parabola kept her airborne for only a moment, then she hit the sloping underside of the tent roof—with a *splat!* audible above the band music—and there she turned from a swan into, briefly, a blue star suspended and glittering, her arms and legs outstretched. But the canvas bounced her off and inward, and she fell into another parabola to hit full-length on the pista curb with another audible noise—this one of sickening finality.

Florian was immediately at pista center, with the megaphone, and Beck hurried his band into the come-out anthem. As Yount and the Turk ran to lift Paprika and pretended to help her "walk" between them out the back door, Florian bawled to the crowd that they had just witnessed a specially staged scene of daredevilry, that no mischance had occurred, that it was all part of the show. He signaled urgently to Sunday, and LeVie and Edge supported her while somehow she smiled and even threw up her trembling arms in the V. Now, Florian bellowed, it was intermission time, time for all to adjourn and enjoy themselves on the midway, and the whole troupe would return afterward, safe and sound, with the second thrilling half of the program.

The next morning, Regensburg was treated to a spectacle as never-seen-before as the two balloon ascensions had been: a circus funeral, and a double funeral, at that. Led by Florian's black rockaway and the steaming but silent calliope, a few of the circus wagons, draped with black bunting, carried all the circus folk. The balloon wagon, its bed covered with a black pall, bore the coffins of Zanni and Paprika. With the bandsmen in their wagon playing the theme from Chopin's "Sonata Funèbre," the train plodded at the dead march from the Dörnberg-Garten to the Katholik-Friedhof.

Although the civic authorities still wanted to ask many questions—and to fill out innumerable forms—concerning the "irregularities" occurring over the preceding two days, there had been no problem about the bodies' getting proper and public burial. Florian had merely shown their conduct books to attest that both Giorgio Bonvencino and Cécile Makkai had been Roman Catholics in life, and the ecclesiastic authorities graciously gave permission.

Nevertheless, the officiating priest looked uneasy at this particular ceremony, and frequently flicked glances up from his missal at the motley crowd of mourners standing about him and his acolytes. Besides the bandsmen in uniform and the crewmen in canvas and denim work clothes, Pater Frederick could count three unmistakable orientals, two blacks, two albinos, a midget, a cloaked and hooded person of indeterminate sex, a giant in a leopard skin and another in a skimpy breechclout, one man wearing as white a face as any corpse in the cemetery and another with a face half-blue, one man in fringed buckskins, five young women in decidedly unsolemn near-nudity. Pater Frederick could approve of only two men—Florian and Goesle—respectably attired, and only one woman—Autumn—who wore a decent dress and veil.

After the spoken service and prayers, and the numerous signs of the cross, and the several aspersings with holy water and censer smoke and the sprinklings of earth into the two graves, Florian spoke the last words over them—once again in the plural: the Latin for "They danced about. They gave pleasure. They are dead." Then, at Florian's signal, the prevailing decorum was riven and shattered and abolished, and Pater Frederick was all but blown out of his vestments, by the calliope's earthquake-volume blast of "Auld Lang Syne."

6

THE FLORILEGIUM and its raggle-taggle tail of midway vehicles followed the Danube downstream, toward Austria again, stopping to show for a week or two in each of the larger towns along the river. Sunday had required only brief rehearsal to take Paprika's place as Maurice's partner, and to do the act exquisitely. Now that she and Monday were star turns, Florian accorded them noms-de-théâtre. For the trapeze act, Sunday become Mademoiselle Butterfly, and Monday, as the ropewalking chimney sweep, of course became Cinderella. (In the backyard, Monday liked to be addressed as Mrs. Fitzfarris, though that union had yet to be endowed with any certificate of marriage.) Major Minim remained in the pugilistic comedy act with Ali Baba, though still grumbling and, even during the performance, trying really to pummel the boy. The circus's new audiences seemed to perceive no scantiness in the program, but Florian did, and yearned to discover new artistes.

On the road between towns, the travelers now found the Bavarian landscape lush to look at. Autumn, in particular, could not get enough of looking at it. Here, as in Italy, the fields of grain and vegetables were interspersed with fields of the bright-yellow colza—here called Raps, said Jörg Pfeifer. But the Bavarian farmers did not till their earth as the Italians had done—with a crude plow drawn by horse or mule or ox; the Bavarians used modern machinery. The entire circus company stopped to watch, in wonder and admiration, the first time they saw a field thus being plowed.

On either side of the expanse of bare ground stood an immense, high-wheeled steam traction engine. Both machines smoked and steamed like the circus's calliope, and made almost as much noise, though not at all musically. A cable was stretched between the two engines, and from it depended a plow more massive and heavy than any man could handle, being hauled by the cable back and forth across the field. The engine tenders moved their machines a couple of feet every time the plow finished one long furrow, to start another, perfectly parallel.

"Just look at that!" said Mullenax, the most impressed of those watching, because he had once been a farmer himself. "Not a single animal doin' none of that work. How can any dirt farmer afford such a rig?"

"The farmer does not own it," said Pfeifer. "The engine men are entrepreneurs. They travel from farm to farm and rent their services."

Another novelty noticed by the travelers was mainly evident in the towns—or rather on the outskirts of the towns: every garbage dump was piled high with tangles and thickets of looped wire. These, when seen close, proved to be great heaps of women's dress hoops. And it was Sunday Simms who was able to explain this curiosity, because she assiduously read every town newpaper, to improve her German, and always translated the society news items for Clover Lee, who liked to keep abreast of the doings of counts and dukes and such.

"The stylish women all over Europe are throwing away their hoops," said Sunday. "I don't know why, but the big crinoline skirts have suddenly gone out of fashion. Look at the women on the streets now. Their skirts are all flat in front, and they use only a sort of little half-hoop to make what they call a crinolette, a flaring, trailing train behind."

Some of the other newspaper reports were of more interest to the older members of the troupe, as when there came the news of the Ausgleich. This political compromise had, after Hungary's years of agitating for independence, at last given that country some measure of separation from the Austrian Empire. By the terms of the Ausgleich, Franz Joseph and Elisabeth would remain emperor and empress of Austria, but now were being crowned a second time—as mere king and queen of Hungary—and that nation, under this new dual monarchy, would henceforward make and administer its own laws, courts and civil statutes.

"Well, it will calm the longtime rumbling of rebellion in Hungary," said Florian. "But Elisabeth will be particularly pleased with the arrangement. She will have more excuse than ever to stay apart from Franz Joseph and spend most of her time being queen in Budapest instead of empress in Vienna."

Just a week or so later, the front-page news in the Deggendorf *Zeitung* was that the tottery French-supported régime in Mexico had completely disintegrated and its Emperor Maximilian—brother of Franz Joseph—had been shot by a Mexican firing squad. A boxed item in that story added that, to express their displeasure at Louis Napoléon's having let such a calamity happen, Franz Joseph and Elisabeth would be the only two European monarchs *not* attending the great World's Fair opening in Paris.

And another news item that Sunday translated from the paper, though it had nothing to do with a royal, a noble or even a man, so excited Clover Lee that she ran to Florian and requested a day off from work.

"The Great Zoyara," she told him, almost dancing, "is giving an exhibition of her equitation in Plattling, and that's only a few miles the other side of the river. Imagine! Ella Zoyara, the greatest équestrienne of the age. My heroine ever since I first got onto a rosinback. Please, Florian, may I go and see her perform? I'll only miss two shows. And I might learn all kinds of new tricks to make it worthwhile. Please, may I go?"

Florian plucked at his beard. "I do hate to lose, even temporarily, another principal from our already depleted program. But I can hardly say no. The fact is, I wish I could play truant and see that splendid lady myself. It wasn't until after I went to America that she made her first reputation with the Zirkus Renz."

"They say she does things no other female rider has ever attempted," said Clover Lee. "Jumps over five flags held horizontally. Somersaults through fifty paper hoops in succession . . ."

"Yes," said Florian. "If we weren't already so well supplied with good riders, I might even go and make La Zoyara an offer. But she would refuse. She must be making a fortune with her solo tours. Very well, my dear. Saddle up Bubbles and go. Only one day, mind. And ride carefully on the way."

But Clover Lee was gone for three days, and Florian was alternately irate and worried. He was about to send someone on her trail when she returned, about midnight of the third day, riding indolently, smiling in a knowing way. Florian and Edge both began to berate her the minute she dismounted, but she went on smiling and, when they paused for breath, she said:

"I know. I overstayed my leave. But I think you'll agree that it was worth it, when I tell you why. Ella Zoyara is not Spanish, as the posters all say. Ella Zoyara is as American as I am. Omar Kingsley-Stokes by name, and even that is probably fancified. I bet it's only Homer Stokes.''

"Omar?'' said Florian.

"Homer?'' said Edge.

Clover Lee nodded. "Small wonder the Great Zoyara can do riding tricks no woman can. It's because no woman has the strength. She is really a man. The secret is closely kept. He even wears female clothes on the street and in private. Wears his hair long, shaves and powders his arms and legs, as well as his face . . .''

Florian said, "It is inconceivable. If no one else in all of Europe has even suspected such a masquerade, how could you possibly know—?''

"Now, Florian,'' Clover Lee said sweetly. "How would you *suppose* I know?'' The two men looked faintly shocked at such blithe shamelessness. "Anyway, this time, I was given more than an embroidered purse and twenty scudi. Maybe my virtue is going up in value.'' She took from behind Bubbles's saddle a paper-wrapped bundle, large but evidently light of weight. "As soon as I've had Maggie do some seamstress work for me, I'll show you what Homer Stokes gave me and taught me.''

She had the new turn ready to add to her act by the time the Florilegium reached the last town in Bavaria in which Willi had booked a tober—Passau, on the Austrian border— and Clover Lee's act was so warmly received there that Florian had to concede that she had made up for her delinquency. While she could not imitate the Ella Zoyara feats that required masculine muscularity, she *could* commence her act the same way La Zoyara did. She told Boom-Boom what new music she would require—quite a variety, and changing in rapid succession—and told Florian how to introduce her entrance, and what to say thereafter. So, the afternoon of her new turn's début, Florian bellowed through his megaphone, "Die Nationen im Prozession!''

The band let loose with oom-pah music and Clover Lee rode into the chapiteau erect on the cantering Bubbles, dancing there a lively Schuhplattler and wearing a Bavarian woman's dirndl and bonnet, and Florian announced, "Beglücken Bayern!'' and the jossers loudly applauded the salute to their homeland. After one circuit of the tent, Clover Lee deftly doffed that garb, but was still costumed. When Edge ran to get the discarded garments out of the way, he discovered that they were made of such fine-denier silk that, though opaque, they had almost no bulk.

Clover Lee was now wearing the next layer: a kerchief and a Colombina skirt of red, white and green. The band now played a saltarello, and she danced it on Bubbles's back, and Florian cried, ''Innig Italien!'' Next she was wearing a flat blue cap and a jacktar's flap-collared blouse, and she danced a hornpipe—''Blühend Britannien!'' Then she wore a tartan kilt and a fuzzy sporran, and danced a fling—''Schottland das Schöne!'' Then she was wearing a small round cap and a toreador's suit of lights, and she was dancing a fandango—''Sonnig Spanien!'' And finally, under all, she wore only her gold-spangled fleshings and her own golden hair, and—''Die amerikanische Artistin, Fräulein Clover Lee!''—went into her accustomed routine of ballet steps, acrobatic poses, the leaping of garters and garlands. From the back door, a roustabout opened the cage so her doves flew after her and did their participation in the act.

Her routine was so popular there in Passau, and everywhere thereafter, that the Mademoiselles Cinderella and Butterfly were a trifle annoyed—also amused—that a mere showy embellishment should have made Clover Lee as much of a star attraction as they with their more hazardous thrill acts. However, no real rivalry or estrangement developed among the girls, and Clover Lee refused to let Florian invent any flamboyant new ''star name'' for her.

''Let Homer Stokes hide his homely name and his sex and his nationality if he wants to,'' she said. ''But I'm quite content to be billed as plain American Clover Lee. At least until I marry a real title to go with the name.''

Passau was a busy crossroads of commerce, situated as it was at the confluence of the rivers Ilz, Danube and Inn. Passau was also currently being host to a citywide trade fair, nearly doubling its normal population. The troupers, in their free time, enjoyed wandering through the pavilions exhibiting the latest inventions, machinery, tools and products—and through the streets crowded with entresorts: slum joints, mountebanks' stands, waxworks stalls, puppet-show tents and the like.

Florian was especially interested in prowling those streets, and hauled Edge along with him, in search of new talent. At one grubby tent, where the proprietor was halfheartedly proclaiming his exhibit in German, though his banner was in some other language, Florian said, "This might be edifying."

Edge looked at the banner—the most prominent words on it were FRØKEN °AL—and hazarded a translation: "Freaks all?"

"No. It's her name: Miss Eel. Danish. A lady klischnigg. A contortionist. Let us buy tickets and see what she is like."

She was good, and she worked hard at being good, although her audience consisted of no more than ten or twelve bored-looking idlers. She was as flexible and fluid as any real eel, but incomparably prettier, and she had delicate curves and shapely limbs that an eel does not, and what she could do with those was simultaneously admirable, amazing and erotic. However, her costume—what there was of it: merely a skintight léotard—was colorless and much darned. She performed on a bare-board platform with no accompaniment but the manager's languid tweedling on a flute. When the act was concluded and the other people drifted out of the tent, Florian stayed to accost the girl and say:

"Jeg vil gerne, Frøken °Al, De har noget bedre. Er De ledig?"

With a glance of contempt, and in English, Miss Eel said, "Piss off, squire."

Edge laughed, which made her give him a look more surprised than contemptuous.

"Er . . . ahem," said Florian. "When I suggested 'something better,' perhaps I phrased it ambiguously, but—"

"If I took every *better position* suggested by every gawk, I should have to know a hell of a lot more twists than I do. What position do *you* want me in? Talk to my manager there.

For enough money, the damned pimp will probably make me turn inside out.''

"Please, Miss Eel, desist. I am not a gawk or a voyeur, and I am not a voyageur forain, like your—er—manager. I am the owner of Florian's Flourishing Florilegium, a highly reputable traveling circus. I come with a legitimate offer of lucrative employment.''

"Oh.'' She looked abashed, and apologized, "Det gør mig ondt. I should have realized, when you spoke in Dansk, that you were not the usual dirty-minded slet menneske.''

"Are you under contract or are you free to negotiate, Miss Eel?''

"Please call me Agnete, Herr Florian. My name is Agnete Knudsdatter. And I can be free in three minutes, if you wish to purchase the banner. That is all the pimp owns of me.''

"We will provide for you a much better banner.''

"Two minutes, then. I have little else to pack.''

When Frøken Knudsdatter emerged from the tent in street clothes, she was followed by the manager, beating his breast, bleating and imploring in several languages. But she paid him no heed, so neither did Florian and Edge. Carrying her meager luggage—two worn carpetbags—they escorted her to the tober and to the caravan now occupied by only Clover Lee and Sunday Simms.

"I am sure the other girls will not mind your sharing these quarters,'' said Florian, "until you can afford to pay your way. Now come with me to our wardrobe mistress. I think, since you are one of the few dark-haired Danes, we will maintain the persona of Miss Eel and dress you in dark, shiny, eel-like tights. We have also on the show a very young and small black boy who is himself no mean posture-master. Not so talented as you, of course. But, since he is already eel-colored, you might wish to work him into your act. Eel and elver, so to speak.''

"I am at your command, Herr Florian,'' said Agnete, looking dazed at the sudden change in her fortunes.

On another foray among the streets of entresorts, Florian and Edge came upon three performers—two middle-aged

men and a young girl—working literally in the street, without
tent, stall, talker or banner. They were garbed, rather rag-
gedly, as clowns: the girl as an Italian serving wench, the
men as loutish Bavarian or Austrian peasants. At the moment
they were performing, to a sizable crowd of strollers who had
stopped to watch, an act that was acrobatic as well as clownish. The men each held an end of a long bamboo pole that
they were whipping and twanging up and down, while the
girl used it very like a tightrope, and almost as skillfully as
Autumn Auburn or Monday Simms, letting it toss her into
leaps and flips and somersaults, but always landing again on
the bamboo.

"The sky pole," Florian told Edge. "These are casse-cou
clowns. The dare-devil, breakneck variety."

After a while of that, the three abandoned the acrobatics,
and the older man and the girl began a loud-voiced repartee
routine. He was a seedy figure—wearing knee-length Leder-
Bundhosen, but without stockings, so his pale and scrawny
calves were bare all the way down to his battered boots—
and he conveyed an old man's impotent and envious lechery.
During the colloquy, the girl simpered and looked coy and
threw flirtatious looks at all the other men nearby. Florian
translated the patter for Edge:

"He twits her about her multitude of beaux and lovers and
suitors, and inquires how she handles so many. She says, 'Ah,
sir, they pass away like the waters.' He leers lasciviously and
asks, 'Pray, Fräulein, do they pass by *the same route?*'"

The crowd laughed heartily as the bawdry went on, and
tossed coppers into a hat being passed by the other man. He
had put an idiotically vacant look on his face and was awkwardly jostling through the onlookers, occasionally stumbling
deliberately off the pavement into the street and nearly getting
run over by passing vehicles.

"These joeys are almost certainly from Vienna," said Florian. "When we get there, Zachary, you will see what a mixture of nationalities that city is. So this kind of clown trio is
something of a fixture there. The evil old man is the Hanswurst—Jack Sausage—a traditional joker in Viennese folklore. The Emeraldina, the comedy wench, appeals to the

Italian population. The other is clearly the dumb yokel Kesperle, a standard comic figure among the Czechs.''

The crowd had begun to straggle away, so Florian approached the clowns and, for Edge's benefit, first addressed
them in English. The girl—who, at closer sight, was somewhat pudgy, but very pretty—turned out to be the only competent English-speaker of the three.

''From Wien we are, yes, ja, sì. We came only to work
this Passau fair, then to Wien we are returning. We work
anywhere we can draw a crowd. I am Nella Cornella. The
troublemaker Hanswurst is Bernhard Notkin. The village-
idiot Kesperle is Ferdi Spenz.''

''I am pleased to meet all of you. I am the proprietor and
this is the equestrian director of Florian's Florilegium.''

''What, the grand circus showing here?'' she exclaimed.

''Yes. We are also on our way to Wien, and I am seeking
to augment my corps of clowns.''

''You think to engage *us?*'' she asked, in an unbelieving
squeak.

''Perhaps. Your ensemble work is passable, and a female
joey I have never had. Do you people possess transport?''

''We travel in caravan together. But not *together*, you understand. I am not the süsse Mädel—not the amante—of either old man.''

''That does not concern me in the least. However, one
thing I would like. Can either of these gentlemen do the Lupino mirror?''

The question did not have to be repeated in any other language. The man named Ferdi Spenz caught at least the one
word and exclaimed, ''Rozumím! Lupino zrcadlo! Ano! Vim!
Dobrý jsem!

''He says yes,'' the girl translated.

''Thank goodness that mirror act is done without words,''
said Edge, as he and Florian walked back toward the tober.
They were trailed by the clowns' extremely dilapidated caravan, drawn by an extremely emaciated horse. ''If we add
many more nationalities and lingos, we're also going to have
to hire a corps of interpreters. Hell, I'll have to start carrying

a little notebook like yours, just so I can remember all our people's *names*.''

The three new hirelings looked as dazed as Agnete the Eel had been when, immediately on arrival at the tober, they began getting "improved." Their ruin of a caravan was turned over to the Slovaks, to be put in good repair and painted. Their ruin of a horse was turned over to Hannibal and Quincy, to be fattened up and revitalized insofar as possible. The clowns themselves were first turned over to Magpie Maggie Hag, to be measured for new costumes, and then to Jörg Pfeifer. He immediately started Lupino-mirror practice with the Kesperle, and meanwhile began rehearsing the Hanswurst to replace little Major Minim in the pugilist act with Ali Baba—and, between times, began introducing refinements into the Emeraldina's casse-cou performance.

''It is all very well, Nella, to be a breakneck joey, but any *man* can do that. I wish you to show off your undeniably saftig femininity at the same time. Now, try it like so . . .''

He worked the newcomers with drill-sergeant rigor and discipline, and worked them late into the night after every evening's show, so passersby would often hear shouting from inside the chapiteau:

''Yes, Nella, do as I just showed you! And no, Nella, do not attempt to improve on my improvements!''

''Madonna puttana! All these yesses and noses!''

When the Florilegium again crossed the border into Austria, continuing on down the Danube, it was apparent that that nation had recovered from its postwar gloom and depression. The Austrians were once more hard at work, looked prosperous and cheerful, and seemed eager for entertainment. When the circus set up in the substantial city of Linz, the very first show drew a sfondone house. By that time, too, the new acts were ready for presentation.

Besides Ferdi Spenz's doing with Fünfünf the Lupino mirror act, and doing it almost as well as the late Zanni had, the three new joeys also did together a King-of-the-Mountain knockabout routine—fighting for possession of a pedestal Carl Beck had built for them. First the Emeraldina would stand atop it, then she would be flung off by the Kesperle, who would be frightened off by the Hanswurst flailing a long sausage, who would in turn be chased off by the Emeraldina wielding a brick. The comic struggle and its weapons escalated: to a stick, to a club, to a ridiculously giant slingshot, to one of Edge's spare pistols, to one of his spare carbines. Finally, when the contest was an anarchic mêlée—and the audience convulsing in hilarity—the contested pedestal itself suddenly became the victor, by sprouting a giant and thorny cactus. This was another Beck contrivance, of canvas and india rubber and spikes, inflated by a hidden roustabout working the *Saratogas*' force pump. When the formidable cactus became king of its own mountain, the Hanswurst, the Kesperle and the Emeraldina all shrugged, threw away their weapons and went off amicably arm in arm.

Miss Eel, in the eel-slinky and even eel-*wet*-looking tights that Magpie Maggie Hag had fashioned for her, became the newest exhibit in Fitzfarris's sideshow. The accordionist played during her serpentine performance on the platform, and Fitz talked all during it—with Florian interpreting in German—"Yessir, ladies and gentlemen, Miss Eel is a good girl, for the shape she's in, and just *look* at the shape she's in! Why, do you know, folks, on salary day she sometimes collects her salary two or three times? Keeps coming to the pay wagon in a different shape . . ."

Many of the other artistes had joined the jossers to watch Agnete Knudsdatter's début, and afterward Mullenax remarked, "Say, Fitz, ain't your part of the show getting a little heavy on the reptiles? You got a snake woman in the annex and an eel woman on the platform, not to mention that maggot, the midget. What next?"

"Well, Abner," Fitzfarris said, mock-seriously, "you haven't done the Crocodile Man for a long time." And Mullenax fled in a hurry.

Another onlooker, Obie Yount, kept coming back to watch Miss Eel's every performance. After a week or so, he got up the courage to go to where she was toweling herself and catching her breath, and to say diffidently, "Miss Eel . . . oh, hell, I can't call a woman that. Miss Kanoods—oh, damn, I'll never get *that* right, neither."

"Can you manage 'Agnete'? What do you wish to say, Herr Quakemaker?"

"Call me Obie. I wanted to say that your act is purely perfect."

"Thank you, Obie."

"But I think Fitz don't talk it up with the dignity it deserves. I've got an idea, if you let me put it to you."

"Havd ønsker De?" She sighed. "Another new position?"

"Well, sort of. I think you ought to be a showpiece in the main ring, not out there with freaks and fire-eaters. So my idea—see, I used to do a pyramid—me supporting a bunch of girls. And, why, you alone, I could hold you over my head with one hand. Could you do your contortions like that, up there?"

She looked surprised and amused, and even pleased. "With some practice, Obie, I imagine so."

"And then, if you want to put the Simms boy into the act, I could hold him up on the *other* hand."

"Are you really so strong? To hold us over your head for so many long minutes?"

Yount did some chest-expanding and muscle-bulging. "Miss Agnete, I'm the *Quakemaker*. I'll go right now and talk to Zack and Florian."

He found them in the red wagon, and they gave him permission to try the act, but they gave it somewhat distractedly, because the office was full of other petitioners. Carl Beck and Jules Rouleau were arguing to Florian that Linz was a city important enough to merit sending up the *Saratoga*, while a delegation of elders from the city of Linz itself waited to speak to him. Florian said, "Very well, Monsieur Roulette, start the preparations and I will get paper printed," and shooed those two out. Meanwhile, Edge was being harangued by doorman Banat:

"Must have tober fencing, Pana Edge, like other Europe circuses. Too much now I see child boy sneak in every afternoon."

"Look, Chief. You know how much those rolls of fencing would cost. I reckon it hurts your professional pride, but how much do we lose in half-ticket sales to the few boys sneaking in?''

"Not boys. Boy."

"All right. One at a time, then. On each one, maybe we lose—"

"Not one boy at a time. Same boy."

Edge gave him a long look. "Alex, you first complained about this somewhere back around Landshut, in another country. Are you claiming that the same boy is still sneaking in and out?"

Banat shrugged.

"Well, it can't be one of our own, doing mischief just to plague you. We've got only two small boys on the show. One is black as midnight and the other is pale as the moon. You'd have recognized them. So are you telling me that for more than a hundred and fifty miles we've been dogged by a kid—the same kid—that keeps sneaking onto and off the tober? You can't catch him, and nobody else has even seen him. If you're not crazy, Alex, the kid has to be a ghost. Now, I've got problems enough with the solid bodies in this company. You either catch that spook or shut up about him."

Banat departed, looking chastened but unconvinced. Edge gave his attention to the delegation of city elders, who were all talking in German. Florian translated for Edge, because the import of this visit was utterly astonishing.

"I told the gentlemen that we were going to favor their fair city with a balloon ascension, but they would rather that we do not. They would prefer to see us pack up and clear out entirely."

"What?"

"I have never in my professional life been thrown out of a city before. But these men are serious. One of them is the Bürgermeister, the other is a high magistrate and the third is the chief of police. They are not at all jesting."

"But, in God's name, what's the reason?"

"They appear strangely reluctant to be specific, but it has something to do with the local children."

"Is our show supposed to be corrupting them? There's been no complaint from any audience. Or—wait a minute—

Banat was bellyaching about boys sidewalling the show. Are we suspected of abducting small boys? Of playing the Pied Piper?''

Florian put the question to the city elders. They replied only curtly, and with some evident embarrassment, but forcefully.

"No," Florian told Edge. "It involves little *girls,* but they decline—on grounds of delicacy—to say exactly *what* it involves. They merely keep repeating that no such thing ever happened in Linz before our circus came to town."

"Well, I'm no lawyer, but this sounds like a pretty thin case to me, Governor. Purely on the basis of coincidence, they're accusing us of some crime they won't even put a name to."

Florian talked to them some more, and again their response was brief, frigid, adamant.

"To judge from their mood," Florian told Edge, "I'd rather not inquire further into the details. Something atrocious has been happening to girl children in this city. Whether or not the coincidence of our being here at the same time makes us culpable, they would prefer that we be gone. I believe discretion dictates that we obey. They could easily make more trouble for us than mere eviction."

"We've been doing damn good business, this while we've been here, but I personally won't be sorry to move on. I'm anxious to get Autumn to Vienna and that specialist doctor there. Do we tear down right this minute?"

Florian again consulted with the men. "They will, albeit grudgingly, let us proceed with tonight's show. Tell the crew to bust the lacings immediately afterward, and we'll hit the road in the morning."

Edge went to convey that message to the company, and an additional one to Aleksandr Banat: "I still don't believe in ghosts, Crew Chief, but there's a sudden rash of coincidences going around. Too damned much of it to suit me. I want that sidewalling kid caught. You tell your roustabouts and I'll tell the artists and the midway folks. Every last man, when he's not on working duty, is to be on the lookout."

Then Edge heard his name called, and turned. It was Major

Minim, and he spoke in his customary voice of snarl, but, for him, almost in a humble manner.

"Colonel, I want to apologize for something." He fingered his little false mustache. "When I got shoved into the pista as a cheap clown, and with a Neger besides, I did not like it, and I know I showed it. So now you have a whole chapiteau full of joeys, and I am back on the midway. But I have to confess, during that time I got a taste for performing in the pista. And now I have an idea for a whole new act, and I would like your permission—"

"I don't particularly give a damn what you do, Reindorf. But if it's a good act, I'll work it into the program."

"I am thinking of a comedy lion tamer turn. Midget tamer, midget lions. You will like it. But I need a prop cage built."

"Then talk to Stitches or Boom-Boom. If they've got the time and the materials, and they're willing, then you've got my permission."

Two other things happened in Linz that night before the circus pulled out in the morning, but they were of concern only to the parties involved. After the come-out of the closing show, the Terrible Turk, for the first time in quite a while had no local widows applying for his attentions. So he wandered into Fitzfarris's blow-off to watch, for the first time, the Amazon Maiden in the toils of the Dragon Fafnir, and he was impressed by what he saw. He gave her time to go and get out of her scale-spangled fleshings, then went to the Vasilakises' caravan and did his usual bouncing of it. Meli came to the door, groaned and said wearily:

"You want money. You must come other time. Spyros went town for buy olive oil and other things."

"How convenient for me," said Shadid, quite good-humoredly. "But I do not want money. This time I come to ask what do *you* want?"

"What I want? I want you leave us in peace. You trouble enough, but what I fear is soon Spyros kill you. Then there be trouble in plenty."

"Bosh! That bull canary kill me? I have no fear, but I do have a proposal. You want me to leave him alone? I will. I promise that. If you oblige me with a fair exchange."

Meli looked wary and clutched her robe closer around her. "What exchange?"

"So simple. You are the Amazon maiden. I shall be the dragon."

She recoiled. "I am married woman and decent woman. You not just greedy and bully. You are vile."

"No doubt," Shadid said indifferently. "But I believe you will find me superior, in many respects, to either a limp snake or that flabby husband of yours. And in return, your flabby husband gets molested no more. Now, none of your Greek haggling, woman. You invite me inside or I come uninvited."

A few moments later, weeping silently, she got out of the robe and he commented approvingly, "Ah, good. You are as bushy there as any Turkçe woman . . ."

Like the Turk, the Quakemaker had no ladies from the seats seeking his services that night, nor had he flirted with any. He and Agnete Knudsdatter were at this moment lying together, naked, under the stars of the balmy night, on the cushiony tarpaulin covering the balloon in its wagon. Agnete ran her hand through his dense beard and then down the almost-furry rest of him, and laughed and said:

"A bear and an eel, making love. Is it a violation of natural law, or is it a fable by Andersen?"

"I don't know who Andersen might be, but I wish you'd stop calling yourself an eel. I never liked the damned things. Always fouling my fishing line."

"But observe my eeliness, Obie. Feel. Here. I am almost as flat as a boy. I do not know why you should be attracted to me. You have many more curves and bulges than I do."

"You feel good to me. I ain't never been attracted to cows just because they've got big udders."

"Do you know something?" She laughed again. "When I was a schoolgirl, and all the other girls were beginning to— bulge there—and I was not, I saw a newspaper advertisement. A guaranteed bosom developer, for just twenty öre. So, like a simpleton, I put twenty öre in the post, and guess what I received in return. *A pasteboard cutout of a man's hand.* Never did I feel so foolish." Yount laughed indulgently. "But, of course, now I am glad I never grew much brystet, as most women do, or got fat, as most Danish women do, for I could not have taken up my contortionist career.''

''And you wouldn't be here this minute. And you wouldn't be mine. And now you are.''

She nestled close against him and murmured, ''Jeg elsker dig,'' and then translated it into English for him.

When Spyros returned from town to the Vasilakis caravan, carrying the supplies he had bought, he found Meli in bed, but sitting up awake, and looking morose.

''What is it?'' he asked. ''Has that ekithiros been pestering again?''

With an effort, she said, ''He was here, yes, but this time we came to an understanding. He will not be demanding money any more, or making us dodge him when we meet, or in any other way making your—making our lives miserable.''

''Indeed? And you took this upon yourself?'' Spyros sounded more offended than pleased. ''How did you do it? A bribe, I assume.''

She hesitated, then said, ''Yes.''

Still sounding hurt and annoyed, he said, ''You might have consulted your husband before declaring any such truce. After all, I am the head of this household and the keeper of its finances. This bribe, did it cost me a great deal?''

Meli looked at him for quite a long while before she said, ''It cost you not a great deal.''

⊷⇒ WIEN ⇐⊷

1

THE FLORILEGIUM STOPPED TO show for some days in the small town of Amstetten, then left the meandering Danube to head directly east toward Vienna, and stopped again to show in the town of St. Pölten. As early as the Amstetten stand, Miss Eel had moved from Fitzfarris's sideshow inside the chapiteau, to do her entire performance uplifted by the sturdy arm of the Quakemaker. Even for a practiced strongman, it was clearly a strain to hold the slender Agnete aloft for the exactly seven minutes it took her to do her amazing convolutions. Though Yount perspired copiously and sometimes trembled slightly, he maintained a stable support of her, and he obviously enjoyed doing it. Those jossers who occasionally took their fascinated gaze off the pretty and infinitely lissome woman could see the Quakemaker's proud smile and the loving glances he gave her from time to time.

Because of that, the circus again had some trouble with the citizenry. After the second night's show in St. Pölten, when the audience was dispersing from the chapiteau onto the torch-lit midway—many of the males heading for the Amazon-and-Fafnir tent—a sudden hubbub broke out in the crowd. There were shouts and curses, and several women shrieked, and the people milled away from the disturbance, leaving an empty space in which two men were wrestling, and not playfuly. Clover Lee happened to be close enough to see them, and she immediately began yelling at the top of her voice, loud enough to be heard over the commotion, "Hey, rube! Hey, rube!"

Edge came running to her. "What the hell goes on, girl?"

"It's a clem! Look! Some fellow is mixing it up with Obie. I don't know what you yell in Europe, but when there's trouble back home you yell 'Hey, rube!' to fetch help."

"Then keep on yelling it," said Edge, and began to force his way through the crowd, for he had seen that Yount was now fighting several men at once.

"Hey, rube! Hey, rube!" Clover Lee continued to shout, and someone somewhere shrilly blew a whistle, and Florian and Banat and numerous roustabouts poured out of the chapiteau, each with a tent stake.

But, before they or Edge could join in the fracas, it was being brought to a quick conclusion. The Terrible Turk had already got there, and, though he and the Quakemaker were embroiled with about a dozen burly locals, the locals were losing badly. In fact, those not being actually flung through the air were limping and crawling desperately from the scene, their clothes torn and some of them bloodied. In another couple of minutes, the fight was over, the losers had fled, and the rest of the crowd quieted down and drifted away. Yount had suffered only a black eye and some damage to his leopard-spotted léotard. He was gratefully shaking hands with Shadid, neither of them even out of breath, when Edge got there to ask:

"What started this ruckus, Obie?"

"Just the one gallinipper at first. I thought he must be crazy to tangle with a circus strongman, but then it turned out he had a whole bunch of toughs to back him up."

"Good thing it was short and sweet," said Florian, joining them. "Before somebody called for the police."

"Hell, me and Terrible could of handled them *and* the

police. Between us, we could take on the devil, and give him an underhold.''

Edge persisted, ''You mean some bully actually came up to you just to pick a fight?''

''Well, no. *I* started the fight. He came up and insulted me.''

''Insulted you how?''

''Never mind. Let me get these duds off so Mag can patch 'em. Then I think I'll go downtown and have a drink.''

When Yount went into St. Pölten to seek a Biergarten, Fitzfarris went with him. After they had ingested several seidls apiece, Fitz felt emboldened to say, ''About that clem and the rube who insulted you—well, it's none of my business. But I've known you for a long time, and I know it takes a Jesusly lot to perturb your temper. It wasn't you he insulted, was it?''

''No,'' Yount admitted, and belched. ''Son of a bitch comes up to me—spoke English, he did. Gives me this oily grin and says something like, 'You and that twister lady are partners, right? In the tent and in bed, too, right? So what's it like—bedding a female as bendable as that?'' Yount belched again. ''So I did my best to show him what bendable *is*.''

''Don't blame you.'' After a period of companionable silence, Fitz said, ''Still none of my business, and I'm not eager to get bent. But, Obie, what *is* it like?''

Yount chuckled, shook his head in marvelment and said, ''Man, it's *something*.''

There was another silence, and the two drank beer and, since it appeared that Yount was not going to elaborate, Fitzfarris said, ''You and me, Obie, we've both got—sort of exceptional ladies.''

''Well, that Simms kid of yours, young as she is, she's got more in her upstairs structure than Agnete does. Not that I'd want Agnete any different, mind, but a fellow can't help noticing.''

''I wish I could tell you what Monday's got in her *basement*. After she's worn me down to a nub, even that's not enough for her. If she watches the lion act, or the elephants clumping around, or anything else exciting, she goes into that spasm of enjoying herself all by herself. I swear, I'm getting fatigued."

"Reckon it is rough on us men," said Yount, with a boozy smile. "But hell, what else is there *besides* women?"

"It's a pity," said Autumn. She was at the caravan stove, frying sausages for dinner. "Obie and Agnete seem so genuinely fond of each other."

"They're even buying a caravan to move into together," said Edge. "But what's the pity about it?"

"That they won't grow old together."

"Why in the world do you say that?"

"The india rubber artistes never have a very long lifespan. They know it, too. It's one of les risques du métier. All that bending and twisting puts such a pressure on the rib cage that their lungs have no chance to develop; they never get bigger than the lungs of a child, so they're easy prey to the consumption. Maybe you haven't seen how Agnete pants and wheezes and coughs after every performance. She hurries off to some private place, so Obie won't notice, and of course she won't tell him, but she's already got the consumption. And don't you say anything either, Zachary."

"I won't." He added, gloomily, "But I will say that I'm getting almighty weary of hearing about people dying young. In wartime is one thing, but—"

"Now you hush," she said. "I was told that I'd be one of those people, but it's been months now, and I'm not dead yet. Probably Agnete is like me—enjoying every day simply because it *is* an extra day. And me, I feel just fine. I only wish I looked as good as I feel."

"Well, let's pin our hopes on that doctor in Vienna. And Vienna is our next stop."

"Then you'd better start pronouncing it the way they do there. Wien. These are Wiener sausages we're going to have for dinner."

"Wien. All right." Edge idly lifted the lid of Autumn's music box. It emitted a few notes of "Greensleeves," in a dolorous, rundown jingle and tinkle. "You don't play this very often any more."

"I'm sorry. I do neglect your sweet gift. Here, let me wind it up again. It's just—sort of a painful reminder—that I'm not out there prancing and strutting in the spec when that music plays."

"Would you like to get out for a while, at least? Dump the sausages. We can join the others at the hotel for dinner."

"Let's not, dear. It's such a chore for me to eat in public, with the veil on. Besides, haven't you heard enough of hotel music? All through Austria, in every dining room, those poor, pathetic, imitation Strausses, with accordions and harmonicas and zithers, playing their poor, pathetic renditions of Strauss."

"True," said Edge. "If there are two things Austria doesn't lack, it's music and clocks. And musical clocks. Even wind harps that play themselves on the house porches. And downtown, a while ago, I came across something I thought unusual, and . . . well, I bought it for you. Today is Saint Anne's Day, they tell me, and here in Austria, they tell me, it's the same as Saint Valentine's Day elsewhere—when a man gets his sweetheart a gift. If you don't mind another gift."

"Oh, Zachary. Mind?"

"I have to confess that it's musical, too, in a curious kind of way. I can always take it back."

"Oh, Zachary."

So he reached outside the caravan door and brought it in. It was a bird cage made of brass wires, with a live canary teetering on a little trapeze inside. It looked like nothing more extraordinary than a canary in a cage, but Edge said, "Wait until he finishes flustering and settles down."

The tiny yellow bird, cocking its head and turning about on its perch, took some while to inspect the two hovering humans and the other visible surroundings. Then, evidently approving of its new home, it serenely preened down a ruffled feather or two, took a sip of water from its little dish, and hopped onto the brass strap that encircled and held together the cage. There it began to hone its beak on one and another of the cage's vertical brass wires, making them twang and vibrate.

"Why, the wires are *tuned!*" Autumn exclaimed in wonder.

"And he'll hop and peck on them all around. He can't play music, of course, but it's nice and harmonious. I thought it was nice."

"Oh, Zachary, it's like something out of the Arabian Nights!" She gave him a loving hug.

"Anyhow, it's not hotel-imitation Strauss."

"Ah, my dear"—she hugged him more tightly—"when we get to Wien, we shall hear the *real* Strauss. One brother after another, conducting hundred-piece orchestras in palatial ballrooms. And there never has been, nor ever will be, any dance devised that is as lovely to hear and watch as the waltz. Perhaps, if the doctor allows, you and I could even go and *dance* it."

"Whoa, woman. I never learned how to dance. I could teach old Thunder his fancy stepping, yes, but I can't do so much as a squaw wrestle."

"But the waltz is so easy." She took the sausages off the fire, came to hold his hand and his waist and began to hum "Light of Heart." Edge, staring down at their feet, tried to match her movements. Autumn said, "Like you're standing in a square box. Step—draw—forward. Step—draw—back. Then we both turn a bit and do it again." She continued humming while they practiced, and the canary plinked and plunked its wires, as if trying to harmonize. "And even more graceful is the Linkswalz—the valse renversée. You simply do that same step, only leading with the right foot instead of the left. It makes for a more gliding movement and less pumping of the arms."

So Edge wore a face of concentrated studiousness, while he lumbered awkwardly about the confines of the caravan, and Autumn wore that lopsided and repellent face, incapable of expression, while her young and shapely body swayed and twirled as liltingly as a flower in a breeze, to her humming of "Light of Heart."

Then there came a knock at the van door, and they parted

abruptly, and Autumn went back to the stove, where she was concealed in shadow. It was Banat on the doorstep, holding a small person by the scruff of the neck. The usually dour doorkeeper was looking almost amused as he announced, "Finally catch our sidewall sneak, Pana Edge. And behold! All time, it was joke."

Edge actually had to look twice at the small person— wearing a boy's school-uniform cap, lederhosen and stockings, carrying some books secured by a strap—to perceive that it was Little Major Minim. He was without his false mustache, and had combed his scanty hair down into boyish bangs across his forehead, and had powdered his face to almost babyish smoothness.

"A joke, ja," the midget said, grinning foolishly. "Wanted to see how long I could run on and off the tober before this dumb Slovak went out of his so-called mind."

Edge, also amused by the little man's grotesquerie, almost said something like "go and sin no more." But then he remembered what he himself had called a rash of coincidences. He said, "Let's you and me go to the red wagon and discuss this *joke* in private. Banat, you find Florian and fetch him there."

In the office, Edge plunked Major Minim into a chair and sat in another, facing him, saying nothing, only eyeing him levelly. The midget fidgeted for some minutes, until he could no longer stand the silent scrutiny, and finally blurted, "Let me put it to you like this, Edge—"

"Herr Direktor to you, Reindorf."

"Ja wohl, Herr Direktor. Every other man on this show has got a woman, even if it's only one of the midway trulls or some trifler from the seats. You've got a steady woman, the Quakemaker has the Eel, the Tattooed Man has got that Neger. Even the plump new girl, Nella—did you know?— she is flirting with that skinny LeVie. She would make two of him. Scheisse! But look at me. What chance do I have? Ach, ja, sometimes a woman has solicited my attentions just out of perverse curiosity. But then, when I undress, and she sees my pale little worm of a hujek, she shrieks with laughter, and that's an end of the episode. True, I have rented a whore

now and then, and paid her enough that she does not laugh.
But a fully-grown woman, why, I just wobble around inside
her. And what did I ever get out of it? From some one of
those whores, I got a dose of the Tripper. So I had to invent
my own way to get my—to get some satisfaction. Am I to
be despised for that?''

Edge said nothing.

''I thought maybe,'' the midget went on desperately, ''if I
tell you the whole truth—throw myself on your mercy—
promise to mend my ways—you might square it with the
Herr Gouverneur . . . ?''

Edge said nothing.

''I am begging you, Herr Direktor. He would throw me off
the stand, make my name a stink with *every* Zirkus, maybe
even hand me over to the Polizei. And—and I told you—I
am working up a splendid new pista act. You would not wish
to lose that . . .''

Florian entered the office just then, glanced at the stony-
faced Edge, stared at the ludicrous other figure and said,
''What in the name of all that's holy is going on here?''

''Nothing very holy,'' said Edge. The midget gave him
another frantically imploring look, but Edge went on, ''Take
a look at those books he's carrying, Governor.''

Minim numbly let Florian take the strapped bundle from
him and undo it. In some stupefaction, Florian said, ''A spell-
ing primer, a hornbook, a school slate. And—and a damp
soapy rag? Zachary, will you tell me what this is all about?''

''It's about our getting thrown out of Linz.''

''What?''

''It's a wonder we haven't got the shove from other places.
Or been tarred and feathered, maybe even lynched. Go on
with your life story, Reindorf.'' The little man looked sullen,
miserable and disinclined to say more. ''*Go on,* or I'll take
you over to the lungia and lynch you myself.''

Minim slumped in total despair and commenced a full con-
fession. ''I already told the Herr Direktor: once I acquired a
venereal infection. Then I read somewhere that a man could
easily cure himself by—by making sex with a virgin small
girl child. So I found a beggar brat—this was in Krakow—

who would have done anything for two coppers, and with me she did that. By the way, I can tell you in confidence, mein Herren, the cure is a myth. Do not try it. I still suffer from the Tripper. But the attempt did do me *some* good. It made me realize how delectable are the little girls. The silky skin . . . why, grown women are like leather by comparison. The bare and tight-shut little coin purse . . .''

"Spare us the slavering," said Florian. "Get on with it."

Minim bowed his head and lowered his voice to a mumble that they had to strain to hear. "After the walkaround of the afternoon show, I make haste. I have just time to go and get—dressed like this—and get into town at the hour that schools are dismissing their classes. I mingle. I look just like one of the Schülers. I choose a pretty little girl, ask if I can carry her books for her—''

"But you *don't* look like a schoolboy," said Florian, with revulsion. "Not when you're seen close. You look like a ventriloquist's painted prop manikin."

"Ach, ja, sometimes a little girl might say, 'Hotte'hü, you have bushy eyebrows for a boy your age.' But usually they come along with no suspicion. And then . . . well . . . I walk her into some alley or some park bushes and . . .'' he shrugged his little shoulders.

Florian said, still unbelievingly, "But surely, a child that age, she must object . . . struggle . . .''

"*She* does not know what is happening—not a child that young, not until it is well along. And afterward she is always crying and trembling, so it takes her a while to put her clothes on again. It gives me time to get clean away, and back here to the tober.''

Florian and Edge sat and regarded him with a look colder than loathing, so Minim raised his voice, as if to propound the most reasonable of arguments. "Herr Gouverneur, Herr Direktor, for a miniature hujek like mine, a girl of five or six years, she is of exactly the proper and enjoyable tightness, and my hujek is for her the right size. Perhaps sometimes even *she* enjoys it. Anyway, I think the little girls seldom complain when they finally get home. They do not know what to complain *about*, except that they got undressed by a schoolmate, and poked in their peeing place.''

Florian muttered, ''My experience of life had been long and checkered. But this is unprecedented. Reindorf, how long have you been—how *many* have there been?''

''Since Poland?'' the midget said indifferently. ''I long ago lost count. Whenever one was required.''

''So you have violated innumerable female infants, and probably infected most of them with gonorrhea, or worse. And I was fool enough to pair you with little Sava Smodlaka in your dancing turn.''

''Ach, nein, Herr Gouverneur!'' Minim exclaimed, with such genuine terror in his voice that he had to be speaking the truth. ''I would not dare. She is pretty, ja, desirable, even unique. But her father Pavlo is a madman. To little Sava, I have been nothing but the perfect gentleman and partner.''

''Perfect gentleman,'' Florian repeated.

''I shall so continue to be, if you will please not dismiss me. I tell you this sincerely. On and off the tober, I shall behave myself. No more little girls, no more trouble. Only give me this chance, Herr Gouverneur, I beseech you. Also, as I have told the Herr Direktor, I am preparing a whole new pista act. You will find it irresistible. I dress as a midget lion tamer, you see. Drive in, with the dwarf horse drawing a midget cage wagon, full of wild midget animals. Only alley cats, you see, I get into it and crack a whip and posture like a midget Barnacle Bill. The audience will wet themselves with laughing. By Wien, I shall be ready. Keep me on the show only until Wien, and then, if I have not redeemed myself''—he made a doleful face—''discharge me, blacken my name, send me to prison, do what you will. I ask only until Wien.''

Florian said, ''One thing still baffles me, Reindorf. The schoolbooks were part of your vile disguise. But the soapy wet rag?''

Minim smiled tolerantly. ''Ach, I am an artiste off the tober as well as on. And art means attention to details. Always, afterward, there is some small blood. So always I wash myself. And her, so she does not go home staining her little—''

"Florian," said Edge. "In my whole life, I have been acquainted with only two midgets. But if every damned one of them is like Russum or Reindorf, I'd say our show can do without any. I suggest we bury this son of a bitch under the pista *alive*."

"Ostrożnie!" Minim snarled at him. "Remember, the Fräulein Eel has left the sideshow. Take me and my dancing act away, and how much of a sideshow does Sir John have? Also, consider *all* the aptitudes of midgets, Herr Edge. I can pry into other places than school yards. I have peeked in a caravan window and and seen your Fräulein Autumn unveiled and in full light. Will you display that monstrosity in the sideshow instead of—?"

Edge came across the room like a projectile, but Florian, with almost equal speed, interposed his body between them.

"Zachary, Zachary, there has been killing enough!" He turned to the midget. "Reindorf, get out of sight and stay out of my sight. Stay out of trouble, too. As you request, I give you until Vienna. Now get out of here!"

Minim did, and Edge stood and glowered at Florian. "We haven't had many disagreements, Governor, ever since we've been traveling together. But now we're butting horns. That runt swine could ruin this whole establishment, and you must be totally insane to let—"

"Zachary, Zachary," Florian said again. "We have only to wait a little, and let him do away with himself, in such a way as to bring no onus on our show, no blot on its reputation."

"How, goddamn it? Wait for him to die of the clap?"

"No. A minute ago, I would readily have killed him myself. But then he mentioned the act he is preparing. You have studied history, Zachary. Go and ponder on what you may remember of Europe's medieval history, especially the most popular entertainments of those times. In the meanwhile, calm yourself, do nothing but your job, give loving attention to your dear lady, and trust that Major Maggot will get what he deserves." Florian added, as a practical afterthought, "Also, we have some dozens of his cartes-de-visite that I bought in Munich, still to be peddled."

2

ON A hilltop at a wide place in the road, the circus train found advance man Willi Lothar and his companion Jules Rouleau waiting in their calash. Rouleau waved a hand expansively around and said, "I know some of you have seen this before, but I never had. Voilà. Here, mes amis, you are on the heights of the Wienerwald. The world-famous Vienna Woods."

"I was just remarking to Autumn," said Edge, "it looks to me more like rolling farmland and vineyards."

"But there are parts of it," said Jörg Pfeifer, "that are more blackly wooded even than Baden's Black Forest."

Edge said, "And I assume that's Vienna—Wien— sprawled out down ahead yonder. Damned big city. Do we make parade, Florian?"

"No, not this time. Too much trouble, what with the emperor's grandiose rebuilding of his capital."

Willi explained, "The work has been going on for ten years now, but the city is still a frightful mess. Streets torn up, excavations everywhere, new buildings half finished, piles of masonry and cobbles and tramway rails, rude laborers, all manner of litter and clutter. But that is all within the Innere Stadt, inside the new Ringstrasse. So our train can detour around through the outer streets. We will cross the river branch to set up in the Prater."

Even in the merely residential and mercantile, not monumental, parts of the city that the circus train plodded through, there was much for the newcomers to see and marvel at— splendid palaces and mansions, triumphal arches, statuary, plazas, fountains. Edge's own first impression of Wien he could have put in one word: "squirminess"—because every bit of stone and gesso and terracotta ornamentation was so tortuously convoluted and filigreed, every building's columns and caryatids and friezes so festooned with carved acanthus leaves and grape clusters and cartouches, every nude statue of a muscular god or voluptuous goddess so very nearly klischnigg in its petrified contortion—and the nudes' nudity not minified but somehow emphasized by a scrap of carved cloth fortuitously "windblown" over nipples or crotch.

The Prater, when the circus crossed the Rotunden Bridge to it, was the most pleasant place the Florilegium had ever yet been assigned for a tober. It was an island parkland of some eight square miles, with the Danube River on the far side and a narrow oxbow branch of the river on the inner. Part of its vastness was still primal wildwood and wild-flowered meadows; other parts were more tailored, with trim flower beds, hedge mazes, strollers' paths and bridle paths and gas lamps. There were numerous edifices here and there, expansive distances apart—a trotting-race track, a huge sports stadium, a gymnastics arena, band shells and benches for open-air concerts, immense and ornate pavilions for indoor musicales and dancing. There was every kind of eating place, from small taverns and coffeehouses tucked among shrubbery to commodious garden restaurants under flower-draped arbors.

The portion of the park near which the Florilegium pitched was the Wurstelprater, the all-summer pleasure resort that was almost a small village itself, of shops, booths and stalls—well-built ones, not gypsily impermanent—advertising entre-sort attractions, exhibits, games of chance, every kind of slum for sale. There was a children's playground, a pony-riding ring, a gaily painted carousel, one of the "swinging-boat" vertical wheels, a target-shooting alley . . .

"And after dark," said Willi, "you will see the red lamps of those establishments which are whorehouses. Even during the day, you will see the brothels' Strizzis—their pimps—on the prowl. Not to solicit customers, but hoping to find and entice, among the maidens strolling in the Wurstelprater, new talent for their houses."

"This sure is as up-to-date as any resort I've ever seen," said Fitzfarris. "Every modern convenience."

"Yes, indeed," said Florian. "Still, some of the old-time fixtures remain. There goes a Buttenfrau, for example."

It was an aged woman, bent and shuffling along in a sort of crouch, almost totally enveloped in a canvas cloak that bulged behind her as if she bore the world's most extreme affliction of hunchback. Even though she was some distance away, she was noticeably smelly.

"What the hell is a Buttenfrau?"

"On her back she carries a Butte, a wooden tub. Should you feel a sudden need to relieve yourself—you yell for a Buttenfrau. Give her two copper kreuzers, she sets down the tub, you sit on it, she covers you with the canvas from the view of passersby, and you do your business."

"All right, then," Fitz said, smiling. "The Prater has every modern convenience, and at least one old one that other resorts might do well to imitate."

The first thing Edge did, next day, was to hail a Fiaker—there were always many of those hire cabs cruising in the park—and help Autumn into it, and hand to the cabman the paper bearing the address of the Herr Doctor von Monakow. They were taken back across the bridge, and then for quite a long ride, because the Fiaker also circled around the construction clutter of the central city.

"You wait here," Edge told Autumn, when they arrived at the house. "I'll ask if he'll see us right away. He's supposed to speak English."

At a desk in the entry hall was a stern and starchy woman who also spoke English. "Three weeks from Tuesday, Herr Edge."

"Er, ma'am—I mean gnädige Frau—we've come a lot of miles and months to consult this particular doctor."

"Then it can scarcely be an emergency call."

"As far as I'm concerned, lady, it's been an emergency the whole time."

"Young Herr," she said, still crisply but not unsympathetically, "there are many others, as worried as you are, anxious for appointments. There is a long list. Meanwhile, the Herr Doktor has patients to attend and operations to perform in the Krankenhaus. Three weeks from Tuesday, Herr Edge, at ten o'clock."

Edge resignedly went and reported that to Autumn, who seemed unperturbed. She said, "Then let us have the Fiaker take us back only as far as the Ringstrasse, and walk for a while. On foot, we will have no trouble making our way through the inner streets. And we've plenty of time before you have to report for duty."

They had only occasionally to sidle around piles of rubble from old structures being torn down, or piles of material for new structures being erected. And plenty of other Viennese—afoot or on horseback, not in wheeled vehicles—were doing the same.

"Everybody comes, almost every day, to admire the improvements," said Autumn. "This used to be the old city's fortification embankment, but Franz Joseph determined to make it a grand boulevard encircling the whole central city, lined with incomparable examples of architecture. Those two tremendous buildings going up over there"—she pointed—"are intended to be the world's most magnificent museums: one of art and the other of natural history. And the people *are* much impressed with all this new splendor. Look yonder. That old country peasant reverently removes his hat before he presumes to cross the Ringstrasse."

"So he did. But a peasant from what country? I've never seen so many different-looking people in any one place we've been."

"Franz Joseph probably rules over more different races and nationalities and religions than Queen Victoria does. Austrians, Hungarians, Czechs, Trentino Italians, Poles, Serbs—I couldn't begin to name them all. And a lot of them congregate here in the capital, if only to market their native wares. That chap there, hawking the fancy silver teakettles—he's wearing a red fez and curly-toed slippers, so I'd guess him to be a Muslim from Bosnia. Those two old gentlemen with the long black robes and big-brimmed black hats, they are Hasidic rabbis. Those other two yonder, with the dark green gowns and the miters, they are Coptic priests."

"It's a cosmopolitan city, all right," said Edge. "Mighty overwhelming for a Virginia hillbilly."

"Ah, and there's the new Opera House," said Autumn approvingly. "The centerpiece of the whole Ring. It wasn't finished, last time I was here, but now at least the outside is.''

''Handsome, sure enough,'' said Edge.

''Franz Joseph wanted it to be, and it is. But poor, dull man, he has absolutely no tact. When he first came to look at the façade, he mumbled something about it seeming too *low* for its surroundings. The architect immediately went off and committed suicide. Ever since then, the emperor hasn't dared to make any controversial comment on *anything*. Whether he attends a ballet or a concert or a monument being unveiled—whatever—he has a stock remark. 'Es war schön. Es hat mich sehr gefreut.' It has been nice; I have enjoyed it.''

''What *I'd* enjoy right now is a morning snack,'' said Edge. ''Every single person we've passed on the street is walking along eating a pretzel or an ice or a hunk of wurst. It's made me a little peckish, too.'' And he steered Autumn into the street-floor coffeehouse of a hotel right behind the Opera House.

''Well, you're a good chooser,'' Autumn said. ''This is the Sacher, probably the most famous hotel in Europe.''

They were seated by an urbane waiter, impeccably attired in white tie and tails even at that hour of the forenoon, who asked in several different languages what he might be honored to serve them. Autumn said, ''Zwei Mokka, Herr Ober. Und die Konditorwaren, bitte.''

So, when he brought their two coffees, he also rolled to their table the sumptuously stocked pastry cart.

''The many-layered dark chocolate thing there,'' said Autumn, ''is the inimitable Sachertorte. You must have that, Zachary. I think I'll have a slice of that walnut strudel.''

''Mit Schlagober?'' asked the waiter.

''Bitte.''

At which, the waiter slathered and smothered her pastry with a mound of whipped cream, artistically swirling and peaking it.

Edge said, ''Girl, if you eat all that whipped cream, you won't be able to walk out of here.''

''I'll manage,'' she said, and laughed, for she had got a

dab of it smeared onto her concealing veil. "You'll learn to, too. Other cities fly flags bearing their civic escutcheons. If Wien has any such insigne, it must be a flying plume of Schlagober."

Edge looked about at the other tables, where extremely well-dressed men and women were having their midmorning confections. True enough, there seemed to be enough whipped cream in sight to have filled the circus pista. He said, "When we first rode in, I thought the local architecture and ornamentation looked—squirmy, you might say. I was wrong. Obviously, it's all designed to be just as puffy and rich and creamy as the Schlagober."

Autumn laughed again. "For a Virginia hillbilly, you are perceptive. Someone else once remarked that every view in Wien looks like the artwork on a chocolate-box lid."

"This hotel is a pretty place, too. But why is it so famous?"

"Oh, my dear, we are merely in the coffeehouse. There are half a dozen other dining rooms inside, and private cubicles where a young man can wine and dine his süsse Mädel. And upstairs is the vast marble-paneled séparée, where rich men have often entertained the entire corps of the Opera ballet. There is even a branch restaurant—Sacher's in the Prater—out there near our tober. Speaking of which, we've time for me to show you one more thing before we have to return. The center and pivot and pride of all Wien."

She led him along the Kärntnerstrasse, a broad avenue restricted to pedestrians only, and blocked to vehicular traffic by immense stone basins placed at intervals and angles, each basin overflowing with petunias or geraniums. On both sides, the avenue was lined with Wien's most exclusive and expensive shops, flaunting in their polished bay windows every kind of rich apparel, haberdashery, millinery and jewelry. At one point along the way, Autumn gestured to a side street and said, "Down there you'll find Auntie Dorothy."

"What?"

"The Dorotheum. It was started as a civic pawnshop for the benefit of the poor, like the Mounts of Pity in Italy. But it very soon became nothing but a fence shop where thieves and burglars sell their plunder. So, if anything of ours gets stolen while we're here, don't even bother complaining to the police. Just go to Tante Dorothée and buy it back. I've always been struck by the coincidence of the name. In London, the same sort of fence houses are all called Dolly Shops.''

The Kärntnerstrasse brought them out into the grand expanse of the Stephansplatz, in the center of which square towered the exceedingly tall, vertical, spiky-steepled and gaudily roof-tiled cathedral of St. Stephan.

"One of these days, Zachary," said Autumn, "we'll go up into the Stephansdom tower—if we don't get blown off by the perpetual wind here. The view is sublime. Stay all day and you can see the sun rise from over the Danube plain and set behind the foothills of the Alps. But we'd better be getting back to the Prater now. There's a Fiaker rank right here beside the cathedral."

They arrived at the tober to find Florian conversing with a young man and woman in spangled bright-red fleshings.

"Compatriots of yours, my dear!" Florian called ebulliently to Autumn. "Cecil and Daphne Wheeler, who—believe it or not—actually do a *wheel* act. Mr. and Mrs. Wheeler, allow me to present Miss Autumn Auburn, expatriate of your own England, who is our principal équilibriste aérienne, though temporarily on leave. And Colonel Zachary Edge, of your American colonies, who is our capable equestrian director, and wears many other hats besides."

"How do you do?" said Daphne, smiling—her smile wavering when Edge smiled back. Daphne was a very pretty young woman, ash blonde, peach-skinned, with a somewhat subdued air about her.

"D'y'do?" said Cecil. He was handsome, sandy-haired, ruddy of complexion and not at all subdued. "Truly, Wheeler is the name—though one might wonder which came first, what?—one's name or one's game. Back in Merrie Olde, Daf and I did a velocipede turn. Then, in Paris, we got our first look at the new skating without ice. So now we do that, as well. Just different wheels, ennit? And one must constantly aspire and improve, mustn't one?"

Florian interrupted to say, "Forgive me, Zachary, Autumn, but I completely neglected to inquire about your consultation in town."

"We didn't have any," said Edge. "But he must be a good doctor. He's got so much business that we can't even get to see him for more than three weeks."

"Ah, well, a heartening commendation, that, though I know you must be impatient."

Edge said, "Right this minute, speaking as your equestrian director from the backward colonies, I wish somebody would please tell me what is a velocipede turn. And skating without ice."

"Spectacular. Sensational," said Florian. "They've just been demonstrating for me. We'll bill them as *The Wheeling Wheelers!* But go ahead, Cecil, you tell the colonel what it is you do."

"Well, old boy, a long time ago there was a machine called the dandy-horse, with two wheels, fore and aft. One straddled a bar between, and scooted it along with one's feet. Then somebody thought to put crank pedals on the front wheel and—"

"Yes," said Edge. "The bone-shaker we call it in the colonies. High wheel up front, small one in the rear."

"Right you are, old boy. The penny-farthing we call it in Merrie Olde. More correctly, the velocipede."

"Since we've been in Europe, I've seen several men riding the things in the parks. It looks damned uncomfortable."

"Dunnit, though. But it's capable of some dashing tricks. I do the pedaling and Daf does postures on my shoulder. Then I close by riding the bloody thing solo, at breakneck speed, stop short and take a header into a vat of flames. Meaning a vat of water with a skim of oil burning on top, don't y' know."

"Bloody hair-raising it is, too," said Florian, as if unconsciously adopting Cecil's mode of speech.

Daphne Wheeler and Autumn had moved off apart, and the new girl hesitantly asked, "On leave you are, Miss Auburn? And seeing a doctor? Excuse the presumption, but are you—would it be a blessed event?"

"Oh, dear, no," said Autumn. "Merely an ailment that has me out of action and all bundled up for a while."

"Ah, one of our notorious female complaints, then. Isn't it bleeding hell, being a female?"

"And you and Mr. Wheeler? Have you a family?"

"No. Ceece isn't much of one for—well, he likes to get about. That's why he applied to Mr. Florian. We've been here in the Prater for two summers now. Doing our wheel acts as fill-ins between the contests in the gymnastics arena. So Ceece is itching to get on a show that will take us moving again."

"Well, while the men are talking, Daphne, come and I'll introduce you around among our female contingent."

Cecil was now explaining to Edge: "When we visited the Hippodrome in Paris, they were putting on this Jolly-Old-Winter spectacle—'Happy Holland' or 'Sweet Sweden' or some such bloody thing—sleighs and cutters and fur costumes and all." Cecil laughed; he had a laugh that was a sort of well-bred snuffle: hnoof-hnoof-hnoof. "But they didn't care to flood and freeze their fine parquet floor, don't y' know. So the whole corps of skater-dancers wore Plimptons instead of blades. Do you know Plimptons, old boy? They're a Yank invention, after all."

"I'm afraid I don't, old boy. I'm not a very good Yank."

"Well, instead of strapping skate blades on one's boots, one straps on these little clogs, each with four tiny boxwood wheels. One simply *rolls* about, as smoothly as on ice. And, with practice, one can cut any caper that can be done on real skates."

"Surely not in the sawdust of a circus pista."

"No, no, old boy. We carry on top of our caravan, in addition to the vat for the flaming-water trick, a collapsible board affair. In the pista it unfolds to a circle. On that, we whirl and glide and figure skate and dance together."

Edge said, and sincerely, "I'm eager to see it."

"Yes," said Florian. "But the Wheelers must give notice to their present employer, so we have plenty of time to decide where to spot them in the program. Now, Cecil, come and meet some others of your soon-to-be colleagues. Right here, for starters, the Quakemaker, Miss Eel and young Ali Baba.''

Yount could only nod and grunt, for he was practicing holding aloft both Agnete and Quincy while they contorted. Agnete, lying prone on Yount's right hand, brought her head out of a tangle of her own limbs to smile and say, ''Welcome.'' Quincy, his rump on Yount's left hand, had his legs straight up in the air, but parted them enough to put his head in his own crotch and shyly say, ''Hoy.''

Cecil said, ''Monkey boy, you must be a source of great satisfaction to yourself. Just be careful not to bite it off''— which left Quincy staring after him, looking puzzled and concerned.

When Cecil was introduced to the Smodlakas, he spoke amiably to Pavlo and Gavrila, and dutifully patted the terriers that Pavlo proudly brought to show him. But he stared in open admiration at the albino Sava and Velja, whom Gavrila was bathing in a zinc tub.

''By Jove, Florian,'' Cecil said. ''You ought to exhibit them just like that: totally nude. Pure porcelain they are— Sèvres biscuit. Never saw any human bodies of porcelain white all over. The little girl's nipples, even the little boy's knob end . . .''

''Stvarno ne,'' muttered Gavrila, giving him a wary look and covering each of the children with a towel.

After meeting Willi and Rouleau, Cecil at least waited until he was out of their hearing before making another crass remark: ''Couple of queans, what?''

Florian said coldly, ''Let's go back, and you can ask them.''

''Oh, I've nothing against queans, old boy,'' Cecil said hastily. ''As artistes, all well and good. But I say, is it the best policy to have a nancy representing you as advance man? I mean, what sort of impression—?''

''Herr Lothar has done an excellent job for us, so far. And Monsieur Roulette is indispensable. Their private lives are *nobody's* business.''

''Quite, quite. They're two full-grown men, after all. Or two full-grown somethings, what? Hnoof-hnoof!''

*   *   *

The tober was thronged with people waiting to buy tickets
for the opening show and meanwhile crowding to every booth
and stall and joint on the midway. The tap wenches were
handing out seidls of beer, the lemonade and Eis butchers
were handing out paper cones of their products, the wurst
braziers were fogging the air blue—and the few Viennese not
eating something were busily buying gimcracks from the
slum stalls. They were buying exactly the same sort of food
and drink and cheap souvenirs that the whole Wurstelprater
had been selling all summer long, but evidently the Florilegium's being itself something new must have lent a newness
to everything about it.

At the entrance end of the midway, the calliope was steaming and smoking and roaring Strauss's "Delirium Waltz"
loudly enough for its own composer to hear, wherever he
might be in the city. Over the front door of the chapiteau, the
florid banners were flapping and thwacking in the wind. At
one side of it, the Gluttonous Greek was erupting plume after
plume of fire; on the other, Fitzfarris was touting his mouse
game, and hordes were elbowing to wager on it. Edge was
making his way toward the marquee when he was intercepted
by Florian and Lothar. "For your information, Colonel Ramrod," said Florian, "a week from today, we will close the
tober to the public for the night time show. Willi has engaged
for us a private audience, and sold out the entire pavilion."

"Well, dandy," said Edge. "A command performance for
the swells?"

"Er, no," said Willi. "I am working on that, and I expect
to arrange it. But no, this private showing will be to celebrate
a beggars' wedding."

Dumbfounded, Edge said, "Since I've been on this show,
we have reserved the whole works just twice. Once for the
King of Italy. Once for a hive of stump preachers back in
Virginia. Won't beggars be kind of a comedown even from
that one?"

"By no means," said Florian. "Viennese beggars stand
considerably higher on the social scale than any backwood
gospel-grinders."

"You see, Herr Edge," said Willi. "Wien is such a very

wealthy city that even cripples do not *need* to beg, but it is an accepted vocation. In this case, the father of the bride has his recognized post at the Stone Bridge, his wife at the Burgtor—as did their parents and grandparents before them. And their daughter is marrying a very up-and-coming young beggar with a stand of his own near the Albertina. The profession is so profitable that these proud parents wish to lavish thousands of kronen on the wedding. The ceremony at Saint Stephan's, the entertainment here at the Zirkus, afterward a gala reception and dinner in the chapiteau—Sacher's will cater the meal—and to that, incidentally, all of *us* are invited.''

''Well, it quizzes me, I'll have to admit,'' said Edge, ''but I can hardly complain. If ever I'm in Virginia again, I'll suggest to the preachers that they contemplate a different calling.'' He broke off to say, ''Hey, Maggot!'' and reached out to collar the midget, who was trotting past, dressed in his sideshow full-dress dancing suit. ''This is Wien. When do we see this great new act of yours?''

The little man snarled, ''Ach, come on, Edge—''

''*Herr Direktor!*''

The snarl changed to a whine. ''Have a heart, Herr Direktor. Stitches and Boom-Boom have built the cage, but I've got to collect the cats—catch them one by one.''

Florian said drily, ''I imagine alley cats are harder to catch than jüngferlich little girls.''

Major Minim scowled, but said only, ''I want a score of cats, and so far I've got only four, and already my caravan smells like a sewer.'' He snatched himself out of Edge's grasp and scurried away.

''We'll give him time,'' said Florian. ''I'm as eager to be rid of him as you are, Colonel Ramrod, but I do hate losing a trouper until we have a replacement. I figure we'll be losing him just about the time the Wheelers join out.''

''Are you still letting little Sava do the dance turn with him?''

''Yes. I think he spoke truly about being afraid to molest *her.* But I've cautioned Gavrila: never to let Sava near him except during the dance act. Or Velja either. The Night Children have permission to fraternize with anybody else in the world except Major Minim.''

After the come-out of that afternoon's show, when the blow-off tent filled with its customary male audience to see the Amazon Maiden's ravishment by the Dragon Fafnir, Fitz-farris was surprised to see that the audience was, for once, *not* all male. Among the men, a pretty girl, in chic bonnet and crinolette, stood holding a sketch pad and busily working on it with a stick of charcoal while she watched intently. When the performance was over and the men went out snick-ering and exchanging ribaldries, as usual, the girl remained. She approached Fitzfarris at the platform, and got prettier at every step. She was in her early twenties, had black hair, violet eyes and an exquisite figure. Then Fitz noticed that she was accompanied by another female, about her own age, but not at all pretty. She had a hanging bush of kinky hair like Spanish moss, and she looked extremely disgusted at finding herself in such surroundings.

''Bitte, mein Herr,'' the pretty one said. ''You are the Herr Direktor of this spectacle?''

''I am, gnädiges Fräulein. Can I do something for you?''

''I should like your permission to speak to the—to the Amazon Maiden.''

''Give her a minute to cram the dragon back in his lair, then I'll call her. May I inquire . . . ?''

She showed him the sketch pad on which, with quick, min-imal and expert strokes, she had limned Meli and the python in several of their erotic intertwinings. ''My name is Tina Blau. I should like to ask the lady if she would consent to sit to me for a painting.''

''Ah, you draw,'' Fitz said approvingly. ''A most ladylike avocation. And paint, too? Watercolors, I daresay.''

''You *daresay!*'' the other female snapped at him. ''What a typically masculine condescension. Why do you not pat her on the head? I would have you know that Tina Blau is no wilting hothouse damsel who occupies empty hours doing dainty water-colors. Tina Blau is a *professional* painter, and of growing renown.''

"And you? Who are you?" Fitz asked, not cordially.

"Please," said Tina Blau. "You must excuse my friend. She is Bertha Kinsky, a leading figure in the Peace Society, in the Young Liberals and in the Anti-Suppression of Women Society."

"And is she your manager, Fräulein Blau? Your keeper?"

"No, no. A friend and patroness. Sometimes Bertha's enthusiasms tend to vehemence, but—"

"I can speak for myself!" said the other. "This whole exhibition is a disgraceful debasement of that poor woman on the platform. But, Tina, if you wish to paint her, I simply want this—this exploiter—to know that you are *capable* of painting her." To Fitzfarris she said, "The Fräulein Tina Blau is a far more accomplished artist than a schmud'l candy-box decorator like the so-famous Herr Makart."

"All right, all right, I'll believe it." Fitz added a wry pun: "I paint myself," then took out a handkerchief and swiped it down his face, revealing the blue half. Tina Blau's violet eyes widened, and the redoubtable Kinsky gasped, then shut up. Fitz said, "I'll fetch the Amazon Maiden for you."

Meli Vasilakis came back into the tent, wrapped in a dressing gown and looking not very happy. Given the language difficulties, it took a while for Tina Blau to convey her request that Meli and the python pose for a portrait.

"Ah, you want dirty picture. Me making zefyos with snake. How you like *real* dirty picture? Me making zefyos with *real* snake. Two, three times a week I must do. Come any time, watch, paint." And she abruptly departed.

"I don't quite understand," said Tina.

"Frankly, I don't know what she's talking about, either," Fitz confessed. "But we'll be here in Vienna for quite a while, Fräulein. Come again, come often, gain her confidence, she'll warm up to you. Anybody would. As for me, I've never met a genuine artist before, and I don't think I ever even *heard* of a female one. I'd be most pleased to see some of your work."

She gave him a long and thoughtful look, then handed him a card. "My studio address: Feel free to call, mein Herr." The Fräulein Kinsky almost yanked at her elbow, to lead her from the tent. Fitz's gaze, following her, collided against the stare of Monday Simms, who stood in the front door opening, regarding him with eyes of anthracite.

That afternoon's show had been so well attended—and so was that night's, and so were the several subsequent shows—that Florian convoked a meeting of his executive managers in the office wagon, to announce:

"This, gentlemen, will be our longest stand yet. We shall stay throughout the autumn and winter and perhaps well into the spring. Much of the Wurstelprater—the entresorts and such—closes down for the winter, and so do the sports stadia and the open-air restaurants in the rest of the Prater. But plenty of people still come out from the city, even on the snowiest days, to sleigh ride or to skate on the river and the ponds, and I trust that some will come to see us. Even if we have only a scant attendance during the winter, I believe we shall still prosper better than by going to the expense and trouble of traveling, setting up and tearing down in smaller communities. Also, Wien offers a wealth of diversions for *us*. We might as well enjoy them. It offers, as well, every kind of supplies and equipment we might desire, in the way of improving our establishment and our program. For example, Carl, you can acquire all the chemicals necessary to send up the *Saratoga* as often as you and Monsieur Roulette may wish."

"Dankes," said Beck. "Might I also some more instruments for the band procure? Woodwinds I should like to add, the band's brassiness to temper somewhat. Also strings, for the more gentle acts, like that of the Fräulein Eel."

"Yes, go and buy as you will. I would suggest that you'll find the best bargains at Auntie Dorothy's thief shop."

"There will be need, then, for more crewmen, Governor," said Dai Goesle. "What with band work and balloon work and routine work and special jobs like that cage for the midget, Banat and the other Slovaks are spreading themselves fair thin. And when we are getting those wheel people, mind you, with their vasty props to handle . . ."

"Quite right, Canvasmaster. Tell Banat to go and recruit. He probably knows the haunts of any Slovaks resident here."

"Speaking of the midget," said Edge, "he now tells me that he'll have enough cats by the time we put on that special show for the beggars' wedding, and he'd like to introduce his parody lion-taming act then."

"No," Florian said firmly. "A wedding should be a happy occasion. We'll save the major's début for some weekday afternoon performance, when the city children will be mostly in school, and the audience will be predominantly adult."

"You want to protect the children from him?" said Edge, a little puzzled. "Hell, he'll be in a cage. But whatever you say, Governor."

At that moment, in the circus's backyard, Major Minim *was* inside the cage, with one of his collection of cats. Abner Mullenax was looking in at them with a mixture of amusement, amazement and skepticism. The cage was a perfect copy of Maximus's wagon, complete to the sunburst wheels, but scaled down to the midget's stature. Right now, Minim was struggling to paint his cat with stripes of black and yellow to simulate a tiger. The cat was understandably flailing and biting and scratching and screaming bloody murder. Minim was cursing almost as loudly, and getting almost as much of the paints all over himself.

"Little man," said Mullenax, "if you think you're goin' to train a bunch of tough old alley cats to do any kind of an act, you're crazy. Me, I'd sooner try trainin' the savagest lion in any jungle."

"Then go do it!" snarled Minim. "I had rather be doing that myself, than having to paint these cursed beasts one by one. Scheisse! I am worse clawed and chewed than I could be in any jungle. But I only want them colorful, not talented. Of this act, *I* am to be the star!"

3

AUTUMN SAID, a little wistfully, "This is the last place, Zachary, that I will be able to strut and swagger as your knowledgeable tour guide." They were standing atop the wind-buffeted north tower of the Stephansdom. "Prince Met-

ternich once said that east of the Landstrasse begin the
Balkans. The Landstrasse is that street you can see down
there by the Stadtpark. Some people claim that he said 'There
begins *Asia*.' In any case, I've never been east of Wien, so
wherever we go next will be as new and foreign to me as to
you.''

''Well, you've done fine, so far, and taught me a lot,'' said
Edge. ''So go ahead. Strut. Swagger. Show me things.''

As they circled the tower balcony, she pointed out the distant Belvedere palace, and the Bösendorfer piano factory, and
the old monument raised in gratitude for the end of the Great
Plague, and the cluster of grand palaces that centered on the
Hofburg, the emperor's own palace.

Edge said, ''There's one Viennese landmark that even hillbilly horse soldiers have heard of. Can we spot it from here?
The Spanish Riding School. I'd sure like to visit there.''

''It's one of the buildings among those of the Hofburg.
Properly, it's the Royal Winter Riding Academy. People call
it Spanish only because its special breed of horses originally
came from Spain. See, your tour guide is showing off again.
But actually I've never been in there. Very few commoners
have. I'm sorry, my dear, but the horses are ridden only by
titled officers of the Imperial Army. And even the spectators'
gallery is reserved to royals and nobles—or to the emperor's
special guests by invitation only.''

''Damn,'' said Edge, looking disappointed. Then he brightened. ''Aha, I was forgetting. We have our *own* resident noble.''

So, when he and Autumn returned to the tober, he sought
out Willi Lothar and put a request to him.

''Well,'' said Willi, ''getting you Eintritt there ought to be
easier than what I am presently trying to arrange—that royal
command performance. I shall see what I can do.''

''Five tickets, if you can,'' said Edge. ''For me, Autumn,
Obie Yount, Clover Lee and Monday Simms.''

That evening was the special show for the beggars' wedding party, and, contrary to most of the artistes' expectations,
it was by no means a ragamuffin audience. The people who
came into the chapiteau—merrily but not riotously—were as

well dressed as any crowd of bourgeoisie attending an opera.
Among the principal figures, the bridegroom did have a peg
leg, but the bride was whole and even rather handsome, and
so were the parents, and the best man and maid of honor. So
were most of the approximately two hundred beggar guests,
only a comparative few of them deformed or mutilated in
some way. A number of legless men wheeled themselves in
on little platforms, and some lepers had to be carried by other
people; but even those wore fine clothes on what bodies they
had, and seemed to be enjoying the occasion as much as did
all their colleagues.

"Hell," said Fitzfarris. "I figured there'd be more freaks
in here tonight than there are in the whole Wurstelprater, and
maybe some I could recruit. Not any of these look like exhibit
material to me."

"The bridegroom, I understand, lost his leg in the recent
war," said Florian, "and was awarded his begging station at
the Albertina Museum by a grateful government, in lieu of a
pension. Most of the long-ago original beggars probably got
their permanent posts in much the same way, but you are
looking at their heirs—children, grandchildren—who are
mostly hale and hearty professional beggars. The few real
cripples are, like the bridegroom, presumably new in the profession."

Kapellmeister Beck and his now much augmented band
gave a lyrical rendition of the "Wedding March"—this time
not to signal calamity—while the guests seated themselves,
or, if they could not sit, found advantageous places in which
to squat or recline. Then the band went into the Schuhplattler
overture and Sir John's corps of midway wenches did their
energetic thigh-slapping dance—and all the beggars who had
hands happily clapped them in time to the beat. At last, Beck
thundered into his rollicking version of "Greensleeves" and
the Grand Promenade began.

· The night's crowd filled hardly a fifth of the chapiteau,
but, perhaps because they themselves were also professional
performers of a sort, they applauded every act as lustily as a
sfondone house could have done—and those spectators who
had feet stamped them as loudly. At intermission, to spare

the cripples the bother of getting outside to the midway, Florian bade everyone remain seated, and the sideshow was presented in the pista. Then, after the closing Grand Promenade, Florian again bade the audience wait, and Sir John brought Meli and her python to do their tableau vivant inside the chapiteau for the first time. This was also the first time it had ever been performed before an audience fully fifty percent female, but there were no complaints; the women whistled and yelled as bawdily as the men.

Next there arrived on the tober the variously stove-heated or ice-cooled wagons from Sacher's Garden. A multitude of tail-coated waiters brought and assembled immense trestle tables in and around the pista, and covered them with snowy linens, stacks of bone-china dishes and heaps of silver tableware. Then they began spreading the trays and platters of food, buffet style, for the guests to help themselves, but there was so much food that the waiters laid it out by courses, the first being oysters on beds of ice. The circus people of course stayed apart until the beggars had heaped their own plates and the plates of their colleagues who could not reach the tables—but there was plenty left over for everybody in both troupe and crew. While the oysters were being consumed, the waiters brought to the tables great tureens of hot turtle soup.

"Christamighty," said Mullenax, as the courses kept coming—lobster à l'Armoricaine, truite au bleu with Venetian sauce—"if the local cadgers eat like this, what do the gentry folks eat?"

"Ach, this is probably a once-in-a-lifetime thing for the mendicants," said Jörg Pfeifer. "Ordinarily, if they dine out at all, it is at the Schmauswaberl."

"The garbage dump?"

"Well, not quite. It is a back-street restaurant—a warehouse, really—originally established to provide the cheapest possible meals for the local students, and its bill of fare consists entirely of leftovers from the emperor's Hofburg kitchens."

But here and now, the superb viands kept coming: quail stew, chicken à la française, salads, four different wines—Chablis, Lafite-Rothschild, Röderer champagne, Sherry Supérieure—and compôtes, ices, chestnut purée, Sachertorten, other pastries piled with Schlagober, coffee, a variety of cheeses and fruits . . .

When everyone—literally, every one of the circus people and their audience—had eaten to satiety, one of the sturdier male beggars waddled heavily into the center of the pista. He belched, then raised his arms, gave a downbeat, and the tentful of beggars began to sing. The song was clearly a thank-you to their hosts, and clearly had been chosen to appeal to "Confederate Americans":

> Oh, Susannah! O weine nicht um mich!

Boom-Boom Beck sent his bandsmen scrambling up to the bandstand to seize their instruments and, after a moment, they were briskly accompanying the tumult of voices:

> Denn ich komm von Alabama,
> Bring meine Banjo nur für mich . . .

"That is the prettiest tribute we have ever had," said Florian, as the beggars came—those who could come, and those who had hands—to shake hands with every available individual of the Florilegium, and to express fulsomely fervent thanks for the entertainment. "Probably," Florian added, "a tribute more genuinely heartfelt than we shall ever get from the high and mighty."

The next day, Willi Lothar presented to Edge five gilt-and-deckle-edged cards, dense with Gothic engraving. "Your Eintritt to the Riding Academy's Exhibition Hall," he said. "I got them from the Graf von Welden, but not so easily as I had thought. After I sent in my card, the damned snob kept me waiting like a peasant petitioner in his reception hall for two hours before condescending to admit me."

"Well, I thank you for going to so much trouble."

Willi laughed archly. "Oh, I took my revenge for the affront. There was in the hall a parrot in a cage. So I occupied my time by teaching it to repeat every filthy word I know in every language I know. Anyway, enjoy yourselves.''

So that afternoon Edge, Autumn, ex-Troop Sergeant Yount and équestriennes Clover Lee and Monday sat, among a number of other and presumably noble spectators, in the pillared gallery above the acre of tanbark riding area, while a string orchestra in the loggia played and eight gorgeously uniformed officers put their eight extraordinary stallions through their extraordinary paces.

Immediately on entry, the riders reverently lifted their bicorn hats to the loggia's unoccupied imperial box. ''They are not saluting the present experor,'' Autumn whispered to the others. ''They are paying homage to the Emperor Karl, who founded the academy some hundred and fifty years ago. Now . . . I have told you exactly *everything* I know about the spectacle. You cavalry-men and horsewomen must explain to me from now on. For one thing, I thought all the Lippizaner horses were white. Some of these are silvery or pale gray.''

''There's not many horses *born* white, Miss Autumn,'' Yount whispered. ''From what I've heard tell, these-here are born charcoal color, and it takes 'em six or eight years to grow through smoke color to pure white. So the darker ones are the younger ones.''

While the orchestra played waltzes, minuets, rosse-ballets, gavottes and karussells, the eight horses walked or trotted or cantered through intricate interweavings, with such ballroom perfection that every horse and rider seemed mirror image of the others. Sometimes the horses would cross legs and advance sideways; sometimes they did an almost pouncing sort of high step. Whatever the dance, whenever any two or four or all eight of the horses met and crossed paths, it was always at some geometrically precise point in the rectangular arena.

''Just *look* how they step,'' Clover Lee murmured in awe. ''If you watch close, it's a kind of soft double action. Each hoof is first placed, *then* stepped on with the stallion's full weight. And they do it at any gait, slow or fast, where an ordinary horse would just go clump-clump. Monday, are you watching?''

''I watchin','' Monday said sullenly. She looked so glum that Edge refrained from asking her what was wrong.

*   *   *

In a high-ceilinged, many-windowed, light and airy studio loft on the Marxergasse, Fitzfarris was saying, "Your paintings are truly beautiful, Fräulein Blau. I don't speak as any expert, but I concede that your tom lady-friend was right."

"Tom? She is not a viragint, if that is what you mean. Bertha merely tries to be as gruff and surly and unfeminine as a man, so her ideas and opinions will be taken as seriously as a man's."

"Well, her opinion of your work can't be faulted. I wish I could buy one of these paintings—except they're kind of, uh, huge. And I live in just a small caravan. What do you get for them, anyway?"

"For that one you are looking at—*Nachthimmel*—one hundred gold kronen."

Fitz gulped and stared. "That's more than the *caravan* cost."

"Here," she said kindly, her violet eyes soft as velvet. "This little crayon of a single carnation, life-size. It is small enough that it should fit in your house wagon. And it is not expensive."

"It's a lovely thing, Fräulein Blau, but—"

"Call me Tina."

"Uh, Tina . . . the drawing . . . how *not* expensive it it?"

"Whatever you wish to give me." She smiled deliciously. "Anything."

"Anything?"

"Anything."

"Are you paying attention, Monday?" demanded Clover Lee. "What that one stallion is doing now is called the 'airs above the ground.' My mother told me all about—" She stopped herself. "Well, look there. That's the levade. The horse squats back on his haunches, lifts his forelegs and holds the position. He probably could stand like that all day, with the rider on his back. I wish some of our nags were as—"

"*Now* look at him!" exclaimed Yount. "I've never in my life seen a horse do anything like that!"

"The courbette," said Clover Lee. "Starting from the levade, without putting his front feet down, he hops on his hind legs like a kangaroo. Only he's much more beautiful than any kangaroo.''

That particular stallion, after graciously nodding to the spectators' genteel applause, was led out of the arena and another brought in. This one, after some warm-up prancing and curvetting, did something even more seemingly impossible for any animal heavier than a goat. At a run, it repeatedly leapt high aloft, and there, with all four feet off the ground, kicked its hind legs violently straight backward. Each time, it appeared to hang magically there in the air, in that graceful pose, like a heraldic horse on an old coin or shield.

"Jesus!" said Yount.

"The capriole," Clover Lee said breathlessly.

Even the glum Monday said, ''Oh, my!''

"I can tell you something about that capriole jump," said Edge. "It wasn't thought up just to look pretty. Unless it's only a legend, that trick dates back to the knights of olden times. If a knight was being chased by an enemy, he would command his horse, at full gallop, to give that capriole kick backward at his pursuer.''

The program concluded with the arena again full of stallions doing another ensemble ballet to the ''Österreichischer Grenadiersmarsch.'' Then the spectators filed downstairs and outdoors, emerging among the vaulted arches of one of the Hofburg's carriage driveways.

Autumn said, ''We've time before you have to get back for the night show. Let us go to Griensteidl's for a coffee.''

When they got there and seated themselves in a plush-upholstered banquette, an ancient waiter, without being asked, silently set in front of each of them a glass of water, a thick mug of black coffee, a dish of cube sugar and a spoon. He also laid on the table a sheaf of newspapers, each clamped in a split wooden rod, then he silently shuffled away.

Edge commented, ''Not exactly as solicitous as the waiters at Sacher's, is he?''

"Oh, much more so," said Autumn. "We could sit here all the rest of the day and night, until closing time, and the Herr Ober would come at intervals to renew our glasses of water—and the coffee, if we ask, or bring anything else we might care to order—and bring other newspapers, when we'd finished these, but he would never *press* us to buy anything. Of all the traditional fixtures of Wien, the Viennese café is the most gemütlich. And each café has its traditional clientèle. Dunel's is for the rich and famous, Landtmann's is for the intellectuals, this one is mainly patronized by young would-be authors, artists and musicians.''

Edge looked around and saw that that was so. At any rate, the café's walls were nearly hidden by unframed paintings and drawings, unmistakably the work of not-yet artists, for even he could see the ineptitude of them. There were posters announcing art exhibitions, poetry readings and such, and there was a corkboard covered with pinned-up handwritten cards and papers. Edge went to look at those. As well as he could make out, most advertised the availability of various students as tutors of music, drawing, dance, essay composition, even penmanship. But some of the notices were merely scrawled communications, done in various languages, including English: "Has anyone a #00 sable brush for sale cheap?" and "Gertrud, when *will* you return my Schiller?" The patrons seated in banquettes or at marble-topped tables were mostly young men and girls, and looked rather seedy, but Edge could not have guessed which of them were would-be whats. Some sat alone, reading the newspapers and magazines that the café provided free, but the majority of them sat in clusters, deep in conversation on topics evidently weighty and earnest. And so many of them were puffing away at pipes or cigarettes that a blue layer of smoke hung midway between the room's ceiling and floor.

When Edge returned to his place, Autumn was saying ''. . . Almost all of Wien's cafés—and this is a rarity among European gathering places—are hospitable even to women without escorts.''

''Good,'' said Clover Lee, who was examining the newspaper on the table. ''I'll come with Sunday, and she can translate these 'personal notices' to me. Maybe some duke is advertising for a wife.''

''Well, me, I ain't go' sit here 'til no closin' time,'' said Monday. ''I got things to see to.''

So they took a Fiaker back to the Prater, where Edge was immediately hailed by Florian.

"Cecil and Daphne Wheeler have finished their stint at the arena, and have just brought their caravan to our backyard. We'll put them in the program at tomorrow's afternoon show. If you concur, Colonel Ramrod, I should like them to have the start of the second half. That will give the roustabouts ample time during intermission to set up the Wheelers' skating board and flaming vat. Then, just for this one show, move Barnacle Bill and his animals to the end of the show, with Little Major Minim coming on right afterward to do his parody of that act."

"You'd snub Monday's 'Cinderella' to give the maggot the close? The star spot?"

"This once only. Indulge me."

The next day being a school day, the afternoon show's audience was, as Florian had predicted, composed almost entirely of grown men and women. There were only a few children of school age; the others were toddlers or babes in arms.

The Wheelers' rolling skates were something unique in a circus, and even those spectators who might previously have seen the couple perform in the Prater's gymnastics arena clearly had not tired of admiring and applauding them. One at a time or both together, Cecil and Daphne did every "turn and change" known to real figure skating on ice—and did them in the constricted space of their circular board—spread eagles, sitting pirouettes, four-cross stars. Then, face to face, joining hands, leaning back from one another, they whirled so rapidly as to become a sequin-sparkling red blur. And then Cecil was holding Daphne by one wrist and one ankle, continuing the whirl while she levitated from the board to fly around him like a red bird at that dazzling speed.

Earlier, Cecil had given the bandmaster the sheet music for that act's accompaniment, and Beck had read its title aloud, with a sort of horror: " '*Oh, Emma! Whoa, Emma!*'—?"

"Don't be distressed, old boy. The lyrics are indeed atrocious—'Emma, you put me in quite a dilemma'—but we don't sing them, after all. The music is cheerful and loud. It *must* be loud, to drown out the rumble of our wooden wheels on the wooden board. And with your chaps making all the noise, so that we seem to skate in silence, well, it makes our skating look the more aesthetic, don't y' know.''

The Wheelers' velocipede turn was done to less vulgar music, more to Beck's taste: the bourrée from Handel's ''Royal Fireworks.'' The velocipede itself was not such a novelty to the spectators as the skates had been. Still, no one—until now—had seen it ridden otherwise than sedately by even the brashest young sports showing off on park drives and bridle paths. What Cecil did with it was considerably different. He did not just ride around and around the chapiteau; he made the high, cumbersome velocipede do right turns in its own length, and frequently roll backward, and sometimes rear up on its small hind wheel—while Daphne stood on his shoulders and struck artistic poses, then inverted herself to do a handstand away up there, never wavering during Cecil's most violent maneuvers.

When she hopped lightly down to the ground to take her bows, a roustabout put a torch to the oil-filmed vat of water, six feet in diameter, that had been positioned for best audience visibility. Cecil pedaled furiously several times around the tent, faster all the time, until at last he steered for a wooden block he had previously spiked to the ground. The velocipede's tall, iron-rimmed front wheel struck it at full speed, with a crash that hardly needed the bass drum's *boom!* for emphasis, and stopped dead. As if from a catapult, Cecil flew over the steering bar and into the flaming and smoking vat, his splash making the flames surge even higher, and there he disappeared—for he stayed underwater during the brief time it took the fire to subside. Meanwhile, Daphne had caught the velocipede when it toppled, so she was beside the vat when Cecil stood up—and the audience nearly raised the roof.

Edge rather wished that the roof could be raised, for the tent was left full of acrid smoke, and people were coughing and rubbing their eyes. So he whistled in the Hanswurst, the Kesperle and the Emeraldina to do their bouncy sky-pole turns as a fill-in until the Slovaks could get the Wheelers' props out and the smoke could clear. When it did disperse, Edge noticed that Florian, near the front door, was standing with a uniformed policeman. Since they appeared to be conversing amiably, Edge assumed that the officer had been posted there by "the authorities" to see that the flaming vat posed no menace to public safety. Edge whistled to bring on the next act—the Smodlakas and their dogs—but the policeman did not depart.

After the last real act had been applauded—Barnacle Bill with his lions, tigers, trumpeting bear and bridge-making elephants—and their wagons were being rolled out by the roustabouts, the band struck up Gottschalk's "Grand Scherzo," and Little Major Minim made his grand entrance. He wore his usual natty full dress and his pasted-on mustache, but had a patch like Mullenax's over one eye. He sat atop his miniature cage wagon, being pulled by the dwarf horse, and was flailing Rumpelstilzchen with a toy whip from one of the midway slum joints.

The cage seemed veritably full of cats, because they all were clinging frantically to the bars, mouths wide open, probably yowling, but unheard over the music and the gale of laughter that greeted them. Every cat's pelt was matted and spiky with the paints that smudgily striped it black and yellow. Minim made a circuit of the whole chapiteau, then turned to the pista and stopped in the center of it. He hopped down from the wagon, gave several sweeping bows, then went to the door at the rear of his cage, slashing with the whip to beat back the cats clinging to it.

The three casse-cou clowns were standing beside Edge, and they exclaimed in their several languages: "Pozor!" from Spenz; "Oy gevalt!" from Notkin; "Porco dio!" from the female joey, and she seized Edge's sleeve. "He will get inside? Signor Diretorre, you must not allow."

"It's his own notion, Nella," said Edge. "And he took a lot of trouble over it. Why should I stop him? Florian said something about this act being popular in medieval times."

She said, so urgently that her English faltered, "In medium-evil times, sì, most popular entertainment was *public execution*. One way of executing was that the criminal be tied inside sack full of cats, and the cats would fight to get out, and—ohimè, too late! He has gone in.''

So he had, and Minim clanged the door shut behind himself. He could dimly be seen, whipping the cats down from the cage bars to the floor, so that he could be better seen. When he had the score of cats all cowering about his feet, he flung up his arms in the V, and the band music stopped on a victorious chord. Then one of the cats sprang high from the pack, raking at Minim's face as it flew past him. With the single slash, it tore off his eye patch and his mustache and left a red scratch across his cheek.

The audience laughed at that, but, over the laughter, a child's voice could be heard shouting clearly, ''Papa! Ist der Knabe! Er brachten mir zum Nacktheit!'' The crowd's laughter became murmurs of puzzlement. Minim stood uncertainly among the snarling and spitting alley cats, his disguise gone, and his face suddenly so pale that the scratch across it gleamed vividly.

''Che cosa c'e?'' said Nella. ''Some little girl cries here is the boy who made her naked. Can she mean—?''

''Goddamn,'' growled Edge. ''The son of a bitch has been at it here, too.''

The child was still excitedly piping, and a louder voice—presumably her papa's—was also audible, and the whole audience was abuzz. Inside the cage, Minim went into a spasm of fury. As if he were beating off his small accuser, he whipped desperately and viciously at the cats. But not for long. Not one cat sprang now, all of them did. Minim stayed upright for a time, but invisible inside a seething, writhing, caterwauling mound of black and yellow, and his own screams were muffled. Then the mound collapsed to the cage floor, but continued to wriggle and scream and yowl. The dwarf horse began piteously to whinny and buck in the wagon traces. The crowd noise became shouts and cries, and many people started shoving to get down from the stands and away from the scene. Then the pandemonium was overridden by the band's booming into the ''Wedding March.''

The policeman came running into the pista and stuck his truncheon between the bars of the cage to beat ineffectually

at the furry, heaving heap. Several roustabouts came running
with sticks to do the same. Florian and Edge ran, too, to
unhitch Rumpelstilzchen before he could run away with the
wagon. One Slovak brought a bucket of water and dashed it
into the cage, but even that did not deter the maddened cats.
They went on with their clawing and rending, and to their
black and yellow coloring was now added blood red.

It was some while, in all that confusion, before one of the
men milling about the little wagon thought to unlatch the cage
door and fling it open. That was evidently all that the cats
had wanted; they poured out in a single surge of black and
yellow and red, then became separate streaks darting in all
directions. Those spectators who had not already been struggling to get out of the tent did so now, when the bloodied
cats exploded among them.

The men at the cage looked in at what was left on the
blood-puddled floor: Major Minim's toy whip, his mustache
and eye patch, fragments of his clothing—few of the scraps
bigger than the eye patch—and a raw, ragged, pulpy, blue-
red slab that might have been freshly delivered cat's meat,
except that it still wore polished black dancing shoes.

When the chapiteau was empty of jossers, and the band
was silent, and most of the circus folk, nauseated, also had
departed, Florian and the policeman conversed solemnly in
German.

"You realize, Brother," the officer said, taking out a notebook, "that I must make a report of this occurrence."

"Of course, Brother," Florian said calmly. "Render the
circle of your duties complete."

"The deceased. Was he of the craft?"

"No. An unhewn stone."

"Has he next of kin?"

"Not to my knowledge. I cannot even say, for certain, who
he was. See, here is his conduct book. He went by many
names—Minim, Wimper, Reindorf, another name in an un-
readable language."

"Hm. With so many aliases, it is possible that he was a
fugitive from justice. In which case, Brother, there could be

many official questions asked. However, the children of the widow must stand firmly together. Also, since you did invite me to the performance, and I did witness the unfortunate episode with my own eyes, I can report—on the level, by the rule—the purely accidental death of a person unknown. That will make unnecessary an inquest."

"Then the tenon is mortised, and the mortise tenoned. I thank you, Brother."

"Unhappily, it will also mean that the deceased must be buried as are the unidentified suicides found floating in the Danube. Without priest or rabbi—whatever his religion—without service or sacrament, without tombstone or even the professional mourner hags, in the city's Cemetery of the Nameless."

"Nameless he was. We cannot repine."

"I will send men from the Bureau of the Coroner. Would you wish to donate a coffin, Brother, or shall he be toppled into the common ditch with the day's others?"

"I herewith donate the cage wagon for his coffin. The coroner's men may simply wheel him away in it."

"Sehr gut. The sign is made, the sign is cut," said the policeman. "With your permission, I go now to make the arrangements."

Florian repeated to Edge in English the relevant parts of that conversation, then called some Slovaks to roll the wagon and its contents to some place in the backyard out of anybody's sight.

Edge said, "Stitches and Boom-Boom aren't going to be too happy. They put a lot of work into that thing."

"They'd be much unhappier if we all got accused of harboring a criminal. Fortunately, I had the officer occupied when that child cried out. And she and her papa decamped with the rest of the jossers, and now there is no criminal to be accused. Pass the word, please, Zachary, that all who care to—troupers and crewmen alike—may dress and join me for a repast before the night show. A good one, at the Café Heinrichshof. To take the bad taste from our mouths."

"To celebrate, you mean. You can be cold-blooded, can't you?"

"It sounds better in French, my boy. Sang-froid. All I did was to stand coolly aside and let fate do its work."

Not everyone accompanied Florian to the restaurant. Autumn and Edge ate in their caravan, as usual; others had quite lost their appetites; others had already left the tober. In a cheap and dirty Beisl on the Rotenthurmstrasse, Mullenax sat at a table with an obese, pink young woman on his lap. One of his hands was under her skirts, the other was repeatedly tossing schnaps down his gullet, and his one eye was rapidly getting red, while he mumbled things she could not possibly comprehend.

"Jesus, them was only alley cats, and look what they done. My cats are a damn sight bigger alongside me than them was to him. Think what *mine* could do. And folks keep sayin', 'Abner, how-come you gotta get drunk afore every show?' Jesus."

"Ja, ja, Gigerl," the woman said soothingly, and suggested, "Du hast etwas Fotze nötig." She pointed upstairs.

"And now that damned Limey has come on the show with a flame-jumpin' act that puts Maximus's in the shade. I gotta invent somethin' better yet."

The woman wiggled her vast bottom and wheedled, "Bumsen-bumsen?" She lasciviously pursed her thick lips. "Pussl-pussl geblassen?" She tried to tug him up from the table. "Kommst du und *Kommst*."

Tina Blau leaned her tousled head on her hand, letting the sheet drop away from her ivory breasts, and asked mischievously, "Do blue men make love only in the afternoons?"

Fitzfarris, lying beside her on the studio bed, asked lazily, "Do lady painters make love only to freaks?"

"Only to blue ones. My name *means* blue. We were destined for each other. But you might sometimes visit after the daylight has gone, so my work is not interrupted."

"I'm sorry, Tina. Between shows is my only free time. After the night show I have . . . duties, responsibilities . . . that I can't get away from."

*   *   *

One of those responsibilities of his was at that moment among Florian's other guests at the tables in the Heinrichshof, and she was the only one silent while all the other circus folk talked about the sensational finale to that afternoon's performance. Monday sat a little apart, looking like a small storm cloud, and drizzled an occasional tear into her plate.

When the artistes and crewmen reassembled on the tober, Banat, who had staunchly stayed there as watchman, took Florian aside to report that "the men of the Leichenbeschauer" had already come and taken away Minim's remains.

"Very good. We have still his horse and caravan—and that probably smells abominably of cat piss by now. Will you and your lads clear all his belonging out of it, Banat, and burn them? Give the van a good cleaning, paint it in our colors, and I shall decide what use to make of it."

4

THE HERR Doktor von Monakow received Autumn and Edge with a welcoming and solicitous small smile. He gestured for them to take the two chairs before his desk, and his expression did not change when Autumn raised the veil from her face. He merely asked, "Gnädige Frau, have you had any previous physician make pronouncement on this condition of yours?"

"Yes, two. One seemed uncertain, and referred me to you, Herr Doktor. The other identified it as a fibroid something-or-other, and told me to expect soon to die. But that was months ago."

Von Monakow shook his head. "You will not die, I think, until sometime in ripe old age." Edge perceptibly brightened; Autumn blinked. The doctor went on, "Tell me. Long before this affliction came upon you—in your earliest youth, did you have much Sommersprosse? Um . . . freckles. Did you have upon your skin many freckles?"

"Why . . . I don't . . ." said Autumn, in some bewilderment. "I never really paid much attention . . ."

"Excuse me, Herr Doktor," said Edge. "*I* paid attention. She never had but a very few freckles, and they were—well—in places where they were no blemish. Hardly noticeable."

"Only in her armpits, ja?"

Edge and Autumn stared at him as if he had been Magpie Maggie Hag making one of her more thunderclap divinations. He continued:

"I do not pretend to be a wizard. I deal merely with signs diagnostic. Had you come to me in your girlhood, Frau Edge, I could have predicted the onset of this affliction—though I could in no way have prevented it—simply from that unusual distribution of the few freckles."

"It *sounds* like wizardry," Autumn said, with awe.

"Nein. This is not even among my particular specialties of myopathy. It is a very rare disease, and only one young physician—von Recklinghausen, of Berlin—has studied it intently. But I do keep up with his monographs and his articles in the medical journals. Perhaps someday he will publish the glad news of a cure. Or prevention. Or reversal."

"Cure of *what?*" Edge blurted. "What *is* it?"

"At present, it has not even a name. In time, no doubt, in the medical tradition, it will be called von Recklinghausen's disease. As of now, all we know is that it is a neural affection, and incurable, and evidently congenital. It is oftenest apparent in the newborn child, but it can lie dormant until the victim is your age, Frau Edge. The nerve sheaths begin to thicken and accrete about them tumorous tissues of both flesh and bone . . . Ach, not to get too technical, it is not a mortal disease. You will not die. Not of that, anyway."

"Then what *will* happen to me?"

The doctor took off his pince-nez and rubbed his eyes. "Unfortunately, the cranial and facial deformity will not go away, but intensify. Eventually, similar distortion will be apparent in other parts of your body—arms, legs, torso, wherever there are affectable nerves—and one's entire body is laced with nerves."

"And there's *nothing* that can be done?" Edge almost implored.

"Very little, I am sorry to say." The doctor turned again to Autumn. "Continue to wear concealing clothing. If and when that becomes inadequate to hide the deformities—the bulges and distortions—we *can* resort to surgical excision of the lesions. To pare away the more obtrusive excrescences. But that would be only a temporary amelioration, you understand, and it would probably have to be done many times during your life."

Autumn said wretchedly, "The last physician I consulted promised me at least an early and merciful death. Dear God, you are telling me that I might live another forty, fifty years? Like this? And getting *worse?* And every so often, like a tree growing askew, I will have to be *pruned?* And all that time, poor Zachary must—"

"Poor Zachary be damned," Edge said firmly. "I've just been made rich." He leaned over, laid an affectionate hand on her knee and looked unflinchingly into her terrible face. "You're alive, Autumn, and you'll stay alive. I won't be losing you. We'll go straight from here to Sacher's and order the biggest celebration Vienna ever saw. I'll even learn to waltz properly with you."

She said nothing, but returned his look. Whether her expression was woeful or grateful was impossible to tell. Then she dropped the veil to hide it.

"If now I might examine you, Frau Edge?" said the doctor. "To assure that there are no collateral complications . . . ?"

"Please, Herr Doktor," she said, in a small voice. "Could I—could we postpone that to another day? I have . . . you have already given me quite a lot to digest. To adjust to."

"Of course. I understand. The Fräulein Voss will give you another appointment. Auf Wiedersehen."

In the Fiaker returning them to the Prater, Autumn said very little, responding mainly in murmurs to Edge's attempts at cheery conversation: "I might even learn to dance before we throw our shindig"—and optimistic suggestions: "Later on, maybe we could go to Berlin, and see that other specialist . . ."

When they got down from the carriage in the circus's back-yard, several troupers and crewmen loudly called and beckoned to Edge from the back door of the menagerie top.

"Here, I'll help you inside, then go see what they want," he said to Autumn, and kissed her through the veil. "You lie down and rest, and I'll be right back."

There was quite a crowd of people in the horses' end of the tent, and Florian, Hannibal and Yount were kneeling in the straw, examining one ribby horse that lay on its side, breathing stertorously.

"It's the old bonerack that draws the caravan of the casse-cou joeys," said Florian, standing up and dusting his knees. "But first, what news about Autumn?"

"She won't get better, I'm afraid. But she'll live, and that's all that matters." Edge bent to look at the horse. "This poor beast won't, I'm sorry to say."

"What you reckon wrong, Mas' Edge?" asked Hannibal.

"I sure hope it ain't glanders," said Yount. "We could lose every animal we got. Maybe one or two of us, besides."

"No. Look at its teeth—what teeth it's got. I'd reckon it's dying of simple old age. What'll get us all, after a while."

Florian said to the clowns, "My regrets, Nella . . . Bernhard . . . Ferdi. Of course we'll get you a replacement horse. But while we're on the subject, Nella, wouldn't you like to move out of that crowded threesome? We now possess a spare caravan."

"Grazie. Danke. Thank you," she said, and blushed. "But I already have moved out. Into the carovana of Signor LeVie."

"Ah . . . well . . . forgive me for butting in. And my best wishes to you both. Zachary, can you do anything to ease the horse's misery?"

"Put him out of it, quick, is the best thing," said Edge, standing up. "My weapons are all in the van. I'll go fetch one."

He was just starting in that direction when they heard the single gunshot from there. Edge stood paralyzed for an instant, then said, "Oh, Jesus!" and would have sprinted, but Florian stepped in his way.

"Best let me go. Obie, Shadid, see that Zachary stays here. That's an order."

Yount wrapped his big arms around Edge, and the Turk stood by, while Florian departed at a run.

"Goddamn it, let me loose!" snarled Edge, struggling fiercely. "And that *is* an order, Sergeant."

"I'm sorry, Colonel," Obie said, "but army orders don't apply no more. Terrible, you better help me."

Edge fought and cursed, and it did require both of the strongmen to hold him, and all the others in the tent looked on wide-eyed while, unnoticed by anyone but Hannibal, the ancient horse lying on the straw quietly expired.

Florian arrived at the caravan to find Magpie Maggie Hag already entering it. "You knew?" he asked, panting a little.

"I dukkered a long time ago, but you never believed. Now you stay out. I see what need doing."

She was inside for only a minute, then emerged carrying Edge's old singleshot Cook carbine, still smoking slightly and reeking of burned black powder.

"This gun short enough, even small girl like her could hold muzzle to head and reach trigger."

"Christ. And Zachary always kept it loaded with bird shot," said Florian, taking it from her. "There must be an unholy mess in there."

"She wanted nothing remain of what she looked like. I attend to her. You send me Slovak—Slovak with strong stomach—to clean walls and all. Also she leave note and sealed envelope. Here."

Florian took them and did not open either. He tucked the carbine under the caravan steps, called to one of the several roustabouts gawking from a distance, told him to fetch water, mops and rags, and returned to the menagerie. Edge's struggling had subsided, but he and the other two men were much disheveled. Yount and Shadid let go of him when Florian entered and wordlessly held out the note and envelope. He also jerked his head curtly at the others in the tent, so they all cleared out.

Edge opened the folded paper; it had obviously been written hurriedly, but without any evidence of tremor. He read it, stony-faced, then said, ''There's nothing in it too private for you to hear,'' and read it aloud.

'' 'Darling. You have been everything to me, and I refuse to be a burden to you. No—that sounds like heroic unselfishness, and it is not. Such a life I would find intolerable, as well. Not long ago I told you—wherever we go from here will be as new and foreign to me as to you. I pray that you will be a long time arriving there, but I shall be waiting. Au revoir, my dearest.' '' He paused, cleared his throat and said, ''Signed with no name, just a little drawing of a heart.''

He tore open the envelope, took out another paper and read the beginning of it: '' 'Darling. I am told that I will soon die . . .' She must have written this one back in Munich, after we saw that other doctor. 'But you have all of your life ahead of you, and I want . . .' '' Edge's voice trailed off, and he read the rest of it silently to himself. Then he tucked the papers in a pocket and said huskily to Florian, ''Now . . . if I could go and see her one last—''

''You would not want to,'' said Florian. ''She would not want you to. Maggie is taking care of her. Please, Zachary, do not make me call for restraints again. Come, get onto my rockaway, I will take you to a good hotel, then proceed with all the proper arrangements.''

Edge nodded numbly and let himself be led to the rockaway. As they drove off the tober, Florian called to Fitzfarris, ''Sir John, you and everyone else who can write, make posters announcing that there will be no show until further notice. Have Banat and his men plaster them all over the Prater.''

A couple of hours later, when Florian returned, he had a different passenger on the seat beside him—that same uniformed officer who had helped dispose of Major Minim—and the rockaway was followed by a hearse, not the city coroner's, but from a private undertaking establishment. As the two vehicles crossed the tober to the backyard, they were trailed by numerous sad-faced or openly weeping troupers.

Magpie Maggie Hag was sitting on the steps of Autumn's caravan while the cleaning-up continued inside. ''Third Slovak working now," she reported. "First one, then another got sick, I had to excuse."

Florian asked, "Is she—is everything presentable enough for this gentleman to examine the scene of the accident?"

The gypsy shrugged and got up to let the policeman go in. He came out again very quickly, with a shudder, took a deep breath of the outside air, and said to Florian in German, "I am sympathetic to your great loss, and to your Herr Edge's even greater bereavement. And of course I am sworn to give aid to any needful brother within the length of my cable tow. But, please, how many more times will you be asking me to bend the rules of my professional office?"

"Brother, you need only certify that it was an accident, so the undertaker can assume charge of the remains. And an accident you can plainly see that it was. As I told you, the young lady was our shootist's partner, and while cleaning his tools of the trade, during his absence . . ."

"A marksman's partner," the policeman said drily, "ought to know better than to try cleaning a carbine already loaded." However, he scribbled on an official-looking certificate, said, "Alles in Ordnung," gave the paper to the undertaker, exchanged a few more arcane remarks and discreet signs with Florian, then again took his leave.

The undertaker directed his men in unloading an extremely ornate mahogany coffin from the hearse, but they were interrupted. Jörg Pfeifer was among the onlookers, and he suddenly cried:

"Nein! Nein! Nichts da!"

Everyone stopped in surprise, and Florian said, "Why, Fünfünf, whatever is the matter?"

"That is but an ordinary civilian coffin, Herr Gouverneur."

"I selected the finest and most expensive in the establishment's stock. What more—?"

"In an ordinary coffin, the Fräulein Auburn can be placed only with her feet side by side. But she was a peerless rope-dancer. I will not allow her to be buried except with her feet placed heel to toe." Without waiting for the stunned Florian to comment, Pfeifer turned and repeated his demand in German to the undertaker.

That gentleman reeled slightly. "Beispiellos! Schändung!"

Florian shook his head. "Unheard of, perhaps, but no desecration. I am in complete accord. You will oblige us with a coffin so constructed."

"Herr Florian, it will have to be custom built," the undertaker protested. "And never in all my experience—"

"Then go and build it."

The undertaker ceased to argue, but kept on muttering remarks about scandalous unorthodoxy. His men brought Autumn's sheet-covered small body from the caravan on a stretcher, gently laid it in the temporary coffin, hoisted that into the hearse and drove away.

During the following day, various members of the company went into town, to the small but elegant Staatsoper Hotel, to give what condolence and comfort they could to Zachary Edge. One of them was Magpie Maggie Hag, who so seldom left the circus tober in even the most enticing cities. She said:

"I know you not believe this, pralo, but have reason be glad. Long time you already know you losing Autumn. You had time, opportunity for be only kind and caring. No need reproach self now for things done, not done. Others have lost loves, after their last little time came and went unguessed. Que en tranquilidad esté."

"Gracias para decirlo, madama," Edge said sincerely. "Que besa su mano." And he did kiss her withered old hand.

Yount and Mullenax came calling together, and Mullenax brought an armload of bottles of Asbach brandy, saying, "Likker's one of the best things I know for gettin' through bad times."

"Thanks, Abner," said Edge. "But if I wanted just to get fuddled and stay that way, this hotel is amply supplied with the ways and means." He went on, somewhat absently, "It's a very accommodating hotel. Autumn would have liked it. In the morning, the hall porter brings up the day's newspaper, freshly pressed with a hot iron. I can't read it, but it's perfectly flat and uncreased, and nice and warm. Even the donnicker here is warm." He opened the bathroom door. "See, that flooring can be raised, and there are stone channels underneath. When you want to take a bath, or just sit on the chamber commode, you pull this bell rope and a hotel maid comes with a shovelful of hot coals and puts them under the floor, so your feet don't get cold.''

"One thing about these maidservants here in Vienna,'' said Yount, "they're prettier than anywhere wc've been yet. And they all *smell* so pretty. They smell of bread and butter.''

"I hadn't noticed,'' Edge said abstractedly.

"You didn't have no reason to, before,'' said Mullenax. "But in time you will. And that's a better way, even, than the jug, for puttin' pain and grief to rest.''

Clover Lee came to tell Edge that she was taking care of Autumn's canary, along with her own pigeons. Jules Rouleau and Willi Lothar came to say that they were occupying his van during his absence, to prevent the theft of anything in it. Willi added, ''The emperor is abroad during this month. When he returns, maybe then I can arrange the command performance we have wanted. I mention this because I wish to give you something to look forward to, friend Zachary.''

"I'll be relieved enough just to get the funeral over with,'' sighed Edge, "and get back to work. I don't think Autumn would have wanted us all to stand around and gloom and mourn.''

Since no one, not even Edge, knew what Autumn's religion had been—if any—there was no church service. The circus company simply gathered in Vienna's Central Cemetery for another grave-side ceremony. Despite the chill of the bright blue autumn day, the artistes again wore their pista costumes—léotards, fleshings, spangles, leopard skin, clown dress—and quaked and shivered rather than hide them under warm cloaks. Edge was somewhat taken aback at first sight of Autumn's coffin, which looked very much like a museum's mummy case. But when the reason for it was explained to him, he warmly thanked Jörg Pfeifer for having thought of it. Then Dai Goesle conducted the service, and he kept it brief and simple, only once indulging in imagery:

"We commonplace creatures stay on the ground, and walk. This lass took to the air, and danced. Now she is dancing somewhere higher yet, on a cloud mayhap, and all the angels are applauding . . .''

At the close, it was Edge instead of Florian who pronounced the old epitaph: ''Saltavit. Placuit''—but he stopped there, not adding the final phrase, refusing to say out loud that she was dead.

When the Florilegium resumed showing the next afternoon, Edge resumed his several rôles of equestrian director, Colonel Ramrod and Buckskin Billy. If perhaps his colleagues perceived that he performed with less zest than formerly, they could not remark that he performed any less than capably. If he seemed somewhat distant, he was certainly not oblivious to anything that went on. At the first opportunity, he called up to Boom-Boom Beck on the bandstand, ''What the hell was that new music you played for the come-in? Nobody sang. Why aren't we promenading and singing to 'Greensleeves' as usual?''

''Forgive me, Herr Direktor, for upon myself taking the decision. But I thought—since your Liebchen's music that was—perhaps painful it would be, and to retire it we ought.''

''No, *sir*. We buried Autumn, but we won't bury every memory of her. You put that music back in your repertoire, and keep it there.''

Edge was again surprised by an unexpected change in the program when it came time for Monday's tightrope turn and he whistled for her to enter. Monday did not appear, and the band did not go into her ''Cinderella'' music, or any other. The only sound to be heard was a sudden small hissing as Goesle ignited his carbide spotlight—although this was late afternoon and the chapiteau sufficiently aglow with sunlight diffused through the canvas. Puzzled, Edge started to whistle again, but desisted when he looked where the spotlight beam was pointed. It shone on the rope-dancer's resting platform, now occupied, Edge could see in the limelight brilliance, by a tremendous bouquet of autumn flowers—chrysanthemums and asters—tied with a wide black ribbon and flowing black bow.

Now from the bandstand there commenced a quiet music—

what Beck had first played for Autumn's performance—
arpeggios on the simple string of tins he had contrived aboard
ship so long ago. As that gentle tinkling went on, Goesle's
spotlight very, very slowly traveled the length of the empty
tightrope, following the remembered antics and graces of an
imagined yellow-clad sprite. Most of the people in the audience probably had heard of Autumn's demise, during the time
the circus had been closed, but few of them could ever have
seen her perform. Nevertheless, they burst into as much applause as if Autumn were really there aloft, and respectfully
stood up as they did so.

When the spotlight went off and the applause dwindled and
the last arpeggio diminished to silence, there was a pause.
Then the band, to end the show in a merrier mood, loudly
launched into the clowns' music, and Fünfünf, the Kesperle
and Ali Baba ran into the pista to do their Lupino mirror act
for the close. But Edge did not see them; his eyes had misted
over. He slipped out the back door and away, to be by himself. Then he wondered why. From now on, he thought, even
amidst the most teeming and busy company, he would be
always alone.

5

GRADUALLY, OVER the winter, Edge cleared his caravan
of what property Autumn had left. He let Clover Lee keep
the canary and its tuned cage, and gave to Sunday Simms the
"Greensleeves" music box, and to Monday Simms-Fitzfarris
the framed and autographed picture of Mme Saqui—"She
was before your time, Monday, but she was a rope-dancer,
too, and a famous one"—and told them and the other women
to divide among themselves Autumn's wardrobe and trinkets.
Thereafter, Edge lived alone in the caravan, declining any
blandishments of the ladies from the seats and the invitations
from Mullenax to join him in "bucking the tiger" in town.

One day, in the backyard, the Smodlaka children came
dancing up to their mother, and the boy said teasingly, "Mati,

can you open your mouth without showing your teeth?''

"Ne znam," Gavrila said offhandedly, occupied with sewing something. "Why do you ask such a question?"

"Man asked *us* it." Gavrila put down her sewing and looked at Velja with concern. "And Mati, I can do it. So can Sava. See?" The boy made a small circle of his pale lips.

His sister chirped, "Then the man said 'just the right size' and he laughed and he gave us each a gulden."

Gavrila snapped, "Velja, stop making that face. Whoever put you up to that was being naughty. The late Major Minim, no doubt.''

"No, Mati, he is long gone. It was just now—"

"Then do not tell me who. I do not wish to know. I wish only that you stay away from this bad man, too. See that you do."

Velja muttered rebelliously, "The Gospodin Florian said we could play with anybody except the Major Minim," as he and his sister shuffled off, chastened and disconsolate.

The artist Tina Blau came from her studio to the tober, and over a span of about a week's work during the intervals between shows, put Meli and her python onto a canvas that she said she would entitle *Andromeda*. To Fitzfarris, who hovered about her easel during most of that time, the artist made one complaint: "I cannot get Meli ever to smile."

"She never does seem to smile any more," Fitz acknowledged. "I don't know why. She used to, a lot. But what the hell, Tina, as far as your painting is concerned, would a woman *be* smiling when she's getting rogered by a dragon?"

"Oh, I think *I* might," Tina said, her violet eyes roguish. "Don't I always smile when I am being rogered by a Tattooed Man?"

That and other such lightsome exchanges were overheard by Monday, who also hovered, unseen, and smoldered at them from behind wagon corners and tent flaps and other concealments. Her smoldering might have flared into flame, but for the cautionary counsel of her sister.

"Don't act ugly," said Sunday. "It'll only make her—or any other woman—seem nicer in comparison to you, and more desirable. But we'll be leaving Vienna sometime, and that woman won't. You'll have John Fitz all to yourself again before too much longer."

Monday said sullenly, "And then what? You got your Mr. Zack all to yourself now, but what good's that doin' *you!*"

"Well . . . he has his grieving and forgetting to get through."

Monday snorted. "Man might remember one woman, up top in his head, but he got a prong below that forgets her real quick. I ought to know."

"Why do you flinch away when I undo your breeches, lad?" the man asked. They lay on a pallet improvised of spare canvas, inside one of the tent wagons tucked away in a remote corner of the tober. "See, I undo mine also. I merely expose our different selves, so we may compare and admire each other. And now you stare, as if you had never seen this part of a man before, but you have one of your own."

"Not big. Not red."

"Because you are a unique color all over, my boy. However, our different complexions do not make our private parts behave any differently. Yours is growing in my hand. And look—so does mine, even untouched. We are precisely alike in our responses, so what is there for you to be shy about? There . . . does not that feel good?"

With a bashful nod, "Um-hm."

"Then come, you must do the same to mine. That's right. Ah-h, yes, it does feel good. Be grateful that I am teaching you something so useful. You *can* do this alone, you realize. And I am sure you often will, from now on. But I am delighted to know that I am the first to pluck such an unusually colored cherry. Now, do just as I do. Tighter. Faster. Yes . . . yes . . ." After a time, "There. Wasn't that divinely pleasant?"

"Um-*hm!*"

"Until next time, then, you may enjoy your new prowess on your own. Or with some other lad. Or—oh, but I do hope not. I sincerely caution you against spending your energies

on any female—even one as close as a sister. I will explain
another day. Go now. And remember, not a word to anyone.''

On a Wednesday, which was salary day for the crewmen,
Edge went to the red wagon, as usual, to help Florian check
off the roster of names and count out the cash. As the men
filed through the office, doffed their caps, took their pay and
grunted respectful thanks or tugged at their low-growing fore-
locks, Edge muttered, ''Every time we do this I find more
new names on the rolls, and faces I don't recognize. For
instance, who are Herman Begega and Bill Jensen? Those
don't sound like Slovaks.''

''No,'' said Florian. ''A Spaniard and a Swede. One is a
carpenter that Stitches hired. The other is Boom-Boom's new
contrabass tuba. They won't be in to get paid today; they are
still on holdback.''

''Where are all these new hands sleeping?''

''I told Banat he could have Major Minim's caravan to
house the overflow. Our Florilegium is becoming quite a populous community. I only wish we could add to our company
of artistes as easily as to the crew. I think I shall send an
advertisement to the *Era*, soliciting applications, when we get
to Budapest.''

In the tent wagon, the boy lay spoon fashion against the
man's back, but moving convulsively. When he gave a last
heave, he groaned in rapture and shuddered all over. Then he
sighed tremulously and began to 'withdraw, but the man
reached backward to hold him there.

''Stay a while, lad. I like the sensation of it dwindling
inside me. And while you rest, let me instruct you further.
Some will tell you that a woman is better equipped to give
a man that kind of pleasure. Do not believe them. Down
there, a woman has only great, slack, slobbering lips at the
portal of a loose, wet, uninviting cavity. None of the firm,
warm, clasping *tightness* you have just enjoyed so much. As
for the rest of a woman, what is she? Nothing but a bosom
of blubber that exudes ogress milk. Are you paying attention?''

Sleepily, "Um-hm."

"If you are quite relaxed . . . well, turnabout is only fair play. Turn over, my boy. And remain relaxed . . . unresisting . . ."

Clover Lee and Sunday sat in Griensteidl's café—of which they had become frequent patrons—with coffee, tortes and the *Neue Freie Presse*, which Sunday had folded to its "personals" columns.

"Anything interesting today?" asked Clover Lee.

"Well, here's one that says something about 'artistic' . . ." Sunday studied it, then translated aloud: " 'Will the charming Fräulein, D. M., who once displayed in my office chambers her artistic Aktentasche, please know that I forever remember her with adoration?' "

"I just bet," said Clover Lee. "I assume a woman's Aktentasche is something, uh—intimate?"

"I have no idea. And I didn't bring my dictionary."

"Anyhow, you know that my initials are C. L. C. If you don't see them anywhere, look for something that *might* apply to me. Preferably signed with a coronet."

"Hm. 'Will the charming Fräulein'—it looks like you've *got* to be charming—'who walked with me through the empty midnight city in a soft snowfall . . . ?' "

"It wasn't me. Damn. Maybe I'll have to put in an advertisement of my own. 'Will some charming and wealthy Graf . . . ?' "

"This time," said the man, "I will teach you how to smoke a cigar."

"Too young to smoke," mumbled the boy.

"Oh, we will not set it alight." The man was much amused. "Dear me—hnoof-hnoof—that would not do at all. No, you will merely learn to take it in your mouth and draw on it properly. I shall demonstrate first on this eager little cheroot of yours. Now, first, one always licks a cigar from end to end . . ."

After some time and some contortions and some muffled exclamations from both of them, Cecil said, "Jolly well learned, my boy, and well accomplished. Now swallow, as I just did. You see, this is another reason for preferring a fellow male to an alien female. A man has only so much of that precious juice to expend in his lifetime. So, if you enjoy these gamahuche games and want to go on enjoying them, you do not wish to waste what makes them possible.''

''No,'' said the boy, with real anxiety.

''Well, there you are. A woman would simply take your dear juice and give you none back in return. But you and I can keep on absorbing each other's—in one aperture or another—and thereby keep replenishing our mutual supply, and never have to fear running dry.''

On a Sunday, some of the circus company went to St. Stephan's Cathedral—along with half the city population, it seemed, from the crush—to hear the renowned Vienna Boys' Choir sing. Afterward, Florian said to Willi Lothar, ''Well, that choirmaster Bruckner is also the emperor's organist at the Hofburg. Is this as close as *we* are ever going to get to that Hofburg?''

''Herr Gouverneur, you know that I am constantly importuning my every remotest relative and least acquaintance in court circles. But, if I may suggest—I think also it would help our case if we volunteered the Florilegium to perform at some civic benefit function.''

''Why not? What had you in mind?''

''Ach, there is the Innkeepers' Ball, the Artists' *Gschnastfest*, the Street-Sweepers' Ball, any number of others. But I thought particularly of the gala at the Brünlfeld Irrenanstalt.''

''The lunatic asylum!?'' Edge exclaimed, when Florian told him. ''Willi has talked a lot about a command performance, but what have we had? First beggars and now zanies. Does it occur to you, Governor, that maybe we're going downhill, not up?''

''This is one of Wien's most cherished traditions,'' Florian said. ''On Carnival Tuesday each year, a gala is always held at the Irrenanstalt. The, er, milder inmates are even allowed to participate, in costumes they make themselves. It is not so much an occasion for *their* diversion, of course, as of the

spectators—who include royals and nobles and other wor-
thies—to amuse themselves by watching the poor loonies cavort. It will not hurt our prospects if such folk see us cavort,
as well.''

"All right. I reckon we're all game if you are. Do we tear
down here and set up in the asylum grounds?''

"No, no. There is a capacious indoor hall between the
asylum building and the adjacent hospital. We will suspend
showing here that day, and take to the Irrenanstalt only what
we can show to best effect. The artistes, the pista curbing,
the band, whatever rigs and props do not require elaborate
handling. Brutus, Maximus, the dwarf horse. No more. We
will not risk frightening the inmates with the calliope or the
more rambunctious acts.''

Other things occurred on the Carnival Tuesday before that
special performance.

"Ah, you are cheating, lad,'' said Cecil, but with good
humor, as he entered the tent wagon at dusk. "You did not
wait for me. But how I do envy you that ability—being able
to double over and smoke your own little black cigar. No,
no, do not uncoil. Go ahead and satisfy yourself. I can wait,
and the sight is ineffably stimulating.''

When Quincy had finished and swallowed and caught his
breath, he muttered, "Druther do it with you.''

"Very well. Let us both take advantage of your elasticity.
See if you can manage this. Insert yourself as usual, but upside down, then bend to bring your head—so. Give *my* cigar
a good smoking while your own enjoys itself back there. Can
you do that?'' After only a little experimenting, the boy
achieved that contortion and began enthusiastically to work
in and on the man, who cooed and crooned, "That's right.
Oh, that is *ever* so right!''

The wagon door suddenly opened, and a dark silhouette
stood there against the twilight outside.

"Confound it!'' exclaimed Cecil, and he urgently shoved
at Quincy, who was still working, oblivious of the interruption.

"So this is where you keep disappearing to," said the intruder, sounding puzzled.

"Daphne!" said Cecil, aghast.

"We are all about to depart for the asylum at—" By now she could see the two naked bodies in the wagon's dim interior and realize what they were doing, and she said hollowly, "Oh, dear God . . ."

"Get off me, boy, *get away!*" Cecil jerked free of Quincy so abruptly that the disengagement made two distinct noises, as of two bottles being unstoppered. Quincy softly said "Hoy!" in bewilderment and disappointment. But Cecil was hastily getting dressed and Daphne had fled from the doorway.

"The people in the boxes and loges draped with bunting are the nobles and notables," said Florian. "Those in the ordinary seats are the lunatics."

He was not being entirely facetious, for there was not a great deal of other distinction to be seen between the asylum inmates and the visitors, except that the costumes worn by the former were perhaps a trifle more haphazardly put together, and of less rich fabrics, but were no more eccentric or bizarre. In both sections of the audience there were numerous identifiable Napoléon Bonapartes and Pallas Athenes, winged angels, horned demons, several apparent Lord Gods and Jesuses, Saint Brigittes and Saint Annes, and all manner of invented nightmare grotesqueries. Florian had said that the lunatics allowed outside the asylum to attend the party were the less seriously afflicted. Still, there was a multitude of uniformed guards and white-garbed nursing sisters scattered about the hall, unobtrusive but watchful.

The circus was minus several of its acts on this occasion, some of them—like the several horse turns—because they would have been unwieldy or too noisy indoors, some others at the tactful suggestion of the asylum's resident physicians. For example, Spyros Vasilakis marched in the opening promenade, but thereafter sat out the show on the sidelines. To see the Gluttonous Greek swallow swords and eat fire, said the doctors, might give their patients unwholesome ideas. They evidently feared nothing unwholesome in any ideas those on-lookers might have got from watching Meli Vasilakis and her serpents do the provocative Medusa-twining and ravished-maiden routines, or from watching Colonel Ramrod do his fancy shooting. Edge did, however, on his own initiative, reduce his powder loads so the weapons made only muted bangs, and entirely omitted the shooting of a ball into his assistant Sunday's teeth.

To make up for the abbreviated program, Florian informed the asylum attendants that at intermission their wards might descend to the pista and take rides around it on the elephant or the dwarf horse, and he left it to those attendants to select suitable candidates. As it turned out, quite as many of the outside guests came to enjoy that privilege as did members of the asylum population. And one man, dressed and peri-wigged and beruffled as Louis XIV, after circling the hall first on Brutus's neck and then on Rumpelstilzchen's back, engaged Florian and Willi in an animated, arm-waving con-versation.

"Bless me, that little notion of mine proved a profitable one," Florian told Edge. "You saw the Louis Fourteenth who spoke to us? He was so excited at having participated in our circus that *he* has promised to secure our invitation to the palace. And he can do it, too. That was Count Wilczek, a particular favorite of Franz Joseph."

"Are you sure?" Edge said skeptically. "I didn't notice whether he came from the deluxe boxes or the guarded seats."

"Oh, it was he," said Willi. "And I am chagrined. After all my efforts, it is an elephant and a pony that may finally promote us into the Erste Gesellschaft."

The show was to resume with Cecil and Daphne on their velocipede—Florian had decided to delete the skating turn as too noisy—so the band thumped into the "Royal Fireworks" bourrée, and Florian announced "the Wheeling Wheelers!" and the equestrian director whistled for their entrance. The velocipede came in, all right, and with Cecil pedaling it, but with no Daphne on his shoulders.

Edge said with annoyance, "What the hell?"

"He and his woman fought una battaglia," confided Nella Cornella, beside him. "So now he is only playing with himself."

"Uh . . . *by* himself, Nella," Edge corrected her. "They had a fight? When?"

"Just before we all departed the tober. I was passing their carovana. I heard her shout, 'You will not ever put that thing in me again. Not after where it has been. You will not ever *touch* me again. Now get of here.' And out he came, scompigliatamente—in haste and disorder. And alone."

"I wonder what that was about," said Edge. "Well, I see he's got at least a temporary replacement. Not anywhere near as pretty as his wife, though."

Ali Baba had come running, in his minstrel-show costume, and Cecil, as he wheeled around the hall between the pista and the front row of boxes, reached down one hand to sweep the boy up and onto his shoulders. Even without practice, Ali Baba did a commendable job of imitating Daphne's poses and handstands and upside-down splits. Since the vat of flames would not cap the act on this occasion, Cecil concentrated on fancy riding—intricate turns, backward pedaling, rearing up the tall machine onto its tiny hind wheel. And one of those sudden rearings caught Ali Baba off balance. He pitched off his perch and tried to twist in the air to make a safe landing, but managed only to turn enough to fall on his head—with a loud crack, for there was no soft ground or straw or sawdust in this hall, but hardwood flooring. The inmate half of the audience immediately began laughing and pounding their fists on their knees in appreciation.

Cecil stopped his velocipede and heeled it over sideways, to dismount and run back. The two other troupers nearest the scene also went running—Florian and Mullenax, who was just then directing the Slovaks in rolling Maximus's cage wagon into the hall. But Ali Baba bounded unaided and spryly to his feet, and threw up his arms in the V. So did Cecil, taking one of the boy's hands in his, to pretend that the spill had been the intended conclusion of the act. So the visitor half of the audience joined the inmates in laughing and applauding.

"Are you all right, Ali Baba?" said Florian.

"Yassuh. Awright."

"Hell, he only lit on his head," Mullenax drawled drunkenly. "Niggers all got heads like cannonballs, ain't that right, kid?" And he playfully ruffled Ali Baba's kinky wool.

"Reckon so, suh."

Florian said frostily to Cecil, "Why this unannounced and unrehearsed substitution, Mr. Wheeler?"

Cecil tried to laugh it off. "Had a little tiff with my storm-and-strife, Governor. Hnoof-hnoof-hnoof. So she played truant, and Ali Baba very kindly volunteered."

Still frostily, Florian said, "I shall have a word with her when we get back to the tober."

The band was beginning to play "Bollocky Bill," so Mullenax whipped a tin flask from his pocket and drained it. Edge, who had joined the group, said, "Let's not have any more surprises. Abner, are you too drunk to go on?"

Mullenax stopped swaying, stood to stiff attention, blinked his lurid eye and said with great precision, "No, sir, Colonel. Just now primed exactly right."

The roustabout had the cage wagon at pista center by now, so Edge hesitated only a moment, then waved him on, and Florian went ahead with the megaphone to bellow his introduction.

Edge kept a wary watch and kept his whistle at his mouth, ready to terminate the act at any time. But it proceeded well enough, though Barnacle Bill conducted the lion through most of it—*platz* and *hoch* and *krank* and *schön'machen* and several more *hochs*—while leaning, as if nonchalantly, against the cage bars and only flubbily snapping his whip. Then the Slovaks brought the oildaubed wooden hoop and handed it in to him through the bars. Maximus backed to the farther wall and crouched low in preparation for his leap. The smallness of the cage always required Barnacle Bill at this point to go down on his knees, while he held the hoop with a long-handled pair of pliers and a roustabout ignited it from outside and hastily fled the heat.

But this time, when the hoop flared up, Barnacle Bill uttered no command. Instead, he slowly toppled forward from his kneeling position, wearily rolled over, stretched out full length on the cage floor and went to sleep. The hoop rolled out through the bars and, flaming merrily, bounced a few times and rolled on across the pista.

"Damnation! Catch that thing!" Edge shouted. Then, "Bring poles! Hold the cat where he is!"

The audience of inmates again briskly applauded—either the impromptu fireworks or Barnacle Bill's insouciant display of bravery. But all the Slovaks had instinctively run to intercept the hoop before it could jump the pista curb and perhaps bound among the onlookers, so no crewman was close to the wagon to fence in or fend off Maximus from moving. And moving he was, now, still in his low crouch, slinking menacingly toward his unconscious master, and licking his lips in apparent anticipation of an unexpected but welcome meal.

Edge himself went running, uncoiling his own whip, as the band struck up the "Wedding March." However, by then, the lion was standing astraddle the supine Barnacle Bill, staring down at him and apparently considering where to taste him first. The animal flicked a sidelong glance out at Edge, curled a lip and gave a low snarl of warning. So Edge still refrained from using his whip, uncertain whether it might infuriate Maximus to an instant attack instead of driving him off. The lion gazed down at his master again, lowered his muzzle to sniff at him and then did something contrary to everything Edge had ever heard about the vengeful ferocity of a great cat with a helpless human at its mercy. Maximus began—it might have been sorrowfully, compassionately— to lick the unconscious man's face.

Edge heard someone behind him shout, "Christ! One of the loonies is loose!" But he did not turn; he watched in mixed amazement and apprehension the lion's ministrations to Barnacle Bill. There was the noise of running feet, then many of them, pounding across the wooden floor, and a hubbub of more shouts, but Edge stayed where he was, ready to wield his whip. The rasping of the lion's rough tongue brought Mullenax awake again. His one eye opened and, fortunately, what he saw with it paralyzed him instead of making him scramble for escape. He stared with horror up at the cat's great jaws and teeth and tongue, and Edge started murmuring—to him as well as the animal—"Steady . . . platz, now . . . platz . . ."

Then, not from either Mullenax or Maximus, there was a sudden flurry of movement in the cage. Its door quickly opened and shut, and there was another person inside—a devil all in bright red, with horns, arrow-ended tail, a domino face mask and, in one hand, a devilish, long trident. Maximus raised his massive head, regarded the newcomer and snarled once more. Edge also snarled: "Get out of there, you maniac. *Raus!* He's protecting his master!" But the intruder ignored them both, coolly touched the points of his trident to the lion's broad chest and told him in a quiet voice, "Zurück . . . zurück, Kätzche . . ." After mulling the suggestion for a moment, Maximus obediently began to back off.

Well, Edge decided, the man might be a lunatic on the loose, but he at least knew the German commands. So Edge also moved from where he stood, slipped around to the rear of the wagon and, when the red devil had stepped over Mullenax, impelling Maximus farther down the cage, Edge growled, "Abner, wiggle your way here, not too fast." Mullenax did so, snakewise, and Edge opened the door just enough to let him slither out headfirst from the wagon sill to the floor. He lay there quivering and breathing heavily. Florian came to stand over him and say, more in pity than anger, "I hope you're ashamed of yourself. The big, bold lion tamer, having to get rescued by a crazy man."

There were also a number of the asylum guards standing by, one of them holding ready a stout canvas strait-waistcoat dangling many straps and buckles. The man in the cage now told Maximus to "platz!" and the cat sat down, yawning as if he had got bored with all the unusual human behavior. The man backed slowly away from the cat, and Edge cracked the door again to let him out. The band immediately ceased its repetitions of the "Wedding March" and swung into the music for the dog act. The Smodlakas and their terriers ran into the pista and the show resumed.

The asylum guards advanced on the red devil, as cautiously as if it had been Maximus that had emerged. But the man reached up and removed his domino, and the guards stopped and gaped. One of them laughed in relief and said to Florian, "Es ist nicht ein Kranke von uns."

"Non," said the devil, also laughing. "No lunatic, messieurs. Jean-François Pemjean, à votre service." He was a handsome man, with a swarthy complexion and merry eyes that went well with his devil garb. "I was but visiting the *medical* hospital, for a minor complaint, when I learned of the gala in preparation. So I borrowed from a cupboard this spare déguisement, in order to attend."

"Fortuitement," said Florian. "Merci, Monsieur Pemjean, merci infiniment. Tell me, are you merely cavalier by nature, or are you a lion tamer by profession?"

"Oui, c'est de mon resort. Of course, I know the old circus saying: that Frenchmen are too temperamental for such work—not Teutonic-stolid enough." He cast a disparaging look at Barnacle Bill, whom some of the Slovaks were assisting from the pista, while others trundled the cage wagon out. "Nevertheless, that is what I am. Pemjean l'Intrépide, most recently of the Donnert Circus in Prague, formerly of the Cirque d'Été in Paris and now making my way thither again."

"Perhaps Monsieur l'Intrépide," said Florian, "you would further oblige me with a few words in private."

Those two went off together, and the show went on without any more interruptions or mishaps. It even included Mademoiselle Cinderella's rope-dancing and Maurice and Mademoiselle Butterfly's trapeze act, for Beck and Goesle had earlier in the day contrived to hang those rigs from the hall's upper beams and columns.

After the closing promenade, the Slovaks swarmed in to dismantle or remove what equipment and props remained, and to give the floor a good cleaning. When Beck and his windjammers left the bandstand, the asylum guards led a number of their wards up there—all harmless, shambling, vacantly smiling idiots, and all carrying musical intruments. But those were clearly not idiots savants; when they settled themselves and raised their horns and fiddles and woods, the music came not from them but from elsewhere. Curious, Edge went

closer to look at the band, and discovered that their instruments were made of papier-mâché, the music being provided
by a volunteer orchestra—perhaps one of the Strausses', since
it was playing Papa Johann's "In the Little Jelly-Doughnut
Woods," from concealment in a curtained alcove. Now the
audience came down from the seats and boxes to the floor
and took partners for the dancing, so commingling that the
outside guests and the inmates were more than ever indistinguishable.

Fitzfarris, watching the scene, remarked to Florian, "Isn't
it possible that after one of these jamborees some counts and
dukes get carried off to the padded cells, and maybe some
cuckoos take their places in the seats of the mighty?"

"I daresay. I also daresay that any such exchange might
never be detected, either in here or outside. Please pass the
word, Sir John, that our artistes are welcome to stay for the
dancing and the food and drink, if they wish. They are already adequately costumed. I hope none will end up in a
quilted cell."

Florian instructed only Abner Mullenax to accompany him
back to the tober, though Edge and some other troupers came
along of their own accord—Cecil Wheeler and Ali Baba
among them—and so did the fortuitously encountered Jean-
François Pemjean, now in street dress. When Florian and
Edge led Mullenax into the office wagon and sat him down,
he had sobered considerably."

"Barnacle Bill," said Florian, "you could easily have got
yourself killed tonight. Worse yet, if you had behaved so in
our chapiteau here, with its floor of sawdust and tanbark and
straw, you could have burned the whole Florilegium to the
ground, and killed numberless innocent people."

"Yessir," mumbled Mullenax. "Reckon you're right."

"What do you think I ought to do with you?"

"Well, you don't have to fire me, Governor. I already decided to quit the trade. I got the nerve scared out of me
tonight for good and all. After lookin' that lion in the teeth
and smellin' his breath, I couldn't never get in no cage with
no wild animal again. Not ever again." He shivered.

"By good fortune, we do have a man willing and able to take your place. But surely you do not wish us to abandon you here in the middle of Europe."

"Nossir. If you could just keep me on as a kind of Slovak, I can nerve myself to swamp out the cages, feed the critters, work like that. Pay me just enough to keep me lubricated, that's all I'd ask, and I'd be grateful for it."

"Very well. Granted. Go now and get some sleep. On your way, please knock at the Wheelers' caravan and ask Mrs Wheeler to come here."

"A sad thing," said Edge, when Mullenax had shuffled out. "To see a man come all to pieces like that."

"I have seen it all too often," said Florian, with a sigh. "Some do it as he did. Others don't hit the skids until *after* they've lost their nerve. But I must unhappily predict, based on those many I have known, that Barnacle Bill will disintegrate further. Somewhere along the road, he will be sodden and comatose when the troupe moves on from one stand to the next. A time or two, he may recover and manage to catch up. But there'll come the time that he won't, and we'll never see him again."

Florian next called in Pemjean, who was idly chatting with Cecil Wheeler outside, to tell him, "The unfortunate dompteur whose place you took tonight has willingly relinquished that place permanently to you. He will, however, remain available—at least for a while—to assist you in caring for the animals. As I told you, we have also three Bengal tigers and two Syrian bears, whose training is not yet very far advanced."

Pemjean said confidently, "I will bring them along with utmost dispatch."

"Good. Now, as to the matter of your persona in the program. I rather liked the effect of that red devil in the cage."

"Aussi moi-même," said Pemjean, grinning. "To my knowledge, no other dompteur has ever worked animals with a trident spear instead of a whip. Therefore, having already pilfered the costume, I took the liberty of keeping it and bringing it along."

"I commend your foresight. We shall make only one

change in it—have our seamstress shorten the devil's tail. It could prove an encumbrance in the cage. And we will bill you as . . . let me see . . . yes! *Le Démon Débonnaire!*"

"Excellentissime!" exclaimed Pemjean.

Edge was studying the company roster, and said, "There's an empty bunk in Notkin and Spenz's caravan, since Nella moved out of there."

"I will speak to them," said Florian. "So, monsieur, you can lodge and travel with our Hanswurst and Kesperle, until we or you can afford better quarters on the tober and the road. Fetch your belongings whenever you like. And welcome to the Florilegium. We hope you will be happy in our company."

"Merci, Monsieur Florian. I like it better the more I see of it," said Pemjean, for Daphne Wheeler had just knocked and opened the door, and to the pretty blonde woman he made the elaborate, deep, sweeping bow of a dancing master before he departed.

She did not smile at that, or speak, but stood alternately wringing her hands and clenching them into fists.

"Be seated, Mrs Wheeler," said Florian and, not too severely, "You missed an important performance tonight, without giving prior notice. A—tiff—with your husband, I understand. I do not customarily meddle in domestic matters, but when they affect the whole establishment, I do like to know—"

"Why don't you ask *him?* He's lurking just outside, fearful that I'm going to peach on him."

"Another thing I don't customarily do is denigrate one partner in the hearing of the other. But I will say frankly that I distrust men who laugh through their noses. I invite equal frankness from you. Go ahead. Peach on him."

Daphne wrung and clenched her hands some more, then blurted a brief but vivid description of what she had seen in the tent wagon.

"Goddamn," grunted Edge. "I thought we'd got rid of that kind of thing when we got rid of Major Maggot."

"This is indeed distressing," said Florian, frowning. "Er,

Mrs. Wheeler, is this the first—uh—disillusionment you have suffered?''

"No,'' she said miserably. "There were plenty of young athletes around the gymnastics arena. But this is the first time he has defiled himself with a . . . with a *tar bucket*.'' She made a face of disgust. "It is the final straw.''

Still frowning, Florian said, "Naturally, my first impulse is to horsewhip your husband off the tober, Mrs. Wheeler, but that means discharging you, too—an innocent victim of my outrage. Also, if I dismiss one pederast, do I in fairness throw the boy into the street, as well? It is a dilemma.''

"Oh, hell, Florian,'' said Edge. "Quincy doesn't have the sense—or the looks—to have seduced anybody. He's a victim, too.''

"And don't concern yourself about me, Mr. Florian,'' Daphne said mournfully. "In the wedding ceremony, Ceece and I pledged to love one another until death. I have ceased to love him. So one or both of us should die.''

"Come now,'' Florian chided. "This is the nineteenth century, not biblical times. There are modern conveniences like divorce, instead of either homicide or suicide.''

"I suppose so. I have already turned him out of our caravan. Because it isn't ours, it is *mine*. Bought with the dowry I brought to the marriage.'' Tears began to trickle down her cheeks.

"At least you have a roof over your head, and transport.''

"Transport to where?'' she said, weeping more copiously. "I have nowhere to go. I might as well let one of the Wurstelprater's brute Strizzis put me to whoring.''

"Come now,'' Florian said again. "Who owns the act's props? The velocipede and rolling skates and vat and board?''

"We bought them together,'' she said, and sobbed.

"Then divide them,'' Florian said decisively. "If you keep only your pair of Plimptons and the skating board, you could work up a solo skating act, could you not?''

Daphne sniffled, stopped weeping and said she thought she could.

"And if later we procure another pair of skates,'' Florian continued, "perhaps one of the joeys could be your partner.

Very well, madame, your husband must go, but you may stay if you choose.''

"Oh, I do choose!'' she said gratefully.

"Colonel Ramrod, will you see if that degenerate is still loitering outside? Conduct him to the Wheeler ménage, stand by while he collects his belongings—only *his* belongings—and then see that he departs. Tonight. I will keep the lady safe here until he is gone.''

Cecil was now at a little distance from the wagon, but keeping an anxious eye on it, while again conversing with Pemjean. Edge, approaching them, could hear Cecil telling the newcomer, ''. . . Do it with the bald-headed end of a broom, that one. Hnoof-hnoof. Yes, indeed, fair game, old boy. Une sacrée baiseuse, as you frogs would say. Let me tell you one particularly favored way . . .'' He dropped his voice to a confidential murmer, and Pemjean's eyes opened very wide. But when Edge stopped and stood regarding them stonily, Cecil broke off to ask, ''Am I wanted, Zachary, old chap?''

"Not by anybody at all,'' said Edge. ''Come to the caravan and clear out your goods and get off this lot.''

"I say, now! You're being a bit brusque, old—''

"I can be a damned sight more so. With a tent stake, if you don't step lively. I'm only surprised that you haven't hit for the tall timber already. You must have known that your wife would tell us the dirty truth about you. Now move!''

Pemjean, appalled, said, ''Sacré bleu? That woman is *your wife?*'' But the other two men were moving off, Cecil plodding with shoulders slumped, Edge walking behind him like a warder.

Edge came back alone, to tell Florian and Daphne, ''He's gone, Mrs. Wheeler. The caravan is yours again. All he took was his clothes and costumes and his personal props—what he could pack in panniers on the velocipede.''

"You didn't hurt him?''

"No, ma'am. He didn't require any rough persuasion. And I wasn't eager to touch him if I didn't have to.''

"Did he say anything? Any parting message?''

"Well . . . he said he was leaving the big fire-water vat. No way to carry it. And besides, he said, he hoped you'd drown in it.''

''Oh,'' said Daphne.

''Good night, sweet prince,'' muttered Florian, and, after Daphne had taken her leave, ''Now . . . about Quincy Simms. I agree that he must have had no notion that he was doing wrong. But he may have acquired a taste for the practice, and we don't want him, in his ignorance, importuning anyone else. I suggest that he be taken off in private and, in a very fatherly way, be told the facts of life.''

''Don't look at me, Governor. No father ever told them to me, and I haven't fathered anybody to tell them to.''

''Nor I. Hm. Grumpf. As far as I'm aware, the only current or former fathers we have on the show are Pavlo Smodlaka and Abner Mullenax. I'd hesitate to inflict either of those on a confused small boy.''

''I know who,'' said Edge. ''Foursquare John Fitzfarris. He's a man of the world, and he once ran a dodge on the solitary vice. At the very least, he'll know how to put the lecture in high-toned medical lingo.''

So Fitzfarris, the next day, without too much recalcitrance, accepted the assignment of reeducating Quincy in the ways of a manly man. He came afterward to report to Florian.

''Well, I took the lad off to a secluded, quiet spot in a grove of trees, and I pulled up a pulpit and sat down and sermonized at him, and he said 'yassuh' every few minutes. At one point he told me he'd only played Wheeler's game because Wheeler said his juices would *dry up* otherwise. I think I set him straight on that, and I think he understood everything else I told him, and I think I've got him turned onto the path of virtue again. But—it's curious—after I'd pumped him brimful of What a Young Man Should Know, I asked if he had any questions. He said 'yes.' I said 'what?' He said, 'Mas' Fitz, does you hear that singin'? All day I been hearin' singin'.' ''

''So?''

''I told you it was a quiet spot. There was nobody singing. Not even a bird, this early in the spring. Do you reckon the kid's bad experience with that buggerous Wheeler has sent him a little bit daft?''

6

ABOUT A month later, there arrived on the tober a grand, gilded, four-horse coach with the imperial arms emblazoned on its doors, from one of which emerged a splendidly liveried steward bearing an ornate staff of office. He wielded that staff to part the crowd of people on the midway as, looking much offended by the sights, noises and smells about him, he made his way to the Florilegium's office wagon, where he rapped the staff on the door. Happily for the man's evident sensibilities, it was Florian who stuck his head out, not Magpie Maggie Hag. The steward handed him an immense envelope and, with an expression of strained politeness, waited while Florian broke the elaborate seal, read the large card it contained and asked of him a few questions.

When the steward was fastidiously edging through the crowd again to return to his coach, Florian was already dashing about to show the card to everybody of the troupe, and to translate for them its elegantly hand-inscribed message:

'' 'His K. K. Apostolic Majesty has condescended—' ''

''What's kay-kay?'' asked Clover Lee.

''Kaiserlich-Königlich. Imperial and Royal,'' Florian said impatiently. ''I'll begin again. 'His Imperial and Royal Apostolic Majesty has condescended, in accordance with his All Highest decision, and in amiable consideration of your contribution to the public welfare in entertaining the unfortunates of the Brünlfeld Insane Asylum' ''—he had to pause to take breath—'' 'most graciously to invite you to present a performance of your company at the palace of Schönbrunn at three o'clock in the afternoon of May third.' ''

''That is all one sentence?'' asked Maurice. ''He is longer-winded even than you are, Monsieur le Gouverneur.''

''Well, you know the bureaucrats. Franz Joseph is popularly known as the Premier Bureaucrat of Europe.''

"And what is Schönbrunn?" asked Edge. "I thought the royal family lived in the Hofburg."

"Schönbrunn is Their Majesties' summer palace and estate, on the farther side of the city. I am glad, now, that he waited to invite us until the family moved from the Hofburg. There we should have had to perform indoors or in a court-yard. On the vast grounds of Schönbrunn we can set up all three of our tops, and also include in the show a balloon ascension. Note, too, the thoughtfulness of the emperor. He invites us on the third of May."

"Why is that thoughtful?" asked Fitzfarris. "It'll be just another Sunday."

"His Majesty is clearly aware that we would not want to leave the Prater until after the first of May, for that is Saint Brigitte's Day. It should be the most crowded and profitable occasion of our whole long stand here. Saint Brigitte's Day begins the Blumenkorso, the festival of flowers, and all the Viennese come to parade in their finery through the Prater. Even folk who never leave the city during the rest of the year would feel mean and disgraced if they did not come out here on that holiday. It is also the day on which all the joints and entresorts of the Wurstelprater reopen for the summer. So we shall do a booming business on the first of May, and the emperor considerately allows the next day for our preparations to set up at Schönbrunn on the day following." Florian gazed fondly at the card he held, and added, "I believe I shall eventually have the billet d'invitation framed, to hang in my office."

"Surely the emperor did not write that himself," said Pfeifer.

"No, of course not. It is written and signed on his behalf by some court chamberlain. But below the message the scribe has appended all fifty-six of Franz Joseph's titles. Emperor of Austria, Apostolic King of Hungary, King of Jerusalem, of Bohemia, of Dalmatia, and so on. A thing worth keeping and treasuring, I think. Now then. We have four weeks to prepare for this command performance. Monsieur Roulette, do any varnishing or polishing the *Saratoga* may require to put it in tiptop shape. The rest of you work on any new acts you may have in mind, and do the ultimate refining of all your old ones.''

The Florilegium had already, and recently, added several new turns to its pista program. Finding and buying another velocipede had been no problem, and Shadid Sarkioglu had volunteered to be the one to learn to ride it. He had soon done that and, though the Turk was too big and bulky to be as nimble as Cecil had been in the trick riding of it, he was easily able to support Daphne while she did her acrobatics on his shoulders—and he just as fearlessly closed the act by hurtling over the high steering bar into the flaming vat. Daphne also did a solo skating-without-ice exhibition, until Goesle found, somewhere in the city, another pair of the wooden-wheel skates. Florian would have given them to the Hanswurst or the Kesperle, to learn to accompany Daphne, but the newest member of the company, Jean-Françoise Pemjean, begged to be allowed to use them to create an entirely novel kind of act.

It was Pemjean, le Démon Débonnaire, who had contrived most of the show's new turns—with some small assistance, not grudging but wistful, from the demoted Barnacle Bill, whenever he was sober enough to assist. Pemjean decreed that Maximus was too old to learn any additional tricks, but he almost magically quickly taught the three tigers to do all the sits and stands and leaps and playing-dead that the old lion had always done. So, in performance, Maximus would be brought on first to do his solo stint—much appreciated by the jossers, as always. Then the jossers would be even more thrilled when Raja, Rani and Siva were brought on to do those same tricks in simultaneous trio—concluding with a leap in sequence, one right behind another, through the fiery hoop.

Further, Pemjean managed to make useful even the two stupid and irascible ostriches. He designed light harnesses for them and somehow got Hansel and Gretel accustomed to wearing them. Thereafter, at the opening and close of every show, the big birds were liberated from their cage and hitched to the managerie's lightest wagon—the one containing the hyenas—and made to draw it around the chapiteau during the

Grand Promenades. Though gawky and graceless, they were definitely eye-catching additions to the spectacles.

But le Démon Débonnaire achieved his greatest success with the two Syrian bears. Barnacle Bill had never got beyond teaching Kewwy-dee to stand on his hind legs and suck sugar water from his toy trumpet while a real windjammer provided his "playing." Pemjean taught Kewwy-dah, the she-bear, to stand on her hind legs *and* on the new-bought pair of Plimpton rolling skates, for which Goesle made and attached special canvas boots. Then Pemjean proposed to Daphne that Kewwy-dah take her departed husband's place as her partner on the skating board.

"Monsieur le Démon!" she exclaimed, aghast. "You must think me feeble-minded. Isn't it bad enough that I am a grass widow? I don't yearn to hurry into a grave *beneath* the grass."

"Fear not, fair lady. Kewwy-dee will be much too occupied with keeping her balance to think of giving you a bear hug. Also, she is muzzled, her claws are blunted, and I will be always standing close by. You simply take her by the paws as if she were a dancing partner, and yourself do the impulsion to make her wheel about in concert with you."

It took a good deal more of his persuasion, but finally, bravely, apprehensively, Daphne made the attempt—and was reassured and surprised and delighted with the result. Though she had to exert all the effort and skill, it looked to the bystanders as if Kewwy-dah really was doing her own skating back and forth and sideways and roundabout. Meanwhile, off to one side, Kewwy-dee with his trumpet apparently helped the band provide the "Oh, Emma! Whoa, Emma!" music for the act. So Daphne and all the other members of the Florilegium—save one—were loud with praise of Pemjean's additions to the program.

"That Pavlo, he behaving crazy again," Magpie Maggie Hag reported privately to Edge.

"Oh, lord, what now? He hasn't been hurrying his act any more, and I haven't noticed him inspecting the audience for spies."

"No, now he crazy jealous. Never was jealous when his dog act followed Barnacle Bill. But now he follows Démon Débonnaire. And that new animal act so good, he says, it makes his slanging buffers look tame and feeble."

"Well, he could be right. I can easily rearrange the program so the Smodlakas come on earlier and well apart."

"I don't know," the gypsy said uncertainly. "Pavlo got notion that Frenchman some kind of *real* demon. Says Pemjean all the time reading in a book. Always same book. Maybe book of sorcery. To make his act shine over *everybody's*."

"Pavlo is crazy, right enough," sighed Edge. "But I'll respot his act and see if that soothes him some."

"Another thing," said Magpie Maggie Hag. "Gluttonous Greek came to me in secret for medicine."

"What's wrong with Spyros? And why in secret?"

"Because he ashamed of ailment. I made purific pills and blue gentian ointment for him. Maybe help, maybe not. But I no tell him what is wrong. Is the gleet, the surge, the pudendagra, or something like."

"A private disease? Hell, then he ought to visit a secret-sorrows doctor. There are plenty of them in Vienna. Why didn't you tell him so?"

"Because, far as I know. Spyros never fool with other women. How he get it, then? Only from wife, Meli."

"Oh, Christ. Yes, I see. Where did *she* get it? I've always thought she was chaste and faithful, too. Have any other men applied to you with the same ailment?"

"No. Other people ask cure for other things. Quincy Simms has headache. Monday Simms pesters me for love potions, make John Fitz love her more, stop his roving eye."

"Well, I can't do anything for Monday. But here—I've got these Dreser's powders left from Autumn's illness. They eased her headaches. Dose Quincy with them. As for Meli . . . if nobody but her husband is complaining of the drips . . ."

"Some men *not* complain. Just wait for gleet to go away. Like having bad cold. Some men have it often, laugh it off."

"More likely, though, Meli caught it from some Johnny

from the seats. And if that's so, Spyros might very well kill her. Do you think you can cure him, without his getting suspicious of what ails him?'' The gypsy shrugged. ''And could you also have a woman-to-woman talk with Meli?''

''She probably not even know she got gleet. Not often a woman does know, until she gives birth to blind baby.''

''All the more reason for talking to her, then. And curing *her*, too. Do what you can, will you, Mag?''

''What I can,'' she said, with another shrug, and went away.

''Ah, there, Colonel Ramrod,'' called Florian, passing by with Willi at his side. ''Would you join me and Chefpublizist Lothar in the red wagon?''

In the office, they all lighted cigarettes and Florian poured for each of them a glass of white wine that had a pale greenish tint to it. ''Another Viennese tradition, Zachary. The Heuriger—new spring wine—fresh from the vineyards of the Vienna Woods. Actually, I've always found it rather raw and meager of satisfaction, myself, but one mustn't cavil at tradition.''

''Tastes pretty good,'' said Edge. ''I've been meaning to ask, Governor. After our performance at that palace, do we come back here to the Prater or move elsewhere?''

''Elsewhere. That is what I wanted us three to discuss. Saint Brigitte's Day should bring out all the people we haven't already performed to, so I imagine we can safely say, then, that we have milked Wien for all it is worth. Now, we *could* take to the road again, but I am disinclined to do so. During this long winter stand, many of our company, the women especially—even the midway nomads—have made their caravans into practically permanent homesteads. It would be a nuisance for them to have to gather up all their belongings, pack them neatly and stow them tightly for road travel. Besides, our next big-city destination will be Budapest, where we shall again settle down for a lengthy stay. I believe it would be easiest for all concerned if we go directly there, and in a manner requiring the least fuss and bother. By river. We can simply roll our wagons and vans onto barges here—

however untidily we have bundled our goods together—and roll off again at Budapest.''

"It sounds easy and comfortable enough," said Edge. "But can we trust that river? Remember what it did to Zanni."

"The Danube is a rushing current only this far," said Willi. "From Wien southward it gets broad and quiet. No hazard at all. A pleasant, scenic journey."

"Then I'm in accord," said Edge. "It *will* make the move less of a chore."

"All agreed. Good," said Florian. "Willi, would you proceed with the arrangements? Go straightaway to Budapest and engage a tober on a long-term lease. Take Monsieur Roulette for company, if you like. Just be sure that you both are back with us before the Schönbrunn show. And either in Budapest or here, book as many barges as you estimate we will need."

"Best to do it there," said Willi. "I shall find some barge-string owner in Budapest who will be bringing cargo to Wien and expects to go home empty. He should be happy to accommodate us, and therefore charge us less."

"Shrewd thinking. Go to it."

On Saint Brigitte's Day, the Prater was indeed, for all its size, crammed with people, some of them simply strolling or riding about to show off their new spring garb, others taking refreshment at the newly opened restaurants, others dancing to the orchestras that occupied every park band shell, still others afloat in bright-sailed little boats on the Danube's loop between the island and the city shore. But most of the holiday crowd congregated in the Wurstelprater, to sample the wares and attractions of the entresorts and game booths and mechanical rides. And of those people such a sufficiency came to the tober that the Florilegium could easily have given four or five shows that day—if the artistes and animals had been able—and every house would have been a sfondone. As it was, the two shows both ran overlong, because the audiences were so enthusiastic and demanded so many encores and bows of every performer.

Everybody of the circus company had to work even harder
the next day. The crewmen tore down the chapiteau and its
seating, the menagerie and annex tents; the artistes packed
wagons with their costumes and rigs and props; the handlers
prettied-up their animals. On Sunday morning, almost all the
circus train, excepting the caravans and the midway people's
vehicles, carried the performers, the bandsmen, the Schuhplattler girls and most of the crewmen back across the Rotunden Bridge. This time, the train did not have to skirt
around the still-torn-up streets of the Innere Stadt, but went
directly west through commercial and residential neighborhoods until those gave way to more open suburban areas, and
then to the high, spiky, wrought-iron fence that enclosed the
Schönbrunn grounds and extended away into the distance,
seemingly to infinity.

Florian, with Daphne Wheeler beside him on his gleaming
black rockaway, proudly led the procession to one of the
massive, curlicued, wrought-iron gates in that interminable
fence. He showed his invitation card to the sentries there—
men of the Hungarian Honor Guard, wearing tiger-striped
capes over red tunics laced with silver—and they hospitably
swung the great gates wide. The train proceeded for at least
half an hour up a gently winding, graveled drive under the
overarching limbs of immense old trees; past velvet lawns
and placid ponds and little cascades; around banks and beds
of tulips, jonquils, daffodils and lilacs; between house-high
walls of dense green hedge trimmed perfectly wall-flat, except where niches were cut at regular intervals to accommodate marble nude statues of every god and goddess known
to antiquity; past a dell in which stood the ivy-overgrown
stonework of what might have been the remains of a Roman
temple: all crumbling arches and broken pillars.

"How old must that ruin be?" Daphne asked, in admiring
awe.

"Less than a hundred years, actually," said Florian. "Only
a folly. The landscape architect built it already ruined, arti-
ficially ancient."

The driveway debouched into a tremendous open rectangle
of greensward and flower beds, many acres in extent, with

three-story-high green hedges and more statues edging both lengths of it. On the lawns, numerous peacocks waddled about, screeching "yeeow!" now and then. One end of the rectangle was closed by the four-story, cream-colored, hundred-windowed façade of the great palace. At the other end of that area, a quarter of a mile distant, was a fountain as broad as the palace, where stone Neptunes and naiads cavorted in a cascade that poured from an artificial mountain of boulders down terraces and walls into a lily pond big enough to float a good-sized ship. Beyond that fountain, the lawns continued, but rising and undulating up a hill, on the high crest of which another edifice was distantly visible, an openwork of arches and columns topped by a spread-winged stone eagle.

"Great day in the morning!" Yount said to Agnete. "This beats even the King of Italy's park!"

Florian immediately began issuing orders. "Mr. Goesle, Pana Banat, we will set up on the grassed areas here, the chapiteau nearest to the palace, the menagerie farthest away. Do *not* set up the donnickers. And be careful not to trample the flowers. Herr Beck, I suggest that you take the calliope some way up the hill, so it won't shatter the palace windows. Take the balloon wagon and generators, too, all the way to the top of the hill. I think it will give a lovely effect, launching the *Saratoga* from in front of the Gloriette." He indicated the eagle-topped stucture up there. "Then, when Monsieur Roulette descends, he can land here among the royal spectators, and that will add to the effect of the vanished and reappearing girl."

"The Gloriette?" said Edge, gazing up the hill. "The name sounds diminutive, but that thing yonder looks pretty impressive to me."

"The Empress Maria Theresa put it there," explained Willi Lothar. "In a war with Prussia during her reign, the Austrians won only a single battle, and that is her monument to it. But Maria Theresa had a sense of humor. She said that, since it had been only a little battle and a little victory, she would call the monument only a 'Little Glory.' Ah! Here comes His Majesty already."

Franz Joseph strolled out of one of the palace doors, wearing a simple loden hunting jacket and knickerbockers, looking more like one of his own gamekeepers than like an emperor. He was a slim man of about Edge's age, and had obviously grown his luxuriant mustache and side-whiskers to lend breadth to a face as narrow as a cleaver and about as expressionless. He was accompanied by two children, also in simple garb, the plumply and rosily adolescent Princess Gisela and the pale, fidgety child who was the Crown Prince Rudolf. They had no guards with them and only a few uniformed courtiers and liveried servants.

Willi and Florian hurried to greet and bow to His Majesty and the Royal Highnesses. Then Florian introduced ''die meinige Zirkushauptpersonen''—Edge, Fitzfarris, Goesle and Beck—who also managed passable bows. While those four and Florian went on with their supervision of the setup, Willi stayed with the royal party as they ambled about and watched with interest every move of the Slovaks erecting the three tents. Franz Joseph, like any ordinary father, frequently bent to his children to direct their attention to this or that instructive detail of the operation.

The other circus people eyed them curiously but discreetly, and Clover Lee said, ''I'm disappointed not to see that beautiful empress of his.''

Maurice said, ''She must be off again, traveling somewhere. It might be untactful to mention her.''

''For such a small family,'' said Agnete, ''they have one meget big house.''

''My dear girl,'' said Pfeifer, ''the family occupies only about sixty rooms of it. The other fourteen hundred or so are for the members of the court and all the servants they each require.''

The royal party remained on the tober to watch even the fixing of the seating in the chapiteau and the tethering of the animals in the menagerie tent. Then Franz Joseph came personally to shake Florian's hand and tell him, ''Es hat mich sehr gefreut,'' before taking most of his entourage indoors again. One courtier stayed behind to say to Florian in English:

"I am the Count Georg Stockau, His Imperial Majesty's deputy marshal of ceremonies. You understand that you are to commence the entertainment at three o'clock. How long, then, will it last?"

"About three hours, Eure Hoheit. An hour of performance, then an intermission during which all adjourn to watch the balloon ascension, to see the sideshow exhibits, und so weiter. Then another hour of performance."

"Sehr gut. His Imperial Majesty graciously invites your entire company to stay to dinner, so I will advise the Küchenchef to prepare to serve at seven o'clock. The laborers will dine in the kitchens, of course. The gentlemen of the troupe in the Vieux-Laque Room, with myself at the head of the table. The lady artistes in the Blue Chinese Room, with the Countess Mathilde Apponyi. The countess and I both speak English, besides other languages, if needed. You and your Baron Lothar von Wittelsbach and your four chief subordinates will dine with the emperor himself in the Konspirationstafelstube. You will be seated on His Majesty's right, Wittelsbach to his left. The Princess Caroline von und zu Liechtenstein will be your vis-à-vis. The Countess Marie Larisch will be the baron's. All very informal, of course."

"Of course," Florian said, somewhat faintly.

"You will none of you be expected to dress, on such short notice."

"We are inestimably honored by His Majesty's favor and regard, Eure Hoheit."

When the royals and nobles emerged from the palace to cross the lawn to the chapiteau, the emperor exemplified the "informality" of the occasion. Though he was now garbed in a crisp, well-tailored uniform of white tunic and red trousers, with an abundance of gold braid on it, he wore only one of his decorations: the red and green band of the Order of St. Stephan. And the little Crown Prince Rudolf wore a miniature version of his father's uniform, with only the chain of the Order of the Golden Fleece. But the other male courtiers and high army officers who streamed out of the palace were impeccably full-dressed in brilliant uniforms—Hussar pink and sky blue, Tirolean Rifle silver green, Arciere Guard crimson and gold—and were very nearly armor-plated with the quantities of medals overlapping on their breasts. The ladies were equally resplendent in modish crinolette gowns of silk and taffeta and brocade. The numerous court children wore not boyish short hosen or girlish pantalettes but scaled-down facsimiles of their parents' full-length finery. When the audience had assembled in the chapiteau—and they were so many that they almost half-filled it, the lesser ranks uncomplainingly taking the tiers of plain board seats—they quite outglittered even the spangled costumes of the artistes.

Everyone stood, the officers at the salute, Franz Joseph and Rudolf with humbly bowed heads, while Beck's band opened the program by playing the "God Preserve Our Emperor" anthem, accompanied distantly but more than audibly by the calliope up on the hill. Abdullah had earlier brought the two elephants into the pista, so, with up-curled trunks, they also saluted the man and boy in the seats of honor. But thereafter, everyone relaxed, and the august audience applauded the dancing girls and the come-in spec and every subsequent act as boisterously as any tentful of commoners had ever done.

The show went with clockwork precision and smoothness and never a mishap. At intermission, the *Saratoga* wafted beautifully from the Gloriette, and dreamily waltzed about the sky. After vanishing "the Fräulein Simms," Fitzfarris presented his sideshow and then to many of the men and women, his Amazon-and-Fafnir tableau vivant. Magpie Maggie Hag went about, reading the palms of Prinzessinnen and Grafinnen and Baroninnen, promising every lady a life of joy and romance and riches. The balloon descended as lightly as a dandelion fluff on the tober, and revealed the reappeared "Fräulein Simms" to general astonishment and acclaim. The pista program resumed, and again went perfectly, and closed with a reprise of the anthem. Then, while the audience returned to the palace, chattering and laughing, there was quite a crush of the troupers at the dressing-room wagon, all eager to get into their best civilian clothes. Florian was prompted to tell Dai Goesle, "Make a note, Canvasmaster. We must soon procure two new tops, a dressing tent each for men and women."

When all were clad in their best—though a poor second-best to their hosts—the deputy marshal of ceremonies came to escort them into the palace. They went, most of them craning and gawking like jossers, through the great Spiegelsaal, where the entirely mirrored, high, long wall opposite the window wall made the hall look twice as enormous as it already was, and twice as full of crystal-cascade chandeliers and golden nymphs holding candelabra. Carl Beck traversed the chamber practically genuflecting at every step and in a hushed voice explained why: "Here it was that the young Mozart his very first court recital gave."

Quincy Simms said, more pragmatically, to nobody in particular, "What dey go' give us to eat? I smells sowbelly fryin'."

"Sowbelly?" said Pemjean. "Qu'est-ce que c'est?"

"Salt pork fat," Rouleau translated. "Darky food."

"Ali Baba, you couldn't possibly smell any such thing," said Florian. "For one reason, the kitchens of every palace in Europe are in a separate building—just so the smells and the smoke are kept well away. Also the flies and any hazard of fire."

Every room of the palace was replete with works of art—statues, busts, tapestries, paintings—the greater number of them portraying members of the royal family, from Maria Theresa to the current occupants. Zachary Edge was not at all knowledgeable about art, and not particularly susceptible to it, but there was *something* about a number of the portraits and busts that gave him a spooky feeling of having seen them somewhere before. He would have made inquiry of their escort, but the count was courteously giving a commentary on the rooms into which he shepherded the separate groups of artistes.

"Meine Damen, you will dine here in the Blue Chinese room. I invite your attention to the scenes of Chinese life inset in the wallpaper panels. The figures of the men and women are painted with a phosphor paint. When the room darkens and the attendants bring in candles, you will see those figures glow and seem to move."

Ushering the male artistes into a room of panels so glossy

that they reflected almost as brightly as the Hall of Mirrors, he said, ''Meine herren, please to observe the perfection of this Vieux-Laque Room. Every one of those panels was done aboard a ship, well out at sea, so that not a speck of dust could mar the immaculacy of the lacquer.''

The last room—the one to which he escorted Florian, Willi, Edge, Beck, Goesle and Fitzfarris—was the smallest they had yet seen, though by no means small, and it was oval, and on that room the count seemed to have no comment to make. But Fitzfarris did, when Stockau had left them: ''The other rooms each had a dining table. This one's only got chairs. Do we eat off our laps?''

''Only wait,'' said Beck. ''Of this room I have heard. In it Maria Theresa in secret with her counselors dined. So not even servants should enter.''

Just then, Franz Joseph came in, with half a dozen women, most of them young and handsome. As the Countess Larisch introduced herself and the other ladies, in English, the emperor gravely pulled a bell rope. The introductions were interrupted by a grinding and grating noise. A section of the parquet floor slowly began to slide—nearly taking Dai Goesle with it, before he stepped to one side. From the considerable gap revealed in the floor, there slowly and majestically rose into sight a damask-covered and fully laid table, complete with its steaming and savory dinner, with napery, porcelain, crystal and plate. There were exclamations and general applause, and Franz Joseph's usually impassive face allowed itself a small smile.

The men brought chairs from against the wall and seated the ladies and themselves in the order Count Stockau had specified, and everyone began immediately to eat, because, the several courses having been served all at once, the soup had to be ingested in a hurry before the rest of the meal got cold. In truth, as the six circus men agreed later, it was neither a very memorable meal nor a very stimulating gathering. The only wine provided was the cheap Heuriger which any least tramp might be drinking in a Wienerwald tavern. And, since the emperor drank only iced water, the others felt constrained to limit their intake even of the mild wine. The meal's pièce de résistance was the common Backhendl, the roast chicken that was certainly on every Austrian bürger's table this Sunday, as it was every Sunday of the year.

The table talk was similarly rather dreary. Florian, Willi and Beck were able to converse in German, and Edge found that he and his vis-à-vis, a young and fairly pretty Baronin Helene Vetsera, had enough French between them to murmur banalities back and forth. But Goesle and Fitzfarris had only English, and their feminine counterparts had little. Anyway, the table talk was much dampened by His Imperial Majesty's taciturnity. On the occasions when he did bestir himself to speak, he did so almost by ventriloquy, directing his remarks to the Princess of Liechtenstein to be passed along.

The first thing he said was, "Wie gesagt—es war schön, der Zirkus. Es hat mich sehr gefreut."

The princess told the others, "His Majesty wishes you all to know that your circus was nice. He liked it very much."

"Besten Dankes, Eure Majestät," said Florian.

Some while later, the emperor told the princess, "Dieser Herr Florian wird Zukunft haben."

"Schönen Dankes, Eure Majestät," said Florian, without waiting for the relay. And later he told his colleagues, "I *assume* it was a compliment—to be told at my advanced age that I 'have a future.' The emperor possesses absolutely no wit or humor, so I doubt that he was being sarcastic. But I swear, I can't remember his making a single other remark during the whole dinner."

Well, anyhow, thought Edge—when the boredom finally ended, and everyone rose, and Franz Joseph again pulled the bell rope, and the table full of litter and picked bones descended into the depths, and the floor returned—if I ever go back to Hart's Bottom, I'll be the only one there who can brag of once eating dinner with an emperor. But nobody will believe it. Hell, probably nobody in Hart's Bottom would know what an emperor is. . .

The mixed company convened in the Spiegelsaal, and a liveried flunky brought a high-heaped tray, from which Franz Joseph dispensed to each of the troupers a keepsake of the occasion: to the females tiny evening handbags and to the males pocket wallets, all embroidered with the imperial arms in the exquisite Viennese petit point. Thanking him in their various languages, the men bowed and the women curtsied— some of them teetering in the process, for those who had dined with lesser personages had clearly not been discouraged from partaking freely of the wine and even more ardent spirits. Then Count Stockau escorted the troupe out to their tober.

They found the Slovaks even more forthrightly drunk; the dinner in the kitchens must really have been festive. Nevertheless, Florian left those men to do the tearing down, as and when they were capable, under the supervision of glum-sober Goesle and Beck. He appropriated only his rockaway and three wagons to transport the artistes back through the midnight city streets. As if the trip had been a sleigh-ride outing, a number of the passengers sang as they rode, and a few snored, and some—Maurice and Nella, Obie and Agnete— gently wrestled and tipsily giggled, and Monday tried hard to make Fitzfarris do so, and Jean-François Pemjean tried the same with Daphne Wheeler, and with better success.

Florian told Edge, who was riding with him now, ''The barges from Budapest are unloading their cargo at the riverfront, and will be ready to load us on the morning after tomorrow.''

''How long will this voyage take, Governor?''

''Um . . . the rest of that day, that night and the next day, I should estimate.''

''That's all?'' said Edge, with some surprise.

''Well, we will be going downstream with the current helping, and with a steam tugboat pulling. It is only about a hundred and fifty miles from here to Budapest.''

Edge said thoughtfully, ''No more than maybe the distance from Hart's Bottom to Winchester in Virginia. I reckon I'm a country bumpkin, yet. I still think of the capitals of Europe as all being tremendously far apart.''

The rockaway and the first of the wagons arrived at the Wurstelprater somewhat in advance of the other two. Those who climbed down from the bed of that wagon, some of them unsteadily, were Magpie Maggie Hag, the Smodlaka family, the Schuhplattler girls, Jean-François Pemjean and Daphne Wheeler. Pavlo Smodlaka was not too intoxicated to take note that Pemjean accompanied Daphne to her caravan, where, after they had done some mutual giggling at the door of it, they went inside together. Pavlo said, under his brandied breath, ''Aha.''

He left his wife and children to make their own way in the dark to their home caravan, and himself scuttled off to the one shared by Pemjean and the clowns Notkin and Spenz, not yet arrived. There was a lantern left alight, hanging on a nail over its door, so Pavlo took that inside with him, and did not have to hunt very hard for the book he sought; it was lying open on one of the bunks, as if Pemjean had lately been reading in it. Pavlo took it up and peered at its cover, having to close one eye so as not to see it double. Even then, he managed only with difficulty to spell out the title, for it was in English. He said again, this time triumphantly aloud, ''*Aha!*''—and ran out with the book.

In Daphne's caravan—in the dark, for they had not wasted any time in lighting lamp or candle—she and Pemjean were already undressed and entwined. For some while, there was mostly silence, except for soft applosions of kisses. But then suddenly the bunk jerked and thumped and Daphne gave a small shriek.

''Eeek! My God, Jean, what are you doing?''

''Aïe, ma chère, am I doing it wrong?''

''Wrong!? What a question! What you are doing is horrid!''

''Hélas. Let me then try it from this direc—''

''Stop that!'' There was a noise of her scrambling to cover herself with the bedclothes. ''What you are doing is disgusting! Immoral! Unheard of! Obscene! It must be Greek!''

''Ma foi, I only wish to do what—''

''I never suspected you were a pervert!'' Half to herself, she said, ''I must ask Madame Hag—under what sorry star was I born, that I attract only degenerates?''

''Mais, chérie, I thought you *liked* . . . well, that sort of thing.''

"Horrors upon horrors! Do you take *me* for a pervert? Whatever gave you such a nasty idea?"

"Eh bien . . . your husband did."

"What!?" The whole caravan rocked and creaked as she violently shoved at him. "Get out of here, you filthy frog!"

"I only sought to please. De bonne foi, chérie."

"Get your clothes on and *get out of here!*"

"You see, Gospodja Hag?" said Pavlo excitedly, breathing fumes at her and waving the book at her. "What I said: the Frenchman is a koldunya, a wizard, perhaps a Vampir. Regard, his book of zabranjeno sorcery. I, even I, can read the terrible name of it. *The Book of . . . Pri-vate . . . K'now-ledge.* You see? I was right to suspect."

The gypsy grunted and took the volume from him. She held it close to her candle and more fluently read aloud the title, all of it: *The Book of Private Knowledge and Advice, of the Highest Importance to Individuals in the Detection and Cure of 'A Certain Disease' Which, if Neglected or Improperly Treated, Produces the Most Ruinous Consequences to the Human Constitution.* Charva! You stupid dalmatinski, this not anything of sorcery. This only . . . medical book."

But Pavlo had comprehended one phrase, and now repeated, with relish, "Certain disease, eh? Aha!"

"Here, imbecile. Put book back before he miss it. And stop sneaking, prying, pilfering where you got no business."

"Da, Gospodja Hag," Pavlo said sweetly. "Forgive me for trouble you." He got the book back where it belonged and got himself away from there, just minutes before the disheveled and disgruntled Pemjean came, muttering, to his own bed.

⇌ MAGYARORSZÁG ⇌

1

"AN AUSPICIOUS COINCIDENCE, I hope," said Florian, referring to the doughty little sidewheel tugboat that towed their string of barges downriver. "Its name, *Kitartó*, means approximately the same as did that of our previous vessel, the *Pflichttreu*—steadfast, loyal."

"I hope it doesn't mean as many misadventures on the way," said Edge.

He and the other circus chiefs were riding with Florian on the first barge in line. The others of the company were distributed in groups on the following barges, riding with their personal caravans or the wagons or animals they were responsible for. Since there could be no visiting back and forth among the towroped flatboats, and no communal cooking, Florian had laid out a good deal of money to have Sacher's in the Prater put up a quantity of "Picknick" baskets for their sustenance on the trip.

So the voyagers were more than merely well wined and dined during the two days and a night that they were afloat, and there were no misadventures, and the river trip was, in still other ways, a very pleasant change from road travel. For one thing, the traffic sharing the Danube was much more various than could be seen on a road—sailboats, rowboats, sidewheel and sternwheel passenger-and-mail boats, fishing skiffs, houseboats, barges and broadhorns laden with every kind of cargo from logs and coal to market produce and even flowers. Also, the surrounding scenery changed more rapidly on the river than on a road. For a while downstream of Vienna, the river flowed at a good clip between reedy banks backed by forests. But then it widened and slowed, and on both sides were farm fields, in which all the workers seemed to be women—heavy, squat, broad-beamed women in kerchiefs and smocks—wielding hoes and spades and scythes and flails. The farmhouses were as dumpy as the women, mere hovels of mud, sometimes whitewashed. Because every house had a thatched roof and was backed by a haystack as wide as the house and three or four times as high, the houses looked from midstream as if they wore straw roofs preposterously too big for them.

Then, on the left bank, the farms gave way to vineyards, interspersed with winery sheds and vats and mountains of barrels. Those in turn gave way to scattered workshops and forges that multiplied and got bigger and more crowded together until they were the industrial outskirts of a city. Then the city itself slid into view, quite a big one, of medieval stone and half-timbered buildings with steep-pitched slate roofs, many turrets and spires, innumerable tall chimneys topped with storks on nests. Behind and above the riverside city towered a splendid old castle on a plateau.

"The city of Pózsony," said Florian.

"Called Pressburg in German," said Willi.

"Bratislava," Banat said firmly. "Capital city of my home province, Slovakia. Once was capital of all Hungary."

"In any event," said Florian, "we are here crossing a border of the Dual Monarchy. Behind us, the Österreich—Austria proper. On our left, Austria's province of die Slowakei. On our right, Hungary—or Magyarország. It is spelled M-A-G, but pronounced as if it were M-A-D. *Madyar*. You will find other linguistic curiosities in Hungary. For example,

Bandmaster, you are now Beck Carl. Or Beck Boom-Boom, if you prefer."

"And I'm F̃itzfarris John Foursquare?" said that one. "Christ. What kind of a country is it that can't spell its own name and flip-flops everybody else's?"

"You will not encounter many problems," said Willi. "The second language here is German. Except for peasants, everybody speaks it. If you could make your way in Bavaria and Austria, you will do as well in Hungary."

"And there are as many delights as curiosities," Florian assured them all. "But what is the matter, Zachary? Are you not looking forward to our next adventures? You appear slightly doleful."

"Not really. I was just thinking: I'm farther east now than Autumn ever got. And her name here would have been Auburn Autumn. Just as melodious either way."

Three or four barges behind, Monday Simms sat on the steps of her and Fitz's caravan, gloomily and unappreciatively watching Slovakia slide past. Nearby stood Jean-François Pemjean, who had likewise been less than effervescent since the night of the Schönbrunn show. Perhaps seeking to cheer them both up, he made bold to ask Monday why she seemed not to be enjoying the voyage.

Without even looking at him, she muttered ungraciously, "Nobody's bizness."

"Eh bien, if it is nobody's, then I am not butting into anybody's. So tell me."

Monday blinked and turned to gaze at him, trying to grasp the logic of that remark, if it had any. Finally she said, "What's gravelin' me is I'm losin' my man."

"Ah. That would be le bleu Sir John?"

She looked away and nodded forlornly. "He found hisself a white hussy in Vienna. And last night, our very last night there, he spent it with her. And now he's not even ridin' on the same boat with me."

"I am not yet too well acquainted with all the—arrangements among the troupe. Are you and he married?"

"No, cuss it. He never got around to that, neither."

"Alors, it is obvious what you must do. En revanche, find yourself a white man."

She said morosely, "I thought I had."

"He is half-*blue*. It wonders me how a jolie fille like yourself could ever have been attracted to him. Also, he is rather older than you . . . and me."

Monday turned again, very slowly, and regarded Pemjean with some calculation. "Fact is . . ." she said, "I wasn't."

"Comment?"

"Attracted to him. I wasn't. He made me take up with him."

"Comment?"

"See, when I first come on the show, Mr. Demon, I was just a White Pygmy in his sideshow. I wanted to learn the high school ridin'—and to be Mam'selle Cinderella on the rope. But he wouldn't let me loose of the sideshow unless I'd . . . well . . ."

"Scandaleux!" exclaimed Pemjean. "I took Sir John to be a gentleman. But what a bestial, what an *unsubtle* way to seduce." He reached out to stroke her hair. "Pauvre Cendrillon."

"So . . . now that I done been ruined for any other man . . ."

"Mademoiselle!" he said sharply. "Do not speak such pre-historic pruderies to a Frenchman! I, Pemjean, do not regard you as ruined. Only awakened to life's pleasures and possibilities."

"Well, anyhow, I ain't like John Fitz. I can't hop from one possibility to—"

"Mais oui, you can. It takes but a little imagination, a little daring, a little *French*ness. The which I can very easily teach you."

She regarded him now with open speculation, and murmured, "You a lot handsomer'n he is, too."

"Perhaps also less fickle." He added, more to himself than to her, "I have never before enjoyed une amourette avec une mulâtresse."

The tugboat *Kitartó* now was leading the barge string in a slow dance through the channels winding among numerous midriver islands, and it may have been the perceptible weaving motion that made Monday begin very slightly to chafe her thighs together. Pemjean noticed that, but made no reference to it. Instead, as if changing the subject altogether, he pointed across the darkening fields of Slovakia and said:

"The sun is down, the night draws on. Hélas, I do dread going to bed, for I must share quarters with the Hanswurst who smells like *wurst* and the Kesperle who smells even *worse*. Voilà, how is that for a joke employing two different languages? Mademoiselle Cendrillon, I am trying to make you smile."

She did. She even laughed. Then she stood up on the little steps and opened the caravan door. "Well, Mr. Demon— tonight, anyway—there's a place empty in this-here house wagon."

All night long, the barge string waltzed its way among the river islands, so all the people in their bunks had their sleep or other activity pleasantly enhanced by that gentle rocking. When they arose the next morning, the islands were behind and the Danube was again unimpeded, taking them directly eastward and between the twin cities of Hungary's Komárom on the right bank and Slovakia's Komárno on the left, both consisting mainly of immense, noisy, steaming and smoking shipyards. After that, there was nothing more to see on the left side except the rolling farm fields dotted with kerchiefed peasant drabs. But on the right there were frequent small but brightly painted and sparkling villages, and then the cathedral-dominated town of Esztergom.

There Florian announced, "We have left Slovakia behind. Now it is Hungary on both sides of the river."

As if to emphasize that fact, the land on both banks now rose into high and handsomely forested hills. And the river, as if to show as much as possible of that scenic landscape, curved back and forth—south, east, north, east again—then made a decided bend to the south and continued in that direction, past several more picturesque villages perched on the heights, and two sizable hilltop towns: the many-castle-towered Visegrad and the many-church-towered Szentendre. But south of Szentendre, the greenery began to be interrupted and blemished again by riverside workshops and forges, and then by big industrial buildings, and the sweet-green-scented air got more and more heavily tainted with the yeasty smell of breweries and the moldy stench of tanneries.

"Ah, the signs of civilization," said Florian. "But give the Hungarians credit. They at least locate their manufactories well away from the city and downwind of it."

"Are we there, then?" asked Goesle. "Budapest?"

"In a sense. There are actually three cities. We are passing Óbuda—Old Buda—on the right. Shortly we shall come to Buda itself, also on the right bank, and we shall have to land there briefly for the immigration formalities. But Buda is so hilly that we should be hard put to find a flat place to pitch. So the *Kotartó* will next tow us across the river to the plains city of Pest, and there we will disembark and make parade to our tober."

The Danube suddenly parted around an island as sharp-prowed as a ship and, like a ship churning upstream, throwing a white bow wave. The tug took the river fork to the right of it and chugged along past the island, which was many times longer than any ship ever built. It was mostly wooded, but here and there a spindly derrick stood higher than the trees, and there were also visible scaffolded big buildings under construction.

"Margit's Island," said Willi. "Saint Margit is buried there. That was the island's chief distinction until just two years ago, when drillers discovered hot and mineral springs. So now there will be grand hotels offering baths to cure every mortal ill. As if there were not already enough spas here."

"Ah?" said Carl Beck, with interest.

The pointed lower end of Margit's Island slid behind, to reveal the great flat city of Pest on the farther shore. And the tiered hillside streets and roads of Buda now loomed on the nearer right bank. The tugboat sidled from midchannel to that shore, lost way and glided up against a tremendously long stone pier, skillfully nestling every following barge alongside it as well. The tug's crewmen jumped ashore to run and do the hitching of all the craft to the pier bollards. Then the circus folk stepped ashore—Pemjean gallantly assisting Monday—to stretch their legs and wait for instructions.

The pier was the river edge of the even more immense, flagstoned Bomba Square, with a church and its appurtenances at one end, government buildings at the other. The landward length of the square was entirely occupied by a great, long, three-story inn, its outbuildings and stables and barns. The main edifice was wavy-roofed, with tiles undulating over its dormer windows, and there was a big, white-painted wooden cross hung for a sign above its central door.

"The venerable and far-famed White Cross Inn," said Florian. "Terminus of the stage line from Vienna, as well as the destination of river travelers. I must report our arrival to the customs and immigration officers in there."

So he went across the square to the inn, carrying the considerable stack of conduct books. All the other circus folk strolled about, taking in what sights they could see from river level. On the other shore, Pest looked to be only ranks and files of ordinary city buildings except where the occasional dome or spire broke the monotony. But on this Buda side of the Danube, above them and a little to the south, rose an immense hill, with stone stairs and bastion walls zigzagging from the bottom to the walls of a massive castle on top. From somewhere near the base of that hill, a graceful suspension bridge arced across the river to Pest. Beyond the bridge, on this side of the river, rose another high hill, topped with a sprawling walled fort.

"This closer height is Castle Hill," said Willi Lothar. "That is the celebrated Chain Bridge spanning the river, a masterpiece of engineering. You will note that it is suspended by chains, not cables. And beyond it is Saint Gellért's Hill, with the Citadel on top."

"As well as I can see from here," said Yount, "that bridge ends right up *against* this Castle Hill."

"It doesn't end," said Willi. "Its roadbed enters a tunnel on this side, whence the road winds upward to the summit and the castle. The locals have a joke. They will tell you that they treasure their Chain Bridge so much that, when rain falls, they draw it inside the tunnel to save it from rusting."

Florian emerged from the inn and trudged across the

square, looking somewhat discomfited, to rejoin the troupe.

"Alas," he said. "Unlike the easygoing new nation of Italy, Hungary appears eager to assert its newly granted measure of sovereignty. It is doing that with a show of fussy officiousness. For one thing, you must each go separately to show your conduct book, answer any questions, radiate good character and so forth. For another thing, these officials are stubbornly speaking only Magyar. So I shall stand by to interpret."

The troupers and crewmen filed through the room off the inn's vestibule that was doing duty as an immigration office. The questioning was not really rigorous or searching, mostly a perfunctory verification of the particulars already set forth in the conduct books: name, age, occupation and the like. For most of the new arivals, the only thing that momentarily caught them off guard was their being addressed hind-name-first. But one of the men had to cope with a little more than that.

"Geezel Dai?" barked the uniformed official.

"Jesus," growled Stitches. "Dai *Gwell*, I mean, excuse me, sir, Goesle Dai."

"Ejha, *Gwell*. Goesle úr, vallás Dissenting Methodist. Mi az?"

Florian stepped in to say, "Ah . . . Methodist jelent metodista."

"És *dissenting?* Elszakadás?"

Florian pretended to hold a quick conference with Goesle. Then he told the officials, in Magyar, "Dissenting means that Goesle Dai is breaking away from the vile Protestant Methodism to return to the forgiving arms of Mother Church."

"Éljen!" all the uniformed men cried enthusiastically, and stood up to pump the mystified Dai's hand and beam at him and wish him "isten hozott!" And they gave barely a glance at the books of the remaining troupers, but waved them cordially past.

Florian consulted his old tin watch and said, "As long as we are here in the inn, and it is getting on for dinnertime, let us dine. Abdullah, run back to the *Kotartó* and ask the captain—you can do it with gestures—if he and his men would care to join us before they take us across the river."

The tugboat crew came with alacrity and appetite. In the vast, smoky, low-beamed dining hall, they and Willi and Florian, who could converse with them, took one of the long trestle tables. The rest of the company disposed themselves around other tables and had their first taste of Magyar cuisine. There was no carte to order from; the handsomely plump waiter girls simply fetched the meal of the day. And the White Cross Inn was accustomed to resuscitating weary travelers, so the meal was rich and ample. It began with Drunkard's Soup, a concoction intended to counter the traveler's long overreliance on his pocket flask.

Quincy Simms took a wary taste of the pale green substance, made a face and said, "Ugh. Fish soup."

"You must be crazy, Quince," said his sister Sunday. "It's made of sauerkraut. You've had sauerkraut often enough to recognize it. And it's good."

Quincy looked puzzled, but mumbled, "Tas' like fish to me," and pushed his bowl away.

Next came Robber's Meat, chunks of lamb, onions, mushrooms, tomatoes and green peppers alternated on a skewer and cooked over an open fire. That was served with little pinched dumplings and potatoes stewed in a paprikás sauce. The meal was accompanied by jugs of black coffee and bottles of assorted wines, from yellow Tokaji to the dark red Bull's Blood. The sweet was Friar's Ears, half-moon tarts filled with plum jam. And afterward more coffee was set on the tables, and more bottles: apricot, apple and pear brandies.

When the company all lurched heavily out of the inn to return to the barges, LeVie remarked to Florian, "I hope, Monsieur le Gouverneur, that we are not now going to make parade. I believe I could not even lift an arm to wave."

"No fear," said Florian. "We shall roll the wagons and vans ashore, attend to the animals, then get a night's sleep and make parade in the morning."

It was full dark now, so the tug's crewmen hung riding lanterns on their own boat and on every barge, and the tugboat's steam horn repeatedly hooted as it towed its string across the broad river on a downstream slant, somehow never colliding with any of the other vessels going up and down and across the Danube. The diagonal course took the circus flotilla under the Chain Bridge, which had become a magically suspended chain of peach-tinted white gas lamps. The long bridge was so high above the water, and so well constructed, that the circus folk gawking up at it could not hear a sound of the horse-drawn carts, carriages and wagons continuously going to and fro along it.

But not everybody of the troupe was admiring the view. Fitzfarris was now riding on the same barge with Monday, and she sat him down on the steps of their caravan and talked to him very earnestly, with many dramatic gesticulations. Then she beckoned for Pemjean to join them, and he also talked very earnestly, with many Gallic gesticulations. Fitzfarris sat and listened, looking slightly stunned but perhaps a little relieved and even a little amused. Only once did he frown, when Pemjean wound up his persuasive argument by saying:

"I think you will agree, ami, that you have no real claim on the young lady—you having employed contrainte to bend her to your will in the first place."

"What exactly is contrainte?" Fitz asked coldly. "Wait, don't tell me, let me guess. Blackmail?"

"Er . . . oui. Duress. Coercion. Denying her the chance to advance her career unless she submitted to—"

Fitzfarris laughed, but mirthlessly. "Yes, that would have been ungentlemanly of me, wouldn't it? That would have been almost Zanni-like, *wouldn't* it, Monday?"

But Monday was suddenly absorbed in studying the constellations of the night sky, and apparently did not hear.

"Il n'importe pas," said Pemjean, a trifle uncertainly. "It will be overlooked. Forgotten. I trust we shall all three remain bon amis and—"

"Oh, I wouldn't *entirely* forget it, if I were you, friend. But I wish you joy of her."

So, before the farther riverbank was reached, Fitzfarris and Pemjean were going back and forth between their two living quarters, shifting their personal belongings.

On a barge farther back in the string, Spyros Vasilakis was urinating over the low gunwale. He would not have done it so publicly, but he had drunk deep of the good Tokaji. And now he was doing it with much groaning and writhing, holding onto the barge's riding-lamp pole for support, and nearly wrenching it from its socket in his agonies.

"Ah, there, Spyros!" boomed Pavlo Smodlaka, abruptly appearing out of the darkness and grinning sympathetically. "You have pain in pissing, da?" Spyros nodded, embarrassed. "Do you not know what that means? You have caught der Tripper, the nasmork, the Parisian head cold."

"Eh?" said Spyros.

"I believe it is called in your language the khonorrein."

"*Eh?*" exclaimed Spyros, galvanized.

"Have you been doing yébla with one of Monsieur le Démon's women?"

"Eh?" said Spyros, horrified.

Pavlo, helpfully, friendlily told him about Pemjean's secret book dealing with "a certain disease." Pavlo went on to expatiate on the filthiness of Frenchmen, and to commiserate with Spyros on his having somehow contracted the demon's shameful disease. But Spyros, with a grimace and an effort, interrupted his painful dribbling and went hastily off, still buttoning his trousers, in search of his wife.

However, just then, the tug and its string of barges glided alongside another long stone pier at Pest, and much bustle and commotion ensued. The crewmen tied up all the craft, then willingly joined the circus roustabouts to roll the wagons and vans off the barges, and to lead off the horses, camel and elephants. It took two hours or so for everything and everybody to disembark and move inland from the pier to the Corso, the big square fronting on it. The vehicles were neatly ranked there, and the uncaged animals tethered, and all the animals fed and watered. Then most of the troupers and roustabouts fell gratefully onto their beds or pallets—Fitzfarris causing Notkin and Spenz to grunt with surprise when he entered their caravan and, without explanation, flopped onto what had been Pemjean's bunk.

*   *   *

The lamp burned long in only one caravan, that of the Vasilakises, and the occupants of other vans nearby were kept awake for some while by the noise in there. Most of the noise was Spyros's rabid shouting, but some of it was Meli's loud weeping, and that was interspersed with violent slaps when he hit her. Spyros was wielding one of his swords, but considerately using only the flat of it, and hitting Meli only between long spates of Greek imprecations, and only in places that would not show when she donned her parade costume.

But finally she stopped him by pleading, ''If I confess my guilt, will you please not hit me again? Then I confess it. Yes, I *did* what you accuse me of doing, but—''

''You whore! When I come back I will use the edge of the blade! I cannot hurt you worse than my poor peos hurts me. But first I kill him!''

''No, no! It was *not* Monsieur Pemjean!''

If Spyros heard that, he did not heed it, but bolted out into the night. It took him a minute or two to find the caravan he sought, and he smashed through the door, felt for Pemjean's bunk, jabbed with the point of his sword and bellowed, ''Get up, French! I bring death!''

''Ow! Je-SUS!'' roared Fitzfarris, scrambling to flatten himself against the back wall of the bunk. There was also scrambling on the other side of the van, and one of the clowns struck a match.

''Sir John?'' said Spyros, nonplussed. ''It was you betray me?''

''What? You crazy son of a bitch! Somebody light a lamp!''

Notkin did that, while Spyros persisted, ''Sir John, it was you beds my wife behind my back?''

''Are you sleepwalking, you dumb Greek? And with a sword? Look, my rump is *bleeding*. One of you joeys take that weapon away from him.''

Neither of the clowns made a move, but watched in terror. Fitz edged out of his bunk—his long underwear now wet red at the back flap—and said, as reasonably as he could, ''Spyros, wake up. You're having a nightmare. This is me, your friend Foursquare John.''

"Yes . . . you friend," Spyros said stupidly. "You not touch Meli. 'Scuse, Sir John. I go find Pemjean and kill him."

He turned to leave. Fitzfarris made a dive, wrested the sword from his hand and held onto him. "You're still dreaming, man. Wake up and tell me—what's all this about Meli? You haven't stuck *her*, have you?"

"Not yet. Later. Pemjean first."

"Have you got some notion that Meli and Pemjean have been . . . carrying on?" Spyros nodded numbly and began to cry. "Well, I'm here to tell you that it just plain is not so. Pemjean's been too busy courting somebody else. I can prove it. He and I made a gentleman's agreement this very night. He's moved in with Monday that used to be my woman."

"Is true, Sir John?" said Spyros, sniffling.

"Is true. If Meli's been cheating on you—which I doubt—you'd better get her to identify the proper party, instead of you running around in the dark sticking innocent people. Here, I'll walk you back and we'll have a word with her. Let me get some pants on."

Meli was standing in the lamplit doorway of the caravan, unkempt, distraught, wringing her hands, looking searchingly out over the Corso, and she leapt for joy as they approached. "Oh, Sir John, you caught him," she wailed. "Has my poor dear Spyros made murder? Please God, say no."

"No, ma'am. Only mayhem," Fitzfarris said. "Let's all go inside and not keep the whole troupe awake and interested."

"I tried tell him," she moaned, as Fitz shoved the now wilted and penitent Spyros in and shut the door. "Was not the Monsieur Pemjean."

"I think I've convinced him of that," said Fitz, tossing the sword into a corner. "And I know, Meli, that you'd never—"

"Was the Terrible Turk," she said, with a sob.

"Meli!" Fitz exclaimed, thunderstruck.

"Woman!" bawled her husband, rekindled. "You did such thing with sworn *enemy?*"

"Oh, Spyros, Spyros . . . so he not *be* our enemy."

"What the hell do you mean, enemy?" Fitzfarris demanded. "Are you both still asleep and dreaming, or am I?"

Meli explained. It took her quite a time, and Spyros erupted at intervals, but Fitz effectively shushed him. Meli concluded, "I thought I did for the best—for us both, husband." And they were all three silent for a minute.

Then Fitzfarris cleared his throat and said, "You must realize, Meli, Spyros—if the rest of us had suspected that Shadid was a menace to you, we sure would have got rid of him in a hurry. Hell, I didn't even know that the Greeks and Turks had been at war. None of this need have happened, or gone on for so long." He cleared his throat again. "But what's done is done. As soon as I get a chance tomorrow, I'll have a word with Florian. Shadid will never pester you again, Meli, I guarantee that. And Spyros, I hope you find it in your heart to forgive Meli—and thank her—for all she went through on your behalf."

Fitz stood up from where he sat, trying to look the staunch and noble family friend, but that fine effect was spoiled when the chair got up with him. Then his bloody seat unstuck and the chair fell back to the floor.

"Idoú!" cried Meli. "You are wounded! Let me fix."

So Fitz had to wait and take down his pants and unflap his underwear and be doctored and bandaged before he could return to his quarters. Notkin and Spenz were waiting awake, with the lamp still lit, and they made inquisitive noises when he came in, but he ignored them and toppled asleep on his messy bunk.

The first circus people to get up next morning were Willi Lothar, Dai Goesle, Aleksandr Banat, the roustabouts and the midway entrepreneurs, so Willi could lead them, and all the vehicles not wanted in the parade, to the tober he had secured in Pest's City Park, a couple of miles inland from the Corso. When the others of the company arose, they breakfasted on what food and wine remained in their traveling baskets, and Florian waited to form the parade until the streets were full of people. When the parade did leave the Corso, it went through some narrow river district streets until it came to the broad Avenue Sugár where the fast-gathering throngs could really see and appreciate it. As usual, Florian led the procession, with the band in a wagon just behind him, playing lustily, and the calliope bringing up the very rear of the train, playing more than lustily. But this time the parade had a new component, and that one did not stay in line.

It was the Terrible Turk, riding the velocipede, and he was everywhere. Maniacally clowning and making faces, he wheeled back and forth along the line of march, sometimes ahead, sometimes behind, often weaving in and out among the vehicles and the flip-flopping three Chinese and the plodding elephants and camel. He made darts at the watching crowds, sending people fleeing and squealing in delighted terror. He sometimes pedaled backwards, frequently rolled along tilted up on his rear wheel, and sometimes rode without holding the steering bar, his arms carelessly folded. He rode in and out of shop doorways and, wherever a building was fronted with streetside low stairs, he bounced the velocipede up and down them.

"He was a tremendous success!" Florian exulted, when the parade disbanded at the tober, and all the city folk who had trailed it there converged on the red wagon to clamor for tickets to the first show. "Shadid must be a regular fixture of the parade from now on."

Fitzfarris said, "I'd like to speak to you about him, Governor."

"Later, please, Sir John. We've already got a straw crowd here. Let's hold them. The midway joints are pretty well ready for business. So get your fire-eater spouting under the banner line, and you spout your German patter. That'll serve to keep the jossers spending until show time."

"You're the governor, Governor," said Fitz, and went off to find his fire-eater.

All three tops were already up, and their banners flapping, and most of the Slovaks were working on the sets inside the chapiteau. The stallkeepers were firing their braziers, setting up their kegs of beer and tubs of lemonade, setting out their slum for sale. The calliope had stopped at the entrance to the midway and was continuing to hoot and shriek until the chapiteau's bandstand should be ready for Beck and his windjammers to climb into it and commence more musical music. The other parade wagons were being maneuvered by their drivers around behind the chapiteau to take their accustomed places in the backyard. The artistes had all scattered to unload their props, rigs, animals, whatever, from where they had been stowed during the river voyage. Fitzfarris assumed that Spyros was unpacking his bottles of naphtha and olive oil and his other implements, and so wandered among the backyard confusion, looking for him.

But Spyros had gone directly to the Turk's caravan, outside which Shadid stood, toweling off the sweat after his long and active velocipede ride. Spyros there confronted him: "Hey, Turk!"

Shadid looked mildly surprised at the brusqueness of address, but only said contemptuously, "Hey, worm."

"You got der Tripper disease, I think."

"Probably," said the Turk, unruffled. "I usually do. So what?" Then he gave a hearty laugh. "Aha! She got it, too? And gave it to you? How terrible. And a puny man like you, it hurts so you weep, I wager."

"Yes, I weep," said Spyros, plucking his dagger from the back of his belt.

Shadid looked at the shiny blade pointing at him. He could probably have snapped off Spyros's whole arm at the shoulder, and then rammed knife, hand and arm right through the man, but he merely said, with scorn, "You will not stab me."

The blade quivered as Spyros tensed for the thrust. But then, ridiculously, he hiccuped. Shamefaced, he let his arm fall to his side. "You are right, Turk. I am not like you." And he turned and went away, hearing Shadid laugh again behind him.

"Spyros! Where have you been?" Meli asked anxiously, when he returned to their caravan. "Sir John is looking everywhere for you."

"I went again to kill the Turk," he said mournfully. "But I could do no more than tremble at him. The very sight of him makes me sweat, gives me shameful hiccups of fear. I could not kill him."

"Of course not. You are a good man, my husband. A good

man does not avenge himself, but forgives his enemies.''

"I wanted not to avenge myself, wife Meli, but you.''

"Only forgive me, too, Spyros. That will suffice for me. I was not really unfaithful to you, and I will not be, ever.''

"I know. I know. You are a better woman than I am a man.''

"Be only my loving husband. I ask no more. And Sir John has promised that we need not fear or hide, ever again. Idoú—Sir John! He want you to hurry and start the fire-blowing at the marquee.''

"Yes. I go.'' Spyros started gathering up his gear. "When I come back, Meli, we start all new again. Everything behind us will be left behind us.'' He hiccuped again, then kissed her, as shyly as a newlywed. She kissed him back. "Go now and give a fine show.''

"Where've you been, Spyros?'' said Fitzfarris. "Even through a megaphone, my German isn't much of an attraction. Get up there and give me some volcanoes.''

"Better than you never see before, Sir John,'' Spyros said happily. He vaulted to the platform, set out his bottles and lighted his little pine splints, while Fitz began trumpeting toward the midway:

"Meine Herren und Damen! Hersehen der gefrässig Grieche!''

Only a few people had turned to look when Spyros took his first mouthful of naphtha, tilted his head back, pursed his lips and lifted the burning splint. But Fitzfarris was looking, and he did see an eruption unlike any the Gluttonous Greek had ever previously done. Just before Spyros was to blow the mist of naphtha past the splint's flame, he appeared to gulp, and his bulging cheeks ceased for a moment to bulge. Then there came from his mouth only a small puff of flame and a muffled *whoompf!* and not only did his cheeks bulge, but so did much of the rest of him. What the balloon *Saratoga* required hours to do, Spyros did in a split second, as if he had been attached to the generator's force pump and it had instantaneously inflated him. His chest and belly expanded so suddenly and unnaturally that his black fleshings ripped open at a seam. His whole face got bigger, his mouth gaping, his nostrils flaring and his eyes bulging out of his head. After that one meager eructation of flame, smoke gushed from his mouth and nostrils and from behind his eyeballs. Then he fell down, but went on smoking for a long time.

Once more, Fitzfarris visited the Vasilakis caravan. Meli was sitting on the steps, stitching something, and she hailed him gaily: "Where you leave my husband, Sir John?"

"He won't be coming home, Meli," Fitz said gently, and he told her what had happened. "Florian called it a backfire. Like Spyros must have swallowed or inhaled the naphtha somehow."

Meli stared at the ground and murmured, "He say he got hiccups from see the Turk . . ."

"Well, I suspected that the quarrel with Shadid might have had something to do with it, and I told the Governor so. I told him the whole story. And the Turk is gone. Florian paid him off like that"—Fitz snapped his fingers—"and Shadid was leaving, cussing fit to turn the air blue, when I came over here. You'll never see him again, Meli. Now . . . if you'd like to see Spyros one last time . . . Maggie Hag has, uh, tidied him up, and he's laid out in the red wagon until arrangements can be made. Maggie'll come back here with you, to keep you company while—"

"No," Meli said firmly. "You lost much of sideshow, Sir John. You kind to us. I not fail you also. Spyros not want that. Like usual, I be Medusa at intermission, and after show I do Maiden-and-Dragon."

"That's brave of you, but it's not necessary. I'm sure Clover Lee would agree to go on as Bathsheba again, and—"

"I Greek woman," Meli said, holding her head high. "Always since Troy, Greek women know how best mourn death. Go on with life."

2

SO, FROM the Florilegium's opening day in Pest, its program was again diminished. During the main show, Yount had to resume his old Quakemaker solo act, and he resumed

doing the tug-of-war with Brutus to replace his contest of
strength with the Terrible Turk. During the sideshow, Sir
John had only two real acts to present—his own ventriloquy
with Little Miss Mitten and Medusa with her snakes—all his
other attractions being merely inert exhibits: the Night Children, the Egyptian Princess mummy, his own tattooed self,
and the Auerhahn, or the siketfajd, as he learned it was called
here in Hungary.

Yount volunteered to spend his spare time learning to pedal
the velocipede—and he did, and got at least as good as
Shadid had been, though never so nimble as Cecil Wheeler—
and soon he was doing the trick riding on it with Daphne,
and before long was even doing the stop-short headlong
plunge into the flaming vat. "Not too much different from
rising horseback into Custer's guns at Tom's Brook," he said
after his first and, happily, successful try at it.

On that ill-starred opening day, Florian had gone to the
nearest police station to report the demise of Spyros Vasilakis, and his report had been received with none of the instant, intense interest and suspicion and investigation it might
have aroused back in Austria or Bavaria. The police only
languidly made a note of the occurrence and suggested that
Florian might tear up the dead man's conduct book, please,
when he got around to it. Then Florian was let depart without
any questions or any demand for an inquest or even any official person's taking a look at the corpse to ascertain that
Spyros was in fact dead. Next, Florian had gone to arrange
for the burial in the local Greek-Macedonian cemetery. And,
with Meli's permission, the funeral had been conducted without any colorful or noisy circus pomp, so as not to attract
public attention and perhaps cast a superstitious pall over the
Florilegium's whole stay in Budapest.

Neither that tragedy nor the resultant abbreviation of the
show kept anybody away; the local folk continued to attend
in sfondone numbers, and applauded unreservedly. The troupers noticed one interesting thing about these audiences: there
seemed to be a tradition in Hungary that pretzels were the
only approved, accepted and fashionable snack to eat at in-

termissions of an entertainment. Every time the chapiteau
emptied out for the interval between halves, everybody in the
audience, young and old, swarmed to the midway stalls selling those big, coarse-salted, brittle twists. Then they all, even
the most dignified and best-dressed dowagers, walked about
munching the pretzels while they shopped at the other midway joints or watched the sideshow or sat down to have their
salty palms read by Magpie Maggie Hag. The males, including the smallest boys, also smoked czigaretta while they ate
their pretzels.

The circus people were as pleased with Budapest as Budapest clearly was with them. Pest's City Park made a delightful tober. It was smaller than the Prater in Vienna, but
contained every kind of landscape from bosky wildwoods to
velvet lawns, brilliant flower beds, ponds with swans, fountains and cascades, bridle paths and walkways. This park, too,
had at one end a small amusement area of carousel, swinging-
boat wheel, children's playground and numerous entresort
booths. At an aloof distance from all that activity stood the
elegant and gracious Gundel's Restaurant. Its several dining
rooms were rich with paneled walls, leather and plush, chandeliers above and candelabra on the tables; its waiters were
tailcoated and unobtrusively efficient; in its kitchens were the
best chefs cooking the finest viands to be had in either Pest
or Buda. The circus troupers dined there as often as they
could take the time to dress as handsomely as these surroundings deserved.

"The Hungarians have a saying," mused Florian on one
visit, after a meal that began with Bugac almond apéritif and
cold sour-cherry soup, proceeding through pike-perch in cucumber sauce, a gypsy gulyás of chunks of many meats, layered asparagus and mushrooms, noodles in cream with
caraway and green paprika, and *Aszú Tokaji* to wash it all
down, concluding with Indianer chocolate-covered cream
puffs, Turkey coffee brewed with rose water and finally apricot brandy. "The Hungarians say, 'If we could afford to live
as well as we live, ah! how well we should live!' "

*   *   *

The circus folk often entertained themselves with the city folk's own favorite diversion: simply strolling about the streets and squares and boulevards. The men of the company did that mainly to admire the many local females strolling to *be* admired. More than anywhere the Florilegium had yet been, there were here to be seen ravishingly beautiful, high-breasted, long-legged women and girls. Even the barely pubescent girl children were as pretty as filly foals. And none of those females, from budding nymphet to full-ripe matron, wore under her summer blouse anything like a corset cover or bandeau.

"Good heavens!" said Daphne, when she first went downtown. "You can make out their very nipples. Not even in Paris have I seen *respectable* women dress so."

Her companion, Florian, said indulgently, "Why should the unrespectable women be the only free spirits?"

Daphne sniffed. "Well, the Budapest women may be gorgeous and shapely from girlhood to maturity. But they must fade quickly after that. See, the old ones are either withered crones or grossly obese."

"Those are peasant women, in from the countryside. You would see the same, my dear, around your Covent Garden market stalls. But do the soignée ladies of London's Mayfair let themselves go to seed or to fat like that? No, and neither do the ladies of civilized Budapest. They grow old gracefully and, after a certain age, do not stroll abroad to be admired, but hold levees at home—well attended by admirers, I assure you."

There were other things to be seen and admired besides the lovely women. Though Pest was a frankly, even flagrantly, commercial city, it was also, as Willi Lothar described it, "a city very livable-in." Almost all the streets were cobbled with stones laid in intricate patterns, and were all lighted at night by decorative multiple gas-lamp standards. There were few tram lines as yet, but there was a brisk traffic of other vehicles, from ox-drawn country drays to imposing four-in-hand coaches. Almost every city square was, by day, a bustling open-air market. From a distance those markets all looked alike—ranks of stalls and carts under bright umbrellas or painted muslin canopies. But they could also be smelled from a distance, and from that distance differentiated as to the wares they sold. One square would waft afar the perfume of flowers brought from the nursery gardens of Margit's Island upstream, and another the fresh aroma of vegetables from the truck gardens of the Csepet Island downstream, and another the less appealing odor of fish hooked and netted from the stream itself.

The numerous cultural attractions of Pest—museums, theatres, art galleries, the Opera—were housed in edifices of magnificently dignified design, and those buildings' walls, columns, arches, cupolas and domes were unadorned by excrescent additions. But the city's far more numerous commercial buildings, though many of those were also architecturally splendid, were much bedizened with flamboyant advertising signs. Every flat wall, even if it was six stories above the street, was a hoarding for ornately lettered, multicolored messages, some of those illustrated with a picture of the product being advertised, or of an eye-catchingly nude female, a winsome baby or a before-and-after bald man and thick-thatched man. Many a building had signs encircling it like ribbons wrapped between every two rows of windows, all the way up its height. And most of the signs were done in duplicate, the Magyar message repeated in German, thus:

OLMOSY FERENC
Gyára
FRANZ OLMOSY
Fabrik

Some of the signboards over the streetside establishments, even if they were written only in Magyar—KAVEHAZ, CZIGARETTA—were comprehensible enough to the newcomers that they could recognize coffeehouses and tobacconists and such, and patronize them. The Kavehaz New-York, actually too palatial and luxurious a place to be calling itself merely a coffeehouse, became the troupe's favorite stop for light refreshment before or after a long stroll through the city. The artistes became known by name to the waiters there, and

eventually got used to being addressed in the Magyar style—
for example, Maurice was LeVie úr, Gavrila was Smodlaka
né, Sunday was Simms kisasszony. The thing they had the
most trouble with, for a time, was the local currency. Hungary
still honored and used the Austrian Empire's kronen, gulden
and kreuzers, but the nation was introducing its own coinage
of koronas, forints and fillérs, so the newcomers—and the
Hungarians themselves—endured some confusion until they
learned to carry the two monies in separate pockets or purses,
and to do quick calculations back and forth between them.

Several of the troupers found other favorite places and
things in the city. Down near the Danube quays, Dai Gocsle
found a raktároz tengerészeti. That was a marine chandlery,
and he could no more pronounce the Magyar name than the
shopkeepers in there could pronounce his, but he and they
managed to communicate in some manner. So there he
bought the canvas, poles, rope and hardware for making the
two new dressing tents Florian wanted. And Dai visited there
frequently afterwards, whenever the circus needed some item
like a shackle, a turnbuckle, varnish, whatever, and he somehow always came out with the exact item he wanted, in the
exactly right size, strength, color or whatever.

The circus women soon discovered the Nagyáruhaz Párizsi,
or Warenhaus Pariser, a kind of emporium that those women
who had not yet been in Paris had never encountered before.
It comprised every kind of shop imaginable, all under one
roof and one management, not divided into separate stores
but into "departments" ranged over the several floors and
mezzanines and interior balconies of the one immense building. There one could buy Scotch whisky, a Turkish rug, a
Romanian crucifix, Sicilian silks—anything from a single
button to the furnishings for a whole house—so almost all
the women of the company found excuse to browse in there
at least once a week. When Agnete bought there some of
Hungary's own matchless Halas bone lace, Yount was heard
to say facetiously, "I don't grudge the money, Lord, no, but
it does seem a lot to pay for a cloth full of holes."

Carl Beck spent most of his spare time trying one after
another of the huge and stately health spas in the locality.

When he was not immersed in some miracle water or mud—
in a natural-rock grotto or a Babylonian alabaster pool or a
balneo-thermo-magnetic vat—he was either swallowing some
patent nostrum or anointing himself with it. He never left or
entered the City Park without pausing for a long drink from
the public tap at the park gate's marble fountain, fed by a
natural hot spring. He forever reeked of the Bánfi Capillary
Lotion or the Kneippkura or the Sámson-balzsam smeared on
his bald head, and, even at Gundel's or the New-York, he
dosed his rose-water coffee with drops from his ever-present
phial of Béres Enlivening Elixir.

Groups of the circus folk also went, now and then, down
to the riverside Franz Joseph Square and from there climbed
the cobbled incline that led between two gigantic stone lions
onto the Chain Bridge. Vehicles using the bridge to cross to
or from the lesser city of Buda had to pay a few fillérs for
the privilege. The tollkeepers could have taken in a lot more
money if they had charged the pedestrians instead, for this
was another favored promenade of all the citizens, but those
were allowed gratis to indulge their pride in the wondrous
structure. Almost all the people crossing it paused for a while
midway between the bridge's high stone towers, and there
leaned on the railing among the suspension chains to watch
the riverboats, far below, going up and down and across the
stream. On the Buda side of the bridge, the vehicular traffic
had to continue on into the hillside tunnel, but walkers could
descend directly onto the riverside quays and streets.

Only in that area was Buda flat enough to provide ground
space for buildings purveying goods and services. But the big
White Cross Inn was the only sizable enterprise. All the other
inns and the shops and markets were small things, compared
to those in Pest, and were patronized mainly by residents of
the neighborhood, meaning the river workers. Mullenax soon
found the Tabán district, where lived all the Danube ferrymen
and assorted other hard characters. He thereafter passed most
of his spare time—and what should have been working time,
as well—sharing with them their preferred potation, a laugh-
ably cheap and horrendously noxious Bulgarian gin.

The slopes of Buda were dotted with peasant cottages, and

they were pretty, with flower bushes growing from their roof thatch, garlands of red and green paprika looped to dry along their whitewashed walls, and every cottage garden sweetly redolent of basil. The heights of Buda were reserved to monuments and monumental edifices: bronze and stone statues, the royal castle, the Citadel, the Coronation Church. Every visiting group from the circus at least once hired a kocsi to carry them to the top of Gellért's Hill and Castle Hill. But the grim Citadel was a working fortress, and the castle was the seat of government, so sightseers were not allowed inside either of them. The visitors had to be satisfied with leaning on the Fisher's Bastion below the castle, or sitting under the walls of the Citadel, and enjoying the view of Buda below, Pest across the river and the long, shining reach of the Danube.

"This Gellért's Hill," said Florian up there one day, "was named for the missionary bishop who first tried to bring Christianity to the pagans of this place. They did not take to it, or to him, anyway. They drove spikes into all sides of a barrel, stuffed the bishop into it, and rolled him down this hillside to his death and sainthood."

"That sounds like a circus act," Edge commented.

"Then I wish we could resurrect Saint Gellért and his barrel," said Florian. "Do you realize, Zachary—counting the eight Schuhplattler dancers, and not counting the men of the band, we now have more females than males performing?"

"Who's complaining? The females or the males? For the first time since I can remember, they all seem at least to have got their private lives straightened out. No triangles or adulteries going on, no secret seductions or simmering jealousies that I know of."

Edge ticked them off on his fingers. Pemjean and Monday seemed satisfied with each other, and so did Maurice and Nella. Obie and Agnete were clearly happy together; so were Jules and Willi. Fitzfarris had begun courting the Widow Vasilakis, to console her in her bereavement. The Schuhplattler girls impartially distributed their favors among the unattached men, including even Hannibal Tyree, the three Chinese and Kesperle Spenz. Most remarkable, even incredible, the old Hanswurst Notkin had lately been making eyes at Magpie Maggie Hag, and she was not noticeably repulsing him.

"And if I'm not mistaken," Edge concluded, "I've seen you squiring the Widow Wheeler to dinner at Gundel's a time or three."

"Purely platonic," muttered Florian. "Paternal."

"Of course," Edge went on, "Clover Lee is still on the lookout for a noble suitor, but in the meantime she makes do with Johnnies from the seats. Sunday, too, I reckon. So who's complaining about the ratio of males to females?"

"Nobody is complaining," said Florian. "I merely say that it is unusual, perhaps unnatural. I have never known a circus where the female artistes outnumbered the male. Also, among all those happy men you mentioned, I noticed you did not include yourself."

"I'm content. That'll do."

Edge was lying. He was not entirely content. In fact, he wondered privately if he might be going crazy. A month or so ago, he had been vaguely disturbed by the apparent but impossible familiarity of some of the portrait paintings and busts in the palace of Schönbrunn. Now, here, in a totally different country, during two nighttime shows of the circus, he had glimpsed an impossibly familiar face among the audience. Was it conceivable, he wondered, that a man's loss and grief and longing, consciously and diligently suppressed by the man's mind, could yet somehow find crevices in that man's mind to leak through and afflict him with hallucinations?

When it happened again, at another night's show, Edge determined to confront whichever it was: his own lunacy or a verifiable phantom. As before, the woman came with another woman, and both were veiled, and both came in late— during the opening spec, when all the rest of the audience was intent on the spectacle—and took their reserved starback seats, and only then lifted their veils. The companion was a plain-faced, middle-aged woman; the other was—

"Autumn?" Edge said diffidently, imbecilically, but unable to do otherwise, when he walked over to them at intermission. They always remained inside the chapiteau during the interval, not mingling with the midway crowd, not beckoning Magpie Maggie Hag to attend them, and they always had been among the first persons to depart at the show's close. Now both the women started with surprise and immediately dropped their veils over their faces. The one he had addressed asked warily:

"Beszél ön magyar?"

Edge simply stared.

"Sprechen Sie deutsche?"

Edge continued to peer, trying to see through the veil. With it down, she could be the Autumn of the final days. But without the veil, she had been Autumn at first meeting.

"Tiens, parlez-vous français?"

Edge shook himself awake, and mumbled, "Un petit peu."

She laughed, and her laugh was Autumn's. "Oon petty pew? Well, here is *one* American with this American circus. I had never heard you speak before, sir, only blowing the whistle."

She raised her veil, and so stunned Edge that he stammered, "I don't. Talk much. Ma'am." No, this woman's hair was more bronze than auburn. But her eyes were the same: brown, flower-petaled with gold flecks. Her always-about-to-smile mouth was the same . . .

"Why did you say that one word at me?"

Edge shook himself again. "It's a name, ma'am. Autumn. Someone I used to know."

She cocked her head, and her mouth did smile, dazzlingly. "Would that someone approve of your accosting other women?"

"I'm sorry. You look so much like her. She was beautiful, too."

"Thank you. If we are going to exchange compliments, we should introduce ourselves. As it happened, you nearly had my name right. I am not Autumn but Amelie, Gräfin von Hohenembs."

"Then I'm even more sorry for my brashness, Your Grace," said Edge, with a bow. "You probably prefer to be incognito in these surroundings. I am Zachary Edge, the—"

"The equestrian director, of course. My companion is the Bárónö Festetics Marie. We are pleased to meet you, Edge úr." She gave him her gloved hand, and Edge bowed again to brush it with his lips. "I myself," she went on, "am an amateur of equitation, and a lifelong circus fancier. But I must indulge my dilettante fancies unrecognized. The common folk might be scandalized or distressed to see their—to see one of us *pompous* folk taking pleasure in something as free and easy as a circus."

"Countess, if you know enough about circuses to call me the equestrian director instead of ringmaster"—he smiled—"then you are no mere dilettante."

"Please do not smile, Edge úr."

"I meant that remark as praise, Your Grace, not impudence."

"I know you did. But you should not ever smile. You are less ugly when you do not smile. Did your Autumn never tell you that?"

"Well, yes. Maybe not quite so frankly."

"A title gives a woman the privilege of frankness. I often tell Ferenc—my husband, that is—I often tell him just the opposite. That he *ought* to smile once in a while."

"The privilege is the count's," said Edge. "To be instructed by so charming a countess."

"My, my!" she said, studying him. "As long as you do not ever try to do it in your Fräuleiny French, you can evidently be gallant. For an American."

"I do my best," he said humbly. "Your Grace, if you would care to linger until all the—the common folk have gone, after the come-out, maybe you would give me the honor of showing you and the baroness the backstage workings of our show?"

She considered, but said, "That might be . . . imprudent. See how Marie frowns at the idea."

"Some other time?" said Edge, almost urging, not wanting to let her go. Go *again*, he thought.

She said brightly, "Un prété pour un rendu. Why do I not show you my circus?" The Baroness Festetics gave her an even more cautionary frown, but she ignored this one. "Can you take a few days of holiday, Edge úr?"

"Why . . . I imagine so. *Yes*. Yes, I certainly can, and will. But . . . your circus, Your Grace?"

"Oh, an ill-favored thing, sir, but mine own. It will probably make you smile your ugly smile. Do you know the town of Gödöllö? I am residing at present in my country house near there. It is only a few hours' fast drive from here. I will send a carriage for you. Dress is casual, except at dinner. Shall we say this day week?"

Edge said that would be fine, and he would look forward to it. Then he remained chatting with them—even the baroness unfroze enough to contribute a few sociable words in English—until the band began playing "Wait for the Wagon" and the common folk came hurrying back into the chapiteau.

Edge resumed his directorial duties with a verve he had not shown for a long time, and he did his Colonel Ramrod shooting with unaccustomed flourishes, and he rode his Buckskin Billy voltige with near neck-breaking recklessness. Each time he took a bow, he bowed directly to Countess Amelie. She applauded with her hands held high so he could see them—noblewomen did not stamp their feet—and Edge had to remind himself not to grin at her. When the performance concluded, the two women did not this time slip out during the spec, so Edge had the chance to say good-bye to them. And when the countess stood up to go, Edge noted that she was also different from his tiny Autumn in being quite a bit taller. But she had just as curvaceous a figure and just as unbelievably slender a waist.

Edge had never mentioned to anyone else what he supposed to be his hallucinations of Autumn encore-vu, and evidently none of the other troupers had noticed the woman, and none of them had noticed him in conversation with her tonight. But all the artistes had observed his sudden new access of gusto, and were pleased but bewildered by it. After the last jossers had departed, Florian approached Edge to say tentatively, almost worriedly, "Did something happen during the interval tonight, Zachary? To make you so, er, unwont-edly vivacious?''

"Something sure did, Governor. I'd like to beg a few days off next week.''

"Mercy me! Are you ailing, lad?''

"I thought I was, but I just discovered I'm not. She wasn't Autumn, after all. She's the Countess von Something-or-other.''

"Oh?'' said Florian, taking a step back from him. "Maybe you do need a rest, old friend.''

"I'm not loco, Governor. Far from it. Never felt better. I've been invited to visit the country house of this countess I met tonight. Amelie—I remember that much of her name. And you're always encouraging everybody to make friends in high places, right? In case they can be useful to the show?''

"By all means, go, my boy. You've seldom had a break from your work since you first joined out. If even the prospect so vivifies you, the actual visit ought to do you a world of good.''

For the next week, Edge spent much of his free time in visits to a tailor Willi found for him, having fittings for a suit of dress clothes. During that time, Clover Lee groused some more about "everybody else finds a prime titled catch except me.'' And Sunday summoned up courage to come to Edge and say:

"The whole troupe is gossiping that you're going to a ren-dezvous with a mysterious countess. Is that true, Zachary?''

"Hardly a rendezvous, girl. That sounds furtive. Only a holiday in the country. And there's nothing mysterious about the lady, except that she looks uncannily like Autumn. If you remember the way Autumn used to look.''

"Yes,'' said Sunday, downcast. "She was a beautiful woman.''

"It takes one to know one,'' Edge said blithely. "You're just as beautiful, Sunday. Only in a different way.''

"Thank you. Are you going to fall in love with this one, the way you did with Autumn?''

"I'd better not. This one's got a husband.''

That encouraged Sunday to say, "Then maybe sometime—if you take another holiday—you'd take me along? For company?"

"Why, sure thing, Sunday. If the countess asks me back again, you come along and use your good looks to lure the count off somewhere, so I can have her to myself for a while."

After a moment of hurt silence, she said, "If you want me to. But Clover Lee could do it better. She'd take the count and keep him. So you could keep the countess forever."

Scarcely hearing, he said, "Reckon that's right." And Sunday went sadly away.

On the appointed day, the promised carriage came: a luxurious, high-sprung, leather-upholstered brougham drawn by matched bay hackneys. There was a liveried coachman on the driving seat and a liveried lackey perched on the rumble. Most of the circus troupe gathered to watch, in some awe, as the lackey leapt down to take Edge's new-bought portmanteau and stow it in the boot, then showed Edge the traveling hamper under the coach seat, full of fresh-prepared food, fruit, sweets, wines and brandies.

"Those are the Festetics arms on the door," said Florian, clearly impressed. "So that's the name you couldn't remember. One of the most distinguished in Magyarország."

"No," said Edge, after consideration. "She was *von* something. I believe Festetics was the woman with her. Well, good-bye, all." He tipped his new gray beaver traveling hat. "I won't be gone long."

3

ONCE OUT of the park gate, the brougham turned northwestward and soon the last suburbs of Pest were left behind. Edge sat back to enjoy the scenery, but the land was so flat and uninteresting along this road—nothing but Kansas-like prairies of high grass, except for the occasional farm of rye or wheat—that he dozed most of the way. Now and then, when a bad patch of the road jounced him awake, he delved in the hamper for a piece of chicken or a dobostorta or a drink of wine, then dozed again.

He was awakened the last time, just about sundown, by the carriage's sudden brisk vibration of rolling over cobblestones, and he looked out to see that it was on the winding driveway of a goodsized park, but not a landscaped one. This was all natural woods and meadows, and twice the horses tried to check when a broadantlered stag went bounding across the drive in front of them. "Her country house," Edge murmured ironically, as it loomed in sight: a handsome castle of fretted stonework and turrets and diamond-paned windows and carved doors, with roses and wistaria climbing all over the high walls.

But, curiously, the brougham did not set him down at the front entrance of that impressive pile; it went through a porte-cochère and around behind the castle. "Servants' entrance? Tradesmen's entrance?" Edge wondered. But he truly was perplexed when the carriage kept on going past outbuildings—handsome ones, but obviously the estate's kitchens, servants' quarters, smithy, storehouses. At last, the brougham drew up before the stables, and the lackey opened the door to bow him out. True, the stables were not a great deal less grand than the castle—but did she *live* here? Had she been putting on airs with that talk of titles and privilege? Was she merely a poor relation of the von Whoevers, or even a scullion of theirs?

Then he heard music. Beside a circular paddock, a man who clearly was a stable hand was playing wheezy but lively cigány music on an accordion. And inside the paddock two graceful Arabian horses, bareback, were going around and around at an easy canter. On the back of each was a slim figure in white shirt and black trousers; in the gathering twilight, Edge could not at first make out whether they were men or women. They were doing an acrobatic and ballet routine almost as good as Clover Lee's: striking postures, standing on one leg, occasionally skipping lightly off the horses onto the paddock fence's top rail and balancing there until the mounts came around again, then skipping back on.

Edge watched with pleasure, and finally one of the riders

vaulted to the ground, slithered between the fence rails and
came up to him, drawing on a black bolero jacket over her
white shirt. Her face was prettily flushed from her exertions,
but she was not breathing hard. Amelie wore no cosmetics—
she needed none—and her bronze-colored hair was tied back
in simple peasant style, hanging in waves to her waist. She
could have been just a stable girl, an exceedingly lovely one,
except that her shirt was of the finest white silk and the jacket
and trousers were of black velvet.

She said chidingly, ''As I foretold, you are smiling, Edge
úr. Kindly desist.''

''Sorry. I was admiring.'' He bowed and she gave him her
hand to kiss. It was ungloved this time, and it was neither
the hard hand of a professional rider nor the rough red hand
of a servant. He hastened to add, ''Your Grace.''

''Berni!'' she called to the stable hand, and motioned for
him to stop playing. She called ''Elise!'' and beckoned to
the other rider.

''Is this your circus, Countess?'' Edge asked.

''A very small part of it. Just us two. I must apologize.
When I invited you, I quite forgot that I had ordered all my
tumblers and clowns to Achilleion. But here—I wish you to
meet the Fräulein Elise Renz.''

Miss Renz was as young and almost as beauteous as the
countess. She forthrightly stuck out a hand to be shaken, not
kissed, and this was the muscular hand of a real équestrienne.

''Guten Abend, Herr Edge,'' she said.

''Elise is the daughter of Ernst Jakob Renz,'' said the
countess. ''Of the Zirkus Renz, of which you may have
heard. Elise is good enough to play truant from her father's
troupe, now and again, to come and instruct me in new bareback routines.''

The Fräulein Renz, with a pretty pout, said something in
German.

The countess translated, ''Elise says, 'But we have no
equestrian director to command us,' and it is true. We lack a
stern disciplinarian. Perhaps tomorrow, Edge úr, you would
crack the whip for us? We much enjoy having a strong hand
to direct us—and chastise us, when necessary.''

"Ja, Strafe!" breathed the other, her eyes shining.

"I would be delighted," said Edge.

"Good." The countess spoke a few words in German to Elise, who giggled happily. "But now, come, my guest. You will wish to refresh yourself after the journey. Elise and Berni will see to the horses." She called once more—"Schatten!"—and an immense, shaggy dog stalked from a stable doorway. As Edge and the countess strolled toward the castle, it paced solemnly along beside them.

"That dog," said Edge, "makes a fair piece of circus all by itself. It's as big as our Rumpelstilzchen. Our dwarf horse."

"Yes. My Schatten is an Irish wolfhound. My faithful companion and bodyguard. His name means Shadow."

"Lucky dog," Edge said involuntarily. Then, to cover the gaucherie, he said quickly, "So it was Miss Renz who taught you equitation?"

"Oh, no. She merely helps me to keep in practice. It was my father who first taught me. He turned his riding school into a miniature zoo and circus, and started me doing fancy riding when I was very small."

"Your father ran a riding school? My father worked in an iron foundry. When there was work."

"You mistake me. The stables and rings and jumps and racecourse of a palace are always called, for the sake of modesty, merely the riding school. My father was Maximilian Josef von Wittelsbach, Duke of Bavaria."

"Oh."

"You have heard of the madness of the family Wittelsbach? Well, my father was mad only in that mild way. He had a passion for the circus life. Once, when I was very young, he and I dressed as vagabonds and wandered on horseback through Bavaria, unrecognized. Whenever we came to an innyard, he played a zither while I did my bareback tricks. Then I would pass my hat among the onlookers." She paused, smiled reminiscently and said, "That was the only money I ever earned in my life. My father, too, I daresay."

Edge chuckled, a little hollowly.

"However, I inherited my father's madness, and some of his circus—the animals, the dwarfs—and I have had them ever since. When my own child was six years old, he was very nervous and shy. So, to teach him fearlessness, I locked him overnight in the zoo full of wild animals. Oh, I left Rudi's tutor hidden nearby, just in case. I would not expose my son to risk, of course."

"Of course. Even so, I expect he had a night to remember."

"He is still very nervous," she said offhandedly. "I am so sorry I did not keep the animals and the rest of my circus here to show you."

"If I had just wanted to see a circus, Your Grace, I could have stayed in Pest with my own."

She gave him a warm look of appreciating that remark, but went on with her small talk. "As I say, I sent them on to Achilleion, where I usually spend my winters. That is my estate on Corfu. I designed it myself, in the Greek style."

They had come around the lawn's white-gravel paths, by now, to the great flagged terrace that fronted the castle, set all about with man-high bronze urns overbrimming with flowers. In each of the weathered stone pillars that flanked the terrace balustrade, a new stone had been set, carved with heraldic arms. Edge noted that the device was different from that on the Festetics brougham, but—again the sense of déjà-vu—he was sure that he had seen the arms somewhere before.

"Ah, you remark that those are recent additions," said the countess. "Yes, this castle was only given to me last year. I am very fond of it, fonder than I am of any of the others. Except in winter. Then I flee to the sunshine."

Edge wondered who had castles to give away, and how many others she had, but said nothing. Footmen swung wide the entrance doors, and they went into a vaulted hall hung with banners and shields and ancient weapons. The Baroness Festetics was waiting to attend the countess and, after curtsying to her, even dropped a small dip in Edge's direction.

"You remember Marie, of course," said the countess. "And this is my chamberlain, the Baron Nopsca." That courtly gentleman bowed and clicked his well-shod heels.

"This is Hirschfeld, who will be your valet. I must tell you that the household domestics speak nothing but Magyar." She dropped her voice to a murmur. "That is so I can speak in other languages with confidence. Even with intimacy." Then she resumed, "However, you will find that Hirschfeld knows his duties, and should require no instruction. He will show you now to your suite. Dinner tonight will be at eight, but not in the big dining hall, in the more cozy Ivory Room. Hirschfeld will also show you how to find that."

In something of a daze, Edge let himself be guided up the swooping staircase, abstractedly noticing that even his valet had servants: a footman carrying the portmanteau and another bearing a tray with a ewer of hot water, a basin, various toilet sundries. The suite—a bedroom with a four-poster bed, a breakfast room and a bathroom—was of a baronial splendor to daze Edge even further. But he did not immediately succumb to sybaritic sloth; he insisted on doing his own washing and shaving of himself, though he almost had to fight off Hirschfeld to do it. The valet went to unpack the portmanteau, sniffing occasionally as if contemptuous of the quality of its contents. Then Edge let the man help him don his dinner dress, for he was unfamiliar with the complexities of false shirt front, collar and studs and such, and never would be capable of tying his own white tie.

The cozy Ivory Room, when Edge got there, turned out to be rather bigger than the house he had been born in. The countess was seated at an ivory-colored—or maybe pure ivory—grand piano in one corner, idly rippling something by Schumann. She stood up and relinquished her place to an unidentified young lady wearing spectacles, who would play, but very softly and sweetly, all through the ensuing dinner.

The countess no longer looked remotely like a stable girl or an équestrienne; she looked like the heroine of some romantic fairy tale. She also still, in the face, looked so startlingly like Autumn Auburn that Edge could not help thinking, "How I wish she were. And how I wish I could have given Autumn such a setting for her beauty." But the Countess Amelie was alive and present, and a gorgeous woman in her own right, and Edge was neither dead nor immune to her undeniable allure. Now her hair was done up in an intricate chignon, and topped with an emerald tiara. There were emeralds about her neck and on her fingers, too. Her dress of darkgreen brocade and ivory lace was cut low to bare her fine shoulders—and her breasts, very nearly to the point of indiscretion. Their luster made all the ivory of the Ivory Room look dusty and dull by comparison. Her waist was so slender, above the flare of the crinolette skirt, that she seemed literally breakable there.

"Seventeen inches," she said, as if Edge had spoken that thought. But she spoke a little regretfully, adding, "My waist was fifteen and a half inches before I married."

Yes, she was married, Edge reminded himself. He said, "Won't the count be dining with us, Your Grace?" There were only two places set at the not-very-cozy table that could have accommodated twelve. "I had"—he could not say "hoped"—"I had expected to have the pleasure of meeting him. And your son."

"My husband is abroad, and the children with him. And Zachary, you need address me formally only when we are in company. En tête-à-tête, I give you leave to call me Sissi. All my friends do."

"An odd nickname for Amelie, ma'am. And I don't believe I could call any woman by a diminutive nickname."

"Amelie, then, if you insist on even semiformality." She touched a bell rope. "Will you take an apéritif? Amontillado? Bugac?" A footman entered and poised himself over the decanters and crystal ware on an ivory sideboard. Both Edge and Amelie took sherry and, when the man had gone, Edge said:

"You mentioned children. I was surprised to hear that you had even one, as old as six. You don't look old enough . . ."

"Rudi is now ten. His sister is almost thirteen. There was another daughter before her, but she did not survive infancy. How old is the Autumn you have compared me to?"

"Not quite twenty-four. When she died."

"Oh, dear, so young! And she is dead? I am sorry. A

younger woman is a rival formidable enough. A dead one is almost invincible.''

''Rival?''

''All women are rivals of each other, Zachary. I might even say enemies. Especially when they are of much different ages. Alas, on Christmas Eve, I will turn thirty-one. Into my fourth decade.''

''From the perspective of nearly forty, I can't see that twenty-four and thirty-one are *much* different ages. Particularly when you don't look a year older than Autumn's twenty-four. And you don't.''

''Ah, well preserved, am I? That is a compliment that fails of gallantry, Zachary.''

''I didn't say any such—''

''Also, I commiserate in your bereavement, but need we talk *all* evening about your lady Autumn?''

''Why, it was you who mentioned—''

''Let us be seated and begin.'' She touched the bell rope again. Flustered and not a little exasperated, Edge was tardy in drawing out her chair for her, and she looked mildly annoyed at that. But, when the first course was set before them, they managed amiably enough to turn to talk of circus matters, with pianissimo tinkle of music for background. Amelie just once more made a reproving remark: ''Do be at ease, Zachary. You sit as ramrod-erect as—as the Count Hohenembs. I am always having to rebuke him, too.''

''I learned my table manners at a strict school.'' He was also being very careful to choose the correct implements from among the array of silver on either side of his plate.

Edge had already partaken of cold prawns in a spicy sauce and now was having hot leek soup, but Amelie had so far only nibbled at a bit of lettuce salad. It became evident, as the dinner progressed, that the castle kitchens had prepared two entirely different meals. His was hearty and varied, but the only substantial thing served to her was a small portion of some kind of pale fish. No wonder she keeps that wasp waist, he thought.

When the footman brought in the sweets—golden dumpling cake for Edge, a few ripe cherries for her—the servants were accompanied by the Baroness Festetics, bearing a silver salver on which lay a yellow envelope. She murmured something in Magyar. Amelie tore open the envelope, read the flimsy enclosure, laughed and said:

"A telegram. In our private cipher. Shall I read to you, Zachary, what it says?" She did not wait for him to answer. "Darling. Arriving tomorrow evening. Wear nothing but your jewels."

The baroness looked pained and closed her eyes. Edge, embarrassed, made a few incoherent noises before he was able to say, "So the count is coming back from abroad, Your Grace? Then he won't want to find a houseguest in—"

"My husband? Good heavens! Ferenc never had such wit—or such arrogant impetuosity. This is from my lover."

The baroness now looked about to swoon. Edge choked out, "Well. Then *he* damned sure won't want to find a stranger in—"

"But here you are, are you not?" She looked at him long and levelly. "Do you wish to be evicted? To make room for him?"

He returned the look. "No."

"I hoped not. Marie, please reply by telegraph to Count Andrássy. Tell him I will be indisposed tomorrow. And perhaps for a day or two beyond tomorrow. Also, as you go, Marie, please send word to the kitchens to serve our coffee and brandy in my chambers."

The countess herself, not a servant, led Edge up there, and they sat down on opposite sides of a low table. "Plus intime, n'est-ce pas?" she said. The huge Irish wolfhound padded in from some other room, nuzzled his mistress, gave Edge the merest look and, with a grunt, lay down close beside Amelie's chair. After a minute, footmen came with a silver coffee service, Sèvres cups and saucers, decanters of cordials and fragile pony glasses. The countess dismissed the men, and herself poured.

What Edge could see of her chambers—the foyer they had entered through and the sitting room they were in—made his own suite, which he had thought baronial, seem fusty and cramped. Her sitting room alone occupied the entire breadth of a castle wing, so that it had at either end a wall all French windows with a spacious balcony beyond. The windows were open, so their gossamer curtains waved lazily in the balmy night wind and let in gusts of fragrance from the roses and wistaria outside. Edge was looking about, not to compare living quarters, but to avoid staring like a lecher at the smooth, billowy, inviting expanse of ivory flesh that Amelie presented to his gaze as she bent forward over the low table to do the pouring.

"You seemed unduly shocked, Zachary," she said, "even for an American, when you heard that I have a lover. No doubt, before you joined a circus, you did suffer from the provincial American puritanism, but surely not afterward. I know circuses." She smiled, as if she might know some things about them better than he did. "But perhaps you still cling to that belief so treasured by ignorant prudes: that we of the upper classes lead purer lives." She touched the emeralds in her hair. "We wear tiaras and crowns and coronets, yes, but only a peasant or a fool would mistake them for halos. Or perhaps you thought—perhaps you flattered yourself—that you would be my first and only lover."

"All evening long," Edge said mildly, "you have been putting words in my mouth and telling me what I must be thinking. If you ever *asked* me what I've been thinking, I would be happy to tell you."

"What, then?"

"I keep thinking that you are a lovely desirable woman and, underneath those jewels and laces and brocades, you are absolutely . . . stark . . . naked . . ."

"Oh!" She blushed all the way from her bronze hair to her dress top. "You are as audacious as Andrássy!"

"Another thing I think is that you have mice."

"I *beg* your pardon!" she gasped, quite off balance now.

"The castle, I mean. I hear rustlings inside the walls."

"Have you lived only in a tent all your life?" she asked, recovering. "Never in a proper house? There are passages inside the walls, naturally, so in winter the servants can stoke those great tile stoves from behind, without disturbing the rooms' occupants. Right now, you hear my maids bringing milk for my first bath.''

"First bath? Milk?''

"And none but Jersey milk. Wherever I travel, I take with me two Jersey cows. Always before I go to bed I bathe in warm milk. You will find that it makes me wonderfully satiny of skin. Afterward, you will hear the maids scurrying about in the walls again, bringing the warm olive oil for the second bath I always take after I have lain with a man. That, of course, is for preventive purposes. I truly do not crave any more children. Afterward, also, you will go to your own suite by way of the wall passages. My servants are loyal and untalkative, but propriety—''

"I'll be damned if I will.'' Edge got to his feet. "Not even a countess is going to *command* me to stud and then make me sneak—''

"I do not speak as a countess!'' she flared. "I—'' She curbed her temper. "I speak as a woman, but not the coy and simpering and swooning sort of woman.''

"Then let me be a man, not a flunky. Does your audacious and impetuous Andrássy have to scuttle out of here through a rathole?''

"How dare you! He is noble born, and the premier minister of all Hungary. You are a *commoner*.''

Edge bowed and said coolly, "Has this commoner Your Grace's permission to take his leave?''

"No. Sit down.'' He remained standing. She darkly regarded him and said musingly, "There was a time—and here in Hungary it was not so long ago—if a commoner had spoken to a noble as you have spoken to me . . . I would have had you set on a red-hot iron throne, with a red-hot crown on your head and a red-hot scepter in your hand. When you were well cooked, but still alive''—she dropped a jeweled hand to touch the dog at her side, and he alertly lifted his head, ready for action—"I would have fed you to Schatten.''

Edge did not doubt that she would be capable of it, then or now, but he simply stood and waited. She stood up beside him and suddenly, amazingly, she no longer looked angry. There was a hint of mischief in her flower-petaled eyes when she said, "Now I do not command, I only ask that you stay in this room until I return. If then you still wish to go, you have my leave."

"Your Grace," he said, and bowed again. She swept out of the room, in an electric sibilance of silks.

Edge sat down, took a cigarette from a lapis-lazuli box on the table and poured himself a pony of Bénedictine. He reflected again on the obvious fact that Amelie was not Autumn and, except superficially, was not anything like her. Amelie was herself, but what that might be, he could not make out, because her moods changed so frequently and so extremely. She was imperious one moment, playful the next; frank and free one moment, frozen and haughty the next.

She was gone long enough that he began to wonder, and not entirely idly, if she were having her minions heat an iron throne for him. But evidently she had only been leisurely taking her milk bath, for, when she returned, she had let down her hair, and its tumbling waves of spun bronze were all she wore. She stood regally proud and not the least bashful, and let him look at her. The lovely face, the ivory glow of her, the tiny waist, the high-carried breasts, their generous dark areoles and already excited nipples, those could have been Autumn's. Below the waist, though, she was different in one small detail. She watched Edge's gaze go all over her, and at last smiled and asked, confident of the reply, "Now, Zachary, do you still wish to go away?"

Edge would never again smell the scent of roses or wistaria, or taste milk, without vividly remembering that night. He had first heard in Mexico, when he was a very young man, the hoary old Spanish proverb, "Por la noche todos los gatos son gris," and even then he had laughed at it, already knowing it to be untrue, knowing that no two women were really alike, even in the dark. But Amelie proved to be truly unique in the act of love, as she was in everything else. She did not, like most other passionate women of Edge's experience, sigh or whimper or moan with pleasure. Instead, from his very first ministrations of lips and tongue and fingers, she began to chuckle with delight, like a little girl being affectionately tickled.

As Edge had already noticed, she was like a little girl in another respect. He said, "You are as smooth as a baby . . . here."

Breathlessly she told him, "The maid who does my hair . . . I have her shave me in that place. I believe it to be hygienic. Now hush. You have already a red-hot scepter. Let me enjoy. Let me laugh."

And that she did. As Edge made her excitement mount, the low chuckle became a merry trill, getting louder and more joyful until, at her convulsive and writhing climax, she erupted in a peal of full-throated, whole-hearted laughter. Then, as she subsided from the peak of ecstasy, so did her laughter, gradually rippling down the scale again, from exultation to jubilation to merriment and at last to the small chuckle of happy satisfaction. That went on for some while, until she ceased it to say urgently:

"No, no, do not slip out. Stay there. I will . . . mine will make yours aroused again very quickly."

And she did indeed use only that part of herself, tweaking and squeezing and inwardly pulsating, to revive that part of himself.

"How in the world do you do that?" Edge asked, with admiration.

"Exercise. I exercise *all* my muscles. Including that one . . . or those . . . or however many are down there. Now hush again. I am . . . I am . . . oh, *yes!*"

More swiftly now, she went from the quiet chuckle up through the gladsome trill until, at the crest, when Edge could feel down there her rapturous spasm, clenched and drenched, she laughed so infectiously that he did, too.

A long time—many times—later, when they lay resting side by side, she was still and quiet for a while, but then she shook with silent laughter.

"I'm not even touching you," Edge said lazily. "What's tickling you now?"

"I was remembering your circus. The joeys' act. You know, that part when the pretty Emeraldina is supposedly the wife of the wrinkled old Hanswurst, and the Kesperle makes lewd advances to her, and she says, 'My husband will not thank you, sir, for making him a cuckold.' ''

''And the Kesperle says, 'But I hope, madame, *you* will.' '' Edge again laughed with her.

''I do thank you, sir,'' said Amelie. ''Perhaps now you are not so disapproving of this faithless wife.''

He said, ''And perhaps now I've convinced you that I am not a puritan. No, I wasn't shocked when you said at dinner that you have a lover. I was just surprised that you *said* it.''

''What harm? Only in Marie's presence.''

''And mine.''

''Fatzke!'' she said airily. ''Even if you were to tell of that—or of anything else—no one would believe you.''

Edge grunted, resentful and a little hurt by her unconscious or uncaring disparagement.

She added, ''And from Marie I have no secrets.''

''And from your husband?''

''I will tell you, Zachary. He is un mari commode. He has to be, for fear that *I* might tell secrets. Seven years ago, and I do not know from whom he contracted it, Ferenc gave to me a . . . a shameful disease.''

Edge grunted again, this time in sympathy.

''You see why I say we people wear crowns—or coronets—but not halos. Anyway, that was when I first traveled incognito and without retinue. To Berlin, under an assumed name, accompanied only by Marie, to have myself cured. And when I was cured, I found that I could be blissfully and unashamedly unfaithful to Ferenc. In fact, I have never slept with him since then, and I avoid his company except on inescapable occasions of state, when we must pretend to be the happy and loving Count and Countess Hohenembs. Now I travel as I please, I have my own estates apart from his, I live my own life. But I do not openly dishonor him or my own high station. I am discreet in my infidelities and I make certain that they do not develop into attachments or entanglements. The Count Andrássy, for example, has a wife and two sons and a reputation to protect, so there is no risk of his wanting more of me than the occasional liaison. Just as you and I, Zachary, will savor this little time together, and then part. Oh, we may meet again somewhere, sometime. But never for long."

Edge sighed. "They say that all is fair in love and war. I've been in love and I've been in war, and I've learned that those have another thing in common. You don't expect any tomorrows. You enjoy, just as much as you can, what is here and now."

"You are wise."

"For a mere commoner?"

"And now you must go. I require my beauty sleep, and first I must have my olive-oil douche and bath. The maids have been long gone from the wall passages; I hope the oil is still warm. Meanwhile, since you were so insistent, I give you permission to depart by way of the door and the corridors. They should be empty at this hour."

"I imagine so. It's nearly dawn. Why don't we sleep a little and then—?"

"No." She sat up in the bed and reached for something from the bedside table. "I sleep in this silken mask—see?— with slices of raw veal inside it. You would not much desire me, seeing me so."

"Good God, Amelie. What's that for?"

"To keep me looking as young as your Autumn. You do not object to *that*, so do not be so appalled at the means I employ."

"I suppose you use only Jersey veal?"

"And do not be impertinent. If this were springtime, now, I would let you remain the night. In the spring, you see, before I retire, all over my face and breasts I crush the ripe wild strawberries fresh with dew. You would find me tasty then."

"I find you tasty right now. I believe I could even ignore the mask and the, uh . . ."

"No. Not again until tomorrow night. Go now." She kissed him and smiled contentedly. "Es hat mich sehr gefreut."

* * *

Edge slept well into the morning, and no one disturbed him. When he awoke, he pulled the bell rope and had not even time to step out of bed before Hirschfeld was there, holding a robe for him, but suggesting by gestures that he remain abed. So Edge complied, and next moment a footman entered with a bed tray of breakfast and coffee, and another brought a freshly ironed copy of the *Pest Világ*. While Edge ate and scanned the smudgy woodcuts, all he could comprehend of the newspaper, his valet and a whole parade of footmen bearing steaming ewers prepared his bath. While he bathed, the valet clucked fussily over the condition of Edge's dress suit—he had removed it in considerable haste the night before, and redonned it only carelessly, and then doffed it again half asleep. So Hirschfeld took it away for some mending and sponging and pressing, but was back in time to help Edge towel himself and dress in walking boots, loden trousers and a hunting jacket that Magpie Maggie Hag had made for him by retailoring and sewing leather elbow and gun-butt patches on his old army tunic.

Edge wended his way down to the great entry hall, and there encountered the Baroness Festetics. She said affably, "You must entertain yourself for a while, Edge úr. Sissi—I mean the Countess Amelie—will not appear before noon."

"She always sleeps so late?"

"Ó jaj, no! She will have been up and about since half past six. But my lady has a strict and crowded morning schedule." The baroness recited it—as reverently, thought Edge, as Homer sang of heroes, and he had to admit that it was a heroic if not Homeric program.

"First, she has her scented bath, and the application to her face of a cream made of Dutch tulip bulbs, and perhaps the washing of her hair in raw egg and brandy. Then arrives the masseur she conscripted from a spa at Wiesbaden. Then, after breaking her fast with herb tea and toast, she dons a léotard and goes to exercise for an hour on the various apparatuses in her gymnastics room. Next comes there her fencing master, to put her through an hour's practice. After those exertions, of course, another bath. When her hair maid has combed and brushed and done up her tresses, the countess selects from her wardrobe and puts on a costume befitting whatever activity is first on her calendar for the day. Then she sits down for another hour to study, with her books and the professor who is teaching her Greek. Then she takes a light luncheon in her rooms. And it is noon, and her public day begins.''

Edge said, ''I feel like going back to bed, after just listening to it all.''

''Ó jaj, do not do that, Edge úr,'' the baroness said, in earnest. ''Come, I will show you about the castle.''

So they wandered through one splendid room and hall and gallery after another, with the baroness explaining the history and rarity and value and mode of acquisition of every last object of art or antiquity. Edge enjoyed best, however, the view of outdoors when they climbed to the top of the castle's highest tower. They could see over much of the surrounding parkland; in one meadow browsed a family of red deer, in another was rooting a sizable herd of extremely sizable and savage-looking black boar.

''Edge úr, have you ever ridden to staghounds?''

''No, ma'am, I haven't. But I've done pigsticking. In Mexico.''

''Ah, then you must do that here, with Her Grace. And perhaps she will initiate you in the chase, as well. She is a magnificent rider, as you know, and a veritable Diana in the hunt.''

When Amelie did make her appearance, riding was obviously the first thing on her day's calendar, for she was accompanied by Elise Renz, and both the young women were again in bolero jackets and slim trousers, this time of dark blue velvet. They and Edge exchanged greetings and some small talk, Amelie translating for Elise, then the three went to the stables and Elise whistled up the stable hand. He led into the paddock the two superb Arabian horses. The girls mounted them, bareback, and began warming them up while the man went back into the stable to bring out his accordion and a long, wicked, braided-leather whip with a tassel like a cat-o'-nine-tails. That was the korbács, Edge learned later, the whip used by the range riders and cattle herders of the Hungarian plains. The man handed it to Edge, and puzzled him by winking broadly when he did so. Then he started playing his rollicking cigány music.

Edge was not puzzled for long. He cracked the whip to start the women and horses circling in their équestrienne routine and, after he had several times cracked it to direct the women to assume one pose after another, and several times gently flicked the horses to make them change pace, Elise shouted something in German. The countess, riding at a stand, called to Edge, "She says do not tap the horses. Tap *us* with the korbács."

"I'm not going to whip any woman," Edge called back. "Damn it, this is a brute of a whip."

"Do as she says! That is my command also!"

"Command, is it?" Edge growled to himself. He gave a smart snap of the whip's tassel directly to Amelie's shapely buttocks.

It made her shriek and start, so she almost lost her footing on the horse. Edge was instantly dismayed at having stung her more sharply than he really had intended. He sincerely hoped he had not marred that perfect little backside, and he half expected the countess to summon the dog Schatten or an iron throne to punish his presumption. But, when she regained her balance, she only called cheerfully, "That is the way! More!"

So Edge shrugged and continued to do as they wished, snapping the tassel first at one woman, then the other, stinging them on their bottoms, on the backs of their thighs and occasionally, when they rode en arabesque, on the thin soles of the upraised riding slippers. After a time, even that was not sufficient to satisfy them. Elise, while riding easily erect, peeled off her bolero jacket and threw it away. The countess likewise doffed her bolero, and both women were riding in the bright white blouses, their unconfined breasts bouncing merrily. Amelie called to Edge, "Now, see if you can do something very delicate. Try to flick our backs hard enough to hurt—hard enough even to make red welts—but not tearing the silk or our skin."

That was tricky, with an unfamiliar whip, and Edge was reluctant, but he cautiously obeyed. And, after he had given them a few strokes, Elise shouted, and Amelie passed it on: "Harder, Zachary! It scarcely hurts at all! Make it sting!" He shrugged again, and laid on the whip a bit more briskly. That brought squeals and whoops from them, but they never bade him stop. Then Elise, carefully watching each time he flung the lash, waited until it was her turn and did a quick pirouette atop her horse, deliberately causing the tassel to catch her right on the tip of one breast.

She let out a long, warbling cry—and Edge, aghast, let the whip end fall—but Elise's was not a cry of anguish. It went on and on, as she spun again, dropped to straddle the cantering horse, flung herself full length along its back, her arms around its neck, and she rode that way, rubbing herself upon it, still uttering that exuberant cry of bliss. Amelie dismounted from her horse, led it out of the way and watched with a smile while Elise went around and around, until—as Edge perceived it—her perversely whipped-up excitement gradually ran down. Meantime, the stable hand grinned knowingly and lasciviously, and went on playing his gypsy music. The Fräulein Renz at last brought her horse to a halt and got down from it, visibly weak and perspiring and trembling. Amelie supported her until she recovered, the two talking quietly and then laughing gaily, and after a moment the countess crossed the paddock to where Edge stood, his whip at trail.

He said, "Your friend is just a trifle strange, isn't she?"

"Then so am I, n'est-ce pas? But you can judge us both for yourself. Elise will be joining you and me in my chambers tonight. The whip is too long to use there. The stable man will find for you a short quirt to bring instead."

And that night, after some initial reserve and modesty on the part of all three—a good deal of it, in Edge's case—their shyness and reticence gave way to familiarity and then to intimacy. Edge, half wondering, half amused, and feeling totally foolish, obliged the women by plying the quirt, but only gently, and they required only enough of that to make their bare backsides rosy and warm—and their insides a lot warmer, he reckoned, from the way the women squirmed against one another. He put the quirt aside, then, and watched them play. When they tired of pleasuring only each other,

they enfolded him, too, and after a while Edge was the only
one silent in the bedroom. Elise did her wildly exuberant
crying and Amelie did her wildly exultant laughing, and they
went on doing so, loud and long and madly, madly. Quite
madly.

4

WHEN EDGE descended from the brougham at the Florilegium midway in a late afternoon, the several artistes, roustabouts and stallkeepers loitering about called to him,
"Welcome back!"—or the equivalent in other languages. By
the time Edge's portmanteau was taken down from the boot,
Florian had popped out of the red wagon and bustled over to
say also, "Welcome, my boy. We have missed you."

"Hell, I've only been gone five days. But it's good to
know I'm not expendable. I see Stitches has got the new
dressing tents up. Our tober is looking like quite a town
now."

"And you are looking nicely tanned and fit after your sojourn among the swells."

"Well, we were out afield for three of those days. Hunting
stag one day, then coursing hares, then sticking boar. The
countess's larder is well supplied with venison for a while."

"Come over to the red wagon and wash the road dust off
your tonsils. Banat, take Zachary's bag to his caravan. And
on the way, ask Tücsök to report to me, please."

In the office, Florian poured glasses of Csopaki wine, and
they both lit cigarettes, and Edge asked, "Anything happen
while I was away that I ought to know about?"

"Why, yes. Several bits of quite good news. Perhaps you
were aware that Maggie Hag has been treating Meli Vasilakis
for her unfortunate malady, with a regimen of camphor and
bromides and calomel ointment. Well, Maggie finally pronounced Meli cured, so she and Sir John have consummated
their courtship. At least I assume so; he has moved into her
caravan."

"I'm glad to hear it."

"And Boom-Boom has hired for his band a talented new windjammer—I should say a string-banger. Gombocz Elemér, a cimbalom player. We had to reinforce the bandstand to hold the instrument, but the melodious music it makes is worth the trouble."

Edge nodded approvingly.

"*And* we've added a new trouper. During your absence, I took over the directing duties and the liberty horse act, but of course we had no substitute shootist or voltige rider, so the other artistes were simply given more time in the pista to pad out the program. But on the second or third day, this unique artiste showed up, in response to my advertisement in the *Era*. I shall not even describe the act to you. I'll let you be as astounded at first sight of it as the jossers are. But this Tücsök is no first-of-May. A seasoned performer, and a fantastic one."

"I heard you say that name to Banat. I thought it must be one of our Slovaks."

"No, a nom-de-théâtre. A Magyar word meaning Cricket."

"Cricket? If that signifies what I'm afraid it does—"

"Yes. A midget."

"Christ, you said you had *good* news. Another damned dwarf? After all the trouble we had with the other little sons of bitches—?"

"A female this time, and she will not be a bitch. I have quartered her with Clover Lee and Sunday, and they are as delighted as if I'd presented them with a dear little sister, although Cricket is as old as both of them put together. She is a darling little creature and—well, here she is now. Szábo Katalin kisasszony, may I present Edge Zachary úr? Our equestrian director, of whom you have heard much praise. Zachary, this is Katalin Szábo, known professionally as Tücsök—Cricket."

She said in a small but not squeaky voice, and in excellent English, "I am pleased to meet you, Colonel Edge."

"Miss Cricket," he said.

He had stood up when the little lady entered. Now he had to bow, deeper than he had ever bowed to anyone royal or noble, to reach down and take Cricket's tiny hand. He had

to concede that she was something new and improved in the
line of midgets. Except that she was a trifle plump for her
height, which was only about thirty inches, she was not mis-
shapen or misproportioned in any way. She was simply a
perfect miniature of a very pretty young lady with curly
brown hair and bright blue eyes—though she was not so
young as her girlish face made her appear at first glance—
and she was smoking a cigarette in a long jade holder.

Florian told Edge, "Katalin does her pista act in the first
half of the program and I guarantee you it's pure magic.
Then, at intermission, she joins Sir John's sideshow. She
rides into the annex on Rumpelstilzchen—bareback at present, but Stitches is making her a miniature saddle and bridle.
She wears the rough garb of a csikos, a Hungarian plainsman,
while she sings some of the bawdy plains songs. Then she
doffs the masculine garments, reveals herself in dainty, colorful village-girl dress and does some bewitching csárdás
dances."

"I'm eager to see your mysterious pista act," Edge said
to the little woman. "And I'm sure Sir John is pleased to
have a real artiste in his sideshow, not just another exhibit."

"I hope to make everyone pleased, Colonel," she said.
"Monsieur Pemjean and I are already starting to teach the
small horse some tricks—head-tossing, rearing, bowing—
that I can put him through. A bantam liberty act right up
there on the sideshow platform."

"It sounds appealing," said Edge. "And I welcome you
to the company." Katalin gave him an elfin smile and blew
a Lilliputian smoke ring.

"As soon as I have a free moment," said Florian, "I will
take you to a daguerrian artist downtown, Tücsök, and have
cartes-de-visite made for you to sell. They ought to sell better
even than pretzels."

Katalin thanked him graciously and took her leave.

"I *reckon* I welcome her to the company," Edge said.
"But I remember Major Maggot and his little playmates.
Governor, this Cricket is delectable enough to tempt full-
grown lechers into lusting for such a novelty."

"I am quite sure that she will repulse any advances," said

Florian. "I will impart to you, and you only, a confidence she imparted to me. Tücsök has but recently recovered from giving birth to a baby. Paternity unspecified, but no matter. It was a normal-sized baby, as frequently happens among the little people, so she straightaway put it out for adoption, to be brought up in a nice, normal, commonplace family. And she is frank to say that that experience of childbirth was so hideously painful—well, you can imagine—that she will never risk it occurring again. No, I think we need not worry about anything like the Reindorf unpleasantness."

From outside there came a sudden whoop and squeal of music.

"There goes the calliope, to herald the night perfor-mance," said Florian. "I must go. But first, tell me. How did you find your countess? Was she still as exquisite as you first thought?"

"Well, I'm no authority on what high-ranking ladies are supposed to be like. But I met Mrs. Jeff Davis once, and she was sure no patch on this Countess Hohenembs."

"Ah, that's her title, is it?" Then Florian repeated, mus-ingly, "Hohenembs . . . Hohenembs. I was there once. Place with a great rock mountain brooding over it. Very near the border of Liechtenstein. And, if I remember rightly, Hohe-nembs is a baronetcy. If so, your lady's title would be only baroness. I fear, Zachary, that you may have been imposed upon."

"It didn't cost *me* anything. Quite the contrary."

"Oh, I could be mistaken. It was a long time ago that I was in Hohenembs." Florian put on his best frock coat and top hat. "Are you too road-weary to participate in the show tonight?"

"No. Let me just finish my wine, and I'll go and dress."

Florian went out and left Edge alone in the office, which was what he had wanted. So many of Amelie's remarks had given him the feeling of déjà-entendu that now he wanted to verify something he vaguely remembered. Muttering under his breath, "Ferenc, Franz . . . Franz, Ferenc," he went to the wall where Florian had hung the framed invitation to Schön-brunn from Franz Joseph, and peered at its long list of that

emperor's other titles. Halfway down it, after the several
kingships and dukedoms, he found ''. . . Landgraf von Habsburg und Tirol, Grossvoivode von Serbien, Graf von Hohenembs . . .''

Edge murmured, ''Florian, you *are* mistaken about Hohenembs.'' He tossed off his wine and went to the caravan.
He opened his trunk and rummaged among his souvenirs—
mostly the few small things of Autumn's that he had kept—
found the wallet he had been given at Schönbrunn and took
it out to look at its embroidered arms of the Empire of Austria. The double-headed eagle emblem was the same as that
on the terrace pillars of Amelie's palace. Still talking to himself, Edge said, ''But you're right, Florian. She's not a countess. Or not *just* a countess.'' Then he laughed. ''Hell, *I*
thought for a while she might be a stable maid.'' He stood
up, took from its hanger his Colonel Ramrod uniform and
began dressing for the show.

By the time he got to the chapiteau, the calliope had hushed
and Boom-Boom's band was playing instead, and the first
jossers were taking their seats. Edge climbed to the bandstand
for a look at the new cimbalom. It was a big and fancily
carved wooden box on carved legs, rather like an old-
fashioned square piano, except that it had no keys and no lid,
so the innumerable wire strings inside were exposed, to be
played on directly with soft little mallets, of which cimbalist
Elemér dexterously held two between the fingers of each
hand. But the cimbalom was no meek and modest dulcimer,
to be overwhelmed by the rest of the band. Though Elemér
could, in deliberately quiet passages, make his music merely
tinkle and twinkle, he could also make it twang and jangle
boldly or even thunder loud enough to be heard above the
massed brasses and drums. He obviously enjoyed his work;
he grinned all the time he played, and proudly tossed his
mane of black hair, and grinned even more broadly whenever
he produced an especially tricky and pleasing musical effect.
Edge did not interrupt to introduce himself by name, but Elemér, without once ceasing to play—and play well—with his
left hand, extended his right for a handshake.

The show commenced, and went smoothly through its usual first-half program. Then, when Monday and Thunder had finished their haute école riding act and taken their bows, Edge got his first look at the other new addition to the company. Florian bounded into the pista with his megaphone to proclaim grandiloquently—in Magyar, in German and, possibly for Edge's comprehension, in English—"A Büvös Gömb! Die Verzaubert Kugel! The Enchanted Globe!" Meanwhile, several Slovaks hauled into the center of the pista a very large apparatus that Edge had never seen before. It was rather like a combination of a circular staircase and a very narrow-gauge tramway. It had two parallel nickel-plated rails that ascended at a gentle angle from ground level, then spiraled upward in easy curves to end at a platform some fifteen feet above the pista sawdust.

The crowd went silent in contemplation of that thing, and in the silence only one band instrument, Elemér's cimbalom, began to play—very softly—the other-worldly opening measures of Josef Strauss's "Music of the Spheres." Then there entered through the chapiteau's back door, rolling between the stands and into the pista, a wooden ball about a yard in diameter, brightly painted in multicolor zigzags. No roustabout had shoved it in and none was pushing it now. The globe was rolling only slowly and sedately, but it was rolling entirely of its own volition. And it did not slow to a stop; it kept on rolling, to make three circuits of the pista. The audience regarded it in silent awe, and the cimbalom kept repeating—quietly, almost eerily—variations on those ethereal opening bars of "Music of the Spheres."

The atmosphere in the chapiteau got even more unearthly as, incredibly, the wooden ball now made a deliberate turn to the nickel-plated tramway, rolled itself between the close-set twin rails and, still slowly but without hesitation, rolled *up* that incline. As it climbed, so did the volume of the cimbalom music, Elemér going on to the crescendo measures of the "Spheres," and playing ever louder and livelier as the ball serenely circled the upward-spiraling rails. When the Enchanted Globe reached the platform at the top, the whole band joined the cimbalom to blare a rousing climax and bring the audience out of its stupefaction to a clamor of applause.

Up there, the gaudy ball did several gyrations in time to the music, and even gave a couple of sluggish hops. Then it opened. Edge had of course early realized the secret of its mysterious locomotion, so he was not surprised when the thing opened like a clamshell, revealing itself to be two hollow hemispheres hinged and with a clasp to hold them together. The zigzag paint pattern served to hide the hardware and also, Edge supposed, some slits to see through. Nevertheless, when it opened and little Tücsök stood up, wearing only a vividly orange-spangled léotard—and smiled and threw up her arms in a V—she was visibly perspiring. Even one as small as she would have been cramped inside that shell, and would have had to walk or crawl laboriously and skillfully to make the globe do all the things it had done. At Cricket's emergence, the band music rose to explosion volume, and so did the audience's cheering, clapping and stamping of feet.

Cricket merrily slid down the spiral tramway like a child on a playground slide, to take her bows in the pista. While the roustabouts removed the props, Edge said admiringly to her, "Florian spoke truly. That was pure magic. And you must be a damn sight stronger than you look for your size."

"Well, I can trundle the ball *up* there all right. But I always conclude the act at the top. Just one time did I try to roll it *down* again. I lost control and it came twirling and bounding down like a boulder in an avalanche, and when I got out of it I looked like a scrambled egg. I won't do that again."

"I hope not. You're too pretty to get scrambled."

"Thank you, Colonel. And thank you, too, for liking the act."

Some of the longtime troupers had added refinements to their routines during Edge's brief absence. Sunday Simms, for instance, had somewhere procured a soccer ball and used it in her act in a breathtaking way. Maurice LeVie had unselfishly helped her learn the trick, declaring himself too heavy and angular to manage it as gracefully as she could. Mademoiselle Butterfly concluded her solo turn by swinging out, seated on the bar, carrying the soccer ball. Then, swooping in long but slow arcs, she stood up, balanced the ball on the bar, then upended herself and *stood on her head* on the teetering ball, her arms and legs extended starfishlike, holding onto nothing at all while she continued to swoop back and forth. Some people in the audience, even grown men, had to avert their eyes in sheer dread of her falling. But Sunday never came to grief, and even told Edge that she found the trick—the taunting of the gods of accident—almost euphorically exhilarating.

Quincy Simms had invented a new contortion. After he and Miss Eel finished their duo act, he provided a nicely horrid coda. In his boneless way he slowly folded to the ground so that his body and arms seemed to disappear, leaving only his crossed legs visible, and between them he propped his chin. Then he grinned a ghastly white grin and bulged his eyeballs. With the grimace, his black face and his angled skinny legs, he exactly resembled the skull-and-crossbones on a pirate flag or on the label of a bottle of poison. Some watchers had to avert their eyes from *that*, too, but most laughed and applauded in appreciation.

"Well, it certainly is gruesome, Ali Baba," Edge told him. "But it's ingenious, and it seems to be generally well received."

"Mebbe dem jossers like it, Mas' Zack," Quincy said, rather grumpily, "but dey don'like *me*. I kin hear 'em in de seats, saying', 'Dat ain't no Ali Baba. Dat's jist a dirty li'l nigger what got hisself in disgrace wid a white man.'"

"Why, Quincy!" said Edge, in surprise and puzzlement. "I've never heard anybody make any such remark. Hell, they *couldn't*. None of these jossers speaks English. You must be imagining things."

At his first opportunity, Edge went to watch Cricket's performance in Fitzfarris's sideshow. Fitz was clearly delighted to have her among his company, and the audience in the annex tent clearly enjoyed her act there almost as much as her Enchanted Globe. When, dressed as a herdsman and assuming a ludicrously deep voice, Tücsök sang the herdsmen's coarse and indecent songs, the men in the crowd roared hilariously and slapped their thighs, while the women pretended to be scandalized and embarrassed. But the women as well as the men beamed at her and clapped in rhythm when, dressed in a colorfully beaded blouse and a skirt of innumerable tiny pleats, to the music of Fitz's accordionist, Tücsök did the age-old, energetic, coquettish dances of the country inns called csárdás.

"She's a jim-dandy, sure enough," Edge said to Florian. "And either she's an exception among midgets or I was ignorant and wrong to condemn the whole tribe in general. But Governor, before I went on holiday, you were complaining about the company ratio of women to men, and the next thing you do is hire another female."

"Well, I can hardly go out and beat the bushes for male artistes. I'll just have to hope that some men come applying, even if they're first-of-Mays, to start correcting the imbalance."

But the imbalance was not soon improved; a week later it got even more lopsided. At an afternoon performance, Miss Eel's and Ali Baba's contortionist act ended, as it always did now, with the boy sinking down into his skull-and-crossbones pose. And today he seemed particularly pleased with the jossers' combined gasps and giggles and applause, for he stayed there like that for so long that the equestrian director finally had to whistle for him to get up, take his bows and make way for the trapeze act. Ali Baba ignored him and sat where he was. Colonel Ramrod whistled more loudly and, when the boy still did not budge, crossed the pista to give him an angry shake. Tightly folded as he was, Ali Baba was rather impervious to shaking, but he would have been in any case, for he was dead. The equestrian director beckoned two Slovaks to come and carry him out, just as he was, still fixed in his now sadly appropriate skull-and-crossbones position. The audience laughed and cheered, taking it to be just a farcical conclusion to the act.

The Budapest authorities would have treated Quincy's demise as lackadaisically as they had that of Spyros Vasilakis. But Florian himself was concerned and curious enough to summon a physician to ascertain the cause of this death. After examining the small body, the doctor reported his findings to Florian, and Florian reported to Edge:

"It appears that, in a manner of speaking, Ali Baba's former gentleman friend, Cecil Wheeler, killed him."

"*What*?"

"Do you recall how, for some time, Quincy had been smelling odors that no one else did, and hearing odd noises, and remarking on strange flavors in quite ordinary foods?"

"Are you saying he was *poisoned*?"

"No. You'll also remember that, at Cecil's last performance, Quincy fell head-first off the velocipede. He has been walking around ever since—and heroically performing—with a fractured skull. If we had known and immobilized him in bed, he might have recovered. But today his poor head simply, finally succumbed to the injury."

Edge went to say a word of condolence and give a comforting hug to Sunday. She smiled sadly and said, "We Simmses are sort of dwindling away. Maybe Tuesday and Quincy would have done better to stay with the Furfews, barefoot and poor and ignorant. Maybe we all would."

"Don't talk such nonsense. You know damned well that they both saw more of life, even in their short lives, than if they'd grown old and gray in Virginia. And you are Mademoiselle Butterfly. There is no limit to how high and far you can fly."

When Edge went to condole with Monday, she scarcely seemed overwhelmed with grief. She said, "Lemme ax you somethin', Mr. Zack, that I can't ax my Mr. Demon. He ain't no Southerner, so he wouldn't know. What it is is this. Now that I ain't got no brother Quincy always in plain sight, do you expect folks might raise their opinion of *me*?"

"Why, Monday, I doubt that anybody ever judged you on the basis of your brother. Not your qualities or your talents or—"

"I'm talkin' *color*. Long as Quince was around, I couldn't be nothin' but kin to a black boy. My Mr. Demon calls me his—some French word, means high-yaller. But s'pose some different man never knowed I ever had a blue-gum brother.

Mightn't that man take me to be somethin' better'n a half nigger?''

Edge said drily, "You don't mean something better, you mean something *easier* to be." He regarded her, estimating. "Well, I reckon you could pass for an unusually handsome Mexican girl. Or some kind of tropical-island girl."

"Hey, now!" She grinned. "Tell me the names of some."

"Hell, you could *claim* to be the Queen of Sheba. But don't expect people just to take your word for it. The Queen of Sheba was a smart woman, and you'd have to work at getting educated and refined and polished. Like saying ask instead of ax." Monday stopped grinning and looked put upon. "Your sister Sunday, now, she—"

"Yeah, her!" Monday said darkly. "She don't mind bein'a buffalo gal, long as she can talk fancy and show off her fine manners. Damn! And any new man could see I'm her sister, just another high-yaller, couldn't he? I can't better myself unless she does, too. Damn!''

Edge sighed, gave it up and went off to help Florian with the arrangements for Quincy-Ali Baba's funeral.

5

"AUGUST TWENTIETH is Saint Istvan's Day," Florian told his chief subordinates at a meeting called in the red wagon. "Or Saint Stephen's Day, if you prefer. Anyway, it is Hungary's highest holiday of the summer, and we will enjoy our most teeming attendance since we've been here. I shall canvass the troupe and, unless there are cries of rebellion, I intend that day to give *three* shows—one in the morning besides the usual afternoon and night performances."

"Nobody object, I think," said Carl Beck. "We circus people. We rather show, get applause, than on our Arsche sit. And Slovaks all day working, anyhow."

"Very well. Plan for three shows that day. Now, after that day, I am sure we would continue to do the same good business that we've been doing all along, and probably would continue to do at least until winter comes. However, after

Saint Istvan's Day, I wish to hit the road again. There is one other particularly beautiful place in Hungary—Lake Balaton—or the Platten See, as Franz Joseph would call it. I think no one should miss seeing that, and the lakeside resorts there ought to provide us with as much patronage as we'd have here."

"Ano, pojd'me na Balaton Jezero!" Alexsandra Banat exclaimed with enthusiasm, he evidently having been there before.

Florian went on, "Then, after a month or so at the lake, when the leaves begin to turn, we will move eastward. We have to cross some four hundred miles of the puszta—the flat, dreary, featureless sea of grass—where there is not even a village big enough to warrant our stopping to show. I want to get to the Russian border before snow flies. I am not eager to make Napoléon's mistake of braving a Russian winter on the road."

"Come you, Governor," Dai Goesle said skeptically. "Russia is one dammo big country, and we will be crossing it as slow as moss. Winter is bound to catch us somewhere there."

"But not on the road and in the open. Although with considerable distaste, I have decided, after long deliberation, to emulate the contemptible Zirkus Ringfedel. From the Russian border, we will travel by railroad train, pausing to show only in Kiev and Moscow before arriving at the destination I have long looked forward to and lusted for—the tsar's grand and shining capital city of Saint Petersburg—where I trust we shall have a long and happy and prosperous stay."

Willi Lothar spoke up. "When all of you leave for Lake Balaton, I shall leave for Russia and arrange to charter a train and engage the first tober in Kiev." He turned to Florian. "Jules will not be accompanying me. I know he will wish to go aloft in the *Saratoga* at the lake. It is a splendid place for a beautiful balloon ascension."

"Hold on," said Edge. "I've had a glimpse of Hungary's prairies—you say they're called the puszta?—when I went to visit the countess. That puszta is dreary, all right. Why should we take the trouble to trudge across four hundred miles of nothingness? Hungary has railroads, too. Why not charter a train here and take it all the way to and through Russia?''

"Because that would be even more trouble," said Florian. "The railroads here in western Europe are what is called standard gauge, if you know what that means. The railroads in Russia are broad gauge, the rails set much wider apart, so the trains are built quite different. We would have to do all our packing and loading and stocking of feed and supplies here, then at the border unpack and unload it all, then repack and reload on a Russian train. It would be more of an inconvenience—and probably take more time—than our going there by road. No, we will head for Czernowitz on the Hungarian border, cross the river Prut and on the Russian side of the river, at Novosielitza, our train will be waiting.''

Edge shrugged. "You know best, Governor.''

"And, incidentally, we will be leaving behind our midway joints and entresorts and their population. They can continue to do a good trade at Lake Balaton—it has winter as well as summer resorts—and God knows they'd do no trade at all on the puszta. Also, the Russian immigration authorities are notoriously suspicious and unobliging; they probably would not even allow entry to such a gaggle of gypsies. Also, and most important, our chartered train will cost me enough. I am disinclined to hire two or three extra cars to transport the hangers-on.''

"Damn," said Fitzfarris. "I guess, like Zack says, you know best, Governor. But I sure will be sorry to abandon my pretty Schuhplattler girls.''

"Then start planning and preparing, gentlemen. Canvasmaster, before we leave Pest, lay in any hardware, spare parts, extra canvas and harness, whatever else you might conceivably need in the future. Such things are hard to come by in a country as primitive as Russia, and we won't find them at Lake Balaton either. Kapellmeister, you do the same—sheet music, horn valves, drumheads, whatever—and, in particular, procure an ample supply of the chemicals for the *Saratoga*'s generator. Crew Chief, you confer with Abdullah and that Slovak assistant of his, regarding the quantities of feed and cats' meat we'll need to get the animals across the puszta.

Once we're in Russia, that sort of thing, at least, we *can* always replenish.'' Florian stood up. ''In the meantime, I will be buying yet another wagon and span of horses. We will need them, and not just for those extra supplies we'll be carrying. We have recently acquired quite a stock of new and heavy appurtenances: the dressing tents, the cimbalom, Tücsök's globe and ramp. Well, anything else to discuss, gentlemen? Then I declare this meeting adjourned.''

On St. Istvan's Day, for the first time ever, the circus presented three shows, and every show was not just a sfondone but a turnaway. Even toward the end of the night performance, no artiste let himself or herself look anything but sparkling and vivacious to the audience, and none of them bungled a single trick in any act. Even the animals seemed imbued with the same spirit, and never once balked or sulked at being overworked. In the night show's closing Grand Promenade, the troupers waved warmly to the crowd and smiled especially brilliantly, proud and pleased at having participated in the best-attended and most profitable day the Florilegium had ever enjoyed. But when the last of the jossers had gone, the troupers and crewmen and bandsmen unashamedly went limp with fatigue, and some did not even take off their pista costumes before falling comatose on their bunks and pallets.

The circus suspended all operations the next day, so the whole company—even the Slovaks, after they had attended to the animals' needs—could relax or rest as they chose. Several of them took this last opportunity to visit their favorite places in the city. Clover Lee, Gavrila and Agnete went for a browse through the Párizsi department store. Carl Beck went to a spa for a final curative soaking and then bought a couple of crates each of the Bánfi hair restorer and Béres invigorator. Abner Mullenax went across the river to Buda to bring back a crate of the ghastly Bulgarian gin, and a quantity of it inside him. Edge, Pemjean, Yount and LeVie went to laze away the afternoon in the New-York coffeehouse. Magpie Maggie Hag and Bernhard Notkin went together to where mostly old people congregated, the checkered concrete tables thoughtfully provided by the City Park, to play a game of chess. Florian spent most of the day in his office, gleefully totting up the previous day's receipts and bringing his ledgers up to date.

The next day was devoted to teardown, cleanup of the tober and loading the circus aboard the wagons. After the loading, every wagon, including the newly bought one, was almost visibly bulging, what with all the extra supplies, feed and bits of equipment Dai and Carl and Hannibal had acquired. Some of the smaller things even had to be stowed in the troupers' living-quarters caravans. Then Florian commanded a number of the Slovaks and the lightest wagon to depart immediately and go on ahead, with a hefty stack of Florilegium posters, to circle the entire extent of Lake Balaton and post paper in every least village and hamlet around its shores.

The rest of the circus train left Pest early the next morning, crossed the Chain Bridge for the last time, climbed over Saint Gellért's Hill, past the gloomy Citadel, and took a road going southwest. Their destination at Lake Balaton was sixty miles and two long days away, so they camped on the roadside that night, near the only building they had seen in several miles: a modest-sized csárda with the signboard Szep Juhászne. "The Fair Shepherdess," said Florian. "With a pleasant name like that, it can't be *too* bad an inn. We will dine there before bedding down."

The innkeeper was delighted to see them; he had doubtless never before had such a mob of patrons squeeze into his establishment. There were not even enough tables for all; they had to eat in shifts. When the first contingent sat down, the landlord immediately, unbidden, set before them immense pewter pitchers of cool dark beer, plus hearth cakes, hot from the fireplace, to munch with it. There was no choosing and ordering of the meal. The diners were simply served huge bowls of what was every Hungarian country inn's standard fare.

"Bográcsgulyás," said Florian. "Kettle stew. What you would call a pot-au-feu, Maurice, or you, Maggie, an olla podrida. Simply a vast iron kettle kept perpetually simmering on the hearth, perpetually being topped up with whatever meat and vegetables come to hand.'' Whatever it presently consisted of, they all proclaimed it singularly delicious and invigorating.

The happy innkeeper hovered about them during the meal, delighted to be able to converse with at least two of them: Florian and little Katalin.

She told the others, ''The fogados—the landlord—says this csárda has been here for ages, and long ago it was the favorite hiding place of the great highwayman Sobri Jóska. He was Hungary's Robin Hood, forever plundering the rich and sharing with the poor.''

''No, is that a fact?'' said Yount. ''And he holed up right here where we're eating?''

''I doubt it,'' said Cricket. ''Every fogados in Hungary will tell you that his csárda once played host to the bandit Sobri, or to the Fair Ilonka, the secret sweetheart of King Mátyás, or to Pál Kinizsi, the Samson of Hungary. In a war against the Turks, Pál killed one of them and then wielded the body like a club to kill a hundred more.''

''Well, such stories make for good advertising,'' said Fitzfarris. ''Like some of Florian's flummeries. I think it's clever of the innkeepers.''

''Oh, we Magyars are clever, all right,'' said Cricket, smiling. ''I like best the story about the puszta farmer who owed twenty kronen to the local Jew, and couldn't pay. When Uncle Isaac kept dunning him, the farmer offered to sell his cow and hand over the proceeds in full settlement. The cow was easily worth twenty kronen, so the Jew agreed. They went together to the market, and the farmer took along a chicken, as well. A man came up and asked, 'How much for the chicken?' The farmer said, 'Twenty kronen.' The man said, 'Good God! I could buy the cow for that much!' The farmer said, 'Tell you what. Give me twenty kronen for the chicken and I'll let you have the cow for just two copper kreuzers.' So the deal was struck, the farmer pocketed the twenty kronen and paid off the Jew with the two coppers he'd got for the cow. Just as agreed.''

All laughing, they got up from the table to make way for the next group waiting to eat.

The next day, as the train got within a dozen or so miles of Lake Balaton, the travelers noticed that the road was bordered by meadows of strange, limp, wild grasses that writhed and whipped like seaweed in just the mild stirring of the air that the passing wagons made. But then, as the train got even nearer the lake, they began to feel a genuine breeze. They were now passing vineyards in which, instead of the mock-human scarecrows common to most countries, long ribbons of bright-colored cloth were hung to flaff and snap in the wind. And they passed haystacks that had originally been cone-shaped, rather like Red Indian tepees, but had been swiveled and swirled by the wind into freer and more graceful shapes, like girl dancers frozen in the middle of a skirt twirl.

"There is always a wind around Lake Balaton," Florian told Daphne, who was riding on the rockaway with him. "I'm inclined to believe that the lake's own configuration must have something to do with it. Lake Balaton is a curiosity in several respects. It's the biggest lake in all central Europe, and not only is it oddly shaped—fifty miles long but only about six miles wide on average—the very lake bed is peculiar. Down at Balaton's southern end, the bottom shelves so very gradually that you can wade out for half a mile before the water reaches your chin. But it keeps on shelving downward, like a fifty-mile ramp, until, at the north end, it is some forty feet deep. I don't know why Balaton's unique characteristics should *create* a wind, but there always *is* a wind, and the water is always choppy. When a real storm comes up— and it generally comes from the south—it acts like a squeegee. It scrapes that shallow water up from the southern end of the lake and tries to pile it on top of the deep water to the north. You'll see waves and billows and breakers on Balaton as impressive as any ocean could offer."

"It sounds frightening," said Daphne.

"Well, there have been fishermen and ferrymen here for generations, and they've developed an uncanny knack for sensing any big blow in the offing. When they do, they fire off rockets that can be seen or heard all around the lake. The boatmen and holidaymakers get off the water and out of it, and everybody runs for cover."

The company finally topped a height in the road from which they could see the lake. Its color was a distinctive milky turquoise, polka-dotted with the little whitecaps of chop. Everywhere about it were bright green reed beds, and everywhere above it flew steel-blue swallows and black-headed gulls, and leaning over it from every bank were the ever-present poplar trees, even this late in the summer still shedding their snowfall of white fluffs, and now and then there would be a visible splash in the water as a fish lunged for one of them. Some sporting sailboats were on the lake, but most of the water traffic consisted of fishing dories and the ferrymen's unwieldy big rowboats. At intervals all around the lake were tightly clustered communities ranging from hamlet to small town in size, but there were long reaches of uninhabited shoreline between them.

The two biggest, most popular and most populous resort towns, Siófok and Földvár, were on this southeastern shore that the circus train was approaching, and the resorts were only seven miles apart, so Florian had already told the crew to pitch exactly midway between them. Darkness was coming down, but the travelers could see their Florilegium posters tacked to trees here and there. And when they arrived at their designated tober-to-be, the earlier dispatched roustabouts who had posted the paper were waiting for them. The Slovaks had, on their own initiative, already lighted two cooking fires, fetched kettles of the clean lake water, and had even bought from the local fishermen a basketful of fogas, the Lake Balaton pike-perch. So Magpie Maggie Hag, with the help of Gavrila, Meli and Agnete—and using also the wood stove in the onetime dressing wagon in which she still rode and slept—pitched in to prepare the first outdoor country meal that the company had enjoyed in many months.

Early next morning, Canvasmaster Goesle, Crew Chief Banat, the roustabouts and the elephants began the setup. Because the lake shore here was all pebbles, they had to move a couple of hundred yards inland to find ground that would hold the tent stakes. And Florian told them to double the number of stakes and guy ropes on the southern side of every tent, as security against the ever-blowing wind. Even that

early in the day, quite a crowd of holidaymakers from Siófok
and Földvár, having seen the poster announcements of the
Florilegium's imminent arrival, came to watch and admire
the setting up and to buy tickets for the afternoon's first performance. That show was a sellout long before the calliope's
overture hooted and squealed and echoed up and down the
lake. And all the shows thereafter were, as Florian had been
confident they would be, as well attended as they had been
in Pest. The jossers came not just from the two nearby resorts;
many made two-day journeys from the farthest fringes of Balaton and the surrounding countryside.

Jules Rouleau had been hoping to make numerous ascensions over that lovely blue lake and the greenery around it,
with which the vermilion-and-white *Saratoga* would make a
striking contrast, but the constant wind kept Carl Beck saying
firmly, "Nein! Nein!" However, the wind did tend to gentle
down to merely a brisk breeze about sundown, so finally Rouleau persuaded Boom-Boom to let him chance it at that hour.
The Slovaks were sent all around Balaton to post paper proclaiming the event, and the tober overflowed with spectators
that day.

When the balloon was inflated, it flailed cumbersomely
about, as if in distress, alternately slacking and straining and
yanking at its anchor ropes. So Florian cut short his usual
magniloquent discourse about Monsieur Roulette's bravery
and the hazards of challenging the heavens. Rouleau clam-
bered hastily into the gondola—and alone; he refused to risk
taking one of the Simms girls—and the roustabouts immediately loosed the tie-downs. The *Saratoga* went up like a
rocket, but on a slant, going northward faster than it was
going upward, and only narrowly clearing some treetops in
its way. However, when it had gained some altitude above
the lake, Rouleau found that the breeze lessened—evidently
Balaton's eternal winds blew only close to the surface—and
at a yet higher altitude he encountered a breeze blowing
southward. So he was able, in his accustomed way of letting
the balloon rise and fall, to cavort about the sky in various
directions.

Then, finally to descend, he took the *Saratoga* toward the

south end of the lake and tripped the clack valve to release enough gas so that the balloon dropped to where the surface wind blew. He came whizzing up the lake, adroitly opening and shutting the valve so that he came in on a long downward slant. He was good enough at the job by now that he did touch down just outside the circus midway—a considerable portion of the watching crowd had to scatter in a hurry—but even though he pulled the ripcord to empty the bag in that same instant, his gondola hit the ground with a mighty thump, and bounced several times before it and the deflated bag both fell over sideways. Rouleau was unhurt, but had to scramble rather undignifiedly out of the toppled basket and the tangle of ropes before he could leap to his feet, triumphantly throw up his arms and receive the roar of the crowd.

He didn't try again; that was his only ascension at Balaton. Nevertheless, the village and country folk for miles around the lake talked for months, admiringly, about that event. They were overjoyed that it had happened in their lifetime, for such a marvel had never before been seen hereabouts, and probably never would be again. From that ascension day on, Rouleau found it impossible to buy a beer, a meal or even a pretzel in Siófok or Földvár; the other customers always recognized Monsieur Roulette, praised him, pounded him on the back and insisted on paying for whatever he was eating or drinking.

At one afternoon show, when Edge rode Thunder into the chapiteau in the ''Greensleeves'' opening spec, his heart gave a little jump. In the starback seats sat two veiled ladies who looked familiar. When they raised and pinned back their veils, they were indeed the ''Countess Amelie Hohenembs'' and the Baroness Marie Festetics. At intermission, when the rest of the audience departed for the midway, they remained inside as usual, and Edge went eagerly to greet them.

He bowed extravagantly deeply and said, ''Welcome, Your Imperial Majesty.''

Elisabeth, Empress of Austria, Queen of Hungary, said, in mock dismay, ''O jaj! You penetrated my modest masquerade. How?''

"I reckon I first got to pondering when you used the emperor's stock phrase to say you had enjoyed yourself."

"Ah, well. I will only remark, Edge úr, that I did not at all *lie* to you. Amelie is my middle name, and I *am* the Countess Hohenembs. And the Duchess of Salzburg and Auschwitz, and the Margravine of Moravia, and all sorts of other things. I could have told you I was something as lowly as the Voivodine of Serbia, and still have been telling the truth. But please, for old times' sake, go on calling me Amelie. I like the tender way you say it—almost as tenderly as you say Autumn."

"What are you doing 'way out here?"

"I am a houseguest at the Festetics palace. I shall be there until the first hint of winter. Then I scurry off to my sunny and balmy and flowery Achilleion."

The Baroness Marie said, "I hasten to tell you, Edge úr, that the Festetics palace is not mine. I have none. It belongs to a cousin, the *Count* Festetics. It is at Keszthely, down at the very southern tip of the lake. Forty miles from here. Even in a coach-and-four, at a canter, we were a whole day getting here. So we put up in a hotel at Siófok last night, and we will do that again before we go back to Keszthely tomorrow."

Elisabeth Amelie said, "I should like to invite you, Zachary, to join us for another holiday stay—"

"Well, I'll feel like a bummer, taking two vacations in one year, but I'm damned if I'll refuse. I'm my own man, and Florian's a decent sort. If it's all right with you, a few short visits would be better than one long one. I could take a day to ride out there, you and I could spend the next day together, then I'd ride back here on the third day. So I'd miss only six shows all together. But, in fairness to the troupe and the audiences, I could do that only, say, at two-week intervals. And I don't know how many times. It'll depend on how long we stay here."

"I am sorry, Zachary. I was about to say that I should *like* to invite you, but Count Andrássy is one of the other houseguests."

"Oh," said Edge, and his face fell. He thought for a few

moments, then said, "Could I make an outrageous suggestion? First, tell me, does the Count Andrássy ride?"

"Why, of course. What gentleman does not?"

"But I don't suppose he does any trick riding like yours."

"No. Except dressage, steeplechase, riding to hounds . . ."

"Maybe he'd like to learn some flourishes. You just saw our équestrienne. Not the dark girl doing haute école. The blonde—she's wearing a scarlet léotard today—who jumped over the banners and through the hoops."

"*Really*, Zachary. The garters and garlands. You forget that I know some of the circus language."

"Well, that's Clover Lee Coverley, and she has a great yearning to get acquainted with noblemen. If you invited both her and me, she might talk your count into letting her give him some lessons in really fancy riding. And meanwhile, you and I could be—doing other things. Clover Lee's only about seventeen, but she's precociously mature for her age, and—"

"Gyula is much attracted to youth," Elisabeth Amelie said pensively. "Even I am fourteen years younger than he is. A girl fourteen years younger than *I* am ought to make him glow like your limelights." She laughed mischievously. "Yes, you truly are outrageous, Zachary. Very well, both of you are most cordially invited." Then she was serious. "Mind you, I should not wish your Clover Lee to displace me permanently in Gyula's affections."

"Affections? That makes me sound like a pimp. I only meant for her to keep him entertained on horseback, and for her to bask in the presence of nobility. Anyway, I'd imagine that a count married to a countess and in love with an empress wouldn't amuse himself for long in the company of a circus bareback rider."

"Be sure you tell *her* that. And for you, dear Zachary, I shall disrupt my regular daily program. Since we will have only one day at a time together, I shall forgo my morning exercises and studies, so we can share the forenoons as well as the afternoons and evenings."

"Thank you, Amelie. Your Majesty."

"Count Festetics, Count Adrássy and I will look forward

to seeing you and Clover Lee, as soon and as often as you can come.''

Edge went back to work as Colonel Ramrod, highly elated, but at the same time feeling that he was becoming a drone and a deserter. When he and Florian occasionally stood together on the sidelines while an act was in progress, he did not broach the subject. Even after the closing spec, as they stood together watching the audience empty out of the chapiteau, he still hesitated to speak up. But then occurred something marvelously fortuitous. Three jossers lingered behind those departing, conferred briefly among themselves, then came over to Florian and spoke to him in Magyar.

The three were men, and they looked very much alike: brute-ugly, tall, burly, sunburnt almost to bronze, with curly black hair and enormous black walrus mustaches. They were also identically dressed: a leather vest over a bright red shirt, much-scuffed leather trousers so broad that they flapped like skirts, heavy leather boots and, atop all, a black hat that looked like a plum pudding set in a wide soup bowl. Most curious, each of the three carried a korbács whip coiled on one shoulder.

After conversing with them for some minutes, Florian turned to Edge. ''These are the brothers Jászi. Arpád, Zoltán and Gusztáv. They are csikosok—herdsmen, range riders of the puszta. They recently lost their jobs when their employer's ranch went bankrupt, so they entrained for the west to have some civilized and cultured diversion in Budapest and here at Balaton before returning to the puszta to seek new positions. Right now, they would like us to lend them three horses so they can give us a demonstration of the csikos riding style. I should like to see it.''

''So would I,'' said Edge. He whistled for a Slovak and sent him to saddle and fetch the three horses acquired so long ago from the ambushing Virginia bummers.

When the horses arrived, the brothers Jászi did not even step on the stirrups, but vaulted from the sawdust to the saddles and had the horses instantly in a furious gallop from a standing start. Then they did amazing things. They performed every trick that Buckskin Billy did, such as sliding under the horses' bellies and up their other sides to the saddles again, at full gallop. But they also turned and rode backward in the saddles, steering the horses by twisting their tails. Then, holding the tails, they slipped off the horses' croups and galloped on foot behind them, going as fast as the horses did. Then they hauled themselves up the tails, leapt onto the croups and bounced forward to the saddles again, and rode standing on them, and then, incredibly, standing on their heads—the horses still going at stretch-out gallop.

Next they resumed their proper saddle seats and uncoiled their korbácsek. First they employed them as whips. Thundering past the front row of starback seats, the first Jászi lashed out and toppled the first chair in the row, the man behind overturned the second chair, the last man the third, while the first man was already toppling the fourth chair, and so on, until the whole row of seats was upended. One of the brothers, careering past Edge, flicked his cigarette from his lips, so deftly that all Edge felt was the swish of wind.

Then they used the korbácsek as lariats. One brother swung at another, not to sting or slash, but to coil the whip around his waist and playfully yank him from his saddle. Another flung his korbács straight upward, at just the right instant to coil its end around a center-pole guy rope. He let that drag him from his saddle and, clinging to the korbács butt, swung back and forth in the air.

After a moment, the whip end loosened from the guy rope, unwound and dropped the man—but at the precise moment his horse had galloped around the pista and was under him, so he dropped neatly into the saddle again.

"Jesus Christ," said Edge. "These boys make my voltige look like a kid on a rocking horse."

"Well, they *are* seeking employment," said Florian, "and *we* have been seeking male artistes." He hesitated, cleared his throat and went on, "Also, for a long time, Zachary, I have felt that you give too much of yourself to our Florilegium—equestrian director, liberty act, shootist, voltige rider, general pacifier when there's trouble. It has somewhat distressed me to feel that we were taking undue advantage of your good nature. Now, I am fairly sure that you possess no professional jealousy, but I will ask this. Would you feel you had been demoted or rebuffed if I hired the Jászi brothers to replace you in the voltige?''

''Not at all,'' Edge said cheerfully, and almost exultantly repeated it, ''Not at *all*!'' The brothers had now dismounted and come over to them. Edge exclaimed, ''Welcome, boys, welcome!'' and pumped the hands of Zoltán, Arpád and Gusztáv, grinning so broadly that he was almost as ugly as they were.

Florian looked a little puzzled at Edge's ardency, but said, ''I'll take them to the office to talk terms, and call in Maggie Hag to talk costumes.''

''Before you go, Governor ...'' said Edge. ''Now that you've got such a spectacular replacement for at least one of my acts, I'd like to ask a favor ...''

He told of the new invitation from the ''Countess Hohenembs,'' this one including Clover Lee, and his notion of their taking only three days off each time, and not too often, maybe every two or three weeks. He wished he could really stagger Florian by revealing Amelie's true identity, but decided he had not the right to do that.

''You'll still have the liberty act that you can handle yourself, and Monday's high school riding, and now these prodigious Jászi brothers. Three good equestrian turns. So the jossers are not likely to miss one lone bareback rider. And one sharpshooter. Anyway, we'll only be absent from six performances each time we go to the palace.''

''Well, I can hardly say no to your consorting with such exalted beings,'' said Florian, who was, however needlessly, feeling guilty at having taken Buckskin Billy's voltige away from him. ''Just please try not to marry off Clover Lee to one of your titled friends. I'd hate to lose her permanently.''

So Edge went and found Clover Lee and told her of the invitation, and the limitations on their visits, and his hope that she could keep the Count Gyula Andrássy distracted with horsemanship while he enjoyed the company of the Countess Amelie. Last of all, he thought to ask if she'd *like* to go.

Clover Lee, whose cobalt eyes had been getting bigger and

bigger all through his recital, gave a whoop like the calliope and cried, "Hell, yes, I'd like to go! Let's go tomorrow!"

"No. I'll be taking Thunder, meaning I've got to give some other horse a double-quick course in fancy stepping, so Monday can go on with her haute école. Meanwhile, I suggest that you go in to Siófok and buy yourself a dinner gown— we high-toned folk dress up to the nines for dinner. Also let me point out that these will be rigorous journeys. Thunder is an old cavalry veteran; he'll do the trips with no strain; but your Snowball or Bubbles won't. I'd recommend that you try out all eight of those polka-dot horses and pick the staunchest and speediest."

"All right. Oh, Zack, I can hardly wait!"

"Yes, I can see you already putting Countess in front of your name. But this Andrássy is forty-five years old and he has a wife and kids. I don't know what other houseguests may be there. There could well be some bachelor noble closer to your age. I don't care how much flirting you do, but whenever the countess and I aren't around, you're to *stick with Count Andrássy* and keep him occupied. Is that clear?"

"Yessir, Colonel," she said, smiling and glowing and giving him a snappy salute.

Then she went immediately, bubbling with pride and delight, to tell all the other circus women of her imminent foray into the world of the high and mighty, and of her almost-*certainly* auspicious prospects there. The women lavished congratulations and good wishes on her, and assured her that she would enrapture every Prince Charming in that fairy-tale milieu. Several of them, with affectionate amusement, pretended to be bitterly envious of her. Only one, Sunday Simms, said not much at all.

And she did not say anything when, later, she and Edge chanced to pass on the midway and he gave her a genial greeting. Sunday petulantly tossed her hair and, head high, walked on. Edge turned and caught up to her and said, "Whoa, Butterfly. Why the frost?"

She glared at him and hissed, "So your countess has already got a husband, has she? So what? It doesn't stop her teasing you on, every time she's in your vicinity. It doesn't stop you chasing her like a coon hound after a bitch in heat.''

"What is this? Why on earth are you concerned about what I do? I don't think a kid should appoint herself the overseer of a grown man's behavior. This is the first time I've ever seen you show a bad temper, Sunday, and for absolutely no reason to do with you.''

"You're falling in love with this one, too, that's why.''

Genuinely bewildered, Edge said; 'If I fell in love with Maggie Hag—or Cricket the midget—or Willi Lothar—why would you *care*? Anyway, all I'm doing is going for another little holiday in the country. I'm even taking along a chaperon.''

Now she spat like a cat. ''You're taking Clover Lee to hoodwink her husband while you and the countess frolic in secret!''

''Well, confound it, girl, even if that's so, it was *your* idea.''

''Yes,'' she said miserably. ''*Damn* me and my ideas!'' And she burst into tears and ran away, leaving Edge shaking his head in perplexity.

6

THE STREETS of Keszthely were empty at eleven o'clock at night but Edge finally spotted a man, perhaps an insomniac, out walking. He asked the man for directions in the only way he could—repeating ''Festetics?'' several times—and the man replied in a way Edge could comprehend—by pointing. Edge and Clover Lee took the road he indicated and, three miles outside town, arrived at the palace. It was a grand edifice, though not so grand as Amelie's—more like a tremendous city mansion removed from the city and set among acres of lawns and flower beds. A butler answered the front door when Edge banged the gold-plated knocker. Edge introduced himself and Clover Lee, but the butler evidently knew no English. He looked haughtily and contemptuously at the man and girl in dusty riding garb, and at the sweat-matted, head-drooping two horses on the drive. So Clover Lee tried her

Rouleau-taught French to tell him that they were guests invited by the Countess Hohenembs.

The butler understood that, but said only, "Attendez ici," and shut the door in their faces.

It was opened again by the Baroness Marie Festetics, who welcomed them most warmly and apologized for the butler's not having been told to expect them, if ever and whenever they might arrive. She and the now obsequiously fawning butler led them to the dining room, the baroness saying, more to Clover Lee than to Edge, "The rest of us are in the drawing room, having a brandy before bed. But I am sure you will not wish to be introduced until the morning, when you are rested and refreshed and presentably dressed. Right now, you must be hungry, so I will have the kitchen prepare a hot meal, and meanwhile have your valet and maid draw baths for you. Where is your luggage?"

"On the horses, Baroness."

"I will have it taken up to your rooms, and have the horses taken to the stables, fed and groomed. As soon as you have had a quick wash, Burkhalter will serve you any drink you might like to have."

"Csopaki," said Edge, and the butler poured them each a large goblet of the wine, then bowed himself backward out of the room.

The baroness must have galvanized the cooks and scullions, or they were paragons of efficiency, for Edge and Clover Lee had barely finished their drinks when footmen were laying their places at the table and setting down steaming platters of mixed grill, hot rolls, silver pots of both coffee and tea, and Burkhalter was refilling their wine glasses.

"Golly," said Clover, her eyes shining. "You take this all so nonchalantly, Zack. Butler and footmen and valet and maid and all." She ravenously attacked her meal. "Well, this *is* the south end of the lake, so would you call this 'southern hospitality'?"

"Just the natural Hungarian generosity and the good manners of highborn folk," said Edge. "I'd better warn you that your maid probably doesn't speak either English or French.

But she'll know her job; you won't have to lift a finger or give a single command.''

When they had finished, Burkhalter led them upstairs to their rooms, where their personal servants were waiting. Edge and Clover Lee had of course not brought their clothes and other effects in portmanteaux, but in ordinary saddle-bags and cavalry-style saddle rolls. So both the valet and the maid were clucking over the wrinkled and rumpled garments. They took them away, indicating by gestures that they would be set to rights overnight and ready for wear in the morning. Edge took his bath unassisted, but Clover Lee was only too happy to have her maid fuss over her, do the soaping and sponging of her, shampoo her golden hair, slip a nightdress onto her and even tuck her into bed.

As she had promised Edge, Amelie shirked her usual morning health-and-strength routine and, like any ordinary empress, came down to breakfast with the others. Introductions were made all around—in English, which everyone present spoke fluently. At Edge's whispered suggestion, and to the amusement of the other guests, the Empress Elisabeth introduced herself as the Countess Hohenembs; Edge did not want an overawed Clover Lee blurting the truth all over the Florilegium. Their host, the Count Festetics, was a widower, an elderly and portly gentleman, but spry, good-humoured and given to long-winded orations; he went on at extravagant length in welcoming his new guests and praising Clover Lee's beauty and grace. Count Andrássy Gyula, first Premier of the new Kingdom of Hungary, Minister of War and Minister of Foreign Affairs, was tall and lean and handsomely hawk-faced, with a sprinkle of silver in his side-whiskers. Besides the Baroness Marie, Clover Lee and Edge, there were no other guests.

Clover Lee and Edge being the newest comers, the others insisted that they go first to the sideboard to choose from among the salvers of various kinds of omelettes, soft- and hard-boiled eggs, bacon, ham, sausage, kippers, calf's brains au beurre noir, racks of toast, bowls of gruel, pitchers of various juices, urns of coffee and tea. They did not serve themselves; they merely pointed, and footmen heaped their plates and filled their glasses and cups.

So Clover Lee and Edge were the first to sit down at the table and, while the others were still at the sideboard, Clover Lee had the opportunity to murmur, "You were right, Zack. It's almost spooky how much the Countess Amelie looks like dear Autumn. *Beautiful*! I'm disappointed that there are no young men visiting, but I can't complain. It'll be no hard task, playing companion to such a distinguished man as the count. He's quite handsome for his age. And he must think the same of me. When he kissed my hand, he practically undressed me with his eyes."

Indeed, when everybody was at table, Count Gyula's interest in the girl gave him the arrogance to interrupt an interminable anecdote his host was telling: ". . . Though clearly guilty, the man was never prosecuted because, you see, he was a mágnás, an aristocratic landowner. And incidentally, friend Edge úr, from that word comes your English word magnate—"

"They tell me," Andrássy rudely overrode him, addressing Clover Lee, "that, in addition to your beguiling blonde beauty, you have a great talent as an équestrienne, Coverley kisasszony."

"Oh, do call me Clover Lee, Your Grace," she said, coyly blinking her eyelashes at him.

"And you may call me Gyula. Or Julius, if you prefer the English rendition. I should like to ask—after breakfast, would you perhaps favor us with an exhibition of your bareback dancing and acrobatics?"

She said modestly, "I should be flattered and honored to perform for such an eminent audience."

"Better than that," said Amelie. "Miss Coverley has graciously offered to teach *you*, Gyula, some manly nuances of trick riding that will astound your steeplechasing friends. I think you should accept her offer." She laughed. "And imagine how thunderstruck your fellow ministers would be if you rode a horse right into the council chamber and began doing csikos leaps and capers. They'd never dare oppose you again on any measure you might introduce."

"Pompás!" Andrássy shouted, laughing and slapping the table. "Very well, Clover Lee. We will all attend your performance and then, when the others go about their other diversions, you and I will practice in private."

Both Clover Lee and Amelie smiled radiantly, and Edge would have, too, except that Amelie had forbidden him to.

While most of the company leaned lazily against the fence around the palace's riding ring, Clover Lee went with a boy into the stables to pick out a suitable horse—not Thunder or her Pinzgauer; they had to rest for the long ride on the morrow. Meanwhile, Amelie announced:

"I have already and frequently enjoyed Miss Coverley's performances, and Zachary must frankly be weary of seeing them. So I shall take him off and show him some of the local sights." And she sent another stable boy to saddle her two Arabians.

As they rode out of the palace grounds, the huge wolfhound Schatten appeared from somewhere and paced along with them. Amelie first led Edge down to Keszthely and the lakeshore, where many family groups were having "piknikek," wading, swimming, rowing or sailing. They halted their horses in a grove of shrubs—the sweet-scented olive, which lived up to its name by being most powerfully and deliciously fragrant—to watch the children wading so far out in the water that their features were indistinguishable, though they were walking on the lake bottom. The swimmers had to go so far out that they were mere dots.

Then Amelie led Edge around the north shore for a few miles, turned inland for a few miles more, to Szent György, to show him the famous lava rock "organ-pipe" formation there. It was a curving and recurving cliff of massive, round, vertical columns; it looked very like a calliope for Titans. They tethered their horses at the bottom and Schatten lay down to guard them. Then Edge and Amelie climbed up and around and among the columns until they found one with a flat and commodious top carpeted with soft grass and mosses. There, undisturbed except by a couple of goats bounding by, they made love, and Amelie's now-familiar crescendo and climax and diminuendo of musical laughter resounded among the rocks as if the columns really *were* organ pipes.

At dinner that night, Edge wore his white tie and tails, and Clover Lee said, admiringly, almost in surprise, that he had never looked handsomer. The two counts, of course, also wore full dress and Andrássy even wore his ministerial sash across his breast. Clover Lee looked angelic in pale-green taffeta with her golden hair streaming down the back of it, and Amelie looked undisguisably imperial in silk the exact color of her ruby tiara, necklace, rings and bracelet. Throughout dinner, Amelie and Edge exchanged looks that Andrássy would have had to be blind not to notice and interpret. However, he *was* temporarily blinded, for he and Clover Lee were exchanging the very same sort of looks. Only the Baroness Marie was aware of both sets of silent communion, and she evinced neither acceptance nor amusement nor disapproval.

Count Festetics was oblivious to any of that byplay, and equally oblivious to the fact that the others at table were quite oblivious of him. He told anecdotes and reminiscences of exceptional prolixity and dullness, untroubled when they elicited little or no comment or response from his listeners. In the infrequent intervals when he had to stop and catch his breath, the guests traded small talk heavily freighted with mots à double entente.

Amelie asked, "How did your lessons go today, Gyula?"

"Oh—ah—very well, indeed. I learned several new things. Unique ways to check. To change gait. To assume various artistic positions."

"And he taught me some things, too," said Clover Lee. She paused for an exquisitely timed beat or two, then added, "To be more graceful at taking the hurdles, for instance."

Andrássy said, "I hope you will soon return for further practice."

Amelie said, "Surely you did not practice riding all day."

"No, no. I am ashamed to admit it, but I took some amateurish falls and eventually got quite sore. So I walked with Clover Lee down to the deer park to show her this year's fawns. Alas, they have lost their dapples, but they were friendly and not at all timid of us.''

''That is because so few people ever go into the deer park,'' Amelie said roguishly. ''It is a private and cozy place.''

Count Festetics, having breathed enough to recharge his soliloquy machinery, launched into another anecdote. However, this one did rouse his guests and make them respond with merriment. Count Festetics was evidently among the many who knew that the Empress Elisabeth seldom took offense when people made fun of her emperor husband. For this particular story concluded, according to the count: ''Well, Franz Joseph told the poor, pleading supplicant, 'I will have it thought about.' Then he turned to his equerry and commanded, 'Think about it, Klaus.' ''

Amelie joined the others in appreciative laughter, and said, ''Ó jaj, that is Megaliotis to the life!'' and the other Hungarians at the table, though they had heard her use the word often before, laughed even louder at the Magyar pun implied in the Greek.

After coffee and Blood Brandy, a cherry liqueur, Edge and Clover Lee said their warm thanks and good-byes to the company, for they were going early to bed and would be leaving at dawn, before any of the others were up.

''Oh, but not *good-bye*,'' said Amelie, looking at Edge.

''Let us hope not,'' said Andrássy, looking at Clover Lee.

Edge rode cavalry style: run a mile, walk a mile—so he and Clover Lee left the palace stable yard at a gallop next morning. When, a mile later, they slowed to an easier gait and could converse, Clover Lee said boldly, ''I hope you and Countess Amelie had as much fun as Count Gyula and I did. When you told me he was getting on in years, I expected him to be all paunchy and wrinkled and withered.'' She laughed. ''*Withered* he is not.''

''I'd be surprised if he was. He's only five years older than I am.''

''Well, I hope the countess properly appreciates *you*. Gavrila Smodłaka once told me that young women and older men make the best combination.''

Edge rode in silence for a minute, then said, ''You and I have come a long way from the pitiful mud show at Beaver Creek, haven't we?''

''All of us have. Except those we've lost along the way.'' Clover Lee hesitated and then said, almost inaudibly, ''I wonder what ever became of Mother . . .''

Edge and Clover Lee were back at work in the pista the next afternoon, and Clover Lee had already regaled all her sister troupers with a detailed description of the Festetics palace—''A hundred and one rooms, a library two stories high, and fifty-two thousand books on shelves from floor to ceiling. The fanciest stables you ever saw. A deer park with tame deer . . .'' She had also given a detailed account—perhaps not *too* detailed—of her entertainment by the nobility, her having a personal maid to dress and undress and even bathe her, plus the particulars of every meal she had eaten there. The other women ooh-ed and aah-ed, and when they expressed envy this time they may not have been entirely pretending.

Clover Lee would blissfully have made the rugged journey again within a few days, and doubtless had the stamina to do it, but Edge said a firm no. ''We've got responsibilities, girl. We can't desert the Governor and the rest of the troupe and the paying public whenever we take the notion.''

''Damn. How many chances in a lifetime does a girl—?''

''However,'' Edge interrupted, ''two weeks from now, so I'm told, there's to be a four-day festival and church doings and street fairs in Siófok. It's to celebrate the birthday of some old fellow named Kossuth, who is a longtime national hero of some sort. So our show will surely draw only scant houses then, and that's when we'll go back to the palace. We'll be able to stay two days this time.''

And they did go—only to find, to Clover Lee's dismay, that Count Andrássy had been recalled to Budapest on urgent government business.

''Some kind of tiresome debate about trade agreements,'' Amelie said indifferently. ''Probably not at all important, but Gyuła *will* do his duty. The message came by telegraph and he departed immediately. I regret to tell you also, my dear, that he will not be coming back to Balaton this year.''

Edge, knowing Amelie's conviction that every younger female was her ''rival,'' privately wondered if she might just perhaps have engineered that urgent summons herself. But he said nothing.

Anyway, Clover Lee was not dismayed for long. It turned out that the palace was now inhabited by a considerable number of new guests: eight young men who were all barons, margraves or counts—or at least were viscounts who would assume those nobler titles when their fathers died—and the wives of six of them. But two of the young men, a Baron-to-be Horvát Imre and a Count-to-be Puskás Frigyes, had no wives, here or elsewhere, and their faces brightened when they were introduced to Clover Lee next morning.

Over breakfast, after the Count Festetics had taken a quarter of an hour to tell of his once having shaken hands with the hero Kossuth Lajos, Amelie announced:

''Zachary and Clover Lee, since you have an extra day to spend with us on this visit, I am preparing a special treat. We shall go to Almádi. Those southshore resorts of Siófok and Földvár, where your circus is pitched, are the most popular on the lake. Everyone flocks to them. But those of knowledge and taste go to Almádi on the north shore. It is quiet, quaint, little frequented by the vulgar city folk, and it has many delights, as you will see.''

''Is it far from here?'' asked Edge.

''Yes, nearly as far as it is from here back to your circus. What I plan is that we leave early tomorrow morning and arrive there sometime after dark. Take rooms in an inn, then spend the next day letting me show you about.''

''But that will be our fourth day, Countess. We have to be back at the tober that night.''

''And so you shall. It is just twelve miles diagonally across the lake from Almádi to your circus ground. The big ferry rowboats can each carry a horse and its owner. With four men at the oars, they make that crossing in only about three hours. So you can leave me and return to the tober as early or as late as you please. Even the next morning, and still be there in time for your show.''

''Oh. Well. That sounds fine.''

''I assumed it would, so I have already sent the Baroness Marie on ahead to engage rooms for us. The inn I have chosen—for a reason I will tell when we get there—is the Torgyöpi. It is quite a respectable inn, not just a country csárda, but it has only five rooms for overnight guests. For me, for Clover Lee, for you, Zachary, for Marie—and one extra. So, Clover Lee, you may wish to invite an escort for yourself.''

''Um-m . . .'' said Clover Lee. Young Horvát and young Puskás immediately put on looks of deep yearning. ''Yes, I probably will.''

Amelie went on, ''I assumed that, too, so I have sent three maids and two valets along with Marie. I dislike being attended by strangers, and even the best inn's domestics are always unreliable. Ours will sleep in the inn servants' quarters, or in its barn, if necessary.''

''And what about us,'' asked Edge, ''if those five rooms are already occupied?''

Amelie flicked him a glance of tolerant amusement. ''Marie will have only to mention my name. Now then. Let us divert ourselves about the palace and the grounds today, and not too strenuously, so we are fit for the long ride tomorrow.''

Clover Lee disobeyed, to the extent of donning her léotard and fleshings and giving another exhibition of her équestrienne skills to the assemblage of new guests, at which the young viscounts Horvát and Puskás cheered and clapped louder than all the others together. When she was dressed again, Clover Lee did spend the rest of the day in leisurely activities. Puskás and Horvát simultaneously requested the honor of showing her the statuary on the grounds, the exotic-fish pond, the lily pond, the deer park. Clover Lee accepted them both, so she was flanked by them as they wandered about the estate, and she flashed coquettish looks at them impartially, and impartially bandied flirtatious small talk. At invervals, the two swains glared go-away looks at each other over Clover Lee's blonde head, while she was wickedly wishing that—like a genuine femme fatale—she could provoke them to a duel for her favor. But they were still a threesome when the company sat down to dinner that night.

Edge did his host the courtesy of spending some of the morning in his company, with the twelve other men and women, and listening, with an assumed air of rapt interest, while old Count Festetics related at tedious length—and sometimes stood up to act out—incidents in his life from boyhood to date. It took him half an hour to get to his thirteenth year, in 1809, when he was initiated by a governess into the Great Mystery. He did not act out that event, but he made it seem as boring and wearisome as his droned account of it; Edge decided that the governess must have been a patient and a desperate woman.

The guest couples, one after another, began to remember errands they had to do elsewhere. Edge stayed long enough to hear about the failed but heroic 1848 revolution against Austria's rule of Hungary, expecting an account of strategies and tactics and battles. But it developed that the count's only heroic revolutionary service had consisted entirely of distributing "Down With the Emperor" manifestos. At which, Edge said he had to go and see how his horses were bearing up after yesterday's long ride.

"God, but that old man is a jawsmith," he said, when he found Amelie cutting long-stemmed roses in one of the gardens.

"That is why you will almost always find a new and different group of guests every time you come here." She added, with a provocative smile, "And there are so many things nicer to do than either talk or listen. Here, help me carry these roses up to my suite."

And there, during most of the rest of the day, Amelie did very little talking but a great deal of her distinctive laughing, soft to loud to soft again, and did it repeatedly, and evidently would have been pleased to go on doing it indefinitely. But they eventually had to pause, to dress for dinner and listen to Count Festetics some more.

Early next morning, the two couples—Clover Lee had chosen Puskás to be her escort; he was handsomer than Horvát—

set out in an elegant but fairly lightweight clarence with a four-horse hitch. The great dog Schatten cantered alongside and occasionally leapt upon the seat beside the coachman for a riding rest. The clarence was followed by another four-in-hand carrying hampers of wine and luncheon victuals, the considerable traveling luggage of Countess Amelie and Viscount Puskás, the considerably less luggage of Edge and Clover Lee, and their saddles. On lead reins behind that coach, Thunder and the Pinzgauer ran unencumbered and easily.

They did not eat their luncheon until quite late in the afternoon, because Amelie insisted on waiting until they could detour southward onto the Tihany peninsula. There the coachmen spread linen tableclothes piknik style, and set out the food and wine, in the middle of eighty-five acres of lavender. Tihany, said Amelie, was the supplier of oil of lavender to every parfumerie in Europe. The gardeners were just then harvesting the blossoms, and it seemed to Edge and Clover Lee that the fragrance must be detectable as far away as Budapest.

They reached Almádi about nine o'clock that night, and that town also was perfumed, but by a more subtle citric aroma. The proprietor of the Torgyöpi Inn, bowing and scraping, and the Baroness Marie met them and led them up an outside staircase, so they need not elbow through the taproom full of tipplers, to their rooms on the upper floor. The innkeeper spoke to Amelie in Magyar, but she repeated his message in English to Edge and Clover Lee. He said that the baroness and his local clientele had already dined, but he was holding the kitchen staff in readiness to prepare a superb meal for the new arrivals—and what would it be Her Imperial Majesty's pleasure to eat?

"On this visit I am the Countess Hohenembs, Juhasz úr. And what else would one eat at a lakeside inn but the delicious fogas in that secret caper sauce of yours? Asparagus. Potatoes stewed with paprika. And to start, I think, a cold parsley soup. And, of course, Somlyó."

"It will be on the table, Your Grace, as soon as you and your guests have refreshed yourselves."

A maid or a valet was waiting in each of the guests' rooms,

and had, with mysteriously prescient timing, already filled the plunge baths with hot and fizzy mineral water—and Amelie's with hot Jersey milk. The Baroness Marie joined Amelie's maid to help attend her. No one dressed for dinner here, but they all changed from their travel-worn clothes into fresh garments.

They convened again downstairs in the big taproom. Its many tables were all chockablock with men, and a few women, convivially drinking, loudly talking and laughing. In one corner, the wife of innkeeper Juhasz was playing a cimbalom. She played nowhere so well as Elemér Gombocz, but none of the patrons seemed to be listening, anyway. Juhasz led the new guests to an alcove off the room, distant enough that the ambient noise was not overpowering, and curtained for privacy, but Amelie told him to leave the curtain open.

"So I can show you something," she said to Clover Lee and Edge and Puskás. "I always come to this inn because it is unique. It is built on the border between the megye—the county—of Veszprém and that of Fejep. Therefore, what you would call the county line runs through the middle of that vast taproom out there. In consequence, this inn is much frequented by highway-men and other kinds of outlaws and fugitives. If, as often happens, the police of one county come in to take a look around, or just to have a drink, the rogues simply move to the other side of the room. That longest table in the center actually straddles the megye line. It may be that the men you see sitting at it are detective policemen on one side and bandits on the other, all drinking amicably together."

As they ate their delicate, flaky, melt-in-the-mouth fogas pike-perch, Amelie told of another curiosity unique to Almádi:

"This wine we are drinking is the local Somlyó, which the Almádi folk claim to be the best wine in Hungary, and I am inclined to agree. The vintners say it is so good because the vines eternally 'see their own reflection in the Balaton.' That is to say, the sunlight reflects off the lake waters, so the vines get the sun on the underside of their leaves as well as the upper."

When they finished dinner and went to their chambers, it became evident that they really need not have engaged *all* of the Torgyöpi's rooms, because, after the servants had been dismissed, neither Edge nor young Puskás spent that night in his own assigned quarters. Edge did, however, get up early and return to his room, so Amelie's maid could be summoned to prepare her olive-oil bath.

The day was disappointingly overcast and gray, but the lakeside vineyards were turning red and gold and seemed to radiate a sunshine of their own, and the air was still scented with that clean, tart citric aroma

"Lime trees," said the Baroness Marie. "Almádi is planted with sixteen different varieties of them, and they bloom at different times, in sequence. So the air here, except in winter, is *always* perfumed."

The town was set within a semicircle of hills, so the two couples went to wander among them, admiring the peasants' cottages—only modest things of whitewashed logs or wattle-and-daub, but every one entwined all about with climbing roses or wearing rose bushes growing all over its thatch roof. Amelie pointed to the highest of the hills in the vicinity, a sort of lopsided cone in shape, which they were approaching.

"This is the Great Nose," she said. "According to Almádi legend, the very last remaining giant of the fairy tales died here. The people respectfully buried him, but they could not scrape up enough soil to cover his nose."

When they arrived there, they found it was a protrusion of solid rock, with no trace of vegetation anywhere on it except for splotches of varicolored lichen. Amelie showed them the numerous but far-apart cells that hermit monks had laboriously chipped out and inhabited, some eight hundred years ago.

"The Nose has always served another function, too," she said. "Perhaps you noticed the boy sitting on its very top. He would be the youngest child of some fisher family. From up there, he can see down through the surface glare on the water, into the lake's depths. When he sees a shoal of fish, he signals its location to the men in the dories."

The atmosphere was getting warmer, grayer and more

muggy when they returned to the lakeside. They settled themselves on a beach of reddish sand and, as Amelie had earlier arranged, their coachmen came from the inn bringing hampers of hot food, wine, table silver, linen cloths and serviettes, plus a tremendous beef bone for Schatten. The four were just finishing the last bottle of Somlyó when they were startled by a loud *boom*! overhead, and looked up to see a puff of white smoke hanging below the gray sky. Another puff blossomed near it and, after a moment, came the *boom*! of that one.

Clover Lee said, "They must be shooting off fireworks at that Kossuth festival over at Siófok."

"No," said Amelie, frowning. "Those are the storm-warning rockets."

Indeed, the sky, which had been a featureless lead-colored dome, was now bulging into pouches of bruise-colored cloud.

"Is it likely to be a bad one?" asked Edge, as more rockets burst up and down the lake.

"The storms are always bad on Balaton."

"Then I'm sorry, Amelie, but I'll have to leave you. This could be big trouble for our circus tops. I've got to get over there before it breaks, if I can. Where do the ferries dock?"

Amelie took him and Clover Lee there, while the coachmen ran to the Torgyöpi to fetch their luggage, saddles and horses. Amelie spoke to one of the ferrymen—who, recognizing her, tugged his forelock and bowed repeatedly—but when he replied, even Edge could comprehend that he was being apologetically reluctant.

"He says," Amelie translated, "that every other boat is coming in off the water, and you'd be a fool—so would he— to go out upon it now for a three-hour crossing. He also says that he certainly would not chance the crossing with a horse in the boat. At the best of times, a horse is always nervous, moving about and shifting the boat's balance. If the storm hits, the panicked horse might kick the boat to fragments. Now, if you wish, I can *command* him, and he will not dare disobey . . ."

"No. Don't call for your red-hot irons. See if you can persuade him to take only me. Clover Lee can stay here overnight—the storm surely will be over by then—and arrange to bring over the horses and our gear in the morning.''

So Amelie spoke again, and rather forcefully. The ferryman looked still reluctant, but cowed. He called his three rowing mates and gave them instructions. They looked frankly apprehensive, but also gave the empress a forelock salute, went and piled oars in the boat and undid its painter from the dock. While they were occupied, Edge gave Amelie a quick embrace and a kiss and said:

"These have been two days to treasure among the best memories of my whole life. If that barge doesn't founder out there, I'll try to see you at least once more before the circus moves on. Or, if the whole Florilegium gets blown away, I may have to settle here permanently."

"Isten vele," she murmured, smiling a little forlornly. "God keep you safe."

With the four oarsmen pulling their hardest, even the big and clumsy hulk of a ferry moved away southward at a goodly speed. Incoming boatmen shouted at them in tones of questioning amazement, or warningly, or derisively, but Edge's ferrymen saved their breath and did not shout retorts. The storm held off for two hours, until they were only four miles from their destination. Then it hit—a fierce south wind, into which and against which the oarsmen had to struggle. It was really less wind than water, what with its deluge content of rain. The lake surface changed from chop to waves, then heaved into billows, then the billows became high, curling combers, which the wind instantly decapitated into blasts of spin-drift.

Within minutes, Edge and the other men were ankle deep in water. One of them shouted to him and jabbed a finger. Edge looked where he pointed and saw a bucket tucked under a thwart, so he quickly began bailing. No storm could have dumped enough water into that big boat to swamp it, but the oarsmen certainly did not want the extra weight of the water, battling as they were directly into the onrushing waves and the battering-ram wind. Though Edge bailed as rapidly and efficiently as he could, he barely managed to keep the water where it had been when he started, at ankle level, because the driving rain and blown spray came into the boat as fast as he threw it out.

The ferry was tossing and lunging and yawing so, and the air was so thick with water, that Edge wondered how the men could possibly be keeping on course, or if they were. Nothing could be seen anywhere beyond a four-or five-yard radius from the boat, except the forks and jags and writhings of blue-white lightning. They lit up the dense air every few seconds, so the bone-shaking, mind-numbing thunder was like a continuous cannonade.

It took fully two more hours to go that remaining third of the crossing, but they did it and almost perfectly accurately. Something suddenly slashed at Edge's neck, and he looked up from his bucket to see that they were entering the lakeside reed beds. Though the reeds thrashed and whipped at the oarsmen on the windward side of the boat, they did palliate the force of wind and waves to some degree. In just a few minutes more, the ferry's blunt bow grated on pebbles. All the men, including Edge, leapt overside and wrestled the big craft up the bank to where it was securely beached. The four oarsmen then collapsed on the pebble beach, so exhausted and already so drenched that they cared not at all that the rain still scoured at them. Edge left them to follow him and collect their fare when they recovered, and plodded on inland against the wind and rain.

Twilight was coming on, but here, where the roiled and thrown-about lake water was not contributing to the murkiness, Edge could see farther. He soon espied the Florilegium some distance off to his left, but its skyline was different from what it had been when he last saw it. He arrived there, and saw why: the chapiteau's canvas and poles and contents were all on the ground. And the ground, having been denuded by the thousands of trampling feet over the past weeks, was now a morass of glutinous mud. Almost every one of the pavilion's roof and side panels had been ripped from its lacings, and the pieces blown far and wide. The roustabouts and most of the other men of the circus were chasing them and trying to roll or fold them to prevent their being blown away entirely.

The two center poles lay on the ground, pointing in opposite directions. The many side poles, the starback chairs, the seating planks, their stringers and jacks were strewn all over the tober. The bandstand had collapsed into an untidy heap of boards, and the cimbalom stood on its legs, but they were slowly sinking into the mud. The tangle that had been the trapeze rigging gleamed from the middle of a puddle. Snarls and knots and snakes of ropes were everywhere. Of the whole chapiteau, only the tent stakes still stood firm in the ground, outlining the immense oval where the pavilion had been, and the pista curbing in the middle of that oval had not budged.

"Blowdown!" shouted Florian, coming up to Edge. He was red-eyed, his hair and little beard disheveled, and his fancy frock coat and stirrup trousers were plastered with mud, but he did not seem unduly downcast. "Could have been worse. Hell, I've *had* worse ones."

"Anybody hurt?" Edge shouted back, to be heard above the roar of wind and the explosions of thunder.

"Nobody important. A Slovak got his collarbone broken."

They put their heads close together, so as not to have to go on bellowing.

"No jossers injured?" Edge asked. "To hold us to blame?"

"No. Only a sparse bianca house—because of the festival, you know. When the rockets went up, soon after intermission, I ordered the top evacuated—the people were sensibly already going, anyway—and Maggie refunded their ticket money. Meanwhile, we rolled all the wagons to the windward of all the tops, beginning with the menagerie, and running extra guy ropes from them to the side poles. The more skittish animals, the camel and the zebras, we tethered in the woods. Carl got all his instruments inside the wagons, except the cimbalom; we couldn't spare men to move it."

"Sounds like you did all you could."

"Well, the menagerie, the dressing tents, the annex, they are all fairly low to the ground—they merely split some lacings here and there. But, even with all our precautions, the high chapiteau could not buck a storm like this one. And a few of the flimsier midway joints and tents got blown to Kingdom Come.''

''Can the chapiteau be repaired?''

''Oh, yes. Have to be dried out and cleaned of mud. Some grommets tore loose and one of the gumshoe spikes snapped off. The lungia boom's yoke tore loose from its center pole. But nothing Stitches can't fix. And we'll need a few miles of new rope.''

Edge's four ferrymen appeared just then, looking weary and bedraggled, but also looking proud of their having bested the storm.

''These are the men who rowed me over here,'' said Edge. ''Ask how much I owe them.''

Florian did, and they named a price that Edge thought so ridiculously little, after what they had endured, that he voluntarily tripled it. Florian spoke to the men again and pointed, and they went off to the wagon he had indicated.

''Mag has made sandwiches and cooked up a huge vat of soup on her kitchen-wagon stove, so the workers can snatch some nourishment on the run. I invited your ferrymen to partake.''

''Well, where can I pitch in to help here?'' Edge asked. ''I'm just standing around like a rube rubberneck.''

''At ease, soldier. The other lads are sufficient. Any more would just get in the way. Besides, when we've got all the fragments retrieved and collected, we'll want one clear-headed and unfatigued boss to oversee the further operations.''

''What operations? We'll be out of action for a good long while. Even if we got the chapiteau up again tomorrow, this sea of mud will take a week to dry out. Nobody would wade through this to see the best show on the planet.''

''I am talking of teardown. As always, Zachary, we must work things out as we go along, and now the Storm God or Mother Nature or something has told us that it's time to take our leave. You just now came through the lakeside reed beds; they were green when we arrived; they are golden yellow now. Autumn is upon us. Since a good part of the teardown has already been accomplished, willy-nilly, I intend that we do the rest of it, pack up and head east. We'll tarry here until Stitches and his men have done the major repairs. Then they can do the lesser work on the road, whenever we stop for the night.''

''Ah, well,'' said Edge, with a sigh inaudible in the storm. ''I sure have got fond of Balaton, but of course you're right. In which case, Governor, I'd like your permission to extend my malingering for a few hours more. I'd like to say a last good-bye to the countess. She's just across the lake in Almádi. As soon as the storm clears, I can go over and back in about seven hours. I'll be here before our men are rested up enough to tackle the teardown or need any clear-headed boss.''

''Of course, my boy. Permission granted.''

The rain stopped shortly before dawn, as abruptly as if a valve had been turned off. The wind dropped to no more than its usual brisk velocity. The lake subsided to its normal chop, and the last clouds trailed off northward in time for there really to be a dawn. The sun came up and set the whole wet world a-sparkle, striking little rainbows from every raindrop on every tree leaf and on every surface of the battered Florilegium. Edge was again aboard when the ferrymen went back across Balaton. They had been much invigorated by the night's rest and Magpie Maggie Hag's provender. They pulled with a will and chattered among themselves— probably, thought Edge, about the devastation they had seen at the tober.

About halfway across, Edge's boat met two others. In one, the polka-dot Pinzgauer horse rocked and swayed and uneasily shifted its feet and walled its eyes. In the other, Thunder rode more serenely, and Clover Lee was with him. She and Edge both managed to tell their oarsmen to stop, and the men let Edge's boat and Clover Lee's drift close enough together that they could converse.

''What are you coming back for?'' she cried, with distress in her voice. ''Dear God, is it all gone?''

"No, no. Chapiteau blew down is all. Nobody hurt. It looks pretty chaotic to me, but Florian is taking it in his stride. Is the countess still at the inn?"

"Yes. She'll stay until the roads dry out some."

"Florian is going to tear down and move on, so I want to say good-bye to her. You go on, and I'll be back in a little while. And thanks, Clover Lee, for bringing the horses and our gear. I'm only surprised you're not bringing the viscount."

She grinned. "He never got around to proposing. Maybe I kept him too busy to propose. Anyway, if he had, I don't think I could bear to have the name of Mrs. Frigyes Puskás. Not even with Countess in front of it."

Amelie, from her upstairs window, saw Edge trudging up the path to the inn and instantly guessed why he had returned. She went down to the taproom and found it empty except for landlord Juhasz and his wife, rearranging bottles behind the serving bar. Everybody else in Almádi was out inspecting the storm damage to his boat or nets or vines. Amelie asked Juhasz úr and né if they would please absent themselves for a little while, and they obligingly did so, as Edge walked in.

He and Amelie embraced and held each other tightly, in silence for some time. Edge did not love this woman and had never entertained any aspirations of ever being anything more to her than an occasional diversion. But he was truly fond of her—and, he would admit it, secretly more than a bit awed and smug and conceited at having been the lover of an empress. And there was also, every time they were together, the illusion that at least the lineaments of Autumn lived again. It was hard to part from her.

"It need not be forever," she said, when he had explained the situation. "Yours is a traveling circus, and I do much traveling myself. This entire continent is but a fraction bigger than your one nation of the United States. So there is every possibility that we will meet again. In Hungary, Austria, Greece, England . . ."

"I'll devoutly hope so."

"Or you may quickly forget me," she said, with a pretense of cheerful teasing. "There are many beautiful women in

Saint Petersburg, among the upper classes, anyway.''

"I'm willing to wager my right arm that I'll never forget *you*.''

"Nevertheless, I do not wish you to take holy orders and vow celibacy. I shall even help you to meet some of those highborn women. Did you know that the Tsaritsa Maria Alexandrovna is of German birth? Before she wed Tsar Alexander, she was Princess Maximilienne of Hesse. Her family and mine have always been close. I was only an infant when she married and disappeared into darkest Russia. But we have had crown reasons to correspond from time to time. I will write for you a letter of introduction to the tsaritsa, and send it by a ferryman before your circus departs.''

"That's kind of you. It will especially please Florian. He is always wanting opportunities to mingle with the élite.''

"And you and I will not say good-bye, Zachary, but viszontlátásra, auf Wiedersehen, 'til we meet again. Now—kiss me once more. Then I will go and I will not look back, for I shall have tears in my eyes.''

Edge's own eyes were a little blurry when he stood alone in the taproom. He reached for a bottle of brandy, poured and drank a substantial glassful, left a coin on the counter and turned to go. Then he paused, surprised. In the cimbalom in the corner, an apparently overtightened string chose that moment to succumb to its long strain, and broke: *kling-g*! Edge waited until its small, sad, last-ever chime had finished echoing faintly around the big room, and then he left.

7

THE CIRCUS train, minus its tail of midway vehicles, made good time going east and a little north across the puszta. The roads were decent, and so was the weather. There was never the slightest hill to climb, and the rivers and creeks were all well bridged or easily fordable. There was only an occasional csárda along the way at which to get a meal of kettle stew, but Magpie Maggie Hag kept her stove continuously banked with coals so it could be fired up in a hurry. She and her women helpers managed competently to keep the whole company fed—if not with sumptuous viands, at least nutritiously—from the supplies stocked in her wagon. She also still slept in there, and everybody suspected that the Hanswurst did, too, since he drove her vehicle and was constantly with her. The old gypsy and the old joey were small people, but they must have been cramped in there, for it had formerly been also the dressing wagon, and still carried, on hangers or neatly folded on shelves, all the costumes of the troupe.

Starting early each morning and not stopping until it was too dark to roll, the circus train made some twenty miles a day, meaning it would take them about twenty days to reach the border at the river Prut. But in less than a week, everybody in the train was thoroughly sick of the puszta—that endless plain of high grass and wild grains, interrupted only at long intervals by minuscule mud villages, where the peasants came out to stare vacant-eyed and slack-jawed at their passing. They also, now and then, passed a farm of domestic grains, where they might see the farmer doing a primitive sort of threshing. A broad circle of mown rye or buckwheat was laid on the ground, and he stood in the center of the circle holding a guide rope while a horse plodded around and around, treading out the grain. There was an infrequent tree or clump of shrub, too, but in this season everything was gloomily colored brown or dun or gray, except for the occasional spangle of bright vermilion wild poppies.

Looking at the flat and uninviting vista ahead, before they took the road one morning, Yount gloomily commented to his Agnete, "Well, this poosta may not be the end of the world, but I do believe I can see it from here."

Standing nearby, Magpie Maggie Hag, who had lately been even gloomier than the others, said, "For some, it *is* end of world."

"Hvad?" said Agnete. "For none of *us*, I hope. We have just lost one companion, not to mention all the midway people."

Abner Mullenax had come to Florian shortly after teardown at Balaton, his one eye bloodshot, and said, "Governor, I ain't no use to you-all no more. I'd like to stay here with the midway folks. One of them shoe-slapper girls is kind of sweet on me, and the whole bunch have offered to pay me a smidgen for doin' odd jobs—carryin' kegs and swampin' out and suchlike—enough to keep me in likker, anyway. Plus peck, if I can live on sausages and pretzels and ices.''

''Well, old fellow, you've been with us for a long time, but you've never been indentured. You are free to go or stay wherever you please.''

''I like this place, and the locals are friendly. I think it'll be a good spot for Barnacle Bill to drop anchor.''

''Won't you be a little hampered by the language problem?''

''Not in bed with my girl. And in a saloon, all you got to do is point at a bottle and crook your elbow.''

''True. But Abner, you should have some money put by, in case sometime you do part company with the midway. The *Saratoga* was your contribution to the Florilegium, and we never paid you a cent for it.''

''Aw, shucks, forget it. You've kept me on the payroll, when I ain't been nothin' but dead weight for months now.''

''No—here—I insist on your taking at least this hundred dollar's worth of forints. Tuck it in a grouch bag.''

''Well . . .'' said Mullenax, thirstily licking his lips, and he accepted the wad of money.

''We all wish you happiness here, Abner. Someday surely we will pass this way again, and we'll hope to see you thriving.'' But Florian sadly doubted that they would ever see Barnacle Bill again, here or anywhere, considering his ever-oftener crooking of the elbow.

Now, far out on the puszta, Florian bawled for the circus train to move out. To Edge's slight surprise, Magpie Maggie Hag climbed up to ride beside him.

''Want tell you something,'' she said, as they bumped from their camping field up onto the road. ''I dukker trouble again with Pavlo Smodlaka. Somewhere. Sometime.''

''Oh, hell, what now? Last time, he was convinced that the Démon Débonnaire was a real demon out to get him.''

''Now he worried férfifarkas get him.''

"Jesus. What is férfifarkas? It doesn't sound any more dangerous than dandruff."

"Don't know word in English. In Spanish maybe hombrelobo."

"Wolf man? A *werewolf*?"

Magpie Maggie Hag shrugged. "Pavlo speak some Magyar. In last csárda where we stop, he drinking with peasants, tell them he going to Russia. They all look horror. Say he brave man, dare go there, because of férfifarkas. In Russia, they say, some men become férfifarkas. In Russian tongue, oborotyen. Come full moon, such man grows hair all over, four legs, tail, fangs, claws, exact same as wolf, goes hunting other men to eat. Or women, children. Easier to catch."

"Godamighty. And he believed this bunkum?"

"Pavlo believe anything, suspect anything, scared of anything. Even nervous of wife, now. Tells me Gavrila wakes him up in middle of night to criticize his *dreams*. She never do any such thing."

Edge made a noise of amused exasperation. "I'll have a talk with him. Try to persuade him there's no such thing as a werewolf."

"Do that, pralo. I dukker very terrible trouble."

By detouring slightly to the south, the circus could have visited Debrecen, a market town at the crossroads of several trade routes and sizable enough to have provided ample patronage for several days of showing. But Florian said he was damned if he'd unpack and unload the tightly crammed wagons until he had to do it at trainside, and he was anxious to get to that waiting train, for the nights were getting cold and even the daytimes were getting nippy. So the only community in which the Florilegium dallied for a while was a village called Nagykálló, somewhat bigger, cleaner and more attractive than the imbecile-inhabited mud hamlets they had earlier passed through. And they paused in Nagykálló only because it happened to be the home village of the Jászi brothers, and Zoltán, Gustáv and Arpád together besieged Florian to plead that the company stop and enjoy the hospitality of their relatives and friends.

Florian might have argued, but he was given no chance. The circus train had halted in the middle of the large square around which Nagykálló was built, and a crowd had immediately gathered. All of them recognized the Jászi boys and began an uproar of greetings and welcome-home. Zoltán waved violently to hush them, then belabored the crowd for at least ten minutes with a bellowed, gesticulating recitation of the brothers' adventures since they had left the defunct ranch outside town.

"Now he's telling them," Florian interpreted to the others of the troupe, "how we rescued them from unemployment, disgraceful idleness and possible starvation. We have given them a job they delight in, and have made them stellar artistes, the toast of Lake Balaton, and soon to be *internationally* renowned. He enjoins the villagers to help him and his brothers show their gratitude by wining, dining and putting us up in their houses, and then turning out tomorrow en masse for a festival in our honor."

The crowd roared again, obviously in wholehearted concurrence, and Florian added, with a sigh of resignation, "We can hardly be so boorish as to rebuff such enthusiastic friendliness. They are poor people—homespun smocks, wooden shoes—and yet eager to share with us whatever they have. Stitches, order your Slovaks to find a field in which to stow all our vehicles and tether the walking beasts. Then, except for attending to the animals, the roustabouts might as well relax with the rest of us. No need even to post a watchman."

The villagers pressed in upon the company, plucking at sleeves and crying, "Gyere! Egy vendeget!" So the artistes and crewmen got rather haphazardly apportioned out by ones and twos—the partnered men and women managing to stay together—and were triumphantly borne off to their inviters' houses. The aged mother and father of the Jászi brothers got not only their sons but also Florian and Edge. All of those except Edge spent the remainder of the day in animated conversation. Then, after supping with the family, Florian excused himself and went the circuit of all the other houses entertaining his company, to see if there were questions or problems that he could resolve by speaking Magyar.

Every guest that night got a potluck meal or whatever the host family had been cooking up for itself—in most houses the standard peasant fare of mutton gruel, cabbage, black rye bread and home-brewed beer. But the women of the house clomped about in their wooden shoes on the hard-packed earthen floor, already at work to prepare a grand feast for the next day. They killed and plucked chickens, brought in slabs of beef and lamb from their barns, brought butter and milk and eggs and vegetables from their spring boxes, began peeling and chopping and stirring things. Meanwhile, everybody in every family happily chattered at every circus guest, not a whit discouraged or desisting when the guest could reply only with a wavery smile.

However, when, with the aid of gestures, the hosts made the guests understand that they were to take the family bed or beds, and the family would sleep on the floor, some of the visitors made polite but firm protest. They seized on Florian when he dropped in and made him tell their hosts that they would do no such thing, but they would sleep in their own caravans or wagons. Most of the company, though, were too meek or too overwhelmed by their hosts' pertinacious generosity to refuse the family beds. Long before morning, they wished that they had.

"Bugs!" said Daphne, with disgust and loathing, when the company convened outdoors next morning. "I am covered with welts!"

"Not just bedbugs! Fleas and lice!" said Meli, scratching. "I feel all crawly. I itch all over."

"Now, now," Florian said soothingly, though scratching himself. "It's an old adage; you're not properly circus until you've been properly lousy. Remember where you are, and pity the people, and try not to be too obviously distraught or displeased by the inconveniences. Besides, this short sojourn will make you better appreciate the lodgings I have hitherto arranged for you, and intend to continue providing wherever they are available."

"But we'll be taking these vermin with us when we go!"

squealed Clover Lee, scratching. "Into our caravans, onto the train, everywhere!"

"No, we won't," said Edge, scratching. "Just don't go near your vans today. Stay in these same clothes. We'll be sleeping here again tonight and leaving in the morning. Ask your chums who did sleep in their vans last night, and didn't get contaminated, to fetch you fresh clothes to put on tomorrow. But not to fetch them *until* tomorrow. Meanwhile, we'll all do an old army trick. I've already been scouting around, and there's an ant hill down yonder by that linden tree." He pointed.

Daphne said, incredulous, "Bugs, lice, fleas aren't enough?"

Edge ignored her. "At bedtime, strip down to your skin and take your clothes—never mind if you have to step over the family on the floor. They won't give you a glance. I've noticed that our hosts sleep buck naked and pile their clothes high on a shelf or something. Before you go to bed, take *all* your clothes and go and heap them on top of that ant hill. The ants will have eaten them clean of the vermin by morning. Just make sure you pop anything still crawling on your skin before you put on the fresh clothes your chums bring."

Some of the more modest of the company were scandalized, and bleated. Others thanked Edge. And even the most modest, after spending the whole day scratching, followed his advice that night, and found that it worked as warranted, and was well worth their blushing nighttime run in the nude through a houseful of strangers and through the village lanes to the ant hill by the linden tree.

However, that day's festival was entertaining and absorbing enough that most of the lousy and flea-ridden company scratched only absentmindedly, all their attention on the performances being given in their honor. The first thing they noticed was that overnight a tremendous wooden platform had been erected in the middle of the village square, supported on posts only about a foot high.

"For the dancing," said Florian.

"What do they need that for?" asked Fitzfarris. "The

ground here is as flat and hard and smooth as any ballroom floor.''

''For resonance. Magyar dancing involves a good deal of stamping and leaping, and on the platform they can thunder more loudly.''

The whole village population attended, and so did hordes of country folk, somehow apprised of the occasion during the night and come from miles around. All those who would not be performing, or not yet, sat or squatted on the ground around the platform, giving the Florilegium guests the places where they could see best. Florian sat with Papa and Mama Jászi, so he could ask questions, and he relayed the replies and comments to any interested others of the troupe.

There climbed onto the back of the platform—to face the honored guests—the village musicians, three men in all, wearing their best and best-kept suits of clothes, as was evidenced by the odor of camphor they exuded. The three heaved up an old and scarred cimbalom, at which one seated himself; the two others went away and came back with an accordion and a zither. They warmed up by playing an overture: ''There Is But One Girl,'' already familiar to the circus folk from Beck's rendition. And despite the paucity of instruments, it was well played. Even cimbalist Elemér was seen to nod in approval of the cimbalist onstage.

Then Carl Beck was seen to confer with little Tücsök, and the midget got up and scampered around behind the platform. When the piece was finished, she reached up and tugged at the coattail of one of the men, and spoke to him. The man nodded with enthusiasm, first to her, then out at the circus people. Tücsök scampered back to Boom-Boom. He beckoned to various of his windjammers—the snare and tenor drummers, the tuba and contrabass tuba, the trombone, clarinets, violins, the oboist, and to Hannibal Tyree, the bass drummer, and sent them running to the wagons to get their instruments.

When all those bandsmen returned, they arranged themselves behind the platform, so as not to detract from the village musicians' distinction of being onstage. Then the audience gave a great gasp of awe and rapture. They had never heard anything like it, when "There Is But One Girl" was played again, and thunderously, joyously, with flourishes, by that massed ensemble. Thereafter, when singers took the platform, Beck kept his band silent, not to overwhelm the voices. But when dancers came onstage, if the accompanying music was familiar to Beck and his men, they played in concert from the start. If it was unfamiliar, they let the Nagykálló musicians do the first refrain and chorus, which was enough to enable them to join in, in perfect tune and time, for the next several repetitions.

If only the prettiest Nagykálló females were allowed or cared to perform in public, then there was in this vicinity an extraordinarily high percentage of pretty women and girls, high-breasted and long-legged. One group of them wore short white gowns festooned all over with little silver beads. Another group wore short, brightly colored dresses that were an infinity of tiny pleats. All wore high, soft, white leather boots. The women and girls had arranged their hair in whatever style best suited or pleased them. By contrast, the men had all plastered down their normally curly black hair, uniformly flat and shiny, with fringes of spit curls across their foreheads, and all wore black bandit mustaches like those of the Jászi brothers. Indeed, the Jászi brothers themselves participated in most of the doings on the platform. All the men were shod in high, soft, shiny black leather boots. For the romantic and comic dances, they wore wide, pleated white linen pantaloons and blouses embroidered all over with flowers of red, purple, orange and green. For the more warlike dances, they covered those vivid blouses with bulky, shaggy, colorless sheepskin cloaks.

"You suppose that we are poor people here," Papa Jászi said to Florian. "And we are, we are. These costumes are brought out only—and tenderly, respectfully—on the most special of occasions."

"My company and I am honored," said Florian.

"But poverty has some advantages, however paltry and pathetic," old Jászi went on. "Our people spend most of their lives stumping about in heavy, clumsy wooden shoes. It follows, then, that when they don the soft, light dancing boots, their feet are feather weightless and fleet and nimble."

"Jaj de szép!" exclaimed Florian. "I can see that."

When only the women and girls danced, the group in beaded white did frisky, laughing, coquettish dances. The group in colored frocks did even brisker, louder-laughing and shouting comic dances. At least one of those was danced throughout on the heels of their boots, their toes never touching the platform.

The men's dances were still more energetic. They repeatedly leapt into impossible caprioles, slapping their hands against their boots behind their backs, in front of them or split wide sideways. In one of their comic dances, the men all sat on low milking stools and danced and stamped their feet in rhythm to the music. Then they lifted their feet and held and galloped the *stools* about the platform in intricate patterns, still in perfect time to the music.

For their warlike dances, the men put on—besides the bulky sheepskins—spurs that they jingled and clashed together, to add a whole new instrument section to the band. Then there was a sword dance. The swords were very old, nicked, some slightly bent but the men must have been up all night polishing them, for they were bright as new. And in that dance, the many ringing, sparkspewing sword fights— each man against another, or one against many, or all against all—added yet another new instrument section to the music.

"Almost all our puszta men's dances," Papa Jászi confided to Florian, "derive from the old verbunkos, the military recruiting dance. The emperor used to send a military band and a troupe of soldier-dancers all about the land. They did such a rousing, exhilarating verbunkos that many of the local young men were stirred to patriotic fervor, and would march off with them to take up military service." He chuckled. "We Magyars are easily moved by emotion."

In between every few dances, the performers stood still to sing—some solo, then all in chorus with the village musicians' accompaniment, then a capella—songs of love, of melancholy, of ancient heroes, anthems from the failed revolution of twenty years ago. They went on like that all day, seemingly tireless, alternating singing and dancing—except for a break at midday, when numerous village housewives went among the crowd, handing out a light repast of little mutton pies and mugs of beer.

The performance concluded at twilight with an explosive climax. A girl singer had just finished a sweet solo about the long-ago lovers King Mátyás and the Fair Ilonka. As her voice and the music trailed off diminuendo, there came a loud rumble of horses' hoofs. Gusztáv, Arpád and Zoltán had gone to get their circus mounts and were galloping headlong around the outskirts of the seated audience, doing their break-neck voltige and shouting war cries as they went. Within minutes, almost every other young man of the village had got a horse from somewhere and joined them, until there was a continuous ring of sheepskin-clad plainsmen doing the vol-tige—and every one as expert as the Jászi boys—around and around the outside of the square. Beck's band boomed into Liszt's "Battle of the Huns," loud enough to be heard above the tumult.

Then the horsemen, still whooping, thundered in single file out of the square and down a lane. The square was quiet again, except for the people's excited exclamations over this unexpected gala day. The musicians left the platform and the housewives brought from their stoves and hearths and ovens the fare they had been preparing since the night before, set-ting out trays and platters and bowls and jugs and pitchers, stacks of clean wooden dishes and tin utensils, until the plat-form was covered all around, to farthest arms-reach, with food steaming and smoking in the cool twilight air. The Flor-ilegium guests were of course urged to go first to the vast buffet. As he helped himself to liver dumpling soup, beef rolls stuffed with mushrooms, cucumber salad, breaded fried cheese, poppy-seed cake and Debröi wine, Florian remarked to Daphne, just ahead of him in line:

"By God, I'd like to hire and take along every single per-son who has performed today, if only we had transport for them."

"And if they'd come," said Daphne. "They seem over-joyed that the Jászi brothers are making good in the great outside world, but I rather sense that most are satisfied with their life here. Even sharing it with the bloody vermin."

Next morning, thanks to Edge's prescription, the troupers were able to leave behind their own collection of vermin and boarded their vehicles or mounts in fresh clothes. When the train filed out of Nagykálló, the villagers again gathered to cheer them on their way. But all the brilliant costumes of the festival had been put away for the next such grand occasion, if any should ever again occur. The people were wearing their everyday homespun garb and wooden shoes, the only distinctiveness in their dress being that unmarried girls went bare-headed and the married women wore coifs or kerchiefs.

Two days later, near sundown, the circus train had to ford a creek. The first ten or twelve vehicles did it handily, the water barely reaching their wheel hubs, and climbed easily up the graded bank on the other side. But the Hanswurst was an inexperienced coachman; he had managed to drive Magpie Maggie Hag's kitchen-and-wardrobe-and-sleeping wagon capably enough so far; however, here, he veered just a little to the right as he crossed the ford. When the horses climbed the farther bank, the left-side wheels were on the grade, the right-side wheels humped-up onto the higher ground alongside, and the wagon slowly, almost lazily but ineluctably fell over on its left side. The two draft horses braced themselves to keep their feet, so there was a loud, splintering crack as the wagon tongue broke.

Yount, driving the red wagon just behind, halted his Lightning in the middle of the creek and let out a yell to alert the wagons that had already crossed.

"Confound it," he grumbled, hooking his reins onto the dashboard and preparing to get down. "I *told* Maggie she ought to let a Slovak drive her cook wagon. But that old fool Notkin is so set on courting her . . ."

"Well, it turned over gently enough," said Agnete, beside him. "They couldn't have got worse than shaken up."

But then they saw the smoke spurt from the crevices of the wagon body. Yount leapt into the water and splashed frantically to the farther bank. Other men jumped from their horses or vehicles in the line behind and hastened forward to help. Yount yanked open the cook wagon's back door and

smoke billowed out. He had to wait a minute or two for the
draft to thin it before he could even see inside, and then he
said, "Oh, Jesus," under his breath before shouting to the
others, "Get buckets! Anything! Scoop water from the creek
in here!"

Yount did not wait for that, though. He crawled inside
among the burning costumes and other flammables, lay down
on the wagon wall that was now a floor, and, with his feet—
feeling the heat even through his stout boot soles—shoved
away the wood stove. It had slid across the room, laid itself
like a lover on top of Magpie Maggie Hag, embraced her
when its iron door swung open, pinned her to the wall and
spilled its live coals all over her. Then Yount hastily scrambled out again, his own clothes smoldering here and there,
his black beard singed and his face and hands blistered. The
bucket brigade took over, and the fire was extinguished and
the stove cooled in just a few minutes.

Outside the door, anxiously wringing his hands, Florian
asked, "Is she badly hurt?"

"She's not hurting now, Governor, I'm sorry to say,"
Yount told him. "She'll never hurt again." Rouleau had
fetched his rudimentary medical kit and was smearing olive
oil on Yount's face and hands.

"Oh, Mag . . ." said Florian, with a heartfelt groan. "Poor
Mag . . ."

Then, from the front of the wagon, someone gave a shout.
Edge and Pemjean sloshed around there and discovered the
other casualty. Notkin had not fallen or jumped when the rig
turned over, or at least not soon enough. He lay at a slant
against the roadbank, on his back, and the edge of the
driving-seat board had knifed into and cruelly pinched his
belly. Perhaps if not everyone had run directly to the more
visible and urgent calamity, someone might have noticed the
Hanswurst's predicament and lifted the wagon to drag him
loose for some kind of emergency treatment. But, for all his
vitality in the pista, he was an old and fragile man. Whatever
the cleaver-like board edge had done to his insides, Notkin
was as dead as Magpie Maggie Hag.

"Old Mag . . . old Mag . . ." Florian kept repeating,

wretchedly, as the bucket brigade finished its work and the last smoke cleared.

"Don't go in, Governor," said Yount. "It ain't no pretty sight. Me and Zack will take care of her."

Someone came and told Florian of the Hanswurst's death, as well, and Florian spared some sorrowful words for him—but Florian was clearly more affected by the loss of Magpie Maggie Hag than by any other tragedy that had occurred in the Florilegium since Edge and Yount had been traveling with him.

"She was on the first show I ever joined out with, when I ran away from home," said Florian. "God only knows how old she was *then*. She's looked the same age ever since. Well, she had a long life, a good run. So did Notkin, I guess. But Mag taught me a good deal of everything I ever learned about circus, and she came along with me when I got brash enough to organize my own. She left a fairly decent outfit to join out with mine—and I'd be stretching the truth to brag that mine was even a mud show when it started." He took a handkerchief from his sleeve and dabbed at his eyes. "Been with me . . . loyal, helpful, hard-working . . . all the years since then. Here in Europe, America, here again. I don't know what we'll do without her . . ."

Then he slogged away from the creek and plodded off into the tall grass to grieve by himself. The other men set the wagon upright and Stitches brought canvases. Edge and Yount tenderly wrapped Magpie Maggie Hag's charred and tiny corpse—tinier even than in life—while Dai shrouded the Hanswurst. The Slovaks dug graves, a toilsome task in the puszta, where the millennia of grass growing, dying, reseeding, growing again, had made the ground an almost impenetrable mesh of roots. But it was done at last, and by then Florian had returned from his solitary mourning.

Edge said, "It's pretty near dark, Governor. Should we put off the ceremonies until morning?"

"No. Maggie always liked the dark. Let's get this ordeal over with. And we'll camp here for the night. Keep them company for at least a little while longer."

At the graveside, some of the people sniffled or wiped at

their eyes. Even Nella Cornella, who had long worked with Bernhard Notkin, and the other women, some of whom had known Magpie Maggie Hag for years, only sobbed quietly. But the Jászi brothers, newest additions to the troupe, barely acquainted with either of the deceased, demonstrated their Magyar emotionalism by weeping openly and copiously.

By torchlight, Dai Goesle preached a short and simple service: "Almighty God, with Whom the souls of the worthy, after they are delivered from the burdens of the flesh, do live in joy and felicity, we give Thee hearty thanks for the good examples of these Thy servants, who, having finished their course, now rest from their labors . . ."

And afterward, as he had had to do all too often, Florian sprinkled a handful of earth into the graves—he also dropped in their conduct books—and spoke the last words, in a choked voice: "Saltaverunt . . . Placuerunt . . . Mortui sunt . . ."

"Zack," Yount said to him, as the Slovaks covered the graves—and doubtless the puszta grass began immediately to overgrow them again—"I don't want to bother Florian with this. He's all broke up. There's several of our women can cook, but it's going to be pretty scant grub from here on. Practically all our groceries was in that wagon. Not too much got burnt, but everything got water-soaked."

"I reckon they can make soup, then, if nothing else."

"Even worse, Zack. Practically all our costumes was in there, too. A lot of them *did* get burnt, or too scorched to be any good any more, or the colors all run or the spangles all ruint by the water. Now, we got cooks to replace old Mag, but I don't think any of our gals can replace her at seamstress work."

"You're right, Obie. Damnation! Well, don't bother Florian with that either, right now. You know what he'd say. We have to work things out as we go along. And it looks like we *will* have to. Maybe we can find a footloose seamstress before we take the railroad train—we're not far from that border town now—and maybe there'll be time before we reach Kiev for her to work up a new wardrobe."

When the other circus women had taken from the wagon some watered comestibles that they could make into soup, and cooking fires had been lit, and Stitches and his assistant carpenters were fitting a new tongue to the wagon by lamplight, Edge climbed inside the wagon by himself, with a lantern, to refold or rehang on the clothes poles what costumes seemed salvageable, and to carry out what other groceries might be dried out and still edible. Then he began to tidy up the personal effects of Magpie Maggie Hag and the Hanswurst, intending to ask Florian—when the Governor was himself again—what disposition to make of them. The two trunks of the old man and woman contained most of their possessions, and they had been scorched and blistered only on the outside; their contents had not suffered from either fire or water. When Edge opened Magpie Maggie Hag's trunk, the first thing he saw—lying on top of everything else, easiest accessible—was a thick, much-thumbed and dog-eared book: *The Ancient Gypsy's Dream Book; or, Every Manner of Omen Mystically Interpreted.*

"Well, I'll be damned," Edge muttered. "Is this what Mag relied on, all this time?"

He tried to recollect some of Magpie Maggie Hag's predictions or onsets of sulking in her bunk. He found himself remembering the very first time he ever heard her "dukker" a dream—that one of Sarah Coverley's, something about falling off her horse and getting enmeshed in a net. And he recalled quite clearly—because it had come so nearly true— that Magpie Maggie Hag had said it foretold Sarah's someday falling into evil doings and being abandoned by her friends.

The *Dream Book* was alphabetically arranged by subject. Edge first looked up Horse. There were a good many dreams that could be dreamt about horses, according to the book, but he found none applicable. He looked under Net; nothing there that fitted, either. He thought to try Mesh, and there it was:

"To a young woman, to dream of being entangled in the meshes of a net, foretells that her environments will bring her into wicked ways and consequent abandonment. If she succeeds in disengaging herself from the meshes, she will narrowly escape public disgrace."

"Well, I'll be damned," Edge said again.

Actually, it had been Sarah who had done the abandoning, but still ... Had Magpie Maggie Hag been a fraud all these years? Not if so many of her predictions had come as near true as this one, but that only proved the *book* right. Edge remembered that she'd had one of her spells of seclusion just before they got the news of Lincoln's assassination. Unless that had involved a dream of her own, the book couldn't account for her clairvoyance on that occasion.

"And she never said or did anything," he muttered, "to predict her own dying. Let's see, what else? She dukkered that Pavlo's going to give us trouble over werewolves."

He riffled through the book again. There was no Werewolf listing, and under Wolf only: "To hear the howl of a wolf in a dream discovers to you a sinister alliance"—which either meant nothing at all or could be mystically interpreted in any number of ways.

Edge shrugged, unable to decided if she really had had some gift of soothsaying, or had cribbed all her omen-dukkering from the battered old book, or had in most cases been just a shrewd old woman exercising the wisdom and intuition and experience garnered over a long lifetime. But then, when he sat down with Yount and Agnete to eat the unidentifiable but not-bad soup that the women had contrived to concoct, and the three of them were glooming over this latest disaster to strike the show, Yount chanced to remark:

"And it wasn't two weeks ago that old Mag told me this poosta would be the end of the world for some folks."

Edge twitched, dropped his spoon into his bowl and had to delve to retrieve it. Surely there could be nothing about the *Hungarian puszta* in that old book. He resolved to keep a close eye on Pavlo Smodlaka and an ear cocked for any wolves howling.

Four days later, they arrived at the border town, by which time Florian had pretty well come out of his funk of misery.

"Czernowitz," he announced, when the circus train had drawn up in ranks and files on an empty lot on the outskirts. "Or so it is marked on maps of the Austrian-Hungarian Dual

Monarchy. But the inhabitants are mostly Romanian, and call it Cernauti. Now, we've been on short peck for quite a while. First we'll have a bangup meal at a good inn. Then some of you women go about the markets and mongers and restock our food supply. Others, please go about the drapers' and mercers' shops and buy every kind of fancy fabrics and sequins and other ornamentation you can find. Each of you take along a Slovak or two to carry for you. Meanwhile, I shall look for whatever street passes as Savile Row here, and visit every single tailoring establishment, in hope of discovering a costumier who yearns for far horizons."

He found one, too. In a cramped family shop of father, mother and daughter, he saw at once that the younger woman was deft with the needle at the gown she was working on. Her name was Ioan Petrescu, she was about thirty, but still a spinster, exceedingly plain of face and broad of beam. So much so, she and her parents agreed, that she had little hope of ever snaring a husband here among the "handsome Romanians." Perhaps she would have better luck in Russia, they all said, where *everybody* was even plainer and squatter than Ioan was. She spoke Magyar as well as Romanian and, living this close to the border, a sufficiency of Russian. Also she was a capable cook, but—she said in some surprise, when Florian tentatively raised the question—no, she could claim no powers of divination that would enable her to replace Magpie Maggie Hag in that department.

"Oh, well," sighed Florian, and he went on to settle salary and terms, including a lump-sum payment to the elder Petrescus for the loss of her services. Ioan said it would take her some hours to gather and pack her belongings, to say her farewells to family, other relatives and friends. So Florian arranged to pick her up next morning in his carriage. Then he went to engage comfortable hotel rooms—they would be the last for some time—for the rest of his company.

Shortly before noon on the day after—it had taken that long to load the wagons with all the new supplies the circus women had procured—Florian's Flourishing Florilegium departed from the Kingdom of Hungary. There were no such finicking formalities at their exit as there had been at their entrance into the country. The guards at the sentry boxes on the near end of the bridge merely waved cordially as the procession went past and crossed the river Prut and rolled into Russia.

To be continued in
Volume III of *Spangle*

The Grand Promenade

⤙══ ROSSIYA ══⤚

1

AT THE FARTHER END of the Prut bridge was a sentry box with a stout barrier pole blocking the road, both box and pole painted in diagonal stripes of white and very dark green with a thin gold line separating the two colors. Beyond was a sprawling guardhouse, flying the Russian flag: a double-headed eagle of dark green and gold on a white ground. Two farm carts heaped with cabbages were ahead of Florian's rockaway, their occupants stolidly waiting for some sentry to take notice of them. So when Florian halted, the circus train stretched behind him all the way across the bridge and some distance back into Czernowitz.

A man ducked under the guard barrier, trotted past the farm carts and came up to Florian, somewhat breathless, agitated and worried-looking. It was Willi Lothar, the circus's "advance man."

"I have been waiting here for the past week," he said.

"We have encountered some delays on the road," said Florian, saving the details for later. "What's the holdup here?"

"The standard discourtesy of every petty administrator in

Russia,'' Willi said sourly. ''The soldiers and inspectors are all having their midday meal. Never will they be persuaded to take turns at the table and on duty. I can tell you, Herr Gouverneur, traveling from here to Kiev and back again, I have learned a good deal about Russian incivility and ineptitude. But I must also confess to some oversights and errors of my own. I can only try to excuse them by pleading that this *is* my first visit to Russia.''

''Perfectly understandable, Herr Chefpublizist. I have no doubt that we shall all be making faux pas along the way.''

''To begin with,'' Willi said uncomfortably, ''I have, at great cost in money and time and interminable red tape and confusion and frustration, procured a special train for us. However, I did not discover until I got here that there is no railway station closer than Khamenets Podolskiy, and that is where it awaits us.''

''How far away is that?''

''About sixty versts. Excuse me—I have begun to think in Russian measures. Some forty miles.''

''Two days, if we push. That is not intolerable.''

''You had better figure on at least four days, Herr Florian. You have not yet seen the condition of the Russian roads.''

''Ah, well,'' Florian said philosophically. ''We suffered considerable damage to our wardrobe on the way here. That will give our costumière more time to work on the new costumes.''

Willi went on, ''During this week that I have been waiting here—and, grâce à Dieu, the commandant and most others of the higher-ranking guards and inspectors speak German or French—I have been doing my best to . . . how would you say? . . . mit Butter bestreichen all of them.''

''To butter them up.''

''Ja. I have at least, in this time, got them to unlock their vaults and give me Reisepässe for our whole company, and I have filled in our destinations, purpose of visit—''

''Passports? Russia demands passports? In addition to our conduct books?''

''Ach, ja. And you will need them to get *out* again, plus a certificate from the police that they have no reason to detain you. I obtained a considerable stock of the Reisepässe, not knowing how many you would be on arrival. Each person has only to fill in his personal particulars—as in the conduct books—and then a stamp of visa will be affixed.''

"Then your buttering-up has had some good effect.''

"But not much,'' Willi said glumly. "You may yet be stuck here for two or three days, perhaps longer, going through the necessary formalities. Not to mention the unnecessary ones. I have tried to convince these louts that your tour through Russia will be of great cultural and economic benefit to their country. That you are not the usual gypsylike voyageurs forains. That you have even chartered an entire railroad train. Und so weiter, und so weiter. I have made you sound like the Second Coming. But these people are even more surly, indolent and indifferent than your typical civil servants anywhere else. For one reason, although the nominal commander of this border post is a colonel of the army, the real director and highest authority here is a civilian official of the Third Section. So no other man on the post dares show the least amiability toward a foreigner, let alone accept a bribe or even a cigarette. He would instantly be sent to the salt mines of Siberia.''

"What in the world is the Third Section?''

"Tsar Alexander's secret police, accountable only to him personally. You will soon learn, Herr Florian, that there is a bland euphemism for everything grim in Russia. A convict trudging off to lifelong exile in Siberia, for example, is said to be merely 'passing through.' However, the blandly named Third Section keeps watch—and not just at the frontiers; its agents are everywhere—not only for illicit immigrants and undesirable persons and contraband, but also for persons evincing undesirable tendencies, political opinions and even objectionable *thoughts*.''

"Great heavens,'' muttered Florian. "And we are an aggregation of certifiable eccentrics. Do you think they will let us *in*, Willi?''

Oh, I think so, but grudgingly. The colonel was clearly impressed when I showed him the receipt for the deposit I paid on the railway charter. We might just pass the word among our company for all to behave discreetly, to do as they are bidden, and not to bridle at any insult. Jules and I, when we meet, must not greet one another too affectionately. The rest of you must be prepared for much interrogation, a search of everything you are carrying, and a generally spiteful dawdling just to cause you delay and distress. Plus a heavy import duty to pay, most likely. I was hoping by flattery and unction to mitigate that, but in vain, I fear.''

"Hm. Perhaps the colonel or that éminence grise of the Third Section is a brother in the craft, and I could—''

"Ach, do not, do not, Herr Gouverneur! The brotherhood of Freimaurerei is, as the Russian euphemism puts it, 'discouraged' here. Every sort of secret society is forbidden. Such societies are rife, of course, but they take care to *stay* secret. Were you to essay any Masonic sign or password, *you* might be on your way to Siberia.''

"Hell and damnation. Anything else I should know?''

"Well . . . everyone might as well throw into the river any books or magazines or newspapers in his possession. It could avert additional delay, for otherwise every page and every sheet of paper must be inspected. All foreign literature, you see, is automatically suspected of being seditious or heretical or at least licentious.''

Florian exclaimed, "This is absolutely incred—!'' But he was interrupted by a loud whistle blast from a soldier at the barrier pole. The guards had finished their meal, ambled idly out of the guardhouse, picking their teeth, and—after stabbing among the two farm carts' cabbages with their needle-like rifle bayonets—had let those peasants pass. Now the soldiers were beckoning impatiently and imperiously for the circus train to move up.

"I'll go first,'' said Florian, "and introduce myself and present our conduct books. Meanwhile, Willi, you go down the line and hand out the passports. And all your good advice, as well.''

The pole was lifted, briefly, for just the rockaway to pass under and beyond it. Florian got down and started for the guardhouse, but a sentry stopped him with his rifle, barked, "Ostavaitye!'' indicated that he was to stay where he was, snatched from Florian the stack of conduct books and himself carried them into the building. There ensued a wait long enough for someone to have read every last word in every last book. Finally the soldier reappeared in the doorway, jerked his rifle in a come-along gesture and barked, ''Void-itye!''

There were several officers in the guardhouse office, all still picking their teeth and occasionally belching. Florian addressed the one who sat behind a desk littered with the conduct books. He was also the officer most heavily bedecked with braid, insignia, medals and flowing beard. In his best-remembered Russian, Florian began, ''Zdravstvuitye, Gospodín Polkhovnik, it is an honor to meet—''

''Qu'est-ce que ça fout?'' growled the colonel, in French rather more fluent than Florian's Russian, and rudely vulgar, and much more to the point. ''No need for the social graces, gospodín. Tak, you are the proprietor of that tsirk and the leader of that canaille cluttering my bridge, are you not?''

''Oui, mon colonel. I am proud to be the owner and general manager of Florian's Flourishing Florilegium. We intend to make a grand tour of—''

''S'il vous plaît, c'est peu nécessaire. During this whole past week I have heard little else, from that lèche-cul Lothar of yours, except the greatness of your tsirk and your aspirations to astound all of Russia with it. Right now, simply be so kind as to verify—without rhetoric—these particulars noted in your conduct book.'' The colonel recited them—name, age, occupation, etc.—and Florian attested that all were truly set forth. The colonel said, ''Tak, I do not read well these barbaric foreign languages, but, so far as I can discern, there are no black-mark demerits cited by the authorities of any of the other places you have visited. Very well, Monsieur Florian, you are admissible. Give me your passport.'' The colonel scribbled in it, then stamped it with an inked brass seal. ''You may wait outside—and fill in the required blanks in your passport while you do so. Send in the rest of your racaille one at a time.''

''Excusez, mon colonel,'' said Florian, with some ill-concealed indignation. ''My rabble, as you keep calling them,

are of numerous nationalities. Not many speak French, and
none of them, I believe, speaks Russian. I may be useful as
an interpreter.''

"As you please.'' The colonel shrugged, then told the sentry at the door, "Odin za drugim.''

The guard leaned out the door—all the wagons and cages
and vans and animals afoot were being let through the barrier
now, and ranked in a field beyond the guardhouse—and
curtly beckoned to the nearest trouper, who happened to be
Jules Rouleau.

Meanwhile, Florian had leaned his passport against the
rough log wall of the room and, with his mason's pencil, was
struggling to fill in the blank spaces with Cyrillic script. He
again said to the officer, "Excusez-moi, mon colonel. Sos-
toyániye means 'estate,' I know, but what do I write in that
blank?''

"Your *estate*, of course. Your status,'' the colonel said
irritably. "There are only five. Tak, which are you? Noble,
merchant, burgher, peasant or cleric?''

"Why, I—I hardly think I fit in any of those categories. I
don't suppose any of us do. We are artistes, entertainers . . .''

"Okh! Put burgher—mestchánye—in all the passports,
then. That will suffice.'' He turned to Rouleau, standing at
attention before his desk, and gestured for Jules to point out
his conduct book among the heap of them. The colonel
picked it up and read, "Yules Rouleau, Français? Nyet. Amy-
erikanyets.'' Then he read, with some incredulity, "Aéronaute?''

Florian translated, "Vozdukoplavatol. Monsieur Rouleau
is our tsirk's balloonist.'' Then, yet again, he said, "Je vous
fais excuse, mon colonel. But would it perhaps be possible,
while you are verifying the conduct books, that your inspectors''—he indicated the numerous other men lounging about,
inside and outside the guardhouse, still picking their teeth—
"might profitably occupy the same time in the inspection of
our train, the calculation of impost and so forth?''

The colonel said negligently, "Skoro budit, gospodín.
What is the hurry? There is no point in making out customs

declarations and weighing poods and funts until we are assured that all of you are admissible.''

Since ''skoro budit'' meant only ''it will happen soon''
and was as deliberately imprecise and noncommittal as the
Spanish ''mañana,'' Florian could only curb his vexation and
seethe silently, and fill out each new candidate's passport after the colonel was done with his routine, and step in to translate when necessary.

''A. Chink?!'' exclaimed the colonel, when one of the antipodists stood apprehensively before him. ''That is no translation of the name he has signed in his conduct book.''

''You can decipher his name, Colonel?'' said Florian, in
surprise. ''We did only the best we could, since none of us
speaks or reads Chinese.''

''Chinese? You dolt. His name is signed in the Korean
alphabet.'' The colonel looked up at the acrobat, who had
begun to tremble slightly, and asked, ''Odi so ososse yo?''

The antipodist was visibly startled. He stammered, ''H-
Hanguk, taeryong. Ch-chip e so Taegu yo. S-sille haessum-
nida.''

''Chossumnida,'' the colonel said affably, and went into
quite a long conversation with him, during which, at the officer's bidding, the Korean separated from the other conduct
books those of his two fellows.

''This man's name is Kim Pok-tong,'' the colonel said to
Florian. ''Please erase that stupid 'A. Chink' and write it
properly in his conduct book and his passport. The other two
are his brothers, Kim Tak-sung and Kim Hak-su.''

Florian hastily wrote in the names, as well as he could,
and said, ''You amaze me, Colonel. I could no more tell any
Orientals apart . . .''

''I have served at Vladivostok,'' the colonel said. ''Tak, I
took the opportunity to cross the Petra Bay and see something
of Korea while I was there. Lovely country, but the people
extremely eremitical. Can't understand how these three
braved the outside world. Wish I had time to converse with
them.''

''Bless my soul,'' murmured Florian.

One by one, the troupers and crewmen survived the interrogation—the colonel noticeably lingered longer in his questioning of the more attractive female artistes—and then, relieved to have that over with, they gathered near their familiar wagons. Only one came out of the guardhouse in high dudgeon, and that was the usually easygoing Hannibal Tyree.

"Cannibal!" he exclaimed, outraged. "Dat ole sojer called me *Cannibal* Tyree!"

"He called me Yules," said Rouleau indifferently. "So he can't read English. So what?"

"Ain't the same thing, Yules don't mean you *eats people!* Jes' 'cause I be's black, dey call me a *cannibal*. Why, even my ole great-gran'pappy back in Afriker wasn't never no—"

"Easy, Herr Tyree, be at ease," said Willi Lothar. "It was an unintentional affront. You see, there is no 'h' sound in the Russian language. They simply cannot aspirate it. So they substitute a velar consonant, usually the 'k' sound. Hence Hannibal—Cannibal."

"Boy, be glad your name isn't Huntley," Fitzfarris said, straight-faced.

But another applicant encountered something more troublesome than mis-pronunciation. The colonel read from his conduct book, "Nom de théâtre: Maurice LeVie. Nom de naissance: Morris Levy. Okh!" He called to Florian, who was filling out Daphne Wheeler's passport, "Attend us here, please, Monsieur le Propriétaire. This man cannot be admitted. He is an Israelite."

"What of that?" asked Florian. "You have some millions of other Jews in Russia, I understand."

"We got them not because we wanted them," said the colonel. "They simply happened to constitute an offensively high proportion of the population of the Ukraine, and later of Poland, both of which Matushka Rossiya motherly took to her bosom. Tak, our so-called Russian Jews still are restricted to the Pale of Settlement—Poland and the Ukraine. They most certainly are not at liberty to wander about the provinces of Great Russia, as you would have this foreign Jew do."

"Monsieur le Colonel," said Maurice, "I am a *Frenchman*. I have never considered myself to be of any other race or nationality, and I have never observed *any* religion.''

The colonel growled, ''Tak khram ostavlennyi—vsë khram.''

Maurice looked questioningly at Florian, who translated, ''An abandoned temple is still a temple.''

''Drop your trousers, *Frenchman*,'' the colonel commanded. ''Show us your quéquette.'' Florian hurried Daphne out of the building. Angry, humiliated, perhaps a little frightened, Maurice let down his breeches and exposed himself. The colonel cried in triumph, ''Nu, z gúl'kin húy! Circoncis, évidemment! And you deny that you are a Jew. I daresay you would also deny that you Jews use the blood of abducted Christian infants in the making of your Passover bread.''

Maurice said miserably, ''Monsieur le Colonel, I have never in my life celebrated the Passover.''

The colonel barked orders to his idling subordinates and they snapped from boredom into eager activity, hustling Maurice into a farther room and shutting the door. The colonel's Russian had been rapid-fire, but Florian caught the gist of it. Maurice was to be stripped and examined for any tattoos or other Hebraic cabalistic markings on his body, any insurrectionary Israelite writings or even phials of poison concealed in his body orifices, and then his caravan was to be just as scrupulously stripped and scrutinized. The colonel turned again to Florian and said threateningly:

''Tak, we will suspend further interrogation of your company for now, gospodín. It may well be, if we find anything of seditious or subversive nature among the effects of this Jew of yours, that you *all* can be charged for harboring an enemy of the state.''

''I assure you—''

''Do not assure me of anything. That decision will be up to my civilian colleague, Gospodín Trepov, a personal representative of the tsar's chancery. Wait outside.''

''Colonel, the Monsieur LeVie is a flying acrobat,'' Florian said desperately. ''I pray that you will not injure him in any way.''

''Such things never happen here,'' the colonel said flatly. ''Not even to poseurs like Monsieur *Levy*. Wait outside.''

*   *   *

When Florian slouched despondently up to the gathered troupers, Edge asked, "*Now* what's the matter?"

Florian explained, concluding, "If we're not all held culpable, and they let us go on, how can we go without Maurice? We can't abandon him to these brutes. Even if we were that hardhearted, it's one more blow to our already diminished troupe. Goddamn it! I knew that Maurice is a Jew. I simply did not know it would matter here, or I would have falsified his conduct book . . ." His voice trailed off dispiritedly.

Edge pondered for a moment, then said, "Well, I had intended to save something as a surprise for you, when we got to Saint Petersburg. But I'll get it for you now." He went off to his caravan and returned with a very large ivory envelope. Florian looked with some stupefaction at the two crowns—imperial and royal—emblazoned on it in gold, and at the flowingly handwritten address:

Ihre kaiserlich Majestät, die Kaiserin und Zarin Maria
  Alexandrovna
Reichspalast
Sankt Peterstadt
Russland

Then, carefully, respectfully, he opened the unsealed flap, unfolded the stiff, handmade paper, and his eyes widened as he murmured aloud, "Gnädige Dame, meine Schwester . . ." He skipped down to the signature and his eyes really bulged. "Deine Schwester von Gottes Gnaden, Elisabeth Amelie, Kaiserin der Österreich, Königin der Ungarn." In breathless awe, he said to Edge, "And I told you she might be no more than a backwoods Baronin. Jesus!" Then he read the body of the letter and went back to the guardhouse at a trot.

He entered just in time to hear a long groan from the back room, and the colonel snapped, "I told you to stay outside!"

Just as angrily, Florian snapped back at him, "Do you read German?"

"Nyet! Get out!"

Florian laid the letter on the desk in front of the colonel, so the embossed crowns could be seen, but prudently kept his hand on it. "Perhaps the tsar's *representative* reads German."

"Um . . . ahem . . . da, I think so," said the colonel. "However, if you hope for conciliation or concession in this matter, I guarantee you that he will refuse. It is what he is for."

Still, the colonel had said that rather uneasily. He got up, went to the door of the other room and cracked it just enough to put his head in. Florian heard him say in Russian, "Desist, men, until further orders. Gospodín Trepov, there is something I think you should see."

He returned with a pudgy man dressed in an ordinary civilian sack suit, with not a single identifying insigne on it. The man's chief distinction was that he was the only Russian that Florian had seen here not wearing a beard. Instead, he had a black mustache like a shoe brush and eyebrows like black caterpillars, seeming pasted there to overhang and hide any expression in his eyes. But when he looked at that deckled sheet of parchment-thick ivory paper—Florian's hand still protectively on it—his caterpillars gave an involuntary leap upward.

Trepov read through the letter, evidently two or three times, then let his caterpillars down again, glowered at Florian and demanded, "How did you come by this?"

"My tsirk's equestrian director—Sprechstallmeister Edge mentioned therein—happens to be a close personal friend of the Empress-Queen Elisabeth. That should be evident, Gospodín Trepov, from the warmth with which Her Imperial Majesty commends him to your Empress-Tsaritsa Maria Alexandrovna. You will also observe that she requests her sister-in-royalty to extend every courtesy not only to Gospodín Edge, but also to *all his tsirk companions.*"

The man from the Chancery Third Section grunted, then drew the colonel aside for a mumbled conversation. Florian strained hard enough to catch snatches of it.

"Forgery . . . ?"

"Impossible. These oafish durákha? Besides, I have seen the writing in official papers. It is her hand."

"Hungary . . . no ally . . ."

"Still . . . addresses her as 'sister.' "

"Tak, suppose . . . disappear . . . them *and* their letter . . . ?"

"Dangerous . . . duplicate perhaps by post . . ."

"If they report . . . complain . . . the tsaritsa . . ."

"Tak, we must immediately atone . . ."

The two of them came back to Florian, each abjectly and oilily rubbing his hands together.

"Had we but known . . ." said agent Trepov.

"Of course, but *of course* you are all welcome, *most* welcome to Matushka Rossiya," said the colonel.

"Including even the Israelite," said Trepov. "I shall this instant make out the special permit he will require at provincial borders."

"There will be no need for further interrogation," said the colonel. "Simply send in all remaining passports, Monsieur Florian, and I will have my own officers enter the particulars from your people's conduct books, and affix the visas."

"I think also, Zasulich," the agent said to the colonel, "considering that these good folk are, in effect, guests of our tsaritsa they might be exempted from customs inspection and duty. Besides—ha-ha!—do you have any scales that would weigh the foods of two elephants?"

"A good point, Gospodín Trepov. I will make out the customs declaration, Monsieur Florian, and will stamp it 'diplomatic immunity,' to avoid your being held up by any officious petty inspector at any other frontier."

"Perhaps also, since it is getting late," said Trepov, "you and your company would honor us by taking dinner at our officers' mess."

"Your ladies, as well," said Colonel Zasulich. "Females are customarily excluded, but we will, for once, have our own wives attend."

"Then, when you depart in the morning," said Trepov, "we will provide a military convoy. There is a company of Kazháki due to repot here tomorrow. They will escort you to Khamenets Podolsky, so that no ruffians or bandits or wolves will molest your train."

"We accept, gentlemen," Florian said smoothly. "And we are grateful for all these favors. I am happy, too, that I shall be able to give a good report to Her Imperial Majesty regarding the efficiency and hospitality of her subject officials at the Novosielitza border crossing."

The two officials beamed at him, and at each other, and rubbed their hands some more.

All but three of the circus company attended the dinner. Ioan Petrescu declined, because she was working assiduously to restore the salvageable bits of pista costumes, and having to remake many of them entire from the measurements and crude sketches Magpie Maggie Hag had left. Maurice LeVie refused to attend because he was nursing bruises about the kidneys and a twisted wrist—and Nella Cornella stayed with him, to rub arnica on his injuries. Maurice was also, of course, still livid at the treatment he had received and the indignities he had suffered. He swore he would never socialize with any such merdeux savages, *ever!*

"I understand, I sympathize, I agree," said Florian. "However, we now have a special permit that will protect you from any further embarrassments or outrages."

"Je m'en fous et m'en contrefous!" snarled Maurice. "Perhaps, if le roi de cons invites me, the Tsar of Russia himself, *perhaps* I might deign to accept."

Colonel Zasulich had laid on an excellent dinner. Even the zakúska appetizers would amply have fed the entire assemblage: black, red and golden caviar, cold sturgeon in aspic, cheeses, pickles, pâté, paper-thin sliced cold meats—and innumerable bottles of vodka imprisoned in blocks of ice. Many of the circus guests, the females especially, discovered that a single glass of that vodka—drunk the Russian way: tossed down so fast that it flashed past the glottis, directly to the stomach, thence to the brain—was very like hitting oneself on the head with a mallet. So thereafter they drank tea, also in the Russian manner, sipping it from a glass by sucking it through a cube of sugar held in the teeth. Some others, however—Ferdi Spenz, Aleksandr Banat and the three Jászi brothers—were so appreciative of the vodka that they had to be helped or carried back to their vehicle quarters even before the serving of the dinner's next courses—borscht, herring-and-beet salad, elk steaks both grilled and tartare, steamed sausages, morels, a great variety of vegetables and unfamiliar condiments, a strong green Crimean wine, bilberry pie, more tea and vodka and a cranberry liqueur.

Most of the officers and their wives—or their female consorts of unspecified relationship—could speak French. Florian got along well enough in Russian, the Smodlakas could make themselves understood in that language, and Colonel Zasulich even spent some time talking to the brothers Kim in Korean. But those troupers who had to stay mute were not deaf, and they marveled at how abruptly the sound of the native speech had changed, from one side of the river Prut to the other, from the bright and brittle Magyar to the catarrhal Russian, so moist that it seemed sometimes to splutter.

"What is all this 'tak-tak-tak' I keep hearing?" Sunday Simms asked Willi. "Even when these people are speaking French, they seem to throw in 'tak' after every third word. They sound like a roomful of clocks ticking."

"Merely a sort of verbal hiccup, my dear. All it means is 'so,' but it is apparently a national habit to employ it frequently and needlessly. I have heard it everywhere I have been in Russia so far."

The mess waiters did not say "tak" or anything else. They appeared to be of no Russian nationality at all and evidently did not speak the language. They looked almost as Oriental as the Kims and went about their serving duties without heeding or needing instruction.

"They are Tatars," agent Trepov explained to Edge. "We import them from the Volga provinces, as does every Russian hotel and restaurant, because they are devout Muslims, hence they do not steal nips from the liquor supply. Tak, we of Matushka Rossiya are fortunate in having such a wide variety of nationalities in our vast land, each with its own peculiar virtues or talents. Our Balts, for example, are known for their honesty and punctiliousness, so they constitute most of our estate managers, accountants, clerks. The Letts are especially skilled in building windmills and water mills. And so on."

What conversation there could be between hosts and guests continued to be amiable, mostly trivial, sometimes informative. Jean-François Pemjean commented to the stout but handsome woman who was his vis-à-vis, "Isn't the weather being exceptionally fine for Russia, madame, this late in October? Are you perhaps enjoying a spell of Saint Martin's Summer?"

"We call it Woman's Summer," she replied, with something of a simper. "Báb'ye léto. Because a woman is here considered most attractive in her late maturity. And yes, the weather is being clement. But, for us, tak, it is still only *early* October. Perhaps you are unaware that Russia observes the Julian calendar, which is twelve days earlier than your Gregorian calendar of the West."

At another table, another handsome woman said to Rouleau, "You speak of serfs, Monsieur Yules. That is actually a word from the French. Here they were called krepostnoyi. *Were* called, tak, because we have no more such peasants in bondage. Our wise and humane Alexander, who himself owned one million of the krepostnoyi, liberated them throughout the land." She added, with frank disparagement of Rouleau's homeland, "That was seven years ago, before your backward and benighted America had to fight a civil war to accomplish the same good for your slaves."

"I don't know that it has accomplished much good for ours," said Rouleau. "When last I saw any freedmen there, they were helplessly adrift, without masters to direct and care for them."

"Tak, I must confess that that is somewhat true even here in enlightened Russia," said the woman. "It will be some time yet before the freed muzhiki rid themselves of their old dependences and their gross unrefinement. Especially their ingrained superstitions." She laughed. "Do you know, if ever a provincial governor or mayor orders a census to count the population that he governs, the muzhiki all flee to the tall timber. Some even commit suicide."

"Par dieu, pourquoi? What superstition can possibly be connected to a census-taking?"

"The muzhiki believe it is done at the instigation of the

Antichrist, who wants all their names so they can be damned. At least that one is a religiously inspired delusion, and perhaps excusable on that account. But the peasants also believe in all sorts of heretical and supernatural things, as well, and live in terror of them. The vampír, the oborotyen . . .''

At another table, Pavlo Smodlaka was anxiously struggling to ask the captain seated next to him for information about one of those very things. ''In Magyar, the férfifarkas. You call, I think, oborotyen.''

''Tak, you have heard of our oborotyen?'' said the captain, putting on a somber expression, though his eyes twinkled. ''Da, we have that thing. And whatever you have heard probably falls short of the terrible truth. Sometimes, at full moon, there is such a plague of men-turned-wolves that even we, the army, must be called out to hunt them down and destroy them. Tak, for that we must use solid silver bayonets.''

The captain went on elaborating, exercising more and more inventive imagination, and Pavlo's jaw gradually gaped until he was spilling chewed morel down his chin.

Colonel Zasulich said to Florian, ''I am indeed glad that we resolved the few minor difficulties, and your establishment is now free to entertain our countrymen. I took a stroll among your wagons, and it is obvious that yours is a respectable tsirk, not a ragtag balagan—what I believe you in America call a tína tsirk.''

''A mud show, yes,'' said Florian. ''You seem well acquainted with circus terminology, Colonel.''

''The tsirk is an honored institution in Russia, Gospodín Florian. We had our first taste of it nearly a hundred years ago, tak, when the Royal Circus of London came to visit Piter—Saint Petersburg. It was warmly received. Partly, no doubt, because Ekaterina the Great immediately took its chief equestrian for the latest in her succession of lovers. Other foreign circuses came after that. Now we have many of our own, from immense spectacles in permanent hippodromes to the shabby balagans that appear at every country fair. But the terminology remains mostly unchanged from that of the West. Tak, our lion tamers give their commands in German. The central ring is the Italian pista. Only a few words are different. What you call a clown or a joey, we call a rizhiy. What you call a midget, like that charming little lady farther down the table, we call a lilliput.''

Florian got out his pencil and a piece of paper. ''Perhaps, Colonel, you would be good enough to assist me in concocting comprehensible translations of some of our people's noms de théâtre. The Quakemaker, Cinderella . . .''

''Tak,'' said the colonel, and they moved their chairs closer together to go through the list.

Later, they two left the others still partying and went to Zasulich's office again, where the colonel generously accommodated Florian by opening his paymaster's safe and exchanging silver Russian rubles and kopeks for Florian's considerable heap of Hungarian koronas and forints, Austrian kronen and gulden. Florian, working the complicated sums in his head, calculated that the ruble was worth about fifty-two cents American and, at one hundred to the ruble, the kopek was worth about half a cent, and he noted that down in his memorandum book.

The next morning, Colonel Zasulich was up and out as early as any of the circus people, and he was a good deal perkier and brighter-eyed than some of them. He arrived at the wagon encampment to announce to Florian and Edge, ''Here comes the company of Kazhák infantry. You can hear their marching music down the road. I shall allow them to rest only while you hitch up your teams and form up your train. They they will be commanded to turn around again and escort you, front and rear of your procession, to the railroad at Khamenets Podolskiy.''

Florian and Edge listened for a military band, but that was not what they heard. Half of the approaching company was merely whistling the Russian national hymn and the other half was singing it:

> Bozhe tsara krani
> Syilni der zharni
> Stsar stvouyna
> Slavouna slavounam . . .

"Well, maybe they don't have a band," said Edge, "but that's a pretty rousing anthem. And I've never heard such warbling whistling. What is it they're singing?"

"Um . . . roughly . . ." said Florian, " 'Our oath to the tsar we pledge with white-hot fervor. Carve it on tree trunks: glory to the Slavic race.' "

As the music got louder, more of the circus folk emerged from their caravans and wagons. When the company marched onto the post parade ground and were halted at attention, still bellowing and whistling, the watchers were able to see how they achieved their peculiarly loud, sweet, harmonic trilling: each of the whistlers had a hole bored between his two front teeth. The company's commander waited for his men to finish a final chorus, then bawled an order that was evidently "Fall out!" The men immediately and efficiently tripod-stacked their long rifles, unslung and let drop their knapsacks, yanked off their tremendous boots, under which they wore no stockings, unbuttoned the flies of their baggy pantaloons and— heedless of the many onlookers, including now all the women of the circus—began pissing on each other's bare feet.

Most of those observing stood stunned for a moment. Then all the women and girls, red-faced, bustled back inside their vehicles.

"The infantrymen always do that after a long march," explained Colonel Zasulich, as unembarrassed as the soldiers. "It rests the feet, toughens them, prevents ringworm and other such foot rots."

Rouleau, restraining a laugh, said to the colonel in French, "I thought the Cossack people were all cavalrymen, real rough riders, like the plainsmen of Hungary and our American plains Indians."

Zasulich said, "You must blame your own Western tsirks and hippodrome shows for fostering that myth about the Cossacks—as you call them. Actually, they are not even one people, or one tribe, or necessarily related in any other way. The word kazhák means only 'brigand,' and in earlier times they roamed and ravaged freely over the steppe. Tak, on the principle that a poacher makes the best gamekeeper, Tsar Pyetr the Great herded them all together and organized them into bodies of soldiers. Very good soldiers they make, indeed. Some, da, are cavalrymen, but not all. Those wild and daredevil riders of whom you speak, da, we have those too, but that sort of horseman is properly called a djigit.''

''Another thing,'' Pemjcan said to Edge, ''which I just learned last night. If you are keeping a calendar, Monsieur le Directeur, of our appointed arrivals and departures here and there, make sure you adjust it to the Russian calendar. Today is not, as you might believe, the twenty-third of October. It is the *eleventh* of October.'' He added, in an undertone, ''Well, Monsieur Florian *did* say this is a backward country, n'est-ce pas?''

For all that the Kazháks were good soldiers, and readily gave voice to their white-hot devotion to the tsar, they grumbled audibly when the circus was ready to roll and they were commanded to go with it back along the same dreary versts they had just traversed. But they did as bidden, pulling on their great boots again, slinging their knapsacks, shouldering their rifles and forming up, two platoons each fore and aft of the wagon train.

''One last word of advice, Gospodín Florian,'' said agent Trepov, as they shook hands at parting. ''When you get to the railway station, you will be inundated by nosíl'shchiki—volunteer porters. Fend them off. Let only your own men do the work. Those station parasites are not entitled to payment, so if you give them even a small gratuity, it amounts to a gift. By our law, any Russian accepting a gift from a foreigner is committing a punishable crime, and so are you in giving it. However, he *is* entitled to *steal* from a foreigner anything and everything he can get his hands on. I thought you ought to know.''

Florian sighed, shook his head in wonderment, thanked the agent, climbed to his rockaway seat and gave the move-out signal. The post officers had all assembled to see the train off, and in unison gave the Russian military salute: the hand snapped to the forehead, then flung high. The Kazháks ahead of the train immediately started marching—now wafting behind them an ammoniac stench strong enough to make Florian's eyes water—while whistling and singing glory to the Slavic race.

2

THE ROAD to Khamenets Podolskiy was made of round slices of log, set close together in the ground like flagstones. Perhaps in mud time when they would be well mired, or in wintertime when they would be gripped solid, the slabs might have made a decent if uneven surface. But now, in late autumn, the dirt road was merely lumpy dirt, and the unsecured log rounds simply lay there at all angles, and teetered and skidded and made a continuous nerve-racking clatter as the circus's animals and wagons went over them. It was a rougher ride than navigating a roiled sea. The Smodlaka children and several of the caged animals were seasick the whole way, and many others suffered bruises and contusions from falling about inside their wagons or caravans. Several times, the whole train had to stop entirely, to repair broken wheel spokes, sprung felloes, torn harness, or to replace thrown horseshoes.

How the new seamstress, Ioan Petrescu, could do her fine stitching in that turmoil was a mystery, but she did, and the journey—it took fully *five* days to go the forty miles—gave her time enough to refurbish all the damaged costumes and make new ones. Those included a set for the Jászi brothers, whom Florian decided to dress in the manner of Edge's former buckskin Billy, since that would look more "exotic" to Russian audiences than the Magyar csikos dress, which many Russians must already have seen. To give Ioan all the time she required, the other women of the troupe did the cooking at meal stops along the way. The escorting Kazhák troops fed themselves, and spartanly. They lit fires to brew tea, but the only other nutriment anyone saw them take was a fibrous dried meat, like jerky, that they carried in their knapsacks.

Because of the terrible condition of the road, Hannibal and his Slovak assistant put the sheepskin boots on the two ele-

phants, and Stitches made another set for Mustafa the camel.
All of those stout boots were shredded and worn through by
the end of the journey, so Stitches made new sets, because
those walking animals would need them even on paved
streets, now that the weather was turning cold. The Woman's
Summer ended when the circus was halfway to its destination. No snow fell yet, but the temperature did. The countryside was exactly like the Hungarian puszta—an endless plain
of now-brown grass, with only infrequent, bare-limbed shrubs
and trees to break the monotony. Every morning the hoar-
frosted grass blades looked like standing armies of glittering
steel bayonets. Then, when the sun got high enough to evap-
orate the frost from the grass, it revealed another strange
sight: any tree in the landscape naturally cast a shadow, but
not a normal dark one; its shadow was silvery-white, because
there the frost had not yet melted.

The circus passed through numerous villages, and the resident muzhiks came out to stare in dull-eyed wonder at the
unaccustomed apparition. The circus folk did not do much
staring in return, as there was little of interest to look at. All
the villages were alike: a single row of one-room izba huts
lining either side of the road, every izba made of rough-cut,
undressed and unpainted logs, their interstices chinked with
moss. Only a few had even one window, and only a *very*
occasional one—maybe the mayor's—would have glass in it;
the other windows consisted merely of oiled paper or even
scraped-thin birch bark.

The country peasants were as ugly as their residences.
Every man parted his hair in the middle, and the lank, tangled, greasy hanks of it hung down on either side below his
shoulders, sometimes as far as the length of his lank, tangled,
greasy beard, which might reach his waist. The women were
distinguishable only because they had no beards and, whatever their hair was like, they wore babushka kerchiefs over
it. Their faces were just as sun- and wind-burned as the
men's, and just as coarse of skin, often studded with warts
and wens or pitted with old smallpox scars. Both sexes wore
thick, gray, graceless belted overcoats of near ground-length
and boots of colorless felt, so huge and shapeless that every-

one looked clubfooted. The boots and the overcoat hems were clotted with mud and manure. The circus company only rarely caught sight of a young girl or any children—probably the elders herded them indoors, safe from abduction by these unprecedented passersby—and those young ones were sometimes very pretty.

The circus folk did see one thing about those squalid communities that piqued their curiosity. Whenever they chanced to be passing through a hamlet as night was falling, they would see at least one housewife setting on her doorstep a crust of bread and a bowl of milk.

"Do the Russians believe in the brownies?" asked Daphne, laughing. "We might almost be in uncouth old Scotland."

"No, not brownies," said Florian. He had lately been spending his evenings with Kapitán Mitiukov of the Kazhák company, learning all he could about Russia and Russian ways. "Oh, they believe in enough other kinds of sprites and elves and such. But those food offerings are set out for 'the unfortunates'—men on the run, being hounded by the police or the army or some other authority. Here, as everywhere, the poor and downtrodden are on the side of the underdog. They have a saying: 'He is no thief who is not caught.' Only if a criminal is caught and officially convicted do his fellow unfortunates shun and spurn him."

Now and then, the train passed other vehicles on the awful road. Most of them were bulky, solid-wheeled farm carts, but some—perhaps the property of local squires—were more graceful carriages drawn by a troika team. The middle one of that three horse hitch proceeded at a brisk trot, overarched by the high, wooden dugá yoke, which was always fancily carved and painted, sometimes hung with jingling bells. The two flanking horses ran at an angle, their heads pulled outward by check reins, and they had to run at a canter to match the "root" horse's trotting speed.

"I don't see any purpose in that," horsewoman Clover Lee said critically. "That high yoke must be heavy, and the flank horses must be uncomfortable, having to run at a slant and a different gait."

"I strongly suspect," said Florian, "that the Russian coachmen long ago designed that complicated harness just so they themselves would be respected and irreplaceable—as the only human beings on earth who can hitch and unhitch a troika."

But the travelers saw more novel things than that. Very often there came along the road a man, less frequently a woman, dressed in rags, most of the rags bunched around the feet in lieu of boots, and holding out a pleading palm. "Religious pilgrims," explained Willi Lothar, "going to some shrine somewhere." And he always threw them a few kopeks. But some of the ragged wanderers came along the road frenziedly dancing, whirling, singing and whooping. "Those are also regarded as devout," said Willi, strewing kopeks, "and are called 'the fools of God,' but they are really only pitiful madmen on the loose."

Willi went on, at the campfire that night, "Even many of the truly religious sects here are so fanatical that we would consider them lunatic. There are the monks called skoptsýi, for example, those sworn to total abstinence from sex. It seems they cannot trust themselves to abstain by willpower alone. So they castrate each other. A monk is said to 'take the little seal' if only his testicles are removed—the 'great seal' if he surrenders his penis as well."

Several people around the fire queasily set aside their plates of food.

"Then there is the sect call the Bozhie Lyudi, or People of God," Willi continued. "They also pledge sexual abstinence, but only in regard to their own husbands or wives. It is quite all right to copulate with some *other* church member's mate. And there are the Holy Ghost Worshipers. They must inhale deeply and frequently while they pray, so that they literally *swallow* the Holy Ghost. Many of them faint from that excessive respiration, and they are considered especially touched by the spirit. One of their late members, I was told, is remembered as the most blessed of all. He actually fell down and died from an overdose of the Holy Ghost."

Just once on that road did the circus people stop to purchase a meal, rather than cook their own. That was in a village called Khotin, a community big enough to have two buildings of fair size. They were even painted and sported a couple of glass windows apiece—and each had a sign over its door. The newcomers gazed at those signs, the first display of Cyrillic writing most of them had yet come upon. The writing seemed bewilderingly to comprise familiar letters of the alphabet, but mixed capitals and lower case, plus familiar letters of the alphabet printed backward or upside down, plus a sprinkling among them of totally unfamiliar characters. Florian read the signs to the others: "Pravityel'stvo Monopóliya Lavka, or State Monopoly Store, meaning it deals in liquor and tobacco. The other sign says Gostínitsa. That is an inn. Let us try it."

The fare they were served—by a buxom, meaty, sweaty and rather smelly woman—was probably no different from what was on the table of every peasant family in Khotin or anywhere else in Russia.

Yount looked suspiciously at his bowl of murky gray-green soup and said, "When she set this down, she called it something like shitsy."

"So would I," said Rouleau, sniffing warily at his.

"The word is 'shchi,' " said Florian, dipping into his without hesitation. "Cabbage soup. Quite good it is, too."

In fact, it was the best part of the meal. The rest consisted of leathery slabs of salt fish, unadorned boiled potatoes, black rye bread like tree bark, raw onions and mugs of what might have been a pale beer, but everyone who tasted it made a sour face and noises of, "Jesus, what is *this?*"

"Kvas," said Florian. "One of the staples of peasant life, I understand. Home-made, and reputedly a most salubrious drink. You merely pour water and a little honey over barley— or even stale rye bread—let it ferment good and rotten, pour off the liquid, and that is kvas."

"By damn," said Yount. "I thought we lived rough during the war back home, when us Cornfeds had to make do with parched-okra coffee and suchlike. But these Russian poor whites . . ." He shook his head pityingly.

*　　*　　*

The wagon train at last arrived at the Khamenets Podolskiy station, to find its railroad train waiting, as promised—and that was an awesomely substantial string of machinery. The Sormovo locomotive was at least four feet higher and two feet wider than any engine the circus people had seen either in the States or elsewhere in Europe. Suspended above its massive black-iron boiler the locomotive had a curious long, thick pipe, almost like a second and thinner boiler, bridging the two bowler-hat-like domes that housed the throttle valve and safety valve. The single driving wheel on either side of the engine was nearly eight feet in diameter, and even the bogie and trailing wheels were nearly the height of a man's chest.

The passenger cars, goods wagons and flatcars were proportionately immense. The coaches did not, like Western European coaches, have a corridor running down one side of the interior, with the passenger compartments opening off it. In this train, the compartments were of a breadth to carry at least ten seated persons in ample comfort on their two facing green-baize seats, for the rooms extended completely from side to side of the coach, with windows and entrance doors on both sides, and narrower doors in the walls beside the seats, opening on the adjacent compartments. For the kondúktor or any other crewman to go any distance along the train without disturbing the passengers, there was a narrow plank catwalk and iron handholds affixed along the *outside* of every car, with gaps between the coupled cars that necessitated the man's making fairly athletic and daring jumps.

The Florilegium arrived at the station about noon. Florian heeded the advice given him by Trepov, shooed away the ragged men and boys vociferously clamoring to be of service and set his own roustabouts to the arduous task of moving the circus from the station platform onto the train.

"If we can do this expeditiously," he said, "we might be loaded by dark. It is only two hundred and twenty miles to Kiev. I should think, since this train will not be stopping at stations along the way, we ought to make that run overnight—and in the dark, so we don't have to look at any more of this dreary prairie."

"Do we sit up all night?" asked Agnete.

"No, Fräulein Eel," said Willi. "I ordered enough coaches that we need put only four persons in each compartment. And, when we are ready to sleep, the back of each seat will be lifted and secured by the train's provodnik, to become an upper bunk. The crewmen, of course, will sleep in the straw with the animals."

So the Slovaks went to work, under the direction of Stitches, Boom-Boom, Hannibal and Banat. It was fortunate that the train's enclosed goods wagons were so big and had broad loading doors, because Hannibal insisted that the circus's horses and the caged and walking animals *not* be ramped onto the flatcars—as were the caravans and supply wagons—but that they ride inside the shelter of the boxcars. It entailed much inching and pinching of wagon wheels and tongues and shafts, and much neighing and roaring and struggling and balking of the animals, and much cursing and frequent cries of pain from the Slovaks, but that was duly accomplished.

Meanwhile, the unoccupied troupers went inside the station and found, to their surprise, that it contained a quite decent gostínitsa—at least far superior to the inn at Khotin—and they had a plain but satisfying meal of sprats, pepper pot soup, pork and dumplings, boiled potatoes and real beer, not kvas. Florian sat Kapitán Miliukov at his table; the rest of the soldiers remained outside, cordoning the train against pilferers or stowaways, and they would eat later, when the Slovaks did. Florian also, after the meal, went into the room adjoining the gostínitsa, another State Monopoly Store, bought twenty bottles of vodka and gave those to the captain. "For your men, by way of thanking them for their services."

"Spasíbo, Gospodín Florian," said Miliukov. "Perhaps, in return, while you wait for your transport to be readied, tak, you and your people will accept my invitation to a fairly uncommon event."

"An event?"

"Da. Come along. It is being held in the square just beyond this station."

*   *   *

The troupe rather puzzledly followed the captain from the station to the square. In its center was an upright stake and stocks, to which a shirtless man was fastened, his arms pinned in the stock openings and tightly roped to stretch all the muscles of his bare back into prominence. He appeared to be a fairly young man, beardless, but his long hair shrouded his face. Several black-robed judges stood about and, at a discreet distance, much of the population of Khameners Podolskiy. Near the stake stood a giant Kazhák soldier, also shirtless, twisting and limbering a stout whip in his hands. Beside him, some iron tools were stuck in a brazier of glowing coals. At the sight, all the circus women except Monday Simms gave a gasp and hurried back inside the station inn. So did a number of the circus men. Florian asked the captain the reason for this "event."

"The man was convicted as an utterer. The local constabulary requested me, as senior to them in rank, to oversee his punishment and to provide my strongest soldier to do the flogging."

"An *utterer?*"

"Of false coins, tăk—a forger, a counterfeiter. He will receive one hundred ninety and nine strokes of the k'nut, then tavró, then shcbitsiki. If he lives through all of that, he will be dragged to the city limits and banished."

Before Florian or anyone else could say anything further, or turn and go away, the k'nut-wielding soldier had backed off four or five yards from the stake. Then he took four or five firm steps forward and sprang high into the air as he brought the whip down with a loud *crack*! That first stroke made only a short cut across the victim's bare skin, from the nape of his neck to his left armpit, but it wrung from him a loud scream. Several more of the troupers and even some of the townsfolk did leave then. Among those who stayed was Monday Simms, and, for the first time in a long while, she was kneading her thighs together.

The knoutmaster backed off again, strode forward, leapt in the air and laid the next stroke exactly half an inch below the first, and parallel to it. He continued like that, each stroke half an inch lower and diagonally longer, until he had striped the shrieking man's back with twenty-five raw red gashes. Then the soldier transferred the whip to his left hand and just as accurately laid on twenty-five more stripes from left to right, crisscrossing the others. When the flogger changed hands again, he laid the lashes perpendicular to the others— changed hands again and whipped horizontally. By this time, the culprit was no longer screaming, and his back was no longer blood red, but a black pulp. During the final ninety-nine strokes, the knoutmaster tried merely to hit any previously unbroken bit of skin remaining among the cross-hatchings, and the victim hung from the stocks, limp and apparently lifeless.

But then Kapitán Miliukov stepped over to him and raised his dangling head, and incredibly the man had life enough to scream again when the Kazhák brought a red-hot branding iron from the brazier and stamped the letter O—for orvyér-zheniy, outcast—on each cheek and his forehead. And yet the man lived, while the knoutmaster took a pair of glowing pincers from the brazier, seized and ripped away each of his nostrils, leaving in the middle of his face only a small pro-trusion of red-gray gristle . . . When that made the victim scream again, weakly, waveringly, piteously, he was echoed by an almost similar noise from the quivering, starry-eyed Monday Simms.

"Christ!" breathed Yount. "That forger fellow is a stronger man than me and the flogger put together."

"And now he's uglier and more freakish than any Tattooed Man like me," Fitzfarris said thoughtfully.

The outcast was loosed from the stocks and let to thud unconscious onto the cobbles of the square, and Kapitán Mil-iukov called for volunteers to drag him to the edge of town. Fitz was the only man who stepped forward.

The train was loaded by nightfall, and the circus rousta-bouts all fed, and the Kazhák company had departed, presum-ably off again to the border, and the engineer and fireman were getting up steam in the gigantic locomotive, meanwhile ringing its bell and hoo-hooting its whistle, evidently just for the pleasure of hearing them. The Slovaks climbed aboard the straw-strewn goods wagons containing the animals, and the rest of the company got into the compartments. A flagman on the platform swung a green lantern, the engine responded with an uproar of ringing and whooping, and ponderously began to chuff-chuff-chuff up to speed and left Khamenets Podolskiy behind.

The roadbed was not particularly well laid, so there was some heaving, rocking and vibration. Monday Simms might well have been doing her sympathetic vibrations, except that her attendance and excitement at the flogging scene seemed to have drained her of such impulses. For the others, the train ride was like riding a swan boat, after the jolting and careening they had endured on the log-slab road. The only annoyance was the oily smoke and soot that drifted in through every least crevice in the carriages.

At the rear of every passenger car was a cubbyhole in which sat a provodnik, tending and perpetually refilling a big samovar of hot tea, and he periodically came creeping along the car's outside catwalk to inquire if anyone wanted a glass of "chai." At intervals, also, the kondúktor or brakeman or an oiler left the crew car at the tail of the train, to sidle up and down the whole length of it, sometimes apparently doing routine inspection, sometimes perilously carrying a pitcher of tea—and once or twice a bottle of vodka—for the engineer and fireman. The passenger coaches and even the goods wagons in which the animals and Slovaks rode were at least moderately heated by steam pipes from the locomotive boiler running under the floors. However, as the night wore on and got colder, the provodnik of each coach came through with lap robes for the passengers to wrap themselves in, and later to use as blankets on their bunks. Each was a patchwork of stitched together scraps of rare and precious furs: mink, sable, ermine. Florian inquired whence came these wonderful coverlets. They were made, said the porter, of bits discarded by the skornyáka workshops that made dress-fur coats, robes and such for Russian rich folks and for export to rich folks abroad.

When the thrill of being again aboard a railroad train had worn off, there being little to look at outside, the passengers began to visit back and forth between compartments. Fitzfarris entered the one in which rode Florian, Edge, Yount and Pfeifer, just as Florian was idly saying, ". . . wonder what will become of that poor wretch we saw beaten."

Fitz said, "Looks like he'll live, Governor."

"Eh? How would you know that?"

Fitz jerked a thumb over his shoulder. "He's stretched out in the compartment that Meli and Jules and I took. Meti and Jules are swabbing his cuts and burns right now, with every medication we're carrying."

"You brought him *with us?!*" Edge exclaimed. "Christamighty, man, what for?"

"What for? Why, to *show*, of course. I'm responsible for recruiting the annex exhibits. I think I'll bill him as the Ugliest Man in the World."

"You'll never get away with it, Sir John;" said Florian. "Those O brands are unmistakable. We'll be swooped upon by the first policeman who sees him. We'll be charged with harboring—abetting—God knows what."

Fitzfarris shook his head. "The fellow was as unconscious as a tree stump when we lugged him aboard. He still is. So I took the opportunity to light up a cigar and doctor those brands some, while he couldn't feel it." The other four men regarded Fitz with horrified awe. "I couldn't make them ornamental, but at least they don't look like O's any more. They could be any kind of wicked burn scars. What I figure, when he takes the platform, I'll talk him up as the survivor of a ruckus with Pemjean's bears. Only man ever to escape from *two savage bears*, ladies and gentlemen, with his life—if not much else."

"Hm-m," said Florian. "In Russian folklore, there is an unkillable ogre known as Kostchei the Deathless. You could call him that."

"Perfect," said Fitzfarris. "And it'll make Kewwy-dee and Kewwy-dah look not so tame, besides. The jossers will be more impressed when Pemjean makes those killer brutes skate with Daphne."

Jörg Pfeifer said, "But that man cannot be just a dumb muzhik. He must have some intelligence, to have been a counterfeiter. How do you know he will agree to becoming a sideshow exhibit?''

"Hell, what better alternative has he got?''

"Sir John is right, Fünfünf," said Florian. "Not even a monastery would take in a branded outcast. His only other recourses would be begging or recidivism. The most charitable almsgiver would be loath to give to him. And if he returns to a life of crime, well, he'll certainly be an easy suspect to identify. Caught again, he would surely be condemned to death.''

"So we're doing him and us both a favor," said Fitzfarris: "Me, especially. Now I can retire from the limelight. A Tattooed Man damn sure can't compete with *him* in freakishness. I can wear old Mag's makeup and look like a normal human being *all* the time. Meli won't have to wince when people stare at us on the street. I mean, if it's all right with you, Governor.''

"Of course, Sir John. Just as soon as Kostchei the Deathless is able to replace you. And I commend your initiative.''

"I swear," said Edge, more in wonderment than reproach. "Florian, you and Foursquare Fitz between you must have cornered the market in brass. Whenever I think I know the limits of your outrageousness, one of you comes up with some new and chancy flimflam. Now we're hiring a convict, an Ishmael, shunned in his own land. The man has no conduct book to give him a circus history, no passport to show to border guards—''

"As it happens," Florian said equably, "secret agent Trepov was so eager to ingratiate himself that he slipped me a couple of extra Russian passports, left blank but properly visaed. It also happens that when the Terrible Turk blew our stand, he left in such a hurry and such a fury that he neglected to take along his conduct book. So our new Kostchei the Deathless—whatever his real name—will henceforth be Shadid Sarkioglu in private life.'' Florian turned again to Fitzfarris. "The man now could pass for any nationality. He certainly no longer has the squat, broad Slavic nose. But take no chances. Cut his hair short, in the Western style. And never let him speak Russian in the presence of strangers.

When you introduce him on the platform, you might mention that the shock of his experience rendered the poor man mute for life.''

"Right, Governor,'' Fitz said cheerfully. "We won't know until he wakes up, but just maybe it *did*.''

The trip to Kiev lasted rather longer than the "overnight'' Florian had hoped for. At every third verst of the way—every two miles—there stood beside the tracks a yellow-painted log cabin in which dwelt a signalman and his family. At the circus train's approaching hoo-hoot, he would pop out, usually accompanied by his whole family—even if they had been in bed, because a passing train was the only event ever to occur in their lives, and the only thing to look at in that desolate landscape—and the man would wave a green lantern to show that, according to his telegraph key, the way ahead was clear. But several times on this trip, the signalman waved a red lantern, the train stopped, its crew got down and swung heavy switch levers, and the train was shunted onto a siding to wait, sometimes for half an hour, to let a regularly scheduled train go by.

There were other stops, some of long duration: to take on water from a tank tower standing stark and lonely on the plain, to take on coal at a division-point railroad town called Vinnitsa. Every time the train stopped, Florian woke up, got out of his fur-blanketed bunk, scattering the soot and smuts that had settled on it and him, and went to inquire, with increasing impatience, what the delay was now, and returned to report to his compartment mates, whether or not they were awake or gave a damn.

At the seventh or eighth stop, when Florian got out, the train was in the middle of a featureless immensity of grass extending to the circle of the horizon all around—no water tank, no coal bunker, no signalman's izboustka, nothing. Clearly something had gone wrong with the train itself, for most of the crew were squatting beside one bogie wheel at the end of one of the goods wagons. The moon was rising just then, full and huge and amber, laying a long, golden, shimmering reflection across the prairie, as if the sea of grass really were a sea of water. Simultaneously, there arose from the far distances all around a chorus of mournful baying and howling.

"Volka," one of the trainmen told Florian. "Wolves."

The circus animals seemed to recognize the noise, too, though they probably never had heard it before, for they responded with anxious whinnies and grunts and trumpetings. Then, almost exactly imitating the wolves' baying, there came a howl from one of the passenger coaches. A compartment side door flew open, a naked figure leapt out and began running up the moon's golden pathway, chest-deep in the grass. That figure was followed by a smaller one, shoulder-deep in the grass; and two figures smaller yet, that quite disappeared in the grass. It took a moment for Florian to realize that the first runaway had been Pavlo Smodlaka and his pursuers were Gavrila, Sava and Velja. Pavlo continued to bay, eerily wolflike, as he ran. But the thick grass impeded his progress, while he left a trampled open swath behind him. So Gavrila soon overtook him, halted him, held him, apparently soothed him out of whatever nightmare had impelled him to that flight, and led him back to the train. They and the children climbed again into their compartment and shut the door.

"I wonder what that was all about," Florian said to himself, then in Russian to the train crew, "And what is wrong here, friends?"

When he returned to his own compartment, he reported to the three recumbent, fur-and-soot-covered, deeply sleeping men, "Now one of the journal boxes, whatever those are, has developed a hotbox, whatever that is, and must be re-packed, whatever that means. It seems it will take a damnably long time."

And so it was that, though the train very occasionally got up to its top speed of forty miles an hour, over the whole run it averaged a sedate fourteen. But at least the penultimate stop was a welcome one, when in the morning the engineer brought the train to a halt at the station of a village called Fastov, so everyone could debark and have breakfast. Even at that small station, the gostinitsa was a good one and provided a hearty and tasty meal.

From Fastov on, there was more to see through the train windows: rolling farmland, fairly substantial farmhouses, barnyards full of goats and geese, villages of houses that had painted or carved shutters and eaves. The railway frequently ran parallel to a road on which peasants were going to the city, astride mules, asses, horses, in lumbering carts, occasionally in light buckboard-style wagons drawn by a troika hitch. Whether the muzhiks were more prosperous in this area, or because a trip to the city was an occasion for dressing their best, they were quite gaily attired. The women wore bright bodices and aprons over long print skirts. The men wore their usual baggy sharováry trousers tucked into boots of felt or birch bark, but added vividly colored shirts and high peaked caps. Another few miles, the rolling land began to bulge upward into real hills and, when the train rounded one of those, the passengers could see the series of wooded heights on which stood the city of Kiev. From this distance, it seemed to consist entirely of onion-domed church towers.

"Well, Kiev is called 'the Jerusalem of Russia,' " said Willi. "It is where Christianity first took root in this country."

The circus train pulled into the Kiev station about eleven o'clock, and was switched onto a siding where the roustabouts could unload it without disrupting other traffic. That job, like the loading, occupied them until nearly sundown. Meanwhile, Florian settled his charter bill, to date, with the various railroad officials in the stationmaster's office, so the train could go back into regular service, but he made arrangements to have it available again whenever he should decide to make the next run, to Moscow. Now the wagon train and animals afoot had to cross some two and a half miles of the city—the circus did not make parade, but attracted a good deal of attention, nevertheless—to the tober Willi had engaged. It was, as it had been so often in Italy, the infield of a racetrack. This one was called the Esplanáda, and it was finely situated on a height overlooking the broad but sluggish and dirty-yellow river Dnepr.

On arrival there, Banat came to ask, "Pana Governor, do we set up first or go and post paper first?"

"Lord, Lord, neither one," Florian said wearily. "First lay fires, Crew Chief, and heat plenty of water. Let us get the grime off us—and off the animals, as well. And anything else that's filthy, which is probably everything. Tomorrow, we will set up just the chapiteau and its rigging, so the artistes can practice. They haven't worked in weeks; they've got a lot of limbering and unkinking to do. We won't paper until we are ready to give Kiev a good show."

"Speaking of bathing, Herr Gouverneur," said Carl Beck, "the Herr Lothar has told me of a most splendid Bad just down the hill from here, and a miraculous healing hot spring it has. On account of so many miracles, there the Lavra Convent was erected—in all of Russia the convent the most highly revered. It is there to bathe I shall go. Perhaps you and others also would care to come."

"Thank you, Boom-Boom. I am too fatigued even to seek a miracle cure for my fatigue. I'll settle for a tub right here. But take anyone else who wants to go."

So quite a number of the company went with Beck down the hill to the spa near the Baptismal Monument. Not until they had paid their fifty kopeks apiece and got to the disrobing room did they discover that it was communally used by both males and females, and that the men and women all disrobed to the skin, and went together into the hot pool in the grotto. So the circus women—except Clover Lee and the equally unembarrassable Nella Cornella—immediately took their leave, forfeited their fifty kopeks and returned to the tober, preferring a private bath to a sanctified but public one.

A couple of the bath attendants spoke French and managed to make Beck comprehend that, besides the simply miraculous healing bath, the spa offered another, *scientifically* miraculous bath, and other invigorating services, as well. Beck decided to avail himself of everything offered, but his companions were satisfied to stay and soak and relax in the communal pool.

One of the extra services was provided by a crone who could easily have been the Russian fairy-tale witch Baba Yaga. She came to Beck bearing a hand basket of huge, knobbly, ugly tree mushrooms. With mortar and pestle, she mashed those into a viscous, pus-like fluid, some of which she spooned into Beck then and there. It tasted awful enough, he later reported, to be the good medicine it was warranted to be, for liver and kidney ailments. The crone poured the remainder of the dreadful substance into a bottle for Beck to take away with him.

Then she led him to a small, private pool of water, scalding hot, and when he had gingerly immersed himself, she brought and threw into the water an entire anthill, complete with its inhabitants. Beck might have bounded right out again, but the ants perished before they could make the situation even hotter for him. The pool instantly turned brown-black and unpleasantly pungent, but the French-speaking attendant made Beck understand that the formic acid in the multitude of little ant corpses, plus the turpentine they had absorbed from living in a pine forest, was far more efficacious than reliance on mere miracles for easing rheumatism, lumbago, muscle strain and backache. Beck's extended stay in the spa cost him four rubles all together, plus a scattering of kopeks in gratuities, but he emerged claiming to feel healthier and livelier than he had in years.

The other circus folk, pleased just to feel clean again and somewhat relieved of their train-ride cramps, had meanwhile ambled about the neighborhood of the Lavra Convent—there were quite a few things to see there—before they went back up the hill.

"Do you know, signori, what they have down there?" Nella Cornella said excitedly to Florian and Edge. "Many, many caves—le catacombe di Sant'Antonio, they are called—and in them are seventy-three saints. All old and dry and wrinkled like fusilli pasta, but dressed in liturgico finery, as if they might get up and say mass next Sunday."

"Then Sir John can give his Egyptian Princess a rest while

we're here," said Florian, "if Kiev already has a surfeit of mummies."

"Wait, that is not all!" said Nella. "Right in the middle of one cave, sticking up from the ground, there is this mummia head of a monk, with one of those tall hats such as bishops wear."

"A miter."

"Si, una mitra. And the rest of him is under the ground. He is called John the Long-Suffering, and he determined to mortify himself to the greater glory of God, so he had himself buried *alive* that way, just his head sticking up, and the other monacchi fed him, and he lived like that for *thirty years*, until he died, and that was seven hundred years ago, signori, and he is still there in the same place! Maraviglioso!"

"Hell, Governor," Edge said humorously. "We might as well fold up and move along. How can we possibly rivalize with such splendiferous native attractions?"

"Bab," said Florian. "You heard Nella. The natives have had seven centuries to get bored with John the Long-Suffering. We will be something new in their experience."